BLACK WOLVES

"Your life is forfeit, which means your life now belongs to me. Why did you climb Law Rock, Kellas? Up the cliff without a rope, at night, with only the moon to light your way."

Through the lattice Kellas sees an aura of light shifting as people move across a courtyard beyond. He hears women singing in a foreign language, their tone as melancholic as sailors dreaming of the lost harbor of their youth.

"Look at me."

The king's gaze is not petty or cruel but you would never turn away from it, not without permission. Kellas's gut tells him this is a man who will not judge him for being a fool but rather for not admitting to it.

"On a dare. To impress my friends. To make a girl sorry she'd scorned me. Because no one has ever climbed Law Rock unaided except in the tales. But now I have!"

The king flicks a wrist. A pale spot flashes. Kellas catches a small, hard object. Opening his fingers, he discovers a carved horse.

"Good reflexes, too," says the king. "What you accomplished is a cursed impressive feat. Now that your life is mine, I have better ideas for how to make use of you than spilling your blood on Execution Rock and hanging your corpse from a pole. If you are interested in becoming a tough and loyal man who will dedicate his honor to protecting the Hundred. Your choice, Kellas."

By Kate Elliott

Crown of Stars
King's Dragon
Prince of Dogs
The Burning Stone
Child of Flame
The Gathering Storm
In the Ruins
Crown of Stars

Crossroads
Spirit Gate
Shadow Gate
Traitors' Gate
Spirit Walker
Cold Magic
Cold Fire
Cold Steel

Black Wolves trilogy
Black Wolves

BLACK WOLVES

BOOK ONE OF THE BLACK WOLVES TRILOGY

KATE ELLIOTT

www.orbitbooks.net

ORBIT

First published in Great Britain in 2015 by Orbit

13 5 7 9 10 8 6 4 2

Copyright © 2015 by Katrina Elliott

Excerpt from *Thief's* Magic by Trudi Canavan
Copyright © 2014 by Trudi Canavan

The moral right of the author has been asserted.

A CIP catalogue record for this book
is available from the British Library.

ISBN 978-0-356-50320-2

Printed and bound in Great Britain by
Clays Ltd, St Ives plc

Papers used by Orbit are from well-managed forests
and other responsible sources.

MIX
Paper from
responsible sources

FIRE

TATTOO DESIGN © STEPHANIE TAMEZ

AIR

EARTH

TATTOO DESIGN © STEPHANIE TAMEZ

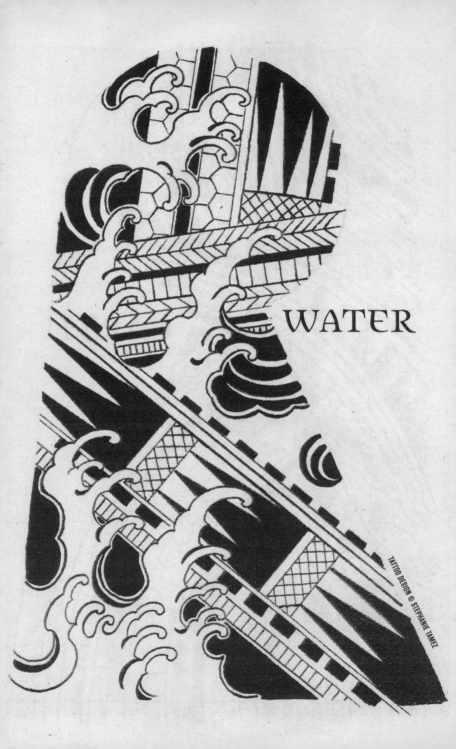

WATER

TATTOO DESIGN © STEPHANIE TAMEZ

Part One

1

The whole business stank of rotting fish.

From his position braced high in the branches of a sprawling lancewood tree that overlooked an unremarkable trail cutting through forested hills, Kellas felt the familiar warning itch between his shoulder blades. Something about this ambush wasn't going to go right, and yet he had a job to do and a secret to hide and no choice except to stick it out to the end. If those cursed smugglers didn't show up, he'd be no closer to the truth than he had been a month ago when he'd joined this company of Black Wolves on the hunt for a traitor in their ranks.

A breeze blew into his face off the nearest height but he smelled nothing except the dense scent of vegetation and the memory of rain. Birds had long ago resumed their chatter and song, no longer disturbed by the presence of six men.

The soldiers had set up an ambush point at dawn. They'd been slipped information that stolen goods would be smuggled down this specific trail under the guard of a demon and its armed confederates. The subcadre commander, Denni, had picked this spot because of the sprawling canopy of the lancewood tree and a flat patch of ground where they'd been able to dig a pit. By now it was midafternoon.

Kellas's vantage in the tree allowed him to study his companions hidden in the surrounding undergrowth. He was certain one of the other five was the disloyal Wolf leaking information to the very outlaws they were meant to capture.

Which one?

Crouched on a branch below Kellas, Ezan breathed noisily. On the stream side of the path, Oyard and Battas shifted around, brush rustling loud enough to almost drown out the gurgle of the distant stream. They were all so cursed loud.

Maybe they were all in on it.

On the mountain side, Aikar whispered to Denni. Idiot. Didn't he know how voices carried on a still day? Maybe he hoped his words would carry a warning on the breeze. Kellas wanted to signal Aikar to be silent, but Denni was senior of this subcadre and thus in charge. Any initiative Kellas took might give away his cover of pretending to be a lowly tailman new to the Wolves.

As if the restlessness of the others made him doubt their careful preparations, Denni tugged experimentally on the pit rope where it stretched across the path under cover of artfully layered ground litter. They hoped to trap a demon on one of the stakes set in the pit and cut off its skin. It was a good plan, if it worked.

A new sound teased at the edge of Kellas's hearing, a slapping that he identified as the thud of feet falling on dry leaves and dusty earth. A moment later a voice floated on the air.

"Sure, the king claims he's sending in his best troops to protect us, but then we're the ones who have to feed and house them above what we already pay in taxes."

Two men strode into view. Both carried hunting spears.

"He's like a baker selling bread for what seems like a good price, only then you discover he's been mixing sawdust in with the flour all along."

"Would the pair of you keep your mouths shut?" said a woman who was not yet quite visible beyond a bend in the path, although movement flashed through the dusty leaves. "You'll warn off the pigs before we have a chance to strike."

As Kellas tried to estimate heads and bodies in an oncoming group that he still couldn't really see through the leaves, a glimmer of pale cloth caught his eye.

The hells!

The most infamous demon of all wore a white cloak. Was she guiding the smugglers in person? He had accomplished a lot of things in the last eight years but he'd never tangled directly with a cloaked demon and its perilous magic. A racing clamor of excitement disturbed his concentration but he calmed it with slow, measured breaths.

The two spearmen in the front passed over the pit without noticing the give in the ground and headed under the wide canopy of the lancewood tree.

And there she was! Wearing a white cloak and armed with a bow and quiver, the demon strode into view and turned to signal to someone unseen behind her. Right on target, Battas and Oyard each loosed an arrow from their hiding place. Both arrows struck her in the chest just as a gaggle of fourteen youths carrying bows and spears appeared on the trail. They had the gawky eagerness of children out on a thrilling expedition, sacks slung over their backs. The ones in front stopped short as the demon choked out a warning. Their stunned, horrified expressions were so heartbreaking that a kick of fury made Kellas tremble even as he held his position in the tree.

The demon was using adolescents to cover its tracks, exactly the kind of cold calculation that made cloaked demons the most dangerous creatures in the Hundred, the true threat to the peaceful rule of the king.

A second woman appeared at the rear of the band. She was also wearing a white cloak.

With a shock Kellas realized both women wore the braided

headbands and ritual white capes common to acolytes of the Lady of Beasts, who was both hunter and healer.

Neither of these women was a demon. They were priestesses dedicated to the goddess, leading a cursed practice hunt for training their youth.

He shouted, "Halt! Halt where you are! Denni, pull the trap now before the kids fall in!"

He grabbed for a rope he had strung from a higher branch of the lancewood, vaulted off the branch, and swung down, gauging distance and depth as he tucked up his legs. He planted the two men with a foot in each chest. The impact slammed him to a halt as they went down. He flipped in the air as he released the rope, and landed on his feet behind them.

Denni snapped up the rope to release the trap. The ground gave way to reveal the pit and its deadly stakes. As the children cried out in confusion, the injured woman staggered like a drunk, then slipped into the pit. She screamed as a stake impaled her.

One of the men Kellas had knocked over scrambled up, jabbing at him with his spear as he hissed out hoarse words. "Cursed cowards! Pissing dogs! You promised us no one would get hurt!"

A pair of arrows—Aikar's reds—slammed into the man's back and he toppled forward.

The wounded priestess was still bellowing, voice ripped raw by pain.

"Run! Run!" shouted the woman at the rear, and the children scattered uphill.

Denni shouted: "Round them all up! They're all under arrest!"

The other spearman rolled up to his feet and jabbed at Kellas's back. Kellas sidestepped with a spin and in the same motion drew the sword from his back. The man thrust again.

Kellas slapped away the haft, cut in, and struck with the pommel under the man's chin. The man staggered back, then cut the point of the spear toward Kellas's head. Kellas ducked under the haft and again stepped inside, striking the man in the throat with the hilt of his sword. With a grunt, the man sagged into him, toppling him back. Kellas let the weight carry him down and rolled sideways out from under as the spearman collapsed to the ground.

Turning, Kellas saw Battas, Oyard, Aikar, and Ezan racing up the path after the children.

He cut a length off the swinging rope and tied the prisoner's feet and hands. Denni slid carefully down into the pit to the woman thrashing below. He stabbed her through the eye; a mercy, seeing how a stake had pierced her raggedly through the belly, a wound no one could heal. Then Denni grasped the cloth of her cloak in his hand and looked up with a shake of his head.

"It's just ordinary wool, not a demon's skin," he said to Kellas.

The hunter shot by Aikar clawed at the dirt, hacking out an incomprehensible word before going limp. Kellas made himself watch as the man's life drained away. Some demons could also see a person's spirit rise out of the dying. Kellas saw nothing except red blood, withered leaves, and gathering flies.

The other four tromped back into view, herding the frightened children, with the second woman trussed so tightly she could barely keep up as Aikar prodded her along. One youth was missing.

"Heya, Kel!" shouted Ezan. "You can't follow orders and help us capture these? What are you doing? Standing around looking pretty?"

"What kind of heartless people march their children into harm's way?" said Denni, which was exactly the question Kellas wanted to ask. Of all the awful things he had seen in his eight years in the king's service, adults abusing their own children or callously using them as bait and bargaining chips disgusted him the most.

Young Oyard scratched his smooth chin as he pursed his lips thoughtfully. He did not look much older than the youths they had just captured. "Someone passed us bad information."

"Throw all your bags to the ground," said Kellas curtly, and of course the youths obeyed, too terrified to do otherwise. They were only carrying a few days' stock of humble food: flat bread, cold rice wrapped in nai leaves, and sour balls of cheese.

"What, you hungry again?" Ezan asked jokingly in his usual ass-witted way, ignoring the dead woman and the crying children as if their grief and pain were of no more interest than the trees.

Kellas sniffed at the pungent, salty goat cheese. "Neh. Just checking to make sure they're not smuggling valuable goods. I think the real smugglers are somewhere else. They purposefully sent this training group along this path guessing it was a good place for us to set up an ambush and figuring the king's soldiers would not attack two priestesses and their pupils."

Ezan laughed mockingly. "Whsst! Where did a small-time criminal like you get so smart?"

Kellas grinned, pretending sheepishness as he decided on a plausible lie that would deflect any suspicion that he knew more than he ought. "Eh, you've caught me out, me and my shameful ways. I got arrested for smuggling, me and a bunch of lads. We used to round up neighborhood children and have them carry the goods while the militia was searching us instead. It worked for a while until one of the kids got hurt and we got beaten up by the neighbors and turned in by them for endangering their little ones."

As he spoke he watched the eyes of the surviving man and woman, hoping they might betray their comrade with a glance, but they kept their gazes fixed to the ground. Both had the stunned look of people who haven't yet made sense of what has just transpired. He had to wonder if they were actually ignorant and had been used as unsuspecting bait. Yet when Denni slapped them, asking what they knew about the smugglers and if they were part of a decoy plan, they stubbornly said nothing.

"I can make them talk," Ezan boasted.

"Shut up, Ez," said Denni. "Let's go."

His words broke the surviving priestess's silence. "What about our dead?"

Denni gave her a glare that made her cower. "We leave them. Chief Jagi will decide what's to be done and whether he'll allow your people to come back and fetch them."

The youths began to cry again, and several, weeping copiously, wrapped the dead priestess in her cloak and arranged her hands on her chest in the traditional custom observed for the dead.

They made an uneasy group as they hiked out of the steep upper valley with the sobbing youths and the two uncommunicative adults. In his capacity as tailman, the newest and supposedly least experienced and thus most expendable member of the cadre, Kellas took the rear guard. He was sure they were being watched and there was in fact still one youth unaccounted for, but he heard nothing and saw no one except, once, a crow perched on a fallen log in a clearing. Its black eyes were trained on them with the inhuman intelligence native to crows. When he swung around and took aim with his bow, it took wing and vanished over the treetops.

He grinned briefly. He'd never have skewered it, as some men might who took pleasure in the killing rather than in the challenge. He allowed himself three breaths to savor the empty path, the fragrant air, and the peaceful forest. A pillar of sunlight cut down through an opening a fallen tree had made in the forest cover. Its lustrous brilliance illuminated a patch of the vivid flowers known as sunbright that had grasped this chance to bloom. Their simple beauty staggered him, like the kiss of an ineffable joy.

A branch snapped, but when he looked that way he saw nothing moving among the trees. As the noise of the others faded, he left behind the sunlight and the flowers to follow them.

After a while they passed a pair of upcountry farms ringed by stockades that protected against deer rather than armed marauders. Their commanding officer, Chief Jagi, waited with his command staff just beyond the village where the path forked in three directions. He took their report, then delegated a different subcadre to fetch the two bodies and haul them down to the crossroads at the market town of Sharra Crossing where the two dead people would be strung up as a warning to others not to break the king's law and trouble the king's peace.

"You think they are in league with the smugglers, Chief?" Denni asked.

Like all of the officers in charge of companies of Black Wolves, Jagi was Qin, a foreign soldier who had arrived in the Hundred sixteen years ago together with the man who had brought peace to the land. In his month with this company Kellas had not heard Chief Jagi raise his voice, not once. But beneath his pleasant voice and mild temper ran the steel of a man who got what he wanted by never slacking. He turned his gaze on the prisoners, who went as still as rabbits sensing the shadow of a hawk.

"As it happens, I just received word that this morning, while we were up here setting our ambush, the king's portion of hides and sinew being stored in a warehouse near Elegant Falls went missing. Someone stole the tithe set aside for the king while we waited for smugglers who never came. Those who participate in a decoy are part of the conspiracy and thus are criminals. Unless you are willing to speak and convince me otherwise I must assume this supposed hunting party was part of the plot, which therefore means the two who died today are guilty of crimes against the king. According to the law, the bodies of criminals shall be displayed after execution as an example to those who might think to follow them."

Kellas could not help but put in, "The local folk won't like seeing one of their holy women hung from a post until her flesh rots away and her bones fall to the earth like so much rubbish. They'll see it as disrespect."

"Then they shouldn't have used holy women and innocent children as pawns in their game, should they? String the corpses up according to the law." Chief Jagi ignored the stony stare of the surviving holy woman and the outraged gasp of the other spearman as he turned to Denni. "Escort the prisoners to the fort. The two adults shall be taken before the assizes, and judgment passed. Assign a steward to find the parents of the children. Tell the steward the parents must pay a fine to get them back. Afterward you and your subcadre can take liberty until your regular duty tomorrow."

They marched the prisoners to the fort and turned them over to the sentinel-guards—regular soldiers under the command of a Hundred-born captain, not Black Wolves under the command of a Qin chief—who were in charge of the cages. Instead of lying down to rest, they washed thoroughly in the tubs while the soldiers who had been stuck in the fort surrounded the washing planks to find out what happened.

"Told you there'd be nothing up in the hills," said one fellow who was engaged in an ongoing duel with Ezan. "But we got some news. Besides the stolen hides, a farmer up by Elegant Falls saw a ghost woman out walking in the night."

"Same as the other?" demanded Ezan. "Cloaked in a pale demon's skin?"

"Think you'll get a chance to kill a demon, Ez?" Denni laughed as he rinsed off his sweaty, sodden hair. "For fifteen years Wolves have been chasing the last four cloaked demons, and never took one down. Heya, lads, what say we go down to that thrice-rotted inn and drink what passes for decent rice wine here in this cold-cursed valley?"

Chief Jagi rarely offered spoken praise to the Wolves under his command, but he had other ways of showing that their performance had met with his approval. So Kellas swaggered out with the others—swaggering was necessary—and they put on their cold-weather cloaks and hurried down the main road to the village of Feather Vale. It was a thirsty walk with dusk sinking down over them.

Chief Jagi had made an arrangement with an inn on the outskirts of the village. His men could take their liberty there as long as they did not fight with the locals and broke nothing, and his steward paid up the bill at the end of each week. The place was nothing special: It had a long porch where folk stowed their sandals and boots before going inside. The inn's single room was floored with old rice-straw mats and made comfortable with low tables and threadbare pillows for seating. Here in the hills it actually got cold at night in the season of Shiver Sky, so the room was cunningly fitted with small, lidded iron pots that had vents and a grated bottom with a plate beneath to catch ash; in these, charcoal burned to warm a man's legs.

Aikar hadn't bothered to wear a cloak. None of the locals gathered for an evening's drink were wearing cloaks, either; it wasn't cold to those accustomed to upcountry weather. The two women who worked in the tavern carried plain wooden trays and poured rice wine into crudely glazed cups, farmers' ware. The smoke from the warming stoves stung Kellas's eyes. Images from the skirmish in the forest flashed in his mind: A fern spattered with blood. Aikar shooting the man who had spoken. The missing youth. The way the spark of life vanished from once-living flesh. How did it leave? Where did it go?

For a region plagued with smuggling and theft, the folk here-abouts were cursed casual about their security, not even building proper stockades or posting a guard at an inn that had a supply of liquor in the back room. He closed his eyes to listen.

The locals at the table behind them were speaking in low voices. "...bad enough to have Wolves hunting in our woods. If they hear about Broken Ridge, they'll never leave."

Broken Ridge. That was better. Now he just needed to figure out what and where Broken Ridge was.

The rice wine had been heated to cure the cloying sweetness of a third-quality brew, and its drowsy flavor went to his head as the day and night he'd been awake caught up with him. He had the knack of dozing lightly, alert to any change in those around him. He could nod out, wake instantly to murmur a pointless comment—"Is that so, Ez? Did you really do that?"—and fade out again.

The locals discussed an upcoming wedding. The door tapped shut once, twice, a third time. A man vomited. Water splashed over the porch outside, rinsing away the mess.

Was that a horn's cry, far in the distance?

He stiffened to full wakefulness, but it had only been a sound chasing through his dream. Often a random sound or sight prompted a reminder of an earlier assignment. A year ago, after he had eliminated the hieros of a Devourer's temple in the town of Seven for plotting sedition against the king, horn calls had chased him for days as he had been pursued by an angry band of locals.

"So the wind came up, and mind you, when the wind comes up, it makes the water that much more dangerous." Ezan was telling the story of a canoe chase across the Bay of Messalia, him in one canoe and a fugitive in another. Ez had a southern way of talking—his vowels twisted wrong and half of his *b*'s turned to soft *v*'s—and a braggart's way of making more of the story than was likely there. But he sure as the hells was impressing the others, who were more drunk than they ought to be with black night to be traversed between here and the fort.

"After ten mey out on the water they were getting tired, I'll tell you." Ezan mimed men panting and blowing as their arms and backs fatigued with the stroke of paddles. "Then we came around the cliffs of Sorry Island right into the swells of the open ocean. Cursed if their steersman didn't lose his nerve and then his paddle. Their canoe flipped right over. Dumped them all into the ocean. Five were smashed onto the rocks before we could come up to the swamped boat. But the gods were with us, for the man we were chasing we fished right out of the water and hauled back to Sandy Port to stand at the assizes for his crimes."

"Hu! Ten mey out and ten mey back, and you never stopped for a rest or a drink? Paddling all that time?" asked Oyard with a snort of disbelief. Although the youngest Wolf in Third Company, he was always the quickest to question whatever everyone else assumed was true.

"What? You don't believe me?" demanded Ezan. He drained his cup of rice wine and thumped it down on the table, daring the others to match him.

Kellas glanced around the tavern. It was very late, and the rest of the locals had gone home, but the two women who ran the inn had not yet worked up the courage to ask the soldiers to leave.

"No one of you can match that feat, can you?" Ezan went on. "A sad day when they had to let your broken swords into the Black Wolves. Haven't you done a single impressive thing beyond surviving training? Chief Jagi's the kindest officer you'll ever serve under, I promise you."

The other men considered this question so seriously that Ezan's jutting chin relaxed as he contemplated his victory in the boasting stakes.

"I grew up in the hills," said Aikar.

"What, like around here?" Kellas asked in the tone of a sloppy drunk.

Aikar hunched up his shoulders. "Anyway, I never saw the ocean until I went to Nessumara for training."

Denni, Battas, and Oyard were plains-bred farm boys who had never done a cursed exciting thing before they'd joined the king's army and then made the cut that elevated them out of the regular ranks into the king's elite soldiers, the demon-hunting, bandit-killing, ruthlessly effective Black Wolves.

"I'll drink to such a hells impressive tale, Ez," said Kellas. "I reckon you grew up there on the shore, neh? Got used to paddling such long distances."

"That I did. It's what everyone does, go out to fishing spots, to the breaker islands to gather shellfish and birds' nests." Ezan was the kind who grew more pleasant the more he felt he had one up on you. "No reason any of you should have spent time on the water. How about you, Kel?"

Kellas had once paddled and swum across half the Bay of Messalia in the dead of night to infiltrate a reeve hall, where he had stolen a pouch of dispatches while his compatriot had murdered the hall's crippled marshal. Then they had swum and paddled back, no one the wiser. But he shook his head just as if he did not know that the distance from Sandy Port to Sorry Island was three mey, not ten.

"I'm just a city boy from Toskala, Ez. You know me. Kicked around awhile, got arrested, was given the choice of joining the army or a work gang. Picked the army, got chosen to run with the Wolves, and they sent me here to serve as a tailman in Chief Jagi's company."

"Aren't you thirty?" asked Oyard, who was eighteen. "That's old to be a tailman."

"He didn't lie about his age to join up like you did, Oyard," said Denni with a laugh.

"I'm a slow learner," allowed Kellas with a lazy smile that attracted the notice of the younger of the women. She came over, ignoring the other men in favor of offering a friendly look to Kellas.

"Are you hoping for one more drink, lads?"

"No cause to keep you up later than you're accustomed to, verea," he said as the others protested that they wanted another drink. "We're the last ones here."

"If you're willing to spend your chief's coin on one more drink, I'll bring it," she said. "I'll say this. Those Qin outlanders are so honest that a merchant could leave his entire chest of leya with any one of them and not have to count the coins when he got it back."

She gave another smile to Kellas and walked back to the counter.

"What is it with you and women?" Denni muttered. "You're not that good-looking."

"I show a little courtesy." For once he was unable to keep a ribbon of contempt out of his tone. "Which you lads would think well on, rather than keeping these two women up all night for your own selfish pleasure."

"Tell me you aren't eyeing the younger one and thinking of keeping her up all night for *your* own selfish pleasure," Ezan said with a coarse laugh.

"I can't take what's not offered."

Cursed if that didn't start all but Oyard in on stories of women they had loved and lost, or temple hierodules who had taken their fancy and milked them dry. There were few things more tedious than arrogant young men bragging about sex, as he knew perfectly well. But there was an edge to their boasting that made him uneasy.

The woman came back with a warmed vase as Ezan was speaking.

"...and then she said, 'No, ver, I don't think I've a mind to,' and I said, 'We've come too far for me to hear no, don't you think, lass?' and so I..."

The woman's expression shaded from tired good humor to scarcely hidden disgust just as Ezan glanced up to see it. Kellas jarred the table with his legs.

"Aui!" The table's edge kicked into Ezan's gut.

"I'm going outside to piss," Kellas said, too loudly, and he made a show of staggering to the door.

As he'd hoped, the others followed, remembering their full bladders. Once they were outside, the stars and the rising half-moon made them consider the lateness of the night and the distance back to the fort, not to mention the rumors of a demon. They set off at a brisk march. He glanced back to see the younger woman standing on the porch of the inn watching them go. He knew that look. If he could slip away, he'd find a welcome.

But the people who served in the secret auxiliary of the Black Wolves—the silent wolves—lived by three rules, the third of which was: No dalliance when you're working. Never. Self-control before all else. It was drilled into them: self-control and the ability to endure pain.

She pinched out the lamp's burning wick and slid the door shut behind her. The men soon left behind the inn and village, Kellas sticking to the back to keep one eye on the man he was by now almost certain was the traitor.

Perhaps whipped into competition by Ezan's story, Denni began telling the tale of how he had earned his subcadre command in a long-running campaign against outlaws in the Soha

Hills. Afterward the well-to-do landowners who had suffered most under the outlaws' depredations had set out a three days' feast. The rice wine flowed freely, the lovers were eager, the music ran like a mountain stream, as it said in the tale. Best of all, their company had gotten a commendation from King Anjihosh himself, who had ridden out with his officers and his son to meet with the local council.

"I will say this," said Denni, "Prince Atani has a shine to his face. The king is an impressive man, truly, but the gods themselves have touched the boy, for he has that look about him. A thoughtful gaze more like that of a full-grown man than a lad just sixteen."

"Never saw the king's son myself," Kellas lied. "Looks like his sire, does he?"

Not much, the others agreed, except maybe about the eyes and hair. Maybe he resembled his mother, but since no one had ever seen her face in public, her being a Sirni outlander with her bizarre outlander custom of remaining behind the palace walls, it was impossible to say. But they all agreed the king's son possessed an essence of special strength and brightness.

"What is it the Sirniakans say of their god?" Denni said. "The Shining One? Like that."

Ezan waved a hand dismissively. "Those southerners can keep their Beltak god on the other side of the mountains. No call for an outlander god to come traveling here."

"I wouldn't say so, not where Chief Jagi can hear you," said Denni.

"Aui! He's not Sirni. He's Qin. None of the Qin worship that shining god, do they? It's those hidden palace women with their peculiar ways who brought Beltak to the Hundred. I've never heard Chief Jagi say one thing about gods, except setting flowers on a rock dedicated to the Merciful One one time, and then because he was with his wife. She is a proper Hundred woman and cursed pretty even for being a few years older than our elderly Kel here, if I may say so."

"I wouldn't, and especially not where the chief can hear you," said Denni.

Having to pretend to be something so his own comrades would not suspect he was spying on them was getting cursed tangled. He changed the subject. "When I was a lad we never called Hasibal the Merciful One. Hasibal is the Formless One. I don't know where this Merciful name came from. Do any of you?"

Naturally Ezan had an opinion. "It comes from the south of the Hundred, from Olo'osson and Mar—"

A horn's cry split the quiet. Three blats, a long blast, three blats, a long blast, three blats. As one, they shifted to a run. Soon after they heard hooves and saw a gleam of lamplight off to their right. Riders were moving through the countryside.

"The hells!" cried Aikar, stopping dead in his tracks.

"A demon!" shouted Ezan. "Eihi! When I'm off duty! My chance for glory, spoiled!"

Abruptly Ezan cut off the road to tear madly across a recently harvested field. Kellas hesitated for only one breath, then raced after him. Crop stubble scraped his calves and crunched under his boots. His eyes had adjusted. He measured the shadows that marked the irregularities of ground and thus kept to his feet when Ezan stumbled and crashed to his knees in a shallow ditch.

A flutter of movement crossed before them like the pale wings of a bird trying desperately to get off the ground with an injured wing. A face flashed into view: a woman, running.

A cloak flowed and rippled around her. The fabric bore a disturbingly bone-white sheen.

With a grunt of effort, Ezan lunged up from his knees and grabbed for her ankle. His fingers grasped the hem of the long cloak. Blue sparks sizzled along the fabric as it wrapped over Ezan's face. He screamed in agony and pitched forward.

She staggered, dropped to a knee to steady herself, and looked up directly at Kellas.

The hells!

Her gaze devoured him, for that was the particular sorcery of cloaked demons. It was the same as being clouted over the head with a hammer and then having knives driven in through your eyes to leak your thoughts into the air.

Her voice was cool and clear. "You are one of the king's silent wolves. Let me see what you know."

So easily she tore through his mind to discover his secrets: the modest wine seller's shop in Toskala where silent wolves like him went to get their orders; the face of the nameless man who had given him his orders for this assignment; Esisha, who had been his partner in several missions and died two years ago; a safe house on the Gold Rose Canal in Nessumara where he had slept for three days in hiding after sinking a ship laden with a cargo bound for Salya...

As if Salya were a beacon and he a moth drawn to the light, his thoughts eddied and trawled him down into a memory from eight years ago. His pride recalled the admiring glance of a beautiful woman on the crowded streets of Salya's busy port. His skin remembered the salty embrace of the warm waters of the Bay of Messalia as he swam to Bronze Hall on his first serious mission. He would never forget the hot pleasurable rush of triumph he'd felt when he pulled himself over the gunnel and into the waiting canoe with the dispatch pouch wrapped in oilcloth tied to his back, although he doubted he would recognize the beautiful woman now if he passed her on the road.

At last he managed to blink, the effort a stab of pain in his head. The king's Wolves were honed for exactly such an encounter, trained to fight demons. With the blink he ripped his gaze away from hers. To keep free of the power of her magic, he forced his gaze to follow the swells and eddies made by the demon's skin, which looked like a cloak. Beneath she was wearing leather trousers and a vest, both garments splashed with mud. She had a body made strong through honest work. She might have been any ordinary woman who had just finished a hard day's labor in a rice paddy somewhere in the Hundred where there was still water in the rice fields at this time of year. That was the glamor with which demons dazzled their prey before they ate out their hearts and stole all their secrets: They made you believe they were just like you.

He drew his sword. The others were calling out, having lost sight of him and Ezan. The troop trotted past some distance away, lanterns swinging.

Sweat broke freely on his brow as the breeze carried away the memories that had seemed so vivid moments before. "Begging your pardon, verea, but I have to kill you."

He thrust the short blade into her gut. It sank hard and swiftly right into the core of her flesh. She grabbed his arms and tugged him closer until they were face-to-face. The cloak whipped across his hair, lighting sparks of pain along his head that made him reel. For all that she had a sword in her belly, she was the one holding him up.

Her eyes were dark with the grip of pain. Yet she mocked him. "Very polite, I am sure, ver. You were well brought up by your mother and aunties. But you will not kill me this night. You have already told me what I need to know. And you'll find nothing at Broken Ridge because we've already cleared out the rice that was being stored there."

She shoved him back with more strength than any human could possibly muster. His sword was dragged out of her flesh. She slammed him across the chest with the palm of her hand. The blow lifted him off his feet, and he hit full on his back and lay there, stunned, as a vast cloud of wings filled his vision. Ez was still whimpering on the ground beside him, face and hands blistered with a fierce burn, but even so the young soldier was trying to roll over to stand.

Kellas climbed laboriously to his feet, dizzy and stumbling, but it was already too late. The demon mounted a winged horse and flew off into the night.

Hooves pounded. Men shouted. The lights swayed drunkenly. Soldiers approached.

With a curse Ezan threw up on Kellas's boots.

The noise of his retching brought Denni, Battas, and Oyard racing up. After them came the mounted troops with lanterns bobbing and swaying. They converged as Ezan, doubled over, heaved out more bile. Kel took a step out of its way. As Chief Jagi himself arrived, Ezan straightened up with a grimace of pain that hurt to see.

"This cursed hells-ridden limp noodle had the demon within his grasp after I took these cursed burns stopping her in her tracks. But she got away from him. Ass!"

Chief Jagi glanced at Ezan, then at Kellas. Like all the outlander Qin soldiers who had ridden into the Hundred in the company of King Anjihosh, he rarely showed emotion. A narrowed gaze was brutal enough. Disappoint your Qin chief, and he'd simply deem you useless to him and cast you out of the Black Wolves.

"Which way did she run?" Jagi asked.

"She flew off on a horse," said Kel, his head aching. Lantern light glittered on the blood and spew that streaked his sword. "I got my blade in her gut. It didn't make a cursed bit of difference."

"Stupid fuckwit," said Ezan, and then he fainted from the pain, thank the gods.

Chief Jagi signaled. The troop broke into four groups and

spread out to cover the ground all around, but they all knew they would find no trace of the creature.

"You kept your wits about you," said the chief to Kellas when they two were standing alone.

"I still failed."

"Next time you'll kill one. But you know the rules. Any man who speaks to a demon must return to Toskala to give full particulars to the king. Anything else you want to tell me?"

"Yes. The traitor is Aikar."

2

"And was the traitor Aikar?" asked King Anjihosh.

"Yes, Your Highness."

"How did you come to single him out?"

"He lied about being local to the area. I knew it from the way he spoke, the way he was easy with the local customs, and how he never got cold when we were all shivering. During the ambush he shot the man who started talking, and did it so quickly I guessed he was trying to shut him up before he revealed anything. In the confusion when Ezan and I encountered the demon, Aikar fled, which sealed it. It turned out that when Chief Jagi emptied most of the fort to chase that demon, two others flew into the fort and released the prisoners."

"So the demon you confronted was another decoy. Did Aikar get away?"

"No. I was able to track him down and turn him over to Chief Jagi before I left Asharat to come here to give you my report."

"What did Chief Jagi do with him?"

"Jagi executed him and hung his body at the crossroads."

"Very good."

The king stood with a sword sheathed at his belt and a knife held lightly in his right hand as if he hadn't decided whom to use it on yet. No one who looked at this commanding middle-aged man would doubt he had spent his life as a soldier, even if he now spent most of his time as a wise administrator of the Hundred, a land he had saved from disorder and conflict.

His gaze shifted briefly past Kellas's face to the garden that surrounded the open pavilion in which the two men met. Walls surrounded the garden, beyond which lay the various wings and courtyards and buildings of the palace complex. Always cautious and alert, Anjihosh valued his security. From where he was seated, Kellas could see two reeves and their giant eagles circling above the palace; there were at least four on palace watch during the day. On the ground, the king's personal guards were all Qin soldiers. Kellas had counted seven such guards stationed in and around the pavilion and garden. An eighth stood directly behind Kellas, who sat cross-legged on a pillow in front of the king. Given that Kellas had been required to relinquish his weapons and be strip-searched before entering the palace, he recognized the arrangement for the soldier's tactic it was. Armed and standing, Anjihosh had an advantage over a seated, unarmed person, especially when his guards were armed as well.

The king addressed the clerk seated at a low table, who had recorded Kellas's report. "The village councils in the Asharat Valley will be dissolved and replaced with a military governor. Taxes will be tripled. The councils and a normal rate of taxation will be restored once the smuggling and theft are halted and those responsible turned over by the locals to the assizes. That is all. You are dismissed."

When Kellas made to rise, the king indicated the clerk, so

Kellas sank back down and waited as the clerk gathered up his implements, stowed them in a box, and departed. Anjihosh waited as well. The king was not a pacer. He had the ability to stand with utter, focused stillness, as if all the pacing were going on in his mind, out of sight to all except demons.

"So, Tailman Kellas, here you are," said the king with a quirk of the lips whose flash of humor startled Kellas. "Ironic that you had to assume the lowest rank for this particular mission, considering that in the last eight years you have become my most efficient and productive silent wolf. I think a promotion is in order."

That Kellas managed not to grin ecstatically or clench his hands to fists in triumph, much less leap up in excitement, was testament to the hardened discipline of his training. He inclined his chin slightly to acknowledge the praise and blinked about five times to bleed off the surge of adrenaline.

"Now that one cloaked demon can identify you, we must assume they all can. I will have to put you on different duty for a while."

"Yes, Your Highness." The flutter in his belly gradually eased as the king sheathed his knife and drew his captain's whip, tapping it thoughtfully against a thigh.

"I wonder what task you would be best suited for..." His intense gaze could not rip into people's minds to expose their memories, but it seemed to Kellas that the king had such a canny understanding of the men under his command that he fathomed all the depths of Kellas's heart and self regardless. "Not a desk job certainly, given my memory of our first meeting? Do you recall it?"

Aui!

Of course he remembered the rash argument eight years ago in a tavern with his equally bored and pathless friends, when he had boasted he could and would climb the promontory called

Law Rock even though it was both impossible *and* against the law. He remembered his reckless disregard as he started up the cliff face where no one, not even the city militia, dared follow. Three times during the climb he had really believed he was about to lose his grip and plunge to a bloody death, but he hadn't. When he had dragged himself over onto the top of the towering rock plateau that overlooked the city of Toskala, soldiers had surrounded him with bristling spears. For a moment he had thought they meant to force him back over the edge to his death. Instead they had marched him to a stone cell. He'd been too exhausted to resist when a sad-faced ordinand had shaved his head for execution. They had swept up the hair, tossed him a clean linen kilt and vest, and marched him out onto the wide plateau of Law Rock as it began to wake beneath the lifting veil of night. The memory had burned into his head so vividly he could taste and feel and smell it all over again.

Air smoky with an oily residue threads up from lamps that illuminate their path. The stern profiles of the soldiers and the gleaming hilts of swords flank him. Wind teases along the stubble of his scalp, all that remains of his much-admired hair. Soon his spirit will be shorn from him in much the same way as his hair was.

He thinks they are leading him to the assizes court for a dawn execution but instead they halt before an ironbound gate set into a whitewashed wall. A pair of soldiers with the foreign features of the outlander Qin take him down a corridor without windows, alcoves, or identifying markers.

The corridor offers no escape route, not even for a young man as strong and agile as he has just proven himself to be. The foreign-born Qin soldiers, although married into the Hundred and living with wives and children just like anyone, have the most fearsome of reputations: It is said they are utterly fair and completely ruthless.

They reach a bronze-plated door and cross a threshold into a simply furnished room whose ceiling is tented with draped fabric. A latticework wall screens one side of the chamber. Morning sunlight stripes gold over rugs piled four deep.

A man sits cross-legged on a brocade pillow watching two children intent on a game involving a large marble square striped in pink and white stone, three bone dice, and a cadre of miniature animals carved to exquisite perfection out of ivory. Kellas does not recognize the specifics of the game they play, but the children's expressions have a charm that can coax a smile even from a condemned man. The older is a handsome boy of about eight years whose smile lights his face like fire. The girl, a little younger, has piercingly intelligent eyes and a robust laugh. She is winning, but the boy finds the turn of play funny rather than upsetting.

"The horse! I knew it would be the horse!" he chortles as she pushes a carved horse from a white stripe onto a pink stripe and crows to mark her victory.

The seated man marks Kellas's entrance before returning his attention to the children at play. The two soldiers halt Kellas beside the door.

"Who is that, Papa?" asks the girl, looking up. "Is that the man who climbed Law Rock? Grandmother says you have to kill him because he broke the law and defied you. Mama says he should live for being bold."

"He is already dead," says the man. He opens a small chest and collects the ivory figures, placing them into tiny silk-lined compartments carved to fit each piece's contours.

The boy's eyes widen as he stares at Kellas. "Is he a ghost? But he can't be a ghost because people can't see ghosts. Only demons can see ghosts."

"Who told you that?" The man's cool voice has a pleasant timbre, but its tone makes Kellas shudder.

"Thinwit," says the girl disdainfully to the boy. "You promised not to tell." She turns an acute and fearless gaze on the man. "It isn't fair if you get mad at someone else because Atani talks too much!"

Trembling, the boy rises to stand as stiff as a spear. "I don't want to tell you, Papa."

"Was it your mother the queen?" says the man, too evenly.

"I will not speak."

The girl leaps to her feet. "Stupid!"

"Dannarah. Sit down." The man does not raise his voice.

She sits.

"Atani, sit down."

The boy plops down as if strings holding him up have been sliced through.

"Enough." The man does not sound angry, merely thoughtful. "Of course any words that pass between you and your mother remain private between you. A son remains loyal to his mother above all things, Atani."

"What about a daughter?" asks the girl.

"Daughters love their mother, but daughters leave."

"I'll never leave! I don't want to leave you, Papa. You won't make me, will you? Not like Mama's brothers made her travel far away from her home."

"She traveled far away from her home in order to marry me. Had she not done so, you would not be here. So what are we to make of that?"

"You won't yell at her, will you, Papa?" asks the boy worriedly. He is really quite uncannily good-looking. His plea makes his features brighten with compassion.

"I never yell at her, Atani. Surely you know that."

"You never yell," agrees the girl. "But sometimes you don't talk to her for days and days and days, and then she cries."

In a shocked tone, the boy murmurs, "Dannarah!"

Kellas sucks in a sharp breath, waiting for the man to slap the girl for her impertinence, but the man merely closes the chest's lid and fits the clasp to its hook. The Qin soldiers seem to be observing the fabric strung from the ceiling. How they manage to keep their faces devoid of emotion he cannot comprehend. For himself, adrenaline has pumped exhaustion out of his flesh. He wants to crawl out of his skin.

But what would be the point? He is already dead.

He marshals arguments, pleas, tears, cocky demands, but when the man rises, all thought flees. The king of the Hundred is a man of medium height and medium build, dressed to perfection in a plain-cut tunic of surpassingly beautiful blue silk whose subtle depths shade to green. He is not handsome like his son; his daughter resembles him, with the same texture of wavy black hair, and a hooked, prominent nose that gives both the look of proud eagles. But he draws the eye as if he has commanded the air and the light to pull every gaze to his person so his wishes may be obeyed without delay.

"You are an observant daughter, Dannarah." He gives her a kiss on each cheek, and a half smile almost indulgent but quickly stifled. He turns to the boy, who straightens expectantly. "And you are a loyal son, Atani. Now go on. Your mother will be expecting you."

"Will you eat with us?" demands the girl.

"Dannarah!" whispers the boy in thrilled disbelief.

The king's narrowed gaze suggests he is turning over distaste at the prospect. Then he touches each child on the head, hands resting on their hair with obvious affection. "Perhaps I will, little eaglet. Do not wait on me, though."

A curtain is swept aside by a woman wearing the bronze bracelets of an outlander slave.

"Take them to Queen Zayrah," he says.

She escorts the children out. The curtain, sewn with bells, tinkles down behind them.

The king touches his own forehead as a man might probe to see if the pain is an encroaching headache or merely the brush of a difficult thought. Then he looks up.

"What is your name?"

An unexpected flare of hope carries off Kellas's tongue, but with an effort he steals it back. "My mother gave me the name Kellas. Dedicated to the Fire Mother at birth. Given into the Herald's service when I was fourteen, just before the war. You are the outlander who saved us."

"As it happens I remember the events of seven years ago. But let us discuss what brings you here today. To ascend Law Rock by the Thousand Steps you must have a pass. To climb the cliff without permission is punishable by death."

In the face of that steady gaze Kellas's careful arguments skitter like mice from a house fire and he blurts out what is true instead of what is prudent. "Before you made yourself king, people rigged up ropes and aided climbers up the cliff face as a challenge in honor of the gods, at festival time. Anyone could ascend the Thousand Steps to visit Law Rock and the assizes at any time. That was the law carved on a holy pillar set atop Law Rock for all to honor."

One eyebrow arches.

Blessed Ilu! This time he really has gone too far. "But I know the law has changed since the end of the war."

"That is correct. The law *has* changed. The Hundred is no longer under the rule of a hundred corrupt town and city councils and a thousand ineffective village conclaves, none of whom were able to stop the demons who with their atrocities almost destroyed this land. Peace is always preferable to war, is it not?"

The king pauses. After a moment, realizing he is meant to respond, Kellas says, "Yes."

"It would behoove you to use a more formal address. *Yes, my lord.*"

"We never had lords and kings in the Hundred before this."

"But you have them now, and with it order, prosperity, safe roads, secure harbors, and farmers who can grow crops and raise animals without fear their hard work will be trampled by outlaws and their children savaged and murdered. Do you want to go back to those times?"

Kellas swallows. "No, my lord. No one would want that."

"This palace is the seat of my power and the home where I raise my children, who as my heirs will maintain my legacy. What belongs to me is mine to control. No one climbs Law Rock without my permission. Is that difficult to understand?"

If he must die, he will cursed well die with dignity. "I make no excuse. I wanted to do it. So I did."

"Why?"

"Why not?" He winces, hearing how petulant and frightened he sounds.

"Is a healthy young man like you not wanted for your clan's work?"

The familiar resentment swells. "Those ivory figures your children were playing with, Your Highness? That fine, delicate carving? That is my clan's work. I'd recognize Auntie Gitla's carving anywhere. It's the horses' manes. She always does them with the bows and flower ribbons. No one knows how she gets the detail so fine."

"They are remarkable for their skill and beauty. A respectable trade any man and woman can be proud of. Yet you say you were dedicated to the Herald's temple at fourteen."

The man is a cursed good listener; he fishes words right out of you.

"I could never sit for more than half a bell without becoming so restless it was like ants crawling on me. They knew I'd never have the patience for carving and they didn't want to spend the coin to make a marriage for me, so they dumped me in Ilu's temple. Sweeping the grounds and carrying messages about the city for the rest of my life! I would rather die falling from a cliff."

"So you climbed Law Rock. Perhaps hoping to fall in truth. Is that the only reason?"

The truth will sound stupid because it is stupid. "I accept the punishment. No one will miss me."

"Not even your mother?"

Shame flames up his cheeks. "What does it matter? You said I am already dead."

"Your life is forfeit, which means your life now belongs to me. Why did you climb Law Rock, Kellas? Up the cliff without a rope, at night, with only the moon to light your way."

Through the lattice Kellas sees an aura of light shifting as people move across a courtyard beyond. He hears women singing in a foreign language, their tone as melancholic as sailors dreaming of the lost harbor of their youth.

"Look at me."

The king's gaze is not petty or cruel but you would never turn away from it, not without permission. Kellas's gut tells him this is a man who will not judge him for being a fool but rather for not admitting to it.

"On a dare. To impress my friends. To make a girl sorry she'd scorned me. Because no one has ever climbed Law Rock unaided except in the tales. But now I have!"

The king flicks a wrist. A pale spot flashes. Kellas catches a small, hard object. Opening his fingers, he discovers a carved horse.

"Good reflexes, too," says the king. "What you accomplished is a cursed impressive feat. Now that your life is mine, I have better ideas for how to make use of you than spilling your blood on Execution Rock and hanging your corpse from a pole. If you are interested in becoming a tough and loyal man who will dedicate his honor to protecting the Hundred. Your choice, Kellas."

He raises an open hand, expecting an answer.

Imagine what adventures a man might grapple with under the command of the brilliant outlander who saved the Hundred from chaos and civil war! Kellas doesn't hesitate before tossing the piece back.

"No, Atani, you can go sit with Mama if you want, if her attendants will even let you in. I'm going to have supper with Papa like we were promised."

Kellas blinked as he shook away the memory of the encounter eight years ago and reminded himself he was standing in the king's presence.

The voice that had broken into his thoughts belonged to Lady Dannarah, now much older than the little girl he'd seen that long-ago day. With the brash energy of a person very confident in herself, she hurtled up the steps of the pavilion in advance of her brother, who was lagging behind to adjust the sash of his silk tunic.

"Here we are, Papa! Stewards are behind us, bringing the food. Atani, no one but you cares if your sash is tied perfectly...Oh!"

She registered Kellas seated to the left in a lattice of afternoon shadow. Her gaze lingered a little longer on him than was appropriate for a girl of fifteen being raised in a palace whose women followed the restrictive customs of the Sirniakan Empire where her mother the queen had been born and raised. With a jerk of her chin she snapped her head around to address her father. "You have heard the news, have you not, Papa?"

The king's calm demeanor did not even ripple. "That your mother's birthing pains have begun, and the midwife has been called to attend her? Yes, Dannarah, I have been informed."

"I should wait with Mama," said Prince Atani as he paused beside his younger sister. At sixteen he already had the graceful, assured carriage of a young man, nothing gawky about him. "She asked me to sit with her. She said the vultures are circling."

With a heavy sigh Dannarah glanced upward at the wheel of red poles that held up the felt roof as if she expected the gods to agree with her impatient scorn. "Mama means Grandmother is the vulture. They've never gotten along. Grandmother bullies her, and Mama cowers."

"Dannarah!" said Atani, then glanced at his father and closed his mouth.

The king tucked the whip between his belt and tunic. His voice was sharper than usual. "Is your grandmother in the birthing chamber now? Does the midwife say Zayrah is to deliver soon?"

"I don't know, I don't concern myself with things like that when I have so many more important skills to learn." Dannarah's color crept high in her cheeks as she sneaked another glance at Kellas. He kept his expression stolid. He could easily recognize that admiring look from girls of her tumultuous age, and it always signified trouble. "I'm never going to marry because I'm going to become a reeve and guard the Hundred from the sky."

Her brother snorted. "Just because you say so doesn't make it true, Dannarah. People don't choose to become reeves. The eagles choose the men and women who become jessed to them.

We don't choose for the eagles." He looked at Kellas and switched from the Sirni language commonly spoken in the palace to the Hundred-speech that Kellas had grown up with. "Greetings of the day, Wolf Kellas. It is good to see you again."

Atani's smile truly deserved the appellation *shining*. The boy who had laughed in delight when his little sister beat him at a game had grown into a youth whose serious demeanor could not conceal a genuine concern for the people around him.

"Greetings of the day, Your Highness," replied Kellas, and hastily added, "and to you, Lady Dannarah."

"Greetings of the day, Wolf Kellas," she answered.

"He is now Captain Kellas," said the king, shifting easily to the Hundred-speech so they all were speaking it. "He has just received a promotion for loyal service in the hunting of demons and other dangerous rebels, outlaws, and malcontents who threaten the peace and order of the Hundred."

"Did Captain Kellas fight a demon?" Dannarah asked with a breathless intensity that caused her father to give her a measuring look.

"Only my officers are privy to the information my silent wolves gather, Dannarah."

"You tell Atani!"

"Atani will become king after me."

She clasped her hands behind her back and lifted her chin defiantly. "Maybe it would serve Atani well to have a sister who supports him in everything because she knows as much about running the kingdom as he does."

"It's true, Papa." Atani did not have his sister's forceful personality, but his quiet manner masked a tranquil steadiness that Kellas admired even if others mistook it for weakness. "I tell Dannarah everything I'm allowed to. Why not treat her as my second in command?"

She elbowed her brother hard enough that he had to take a step sideways to balance. "You don't have to ask for me!"

"I'm not asking for you," he replied without the least sign of anger. "I'm asking for myself. There's no one I trust more than you, Dannarah."

"Hu!" exclaimed the king, more to himself than to either of them. "I may as well tell you that we have begun discussions about betrothing Dannarah to a Sirniakan prince and sending her south to the empire as a seal to a treaty between the Sirniakan Empire and us—"

"I won't go! Atani, tell Papa I won't go!"

She nudged him again but he said nothing, only frowned.

"We will discuss the matter another time when we aren't waiting to eat. Captain Kellas, you will join us."

The king beckoned to a file of stewards who had paused outside the pavilion. They swiftly unfolded trays, set them beside cushions, and arranged platters of food along a thick embroidered cloth. Others hung unlit lamps around the circumference in preparation for dusk. Only a few things would have made Kellas more uncomfortable than the prospect of dining with the king and his two eldest children, as Anjihosh's Qin officers often did, but of course having been given the order he could not excuse himself.

King Anjihosh seated himself on a cushion with Atani on one side and Dannarah on the other. Each had a tray placed to one side arranged with particular delicacies. "Very well, Dannarah, let us see how well you have paid attention to your lessons. What is a demon?"

Atani began to eat from a tray of freshly slip-fried noodles and vegetables with the air of a person who is both hungry and fairly certain he won't be disturbed for a while.

"There are two kinds of demons, ordinary demons and cloaked demons." Dannarah had her father's intensity of manner, although where his charisma was a contained and smooth vessel, hers always seemed on the verge of bursting out all over. "Demons look like people but they aren't really human, not like we are. In the tales told in the Hundred, ordinary demons are also called demon-hearts to distinguish them from blind-hearts. Blind-hearts is what humans are called in the old songs that describe the Eight Children of the Four Mothers—these are the eight children of the Hundred, the dragonlings, the firelings, the delvings, the wildings, the lendings, the merlings, the demon-hearts, and the blind-hearts—which I will not relate to you at this moment even though I have learned all eight of their songs by heart."

"My thanks," muttered Atani between mouthfuls. "You sound like a cat wailing when you sing."

"I do not, you pig!"

Anjihosh coughed, and both children immediately fell silent. He looked at Kellas. "Is the food not agreeable, Captain? Are you not hungry?"

"My apologies, Your Highness. I am honored to be asked to dine with you and to be honest rather overwhelmed."

"The chicken cooked in a sauce of ginger and pear is particularly flavorful today." The king nodded as if giving an order, then turned back to his daughter. "Go on, Dannarah. But confine your recitation to information about demons."

She absorbed this mild criticism with a fierce nod, a soldier eager to gain mastery as she drills. "Ordinary demons are called demon-hearts because they have strange abilities. Some can see or hear the wandering ghosts of the newly dead before their spirits pass to the other side. Some can hear the whisper of the earth's secret passageways or sense the changing patterns of the weather before the wind shifts. Some can understand the language of birds, and so on."

The pear-ginger sauce melted on Kellas's tongue, and he finally began to relax.

"Here in the Hundred these demon-hearts are called gods-touched and are granted wary respect. Usually they are dedicated to one of the temples of the seven gods. Some hide themselves, preferring to live an ordinary life. However, in the Sirniakan Empire, boys of twelve are tested for such sensitivities. Those who exhibit them are taken into the priesthood of Beltak the Shining One."

With a wry smile, the king considered the dumpling sitting plump on his spoon. "Although not every family wishes its sons to serve in that way. But that is neither here nor there, is it? Have you tried the custard buns, Captain? Go on, Dannarah."

The king signaled a steward to carry a platter heaped with warm buns over to Kellas.

"There are only nine cloaked demons. They were once known as Guardians. In the Tale of the Guardians they are said to have been born in the distant past out of Indiyabu, a mysterious lake, during a time of endemic war. They ride winged horses, can walk on the magical labyrinths called demon's coils, and can speak to other demons through the coils. The coils also give them nourishment, a liquid that is poisonous to humankind. The demon's skin they wear appears to our eyes as a silk cloak. It makes them impossible to kill unless you can cut the cloak off their body, which is very perilous because the cloak burns human flesh. But that's not what really makes them dangerous. People fear them because they can peer into the mind of any person and see their thoughts and dreams and memories. With their lies and lures they can coax people into any sort of terrible criminal act and rebellion. They hate your rule, Papa, because you have brought peace and prosperity and order to a land they once crushed under their evil gaze. But with patience and vigilance, and through harnessing the skill and loyalty of your Black Wolves, you have killed five, and driven the last four and their deluded followers into hiding."

When Kellas bit into the bun, custard gushed into his mouth and he had to close his eyes to savor the sensation.

"They are excellent, are they not?" remarked the king.

Kellas opened his eyes, embarrassed for feeling so out of place, and yet how could he not? Son of common artisans, he was eating with a man who was the exiled son of the previous Sirniakan emperor, now deceased, and also the nephew of the current ruler of the united Qin tribes and armies out in their grassland kingdom.

"Please understand that it is Qin custom for a commander to consider his loyal officers as kin," added the king, leaving Kellas with a sudden rarefied sense that his entire life had changed in a moment. If the king noticed his stunned expression he made no show of it, merely returned his attention to his daughter. "Now, Dannarah, is there anything else you wish to add? No? Atani?"

"Oh," said Atani, putting down his spoon, for he never disobeyed his father in the slightest particular. Over the years Kellas had come to consider the boy too determined to do everything without flaw in the hope of pleasing a daunting father whom everyone but the child could see doted on his son. "Let's see. The cloaked demons were once called Guardians—"

"I said that already," remarked Dannarah.

"But you didn't state why they used to be called Guardians. It's because they once claimed to be judges who flew a circuit of the Hundred on their winged horses, judging difficult criminal cases by means of looking into the hearts of the accused. That's how they gained so much power. By digging secrets out of the minds of unwilling people they could control them, and by this means they ruled the Hundred. That is why Papa had to overthrow them, because they used their cruel insight to foster disorder and injustice rather than to impose order and justice. That is why the Black Wolves are always on alert, trying to hunt down and kill all of them so they can never rise again."

Atani glanced at his father, clearly hoping for an approving word, but the king was frowning at a sight outside of the pavilion. He rose as a boy of about the same age as Atani and Dannarah, half Qin by his features, ran up and handed a slip of paper to one of the guards. The man examined it, sniffed it, and brought it to the king.

The king read its words. "It seems your mother's childbirth is proceeding more quickly than anyone expected. Captain Kellas, guard my two eldest children."

He descended the steps and strode off with all eight of his guards. Two Qin soldiers lingered, the personal bodyguards of Prince Atani. Dannarah had managed to shed the Sirniakan eunuch from the women's wing who was meant to attend her at all times. Yet the king had not left his children unguarded. It seemed that the disgraced young malcontent of eight years ago had, without intending to, climbed Law Rock into the very heart of the palace.

3

Atani covered the platters of uneaten food and got up. "I'm going, too."

Dannarah edged a glance toward Kellas, then shoved a dumpling around her tray with intense concentration.

"We shall all go," said Kellas, hoping he hadn't smeared any custard on his chin. He turned away for long enough to eat the rest of the bun because it was so soft and so delicious.

Shepherding the two young people out of the pavilion and across the spacious garden with its trimmed trees and blooming flowers put him in mind of being a cursed teacher at a temple filled with novices. This was a far cry from his recent mission in the western hills, but the king had elevated him to a position of trust Kellas could never betray.

Guard my two eldest children.

The palace was a sprawling compound remodeled from a council hall, emergency grain storehouses, and militia barracks built atop Law Rock, the promontory that overlooked the prosperous city of Toskala. When Queen Zayrah had arrived as a young bride for King Anjihosh sixteen years ago, she had brought her Sirniakan customs with her, which meant the palace women lived in a separate wing. Men like Kellas could never advance into the women's wing farther than the queen's formal audience chamber. Here, palace women like Zayrah who followed the Sirniakan custom seated themselves behind a lattice screen to receive visitors and to pray with the Beltak priests.

This chamber had been overrun by the children being raised in the palace, including the four younger daughters of King Anjihosh and Queen Zayrah. As soon as they entered, the three older of the girls swarmed Atani, calling his name, plucking at his sleeves, and talking all at once in Sirni. They were so close in age they seemed like triplets. Kellas found it difficult to tell their voices apart.

"Mama is sick and crying and they won't let us go in to see her. Is she going to die? Is the baby going to die like the other three did?"

The littlest girl—the fifth of the king's surviving daughters—wasn't yet old enough to speak. She attached herself to Atani's legs so tightly he couldn't walk.

"No, no, Mama is healthy. All will be well," he said, touching each one on the head, but his gaze met Dannarah's.

She gritted her teeth, and when he kept that steady stare fixed on her she made a face and, with a final, cutting glare as if to say she would despise her brother for the rest of existence, scooped up the toddler and carried her toward a private courtyard reserved for women. "Come with me, girls. We will go outside and practice our recitation. That will make the time pass."

Kellas watched them go. She certainly took after her father in her ability to command. When he looked back around Atani was dodging around the other overexcited children to get to the closed doors that let into the inner rooms. Kellas followed in time to see the prince halted by two Sirniakan eunuchs on guard duty.

"But I'm her son!" Atani was saying.

"Your Highness, we obey King Anjihosh and his gracious mother, Lady Irlin, who rules the women's quarters. The king himself gave us the order to allow no one in until the matter is resolved."

Atani opened his mouth to protest, noticed Kellas waiting at his elbow, and abruptly acquiesced. It was so typical of Atani. Dannarah would have pushed, but the young prince gave way.

"Wait here for me," he said to his two bodyguards. "Captain Kellas will walk me to the privy and I will return directly."

He walked back into the garden but instead of going to the privy he strolled along the perimeter with Kellas, walking a slow circuit as shadows crept over the ground. On their second round the prince halted where a stretch of hedge abutted a modest gate set into the garden wall.

"I need your help," he said in a low voice. "There's a way to climb in that Dannarah figured out. I need you to lift me up."

Who would have ever expected such defiance from Atani? But Kellas knew his duty.

"Your Highness, according to the custom of the palace you are a male who is now too old to walk in and out of the women's wing without permission from your grandmother. Furthermore the king has closed access, so you must obey him and stay out."

With flushed cheeks Atani lifted his chin, his dark gaze stormy and determined. "Mama is the queen and it should be her permission I need, not Grandmother's. Yet Grandmother rules the women's quarters. Besides that she is rude and dismissive toward Mama. It isn't right I'm not allowed in to give Mama support when neither Grandmother nor Papa love or respect her as they should. I am sorry to say such a thing, Captain Kellas. It is unfair to inflict on you my poor opinion of their affection. You know I love my father and admire and respect him above all other men. But it would be a lie to pretend my mother is not scorned by the very people who should care for and appreciate her the most. They believe her to be dull-witted because she is retiring and quiet, but anyone who studies the intricacy of her embroidery ought to be able to see the keen mind that lies beneath its patterns."

As this was the longest and most passionate speech Kellas had ever heard Atani give, he was too astounded to reply.

Nor did the prince wait. "I command you to help me. No fault will fall on you."

"Unless the king discovers all."

"What you say afterward I leave to your discretion, but you cannot refuse a direct order from me. Dannarah and I know a hidden way to creep through the women's wing. We do it all the time. You of all people should be able to sneak around where you aren't allowed without being caught."

What hidden mischief lurked in the boy! Kellas's resolve wavered. The hells! He could never resist a challenge, the more foolhardy the better.

"Very well, Your Highness."

"Don't worry, I will protect you," said the boy with all the certitude of a youth who has never suffered more than a skinned knee. He glanced around the garden. With all the anticipation fluttering around the entry to the women's wing, no one was looking their way. Besides that, he had cleverly delayed until twilight shadowed the garden.

A puzzle lock bound the gate's latch. Atani made quick work of it. They slipped into a large deserted square whose only building was a round four-story tower with windows shuttered and front doors chained shut: the old Assizes Tower. Next to it a long granary once used to store emergency rice had been converted into the women's wing. Kellas gave Atani a boost up onto its lower roof, then easily pulled himself up after. It was almost dark but Kellas had infiltrated buildings so often by roof that he had no trouble edging after Atani's dark form. Bars blocked the ventilation gaps between the eaves of the upper and lower roofs, but Atani shifted aside a set of bars and squirmed in. Feeling his way, Kellas followed him into a crawl space just high enough for a body to fit through.

Voices murmured from all sides. The faint glow of lamplight drew horizons on the crawl space and the even narrower ventilation shafts. Warehouses had to be built with a good flow of air, but this easy security breach was outrageous.

He bumped into a sandaled foot, and slid forward beside the prince. A barred gap gave them a view onto a lamplit chamber below. A set of doors opened onto a farther room, out of which Kellas heard a woman murmuring encouraging words and the occasional gasp and hoarse comment from the laboring queen.

In the room below Anjihosh faced his mother, Lady Irlin. A princess of the Qin, she had survived over thirty years as a foreigner inside the Sirniakan palace with its deadly infighting among the emperor's wives. She was the one person Kellas hoped he never, ever had to take orders from.

"According to Qin custom, a father does not see his newborn child until seven days have passed," she was saying in the Qin language. "You should not even be here, Anji."

"You have forced this breach of custom on me, Mother."

"How can you accuse *me* of misdoing?"

"Because I have the right in this matter. Qin custom gives the *father* the obligation to judge if his children are whole and without blemish. On my head falls the burden of whether my children live or die. It is not yours to choose."

"You are too softhearted, Anji. It is a good thing you were away from the palace when the first boy was born or you might have let him live. Fortunately I was here and did what is necessary."

"I do what is necessary," Anjihosh retorted in a defensive tone so unlike his cool and commanding demeanor that Kellas winced. "When the deformed girl child was born, I smothered her with my own hands as is a father's obligation."

"And the second boy? Did you kill him, too, according to our agreement that any male child out of Zayrah has to die?"

"Do not accuse me of weakness. Need I remind you I would be dead, or a wandering exile, if I had not carved a home here in the Hundred?"

"Need I remind you that you are alive at all because I gave birth to you? Because I smuggled you out of the emperor's palace when you were twelve, and sent you to be raised by my brother?"

"Yes, Mother, I am alive because of you. That is why I did my duty in the matter of marriage, according to your command. That is why I gave up the finest and most valuable treasure I ever possessed, because I am an obedient son."

"As I recall the treasure insulted you most egregiously and took herself off."

"Because you refused to respect her and then tried to kill her. She would have stayed with me if you hadn't interfered. I could have smoothed a path and worked it out. I could have made the marriage alliance with the empire *and* kept her."

"Believe the story you tell yourself if it soothes your pride.

I wish I had destroyed that impertinent fruit seller when I had the chance."

"You certainly tried! The day I hear she has been tampered with in any way is the day I send you to live alone on a country estate. She will not be touched by you or anyone. No one but me determines death and life in the Hundred."

"Ah, I see it now. This is about your vanity, not your pride. You have decided that if you cannot have her then no man can."

An abrupt silence from the far chamber caused the king to turn and Lady Irlin to take a step toward the open doors, which the king blocked by moving in front of her. Atani's hand came to rest on Kellas's fingers, squeezing so hard the lad began trembling.

Kellas had too much experience to be shocked, or at least not while he was in action. His training had kicked in, neatly sorting the conversation away to be considered later.

A newborn wailed.

The king hurried into the birthing chamber.

In a ragged, frightened voice, a woman in the far chamber said, "It is a girl, is it not? Let me see her. Pray let it be healthy and a girl so you do not kill this one, too."

Lady Irlin turned to beckon to one of her eunuchs, a richly dressed man Kellas recognized as serving high in the palace hierarchy. The light fell full on her face. She was Qin through and through, unlike her son whose features blended his mother's wide Qin cheekbones and distinctive eyes and his father's Sirniakan complexion and curly black hair. Her face wore its lines of age easily, as if her seventy years dwelled restfully with her. She had square shoulders as yet unbent by care or age, a woman entirely sure of herself and her place in the world.

She switched to Sirni, the language most often used in the palace, speaking in a low voice so as not to be heard in the birthing chamber.

"I have wondered for years if that second boy-child born to Zayrah was really stillborn, or if Anji only said he was and instead had him smuggled out of the palace to escape his ordained fate. I have excused my son's sentimental whims for long enough. They have become a danger to Atani. It is time to act. Send a trusted agent."

"The second boy was born eight years ago, Lady. How can we know where to look after so much time has passed?"

"Start in Salya. If your agent finds the boy alive, kill it. But leave all else alone."

"A girl, by all appearances whole and without blemish," said Anjihosh from the far chamber, and the queen began to weep with exhausted relief.

Atani scraped backward, noisier than Kellas was as he cautiously followed. By the time they reached the garden it had fallen into full night illuminated by fragile beacons of lamplight. Atani tugged agitatedly at his rumpled clothing.

"Did you hear what they said?" the prince hissed. "Everyone knows Mama has had three stillborn children. I remember the girl because I was nine that year. Father took me to look at her corpse. Her head looked wrong, and he told me it was merciful for such a child to die quickly rather than suffering. I thought that was what must have happened with the two boys, too, that I just wasn't old enough when they were born to be allowed to see them. But Grandmother just said *she* killed the first boy only because it was a boy. She told her attendant she thinks the second boy is still alive. Isn't that what you heard?"

"I only learned to speak Sirni and Qin when I began training as a Wolf, Your Highness. I don't always catch the nuances."

"They discussed a woman. I've never heard of there being another woman. Father called her his 'treasure.'" Atani glared at the ground, hands clenched as he whispered indignantly, "Mother should be his treasure."

"Your Highness?"

The boy rubbed his face, then looked up with an angry shake of his head. "Grandmother told her servant to send an agent to track down and murder this second boy if he's found alive. Why would an eight-year-old boy be a danger to me? It's not as if I'm the heir to the Sirniakan Empire and have to kill all the other contenders for the throne!"

"Quietly, Your Highness." Kellas had most of his attention on listening: Celebratory choral singing in the Qin style. A rumble of festive drums in the Hundred manner. A priest's voice raised in a flowery hymn of praise to Beltak the Shining One in whose mercy the innocent and frail are sheltered, as the Sirniakans who had come with Queen Zayrah made their prayers. No sign of alarm about Atani. No one had noticed their brief disappearance. He temporized. "I don't know these things. I am only a Wolf."

"That's right, this is my responsibility and I will take care of it," said the prince with a quiet assurance that made Kellas feel he had badly underestimated the youth. Atani met his gaze, held it. His dark eyes seemed as deep as oceans. "You will say nothing to my father of what just happened."

Before Kellas could think of what to reply, the prince's Qin bodyguards trotted up, looking exactly as alarmed as they ought, having lost track of their charge in a most shocking way. Really, anything could have happened to Atani! Kellas was a captain now and had the right to say whatever he pleased to the lower ranks.

"I have just conducted a test of how well you guard the prince. Both of you have failed."

Atani cast an unfathomable glance at Kellas before addressing his guards. "I was too nervous to remain inside with all the incense and chatter. Captain Kellas kept me occupied out here.

I will go see my mother now, if they will deign to let me in. Captain Kellas, you have your orders."

He walked away, flanked by his guards.

The hells! He admired Atani's subtle reprimand, even if he could not agree with the prince's leniency toward men charged with protecting him. He looked around the lit courtyard. Servants were laying tables with food and drink, and the celebration looked ready to go on all night. Surely he had not heard the king and his mother discussing the murder of innocent babies. Queen Zayrah had given birth to seven daughters and three sons, and it was in no way remarkable that three infants had not survived their early days. His own mother had lost two of her seven children.

The many days of travel from Asharat Valley to Toskala had fatigued him. He was losing his edge, and needed to rest, but had no cursed idea who a newly coined officer reported to.

"Captain Kellas?" A Qin officer who walked with a marked limp approached him. "I'm Chief Seren, quartermaster for the Black Wolves. You're being assigned new quarters. You'll be moving from the barracks to the palace."

"As captain will I be allowed a staff? There is a clever young Wolf named Oyard I would like to have assigned to me, if that's possible."

"We'll discuss it later. For now, come with me."

Kellas had so few possessions that the move to a tiny closet of a room all to himself was quickly managed. He slept deeply and without remembering his dreams.

In the morning he sought out the on-duty officers' mess, where the on-duty officers—all Qin—greeted him politely enough but with astounded disbelief when he informed them he was thirty and not yet married. Like Chief Jagi, the Qin who had come to the Hundred with Anjihosh had married local women, and they immediately began suggesting relatives of their wives who might be interested in a man elevated by the king himself to an officer's rank.

"The king likes his officers to be married," said Chief Seren when Kellas met with him later that day to discuss Kellas's interim duties. "But I know your Hundred customs are different."

"Given the nature of my work I have simply not had time to think about such matters." He considered his next statement carefully, wanting to protect Atani and Dannarah without getting them into trouble. "If you don't mind my saying so, Chief Seren, I would like to do a security check of every foundation, wall, and roof of each building in the palace complex to make sure there are no overlooked gaps."

Seren wasn't that much older than Kellas, but his status as one of Anjihosh's original Qin company made him a dangerous man to annoy.

"Do you think we aren't capable of protecting our commander, Captain Kellas?"

Kellas favored him with his friendliest smile. "I'll stake you a year of drink at your favorite tavern if you or your men can find a physical breach before I do. You can start—I don't know—with the women's wing since I'm not allowed there anyway, and I'll start with the barracks."

"You're very sure of yourself."

"I think I've earned that right."

Seren stared him down, then laughed and leaned over to slap him on the shoulder. "You are the man who climbed Law Rock without a rope and at night. Very well. I accept your wager."

Thus it was that a week later Kellas was buying drinks for Seren, and hearing the story of how he had gotten the wound that crippled his leg, when one of the king's personal bodyguard approached their table.

"Captain Kellas, the king wants you right now."

As night fell the two men climbed the Thousand Steps that led from the city up Law Rock to the palace. From the steps Kellas could see the cliff face he had climbed eight years ago, not that there was any trace of his effort. Guards descended to meet them, bearing lanterns. In the city below gleams of light flared to mark night-watch stations, and handheld lanterns bobbed along the streets as folk hurried about their early-evening business.

King Anjihosh waited for him in the garden pavilion. His gaze would have struck an unprepared man dead.

"My son and his two personal guards have gone missing. I understand that at your insistence we have discovered certain breaches in the security of the palace structures. Most specifically entry to a crawl space in the women's wing. Lady Dannarah has confessed to me personally that she and her brother created the entry. How is it you suspected and did not tell me?"

Kellas wondered if this was how death would come: He would tell Anjihosh what he should have told him seven days ago and then he would be executed and have his body hung from a post as a reminder that you did not disobey the king even at the order of his son. His cursed life belonged to the king regardless. The hells! Death would come, and then it would be over.

"I was trying to protect Prince Atani and Princess Dannarah, Your Highness."

"From my wrath?"

"Something like that. Once I discovered the breach I thought it best to close it without implicating the prince or his bodyguards. Do you think Prince Atani was abducted, Your Highness?"

"Do you have any reason to believe he was not? You know who my enemies are."

Kellas checked his topknot, suddenly wondering if it was

fixed correctly, no hair out of place, the way the king's hair and clothing always were. The nervous gesture betrayed him.

"If you think there is any chance Atani left for reasons that would cause him to hide his departure not only from me but also from his mother and his sister, let me know now. Because if he was abducted by demons, I will tear apart the Hundred to find my son, and I will not be merciful."

Kellas caught himself before he took a step back. "Atani and I overheard a conversation between you and Lady Irlin, and another afterward between her and her steward."

As he related the exchange, the king grew more still and more ominous.

When Kellas finished, Anjihosh drew the whip from his belt and pulled it through his fingers as if each knot were a whisper of memory. Like all his Black Wolves, like Kellas, the king wore a ring formed into the shape of the head of a wolf.

Touching his ring, Anjihosh gave a little nod, as to himself, then looked at Kellas.

"Atani can be more persuasive than he realizes so I don't fault you for obeying him, this time. From now on, come to me immediately. As for Atani, I know where he will end up. It's likely he's gone overland to the province of Mar, to a port town called Salya. Find Atani, and kill my mother's agent before he has a chance to carry out her orders. I expect you will find those two matters can be achieved in the same place. Return here immediately. All that you learn you will share only with me."

He went on with the relentless cold dispassion of a man who is furious but will never let you see it until the moment he decides to kill you for crossing him.

"Captain Kellas, I assign you now and permanently as captain of my son's personal guard. We are never safe. Demons walk boldly among us, hiding in plain sight. Rebels and agitators work with those demons to overturn the peace and order we restored with so much blood and toil. As one of the Black Wolves you have devoted yourself not to glory but to maintaining order in the Hundred. Beyond that and most especially, I now command you to dedicate your life and indeed your honor to protecting my son."

4

Dannarah endured her mother's weeping until she was ready to scream with frustration. How she hated having to sit and wait as others took action!

Queen Zayrah reclined on a couch with her daughters and attendants clustered around her while Dannarah stood poised by the door ready to take flight the instant she had a chance. From behind a screen, the queen's favored priest chanted a prayer to Beltak, the Shining One Who Rules Alone.

"Let all who pray to the Resplendent, the Glorious Beltak, discover the strength to walk the path of right action and the courage to stand upright for justice. We are humble before the Shining One's gracious majesty. We are small yet each one held within the shelter of His righteous power. We are afraid but in His hands we are given courage."

The priest's melodious voice faltered when the queen drew in a shuddering breath as prelude to a sob.

Everyone tensed and looked at Mama, just as if she was the only one suffering the pain of Atani's disappearance. Not one person had asked Dannarah how she felt or if she cried in her bed at night. No one thought she cried at all, but to contemplate the palace without Atani made tears sting in her eyes even here where anyone might see and comment. She didn't want their sympathy!

The queen did not sob after all. Instead, she gathered two-year-old Sadah and the newborn girl—still unnamed—to her breast and embraced them tenderly as the older girls knelt before her to pat her arms and kiss her face. Crying had turned her mother's nose red, and her hair was tangled and unkempt like that of a mourner instead of elaborately coiffed and adorned by a tiered headdress appropriate to a noblewoman.

Yet her mother's disarray felt righteous to Dannarah. Every time she had seen Papa in the last three days he had looked exactly the same as always: clothes neat and tidy, hair perfectly done up in a topknot, face impassive. Whatever else she might be, Mama did not really care what people thought of her because she assumed they did not think of her at all.

A sudden rush of affection surprised Dannarah. She took a step toward the couch but halted when the priest unexpectedly spoke.

"Take heart, Gracious Queen. The prince will be found. I am sure of it."

His kind voice made Dannarah feel heartened for the first time since Atani had vanished. Papa would never let Atani be stolen from them.

With every gaze fixed on the couch, Dannarah saw her opening. She slid sideways into the servants' passage, mercifully empty at this moment, and ran along the narrow corridor to the entry into the bedchamber she shared with her sisters. Normally an attendant worked in the spacious chamber at all times, sewing or cleaning or ready to run errands, but the emergency had torn everyone's attention to the queen for once. At fifteen, Dannarah was allowed a single small locked chest, a privacy her younger sisters had not yet earned. Mostly she kept her school-books and writing implements there, away from the disapproving gaze of her mother and the other Sirni women. In Sirniaka, noblewomen did not learn to read and write, but Papa had allowed her to be tutored alongside Atani despite Mama's endless complaints that such masculine learning would make Dannarah unsuitable for an advantageous marriage in the empire.

As if she wanted to get married, hauled off like a cow to be bred to some tiresome bull of a man!

She lifted out the books, then opened the cedarwood box nestled beneath them where she stored a set of exquisitely carved ivory playing pieces. She traced the tiny bows and ribbons and filigrees as her tears dripped onto the miniature animals she and Atani had once spent so many hours playing with. With a hard sniff, she roughly wiped her cheeks with the back of a hand and was about to close the box when she spotted a black braided cord wrapped around one of the carved horses. A flush warmed her cheeks. It was one of three cords that had come loose from Kellas's formal uniform last year when he was making an official report to the king in the King's Audience Hall. Papa had reprimanded Kellas for sartorial laxness while Dannarah, allowed to sit with Atani when Papa heard reports from his officers, had managed to sneak her slipper over one of the cords and slide it away with no one the wiser.

No one but Atani, of course, but he knew everything and would never tell.

She doubled over as if she had been kicked in the gut, her head coming to rest on the rim of the chest. She couldn't find a way to breathe. If he had been kidnapped by demons she would stalk the Hundred until she had torn his murderers to pieces and scattered their bones to the four winds.

Calm. Find calm. Draw a lesson from those who accomplished their work to her father's exacting standards.

She picked up the braided cord and touched it to her cheek as if it carried the essence of Kellas in its threads. But after only a moment, grimacing, she set it aside, angry at herself for having such a stupid infatuation with a man who never even looked at her except because he served Papa.

A full set of servant's clothing lay folded at the bottom of the chest together with one of the special brass tokens only the palace servants were allowed to carry. She stripped out of the long embroidered jacket and belled silk trousers that were everyday wear for palace women and pulled on the light servant's garments: baggy cotton trousers and a knee-length muslin shift over which she bound a vest fitted for a woman that she was just beginning to fill out. She wrapped her hair under a scarf and kept its ends loose over her shoulders in case she needed to conceal her face.

She picked up a hand mirror from a side table to look at herself, but a glance was enough to make her hastily set the mirror back down. At the last minute she looped the black cord onto her belt, like a woman might who was carrying a memento of her lover. She could pretend just for now, couldn't she?

After layering everything else back into the chest she locked it and hurried out the servants' passage past the indoor kitchen, the outdoor kitchen, the weaving house, and the grain storage. Here she grabbed a basket from an unattended shed and stuffed it full of random items. Because she was dressed as a servant and few men ever saw the faces of the palace women, she had no trouble flashing the token and walking out the palace servants' gate as if she were a commonplace girl about a commonplace delivery. Servant women could walk about as they wished. Down in the city women went about just like men. No one remarked on it at all. That was the custom of the Hundred.

Everything was different in the palace because the women had to abide by Sirni tradition even though they all actually lived in the Hundred, not in the empire.

After her father had saved the land known as the Hundred

from the terrible demon war that had almost destroyed it, he had established his palace and thus his base of power atop the famously unclimbable Law Rock. Bounded by cliffs on all sides, Law Rock was a rocky promontory at the confluence of two rivers. Its flat plateau had long housed the city of Toskala's Assizes Tower, council house, emergency grain warehouses, the actual rock stele on which the old laws of the Hundred were carved, and a reeve hall from which a chief marshal administered the six reeve halls spread throughout the land.

The sun shone hot on the wide, dusty plaza at the center of all the buildings. Striding across the open space with the wind in her face and the sun in her eyes made her spirit swell. The air smelled better out here, fresh and new instead of dense with spicy fragrances that got into her nose and made her sneeze.

In the distance, toward what everyone called the "prow" of the promontory, workmen were laying in stone patios and walkways in preparation for erecting a formal Beltak shrine, Papa's gift to placate Mama. Over toward the broader "stern" end, near the gate to the Thousand Steps, a company of one hundred Black Wolves drilled, but she didn't dare pause to watch for fear of drawing attention to herself. It wasn't that she wanted to be a soldier, but every morning she woke up with a yearning. Why was it too much to ask that she be allowed the same choices Atani had? He trained, and in private showed her the drills he'd learned. How she hated living her life secondhand!

As she approached the huge double gates to the reeve hall she gripped the basket more tightly against her hip. Her breathing came faster, and she bit her lower lip. She had sneaked out of the palace numerous times with Atani but never alone. Everything was easier with him because he knew how to smooth things over with people, how to guess their intentions and nudge them along the path he wanted them to go. Even Papa underestimated Atani's skills because he was so quiet and thoughtful.

A boastful, arrogant brother would have been unendurable on top of everything else.

"Verea?" A guard at the reeve hall gate gestured to her, asking a question in the lift of his fingers.

She smiled—that was simple!—and showed the token and the basket.

"Delivery," she said in the language people spoke in the Hundred, which she had insisted on learning even though Mama could still only speak Sirni after sixteen years living in the Hundred.

The guard chuckled as at a shared joke. "Pass through, verea."

Victorious! She sauntered under the massive wooden lintel with its carved eagles and immediately cut right to a little passage she and Atani had discovered the second time they had sneaked into the reeve hall pretending to be servants. She ditched the basket in a closet and climbed a dusty ladder to a niche in the wall where she could crouch and look over the reeve hall's parade ground.

Several eagles circled high overhead. At least four reeves flew sentry duty at all times during the day. They soared so effortlessly, the way she wished she could, if only she had wings.

Fortune was with her. Just as she settled more comfortably onto her haunches, prepared for a wait, one of the giant eagles descended for a landing. The speed with which the raptor dove caused the hairs on the back of her neck to stand on end with excitement. At the last possible instant it spread its wings to brake and thumped down on a huge perch.

Its reeve—a woman!—dangled below the eagle's body in a harness that wrapped hips, torso, and shoulders. The reeve unhooked and dropped to the ground with practiced confidence. Fawkners—the brave people who helped care for the huge eagles—approached with whistles and signals from their batons, so the eagle wouldn't be surprised and strike.

The reeve had a pouch of dispatches buckled on her harness,

bumping against her back beside a quiver packed with signal flags and reeve's baton, and she hooded the eagle and traded words with the head fawkner before hurrying off to make her delivery to the hall marshal.

"They are impressive creatures," said her father in a low voice, settling cross-legged beside her where Atani usually sat.

She jerked so hard he grabbed her arm reflexively, then let go.

He went on. "But I believe the fawkners are the bravest of all. Reeves have a bond with their eagles—"

"They are jessed to them," she said eagerly. "That's what they call it."

"I have seen enough of eagles and reeves to believe it is true some kind of intangible thread binds the one to the other. Fawkners have no such jess. They do the work even knowing an eagle might turn against them. It's dangerous, as anyone can see by the scars most fawkners bear."

"Eagles never kill their reeves," she added, forgetting her surprise over her father's presence as she leaned forward to get a better look while a big door was shoved open in one of the tall buildings called lofts.

Was there a hooded eagle at rest inside?

"Sometimes eagles do kill their reeves, but it's rare. Could you risk that, Dannarah?"

"I want wings," she breathed. "Can you make me a reeve, Papa?"

When he did not reply she glanced at him. The way he wrinkled his brow made him look pensive, and that surprised her enough that she shifted, and accidentally bumped his knee with hers, and he shook himself.

"Alas, no, little eaglet. Some things even the king cannot command. If an eagle jesses you, you will be a reeve. If one does not, then nothing I do can change that."

She sighed with a great heave of her shoulders. "How did you find me here?"

He copied her sigh, and that made her smile just a little, and only when he saw the smile did he go on. "Dannarah, do you think I don't know everything that goes on in the Hundred? What do you think my Wolves are for? I know about all the mischief you and Atani get up to."

"You didn't know about the secret way Atani and I made into the roof of the women's wing."

"That I did not, and I wish I had. I'll have to be more alert."

"Did I outwit you, Papa?"

His rare smile flashed. "That you did, little eaglet. Now I think we need to get back before your mother thinks you have also gone missing. She has enough to weep over."

"She doesn't care about me!"

"You are quite wrong about that, Dannarah. It's just you are so different from her that she struggles to understand you."

"How am I different? I'm like you, Papa!"

"Yes, you are."

He did not move to leave, though, instead watching the fawkners' careful examination of the eagle's feathers as they shucked the raptor out of its harness. So she did not move, either, savoring the unusual opportunity to sit with him alone, to be the sole center of his attention. He could bide in perfect silence, thinking about what she could not imagine, although right now by the frown that kept tugging down his lips she supposed he was thinking of Atani.

In a low voice she said, "Maybe it would have been less cruel to refuse me all these things you've given me, Papa."

"What do you mean?"

"If you had agreed to Mama's strictures in all their measure then I wouldn't dream of things I can't have. Like you taking Atani on a circuit of the Hundred next season while I, as always, will be left behind and stuck here. I mean—"

Suddenly she realized what an awful thing she had said. A

miasma of dread seized her. She tried to swallow but it was like choking down rocks.

"I mean…Atani…if Atani isn't…"

Dead.

Instead of replying his eyes narrowed with a look that always indicated his displeasure. He reached out and between two fingers caught the braided cord, tugged on it just hard enough to note how it was looped to her belt, and finally raised his eyes to meet hers.

She flushed, a blaze of heat in her cheeks.

He released the cord. "I've already let your mother know, and now I'll tell you. I've sent Captain Kellas to track down Atani."

She clapped both hands to her chest. "Captain Kellas will find him!"

His eyes were still narrowed. "If anyone can, he can, yes."

"Do *you* think he'll find Atani?"

He shrugged one shoulder. "Let us never tempt fortune by claiming we know what the future holds. But I think it likely."

She covered her face with her hands so he wouldn't see her tears, and he allowed her the silence to compose herself. But when at length she lowered her hands and sniffed, he did not wipe away the tears as Mama would have done. He considered her gravely.

"Dannarah, never forget that a king wields many weapons, and some of them are men. The soldiers I command are sometimes kinsmen but most, however valuable, are expendable in the service of victory. Do not deploy them lightly, or incompetently. Do not waste them, because the best ones take far more time to train than they do to die. But never mistake them for something they are not. Do you understand me?"

She stared at her hands and wondered how red her face was and if he was going to take the braided cord away and embarrass her even more.

Instead he coughed slightly, as at a change of subject.

"As for riding a circuit of the Hundred, yes, I think after all I will take you and Atani together. How would you like that?"

"Papa!" She grabbed his hands and surprised another smile from him, then hated herself for being happy at such a time.

"When Atani returns," he added.

Even her brave father would not say the word they all feared. If Atani returns.

If.

5

Even traveling at speed, carrying an official pass that allowed him to trade off for a new mount whenever he needed one, it took Kellas twenty days to ride south to the province of Mar. None of the way stations or village inns along the route revealed any trace of the prince and his guardsmen, but he collected stories of a solitary foreign traveler with a taciturn disposition and plenty of coin who might be Lady Irlin's agent. Kellas was running seven, then six, then five days behind the man.

Upon arriving in the port town of Salya, Kellas scouted the many inns along the waterfront. He wanted the agent to get wind someone was asking after him; it might flush him out or impel him to act precipitously and thus clumsily. By the time he had worked his way up and then down the main street, called Drunk's Lane in honor of the sailors who frequented the town, he had identified and dismissed several suspects. Finally he settled on the spacious veranda of an inn overlooking the scenic harbor, considering his next move.

The view over the Bay of Messalia had such a calming beauty that it distracted him when he ought to have been most alert. The wide waters shone with the vivid blue-green facets of a molten jewel. Scraps of clouds hung like tantalizing wisps on the horizon where they piled up over the outer islands, too far away to see with the naked eye. He had run his first assignment as a silent wolf here, eight years ago. Together with his senior comrade Esisha, he had paddled and swum across this bay to an island, unseen from here, where lay the reeve compound known as Bronze Hall. Then, after he had stolen a dispatch pouch and Esisha had murdered the marshal of Bronze Hall, they had swum and paddled back. Afterward on this very street he had noticed a woman...

As if thoughts could summon substance—or as if his mind had registered her presence and caused his memory to alert him—she appeared.

She wove confidently through the bustling crowds of people moving up and down the main thoroughfare that ran from the harbor up into the higher hill terraces of the town. Because she was an outlander her features stood out, but it was her striking beauty—the astonishing symmetry of her features, the perfect bow of her eyebrows and lustrous darkness of her eyelashes, the slim pillar of her neck—that fixed the eye.

A passing string of pack mules cut her off from his view.

Setting down his barely touched mug of ale, he passed a coin to the server, pulled a faded laborer's cap low over his head, and descended steps from the veranda onto the street. King Anjihosh had given the mysterious woman no name; he had refused to give any details at all, only that he was certain Atani would by one means or another end up at her household, called Plum Blossom Clan.

Until this unexpected glimpse of her Kellas had not fully put together the obvious fact that the woman he had glancingly met eight years ago was the same woman the king and his mother had been talking about, the finest and most valuable treasure Anjihosh had ever possessed if his claim was not merely an exaggeration meant to annoy Lady Irlin.

When he considered his relationship with his own demanding mother, Kellas felt a fair bit of sympathy for the king. He'd been scalded by his mother's blunt assessments of his failures more than once. No wonder he'd developed a habit of reckless risk taking.

The treasure had been in the center of the street, headed uphill, and because she was walking with four companions who included two children they weren't moving fast. Falling neatly in behind a man pulling a cart loaded with bolts of cloth, he got a better look at her from behind. Her thick black hair curled like a shell onto the back of her head, adorned with a cleverly woven five-petaled wheel of plum-colored ribbons. She wore the typical dress of Hundred women, called a taloos, a length of cloth wrapped with cunning twists and folds around a body to best emphasize the curves of the female form, or so he always thought. Certainly her hips twitched side-to-side in a pleasing way as she climbed the steepening avenue. The spectacular quality of the weave and its rich emerald-green hue suggested a woman who had the taste and coin to dress herself in expensive silk even for an everyday expedition to the market. Given the net bags filled with fruit and vegetables she and her companions carried, they had just been buying food for the day's supper. With her walked a taller woman midway through pregnancy, and a boy and a girl each about eight years of age. The boy had curly black hair and an eagle's nose; except for the laughing smile on his brightly cheerful face he looked a lot like Dannarah. The group was so cursedly vulnerable, walking along without the least idea someone was stalking them. Lady Irlin's agent could leap out from the middle of the crowd and easily stab the boy.

Only then did Kellas really look at the fifth person in the little group.

Only then—so late!—did he recognize the youth who strode beside the woman, head bent toward her and listening in the intent way that endeared Prince Atani to so many.

The hells!

A single look at the youth and the woman, profiles side by side, revealed exactly what King Anjihosh had kept secret for so many years.

As if the woman felt his gaze on their backs, she turned her head to glance behind. Kellas ducked down so the cartman's stout form obscured him. He retreated to a side street and stood there on the shade side of the street trying to take slow, steadying breaths, but his heart still pounded and his pulse roared in his ears.

The hells.

Unless he was badly mistaken, Atani was this woman's child, not Queen Zayrah's, even though everyone called Atani the eldest child of Anjihosh and Zayrah.

Well, and after all, why did it matter? Anjihosh was king. His son would become king after him. As far as Kellas could make out, in the Sirniakan Empire a child's father and his kinship line were of paramount importance, not like here in the Hundred where a person was known equally by kinship from both mother and father but a mother's claim came first.

When he thought about how calmly Lady Irlin had spoken of the need to murder any boy-child born out of Queen Zayrah, sweat broke down his neck and back. He had killed a few people on the king's orders, but never children. What would he do the day the king ordered him to kill a child? How could he be sure he would never be given such an order by a man who had smothered his own newborn daughter, whatever excuse he had made?

Who was to say he had not already been the agent of a child's death? What happened to the children of the people he silently executed in the king's name? How did their lives proceed afterward? Death was not the only way to destroy a life. He hadn't bothered to think about it quite so directly before. Serving the king on behalf of order and prosperity had been enough.

He gave up on the usual disciplines he used to focus and sought out a street vendor selling coconut milk flavored with cinnamon. The sweet, cool liquid drained the last of the rush out of him and he could at last breathe normally.

Afterward he went to the market and from a stall that sold used clothing bought a pair of loose sailor's trousers, faded, and a mended cotton sleeveless laborer's vest. Laborers' clothing in the city of Toskala had tiny differences from what men wore here in the south. Little details mattered. If Lady Irlin's agent heard a man had been asking questions in the inns, he would be looking for a man dressed like a city man, not a sailor. People got stuck seeing what they expected to see and often did not look beyond hairstyle and garments. A good infiltrator disguised himself in plain sight.

Returning to the inn he was actually staying at, he took an early meal of spicy fish and noodle soup in a tamarind broth garnished with mint. As he ate he struck up a conversation about his travels with the congenial server.

"Cloudy today."

The old man gestured to the clouds pushing in from the east and inhaled deeply. "It'll rain hard tonight, mark my words. Maybe high winds and a storm, too. Feel the pinch of that breeze?"

"Last time we came into port we got caught in a storm out past the islands that tore our sails to ribbons."

Because it was midafternoon and custom was slow, the server lingered, clearly bored enough to find Kellas's tale more engaging than washing dishes in the back.

"We barely limped into port, and we were just fortunate our cargo chests held tight because we were carrying silk, and water getting in would have ruined the cloth. We sold the cargo to one of the merchant clans here... I can't recall the name of the clan although I remember they flew a banner with flowers on it. I could scarcely forget the woman who did the negotiating because she was so young and pretty."

"Whsst! You must mean Plum Blossom Clan. That would be Mistress Mai. *Mai.* What kind of name is that for a woman, I ask you? Sounds more like the number 'one' in the trade language outlanders speak. I wouldn't call her pretty, though."

Kellas blinked out of sheer surprise. "You wouldn't?"

"Neh. My granddaughters are pretty. Smart girls, too, I'm that proud of them. But that woman is beautiful. Not just in her face, in her spirit as well. The gods may favor any person with attractive features but what lies beneath is the true measure of them."

"True enough!" agreed Kellas, and used the opening to veer the conversation onto a girl he'd once fallen for who had turned out to only want his coin, a story he made so tedious that the old man excused himself.

"I've got to get the awnings rolled out if there's rain coming."

Kellas thoughtfully finished his soup. He spent coin for a bath, tied his hair up in a club, dressed in the sailor's clothing, sheathed one knife at his belt and two more in his boots, and strapped on a pouch containing various small tools. At dusk he made his way up the main thoroughfare to the highest terraces, where the wealthier people had their homes. Like all residential streets in Salya the quiet lane where she lived had walled compounds on either side, the walls high enough to hide their buildings and gardens. The public face of each household was a long veranda where visitors could meet and visit without entering the intimate private chambers within. These verandas boasted splendid views over the lower city and the bay although no one was sitting out on them now. At dusk people were inside eating their last meal of the day.

The only other piece of information the king had volunteered was that the compound was guarded day and night by special agents under personal order from the king, identifiable by their red caps. The first thing Kellas had done after arriving was to scout out the red caps: One kept watch over the alley that ran along the back walls of the compounds, while another stood right out in plain view of the veranda to mark who entered and left.

Setting a guard on a woman's household was a cursed odd thing, when he really got to thinking about it.

Kellas strolled up to the red cap on duty. Dusk made it impossible to make out his features until he got within a few paces. Abruptly recognizing the man's frowning face, Kellas shifted tactics.

"Heya, Feyard. How are things?" He smiled, trying to remove any sting of pity. "I didn't know you'd drawn this duty."

Whatever the hells this duty was.

"Have we met?" The man had a way of hunching his left shoulder that made him look like he was about to duck. "I don't know you, do I?"

"We trained together in Nessumara, in the Year of the White Crane. I'm Kellas."

Feyard squinted, then said, "Hu! So we did. I remember you now."

"The basket moon breathed her last under the Shiver Sky." Kellas trotted out the code phrase and waited as the other man's eyes narrowed.

"Then the sun rose," Feyard answered, then shook his head disbelievingly. "You're a red cap now? I thought only those of us too good for the regular army but not quite good enough to make the cut as silent wolves got stuck with this duty. Everyone was sure you were destined for great things. I never saw anyone who could climb like you."

"I'm not here to relieve you. I'm here about that youth who is in the house now. Have you seen him? A good-looking boy, sixteen."

"Ah. That one. Handsome lad." He clucked his tongue mournfully.

"Does he have any companions with him?" Kellas still had not found the two Qin bodyguards.

"Neh. He showed up alone. Took me by surprise but you can tell the lad's an outlander, can't you? I'm surprised she let him in the house. Usually she's more careful. And I wouldn't have thought her to have a taste for the young ones. A shame he has to die but there it is."

The confusing spill of words muddied Kellas's thoughts. "What do you mean? Let him in the house? Careful? He has to die?"

The hells! What if Lady Irlin hadn't sent an agent at all but rather bribed one of the red caps to carry out the deed?

Feyard gave him a curious look. "Surely you were given the same instructions as the rest of us?"

"Which are?"

"We have standing orders to kill any man who is alone with her. Excepting the man who is married to her sister, the boy-children who live in the house, and the current reeve marshal of Bronze Hall because he's not fashioned that way."

Kellas stared at the lamp burning on the household veranda, a beacon welcoming late visitors. A gust of wind caused the flame to flicker. A spray of rain spattered the street before tailing off. He turned back to Feyard.

"I don't understand what you mean, kill any man who is alone with her. That doesn't even make any sense."

"Why does it have to make sense? The king came from outside the Hundred. Those outlanders keep strange customs, if you ask me. One god instead of many gods—busy work for only a single god! Think about how the palace women live in separate buildings from the men. I guess this is something like that. She's to live in a separate room and no men are to enter it."

Kellas did see. He found it an ugly sort of picture. "If he can't have her then no man can."

"If the king wants to keep her sealed up like a bird in a cage it's not my part to question it. I remember the war. I lost a brother, a sister, an uncle and aunt, and five cousins to the demons. I'll happily serve the man who conquered the demons and saved us. There is something uncanny about that woman anyway. Makes you wonder why we never heard a whisper of this in the army, doesn't it? I never knew anything about this household until I was sent on this assignment two years ago."

"I certainly never heard a breath of this in the palace or among the Wolves." The situation dizzied Kellas, like he'd been dropped into a spinning wheel and had nowhere to go except tumble.

"Folk in Salya won't speak a single bad word about her, though. She's held in great respect. But there's a few who will talk if you get them drunk enough. A man told me she's a demon who bewitched the king and then abandoned him. Said the king tried to win her back but she insulted him instead. After that the king swore if she would not return to him, she could cursed well live alone and never take another husband. By which he meant not even a lover."

Words died on Kellas's tongue. He licked parched lips as his thoughts mired in a morass of disbelief.

"You're not here guarding the child?" he asked, thinking of the infant smuggled out of the palace and brought here to be raised in secret.

"The child? You mean that lad you spoke of? No, there have been red caps guarding this household for fifteen years, which if you ask me is a cursed long time for a man—even a king!—to hold a lover's grudge like that. Still, we have our orders. Thus, that lad will have to die. We're just waiting to get him alone. So far he hasn't left the house except in company with Mistress Mai."

"Oh the hells, you cursed fool." Anger boiled up to oil his speech. "That lad is Prince Atani. I'm here to fetch him back to the palace. None of you will touch him."

"Huh." Feyard scratched his chin as he eyed the house with all the suspicion of a man who is sure his rival has just scarfed down the last of the custard buns. "I thought he looked familiar but I've never seen the prince up close. What an odd thing he should come down here."

"The king sent me to bring him back."

"That's all very well, then, but how are you going to fetch him? He's staying in the household. If you go inside, I would have to kill you."

Kellas laughed.

"I would!" objected Feyard, squaring his shoulders. "No exceptions."

Kellas stared the other man down until Feyard recoiled a step, touching the hilt of his sword as if to remind himself he was still armed.

"I'm here to collect Prince Atani and take him back to the palace," Kellas said in as mild a tone as he could manage. "You will not interfere."

Feyard looked him up and down with a pitying sneer. "You think you're safe because you can take me in a fight, and you're right about that. But here's what you can't do. You go in that house and I or one of the other red caps will report it. Once the king hears, you're dead. It's that simple."

You are already dead, King Anjihosh had told Kellas on the day he climbed Law Rock. *What belongs to me is mine to control.*

Kellas had not succeeded as a silent wolf by being slow to adapt to a sudden change of circumstances. "Very well. I obey the king. Do they go to the market every day?"

"Usually, yes."

"Then I'll pull him from the street. One other thing."

But he hesitated. If that eight-year-old boy he had seen was Anji's son, then he had no authority to reveal that particular secret to Feyard and the red caps if they did not already know, as it seemed they did not. He would have to take care of Lady Irlin's agent without their help.

Feyard, strutting a little from the rush of having bested a silent wolf, said cheerfully, "What's the other thing, then?"

Kellas shifted ground easily. "I'd like to find out if Prince Atani's two personal guards are somewhere in town. If you red caps could help me with that, without giving away my presence here, I'd be in your debt."

"We'll find the guardsmen for you. Just because we're not silent wolves doesn't mean we are incompetent fools. What we do here isn't a trifling duty, I'll have you know."

Kellas did not have to fake the uneasiness building in his heart. "I can imagine. I want to take the prince with as little fuss as possible, so I will give you an alert before I move. It may be tomorrow or in a few days."

They parted on amicable terms, for they were, after all, comrades in arms about the same mission: soldiers protecting the Hundred so it would not fall back into the war that had almost destroyed it sixteen years ago. People remembered those awful days. People liked to be able to walk the streets safely at night, to go about their business without being robbed, to raise their children without fear they would be enslaved or raped or murdered, and to eat, drink, and celebrate all of life's festivals.

King Anjihosh had returned peace to the Hundred.

Kellas walked back along the lane, counting gates as he went. Night settled as the rains came in. There were five substantial compounds between Plum Blossom Clan and the main street headed down to the harbor. Unlike Toskala, where the king mandated night-lanterns be posted on every corner, the thoroughfare was dim, lit only here and there by lamps burning on verandas. The darkness protected him from the red caps' watch. The way all the compound walls ran together made his task simple for a deft climber.

He tested handholds and finger's-width ledges in the mortared brick of an outer wall, then stepped back as a small lantern bobbed into view up the street. Four people ran past, poorly sheltered beneath a single umbrella; they called out a laughing greeting, a friendly jest about getting soaked, and hurried on without stopping.

He scrambled up the wall as the rain washed over him and tipped himself over into a garden. There he crouched in silence under the branches of a jabi bush as a woman rolled down screens over rice paper windows in the nearest building. After she finished he crept through the unlit garden to the next wall. By this means he worked his way through five compounds until only a single very high wall separated him from Plum Blossom Clan.

A work shed's shingled roof got him up high enough to swing

over onto the adjoining wall. Dogs whined on the other side. He lay motionless atop the wall in the drenching rain as the dogs thrashed through bushes planted along the wall as a clever means to detect an intruder: Anyone climbing down from the outer wall would make a great deal of noise in the branches. The dogs sensed something was wrong but in the rain could not catch his scent. A whistle from inside the house caught the animals' attention and they loped off.

Lightning flashed in the distance, revealing for an instant the tiered and tiled rooftops of an expansive building with several wings and a spacious garden wrapped around the back. The dogs were now sniffing along a covered walkway a stone's throw away.

Thunder boomed, and the dogs yelped and bolted away around a corner, out of his view. He calculated the distance from the wall to the nearest roof and waited.

When lightning flashed again he counted, then leaped blind into the darkness as thunder rolled. Its rumble covered the thump of him hitting the roof. He slowed his slide down the slope by splaying his feet and hands and pressing his knees against the tile's ridges. Reaching out to give himself as wide a span as possible, he eased up the wet tiles until he could hook an arm over the long ridged apex of the roof.

He rested there as he waited for another flash of lightning so he could plot out a route into the central building, which had a multilevel roof he could surely squeeze inside as he and Atani had in the palace.

The rain slackened. No lightning came. Children shrieked with laughter, and little footsteps pounded as they trampled around in some kind of game. A comfortable babble of adult voices rose from below, punctuated by more laughter and then a woman's voice raised in song.

A cheerful home, it seemed.

From this angle he could see down onto the covered walkway the dogs had been sniffing along. The raised plank walk led from the central building out to a little gazebo set within the shadows of the garden. To his surprise Atani appeared on the walkway beside a pretty girl about the prince's own age. They weren't touching but every line of their bodies, the way their heads were canted, the heat of their smiles, told him more than he needed to know.

"The hells," he murmured under his breath.

"That's what I said."

The shock of hearing a quiet feminine voice not an arm's length away actually caused him to flinch hard enough that he lost his grip on the roof. Tile scraped under his knee, and he caught the ridge barely in time to stop himself tumbling.

Then he looked up.

An adolescent girl dressed in humble clothes similar to his own sat cross-legged in the most casual manner on the roof's rounded ridgeline.

How in the hells had she gotten there without him seeing or hearing anything?

Her sigh held all the weight of the world. She had a soft voice that seemed to crawl right into his bones. "Once they get to the gazebo and think no one can see, they'll hold hands. They've even started kissing."

Unable to help himself, he looked toward the gazebo just in time to see Atani and his companion sit on a bench under a flickering candle and, indeed, share a tentative kiss with all the adorable sweetness of first love.

"It's nauseating, don't you think?" said the girl on the roof. "Mama says I mustn't be jealous of Eiko. That's her name, my cousin Eiko. She's not really my cousin because her mother and my mother aren't really sisters, they just say they are, so everyone says Eiko and I are cousins. But don't you think it's unfair that she and I have grown up together side by side and then he walks in and suddenly she has eyes for nothing but him?"

Strangely, it seemed like a reasonable question.

"It never feels good to be left out."

"Oh, they don't leave me out. They are both far too kind and thoughtful for that, which is the worst part of it. Oh my dear Arasit, come sit with us. Shall we walk in the garden together? Do you want to play a game of khot? I would rather stab my eyes out with a knife than watch them melt at each other. No one else understands."

"I understand."

"Do you? You must be pretty old."

"That could be, as I have it on my mother's authority that I am thirty."

"You're almost as old as my mother! She's a Blue Ox. That makes her four years older than you. She says I should be patient with them because calf love only happens once."

"It must have happened awfully fast," he agreed. "Atani can't have gotten here more than three or four days ago."

"Three or four days? He arrived here *twenty* days ago, and I have counted every single one! Look at me." Even though it was night without stars or moon he could see a flickering blue gleam deep in the black pools of her eyes.

Before he realized what was about to happen, she struck. The attack felt like a tickling behind his eyes, like the stroke of a feather brushing through the tangled foliage of his thoughts.

Memories and emotions cascaded, a rain of images soaking him to the bone.

His mother berating him for climbing up onto the roof when he was six.

The carved horse in his hand, tossed to him by King Anjihosh.

The king's crisp order: "Kill Lady Irlin's agent, find Atani."

Him walking up this very lane eight years ago with the stolen Bronze Hall dispatch pouch slung over his back, after he had been unexpectedly ordered to deliver it to the woman who lived here instead of taking it back to the palace. Finding her awake on the veranda. The brief conversation he and the beautiful woman had engaged in while her two children slept. Their words and interaction had the flavor of foreplay that would never be consummated. The way she had precisely studied his body, and the way he had noticed how the fabric of her taloos emphasized the curve of her breasts...

"Sheh!" the girl hissed. "Aui! That's my mother. I don't want to see *that*."

He blinked and found himself atop the roof, clinging to the ridgeline in a darkness that swallowed his sight so all he knew was what he touched, smelled, tasted, and heard.

"So *you* are Captain Kellas! Atani must have mentioned you a hundred times since he got here. He thinks you can do anything."

An ache began to throb behind his eyes as she kept talking. Had she blinded him?

"Don't worry about that man who came to kill Hari. Mama got rid of him the day he got to town. You'd better come down and talk to her."

"You are a demon," he whispered hoarsely. "But you wear no cloak."

"I'm not a Guardian, if that's what you mean. And because I have no cloak you can't kill me so don't bother to try." She sniffed audibly several times, testing the air's scent. "Storm's moving off. The clouds will blow away and the red caps will see your shadow up here once the stars and moon come out. Climb to the end of this roof and drop down into the inner courtyard. I'll go get Mama."

She stood up and took a step right out onto the air as if on an invisible bridge. It wasn't that she glowed; rather he could sense her presence as if it were the warmth of a fire.

"The dogs," he whispered because he needed an ordinary thought to allow himself to process the dangerous situation: He had just met a demon in whose home Prince Atani had become trapped.

Yet out of the darkness her voice sounded like that of any relaxed adolescent girl who has just greeted a visitor to her family's welcoming house. "I'll bring them to meet you so they won't bark."

Then she was gone.

6

By the time he crept along the roof and dropped into a small interior courtyard, his head was really hurting. Lit by a glass-walled lantern at each corner, the courtyard had two benches, two troughs of flowers, and two posts for anchoring a loom, but mostly he guessed the square courtyard was a light well to feed sunlight into the interior rooms.

"So you are Captain Kellas." The voice had a foreign lilt that fell like music.

He turned as the woman stepped into the glow of lamplight. Up close she was more beautiful than he remembered, no longer young but rather as rich and sumptuous as finest silk.

Her gaze wandered down his body and back up to his face as her lips curved. He glanced down, wondering what would cause a woman to smile with such pleased admiration. The drenched cloth of the thin cotton vest and trousers clung to his body, revealing everything.

Aui! He had nothing to be ashamed of.

Her smile widened as if she could guess his thoughts. "Captain Kellas, I believe we have met before."

"Yes, verea, we have although I was not a captain then. I believe your name is Mai. Is that how you pronounce it? I like to do things correctly."

"Do you?"

That smile of hers would make any man's headache vanish.

She added, "My daughter Arasit says you are one of Anji's silent wolves. You call him Anjihosh, I suppose."

"I call him King Anjihosh."

Her nod granted him the point. "You've come about Atani. I need to make clear I was as surprised as anyone when he showed up here twenty days ago looking for a younger brother. I didn't know Atani even realized we existed."

"He didn't know you existed until he overheard words not meant for his ears. I'm here to take him back immediately."

A faint crease appeared in her brow. She held a fan in one hand and snapped it open like the offended echo of her thoughts. "Atani is perfectly safe in this house."

He thought it prudent not to disagree with her. "That's not the only reason I've come. The king also sent me to make sure the younger boy is safe."

"Ah." She tapped the fan closed against a hip. His gaze skimmed the slope of that hip, the way the wrapping of the taloos drew the eye up along her waist. "The man Lady Irlin sent to kill my son Hari will no longer trouble us."

The statement yanked him out of his distraction. "He won't?"

"When next he sets foot on land it will be in a very distant foreign country. It could take him years to return if he even manages to find a way to pay for such an ocean-spanning journey. I am sorry to have been so ruthless to a man who was simply obeying orders. But I do intend to protect my children."

She delivered the warning in such a pleasant tone and with such a neutral smile that he was suddenly certain *she* had indeed rejected both Anjihosh and the wealth and power of the court, never the other way around.

"Arasit and Hari are the two children I saw you with that night eight years ago, aren't they? The girl would have been about seven then, and he would have been the baby you held in your arms. He is the king's son out of Queen Zayrah, is he not? Not yours."

"Of course Hari is mine. I am his mother."

That was a tone meant to correct, although it had nothing of his mother's blunt hammer. "Aui! I meant no offense, verea."

"Let me be clear about this, Captain Kellas. Although I did not give birth to him, I am Hari's mother. In this same way, Queen Zayrah is Atani's mother. Please assure Anji that Atani thinks of Zayrah as his mother. Nor will I interfere with the bond that has grown between them. Whatever may lie between Anji and myself stays in the past."

"Eiya!" The exclamation slid out of him with more pity than he intended. "You gave up Atani to the king."

"Something like that. I am not an emperor's sister, as Zayrah is. A woman of humble origin like myself brings no valuable alliance to a new king who needs allies. I rejected the offer Anji made me. I want no part of his court or his palace or his attention. Do you understand? I am satisfied with the life I have built for myself and my family here in Salya."

Kellas had become adept at interpreting emotion and expression. She had the steady, assured stance of a person who means what she says. After a moment, she opened a hand toward him as if inviting a reply.

"What I don't understand is why Lady Irlin thinks any male child Queen Zayrah gives birth to has to be killed," he said.

"Because that is the custom of the Sirniakan Empire. Lady Irlin fears Zayrah would kill Atani to pave the way for a son born of her own womb to become Anji's heir. Thus Zayrah's sons must die, so Atani can never be challenged."

"But the king does not fear that the boy Hari is a danger to Prince Atani?"

"Among the Qin, where Anji came to adulthood and became a soldier, brothers are seen as allies who can support each other as co-rulers throughout the Qin territories. Anji is a complicated man. He does genuinely care for his children. That is why he saved Hari and sent him to me."

"In exchange for the child he took away many years earlier."

"Perhaps. He believes in the appearance of justice. But primarily because he knows I will raise Hari to never make any claim on the palace. Remember that Anji is both Qin and Sirniakan. He spent his early years in the Sirniakan imperial palace, one of the sons of the emperor and thus a potential heir. That is why his mother sent him to be raised among the Qin, to get him out of palace politics. In the empire only one prince can ascend the imperial throne, so all other male contenders must be eliminated. Those who are not killed in battle are generally poisoned at the command of the victor's mother. Obviously Lady Irlin favors Atani and is taking no chances with Zayrah."

"The Hundred is not Sirniaka!"

"Not yet."

"Do you think it will ever become part of the empire? We are separated from the empire by a high mountain range. They can't easily attack us."

"Does it matter if we become the legal subjects of the emperor if, in the end, the customs of the empire creep in and smother the traditions of the Hundred?"

"You are an outlander. Why would you care?"

"For one thing, I am not of Sirniakan ancestry and have never followed their way of life. Regardless of where I come from, the Hundred is my home now. I love all that it is. Surely I am no different from you, Captain. Would you want your gods to be forgotten and a foreign god to take their place? Would you want your grandchildren to become Sirniakans in all but name? To forget all the customs and songs and relationships you take for granted?"

He said, "I am not married nor do I have children, verea."

"You are not married?" She tilted her head to one side, absorbing a statement that clearly surprised her. After a moment and with a deliberately flirtatious smile, she opened the fan and fluttered it back and forth below her chin as if to cool a face heated by desire.

The gesture provoked him; she meant it to. For several breaths he found himself unable to speak. Fortunately a spatter of rain cooled his cheeks.

"Are you a demon, too, like your daughter?" he asked, knowing he ought not to laugh, but he did anyway.

She walked several steps closer. Her perfume of musk vine and heady stardrops made his head swim. The lamps burned brighter, and the whole world seemed to hold its breath.

"I can't see into your thoughts or walk on air. I wear no cloak, can't walk on a demon's coil, nor does a winged horse come at my command. I was born an ordinary girl and grew up an ordinary girl in an unimportant desert oasis so far from here that no one in all of the Hundred could possibly have heard of it."

"Never ordinary, I am sure," he blurted out.

She chuckled. "Beauty is nothing more than the random thoughtlessness of the gods. It is not what I value most about myself."

He took a step to close the gap between them. His chin came to the level of her forehead but as she tipped her head back to look up at him, all he could see was her pink lips, parted slightly, and the teasing confidence of her gaze. Nothing coy about her. She was enjoying this. He could easily have embraced or kissed her, but in this sort of situation he would never touch a woman without her invitation.

Instead he murmured, "What do you value most about yourself, Mai?"

She leaned so close he had to brace himself and clasp his hands behind his back, a soldier at attention facing down a perilous foe.

Her whisper coursed through his flesh like the snap of lightning. "My honor. My generosity." Her gaze grew as acute as a well-honed knife's edge, and her tone sharpened. "And my intelligence, Captain. Never forget *that* while you admire my beauty."

Children's laughter broke like a wave between them.

She stepped back. His heart raced crazily, and it took him several measured breaths to calm it. People emerged from the house into the courtyard: three women, a man, and twelve children ranging in age from a hulking lad with a burn-scarred face to a babe in arms. All, even the thumb-sucking baby, examined him with amused approval, as if they were pleased when strange men secretly climbed into the house. He hastily tugged at the cloth plastered against his body, peeling it up.

Snickering, Arasit paraded over with three large dogs. They sniffed around Kellas's feet, smelled his hands, and yawned wide enough to show him their teeth before circling away.

"Captain Kellas!" Prince Atani stared, eyes wide and a hand pressed to his chest. "How are you come here?"

"I have been sent to bring you back to the palace, Your Highness."

The lad's answer was to glance at the pretty girl standing beside him and, right there in front of everyone, grasp her hand. Had the prince no idea the degree of trouble this inappropriate relationship would inevitably cause?

Kellas went on more sharply than he intended. "I admit I am puzzled by how you could have gotten here so quickly, Your Highness. A ship would have taken longer than the fast riding stages I managed. Yet you evidently arrived here the day I left Toskala, two days after you vanished."

Atani glanced at the sky. The wind had started to rip holes in the cloud cover, and a star winked into view. A triumphant smile teased up the corners of Atani's lips. That smile made him look a cursed lot like Mai.

"Tell him," said the girl whose hand he was holding. "What you did was so clever, Atani."

The two eight-year-olds—boy and girl—giggled, nudging each other in the way of comrades accustomed to sharing a joke. Arasit let out a gusty sigh.

Atani drew himself straight, with just a hint of cockiness so unlike his usual modest self that Kellas had to believe he was showing off for the pretty girl. "I commandeered a reeve and his eagle, and had the reeve fly me here. Of course he couldn't refuse when I gave him the order, and I didn't give him time to tell his superiors. I'm afraid I tricked my guards and left them behind in a place they couldn't alert the king. I hope you will help me make sure they aren't punished, Captain."

"Your Highness! I hope you understand that given the orders I received from your father the king, I cannot be easy about guards who are so easily tricked. Their job is to protect you. If that means to protect you from your own foolish, impulsive, and reckless choices, then they have failed."

"I was just trying to act as I thought you would, Captain. It's exactly the sort of thing you would have done. Isn't it?"

"A fair question," said Mai, "if all the stories Atani has told of you are true, Captain. Did you really climb Law Rock at night without a rope?"

Kellas pressed a hand against his forehead, but the headache had passed. A dream would have made more sense with its elaborate twists and erotic—no! erratic!—turns.

"I have my orders," he repeated, clinging stubbornly to duty.

Atani released the girl's hand. "Of course you do, Captain. You are my father's most prized Wolf, are you not?"

Was he? The praise scalded him, made him wonder what Mai thought of a man described as the king's best spy and assassin. No! Mai's opinion must not sway him. The hells! Her own daughter was a demon, and she herself spoke words that held the taint of rebellion.

"Anji has another child in this household, a second child born to him and me," Mai added. "You have seen the truth of what she is."

Seen under lamplight Arasit did indeed have curly black hair and a rather prominent nose, although otherwise she had her mother's round face and slight stature.

Mai went on in the relentlessly cordial voice of a fruit seller in the market dependent on her customers' goodwill to make a living. "Will you return to the palace and tell him that the infant daughter he acknowledged many years ago is what he would call a demon? When you know he has sworn to kill all demons in the Hundred?"

Atani crossed to Arasit and grasped her elbow. "I won't let that happen. I'll go back to the palace with you immediately, Captain. But you must not speak of any of this to my father. Let me handle him."

"You handle him, Your Highness?"

"I know everyone thinks only Dannarah can talk him around, but I have learned a great deal in my time here. I understand things I did not comprehend before. I know what I have to do."

That Atani glanced first at Mai and only afterward toward Eiko betrayed something, but Kellas could not know what it was. Not without gaining Atani's full trust.

"I should go back now anyway," the prince added. "Mother will be sick with worry."

Atani was still looking at Eiko as he said the words so did not see the wistful smile that touched Mai's face, as swift as a bird's passing under the shadow of night. A woman who is generous enough to let go of something she desperately loves because she sees another may have greater need of it would smile like that.

A spark of bright hot emotion flared in Kellas's heart. The hells!

A man could willingly die for a kiss from those lips.

A man *would* die from that kiss.

The mere thought of its risk was so cursedly tempting.

Mai caught him looking at her and, guessing he had recognized the emotion her smile had betrayed, she gave a tiny downward gesture of her hand to indicate he should say nothing and show no sign so Atani would not know of her feelings toward the boy. The intimacy of the communication, the casual way she assumed Kellas would understand her, took his breath away.

"Dannarah, too," Atani went on obliviously. "It's hard for Dannarah at the palace. Mother wants her to be brought up the same way she was in Sirniaka, but that isn't right for Dannarah at all, especially not here in the Hundred. Besides me, no one really understands Dannarah except Father, and he thinks he has to send her away to please Mother, but that is only because he never really talks to Mother, he just talks past her. You and Dannarah will get along well, Eiko. I know it! I'll go back, and sort things out, and then I'll send for you."

Ever attuned to the nuances of emotion, Atani took hold of Arasit's hand.

"It's all right," the demon said curtly, blinking back tears.

"I understand why I can't go. You can come visit me here, when you can take out time from your glorious and princely life. But I guess it all depends on what your hero Captain Kellas decides to do, doesn't it?"

That was when it truly hit him.

All that you learn you will share only with me, King Anjihosh had said.

You will say nothing to my father of what just happened, Atani had commanded him.

"Your choice, Kellas," he murmured to himself, just to pretend he hadn't already decided.

Part Two

Forty-Four Years Later

7

"Marshal? Marshal Dannarah, wake up. News has come in from the king."

Dannarah allowed herself one last inhalation to enjoy the heat of the sun warming her body, then opened her eyes. "I wasn't asleep."

"No, of course you weren't, Marshal." The reeve standing before her grinned. "That's why you have this couch positioned to catch the afternoon sun. People basking in the sun don't ever get drowsy when they lie down for a few moments to fret about their manifold responsibilities."

Dannarah swung her legs off the couch and winced as her back tightened, the familiar tug of age. "It's why they send you to wake me up, isn't it, Tarnit?" she said as she reached for her reeve's baton.

"Because I'm still nimble enough to jump out of the way before you can hit me?"

Dannarah laughed and shook the baton at her. "You're only seventeen years younger than I am. You'll be feeling these hells-bitten aches soon enough. Anyway I never fret."

She stretched to feel out her back and decided it was fine after all, no worse than usual. Tarnit walked over to the side table and poured water from a pitcher into a basin, a gesture the woman made not as a subordinate but because Tarnit was the sort of person who never thought twice about performing small kindnesses.

It was one of the things that made Tarnit a good reeve: People found her easy to trust.

"Go on, Tar. I'll be right out."

Tarnit gave her a swift, assessing look, nodded, and pushed past the curtain that led into her study. Dannarah could now hear the voices of people chatting as they waited for her. She washed and dried her face and hands, then walked out onto the rock-hewn balcony of the suite of chambers that belonged to her: the marshal's cote.

The Hundred had six reeve halls—Horn, Bronze, Gold, Iron, Argent, and Copper—as well as Palace Hall in Toskala atop Law Rock. Reeves favored eyries that were hard for people to reach if they could not fly, and Horn Hall was no exception. It had been established countless generations ago atop a stony ridge at the edge of an escarpment that marked the westernmost edge of the Ossu Hills. Except for an easily defensible switchback trail that worked up the back of the ridge, the hall could only be reached by air. While the landing ground, lofts for the eagles, and gardens lay atop the ridge, the living areas were carved out of the rock. From her balcony she looked onto a gulf of air, the ground a hazy gold far below, the onion-like circular walls of the prosperous city of Horn laid out as neat as a map drawn by an expert hand, two main roads splitting east and west, and the spectacular peak of solitary Mount Aua in the far distance, half obscured by clouds.

The sight never failed to wash a momentary sense of peace through her:

She had come here often with her father and had often stood in exactly this place with him, looking over the land he ruled.

Tarnit waited in the marshal's study along with Horn Hall's chief deputy and reeve instructor, chief fawkner, and chief steward. The messenger was a startlingly good-looking young reeve wearing the green stripes on his leather vest that marked him as assigned to Argent Hall. Cursed if new reeves didn't look younger every year. He was well built and confident in the way she remembered Captain Kellas being when he was young. Although why she was reminded of Kellas after all these years she could not imagine. The hells! She hadn't even seen Kellas since that terrible day twenty-two years ago.

"And you are?" she said more snappishly than she intended as she walked to her writing desk.

"I'm called Reyad. My eagle is surly."

"Bad-tempered?"

"No, her name is Surly. Sweetest-tempered raptor in the Hundred."

Everyone chuckled. Reyad's smile was a sweet one, sure to be a lure to questing eyes. She glanced at Tarnit and, indeed, Tar was examining him in her usual appreciative way.

Dannarah bent over, touched a hand to the ground, and used the support to lever her aching knees down. She settled cross-legged on the pillow in front of the low desk, pleased that she managed it without looking too clumsy. "You've got a dispatch for me from Chief Marshal Auri about King Jehosh?"

"No. The dispatch is about something else." He held out a message tube, a length of bamboo sealed with wax at either end. Tarnit took it, melted the wax over a lamp flame, and shook out the rice paper with its neatly brushed words.

Dannarah read quickly with mounting irritation, then summarized for the others. "The dispatch is a request for Horn Hall's aid in tracking down criminals who escaped from a work gang when a ferry transporting them across the River Olossi capsized. A company of the King's Spears have tracked the fugitives north into the province of Sardia. The chief marshal explains that Argent Hall is overextended right now and needs Horn Hall to assist." She glanced toward the large map table placed in the center of the chamber, built to the exact dimensions of the exceptionally detailed map of the Hundred she had inherited from her father when he'd died. "Argent Hall wouldn't be overextended if that ass Auri hadn't decided to transfer Sardia out of Horn Hall's patrol territory to Argent five years ago."

"Sardia hasn't always been part of Argent Hall's patrol territory?" the young man asked.

"How long have you been a reeve, Reyad?"

"Three years."

"Always at Argent Hall?"

"Yes." He did not sound happy about it.

She opened her mouth, caught Tarnit's warning glance, and remembered prudence. "Since King Jehosh appointed him to the office, Chief Marshal Auri has made a number of changes in reeve hall protocol and administration that some of us are cursed sure..." Tarnit coughed. "...are ill advised," Dannarah finished, although the kindlier word left a sour taste on her tongue.

The others smiled, amused by her restraint. Reyad's cheek twitched at a strong emotion she could not interpret. If only Atani were here, he would uncover the young man's entire history over a cup of tea.

But Atani wasn't here and never would be here again.

The grief always hit without warning like a gust of wind knocking you off your feet. She shut her eyes. Her hand groped up the right-hand edge of the desk to the lacquered tray at the corner where she kept the carved ivory playing pieces, and she gripped one of the little animals so tightly its ridges dug into her palm.

The swell passed quickly. She hoped no one had noticed, and smiled bitterly as she opened her eyes and her hand to see she had grabbed one of the wolves. She set it down sharply.

"Then what is this message about King Jehosh I've been promised?" she asked, proud of how ordinary her voice sounded.

"It's just something I overheard while I was waiting for this message to be written out. A reeve wearing the blue stripes of Copper Hall came in and told Chief Marshal Auri that King Jehosh has returned unexpectedly to the palace. Before he was expected back, I mean."

"So the king has arrived safely home from his latest war in the north?"

Reyad nodded slowly. Dannarah could almost see his mind pacing through the words he had heard so he could report them precisely. Patience and precision were good traits in a reeve. "The Copper Hall reeve said the king reported he'd had a monumental victory over the northern rebels in the country of Ithik Eldim and restored the Hundred's military governor there. Then the reeve handed Chief Marshal Auri a dispatch and said he had orders from the palace that the chief marshal needed to speed things up."

"Speed things up?"

"Then the clerk gave me my message and I had to leave."

"Why are you telling me this, since it wasn't part of your official dispatch?"

His gaze shifted guiltily side-to-side so quickly she almost missed it. "The reeves protect the Hundred. So isn't it the duty of all six marshals to know the whereabouts of the king they serve?"

She lifted a hand and caught his gaze, using the pressure of her stare to pin him to her will. She had learned this look from her father. "Tell me what you are leaving out."

The barest hint of a smile flashed, then vanished, like a man biting down his triumph so no one else will see it. "You are the daughter of King Anjihosh the Glorious Unifier, of blessed memory, is that not right?"

"Yes."

"The sister of King Atani the Law-Giver, of blessed memory."

She nodded, picking up the wolf again.

"Therefore the aunt of King Jehosh the Triumphant, conqueror of the northern barbarians of Ithik Eldim. So when Chief Marshal Auri told that Copper Hall reeve not to let anyone else hear the news of the king's return yet, I just thought he couldn't have meant you."

Dannarah spun the wolf piece through her fingers, then set it down amid the others, exactly in line. "I like how you make your decisions, Reyad. I'm going to take this patrol myself. Tarnit, put a wing of reeves together. Reyad will accompany us as Argent Hall's representative. We'll depart at dawn."

Wind rumbling in her ears, Dannarah soared over the Westhal Hills, scouting for the escaped prisoners. Even after forty years as a reeve, patrolling never got old: high above the land, the wind in her face and the sun in her heart.

She had gotten her wings after all, to everyone's surprise. Even her own.

Reeves did not sit astride eagles, of course. Hitched in front, they dangled as from the bird's breastbone and thus had the land laid out below their feet. There was very little a reeve could not see from the air, and nothing that blocked her vision except her own blindness, her own fears, her own secret desires and thwarted aspirations.

She reined Terror into a circling pattern. Together with a company of King's Spears, she and her wing of nine reeves had tracked the fleeing criminals through Sardia to these rugged uninhabited hills blanketed with thick forest cover. It was a good place to hide. An animal trail snaking through a clearing made by a tumble of rocks caught her eye. A sunbeam flashed off a slash of polished metal. Some idiot had dropped a machete in the grass, maybe while running to get out of view.

A nod of satisfaction was the only gesture she allowed herself. A quick survey showed the other two reeves in her triad, Tarnit and Iyar, flying north and south of her position respectively. She quartered the area, focusing her attention on the trees that ringed the clearing, and glimpsed lines and shapes that might be huts or lean-tos so well hidden beneath the forest canopy that a reeve on regular patrol would never notice them.

Leaves thrashed at the crown of a stately oak. They bent and rustled with too much weight for a bird: Someone was climbing. She reined Terror to the right just as an arrow spat out of the tree, shot by a desperate fool. The missile fell harmlessly back into the branches and although she circled once—out of arrow range—she saw no sign of the archer.

It was time to alert the troops.

She gave three quick tugs on the central jess, and Terror caught an updraft. The view from aloft always exhilarated, that sense of having it all in her grasp. She noted her landmarks: Demon's Eye Peak to the south; a waterfall to the north; an ancient Ladytree whose canopy marked an old way station on a hill path entirely concealed by forest cover; the clearing with the machete. By the dark clouds piling up in the east along the Westhal Hills it was going to storm soon. Like all reeves she had four signal flags in her quiver. She slipped out the striped flag that meant "Watch and Hold," and signaled Tarnit and Iyar to remain over the area.

Leaving them behind, she glided on an air current down to the staging point in the upper reaches of the valley of the River Elshar. From the air the camp of the King's Spears had the efficient look of a place well guarded by sentries and easy to break down when they needed to move out. She thumped down a prudent distance from the tents. Even so Terror opened her beak and fluffed her feathers to make herself look even larger than she already was, as if the eagle were worried these trifling soldiers wouldn't respect her. Dannarah hooded her and, stepping out of range of her talons, beckoned to the nearest soldier.

The brawny young man had the look of the palace about him by the evidence of his curly black hair and a prominent nose not unlike her own. He hesitated before sauntering over, examining her as if surprised to see a woman with gray hair dressed in reeve leathers and carrying a reeve's baton just as if she were actually a reeve.

"I need to speak to Chief Tuvas immediately," she said.

"Who are you to demand the chief come when you call?" he retorted with a sneer. "You reeves are meant to attend him, not the other way around."

"I'm surprised a man who trained hard enough to gain the honor of serving in the king's elite Spears is so unobservant that he hasn't noticed me consulting with Chief Tuvas the last few days. Not to mention the marshal's wings sewn right here on my vest in plain sight of your lazy eyes. Be quick about it."

His eyes opened wide as he took a step back, touching two fingers to his forehead in the sign used by worshippers of Beltak to show obedience to the god. He muttered words that she didn't catch. She tapped her baton onto her open palm. He hustled away.

It didn't take long for Chief Tuvas to stride up. He greeted her with proper respect, fist to chest. She shouldn't have cared that the young soldier who had been rude to her witnessed the gesture, but he did, and she was glad.

"Marshal Dannarah! You must have news."

"I've spotted an encampment in the forest."

As she described what she'd seen, she studied him. The chief had the broad, flat cheeks and straight black hair of a man descended from one of the Qin soldiers who had guarded King Anjihosh. Theirs were the faces and presence she still trusted most after all these years, because they reminded her of the men who had unstintingly served her father when she was growing up.

When she finished her description, the chief nodded. "We'll strike at once."

"They betrayed their position, so they'll run."

"The quicker they scatter, the more chance your reeves can follow them."

She got back into the air and became the banner the soldiers tracked as they moved at speed up over the back ridge of the valley and into the wilderness beyond. The site was maybe two mey distant, which they made in half the time ordinary folk would have taken to walk there. A cloudburst swept through but barely slowed the soldiers, although Terror gave a few huffy chirps of displeasure. When the Spears reached the area they went in fast. The heavy tree cover hid the attack from her and wasn't her responsibility anyway.

She circled, looking for any sign of people running away from the Spears' attack.

But she saw nothing, only a deer and a flap of wings from a disturbed bird. Her instinct for trouble tingled. For days the escaped prisoners had eluded them despite the advantage reeves had in being able to track by air. It was clear they had help from disloyal elements within the local population or, worse, from the demons who were still trying to tear down the peaceful administration her father had set in place sixty years ago.

She would never let the demons and their allies destroy her father's legacy. Never.

On alert for a possible flanking attack or an as-yet-unseen escape route, she made a wide loop south over the hill called Demon's Eye Peak because its flat crown had a demon's coil carved into the rock. It had been years since she had patrolled this area, but when she had become a reeve her father had given her the special duty of locating as many demon's coils as possible, since many were impossible to find unless you were flying.

Clifflike slopes protected the summit of Demon's Eye Peak, but from the air the maze was easy to trace: a hexagonally shaped spiral path etched into the rock around a central bowl-like depression. Its twisting lines resembled veins of gleaming copper, and from a height it appeared painted onto the ground. At the coil's center shimmered a pool of polished blue like palest turquoise that had something of the texture of water even though no one actually knew what it was. No person could walk the maze; only demons could. She had tried once many years ago on a different coil and come within a handbreadth of dying when the coil had expelled her with a jolt that almost flung her over the side of a ledge.

On this patrol she'd not seen any demons or their winged horses although she always watched for them. Yet she could not help wondering if it was merely a coincidence that the prisoners had taken cover so close to a demon's coil. Helping criminals escape the king's justice was exactly the sort of thing demons would do to destabilize the king's rule.

She reined Terror back around for one last look at the coil, then glided down into a narrow spur of the Elshar Valley that tucked right up against Demon's Eye Peak and a neighboring hill.

In this secluded vale lay a substantial estate whose forecourt overlooked the headwaters of the River Elshar. The main building with two wings and a tower marked it as the country estate of one of the Ri Amarah clans, a secretive people who had immigrated into the Hundred about five generations ago although most Hundred folk still thought of them as foreigners.

She admired the extensive garden enclosed within walls as thick and high as those of a fortress. Seen from the air, the vast grounds had a precision that would have appealed to her father, each section tidy and discrete: a terrace abutting the back of the house, a fountain of flowers, a slope down to the lower garden shaped by shrubs and trimmed cypress hedges, a court of grapes, several workshops and garden sheds, and herb beds that gave way to an orchard. A woman walked out from the back portico of the house, spotted her, and ducked back inside in the usual way of Ri Amarah women who, according to their peculiar foreign customs, never bared their faces in public.

As she turned Terror to head back, a flash caught her attention. She twisted in her harness in time to see three more spasms of light flare in a rhythmic pulse from Demon's Eye Peak.

The hells!

Yet when she flew back over the peak it lay as quiescent as before, nothing to see except the faintly shining thread of the coil embedded in rock like a ribbon pressed into the earth.

8

The months when her city cousins came to rusticate at the estate to escape the heat and Flood Rains in the city were the worst part of Sarai's year. When they were here she couldn't pretend she wasn't an outcast among her own people. She concealed herself in the shadows at the top of the stairs until no one was in sight, then quickly descended and hurried along the central atrium that ran the length of the main building. The men still sat at breakfast in their wing of the house. Women and children ate first, and she heard their genial talk and careless laughter from the kitchen along with the squeals of children playing in the kitchen yard.

Doors at either end of the atrium had been slid open to let air through. Sarai went out the back onto the portico that overlooked the estate's grounds. As she stepped out from under the portico a huge shadow rippled across the upper terrace. She ducked back under cover to avoid being seen. Overhead, a giant eagle flew down the valley. Sarai could just make out a reeve strung from a harness and dangling beneath the eagle, one of the wardens of the Hundred, the loyal servants of King Jehosh the Triumphant, son of Atani the Law-Giver, son of Anjihosh the Glorious Unifier.

What would it be like to be able to travel wherever you wished with no one telling you what was permitted and what was forbidden?

A glare of sun flashing out from behind clouds piled up along the eastern hills hid reeve and eagle from her sight. But it wasn't the sun. The flash winked three more times in a steady, intensifying pulse like a soundless boom Boom BOOM. Her breath caught in her throat as she shaded her eyes in the direction of Demon's Eye Peak.

What did the flash mean? Was the reeve on the trail of a demon?

A bright voice sang out from the atrium. "I saw Sarai go outside."

She hastily stepped into the shadowed corner of a decorative latticework screen. Three of her city cousins strolled out onto the portico. Waving painted fans against the heat, they shaded their eyes into the glare of the rising sun.

"I don't see her anywhere, Garna."

Garna was a pretty girl four years younger than Sarai. "I am sure I saw her. I need her to pick out the embroidery on my new silk shawl because I don't have time now that I'm betrothed. She has very deft fingers. She's quite clever."

"I'm surprised you would let her touch your bridal shawl, considering how she is tainted," said the girl who had first spoken, a friend Garna had brought as a guest to the estate and with whom she spent all her time. "Just to look at her you can see it."

"It's unkind to speak of something she can't help," objected Garna with more graciousness than Sarai expected from a girl who had mostly ignored her all the years she had been visiting the family's country estate.

"Is it true what they say?" asked the third girl, a younger cousin just this year old enough to be allowed to sit up late in the hall after the children under thirteen were sent to bed. "That she hasn't left this estate since she was brought here as a baby? My brother told me that wolves carried her out of the mountains in their teeth and dumped her by the back doors because even wolves didn't want someone tainted like her."

"People tell such stupid stories!" Garna clucked her tongue in displeasure. "The Black Wolves aren't wolves, they were terrible soldiers who lived in the old days and were so cruel the king finally had to get rid of them all."

"Did those terrible Black Wolves kill Sarai's mother?" asked Garna's friend in a tone of quivering eagerness.

Sarai wanted nothing more than to run so she didn't have to hear, but if she moved they would see her and their embarrassed apologies would be worse than their gossip.

The younger girl broke in. "Yes! Black Wolves killed her mother, while her mother was holding her in her arms!"

"For shame!" Garna cut the girl off so sharply that a stab of gratitude lanced right through Sarai. "It is women's business, not for the ears of ignorant girls. If you understood anything you'd know that our history and magic must be kept secret. Always!"

"You are so high and mighty now you are about to be married, aren't you?" muttered the young cousin, and she stomped back into the house.

"The truth is I pity poor Sarai," said Garna to her friend. "No one will ever be able to marry a son to her, even though she has a rich brother living in the richest clan of all. Not that she is ever allowed to visit him. She's four years older than us, and yet because she'll never be allowed to marry, she'll never learn women's knowledge. She'll be a girl all her life. Stuck living out here, never to leave. Don't you think that's sad?"

Their voices faded as they went inside.

Poor Sarai! Usually she could shrug it off but today she counted by prime numbers until the mental exercise calmed her irritation. The moment she was sure they had left the atrium, she dashed across the drive. As she descended the terraces into the garden her tension twisted out of a knot of humiliated frustration and into a brisk stride of expectation. There was nothing she could do about her lack of marriage prospects. But maybe she could discover what a flashing light from a demon's coil portended.

The dark clouds boiling up from the southeast would keep the other women indoors. The outside gardeners didn't come until afternoon. So no one was around to see her unlock the forest gate painted with the four-tiered tree that was the badge of their clan. She slipped outside the estate wall, as Ri Amarah women were never meant to do alone or with their faces uncovered.

Stone steps led up through the trees to the top of Vista Hill. Metal posts lined the path. On festival nights lamps would light the way. In the rainy season the lamps were taken down, and even though the path was paved with stones its surface was slick with puddles.

She climbed quickly toward the long hillside pergola overlooking the estate where in good weather the women of the house would eat an outdoor dinner or celebrate a festival. When she reached the terrace with its pillars and lattice roof woven with heavy vines, she climbed steps carved into the rock face, meant for the gardeners so they could reach the vines growing along the roof beams. On Vista Hill's rocky crown a narrow trail curved along the steep hillside through blooming curtains of blue and white starfall. No one ever went this way, because everyone pretended Demon's Eye didn't exist. But demons were like poisoned threads in the tapestry that was the Hundred: They were woven through the land, inescapable.

Yet nothing was inexplicable, not if you could learn enough about it. She had long hoped to climb the cliff and reach the coil but could not manage the climb alone. The one time she had suggested such an expedition to Elit, her beloved had rejected the idea with such impassioned horror that Sarai never mentioned it again. But after Elit left the village four years ago, Sarai had nothing to lose.

She crept under an overhang of wild fistir into the shelter of a shallow cave from whose lip she could look across the deep cleft that separated the two hills. The sight of the coil's mysterious shimmer never failed to bring out a dizzy smile. She would uncover its secrets.

As her beloved great-aunt Tsania often told her, *If your mind has wings then you can always fly.*

Using a large square board and surveying instruments hidden in the cave, Sarai measured the coil whenever she had a chance. Setting the board on the ground as her table, she unrolled a fresh sheet of rice paper and weighted its sides with stones. With a ruler and compass to calculate angles and dimensions across the gap, she outlined the pattern of the labyrinth onto the paper with brush and ink. Through repeated observation she had discovered occasional changes in the path: a shift in the tangent of an angle, or a lengthening or shortening of one of the straight sections.

Today's drawing shocked her.

Four angles into the twisting path one of the branches had been entirely erased, gone as if it had never existed except for a murky patch of what looked like silvery mud dried into ripples. The path forked around the absence to stay unbroken.

She bounced in excitement. Was the four-part flash related to the disturbance?

The scuff of a foot on stone startled her.

"Who in the hells are you? What are you doing?" said a youthful voice.

Jolted, Sarai dropped both ruler and brush and looked up.

A woman stood on the lip of the rock overhang, above Sarai, poised like a person on the verge of plunging to her death over the cliff. Not much older than Sarai, she wore a laborer's short kilt fluttering around her thighs and a sleeveless vest barely laced closed over full breasts, their half-glimpsed curve like an invitation. An iron ring depicting a wolf's head hung from a chain around her neck. Her feet were bare, smeared with a red clay dirt that Sarai had never seen in these parts. Her curly black hair was wildly blowing in the stiff wind, strands obscuring her brow and then whisking away to reveal beautifully lashed brown eyes. She was magnificent. The recklessness of her stance and the air swirling around her, flashing with threads like strands of blue fire, made her look like a character from one of the tales Elit had often sung and danced in the outside servants' parlor at night:

> *The firelings kidnapped the girl and made her a demon of fire and air*
> *never more bound to earth!*

Just as Sarai opened her mouth, trying to force out any word, the young woman caught her gaze as with a hook.

"Not that cursed song again. Don't sing it!" She didn't look one bit like the locals, and although her speech was perfectly intelligible it was obvious she came from somewhere else in the Hundred. "You are Sarai."

"Who are *you* and how do you know who I am?"

"I'm a demon, of course."

Sarai was too stunned and curious to be frightened. "Did you just walk on the coil? Is that why the maze changed? Of what substance are coils made? What do they do?"

"Are you always so full of questions?" retorted the young woman with a laugh.

"Yes."

"No time to answer. There are reeves on the hunt and we have to clear the area. Hurry home, Sarai. Go by the garden shed on your way. You'll find someone you know. As for me, remember nothing." The voice slammed right through Sarai's head as though the vision had fixed fingers into her eye sockets and tugged her skull open.

The earth jerked beneath her like a bucking horse.

She woke lying facedown on the pergola terrace, cheek resting against stone pavement made damp by a spray of rain. A headache gnawed at her eyes. Flies buzzed around her face. She waved them away, then sat up. It was already halfway through morning.

She tried to rub the headache out of her brows as she retrieved her shawl, which was draped over a stone bench. The city girls had been giggling all night in the dormitory so she hadn't gotten much sleep. It was just odd she hadn't used her shawl as a pillow, and now it was too late to make a measurement of the demon's coil. She had to get back before Aunt Rua wondered where she was.

Wind skittered through the eaves of the pergola. Overhead an eagle glided closer, as if looking for someone. She hurried down the path, through the gate and the garden, and dashed into the workshop just as rain broke over the valley. Its downpour rolled thunderously on the roof. She shook off her damp sandals and climbed the step to the raised plank floor. The glorious smell of rain wafted along rows of troughs and counters crowded with plants.

Aunt Rua sat on a stool at a table, bent over a dead, plucked sparrow whose wings were spread out and pinned to a board. She was teasing apart the musculature with tweezers and a scalpel. The work so absorbed her that Sarai was able to tiptoe past without her looking up.

The potting room had its own sliding doors screened with opaque rice paper. Her great-aunt had insisted on it, for the potting room was Tsania's only domain since she had never married. As Sarai quietly slid the screen shut behind her, her great-aunt turned in her chair, head bobbing with the effort. Tsania's twisted back and palsy were all many people saw of her, but Sarai had flourished under an intelligence and affection that were as nourishing as sun and rain. As always her smile made Sarai grasp her aunt's hands and, with an answering smile, kiss her gaunt cheek.

"There you are. The rain." These days Tsania's voice was a whisper.

Sarai waited out her aunt's coughing fit before she replied. Overhead the rain was already easing. "Aunt Rua didn't see me. Verea Yava, a good morning to you."

"A good morning to you, Sarai." Yava was a Hundred woman from the neighboring village, not Ri Amarah. Powerfully built and strong enough to lift and carry Tsania, Yava had acted as Tsania's attendant for over thirty years. She was also Elit's mother. "I will go fetch tea."

She closed the screens as she left.

"Are you cataloging Uncle Abrisho's seeds?" Sarai asked, for the oversize ledger was open.

"Waiting for you. His factor sealed the packets too tightly."

"I'll undo them." Sarai sorted the seed packets by the names Abrisho's factor had written on each envelope. "The girls were talking all night in the dormitory. I was going to make a measurement of the coil but I fell asleep instead."

Illness had pared Tsania to skin and bones, yet she pinched her lips with concern for Sarai. "Are you well? You have shadows in your face."

When Sarai shut her eyes, flashes of light made her woozy. For an instant she glimpsed a woman standing atop the rock as if about to walk across a bridge woven out of air. She grasped the table to steady herself as the image faded. "Just tired. Is this sunspear?" She pushed a packet toward Tsania. "We've never grown this before."

"Sunspear has eight varieties. I want to produce new color varieties..." She coughed.

Aunt Rua's voice carried from the other side of the closed screens. "Tsania? Have you seen Sarai? She never came in. I don't trust what she might be about, the sly girl."

Sarai looked down at her betrayingly wet clothes. "I'll go down by the garden shed. You can say I've been thinning the ruvia all morning in the rain."

She grabbed clippers, canvas gardening apron, and wooden clogs from a hook and fled into the lower garden. The rain had stopped except for spatters. Sunlight slashed open the clouds, streaming over what everyone called the women's garden because these plants had a special efficacy for women. The rows were marked with Aunt Rua's tidy labels: Bright Blue to stem bleeding; muzz to bring on menses; lady's heart to ease cramps; moro to bring in milk. Ruvia was mashed and eaten to strengthen pregnant women and elders so they tired less easily.

The ruvia plants were too crowded to grow to their best size. When she had an apron's weight of trimmings she carried them to the compost beds that lined the wall.

Because the estate was so huge, the clan employed outside gardeners. These men came only in the afternoon, at which time Aunt Rua and any other Ri Amarah women would leave the garden. They had their own garden shed on the outside, and entered the estate through a locked gate. Because Aunt Rua often consulted with the outside gardeners, their shed was built into the wall, abutting the gate; that way Rua could speak to the men without being seen by them.

To Sarai's surprise she heard a man singing even though it was well before the usual time for the gardeners to come. His deep and mellow voice intoned the words of a song Elit had often sung to her, "The Sad Girl and Her Happy Lover."

She frowned so deep that her heart became a crater
But when her lover smiled the dry bowl became a lake.

How her heart beat hard at the sound of a friendly voice! She was so lonely since Elit had left the village. She glanced toward the workshop to make sure the doors were shut and no disapproving aunt was looking this way.

"Ver Zilli?"

He broke off. "Ah! Blessings of the day to you, verea." He always addressed her with the polite title used among the people of the Hundred for women, just as she used the correct polite address for men.

"Blessings of the day to you, ver. Is your family well?"

"They are indeed. Thank you for asking."

"My uncle brought sunspear seeds from Toskala. Do you have any advice?"

"Yes. Those will flower brightly in the dry season but it's too wet for them now. Start the seeds in pots and coax them along until Whisper Rains. Then plant the seedlings outside—at night, mind you—where they'll get full sun."

"I'll do that!" It was so hard to let him go. "I wanted to ask you about the fistir hedge. Cousin Beniel insisted our hedge ought to be trimmed no wider than a hat's brim, just like the one he sees in the city garden of the Herelian clan that has some kind of connection to the palace. But in truth I think he just wanted a chance to brag about what a man of the world he's becoming with his new palace friends."

Zilli cleared his throat. After a pause during which she realized abruptly that she had compounded the crime of being an unmarried girl talking to a man who was not Ri Amarah with the worse transgression of gossiping about family to an outsider, he went on. "A sudden trimming like that will only traumatize the plant. But let me see what applications of compost and lace-berry juice can do. Oh here now. Who is this?"

From beyond the shed a new voice broke into song, the husky tone and familiar refrain staggering Sarai's thoughts so thoroughly she could neither move nor speak. She knew that voice as she knew her own soul.

The sad girl and her happy lover
What a striking pair they made.
One in shadow, and the other in light—

The voice broke off as the servants' bell chimed from the direction of Rua's workshop.

"Best you go, verea," Zilli said in a sharper voice, for he knew as well as she did that they weren't allowed to speak. His footsteps stomped to the far end of the shed. Pushed hard, the door slammed back, and he called, "Heya! You, lad, hurry! Curse it! I told them to send a woman because it looks suspicious if men come up here too early in the day. Get inside before someone sees you."

"Greetings of the day to you, ver!" replied the new arrival

with brisk cheerfulness. "May the Merciful One greet you on this fine morning when we are graced by Hasibal's Tears."

"Ah. May the world prosper, and justice be served. Are you my contact?"

"Yes, ver. We need to move everyone out now before the reeves get here. Go on. I'll lock up."

A door slapped shut as one or both of them left.

Sarai could not catch her breath. With another glance back at the workshop to make sure no one was in sight, she fumbled at the multipronged lock. She shifted the gate open and peered into the dim confines of the shed. A person stepped into shadowy view.

"Elit!"

Two steps brought them into each other's arms. The embrace was tight, comforting, and yet painful after being apart for so long. She never wanted to let go.

"I wasn't sure I'd ever see you again," she whispered, looking up to give her beloved a kiss.

Elit pressed fingers to Sarai's lips. "You're not supposed to know I'm here. You mustn't tell my mother or anyone, not even your great-aunt."

"Why are you here, then? If it's a secret even from your mother?"

"To take a delivery of rice."

"Is that a euphemism for something else?"

"It's the gods' business. They sent me because I'm from here and know my way around. I can't tell you more. I'm sorry."

Elit had cut off her beautiful long black hair into a short, spiky mess, in the fashion worn by many Hundred boys and men. On her lanky frame the hill country tunic and trousers commonly worn by men hid her small breasts and narrow hips, and her shoulders looked broader than they had before, as if she'd been at hard labor. If Sarai hadn't known her she might well have mistaken her for a lad, as Zilli had.

"It's to do with you being one of Hasibal's pilgrims, isn't it?"

"It is." Elit lifted Sarai's hand to her lips and tenderly kissed her palm. "I don't have much time. I shouldn't have volunteered to be the one to come to the shed, but I was hoping I might see you. And here you are!"

She caught Sarai's face in her hands and stared at her so hard, tears in her eyes.

"It was my idea to make that song the signal we use to alert our allies that it's safe to approach. It always makes me think of you. Are you well, Sarai? How is it with you?"

A lump in her throat made it hard to speak calmly, but she did not want Elit to see her cry.

"Great-Aunt Tsania and I always have some project going. I've read all of Aunt Rua's medical books, and I'm allowed to sit in when villagers bring her their difficult medical cases. I've read all of Uncle Makel's history and geography books. I can tell you in great detail about the towns and regions and customs of the Hundred, and I am well versed in the geography of the Sirniakan Empire in the south and the kingdom of Ithik Eldim in the north, all the places I will never see except to read about them in a book."

Her desperate babble began to embarrass her.

"I'm going to begin writing my own pharmacological study," she finished. "That's all."

Elit released her, glancing away with such remorse that Sarai could not bear to leave it at that.

"I have some ideas about better recipes for medicinals, prepared through sublimation and distillation, with special attention to compounds of plants and minerals that can alleviate illnesses particular to women..."

She couldn't go on.

"I didn't mean this to be so painful," whispered Elit, letting the tears flow.

"No, I'm glad you came. Are you glad you dedicated yourself to the temple?" Sarai asked, not sure which answer she feared more.

Elit's face lit like fire. "Oh, Sarai-ya! I am so glad! Hasibal's service is more even than I had imagined! I wish I could tell you everything but I can't."

She clasped Sarai's hands again. Hers were callused and strong like iron. This time they said nothing because there was nothing to say. The honk of a salt-goose broke the silence, although it wasn't the season for salt-geese to pass over these hills.

Elit released her hands and stepped back. "I miss you, my dear one. But that's the signal I have to go."

Sarai stood there, dense and stolid as a tree, stuck in one place until death felled her. "When will I see you again, Elit?"

Even in shadow Sarai could absorb every delicate nuance of Elit's expressions because she knew them so well: compassion, impatience, excitement, pain, love, and the final stamp of regret accepted as inevitable. "I don't know. Probably not for years. We won't be coming back here anytime soon. You know how hard it was for me to leave you the first time, and there isn't anyone else, Sarai-ya, I need you to know that."

"No one but the god."

Elit nodded. "I walk in the service of Hasibal the Merciful One now. I wish…"

I wish I wasn't a demon-touched Ri Amarah girl whose clan will never let her go. I wish I could worship your god so I could go with you, but I can't. Sarai had already said the words four years ago. No point in repeating them now.

"…I wish you can find a path that makes you happy, that brings you what you need and what you deserve. Whatever you must do to find fulfillment and a life you can bear to live, please do it. You're in my heart always. I'll return when I can, but I'm the god's servant now and I don't control my own movements. Please don't wait for me if you find another path. You deserve more than this, Sarai-ya." She kissed Sarai hard one last time and left, shutting the shed's door behind her.

Sarai stumbled backward into a light and air that seemed stifling, here inside the estate wall. A shadow rippled over the ground. An eagle flew so low over the garden she could trace the feathers on its wings and see the creases in the leather trousers worn by the reeve. She shoved the gate closed and clicked the lock's complicated pegs and levers back into place.

What if the reeve had noticed the open gate?

She reached the back entrance just as Yava slid a screen aside, looking for her.

"Didn't you hear the bell?" Agitation wrinkled Yava's brow, at odds with her normal good humor. She said nothing about the tears on Sarai's cheeks as she looked past Sarai toward the locked gate. "Do take care, mistress. The new gardeners your uncle hired aren't from around here and may not understand your family's strict rules."

Sarai bent her head over the clippers, wiping them on the apron. Her lips burned, and her heart had shattered. But she could still think straight and speak in a falsely calm voice. "I was all the way in the back where the ruvia is thickest. I got some nettle on my foot and it really stings."

Yava coughed. "Your uncle is here."

"Uncle Makel is here?" He never came down to Aunt Rua's workshop.

"Cover your face. There is a stranger with him."

Sarai was grateful to have an excuse to pull a corner of her shawl up to conceal the lower part of her face. As she and Yava hurried down the back corridor, she recognized Makel's approach by the familiar hitch in his walk. A second set of footsteps paced him.

"This way," her uncle said in a stern voice.

She and Yava slipped inside just as the far door rattled with a knock and was slid aside. Uncle Makel entered the room followed by a stranger. Except for the outside servants, people who were not Ri Amarah never entered any part of the estate except the audience parlor.

The man wore leather trousers, a close-fitting leather vest, and leather gloves and boots, clothing sewn from the skin of animals and thus forbidden to Ri Amarah. A harness wrapped his torso and hips, like a plow ox's rigging. His bare arms were sheeny with sweat and tight with muscle. Hundred men did not cover their hair as did Ri Amarah men. His black hair was shaved so short that the shape of his skull was a lure to her eyes. She knew she was staring but after the shock of Elit's sudden appearance and departure she just did not care.

"My apologies, Aunt Tsania," said Uncle Makel. "This is Reeve Reyad. He says he was sent to keep watch on the demon's coil, and he saw a woman standing on Vista Hill." His gaze marked Sarai. "Your aunt says you did not come to the workshop this morning, niece."

"She has been here all morning," said Aunt Tsania. "I sent her down to thin the ruvia."

"My wife says she wasn't here."

"Makel!" Tsania had been born on the estate while Makel had merely married into the family through his alliance to Rua, who was Sarai's mother's sister. "I cannot help what your honorable wife does not see when she is busy. Why do you permit a strange man to intrude into my private workshop?"

The question raked so accusingly that Makel retreated to the door, but the reeve did not budge. He examined Tsania with no sign of the disgust with which her own relatives often treated her, instead giving her a respectful nod. Then he studied the long shawl that draped Sarai from head to halfway down her skirt. Her clothes were ordinary, nothing fancy like the other girls liked to wear, and for once she was happy for it because it made her harder to identify. His gaze dipped to where her bare toes peeped from beneath the hem of the skirt. They were damp and dusty, smeared along the tips. With a lift of the eyebrows, he looked up directly into her eyes, and she stared belligerently back, knowing her expression was concealed.

"My apologies, verea, for intruding where I am not wanted," said the reeve. "But I have my duty. Can the girl speak? I have questions for her."

Makel's lips pressed primly together. "It is not Ri Amarah custom for unmarried girls to speak to men not of the clan."

"Very well. We reeves are told to respect your foreign customs. I'll tell the marshal. I'm sure she'll send a woman to the house to interview the girl."

He left.

"Yava, bring Sarai and my honored aunt up to the house at once." The glare Makel flung at Tsania made him look like a baby on the verge of a squall but Tsania merely smiled. He flushed. "Sarai, go sit with the girls at Garna's jubilee. Do not mention a reeve was here, do you understand?"

Without waiting for a reply he stamped out the door.

"Did you see anything?" whispered Tsania.

She thought of Elit, and for the first time in her life she lied to her beloved great-aunt. "No. I didn't see anything."

9

The lack of fleeing criminals nagged at Dannarah as she flew sweeps and yet still spotted no suspicious movement on the ground. Finally she returned to the clearing where the discarded machete had caught her eye. The "All Clear" flag had been planted in the dirt, and a hooded eagle waited on the ground. She landed at a prudent distance and hooded Terror.

Walking through the wet growth with the tall grass dragging against her leathers made every creaky joint and tight muscle pop and pull. Her left knee ground with each step. Her right shoulder hurt. Everything hurt. Eventually she would get frail enough that Terror would snap her head off to be rid of her and thus acquire a younger, stronger reeve. But not today.

A temporary settlement had been constructed beneath the trees. Goats had grazed back undergrowth but were absent now, which struck her as strange. Soldiers picked through remains of crude huts and stone-built hearths.

Reyad beckoned to her. He was standing beside a scaffold on which lay a dead woman with her long hair unbound and her body wrapped in a length of undyed linen. She had a work gang mark inked on her cheek.

"Marshal Dannarah!"

"Didn't I set you to watch the demon's coil?" she asked as she came up.

"Yes, and I saw a woman on Vista Hill. I landed in the estate and tried to interview a girl who may have been the one who was outside. But they'll only allow a woman to talk to her, a cursed unpleasant custom, if you ask me. She kept her face covered, too, although that did make me notice what pretty eyes she had."

Charming men were so full of themselves, but his grin amused her anyway.

"That's what I flew back to report," he added.

"You did well to seek me out, then." She studied him to see how he would react to praise; he merely nodded to show he'd heard, neither modest nor arrogant. "Was this person killed in the raid?"

"No. The soldiers told me the camp was deserted when they got here, except for her body."

"If there was a demon helping the fugitives, it could have warned them before we arrived."

"These folk may be outlaws and criminals, but look how they've done their best to build a proper Sorrowing Tower for the corpse, and how she's been washed and laid out respectfully."

She looked at him with more interest. "Where are you from?" she asked, trying to sort out the odd pronunciations in his speech.

"I'm from upcountry Mar, the Suvash Hills." The reeve's left forearm and right calf bore the inked patterns marking him as a child of the Earth Mother. "My clan grows rice and bitter-leaf."

"Ah. That explains it."

"Explains what, Marshal?"

Like many countryfolk he was impertinent, speaking just as if he were the equal of anyone and even her. "You're inked in the old-fashioned way. In the cities the old custom of the Mothers' mark inked onto forearm and calf began to fall out of fashion twenty years ago when King Jehosh decreed all war captives be inked on the face. Now that work gang criminals are also marked in the same way, only people who live in the country still ink their children. Just like most folk no longer follow the old death customs of building a Sorrowing Tower and binding the corpse."

"More the shame to them! It honors the Four Mothers to ink each of us with the symbol of which essence we bear. I've seen that outlander custom of trapping dead flesh under earth when bodies ought to be washed and laid out for the vultures to pick apart and the wind and rain to scour clean. It's impious." Abruptly he drew his shoulders up his ears exactly like a boy being scolded. With a breath he forced his shoulders down.

"No offense meant. I know you are of the lineage that worships the southern god and his spirit bowl and stone tombs."

"Hard to offend me, lad. I've heard it all and worse. Honesty serves better than lying smiles."

Reyad touched a bronze armband on his upper right arm as if it were a talisman. He glanced around to make sure they couldn't be overheard. Since the soldiers had widened their search for any trace of the vanished inhabitants, most of them were now out of sight among the trees. "Is it true you were chief marshal? When King Atani was alive?"

"I was."

"Do you have any influence over King Jehosh?"

She had been as good as exiled from the palace twenty-two years ago, but she was not about to confess that to this young bantam. "I find being demoted to marshal of Horn Hall preferable to being leashed to the palace under my nephew's rule. Why do you ask?"

"I just wonder how an ass of a man like Auri gets to become chief marshal over all the reeve halls." He paused, looking taken aback at what he had just said.

Young men held no mystery for her. "It's no wonder you're glad to be out of that cesspit of backbiting and foot licking in Argent Hall. Every reeve who wants to catch the notice of Chief Marshal Auri begs for a transfer there, so they are all stewing in one foul-smelling pot that has as much shit and piss in it as rice and greens. Anyway, that ass Auri only gained the post of chief marshal because he's an old crony of Jehosh's. It was sheer luck for him that he got chosen by an eagle although I swear an oath no one can understand why. He can't even trim his own eagle's talons, leaves all that care to the fawkners because he fears the bird."

Reyad snorted. "It's true! Everyone knows he's afraid of his own eagle. Who is called Slip because he's a slip of a thing, small and gentle. It's a cursed shame any eagle is wasted on a strutting cockwit like him. Although that explains why he's chief marshal when he's the very kind who uses his position to grab for things he wants instead of working to make the reeve halls well run."

"An opinion I agree with but which you'll do well to keep quiet."

He took a hasty step back, ducking his head. "My apologies, Marshal. I forget myself."

When she was young she had never given a second thought to her status as King Anjihosh's daughter. Now she found that it put distance between her and people. "I'm not scolding you. Around me, do not ever hesitate to speak your mind."

"I poked around while I was waiting, and I did see something odd over in that hut." He pointed with his elbow toward a hut woven of sticks and tucked against the bole of a red pine.

They walked over together, and she saw the odd thing immediately: Over the crude lintel hung a wreath woven of supple branches bearing slender red leaves.

"A redheart wreath!" she exclaimed. "How did that get here?"

He squinted at the lintel. "What is a redheart wreath? I thought that was just decoration."

"You probably have never seen them in Mar because you're too far south. In the provinces of Istria, Herelia, and Haldia, a redheart wreath is a decoration set over the door of a recently married couple to bring joy and good fortune. The branches come from a tree called redheart, which only grows in the Wild."

"The Wild? Oh, the Weldur Forest, you mean, like in the tales."

"Yes. This wreath is fresh. But the overland or river journey from the Wild would take more than ten days. Which means either someone has planted redheart outside the Wild, which would be a matter of interest mostly to the mendicants who wander the roads with their healing potions—"

"Atiratu's healers, you mean? Those are the only mendicants I know."

"That's right, they used to be priestesses of the god."

"The Lady of Beasts, Marshal. Begging your pardon. Atiratu the Lady of Beasts is one of the seven gods and goddesses. Many mendicants and healers still serve Her. I must admit that when I was assigned to Argent Hall I was shocked to see all the seven temples have been closed in the city of Olossi in favor of a Beltak shrine. I mean no offense. I'm just a country lad."

He wasn't belligerent, just persistent and proud.

"Fair enough. The point is, either a reeve or a demon must have brought this wreath here."

"If demons are so cruel, why would they bring a wreath to celebrate a marriage?"

"Demons use lies and lures to snare people into their service. Lures can include seeming kindnesses. It's easy for a young man like you to forget that sixty years ago demons destroyed the peace of the Hundred. Villages burned. Children abused. Adults barbarously murdered, or enslaved into unspeakably brutal servitude. People starving. All of it enforced by demons' monstrous ability to rip into your very thoughts and compel you to obey them. It was my father King Anjihosh who defeated them."

"Wasn't it demons who killed King Atani?"

She found she couldn't bear to discuss Atani's death with someone she barely knew. To avoid answering she pushed past a barkcloth curtain into the hut's interior. An unrolled sleeping mat lay abandoned on a low plank platform, a pair of lovers' pillows stacked atop, waiting for two people who would never return.

"It's a sad thing to see." Reyad picked up a rice basket that someone had kicked aside and fixed its woven cover back over the top. "Makes me miss my own wife."

"You're married?" She eyed him askance; he looked so young.

"Three years ago." He did not smile as he said so.

She said nothing.

After a hesitation he went on. "She came with me to Argent Hall but she hated living there so she went back to her clan in Mar."

"Was it leaving home she disliked? Or Argent Hall in particular?"

"Argent Hall in particular." His hands clenched to fists.

"Several women transferred to serve under me at Horn Hall because of a sour trial of duty at Argent. But then they stopped coming so I thought things had improved."

"The last of the Argent Hall reeves who were women transferred out a few months ago. I don't know where they went."

He crouched to peer under the low platform. In profile his frown made him look worn, fretful, discouraged. When he made no reply she thought him distracted by his troubles but after all he was scraping under the platform. He sat back with a grunt of satisfaction.

"Here's what I saw." He held out a tin pendant strung from a leather cord. The pendant had the shape of a branch studded with seven five-petaled blossoms. "Hasibal's Tears."

"A common enough thing for a person to wear who gives offerings to the Merciful One." She plucked the cover off the rice basket and looked inside. "It doesn't seem they were starving."

"See, that's what I wonder. They had to get that rice from somewhere." He swept up a few grains. "Look how short the grain is, and its speckled red color. At the Spears' camp we've been eating rice the soldiers buy at the local villages. This isn't the variety of rice they grow around here."

"Spoken like a farmer."

"Proud to be so! My clan grows long grain, both green and black. This rice is so distinctive we should be able to narrow down where it comes from. Then, like the redheart wreath, we just have to figure out how it got here."

"That's an excellent observation." She set down the basket before stepping outside and directing a soldier to fetch Chief Tuvas. Going back in, she caught Reyad's attention with a lift of her hand. "If you're interested, I have the authority to assign you to my own flight."

"Do you mean…" He hesitated before going on. "…a transfer to Horn Hall?"

"Will you take a transfer? If it suited her to join you, I can assure you your wife will not face any troublesome incidents at Horn Hall. Not under my watch."

He rocked back. "The hells! If she would… It might… To be out of Argent Hall… Withering Taru! My thanks, Marshal! You won't regret giving me this chance!"

He grinned brilliantly. He was so full of the confidence that no matter how deep the pit there is a way to climb out. Not like her, embittered and weary. Losing Atani had been like losing pleasure in food: Everything tasted flat.

Chief Tuvas arrived, flanked by soldiers. "Marshal, your report?"

"Was the settlement abandoned before the raid?"

He nodded. "Yes. We found the one corpse, that's all. They even took their goats."

"I'd wager the machete I saw in the clearing was a deliberate lure to draw us here while people were escaping elsewhere, warned by demons."

Tuvas's eyes widened. As a grandson of one of Anjihosh's Qin company, he had no doubt grown up on tales of those dreadful days. "Demons? Do you think so, Marshal?"

"I do think so." She shook grains of rice into his hand.

"What good does rice do us?" The grains dribbled through his fingers.

Reyad kept his expression blank although his mouth twitched.

She brushed the last few grains off her hands. "We discover how and where they got their supplies. But first I want you to come with me to interview a woman at the local Ri Amarah clan. She may be implicated."

10

Sarai watched with a false cheer sewn onto her face as the new bride was escorted from the girls' corner over to the women. All smiles, they greeted Garna with necklaces of flowers.

"Here stand now as a woman and receive your mirror and your Book of Accounts." Aunt Rua offered Garna a cup of the wine reserved for adults.

A polished bronze mirror reflected Garna's beaming face before she hooded it in a silk bag and looped the handle to her belt. The thick ledger was so new, Sarai could smell its freshly cut pages and scarcely dried glue. Garna opened it to display the blank pages, for it was here she would keep track of household finances, trading ventures, and the secret knowledge, written in code, that each woman learned as her part in the upkeep of the clan. Day by day and year by year the mirror would show her the truth of who she was while the book would become the record of her life. Meanwhile Great-Aunt Tsania would die as if she had never lived, unwritten except in the catalog of seeds and plantings that no one would remember as her handiwork.

The women began singing an ancient song brought from across the ocean generations ago. Rain rolled a counterpoint along the roof.

Now the parched land drinks.
For this one season the land will flower.
A rose is blooming in the garden.
For this one breath the heart will sing.

When trays of jubilee cakes were brought Sarai helped Tsania eat a pair of plum cakes, her favorite, but for herself she had lost her appetite.

Tsania squeezed her hands. "I hated it, too, when I was your age. Seeing younger girls cross over and knowing I would never be allowed to take on the full measure of the women's work that keeps our people safe and secure."

"It isn't fair!"

"You can't breathe in here, Sarai-ya. Say you are going to fetch me some of Rua's spread-wing tea for my lungs."

Sarai kissed her great-aunt's soft cheek and crept out of the parlor into the central atrium. Standing alone in the empty hall she saw the unwritten life that stretched ahead of her: Elit was gone. Tsania would die, and Sarai would pick out other women's embroidery stitches, catalog seeds, and grow old alone.

Despair battered her in waves. She did not want to sit for the rest of her life at the back of the room, ignored and pitied, still called a girl when she was sixty. Yet wasn't it shameful to pity Tsania, the woman who had raised her with care and affection and who went about her life with no sign of bitterness?

How she hated feelings! It would be better to be the wind, never pinned down, free of the burden of all these terrible emotions.

A bell rang at the front of the house. Uncle Makel hurried

into view from the men's wing, which faced the front drive and the grand entrance. Men's voices rose like the river in flood, churning and foaming.

"Sarai! There you are! Come along!"

To her surprise he led her to the tower stairs instead of the audience parlor.

The two-story compound had a four-story tower rising at its center. With each step up the tower stairs her thoughts turned and turned over the mystery of Elit's unexpected appearance. Rice and reeves: She couldn't fit the two together.

She and her uncle passed the first landing, which let onto the women's room of records, and then climbed past the closed door of his study on the second landing, and up the last long set of steps to the tower's crown.

He halted by the curtained archway. "Wait in the women's crown until I call you."

He went back down.

She pushed past the curtain, as every girl was allowed to do although no man or boy could enter this space. The top story was open to the air, protected by a railing and sheltered by deep eaves. The space housed a huge glass vessel shaped like a teardrop and almost as tall as she was. Inside the thick glass rested the sacred flame of the house.

The twisting blue fire was lively today, as passionate as if celebrating Garna's passage. The blue light wasn't really a fire. It gave off no heat. Once a month at the dark of the moon the women fed it with a thimble-cup of menstrual blood. Men were forbidden from invoking the flame because males risked waking the slumbering Imperators who, in the ancient past known to the ancestors, had worn the flame as their crown. Only married Ri Amarah women knew its secrets, for it was women's sacred duty to tend the fire that protected the clans from the pitiless Imperators who, as it said in the children's tale, had once enslaved their people and would do so again if they ever found them.

Usually the flame's writhing dance soothed her with its endless variations, but tonight she glimpsed a young woman's face in the fire: sharp brows, a bold nose, dark eyes, a ring hanging by a chain around her neck stamped with the likeness of a wolf's head. The face was that of a stranger.

She shut her eyes against an encroaching headache. Each Ri Amarah household cut a unique layered pattern of slits in the eaves of its sacred tower so that by the tune of the wind you could hear which clan owned which house. She listened to the wind singing through the roof, its whistles and humming acting as herald to the storm blowing in from the east.

A door shut below, startling her. Although the floor beneath the vessel was solid, a latticed square in each corner gave added ventilation to the room below. Kneeling at one corner, she peered down into the study. Two men had entered.

"I have other urgent business, Abrisho. This interruption comes at a poor time."

"My apologies, Makel." Abrisho was Aunt Rua's cousin. "I'm sorry I have to leave just as there is this trouble with the Spears and reeves, but Beniel and I must return tomorrow to Toskala. I urge you to favorably consider the offer I have brought. Such a chance will never come again."

"It is impossible to accept."

"How can we pass up a chance to place one of our children into a family as well connected as the Herelian barons? They are the descendants of General Sengel, who was King Anjihosh's most honored soldier of all his original company!"

Makel halted by an open window just below Sarai, staring toward the river. Fortunately he did not look up. "You walk too much among the courtiers, Abrisho. Your son Beniel walks with a foot outside our people already."

"His friendships with the young men of the court aid us with information and preference. He has more than once received the courtesy of a friendly word from King Jehosh's third son, Prince Kasad."

"Be careful lest he stray into error and forget who he is. We need not curry favor."

"Of course we need the palace's favor if we wish to protect ourselves in these uneasy times! Do you think the wave of violence against our cousins in High Haldia an isolated incident?"

"We must not act precipitously."

"Do you believe their compound was half burned and their furnishings smashed because of a freakish storm instead of by the suspicion and envy of their neighbors?"

Burned and smashed! Sarai pressed her ear to the lattice. She had heard nothing about trouble for Ri Amarah in the city of High Haldia. News of such a frightful attack was the sort of thing only discussed among the adults.

Abrisho went on, so worked up that he was shaking a hand almost in Makel's face. "We are vulnerable because we are still seen as foreigners and outsiders even though our clans have lived in the Hundred for five generations. In the past King Jehosh has been an advocate for our people, like his father and grandfather were. But his humor is famously known as changeable weather. Anyway he has been absent so much these last few years fighting in the north that it is hard to know what he intends now. His two older sons are in thrall to the Beltak priests, and they emphatically do not trust us. Don't you see? The goodwill of the Herelian clan can protect us."

Makel said nothing. Sunlight wove a sheen along the folded silk with which he covered his hair.

Abrisho went on. "Gilaras is the youngest of the six sons of Sengel's elder son, Lord Seras."

"A son of Lord Seras! Are you daft? How can allying ourselves with the disgraced branch of the family help us? Lord Seras murdered King Atani!"

"That was twenty-two years ago. Seras died in the attack as well, and nothing came of his demon-inspired conspiracy to place himself on the throne. Meanwhile his two oldest sons grew up to become notable generals in the army and have served loyally and with honor. As a clan the Herelians are still connected to some of the most powerful people in the palace. Furthermore, the peculiar nature of their menfolk and the complete destitution of their clan's coffers means they are desperate. They need our money to restore their fortune and they are willing to seal a marriage alliance even with a Ri Amarah girl to get it."

"If this Lord Gilaras is the youngest, then any girl he marries will become least among the women of the household," objected Makel.

"Quite the contrary," said Abrisho. "Her position would be paramount. You see, Gilaras is the only one of the brothers who still has his testicles. After their father murdered King Atani, the boys were all castrated in punishment for his treason. This is why it is of paramount importance to the family that the young man marry and give their branch of the clan a future."

"The old Hundred families do not care whether their heirs come through the male or the female line. What of his sisters?"

"The lad has one sister but because of the family's lack of fortune she remains unmarried as well. They hope to restore all with our help."

Makel walked away from the window, out of Sarai's sight. "A young man from such ill-favored seed may have grown up twisted and perverse."

"Do you think I have not already considered this aspect? The money will be settled on the clan through the girl and thus will remain in her keeping, as is our custom. Any abuse or trouble heaped upon her would result in an immediate dissolution of the contract. Their desperation will protect her because if they anger or abuse her she will leave and take the money with her."

Makel's pacing halted. His tone cracked. "To marry a child outside our people is the same as killing the child. I will not allow it."

Abrisho wore city clothes, festooned with beads, and the silk that hid his hair was a shimmering gray. Silver bracelets hid his forearms, the mark of his success as a merchant. "I will give my own second daughter to this venture because I believe it is that important. I have taken the step of asking her if she will consent to the marriage, and she has agreed. But I need your permission."

"No. As head of the clan, I refuse it. I refuse it. I refuse it."

The rain died off as the wind dropped abruptly. Voices rose from the front of the house. Sarai crept to the railing where she could stand hidden in the corner by the eaves and see the graveled forecourt. Four carts escorted by soldiers rolled into view.

Young men of the house ran to open the gates of the carriage house just as a pair of eagles plummeted from the sky and landed with a rousing thump on the grassy riverbank. The speed of their descent made her clutch the railing and stifle a giggle born of excitement. She had never seen reeves and eagles so close before today. One was the good-looking young man she had encountered earlier. The other was a much older woman. Her hair was shaved as short as the man's, her ears were unadorned with a woman's earrings, and she carried a baton in one hand and looked ready to use it.

The first three wagons were piled with objects. In the last lay a woman as limp as if she were dead; she was jammed in beside a covered basket. The sight of woman and basket hit Sarai like a fist to her gut. According to Tsania, Sarai had arrived at the estate as an infant twenty-two years ago, in a basket wedged into the bed of a wagon between a bundle of ragged garments and her mother's decaying corpse.

The sky opened up, rain drumming so hard that the people caught out in it could only laugh as they ran for cover. A gust of wind made the roof howl. The sacred flame leaped, although no wind touched it.

Footsteps hammered up the steps and the door slammed open below as two strangers walked into Uncle Makel's private study as if they needed no permission, and probably they did not. Peering down through the lattice, Sarai glimpsed the silver-streaked black hair of the woman. A soldier wearing his hair in a topknot glanced at the ceiling as if he sensed her. She froze, suddenly sure the Black Wolves had come to kill her as they had her mother.

Then she remembered that the Black Wolves were no more. King Jehosh's elite soldiers were known as the King's Spears.

Makel and Abrisho had given up their disagreement to stand together in solidarity by Makel's writing desk.

The reeve spoke in the tone of a woman accustomed to obedience. "I am Marshal Dannarah of Horn Hall. This is Chief Tuvas of the Spears. You are Headman Makel. Your house is recorded in the covenants as the Fourth Branch of the Tree of Heaven. Is this correct?"

"In the language spoken here it is a decent approximation of what we call ourselves. I am Makel, who stands as headman of this branch."

"Who is your companion?"

"This is my cousin Abrisho—you would say Abrishon since Abrisho would be a woman's name here in the Hundred. He lives in our household compound in Toskala, where most of our trading ventures take place. I mean no offense, Marshal—"

"One of our reeves saw a woman up by the demon's coil," the reeve broke in, clearly unwilling to waste time. "I have come to interview her according to your custom, for I know you do not like your women to speak to Hundred men. If you would fetch her, I would be most obliged."

Makel scratched his neck. "It would be most irregular. I must object—"

"I think it best you do not object, ver," she said over his words. "We have reason to believe a group of fugitive prisoners settled in the hills nearby and have now escaped us, most likely with the assistance of a demon. One of your women was seen atop Vista Hill, next to Demon's Eye Peak."

"Impossible!" cried Makel. "None of our women would walk outside our walls alone."

But Sarai felt dizzy. The reeve's accusation suddenly made Elit's mysterious errand seem ominous. And yet the Elit she knew would never do anything criminal.

"In fact, as I recall," the marshal went on in a voice that had an edge like honed steel, "your clan was implicated in the murder of King Atani. One of your women was found with the outlaws who ambushed and murdered him."

Makel's voice spiked higher than normal. "We had nothing to do with that! It's true my wife's sister was found with Lord Seras and his traitors. But her presence there had nothing to do with us. She disgraced us by running away from her husband, taking her infant daughter with her and leaving behind her five-year-old son. She ran away with a wagon driver! You can't imagine we would have humiliated our clan by agreeing to any such thing!"

Abrisho coughed. "Marshal Dannarah, we who are Ri Amarah know very well that we are beholden to the original covenant made between King Anjihosh and our clans that has been upheld by his son Atani and now his grandson Jehosh."

The marshal studied the two men until they began to shift from foot to foot uneasily. "A covenant that protects your people, whom many in the Hundred consider to be untrustworthy outlanders. As long as you understand, and report any suspicious activity, you will remain under the king's protection. Where is the girl I wish to speak to?"

Uncle Makel held hard to the old traditions, and in his hesitation Sarai read his absolute belief that to expose an unmarried girl to outsiders was to taint her irrevocably. He was not an unkind man. He treated her respectfully because she was dutiful and quiet and because she helped him catalog the scrolls and books he had shipped up from the city to fill his collection. He did not avoid Tsania as some did, and for that she could forgive him a lot.

Yet like everyone else he said that her mother had been a selfish and wicked young woman who had betrayed her husband, her young son, her siblings and parents, and indeed her entire clan to run away and join a criminal who then helped to kill the beloved king.

The tower shuddered as the gale swept over them. Rain misted against her face, driven sideways by the wind. The storm's voice tore into her heart.

Beyond the estate walls lay the Hundred, the village where Yava and Elit had been born, all the rivers and cities and provinces she had read so much about. The Ri Amarah called this land Exile even though it was the only home generations of their people had known.

Reckless fancy had never suited Sarai. Not for her the daring story of a bold girl setting out with a single rice cake and a change of undergarments to make her way in the world on a dashing escapade. Better planning beforehand would make the journey far more likely to succeed rather than ending in misery, starvation, abuse, and death.

Her mother had run away and been brought back dead.

But she was not going to die in this cage. She deserved better than this.

She hurried down the steps, treading hard so they would hear her coming. So it was that Makel had not yet replied and the others were looking with curiosity toward the door as she entered the study with her shawl pulled up to conceal all but her eyes.

"Why have you called me away from the jubilee, Uncle Makel?" she asked, speaking in the language of the Hundred, which she had learned to perfection in the servants' parlor and in the comfort of Elit's arms. "Garna and I have just begun to sing our betrothal songs."

"Your betrothal songs?" Makel's silver bracelets jangled as he gestured in confusion.

Abrisho gaped, then clamped his mouth closed as the skin around his eyes wrinkled like that of a man acquiescing to a cunning plan.

The reeve had a hawk's gaze and features very different from those of Elit and Yava. "You are the girl Reyad saw up at the demon's coil?"

"I was with my great-aunt in her workshop awaiting the jubilee and celebrating my good fortune. I have just become betrothed to Gilaras Herelian of the Herelian clan. He's the grandson of General Sengel, of whom you may have heard."

The soldier snorted and, for the first time, spoke. "Gods and hells, that will put the swan among the feral dogs in all their mange."

Sarai pretended not to hear this rude comment. The reeve watched her with steady eyes. It was disconcerting to see her dressed in the same sleeveless vest as a man. Up close, Sarai saw that the woman was older than she had guessed from a distance because her muscular shoulders and arms and her confident stance gave her a physical authority Sarai associated with soldiers.

"Lord Gilaras is the youngest son of Lord Seras the traitor, who murdered my beloved brother," said the reeve in a tone whose implacable contours made Sarai shiver. "What an unlikely coincidence."

She ignored it as best she could and traipsed gaily on, pretending she were Elit playing the part of The Oblivious Girl in a tale. "It is a terrible story, I know, but it all happened so long ago, when I was only a baby! The women are singing the jubilee now. We will feast tonight. In the morning I journey to Toskala with Uncle Abrisho and Cousin Beniel. I am sorry if I have caused any trouble for being quite with my head in the clouds this morning for the excitement of my change in circumstance."

Uncle Makel blinked.

The curse of longing that Sarai had spent all her life crushing into silence burst so hard in her heart that it hurt.

But she waited.

To deny her claim would make Uncle Makel look foolish and a liar.

So he did not deny it.

"You have discovered us at an unusually busy time, Marshal, with much celebration afoot," he said as Abrisho fought down a victorious smile that tugged at his fleshy lips. "I do not know what your reeve saw up at Demon's Eye Peak. I wish I did. But I make an oath no betrothed girl of this clan left our estate this morning. The oaths of my people were honored and embraced by your own father King Anjihosh the Glorious Unifier. Indeed, it was our people who gave him the assistance he needed to mount his campaign to drive out the army that was laying waste to the Hundred."

The reeve's glare probed but the shawl hid Sarai's expression.

"It is true my father considered the oaths of the Ri Amarah to be honest and unshakable. Very well. If I find evidence you are involved with outlaws or demons I will destroy your clan myself."

Without the courtesy of a proper farewell the reeve and soldier walked out. Thunder rolled along the heavens, drowning out their footfalls as they descended. It was getting dark.

Sarai dropped the shawl to face her uncles.

"This will do very well, Makel," said Abrisho. "In fact, it is a brilliant idea. My daughter can expect an advantageous marriage within the clans. But Sarai is of no use to you as she is. Her birth shames her but there is no way the Herelians can know that if we do not tell them. Except for the stain in all other ways she looks a healthy girl. She is certainly intelligent enough, and would suit our purpose well in that regard."

The flickering light chased the shadows from Makel's face. He was so sure of himself and his place. "They are not our people, Sarai. They are not us."

"So was the man who fathered me not one of us."

"Your mother is dead and in shame for all eternity for what she did!" he thundered. "You do not understand what this will mean for you. To marry a man who is not Ri Amarah. To live in the world outside the walls, a dreadful thing for a woman. You will be cut off from the heart of your people...the sacred fire tended by women's magic...the curse..." He dragged a hand across his brow as Abrisho shot him a stern glance. "The curse of living outside the household for the rest of your life."

"I am already cut off. If I stay here I will never be allowed to learn the woman's magic that is our sacred duty. Here in the clans you would not even allow me to bear a child, should I want that! I understand it is preferable for Uncle Abrisho's daughter to marry within the clans. You cannot give the best fruit to the swine, I understand that. But the fruit that is too bruised and rotten to be eaten, that you may feed to swine."

Abrisho whistled under his breath. "I would not call the people of the Hundred swine," he said with a hint of asperity and quirk of his eyebrows.

She nodded politely but with a flare of her eyes. "A figure of speech, Uncle Abrisho. I mean no insult by it."

He chuckled. "The court appreciates the blade of cool sarcasm."

Uncle Makel shook his head. "I cannot allow it."

Storm wind shook the walls. Rain hammered the tower. She gave way to the gale of emotions ripping through her.

"Let me go, Uncle Makel. If you do not, I will run away as my mother did."

"You would shame the entire house with such selfish conduct!"

"I have never done anything wrong. But I will not live in this house as a girl for the whole of my life, not as Aunt Tsania has. You are cruel to condemn me to that life."

"She is right," said Abrisho, pressing his case. "She is not crippled as Tsania is."

"Shame cripples her."

"No. We are the ones who visit shame on her. She has done nothing. So the Hidden One exhorts us, Makel: Do not visit the wrongdoing of the parent upon the child. Do not smother a spark before it has a chance to burn."

"Let me go." She would not let Uncle Makel look away, would not let him allow his scruples and Ri Amarah custom to trap her.

His stare met hers, but then it wavered.

"Let me go," she said.

When Uncle Makel glanced down at the rug on the floor, she knew he had given in.

Abrisho's smile flared, thrown at her in shared triumph. "We leave at dawn. Will you be ready for whatever comes of this decision?"

She thought of Aunt Tsania, left behind. But she knew her aunt would demand that she fly.

Was this what anticipation felt like, surging up from her feet to flood her head with giddy smiles? Lightning flashed outside, and thunder boomed in answer, cracking her open with hope and possibility.

"Yes. I will be ready for whatever comes."

11

Long past the seventh bell, in the dead of night, the three young men were kicked out of the brothel. They stumbled out the door into the teeth of a storm. Rain poured in sheets, driven sideways by the howling wind. Their hired coach rocked in the gale, windows shut tight. The poor horse shivered in its traces with only a thin blanket to protect it.

Gilaras Herelian hammered a fist on the coach's closed door. "Open up! We want to go somewhere we can get a drink!"

The door remained shut.

When his friend Tyras tried the handle, it stuck. "I cursed well paid the man enough that he ought to have waited for us!" Tyras had to shout to be heard above the cloudburst. "I hope the Devourer bites off his cock!"

The third man edged down the rain-slicked steps. "That's what we get for hiring a Ri Amarah coachman. Everyone says Silvers can't be trusted. He delivered us here and then abandoned us to this foul weather. The poor horse, too."

"If you call that a horse," said Gil, wiping rain out of his eyes.

"It looks like a horse to me, Gil!"

"You look like an intelligent man to me, Kas, but that doesn't make you one."

Kasad was drunk enough to swing at him. Prince Kasad might be graced with such magnificent titles as Third Lord of the Bow and Fifth Exalted Master of the Hunt, but when he slid on the wet ground and pinwheeled his arms to keep his balance he looked as ridiculous as anyone.

"Oh shut up, Gil," said Tyras, but he laughed as Kasad went down clumsily on his ass, biting out several ripe curses.

Gil looked up and down the empty street. He was in a mad, bad, dangerous mood, and not nearly drunk enough. But something about this situation made his skin prickle. "Don't you two find it odd that the coachman is missing but his coach and horse are still here? Where would he have gone if not inside the coach? Why would he abandon the very animal he relies on for his livelihood?"

Every shutter along the facade was closed tight. The building had seen better days when it was part of a respected temple precinct, dedicated to Ushara the Merciless One, the All-Consuming Devourer, mistress of love, death, and desire. Yet even the oldest scribe in the city recalled the days of his youth through a misty haze, back before the Righteous Victory of King Anjihosh the Glorious Unifier, sixty years ago. Now the place was a brothel staffed with listless flower girls. Since it annoyed the hells out of his family that he went there, Gil kept going back.

He ran back up the steps and pounded at the entry, but the door didn't budge and no one answered. They had been the last to leave. The flame in the street lantern farther down the avenue blew out. Its glass and brass door, having come unchained, banged and then shattered. Only two other lanterns kept the shadows from engulfing the street. For an instant Gil thought he saw a person move along a wall but when he blinked water out of his eyes there was no one there.

Kasad staggered to his feet. "An intelligent man keeps a hierodule in style instead of cocking about with cheap flower girls. My mother says she'll advance me the coin to hire the Incomparable Melisayda."

"Fat chance the Incomparable will accept a contract with you," said Gil as his hands clenched.

Kasad's upper lip curled in a gloating sneer. "You'll be jealous, won't you? You've lusted after her ever since she took up with your brother although I don't know how the hells he can afford her. How he manages the deed with no balls is a mystery to everyone."

"Gil, don't!" Tyras grabbed Gil's arm.

Gil shook off Ty's grasp, swung, and connected. Kasad went down hard.

"Leave him be, you ass-witted cow," said Tyras. "Help me get this door open. Neither of you will have any use for your cocks now or later if they freeze off like mine's about to!"

Together they wrestled with the handle but it wouldn't give.

Teeth chattering, Tyras looked up and down the street as if expecting some helpful servant to appear. "Gods, I'm soaked. I wonder how long I'll linger before the rot sets in with fever."

"Not long, I hope, if it will spare us your moaning." Gil tapped at the door thoughtfully. "Does either of you have a knife?"

"Your family doesn't even allow you a knife when you go out?" demanded Kasad, getting to his feet again as he rubbed his chin.

Gil said nothing as the old anger roused in his gut.

Kasad's laugh was as good as a punch. "It was that incident with your cousin, wasn't it? Lord Vanas's oldest son."

"My uncle Vanas is always lording it over us, how our branch of the family fell while his rose. His snot-nosed son thought he could taunt me with some limp jest about cocks."

Tyras sighed as he fumbled at his sash, fingers clumsy with cold. "Getting into a knife fight with your rich cousin is just the stupid kind of thing you always do, Gil. Especially over some cheap flower girl. I heard your cousin will sire children but always walk with a limp. It was a close thing."

"It wasn't close at all." Gil laughed, because if he didn't laugh he would break something. "I knew exactly where I was cutting."

"So you say." Tyras finally produced a small knife and thrust it into Gil's hands. "For the love of the Opener, could you get on with it?"

Gil worked the knife's point against the door's lock. "Careful. People at court are only allowed to curse in the name of Beltak the Shining One."

"Go fuck goats, Gil!"

"Quiet!" When Gil used that tone, his friends always obeyed.

A gust of wind blew a drenching burst of rain over them. They waited, shuffling restlessly while wind and rain did their worst. Gil gave a grunt of satisfaction. He pulled out the knife, turned the handle, and swung the door open.

A body tumbled out.

"Drunk!" proclaimed Kasad sagely.

"Dead," said Gil as blood from the blow that had stove in the back of the coachman's head melded with rainwater in the gutter and flowed away down the street.

The dead man's silk head covering had begun to unravel. The fabric swirled around the man's pale fingers and caught over his gaping mouth like a gag. His lips and face were contorted in a grimace of agony. Dead, the man looked horrifically gruesome. But the two silver bracelets on each arm had a glamor that drew the eye, as if something alive were caught inside them.

"Oh, piss." Kasad vomited onto the street.

Tyras pulled his feet away from the body. "Oh the hells!"

Gil set a foot up on the carriage and stuck his head into the interior, probing around with a hand. "How did he get himself killed on the inside of a locked door? There's blood greasing the floor. Ah! It's on the forward-facing seat as well. It looks as if he was killed and then fell forward and knocked the handle askew. But the door was locked. He can't have locked it after he was dead, so who did and where is the key?"

Tyras peered into the dark interior. "A strange turn of events, truly."

Gil grabbed a coin pouch from the damp floor of the carriage and shook it, then opened the strings and peered inside. "Whoever killed him didn't steal his coin."

Kasad stumbled up to them, leaning against the carriage. Rain sluiced down his body. Water streamed past his boots as it ran along the stonework paving of the street. "What are we going to do now, Gil?"

Tyras glanced at the brothel. No one had come out to investigate. He shivered as rain slammed into the pavement. "We'll walk until we find another conveyance. Then go to my house and send out a servant to alert the constabulary."

Gil shook his head. "We're not walking anywhere at night, in this weather, with a prince in tow. Anyway, where's your sense of fun? Ty, you grab his feet and we'll heave him back inside. I think we should sell his bracelets."

"You're already in trouble with your family," objected Tyras.

"How much more trouble can I get into? I'm the only male in the house who has balls. They have to keep me for stud service. Anyway, I desperately need coin."

Kasad stared at the dead man. He looked ready to retch again. "No one will redeem his bracelets. Ri Amarah silver is cursed."

"You're right. The bracelets are nothing without the man. So we'll sell his corpse, too."

"Sell his corpse?" echoed Tyras, gaping like a fish.

"How can you get coin for a dead man?" Kasad asked.

The idea unfurled in his head with lightning swiftness. He

grinned, and as if his smile was a threat, his friends took a step away from him. He didn't blame them. They knew what he was capable of when these stormy moods overtook him. He tucked fingers under one edge of the cloth and pulled it away from the man's head.

"Gil!" cried Tyras in a shocked tone.

"Haven't you always wondered if they really have horns?"

The dead man's hair was as black as their own. That wasn't what made them fall silent just as the rain and wind slackened.

"I'll be cursed to all the hells," murmured Gil, eyes wide. "It's true."

Peeping through the thick curls were two horns each no longer than a woman's thumb.

"Enne preserve us," mumbled Kasad. "Now we *are* cursed for seeing what is forbidden."

"Are you asking to be arrested and condemned to a work gang, Gil?" demanded Tyras. "I want no part of this."

"You two have the nerves of old men." Gil tugged the silk roughly back into place, concealing the horns. "Help me! I'll bet we can find someone in the night market who'll pay good coin to see what we just saw. I heard people pay a bounty for dead Silvers. Maybe they grind up the horns for medicinal potions or maybe they just hate them because they're rich and foreigners."

"Like our grandfathers?" asked Tyras with an unusual snap in his tone.

"Our grandfathers were soldiers who saved the Hundred from a terrible war. That's the difference, isn't it?"

He and Tyras swung the dead man back into the carriage and laid him on the blood-soaked rear seat with his head lolling forward and his knees bent and legs twisted to brace him so he wouldn't slide off.

"Get in, Kas," said Gil cheerfully, warming to his plan.

"I can't," said Kasad. "If my mother finds out I've touched a Silver's corpse and seen such an impious thing…"

"Then you're on your own."

Being on his own was always the situation Kasad avoided. With a groan, he climbed in to huddle on the forward seat.

"I'll drive," said Gil.

"The hells you will," said Tyras, who had already anticipated this suggestion and gotten hold of the reins. "We can leave Kas to keep company with our dead friend here, but I'll drive and you'll tell me where we're going."

"I don't want to stay in here alone!" shouted Kasad. "Their corpses give off noxious fumes that choke any but their own kind."

Gil laughed. "That's the stupidest thing I've ever heard. What I wonder is why this fellow was stuck driving people around the city instead of making his fortune in trade like the rest of them. Maybe the Silvers have poor as well as rich folk, just as the rest of us do. Let's get out of here before whoever killed him comes back looking for us."

He slammed the door and clambered up onto the driver's seat.

Tyras flicked the coachman's discarded whip over the horse's back. The nag was eager to get moving.

"Where are we going?" Tyras asked once they had negotiated the first corner and rumbled down a deserted avenue lined by compounds shut up for the night.

"Like I said. Wolf Quarter."

"I don't know, Gil. You're in so much trouble with your destitute family they don't even let you carry an eating knife when you go out. Why should I just do what you tell me?"

"Go home to your mother, Lord Tyras. Have a posset of sweet tea and some bean-curd cakes so you won't crack your teeth on anything hard."

Tyras stiffened, then shook out the reins as the horse faltered at a corner. "May your balls wither and fall off, Gil. You'll kill us all someday." He grinned, angling the coach to the right. "Let's go."

By the time they reached Canal Street and Four Quarters Bridge, the clouds were clearing off. Four Quarters Bridge was a lovely span, built up on pilings with a bridge from each quarter meeting over the wide intersection of the two canals. At night the entrances onto the bridge were closed by gates.

They pulled up beside the Bell Quarter guardhouse. Although it was no longer raining, they looked drowned, clothes bunched in wet ripples down their bodies. Tyras's curls were utterly gone; hair twined down his neck like tendrils of waterweed trying to choke him. Two guards strolled out, irritated at having to come out from under a roof. One carried a truncheon and the other a whip.

"We'll get arrested," muttered Tyras. "Then I can say I told you so."

"Let me do the talking."

The guard with the truncheon halted at the horse's head, looking over the nag with an expression of almost comical disbelief. "Your names?"

"I am Lord Gilaras of Clan Herelia. This is a man I've hired to drive, no one important. And a cursed poor driver, too, if you take my meaning."

Tyras groaned under his breath, hands tightening on the reins.

"Where may you be off to, my lord? At this untimely late hour when most folk obey the curfew?" The guard had a firm grip on his truncheon and no patience for youthful nonsense.

Gil smiled. "Wolf Quarter, ver. Where else?"

The man snorted. "You'll lose all your money."

"Haven't got any to lose," replied Gil cheerfully.

The guard with the whip saluted him with a mocking flourish a hair away from insult. "This is a Silver's coach. How'd you come by it?"

Tyras stiffened.

Gil almost laughed aloud at this predictable interrogation. "A friend of ours gave us the name of a coaching establishment. We spent all our coin renting the coach, on a dare."

"Did you now, my lord?" said Whip. The lamps burning at the guardhouse porch and hanging over the gate gave plenty of light with which to observe the meaningful glance the man shared with his comrade.

Truncheon hefted the truncheon. His bare arms looked strong. "I never heard those cursed suspicious Silvers rented out their livelihoods to honest Hundred folk like us. But maybe they can't refuse a lord."

"Very true." Gil looked the man straight in the eye, holding the gaze. "My grandfather was General Sengel. People just don't like to say no to me."

Truncheon tapped the other guard on the arm. "No sense getting a foot in the antics of palace lads." He turned back to Gil. "You may proceed, my lord."

The guards retreated to the guardhouse. Bells tinkled along the length of the bridge as the Bell Quarter gate swung open. Tyras drove across toward the Wolf Quarter gate. From high on the span they had a clear view of Law Rock, the massive promontory that rose above the city.

"Do you believe the story about how Law Rock came to be?" asked Gil.

"What story?" Tyras kept his eyes on the bridge.

"Back in ancient days, so long ago that the seven gods had not yet come into being, the Four Mothers shaped the land. Being so different, they went to war. When the Water Mother sent her watery dragons against her sister Earth, the Earth Mother flung a spear of stone at the beasts. The Fire Mother intervened with bolts of lightning and broke the stone shaft into pieces. One fragment pierced the body of the larger dragon and pinned it to the earth. The dragon's watery essence transformed into the River Istri. And the fragment of the huge spear became Law Rock. The thousand stairs by which we ascend to the top were carved in later."

"Where do you hear those ridiculous tales?" Tyras said with a snort.

"My grandmother sang them all to me, Ty. You want to make fun of her?"

"No, no, not at all."

As they passed the Wolf Quarter gate and rattled away along a lantern-lit street, Kasad began retching noisily.

"No worries, Kas, I got through the gates without a mention of your name," Gil called back. "No one will know you were with me."

"The scent in here is sickening." Kasad's muffled voice broke off into a string of gargling coughs. "...just not got anything left to heave."

"No need for details." Tyras shuddered. He nudged Gil hard with a boot. "Now where?"

"The night market at the docks."

Tyras gave him a wild look but fortunately did not argue.

Most of the compounds in Wolf Quarter were closed up tight against the night, and the only lights burning were watch-lights mandated for each neighborhood. Things got livelier down along the dockside streets, where everyone knew the king had agents skimming off the top of the unregulated markets that flourished at night despite the tax reapers and toll agents. Groups of loitering men watched the coach pass. Slurs and curses drifted their way, but no one molested them.

Gil directed them to an open gate flanked by a pair of wood statues, dragonling guardians with sinuous bodies and weeping eyes. A sign swayed in the wind, marked by a snake with a head at either end. The place had once been a temple dedicated to the Lady of Beasts but now was a tavern.

"The hells," exclaimed Tyras. "We could get arrested for going into a place like this. Isn't this a nest of poisonous agitators who call for the overthrow of the king? Are you insane, Gil? Do you want to get your balls cut off like your brothers did?"

"My brothers were children when that happened, not traitors. Anyway, we can't get arrested. We're too highborn. Haven't you figured out yet that our rank protects us no matter what we do? Why do you think I went after my cousin? The law was never going to touch him for what he did to that flower girl."

Men armed with cudgels allowed them to pass. Gil wasn't sure what part of the sprawling building had been part of the temple compound back in his grandparents' time. The tavern now was a series of roofs supported by stone pillars and wood posts. The place was crowded with people drinking, men and women mixing together in the way common to the Hundred but which was never allowed in the palace.

At the sight of a Ri Amarah carriage come to a halt, all the talk ceased.

Gil was genuinely startled when every person in sight rose in silence and stared.

An elderly woman limped out, leaning on a cane. She looked so old she might have once worshipped at this temple before it was shuttered.

"What is this, my lords?" she asked without blinking an eye. "I am surprised to see palace youths at my humble establishment."

Tyras shifted uncomfortably. From inside Kasad said, "Where are we?"

Gil swung down from the driver's bench and made a polite curl of the hand for greeting in the sign language once known by everyone in the Hundred.

The old woman's eyebrows lifted. "I'm surprised a palace lad like you knows the hand-talk, since there are folk who live their whole lives in the upper palace without ever learning a single word of the Hundred-speech we Hundred folk have spoken for generations down here."

"I learned the hand-talk from my grandmother. Her ancestors have been in the Hundred as long as yours, I daresay, verea. Her people just happened to be so wealthy and well connected that one of King Anjihosh's Qin soldiers married her." He grinned his sweetest grin. "You can't blame me for that."

Her stare did not soften. "What do you want?"

"I hear there are folk who will pay a bounty for dead Silvers," he said in a low voice.

"Is that what you hear?"

"Why would I say so if it were not?"

"Hard up for coin, are you? Or just bored and looking for a fight you'll never be brought before the law for starting, while our lads will be arrested and sent out on work gangs if they throw even one punch at a lord like you?"

"I really have a dead Silver in the coach," he retorted, annoyed at her shrewdness. "Give me the bounty, and you can have the corpse."

"If you killed him I suppose you've a need to pass off the crime onto someone else. Onto people like us."

"We didn't kill him! We hired him for the night to drive us about on our diversions. He was killed while he was waiting on the street. We saw nothing, only found him afterward with his head smashed in."

"If one of my grandsons were to tell that story to the constabulary, what do you suppose the constabulary would say?"

He glanced around to see that men had taken up stations all around the courtyard. "What were we to do? I hear people say Silvers are bootlicking flatterers who keep the king happy with monthly infusions of coin. People have little enough love for them and their closed doors and their hidden women and their heaps and heaps of coin. We couldn't help that unknown and unseen criminals decided to murder the man. But I've heard rumors of bounties for their silver bracelets, for I hear there's a magic laid on them that people covet. I've heard owning even one bracelet can turn a clan rich if they burnish themselves with spell-wrapped silver. I've heard other things about them, too. Things I don't want to speak out loud. So. What's it to be? How much?"

"How much?" She offered a rude two-finger salute. "How much time will I give you to get the hells out of my respectable establishment? As much time as it takes you to turn around and drive right back out of here."

Gil knew better than to confront an old woman with that look in her eye and tens of thugs awaiting her order to bash his head in.

He swung back up. "Let's get out of here, Ty."

Tyras was clearly rattled as a snared bird, for he made a terrible mess of getting the coach around and finally out the gate while every gaze there watched them with a hostility so thick, Gil felt it as waves of hate on the air.

"I told you we should have left the dead man," Tyras muttered.

They hadn't gotten a block down the dark street when six men stepped into the street, forcing Tyras to drag the poor exhausted horse to a stop. Armed with staves, the toughs slouched forward. One of their number took hold of the horse's harness. Another stepped right up beside the driver's bench and grasped hold of Gil's sandaled foot, offering him a gap-toothed smile.

"Heard you palace boys had a bit of trouble. We'd be glad to take the stink of that dead Silver off your hands."

Tyras sucked in a sharp breath.

"How much?" said Gil coolly.

"We won't beat the shit out of you." The gap-toothed smile vanished into a gaze as emotionless as a slab of stone.

"Gil..." Tyras muttered.

Gil shook his head. "Not enough. I'll accept a gold cheyt for the coach and the dead man and his bracelets. That would be a bargain for you."

The man's grip tightened on Gil's ankle. "A bargain for you would be going home instead of lying on the street with your head stove in."

Gil smiled down on him, leg tensed, ready to kick. "I'll take fifty leya. Still a bargain for you."

"You've got cheek, I'll give you that. But there are six of us and two of you. You should have known better than to drive into Wolf Quarter this time of night with a dead Silver on your hands. Run away, little man. But leave the stinking outlander with us."

"The hells I will! I need coin—"

Gil felt the moment the man made his move, the pinch of his fingers against Gil's skin, the tug of weight as he went to drag him off the driver's bench. With a twist, Gil punched him square on the nose and kicked his heel into the man's chest.

"Go!" he snapped to Ty as he ripped the attacker's steel-tipped stave out of his hand.

Tyras knew when to stop whining and start moving. The horse did not like the armed men any better than they did. Its surge forward had real power.

Gil thrust at the men with the stave, poking one in the shoulder and another in the thigh so they fell back. One fellow leaped up on the runner. Gil swung the haft in a move that slammed the man's head into the shuttered window.

"Open the door, Kas!" he shouted.

From inside Kasad opened out the door so hard that the intruder lost his grip and tumbled to the cobblestones. The leader clambered up the back, barely holding on as Tyras swung the coach around a corner. Gil climbed up onto the roof of the coach as it lurched along and, clinging to the top, pummeled the man in the chin and forehead with his heels. The thug thudded heavily onto the street as the coach rolled on.

"What in the hells is going on?" Kasad shouted.

Tyras swore.

"Who in the hells thought that was a good idea?" Gil could not stop laughing as he hauled himself back down to the driver's bench. He had lost the stave. His right hand was bleeding, and one of his sandal straps had gotten cut so the toe flapped.

"Can we just abandon this cursed vehicle and walk home now?" said Tyras.

"No! Leave this noble horse to any common ruffian? The beast saved us with uncommon loyalty and steadfast courage. We must take him to a fine stable in thanks."

"To what fine stable? We can't leave the city at night because all the gates are closed."

"You sad man, we're in Wolf Quarter. We go to the House of the Dagger."

"Oh no, Gil. No. You're not to bother the Incomparable again. Your family ordered you to stop going there."

"How will they know if you don't tell them?" The reckless urge had a grip on his heart that would not let go. "Take us there, Ty, or give me the reins."

Tyras never defied him. But he groused as he drove the coach through the quiet streets, his face woven on and off with shadows as they passed lantern posts.

"Do you know what, Gil? I hope you get married off to a

woman richer than you so you have to bow and scrape to the tune she commands. You'll just be another one of her gallery of musicians, fiddling with your pipe when she wants music!"

"You wound me, Ty. How you must hate me!" Gil pounded on the roof. "Kas? How are you doing in there? Has the Silver woke up yet?"

"That's not funny." Kasad's voice was muffled, as though he had cloth over his mouth, but at least he had stopped that horking retch. "What in the hells happened? Let me out!"

"No, no, you have to stay there to keep our friend warm and tidy."

"My feet are all over blood, Gil! Have pity!"

"Kas! Shut up! If I do not win a kiss from the Incomparable Melisayda, then you can both kiss my ass for a month."

"And you'll kiss ours if you do get a kiss?" retorted Kasad.

Gil cackled. "Rare wit from the prince! Hush, now, here we are."

They rolled up to the House of the Dagger. Four burning lamps hung from the wooden lintel set above the closed gate. Through thick latticework shutters set into the gate they could hear music playing, a woman singing, and the complex rhythm of dancing sticks plied together in accompaniment. Just the thought of the most beautiful woman in Toskala aroused Gil, and he had to shift on the driver's bench and force himself to consider the dead Silver hidden in the coach to stop himself from getting hard.

A woman walked a balcony set alongside the gate, wearing a body-hugging taloos, the cloth tightly wrapped around her shapely form. The lamplight made its metallic embroidery threads shimmer as if she were garbed in a web of spun gold. She leaned over the railing to study them more closely. Her face was pretty but she was not the Incomparable Melisayda, only some lesser hierodule. Yet Gil saw how she noted and dismissed him and Tyras before closely studying the distinctive sigils carved into the coach's doors. Her dour frown made a dark night darker.

He stood on the bench, which made him tall enough to reach the lower span of the balcony. "We are here to pay our respects to the Incomparable Melisayda."

She set a hand on a hip. "Are you, now? She can't be expecting you. Nor can I invite you in if you have no invitation."

"Tell her that Gilaras Herelian is here to see her. I have brought a noble horse, a sturdy coach, and a dead Silver as offerings to lay at her feet—"

The coach door burst open and Kasad stumbled out, cloth pressed over his face and mostly concealing his features. His gagging completely ruined the drama of Gil's speech. With a wince of distaste, the woman vanished through a curtained doorway.

"I'm going home," said Kasad in an altered and unusually decisive tone. "I've had enough."

Tyras tossed down the reins. "I'll go with you! Gil, I'm not staying one breath longer with you when you're in one of these careening moods. You're just asking for it."

"Go on home," he said, not even looking their way because he already had a new idea.

When Tyras jumped down, the coach rocked, and Gil leaped, grabbed the bottom of the railing, and hooked himself up. By the time he swung onto the balcony, Tyras and Kasad had raced away into the gloom of the night streets, leaving him with the damning evidence. It was certainly for the best that they'd left. Anyway he had more pressing interests. He blew on his left hand, which was stinging, and wiped the blood on the curtain. Then he pushed inside.

Bells tinkled all around him, their chime the sound light would make as it glistened, if light had noise. Golden netting spilled over him. A weight slammed him atop the head, and all the lights went out.

The next thing he knew, he was lying on his side on dirt and throwing up all the cheap rice beer he had drunk earlier.

When he stopped heaving, he pushed up to his hands and knees for a few breaths until he judged he could raise his head without passing out.

His brother Shevad was standing over him, dressed in a linen kilt and nothing else, as if he had only wrapped the kilt around his nakedness to deal with an intruder. His expression was one Gil had seen a hundred times or more over the years.

"What in the hells are you doing, Gil? You have been expressly forbidden from coming here."

"Can I have something to drink?" Gil croaked as he staggered to his feet. His head ached and his legs quivered, but cursed if he would kneel in front of either of his brothers with their sanctimonious sneers and beardless faces.

"You've already had enough to drink. As you might have noticed while you were puking it all up."

Gil had no memory of how he had gotten from the balcony to this small interior courtyard adjacent to a lavatory. His spew made a stain on the ground but fortunately he hadn't eaten anything recently so it was only sour wine. Music floated over the wall. In an open gate a woman stood in shadow, half seen, watching them, but he would know her anywhere by the sly tilt of her shoulders and her scent blended of musk vine and heady stardrops.

"I brought you a present, verea," he called to her. "A secret no other Hundred man can possibly tell you."

Her low laugh teased him but she did not step into the light.

Shevad slapped him so hard that Gil stumbled and would have fallen if he hadn't hit a wall.

He steadied himself as he rubbed his cheek. "What was that for?"

"So many people have seen the coach and heard news of a dead Silver that the city watch was called. Don't you understand, you ass? They are coming to arrest you for murder."

"I didn't kill him! But I'll tell you this: You ever wonder if Silver men really have horns?" He glanced toward the gate to make sure she was listening, but she had gone.

His brother grabbed him roughly by the shoulder. "Do not fuck with me, Gil, you stupid shit. Now sit down."

Shevad was a general in the army who had proven himself the hard way and earned an impressively crude nickname despite his inability to sire children. Right now he was so tremendously pissed off that Gil decided to wait a bit before pissing him off even more. But he did not sit down. As his brother paced, Gil passed the time by practicing the story-talk his grandmother had taught him, the hand gestures used to accompany the tales everyone in the Hundred used to know: a hand moving open and shut for the barking dog; fingers bending at the knuckles as the hand recoils at the wrist for the man who walks in on his friends making love; the stumbling merchant disguised as a beggar, the impatient reeve, the dragonling's laughter, the merling's bubbling sigh.

Thus he was taken by surprise when the supreme captain of the King's Spears walked into the courtyard's lamplight. "General Shevad? Even I am shocked to hear your reckless young brother has been accused of murdering a Ri Amarah man."

Gil's legs gave way and he sat down hard on a bench.

Even General Shevad had to bow, fist-to-chest, before the man who commanded the elite Spears as well as a rumored secret cohort of spies and assassins called Knives. "Supreme Captain Ulyar. I did not . . . I expected the watch captain."

For all his ordinary appearance, Ulyar was the second most dreaded man in the Hundred. His word alone could condemn a man to servitude in the naphtha fields or salt panning in the Barrens, or he might offer a more merciful impaling. In fact he was the man who had ordered all five of the young sons of Lord Seras be castrated on the day King Atani's corpse had arrived back at the palace.

"Stand up, Gilaras Herelian," he said.

Gil stood.

Supreme Captain Ulyar studied Gil as if deciding which testicle to cut off first. "This exceeds all the rest of the tiresome mischief and lazy troublemaking perpetrated by you and your useless friends. Did you kill him?"

"No, Supreme Captain, I did not kill the Silver. I hired a coach and driver for the night, and found him dead after he'd been waiting on the street while I was inside an establishment."

"What of the two who were with you? Might one of them have done it?"

Gil cursed himself inwardly for giving the man a possible hook to make serious trouble for Kasad inside the palace. "No one was with me, Captain. I was alone."

Shevad sighed.

Ulyar had an excitable eyebrow. It leaped now. "Strange. I've heard numerous reports that you were accompanied by two men on your sad little escapade."

Gil shrugged. "Trick of the light maybe. I'm the only one here."

"Might we take care of this at home, Supreme Captain?" asked Shevad. "I have served the king well and honorably—"

"I don't like you and your traitorous family, General Shevad. Even if I did like you, it wouldn't matter. Palace lads can get away with a lot but not with this. By itself murder is a grave charge punishable by a public lashing and seven years on a work gang. But the old covenant sealed between King Anjihosh and the Ri Amarah means I have to attend to any death of a Ri Amarah personally and treat it as a much more severe charge. Which if you ask me is a courtesy Silvers don't deserve, but I am a man who follows the law."

Gil curled his lip to a careful sneer. "The rumor I hear is that you follow the coin to wherever it smells sweetest."

"Gil!" snapped Shevad.

Ulyar had a whip with three knotted lashes. He laid the whip across Gil's chest so the knots dug painfully into his flesh. They were of a height, but although Gil was twenty years younger, Ulyar had the strength and authority of a man used to getting his way. "You don't want to make me angrier than I already am. Tell me what happened."

Gil did not wilt. *Give them enough truth and no specific lies.* "Just as I said. I hired the coach because I wanted to visit a flower girl over in Bell Quarter. I went into the establishment for several hours, drank and sang although I must say none of the flowers convinced me to pluck them. When I came out the Silver was dead inside the coach. So I thought I could sell the coach and the dead man in exchange for enough coin to pay for a single night with the Incomparable Melisayda to slake my other thirst. But no one was buying, more's the pity."

"Is that the story you'll tell when I have you publicly whipped to get your confession?"

Shevad broke in, which was far more than Gil expected. "Supreme Captain, I and my brother Yofar have served honorably in the army since we were younger than Gil here. Yofar died in the service of the king. Out of consideration for our loyalty—"

"What is it worth to you not to disgrace this fool in public?" Ulyar took a step back, lowering the whip. Gil sucked in a painful breath and with every grain of will he possessed he managed not to rub his aching chest. "I imagine the disgrace added to the household's destitution and reputation will ruin you permanently, will it not, General? Unless you convince me otherwise."

A fist of suspicion clenched in Gil's belly. What if Ulyar had had Gil and his friends followed, had the Silver killed, and then waited like a spider to eat up the hapless creatures now caught in his web?

"How much?" asked Shevad.

Ulyar laughed in a way that made Gil's skin crawl. "Let me see. If I tell you five hundred cheyt to see the young man left alone, what would you say to that?"

"You're mocking us!" cried Gil. "We'd have to sell our compound to raise that much gold."

Ulyar scratched an ear. "What a pity that would be. A clan without a house is no clan."

"Done," agreed Shevad with a curt laugh. "Five hundred cheyt, as I have just heard you speak with your own mouth now, and Gilaras is free and clear of all suspicion in the matter. Nor will he and any supposed associates ever be blamed or accused again of this crime."

Ulyar blinked, so taken aback that Gil had to admire Shevad's gloating smile. The captain opened his mouth and then closed it.

Shevad dusted off his hands. "In fact, Gilaras shall become the hero of the piece. He will deliver the poor dead man, whom he discovered murdered on the street, back to his grieving family as a mark of respect to a distant cousin of the woman he is about to marry."

"What?" demanded Gil, sure Shevad had begun babbling in a foreign language.

Ulyar's calm anger was legendary; the way he stared at Shevad would have turned a lesser man to stone, but Shevad had, after all, survived worse than an ugly glare. "Now, that's something I thought could never be done. Convincing the Ri Amarah to give up one of their women in marriage. I'm impressed, General. I've heard not even a whisper of the negotiations."

Shevad nodded. "My thanks," he replied with a slim edge of mockery. "I just heard at dusk today that the alliance can go forward, which is why I came here to celebrate. They give us a fortune, and we give them entry into the palace. A fair trade, don't you think?"

Ulyar fingered his whip. "Deliver the coin to my office personally, General Shevad. I want you to bring it with your own hands."

Gil looked Shevad over one more time. Shevad's bare torso gleamed in the lamplight with a thin skin of oil, as if he had been interrupted in the midst of being rubbed. No doubt by the Incomparable Melisayda.

Without another word Supreme Captain Ulyar left, walking out through the gate in which the Incomparable had, so briefly, waited and watched.

"I would not be one bit surprised to discover Ulyar had the Silver murdered to get at Kas," Gil murmured.

"What do you mean?" Shevad strode to the gate to make sure the man had truly left.

"It seems suspicious that it happened so conveniently on a deserted street."

"It was a Silver, Gil. One of their clan houses was attacked and burned in High Haldia last month. People resent them. They are rich, and they hoard powerful magic in their households."

"Maybe. But if I had a means to slip a warning to King Jehosh that his youngest son is in danger, I would. I can't keep an eye on Kas all the time. Even I have to sleep." He yawned as the events of the night caught up to him.

"Is someone paying you to befriend Prince Kasad? Is that how you get your drinking money?"

"Gods, you are such an ass, Shev. Is it so strange that I might have friends? By the way, you can be cursed sure I'm not marrying to fill the clan coffers. I may be the only bull you have but I won't be put out to stud."

The look Shevad turned on him bore a hostility as ugly as that Gil had seen in the Wolf Quarter tavern—but it was made all the worse because his brother was usually at pains to hide his dislike, whereas the strangers at the tavern meant nothing to him.

"Either we pay the bribe to Ulyar, or you get whipped until you faint. Then if you don't die of pus and inflammation you'll be sent into indentured servitude at hard labor for seven years. The point is, Gil, we don't have the coin to pay the bribe unless you marry."

"Oh the hells, you're right," said Gil, and there was nothing he could do but laugh.

12

The Ri Amarah were a practical people above all else. When Uncle Makel called Aunt Rua out of the jubilee and explained the situation to her, she accepted his accounting of how the alliance would benefit the clan. Garna gladly welcomed Sarai into the center of the celebration, for among the Ri Amarah everything was deemed better if it was shared.

"Isn't your brother in Nessumara? Isn't he one of the heirs to the household of the First Branch of the Tree of Heaven?" Garna blurted out. "Maybe you can travel downriver from Toskala to Nessumara to visit me at my new home in the Seventh

Branch. Then you can finally meet him, now that you will be respectable."

The disapproving silence that met this innocent statement made poor Garna blush.

"I have met my brother, even though I don't recall it," said Sarai, emboldened by her new status. "He was a young boy when I was a newborn. He and I have corresponded for years; didn't you know that?"

"But he's never been allowed to visit you here," said Garna. "I always thought that was odd."

"Sarai is leaving us," said Aunt Rua with a stern glance at Sarai to remind her of her place in this new scheme of things. "Her life at court will keep her busy, away from the clans."

Aunt Rua dug up an unbound virgin Book of Accounts to present to Sarai. After the book was hastily inscribed with Sarai's name and lineage and an ancestral poem for good fortune, the pages were sewn up. But since she would be living outside a Ri Amarah household they would not give her one of the enchanted bronze mirrors.

She was done with living inside their walls.

She left the jubilee as soon as she could and pretended to go to bed. Instead she lay awake under the covers as the other girls filtered into the dormitory with songs and giggles. At length everyone settled down and the lamps were extinguished. She breathed into the darkness until the last whisper died away. A moon-spark cooed outside. The soul bell rang to chase away night-walking evil spirits, a relic of the life the Ri Amarah had escaped from in a distant land far away across a vast ocean that she would never see.

At last she judged it safe to creep barefoot out of the dormitory room and through the atrium to the side porch that let onto the kitchen courtyard. A single lantern burned by the gate. Slipping outside, she felt her way along a stone-paved path to the tomb east of the house. A lamp in the shape of a globe pierced with many holes burned at the entrance. She lifted it off its hook and, with its splintered light to guide her, went inside.

The building was a miniature copy of the main compound. The Ri Amarah believed that each burial vessel must be installed in its fitting place: the men in the men's hall, the women in the women's wing, unmarried girls in the girls' dormitory, and boys who had died before manhood in the anterooms of their fathers' suites. Small jars containing the bones of infants and stillborn babies were placed in the tiny forecourt, a sad reminder of souls who had not fully entered the household. Fresh flowers wreathed every jar so their fragrance would sweeten the long silence.

The remains of Sarai's mother had been placed within a stone ledge on the back portico, away from everyone else, under the roof as required by her birth but alone as befit her shame. The large jar had a sealed mouth and no decoration, unlike all the others with their painted filigree and splashes of color-fully painted vines and ripe fruit to remind the grieving of the joys of life. Sarai brought a necklace of fresh flowers every week, but no one else did. Her mother's mirror was hung around the jar's waist in the proper way. The family could not take that courtesy away from her.

She rested her forehead against the ceramic. Inside lay jumbled her mother's bones, dust in the dark of the grave. Her soul had flown to the Hidden One's heart. The scent of flowers faded in the sleepy air like the last trace of her passage.

The hard surface told Sarai nothing of her mother, just as the past was an opaque shell that sealed her mother away from her. *We were well rid of her,* Rua had once said when she hadn't known Sarai was close enough to overhear. They littered scraps of memory at her feet: Nadai had been vain, selfish, unkind, the girl who ruthlessly demands loyal obedience from the other girls her age and scorns and mocks the ones who refuse to follow her lead. Nadai's betrothal to the prestigious Aram Elder of First Branch had been a triumph that she had flaunted in the faces of her less pretty and less fortunate cousins. She had warned them she would be too busy in her prosperous new life as the wife of the richest Ri Amarah man in the Hundred to communicate with those she left behind, and she had kept that promise.

But Nadai had not left Sarai behind. She had fled her home with her daughter in her arms.

"Mother, I am leaving to make my own way, just as you wished for me," Sarai whispered, although she did not believe souls could hear the voices of the living. They drowned in the light of the Hidden One, awash in the brilliance of eternity. "I wish I could see your face just once. It seems cruel I don't remember it at all."

Like the other girls Sarai had a cheap bronze mirror whose cloudy surface was hard to polish and easy to scratch. She glanced around, sure that the ghosts of the dead were watching in the glimmers thrown across the floor and walls by the lamp's hatch-work of light. The tomb lay utterly silent. Even the wind had died, and all she heard was the tick-tick-tick of water dripping from a tree.

Because it was the same size as her mother's mirror it was easy for her to replace the one with the other. By the time anyone noticed, if anyone did, she would be established in a new life.

The final leave-taking from Great-Aunt Tsania took place at dawn in her aunt's tiny alcove off the girls' dormitory, where Tsania had slept all her life. Sarai sat on the edge of the old woman's bed, holding her hands and not sure she could bear to let them go. Yava had stayed all night. It was she who held a lamp to illuminate their parting.

"It is possible we will never see each other again," said Tsania, wheezing between words, "but I need you to go without regret,

Sarai-ya. You have brought me more joy than I can tell you but now you must leave. It is the right thing for you."

"I love you." Sarai's tears fell from the ache that overflowed in her heart.

Tsania looked so frail but so had she always been, and yet there was steel within her. She coughed up a bubble of mucus, which Yava efficiently wiped away.

"Make your way by observing and asking questions. Look and examine, then make your decisions. You will build a home for yourself and make allies and perhaps even friends. Do not be afraid to let yourself open to another when it is your own fear that troubles you. Find your generous spirit, Sarai-ya. Generosity is the ship that will carry you out of the dark heart you have struggled against."

"I've not been unhappy here, with you." Sarai clutched her aunt's bony fingers. It was hard to speak without crying. "I will miss you so much."

Tsania's gentle smile soothed her. "I expect lengthy letters and minute descriptions of all you see and do. Through words we will speak and answer, Sarai-ya. We will always be together."

Sarai kissed her, released her hands, and walked away on the path she had chosen.

13

Dannarah sat on her bedroll eating a hasty breakfast of rice boiled in moro milk as she conferred with Chief Tuvas. "I'm going to the Weldur Forest to see if I can track down that red-heart wreath."

He scratched at his beard, looking at the bulge in her travel pack where she had crammed in the wreath. "Do you think you can find anything? It's a huge forest."

"As I remember there are only two markets where you can buy redheart, because it's so dangerous to harvest. Only two clans living at the forest's edge even do that work. If the wreath was bought less than ten days ago, someone might recall who purchased it. It's just a hunch."

He nodded. No fuss or second-guessing with him. He was smart enough to figure things out. "I'll make one more pass through this area, but my guess is the fugitives have scattered. It gripes me to lose them, though."

"They can't have gotten far yet. I'll take only a triad with me and leave you the rest of this wing, under the command of Iyar. You can be sure he's good at his job."

"I can't imagine you keeping him under your command if he wasn't." The chief had a habit of quirking his lips in ironic acknowledgment, an expression she associated with the generation of Qin soldiers who had so loyally served her father. Those men had been the landmarks of her youth. All dead now, every last one.

"Have you anything to add before I leave, Chief?"

He glanced toward the hills. A thread of smoke could be seen in the distance where a detachment of Spears was burning the abandoned huts and tents. "I think there are more people than we know moving about the countryside, uprooted from their homes, walking the road to somewhere else as they seek work and food. It wasn't like this five years ago, before the king started spending most of his time up in Ithik Eldim. Hard to say if these people are organized by demons, as you suspect, or simply have become discontented with the work gangs and the new taxes and harsher laws."

"King Jehosh is back, so I hear. Maybe he'll see the wisdom of staying home for a while."

His gaze returned to her. "Maybe he'll listen to advice if it comes from you, Marshal."

"I'm doubtful. Jehosh demoted me from chief marshal to marshal as soon as he realized I wouldn't grovel at his feet as he likes his cronies to do."

Tuvas didn't even flinch at this blunt statement. What a pleasure it was to speak to a competent, mature person whose feathers she didn't have to smooth!

"Maybe I'll try one more time," she added. "I've always felt free to speak my mind to him, considering I remember when he was a squalling babe-in-arms. Our relationship has been... complicated, but I can never forget that people like you and me serve the peaceful and orderly kingdom my father built, Chief. That is our primary duty."

He clapped fist to chest in answer. They made their farewells. As he left, Tarnit strolled over with her bedroll tucked under an arm, pack and bowcase hitched over her back, and baton dangling from a sling at her belt. Tall and rake-thin, she had been eighteen and a newly jessed reeve when she had first been assigned to Dannarah's flight twenty-four years ago. Her sunny smile hadn't changed at all over the years.

"Is it true you've attached Reyad to Horn Hall, Marshal?"

"Yes. He deserves better than whatever sour wine they're serving him at Argent Hall."

She whistled softly. "Chief Marshal Auri wouldn't approve, or give permission."

"Certainly the thought of Auri's disapproval is enough to make me sure I must do it."

Tarnit's grin turned even sunnier, if that was possible. "I'm not complaining, mind you. I'd wager he looks as good out of his leathers as in them."

"Don't complicate things for me, Tar."

"Too late. I propositioned him last night but he politely

turned me down. He's so polite he made it seem he was sorry
to have to do it, not like I'm too old or not pretty enough. Then
he mentioned five or ten times that he has a wife. Very casually. Like beating a person over the head with a stick. As if that
ever stopped anyone when they were stuck on isolated duty with
nothing better to do to pass the time!"

Dannarah gave Tarnit a look of exaggerated disapproval.
"I only keep you around because you amuse me. Not because
you're any good as a reeve."

"Yes, you're certainly famous for tolerating incompetence!"
Tarnit's smile turned wistful as they watched Reyad hurry over.
"He makes me miss my Errard. Even though Erry was a soldier
I never really imagined he would die in war."

After so many years serving together Dannarah said nothing,
for there was nothing to be said. She touched the other woman
on the arm and allowed the moment of connection, her fingers
warm on Tarnit's skin, to bring what she hoped was a sliver of
comfort.

Grief trod so hard upon the heels. Life went on, and yet the
dead paced alongside like shadows.

Reyad trotted up, so excited he was beaming. "I can't believe I'm
really going to see the Weldur Forest! Wait until I tell my wife!"

Tarnit mimed beating her head with a stick.

Dannarah bit down a laugh, then realized what he had said
and frowned at him. "Do you mean you've never seen the Wild?
At the end of training it's traditional for all new reeves to make
a circuit of the Hundred so they know all the major landmarks
and demon's coils, and can find all the reeve halls, refuges,
eyries, and assizes."

"At Argent Hall we only learned the territory we were assigned
to patrol."

"Was that by Chief Marshal Auri's order?" demanded
Dannarah.

"Marshal," said Tarnit lightly but with a warning.

"He claimed that way we could know our patrol territory well, not get distracted by new sights." Reyad glanced at the ground. "It seemed strange to me."

"Never mind, Reyad. You'll get proper training now."

Tarnit shook her head but it wasn't clear whether she was skeptical about Reyad's ignorance, the chief marshal's incompetence, or Dannarah's decision to attach Reyad to Horn Hall without clearing it through the chief marshal and Argent Hall first. Probably all three.

Leaving the rest of the wing, Dannarah, Tarnit, and Reyad took flight. They had not gone more than two mey down the Elshar Valley when she spotted a troupe of Hasibal's players striding along the road in their distinctive formation. Two walked a spear's throw ahead of the main group, two just out of sight at the rear. Banners aloft, the rest paced in a shifting formation, rows that turned into columns as individuals took sideways steps to form into new ranks. They wore cloth in all colors and so many ribbons and scarves in adornment that one person's garb seemed to flow into the next. From above the party had the look of an unfolding pattern, writing brushed from one letter into the next. They sang in time to their march, stamping their walking staves on the ground to punctuate certain phrases.

The Merciful One's players—called pilgrims—walked the length and breadth of the Hundred to perform the old tales wherever they could get food for the night. It was a hard life but those who dedicated themselves to it seemed content. Tradition mandated a troupe consist of seven players, or multiples of seven. This troupe was so big it seemed a lot of mouths to expect isolated villages to feed. She circled Terror back, trying to count and yet continually stymied because every time she had everyone accounted for, the pattern shifted. Were there thirty-two? Thirty-nine? Either was a suspicious number.

She flagged Tarnit and Reyad to stay aloft while she went down. Terror was feeling playful today, so she took the descent at a steep dive, pulling up on the road with a thump as if the road were a gigantic snake the eagle had just caught. An older man and a younger woman walked into view just as Dannarah unbuckled her harness and dropped. The young woman halted dead in the middle of the road, but the man ambled up with a wide grin like Dannarah was his long-lost aunt: Hasibal's players were always acting a part. Dannarah sauntered forward to meet them, knowing how impressive Terror looked at her back.

"Greetings of the day, Marshal!" The man cut a sweeping arc with his walking staff and followed it with an elaborate bow that might have been respectful and might have been mocking. Strands of gray in his hair made her think him older than Tarnit but not as old as she was. "I'm Pilgrim Gani. Behind me walks my shy companion Arasit."

The woman called Arasit did not meet her gaze. A linen scarf covered her hair and half concealed her face in its shade. She was dressed in worn laborer's clothing, a short kilt wrapped around her hips and thighs and a sleeveless vest tightly laced over full breasts. Where the others were colorful, she was strikingly drab.

"I'm Marshal Dannarah of Horn Hall. We've been on patrol with a cohort of the King's Spears. You must have seen them."

"We performed one night for them and they fed us a most excellent rice porridge!" said Gani so heartily that Dannarah reflected on how quickly his enthusiasm would start to grate.

"Did you perform at the Ri Amarah estate, Holy One?"

He smiled in a kindly manner, as if to wonder when Dannarah would stop pretending and get to her real question. "The Ri Amarah do not welcome Hasibal's pilgrims into their homes, for we speak of the seven gods of the Hundred and that is not pleasing to them."

"Then you've made a long trip uphill to so small a village as the one near the estate."

"Indeed, so it was, but such good exercise!"

The young woman snorted, and Dannarah had to smile at his exaggerated tone of pleased surprise. The rest of the troupe came into view, their robust voices raised in a familiar song: "*The sad girl and her happy lover, What a striking pair they made.*"

The troupe's singing ceased between one footstep and the next as they took in the size of Terror. Most had the look of casual confidence that in her experience marked people who really knew what they were doing. Yet she counted at least eighteen individuals whose skin was inked with the brand given to criminals. Several shifted nervously from foot to foot.

"I see work gang brands," she said, turning back to Gani as her heart raced with sudden expectation. "You wouldn't harbor escaped prisoners, would you, Holy One?"

"What makes you think any of us are criminals?" Gani smiled with the patience of a man who likes to tell a long story. "Heya! Elit!"

A lanky young woman trotted forward. She was dressed in the trousers and tunic commonly worn by highland men. She wore her hair short, and had a work gang mark on her cheek.

"Show the marshal." He tossed a leather bottle to Elit, who caught it deftly, poured liquid on her hand, and began rubbing at her cheek. Stubbornly the mark began to stipple and fade. "It's paint, Marshal. We're performing a tale about a lad who gets charged with a theft he did not commit and yet is condemned to seven years in the work gangs, and dies there without seeing his sweetheart ever again."

His mild tone wrapped like a warning around her thoughts. "Holy One, I hope you are not spreading tales that criticize King Jehosh and his laws. I do not like to trouble people who have dedicated their lives to the Hundred's seven gods, but if the palace hears of it, you'll get remanded to the work gangs yourself. Let me see each person wash the paint off their faces."

Arasit stepped assertively past Gani, tugging off her scarf. "We don't have time for this."

Her curt tone set off all Dannarah's alerts. She glanced around, half expecting an archer to dart out of the trees and loose an arrow into her back. Instead she saw that Terror had tucked her head against a wing to slumber even though Dannarah hadn't hooded her.

Demons had that effect on eagles.

"The hells!" She pulled her baton from its loop, swung back to face the pilgrims, looking for anyone who was wearing a cloak. Instead she looked straight into a face that made her thoughts stumble.

Seen full on and close up, the young woman Arasit looked rather like King Anjihosh in having that odd blend of the wide cheekbones common among the Qin and the distinctive hawk's nose that came from his Sirniakan father. She had even bound up her curly black hair in a topknot in the old Qin style still popular among soldiers and palace courtiers. From a cord at her neck dangled a wolf's head ring exactly like the one Atani had always worn, with a chip flaked out of one of the wolf ears. After his death Dannarah had never seen his ring again.

She had a brilliant flash of stunned recognition.

"That's my brother's ring," Dannarah cried. The whole world narrowed down until all she could see was the woman and the ring. "Who are you?"

"I've always suspected you were behind Atani's murder," said the woman, meeting her gaze as with a blow. "You were in charge of the reeves but you left him vulnerable the day he was killed."

"Me! How could anyone think I ever wanted Atani dead?"

"You wanted what he had. You wanted to be king."

Dannarah grabbed for the throwing knife tucked onto her harness. Too slow. The demon's gaze punctured her. With nerveless fingers Dannarah released the knife and heard the thud of the weapon hitting the dirt. The demon prised open her mind and exposed her memories like the guts of a slaughtered soldier.

Platters decorate the center of the table: fish stewed in a mango sauce; a spicy barsh stew from Mar that her father favors and Atani refuses to eat because it burns his tongue; slip-fried vegetables that came to the table hot and crisp but have begun to sag as they cool. She sits on a cushion, trembling with defiance beneath her father's stern eye. Atani stares at the table, fingering that cursed wolf's head ring he wears on a chain around his neck, the one he never used to have before he ran away and returned without ever telling her what he had seen and what he had done. He is playing with the ring to avoid looking at her. Coward!

So be it. She will not go down without a fight.

"I'll run away like Atani did, only I'll never come back! I won't go south to the Sirniakan Empire and be locked in a palace and wither away like a flower without sun or water!"

"It has already been arranged, Dannarah. You have been betrothed to an imperial prince, your own cousin. You will leave next month for the empire."

She studies her father's impassive expression, seeking any glimmer of hope, any sign of the affection he has always lavished on her. He cherished her bold speaking and brash spirit before.

"How can you betray me like this, Papa? I will be trapped in a cage, never to be free. They will hate me and never, ever trust me."

"It is what your mother wants. This is marriage to her sister's son, an honorable alliance for you."

"Can't you send one of the younger girls when they get older?"

Atani looks up with a rare sharp glimmer. "You would condemn the little girls to a place you refuse to go because you fear you will hate it there? If you might dislike it so much, and think it so horrible, then why volunteer them to go instead of you? That's positively selfish, Dannarah! Even for you!"

"Easy for you to be the fish complaining of water! I can't believe you of all people would turn on me like this. Our kinsfolk will send some tongue-tied, milk-witted princess north for you to marry. You can stow her in the women's quarters and visit her when you want or maybe only when you must." The barb makes her father's lips tighten but it does not wound him because he is beyond her hooks and blades. In frustration she snags a spear of turnip off the platter with her eating sticks, but it sags limply, a broken weapon. "I won't go, Papa. I respect Mama as I ought, but I won't accept what she was forced into. I won't be married off! I won't!"

"Eat your food before you drop it on the table." Her father never loses his temper but she feels his mounting anger in the way the air in the dining pavilion snaps as with the sting of lightning.

Suddenly terrified and furious, she tucks the stalk into her mouth and swallows with one gulp. Atani says nothing, and she hates him for being the only son and thus the heir.

Their father speaks. "You are the price we pay to keep the peace, Dannarah. The empire knows that the Hundred exists. The imperial traders covet our spices, slaves, and precious oils. Most of all they desire our naphtha, which the priests and princes of the empire treasure more than anything. The Hundred cannot stand against the empire's armies, should the emperor send them against us. So we make alliances. That is how the game is played."

She will not give up. "The Sirniakan Empire would not care at all about the Hundred if you yourself did not have a claim to the Sirni throne."

"One I have renounced by claiming a kingdom of my own, outside the empire."

"That doesn't change my point," she cries, eager to press her way to victory. "Yours is a circular argument, as you taught us. Because you came here, the imperial eye is turned this way. That they threaten us justifies your position as the king who protects the Hundred, a position that fell into your hands because you came here as an exile fleeing from people who wanted to kill you because you were one of the claimants to the throne in the last imperial crisis. Thus the imperial eye has now turned this way. It isn't fair to throw me to the vultures when you are the carrion they seek!"

He rises abruptly, and she stiffens, knowing she has gone too far.

"Enough, Dannarah!" says the father she loves in a tone that scalds her to the bone.

Atani jumps to his feet because he knows better than to sit when his father stands. Quite to her shock, he speaks.

"You don't want her to go, my lord." He speaks in the formal style he has come to affect in the months since he returned from his mysterious adventure. "But you don't know how to say no to Mama because you can't give her the affection and respect she craves. You don't love her the way you love me and Dannarah, so you're giving up Dannarah as if to make it up to Mama. But you will never make it up to Mama. That is the peace you crave, the one that will keep Mama's reproaching gaze from your face that is always turned away from her."

Her mouth drops open as the words spill from Atani like

blistering flames, although his voice is quiet and almost apologetic. She thinks their father will break into drastic and violent action, not that he ever has before because he is not a violent man. Still, she hurriedly scrambles to her feet because she will not be a coward who watches passively while her brother is punished for defending her in a most courageous and dangerous manner.

But her father surprises her. He walks over to Atani and slips the wolf's head ring onto the tip of his finger to study it more closely. After a moment he meets Atani's gaze.

"Have you more to say on this account, Atani?" he asks in a calm voice.

"Yes! You have decided it is better to be rid of Dannarah than to regret she was not the son you wanted. You worry because you are not quite sure I am strong enough to take the reins you mean to pass to me. So let her stay. Let her and me rule in partnership even if I am the one who will wear the title."

She waits for their father's fury to break over them and obliterate them. But there like the sun emerging from the clouds shines the king's rare smile...

Sunlight slanting out from broken clouds made her blink. She had dozed off. A headache chased behind her eyes as she looked around to orient herself.

She and Terror were high aloft, gliding south, the River Istri a thread far below. Tarnit had taken the lead, Reyad off to the north as the third point. From the upper Elshar Valley to Horn Hall was about a hundred mey as the eagle flew, a twenty-day journey on the road but one an eagle flying at speed by rising and gliding along the thermals could manage in half a day.

For some reason her thoughts had mired in memories of her father and brother. Memory made her smile wryly. How she had cursed Atani that year, when he was sixteen, for running off to have an adventure without taking her along. She had hated him for a while, especially since he had never told her anything about his journey except scraps.

But then, three years after Atani's escapade, Terror had landed in the palace garden and jessed her. That had been the best surprise of all. Once she became a reeve she had left the women's palace and never looked back.

She rubbed her cold hands, having forgotten to put on her gloves. Funny that she never wore rings. They got in her way. Spending time with Chief Tuvas reminded her of her father's loyal Black Wolves and the wolf's head rings they had worn. At his ascension Jehosh had disbanded the Wolves in disgrace for the crime of allowing King Atani to be murdered under their watch. Had some of them held on to their rings, or had they all cast them away out of shame?

Ahead, Tarnit flagged an alert.

They were gliding down the updrafts coming off the North Reach of the Soha Hills. The wide expanse of the Istri Plain opened to her left, a landscape of green fields and orchards ornamented by copses of trees and the sparkling water of irrigation ditches and reservoir ponds. They flew south straight toward the magnificent glittering peak of solitary Mount Aua. The powerful thermals streaming up the mountain would give them the last boost they needed to glide east across the Aua Gap to the city of Horn and Horn Hall beyond.

Just at the edge of her sight she saw what appeared to be a full wing of eagles circling where the plain narrowed to become the broad pass called Aua Gap. She'd received no message that there was trouble in Horn Hall's territory, so naturally she altered course and headed that way.

Soon enough they spotted the commotion. An army marched

on the road below, soldiers in their ranks, the banner of the King's Spears, wagons, and men riding attended by the red and gold banners of the palace. In other circumstances she would have called it half an army on its way to war. It was such a long column that the vanguard had already halted and started setting up camp.

A triad of reeves broke off and headed their way. All reeves wore colored stripes on their leather vests to mark hall affiliation. What in the hells was Argent Hall doing this far north without a single message to let her know they would be passing through Horn Hall's patrol territory? And after demanding Horn Hall take over the pursuit in Sardia?

The lead reeve flagged preemptively for them to land. Their aggressive circling caused Terror to tug so hard against the jesses that Dannarah thought it better to descend than risk her eagle going after one of the other raptors while they were still aloft. She flagged Tarnit to stay aloft with Reyad and went down. When they landed Terror was in a foul mood with so many strange eagles too close.

She was in a pretty cursedly foul mood, too.

She unbuckled and hooded Terror before the eagle could do something rash. Tents were going up about a hundred strides away on a strip of roadside field whose massive Ladytree offered shelter to impoverished travelers. She shaded her eyes against the afternoon sun to study the main tent, an elaborate structure with painted canvas walls and three banners flying from the center pole: the chief marshal's eagle banner, the Second Company of the Spears—which only accompanied the princes—and a red and white banner marked with a sword. One of Jehosh's sons was here.

"The hells!" she muttered.

The guards gave her a startled glance as she approached.

A pair of reeves emerged from the tent and stopped dead. She thought they would move aside but instead they blocked her path.

"Is there a problem, reeves?" Even having to say that much got her wishing she had feathers to fluff up like an angry eagle.

Cursed if the men did not glance at each other and then toward the cloth entrance, seeking orders from an unseen authority inside rather than obeying her instantly.

She slipped her baton from its loop, feeling the headache throb back into life. "Maybe you're too blind to see my marshal's wings but I'm not too blind to whack you both on your slow asses. I'm going in."

Like startled grouse they hustled back inside.

The guards crossed their spears across the entrance to stop her from following. "You need permission to enter the presence of Prince Farihosh."

Dannarah rarely found herself taken aback, but the long flight and this unexpected hostility left her blinking for just long enough that the entrance curtain swept up again to reveal a man she knew.

Chief Marshal Auri smirked at her. She'd hated the prick for years, and he knew it. "Marshal Dannarah. What brings you here?"

She gestured toward the area where four eagles besides Terror were hooded and waiting. "I might ask what brings you here since I don't see your eagle. Perhaps you prefer to walk rather than risk yourself to an eagle's talons and beak. I'm sure it's safer to walk even though you jessed the Hundred's gentlest bird."

His flush entertained her, but he was still chief marshal and she was not. "I am come from the palace with a private message for the prince from his mother Queen Chorannah. Certainly I did not expect to see you here as you are never invited to the palace."

"Your reeves flagged us down. My flight is returning to Horn Hall from a patrol in upper Sardia. One you requested us to take on, as I recall."

"And did you catch the fugitives?"

Her expression must have betrayed her because Auri relaxed, seeing her in a weak position.

"They were being aided by a demon," she added.

Auri's smirk widened. "A poor excuse to cover up your failure to capture the prisoners."

Had she feathers she would have fluffed up now to signal her displeasure. "Wasn't that the excuse the Black Wolves used when King Atani died and a demon was involved? As I recall, you were part of the company assigned to protect him that day. But maybe you were lurking in the rear guard waiting for the danger to pass."

Now she'd really made him angry.

"I can have you stripped of your marshal's rank, Lady Dannarah. Don't think King Jehosh won't support me over you."

"Since he already did, why would I think that?"

He took a step toward her. He was taller, and he still had the build of a soldier although with more flesh now he was twenty years older. "I suggest you return to Horn Hall. Don't trifle with me."

"It's difficult to resist such an easy target," she said, but it was a cheap shot and they both knew he had won the day, years ago, when Jehosh had named him chief marshal in her place. Her inability to dwell in a nest of calm had always been her flaw. Things just pissed her off.

Just as she was about to take a grudging step back, a young man emerged from the tent to stand at the chief marshal's side.

He gazed quizzically at her. "Lady Dannarah? Has no one invited you inside to take refreshments with me?"

The clean and pleasing lines of his face so resembled Atani's that seeing him startled her. She flashed to a memory of Atani standing at a tent entrance, surprised to see her when she had come to cry on his shoulder after the reeve who'd trained her had unexpectedly died. At the time Atani hadn't been much older than this young man, twenty-four at the most. Was the young man wearing a wolf's head ring on a chain at his neck? No, that was just her memory of Atani.

Prince Farihosh wore a soldier's practical tabard, no rings, no necklace, no embroidered hems on sleeves, no ornamentation except the braided ribbons that decorated his topknot.

The headache pulled at her eyes; she rubbed her brow.

"Lady Dannarah, please sit with me for at least a cup of khaif before you go on your way. Chief Marshal Auri? I believe our conference is complete. You may go."

She could not help but laugh as Auri's smoldering resentment at being dismissed took itself off toward the eagles. Probably one of them *was* his eagle, and he had certainly flown here, but she had enjoyed needling him. Pushing people until they got angry was a bad habit, she reflected as the young man escorted her to a lovely set of cushions tossed down atop several layers of rugs.

"My thanks, Prince Farihosh," she said with careful politeness. "I think we have not met for many years. You are certainly grown since the last time I saw you."

"It is a pleasure to meet you again, Aunt Dannarah. Great-Aunt is more correct but Aunt is less formal, don't you think?"

The moment she seated herself a servant appeared with a basin of water and a towel for her to wash her face and hands. A second man succeeded the first with a steaming cup of freshly brewed khaif and a platter of bean cakes, ginger-soaked sweetened rice balls, and buns flavored with coconut. Patrol rations had left her hungry for delicacies.

"Your mother Queen Chorannah is well?"

"She is well, my thanks for asking."

"And your father the king?"

His gaze flicked sideways toward the soldiers, servants, and reeves in attendance, then returned to her. "He is well, Lady Dannarah. My younger brother Prince Tavahosh flourishes."

"All blessings be upon Beltak, the Shining One," she said with the correct formula, grateful that he had reminded her of his brother's name, which she had forgotten.

"As for my half brother, Kasad, Queen Dia's son...Let's just say I am glad to be out of the way of the two queens as they steep their bitter rivalry like a nice cup of tea."

With an effort she managed not to laugh, but oh the hells how she wanted to. "A striking phrase. I have stayed away from the palace for many reasons, that among them."

"So you have. Are you returning from patrol?"

Like Atani he had a solemn demeanor but a way of listening as if he were genuinely interested. So she spoke concisely of what had happened in Elsharat, the valley of the Elshar. "Beyond anything to do with demons it seems there is genuine and increasing discontent with the work gangs," she finished.

He nodded, as unruffled as still water. In this same way Atani had absorbed information without any sign of agitation. "Yes, it is a concern of mine."

"Is that why you travel with such a large company?"

Again he glanced at the men in attendance, then back to her. "No. This is more in the way of an honor guard. I am on my way south to the province of Olo'osson. My mother the queen expressly desires me to stand in attendance on her behalf when the new Beltak shrine is anointed. It has taken five years to build."

"The first of several holy complexes going up these past few years," she said. "Your great-grandfather Anjihosh and your grandfather Atani confined Beltak shrines to a few major cities.

I can understand building a shrine in Olo'osson since it is near the border with the empire, but I hear shrines are being built even in market towns like River's Bend by the Weldur Forest where most people still worship the seven gods."

He opened his hands in a gesture of peace. She was not quite sure if he was mocking her or sharing his mockery with her. "My mother and my brother concern themselves with religious matters. Queen Chorannah, my blessed mother, is a very holy woman who prays devoutly and listens to the wisdom of the Beltak priests. She wishes to bring the peace and righteousness of Beltak's worship to people who do not yet know of the Shining One's kindness and truth."

Dannarah looked around the tent. Four servants waited nearby. The two reeves she had confronted loitered by the entrance. The shorter one looked so Sirniakan that Dannarah was pretty sure he had no Hundred blood in him at all, not like the other who looked as Hundred-bred as Reyad and Tarnit. The reeves wore Argent Hall green. Two soldiers stood guard inside the tent. A clerk sat in the back with a portable writing desk atop his lap, brushing words onto a scroll. Where Jehosh always traveled with his friends and cronies around him, Farihosh appeared far more isolated, or maybe he just had a more solitary nature.

"For a man who travels to represent the king at the dedication of the holy shrine, do you not find it curious that you have no priests in your retinue?" she asked.

His smile killed. The hells! The young man had a dimple, and a surfeit of charm, just like his father, Jehosh. "I pray you, Aunt Dannarah, never mention it within the palace, but I am one who grows weary of preaching. Not like Tav. He can't hear enough of it."

"Then why not send Tavahosh to the Olo'osson dedication instead of you?"

His shrug revealed an unspoken message, but since she did not know him she could not guess what it might be. "I am obedient to the command of my blessed mother, Aunt. Does that not meet with your approval as an honored elder?"

What a sly dig. Oh, he was a clever one, and she liked him already. That was her problem. She made up her mind about people within a few breaths of meeting them and thereafter could not shake her opinion no matter what other side of them she saw.

She took up a rice ball and popped it in her mouth. It was delectable, moist, and with enough burn to really savor. "I can see a great deal of my brother Atani in you, Prince Farihosh."

He inclined his head. "I've heard it said that I sat upon my grandfather's knee and was quite attached to him, but I fear I do not remember him at all."

Such a rush of painful recollection assaulted her that she sucked in a breath, wincing.

"Aunt Dannarah? Have I offended you?"

"Not at all. I do recall it. Atani cherished you, Farihosh. He liked nothing better than to make you laugh."

"They say he was a good king, fair-minded, patient, and able to tell if any person lied to him. Is that true? It would be a vital skill for a king to have, do you not think?" He refilled her cup in a gesture appropriate for any young person toward their elder. "But perhaps I talk too much about things you do not wish to remember."

"No, you do not talk too much. It is true that Atani knew when people lied to him." Except when she had lied to him, on his last day.

He tapped fingers together, then glanced at her. "Might I persuade you to take supper with me, Aunt Dannarah? Tell me stories of my grandfather Atani? My father rarely speaks of him, and since he does not, no one else in the palace will."

He might as well have stabbed her and been done with it, for she could not move from the gush of emotion that flooded through her. "Of course I will stay."

So she did, sending out one of the reeves to flag down Tarnit and Reyad for the night. Farihosh proved to be an excellent listener, plying her with questions that loosened her tongue. His genuine interest freed an old ache in her heart. For once she could remember Atani with love and generosity instead of with the endless caged pain.

"With what respect you mention your father, the great Anjihosh!" Farihosh remarked. "You knew him, spoke to him, were taught by him! Is it really true he rode as an exile into the Hundred with only two hundred Qin soldiers and yet single-handedly defeated the demons who were burning and murdering the population? That he brought peace to the land, and made himself king?"

"It is true. He and I often discussed the campaign and the choices he made."

"He must have been a brilliant strategist to accomplish so much with such modest resources. How did he do it?"

His enthusiasm was irresistible. She hadn't spoken so much about her father in years.

Very late she refused a pallet in the tent and went to sleep outside with her reeves, as was always her custom when out on patrol. Reyad slept but Tarnit was still awake, chatting with a reeve she had trained with as fledgling reeves twenty-four years ago.

She left the fire to join Dannarah under a rough lean-to of canvas set up in case it rained. "So I was talking to my old friend Herard. You've met him once or twice. He's been posted at Argent Hall for years. He says in the last few years everything at Argent Hall has been turned upside down. Most of the veterans have been sent elsewhere, and Herard says he lost track of a number of them. Herard himself was attached two years ago to

Palace Hall atop Law Rock. Besides flying patrol around Tos-kala he has mostly flown messages for the palace ever since. He's not happy about being turned into a courier. Maybe you should see if you can attach him to Horn Hall, too."

Dannarah rubbed her forehead, wishing the last of the head-ache would dissipate. "Argent Hall has taken a turn for the worse since Auri moved his headquarters from Palace Hall to Argent Hall, that's for certain."

"What's even more interesting is that the chief marshal pulled an entire flight of eighteen reeves to escort Prince Fari-hosh on this trip. They wear Argent Hall green but with two extra gold stripes to mark them out, like an elite flight. Don't you find that odd?"

Dannarah glanced toward the tents and their pacing sen-tries. On a cloudy night like tonight the sky breathed darkness the way palace alcoves breathe gossip. "I was never given notice that a prince would be moving through territory Horn Hall is responsible to patrol. What do they fear on roads that have been safe since my father made himself king? Surely they don't need so many soldiers to guard against a few disgruntled escapees from the work gangs."

"What did those Hasibal players say?" Tarnit asked as she rolled out her bedroll with the ease of long practice.

"What Hasibal players?"

Tarnit paused, giving her an odd look. "The ones you landed to talk to as we were flying out of the Elshar Valley? Reyad and I remained aloft, and then you joined us afterward?"

"Oh. Ah." She rubbed her forehead again as the ache intensi-fied. "Nothing of interest. They performed for the village and the soldiers. The Ri Amarah don't hold with that sort of enter-tainment. They hadn't seen any criminals or had any trouble."

Tarnit relaxed, and sat on her bedroll to pull off her boots. "That's good. What is the prince like?"

"He reminds me of my brother."

"Ah." Tarnit's fingers brushed Dannarah's arm, a gesture few would have dared make.

Dannarah smiled at her. "My thanks, Tar. Funny how much it still hurts."

After a silence, Tarnit asked, "Do you think we'll find anything in the Wild?"

"The Wild? Why would we find anything there?"

"You said we were going to the market towns by the Weldur Forest to look for redheart wreaths."

"Did I?"

Tarnit's hand closed around her wrist. "Are you well? We should go back to Horn Hall."

Wind tore apart the clouds, revealing moon and stars. "That's right, the redheart wreath," she said, wondering why the moon looked so bright. "I'm tired today. Never mind it. We will go to the Wild. I have a hunch we're going to find something important there."

14

The very best days were when Lifka and her papa, just the two of them, left at dawn for the skirts of the Wild to collect wood. First there would be an exhilarating argument with Mum as they got ready to leave.

"Pull back your hair! You're not fit to be seen with it all sprung out like a bush! What will people say?"

"What people always say! Why does it coil up like that? Can I touch it? That never changes!"

"That's not what I mean, which you know as well as I do, so watch your tongue, young woman, just because you're taller than me now! You will be neat and you will be clean when you go out of this compound. We don't concern ourselves with other folk's bad manners. We do what is right."

"I'll shave it all off!" Lifka threatened.

Mum kissed her on each cheek, which always disarmed her, then slapped her so hard on the butt that she jumped. "You will not cut your beautiful hair. Do you want me to tie it up under a scarf for you?"

Lifka was too old to admit that she did so she yanked her hair back and wrapped it with leather cord.

Mum shook her head with a wry smile. "Before you reach the river you'll be regretting you didn't let me fix it properly. Go on, then!" She handed Lifka her staff because no one in the family left the compound without the means to defend themselves. "Your father's waiting."

Papa had already loaded the hatchet, the ax, the sledgehammer, and three wedges into the empty bed of the wagon. She climbed up on the driver's bench beside him. The cart dogs Yap, Goblin, and the Runt leaped up. The mules, Courageous and Steadfast, were eager to go. She rubbed her forehead because her hair was pulled so tight it strained her skin.

"Might as well cut it short like the lads," remarked Papa.

"Girls and women don't cut their hair short. Mum would have a seizure."

"Wish you could, though, don't you? Strange to think you can't, when all it would take is a razor." He whistled a brisk "hee-up" and flicked the reins. The mules ambled forward, taking the measure of the cloud-ridden day.

"You give a thought to what you want to do, now you're a young woman? You want to go to your mother's clan and walk the roads as a caravan guard with your aunties and uncles? See the Hundred? I thought for sure you'd go with Ailia last year when she went out to them."

"No."

"Any lads you've a mind to marry?"

"No. I like the lads well enough but I don't want to marry yet."

"We might apprentice you out, if there's a trade you want to learn—"

"Papa, I'm happy at home. Can't I just work with you like we always do? Are you trying to get rid of me?"

His smile teased her, as if he was about to say he was, but after a moment his gaze softened. "Never that, Lifka."

"Heya! Heya!" Her brothers Alon and Denas and cousin Nanni came running. "You said you'd let us ride to the work site!"

"I didn't say I'd wait for you laggards." Papa did not slow down but he did not speed up, either. The lads slung their tool bags and staffs into the back and swung on, laughing.

"Leaf, you look like your face is being pulled off. Let me do it over." Denas scooted up.

The Runt bared his teeth at him, and Denas showed teeth back. Ears flattening, the Runt curled his upper lip back a bit more. Lifka and Alon and Nanni all watched with interest to see if the young dog would snap but he gave way by pressing against Denas's leg, stub tail wagging apologetically.

"You're so impatient, Leaf." Denas unwrapped the cord, got her hair under control, and braided the leather cord into such a clever loop that Nanni and Alon praised the ornamentation although just by feeling at it she couldn't quite suss out what he'd done.

"Think there will be work today?" Papa kept his eyes on the road, careful not to seem like he was pressing his sons and nephew over a problem they could not influence.

"The usual promises, now the rains are fading." Alon rubbed

a hand over his shaved short hair in the nervous habit he had when he got to thinking about things that worried him. "Digging out the ground for foundations for forty vey for the day, a day's labor in the brickworks for thirty, or twenty for hauling dirt."

Papa's rare frown flared. "Tssh! Same wage my father got when he was my age. Yet rice costs twice what it did then. How is a family to eat with the king's tithe to hand over out of what little we manage to earn?"

None of the lads answered. The wagon moved alongside a stream of local men walking toward town for work, so it wasn't safe to say the things they might speak inside their compound. No one wanted the Beltak priests to get wind of complaining. Complaints could get you rounded up for a work gang and sent away to another part of the Hundred.

Men who could afford a vey for a ride clambered up into the back and pressed the copper coin into Alon's hand. Yap and Goblin ignored these passengers; they kept their gaze on the countryside and their noses to the wind, proper guard dogs seeking wicked bandits just like in the Tale of the Carter and His Barking Dog. The Runt eyed each new interloper with a quiver of his muzzle but pressed closer to Lifka until his head was practically buried against her leg.

Men talked about the weather and the fields. The rice fields were draining as they did at this season with the stalks growing tall. Lantern-berry shrubs and mulberry trees lined the embankments, bright with flowers or green fruit. It smelled like promise, the hungry weeks of the Flood Rains finally passing and the hope of a few hearty meals and extra vey coming into each household from day labor. That would happen only if the men could snag work at the new building site on the other side of the river.

"I hear they're not hiring because they brought in a new

work gang, all of them criminals from Toskala," said a neighbor youth, one of Lifka's occasional lovers. He was all frowns now. "How are we meant to eat if we can't work? Yet the Beltak priests grow fat while we starve."

Papa stiffened. "The wind hears all."

Lifka knew he was thinking of how badly Aunt Ediko had died.

In silence they reached the ferry crossing. Each man paid a vey to board. Lifka and Pa held the mules' heads as the barge was hauled across the river on its cable. Downstream beyond the river's curve rose the town of River's Bend, where the district archon lived.

Midway across the old ferryman left his nephew at the windlass and made his way over to Papa. The noisy slap of water against the hull drowned his words from anyone more than a step away. "Just a word of warning, Geron," the old man said to Papa. "Yesterday the archon called me into town to tell me the priests are taking over both ferries as soon as the shrine is completed."

"How will your clan live?" demanded Papa. "Your people have always maintained the ferries."

The old man looked weary and defeated. "Maybe they will sell us a license to operate it. I don't know."

"We lost our livelihood because of the new licenses needed to transport goods on the roads," muttered Papa. "The king's officers and the Beltak priests are grabbing everything for themselves."

"Hush, talk is dangerous," said the old man as the barge bumped onto the landing on the eastern shore.

The Weldur Forest with its ancient trees and impenetrable depths rose before them. The interior was accounted sacred by the people who had lived in this area since time out of mind. People known as wildings lived there as keepers of the forest's heart. But the Beltak priests had decided to build a shrine right up against the forest.

In the old days the archon was elected by the town council, but now he was appointed by the king, and their current archon had no interest in respecting the old customs kept by those who worshipped the Hundred's seven gods: Hasibal the Merciful One, Kotaru the Thunderer, Sapanasu the Lantern, Taru the Witherer, Atiratu the Lady of Beasts, Ilu the Herald, and Ushara the Merciless One Who Rules Over Love, Death, and Desire.

The building site cut a scar into the earth with turf cut up and underbrush slashed back. Fires smoked where stacks of wood were being burned for charcoal. The shrine grounds were marked out by rope and posts. Ditches marked the foundations. The outer wall was going up first, to hide the mysteries of the god's architecture from those who could not be admitted within the walls. A file of men roped together waited at a food line. Each had a criminal's brand inked on his right cheek so no one could mistake him for a free man.

The men hopped off. Her cousin and brothers left last with farewells that rang in her ears with false cheer.

"Do you think they'll get work?" she asked Papa. "Or have to walk home empty-handed?"

"Don't stare, Lifka. The priests don't like it."

"Will we have to give offerings at their shrine when it's finished? Will the priests stop us from giving offerings to the seven gods?"

"Shh, lass. Not here, where the wind may have ears."

Too late she remembered that the wind *might* have ears. Aunt Ediko had a bit of demon's blood in her, just enough that she could see things others couldn't. She had claimed the priests used the tethered ghosts of the dead as spies. The mules plodded stolidly on. They did not like the stench around the shrine

and wished to reach greener pastures north of the ferry landing,
where local people were permitted to forage for downed wood.
As the building site began to fall behind, Lifka let out a held
breath.

Yap and Goblin flattened their ears. The Runt tensed.

A man at the head of a cadre of soldiers waved them down.
Papa brought the mules to a halt.

"Ver, greetings of the day," Papa said politely.

The twelve soldiers were not from around River's Bend. For
one thing, they wore their long hair up in clubs behind their
heads, as only soldiers, courtiers, judges, favored merchants,
and the archon and his council were allowed to do in imitation
of the men of the palace. They stared at Lifka and she stared
right back until Papa nudged her with a foot.

The captain of the group caught the exchange. "Your slave
has a belligerent look about her, ver."

"She's my daughter," said Papa in the tone of a man who has
spoken the words a thousand times.

"Your daughter? She can't be your daughter," said the captain
in a mocking tone. Some of the soldiers laughed.

Papa kept talking in that even voice. "So unless there is some
trouble, Captain, we'll be getting on to our usual work of the
day. We're off to bring in wood for the charcoal pits."

The man fingered the whip he carried. "By my authority as
the king's man, I am commandeering your wagon and your
labor. We have a cargo for you to take."

Yap rumbled, preface to an outright growl, but Papa rested a
hand on the dog's back to calm her. Goblin gave a single short
bark to remind the men that he did not like the way they were
looking at his people. The Runt was quivering, lips pulled back
to display his impressive teeth. They weren't big dogs but they
knew how to fight.

"Good-looking dogs." The captain gave a pointed glance to

those of his men who carried crossbows. "I'd hate to see anything happen to them if they get too aggressive."

Papa sighed in defeat. "What manner of cargo and what distance? We're prepared only for a day's work."

"Just some rubbish to bury in the forest."

The captain pointed with his elbow toward a midden over by the latrines. What looked at first like logs Lifka realized were corpses. "They're starting to stink."

Papa's calm reply disguised the anger in his gaze. "There is a Sorrowing Tower in River's Bend as in every town, where the dead are properly laid to rest in the eyes of the gods."

"Once the shrine is finished the priests will close down your vulture tower. Anyway, the head priest has decreed that the dead bodies are defiled because they died on holy ground. They must be buried so their poison will not infest the god's habitation."

The droop of Papa's eyelids gave him the expression of a man already in mourning. "The dead are meant to be laid out on Sorrowing Towers and their flesh scoured clean by the elements. To bury a corpse is an affront to the gods."

"It is the law," said the captain. "And I am telling you to do it."

"Will we get payment for the work?" Papa asked in that slow way he had that made the question seem more like curiosity than demand.

The captain hesitated. Lifka had a feeling the man was wrestling with himself, as if he knew he could easily say no but felt it unfair.

"Ten vey for your trouble," he said finally, "but no more, since you're already going that way and can come back with a full wagon of firewood. If you've any to sell, we're buying. Can't seem to get these work gangs to cut enough for the barracks' cook fires. Laziest asses I've ever supervised. And they keep having accidents."

"They having trouble in the forest?" Papa's gaze lifted toward the trees. Sunlight made the dense crowns shimmer as with the breath of a vast and mute beast tending its wounds.

The captain touched two fingers to his forehead. "Cursed nasty place, that forest. Ought to chop it all down, and maybe that's what the priests mean to do."

His men laughed uneasily.

Papa shook his head. "The Wild and its guardians are not to be trifled with. Nor is it proper to insult the seven gods, and the Four Mothers who gave birth to the land before the gods came, by even suggesting such an impious thing."

"You can do as I ask, ver, or you can talk to an exalted priest and see if you wish to trifle with the shrine hierarchy."

"As you say, Captain. I'll do as you ask."

Papa guided the mules toward the latrines, his lips moving in silent prayer: *Be merciful to your children who are forced to walk into a place they know they ought not go.*

He turned to her as they approached the corpses. "My apologies that you are forced to witness an offense against the gods, and that I cannot refuse to be party to it. May the gods be merciful to this spiritless flesh about to be handled with such disrespect."

"It's not your fault, Papa."

She hated the lines that furrowed his brow, as if he thought he could put a stop to it. The five bodies were naked. Three had crusted and festering wounds. One had a cracked skull. The fifth had no mark beyond the hollow cheeks and bony limbs of a man worked in constant hunger.

"You take the feet, and I'll take the hands," Papa said.

She grabbed a pair of cold ankles. The skin was scaly dry and dappled with unsightly bruises. They quickly swung all five corpses into the back of the wagon as the dogs watched with puzzled interest. She could imagine the Runt trying to sort out the change of plan, for he sat there with head cocked to one side,

one ear up and the other down. He was a dog who liked his rou-
tine: the ride, the chopping, the logs, the delivery, then home.

As they headed north along the cart track they passed a work
gang shuffling past toward the building site. Most kept their
eyes averted from the dead men but several stared angrily their
way, as if she and Papa were somehow responsible! What were
they to do? Refuse orders and be punished themselves? Be executed like Aunt Ediko when she protested the wrong thing at
the wrong time?

She studied the living men's gaunt bellies, haunted eyes, and
disturbing silence. Laborers usually sang as they worked to
make the time pass, but these men could just as well have had
their tongues cut out. She looked back farther down the road in
the hope of seeing her brothers and cousin but all she saw was a
veiled priest standing at a gap in the walls that someday a gate
would close. He was looking their way, holding a priest bowl. A
finger of wind stroked her eyes as if a ghost sought a way in to
discover the truths hidden in her heart. She scooted closer to her
father.

"Lifka?"

"Nothing. Let's sing."

So they sang their favorite songs as the mules plodded along.
Lifka accompanied the stories with the hand-talk that punctuated the words with extra meaning, but the lilting melodies fell
like stones instead of leaping into the sky. Clouds covered the
sun. Shadows clotted their path.

Once they were out of sight of the shrine, Papa turned the cart
onto an overgrown wagon trail where years ago men had hauled
out logs. Lifka said nothing, troubled by his grim expression.

"Hop off and make sure we're hidden from the track," he said.

She grabbed the Runt under an arm and with him holding
himself rigid—for he hated the indignity of being carried—she
scrambled off and set him down. As he snuffled through the

brush, she tidied up broken branches as Papa drove on, out of sight. When she had concealed their passage to her satisfaction, she followed the wheel ruts into a spur of uncut forest where a copse of towering redheart stood like an outpost on the borderlands. Even the priests did not order the heartwood to be hewn down; axes could not cut into it.

"I will not bury any child of the Hundred," Papa said as she walked up to him. "We'll weave two ladders out of branches and call them Sorrowing Towers. This is as good a place as any, close to the redheart."

"It will take half the day to weave funeral ladders, Papa. What about gathering and cutting wood? We need the coin, and besides that we need to replenish our own wood stores at home."

He began trimming ash saplings for ladder legs. "We must do what is right for the dead, who cannot do for themselves."

She nodded and set to cutting branches to make rungs, the only sound the thunk of their tools. The dogs fanned out to sniff and scout.

"Papa, I know the Qin and Sirni outlanders brought their own ways and their own king with them, but why do Hundred folk like us turn their backs on the seven gods?"

His gentle frown made her uneasy. "Because they want the wealth and position the king and his court can offer them. I hear this isn't the only place where they are building Beltak shrines. The temples to the seven gods were closed in the big cities years ago."

A twig snapped. Yap and Goblin growled. The Runt came pelting out of the brush to take refuge at Lifka's feet. Branches rustled noisily among the redheart. Papa set down his ax and nodded at Lifka to do the same.

He faced the trees and gestured *greeting and peace* in sign language. As he spoke with his lips he also spoke with his hands.

"Cousins, we stand in peace. Forgive us if we walk where we are not allowed. This spiritless flesh we bring only to offer to the Four Mothers."

Lifka was sure she saw people hidden in the shadows of the trees but she could not be sure. The guardians of the Wild killed anyone who crossed into their territory yet the priests of Beltak demanded more logs for their shrine, forcing people to push ever farther into the forest.

A shard of darkness slashed the air. A javelin thunked into the ground right between Lifka and her father, quivering from the force of the impact. A file of soldiers trotted into the clearing, the same group who had ordered them to dispose of the dead men. In their midst walked the veiled priest, most ominous of all because only the high exalted among the Beltak priests were allowed to conceal their faces as a sign of an exalted spiritual power mere mortals could not look upon.

From the priest's belt hung a small wooden bowl. Its rim gleamed with such a sheen of despair that Lifka took a step away as he confronted her father. "You were commanded not to lay them out, for that blasphemy is forbidden to men who have died on holy ground."

"All the land of the Hundred is holy ground." Her father looked ready to spit. "We are enjoined to return our flesh to our ancient Mothers. Here in River's Bend we follow the customs we have always followed. It is not forbidden to lay the dead on a Sorrowing Tower. Even if we must build a simple weaving of branches to serve the gods' holy purpose."

The priest's gaze burned. "I arrest you on the charge of blasphemy. These soldiers will escort you to the assizes. The punishment for blasphemy is seven years' service in a work gang so you may labor in the gods' holy service and see the error of your rebellion."

Yap and Goblin stared fixedly at the soldiers, shivering with unvoiced growls. Lifka tightened her hands on her staff, but her father gave all of them the gesture to stay. She was so angry she wanted to hit something. The breeze shifted. A rotten stench drifted out of the trees.

"Let's get out of here," said the priest with a nervous glance toward the redheart trees. "Come along, prisoner."

"What of my daughter? What of my wagon and beasts?"

"A slave cannot be your daughter. Why is she not marked with ink as the law requires? Send her home with your wagon and beasts but I expect her to appear at the assizes tomorrow when you are sentenced so she can be properly marked."

She was as tall as half of the men; she could fight with the staff as Mum had taught all the children, and thus give Papa time to run. But Papa again made the sign that she must stay quiet. In his eyes she saw his haunted memory of his sister Ediko's horrible death. In his eyes she saw him wondering why the priest had followed them, how the man had known.

So she imagined herself a sapling, rooted to one spot. Papa whistled the dogs over to her. Then he walked away under guard. The soldiers at the rear measured her as the others strode out of sight. She tightened her hands on the staff to let them know they would not trouble her without an ugly fight. But there were five of them and only one of her. No man in the village would ever have assaulted her, but these were not village men, and the priest had just named her a slave. According to the law, slaves did not have the same rights as people.

Behind her came a rustle, a thump, and an ominous scrape. The soldiers looked toward the trees. Recoiling from a sight she could not see, the men thrashed away through the undergrowth after their comrades. Her back prickled as if a monster were breathing on her neck. But she did not move until the noise of the soldiers' passage faded.

Then, almost weeping with fright, she turned to face whatever was behind her.

One of the dead men had been pulled by means of a leafy green rope up off the ground to dangle horribly by his feet from an overhanging branch. The body swayed, arms dangling, genitals exposed, a mockery of what he had once been. No one else was there, just the dead man hanging.

The forest people had hung up the corpse to warn away the soldiers.

Fear pulsed through her skin, wiping away all thought. Yet as she stared, the rope let out and the body was lowered to lie on the earth like the stroke of a broken letter.

Yap and Goblin stood, tails raised, ears high. The Runt subvocalized a tentative growl.

"I ask you with all respect, brothers and sisters, let me attend to the dead flesh of these people according to the will of the gods." She spoke with her voice and her hands to the unseen watchers. To the gods. To herself. To Papa.

Oh gods. *Papa.*

But she knew what he would want her to do. So she set her staff aside and finished constructing the crude platforms. The bark rubbed at her hands. Her thoughts rubbed at her heart. Papa couldn't possibly survive seven years in a work gang! How would Uncle react, considering how delicate his nerves already were? What would her brothers do? How would she tell her mother?

The trees swayed. She froze as three people emerged from them into the clearing. They were shorter than she was, with elongated arms and hairy bodies, but when she signed the hand gesture for *peace and greetings* they all three signed it back in the sign of the Hundred, which was also known as the speech of the Mothers.

Their eyes examined her silently. She smelled no threat; she tasted none. Yap and Goblin remained standing but they did not growl. The Runt hid behind her legs. So she kept on building.

One of the forest people ventured over to the wagon, sniffing cautiously at the beasts. The dun mule crooked one leg, threatening to kick. The other two forest people bent to the bier Papa had been forced to abandon. Lifka's breathing quickened, but instead of ripping it apart they set to work. Their strong hands wove a platform from stiff branches far more quickly than she could. In an oddly companionable silence they worked until two platforms were finished and braced off the ground. With their aid, she slung the naked men onto the ramshackle Sorrowing Towers.

She chanted the death prayers over them, prayers she had last sung at her aunt's passing. She wept, not for men she did not know but for the indignity of it. People were meant to be given to the Sorrowing Tower in dignity, wrapped in a light shroud, with a proper mourning procession and a feast afterward, not tossed into the woodland like rubbish or confined by the priests in their stone tombs and with their foreign rites.

When the last note faded and she looked around, the forest people had vanished. The dogs wagged their tails. The mules flicked their ears at flies.

She wanted to beat at the earth with her staff until everything broke. But she had to stay calm. In the end, she collected enough wood that Mother could afford to buy another week's worth of rice. That's what Papa would have her do because, he would patiently explain, they could do nothing until the morning so might as well not waste the day when it could be put to use.

When the wagon bed was filled, she lifted the dogs up onto the driver's bench and turned the mules toward home. A shadow rippled over the path. The dogs cowered.

A huge eagle glided overhead, quartered back, then vanished over the trees.

Were the reeves scouting for people like her who were breaking the priests' rules? Had Papa escaped and made a run for it?

But when she arrived home the worst had come true: The archon had sent word that Papa was to be condemned tomorrow. Uncle wept. Her sisters and brothers and cousins wept. Gray with shock, Mother trembled over their dinner of watery rice porridge and a few soggy dandelion leaves. Lifka felt too sick to eat.

What memories she had from her earliest childhood were nothing more than flashes: A plank floor that swayed beneath her as she played with a tinkling brass ball by rolling it as the floor tipped. A solemn space with a roof where people were singing while she wept; she had been so small she remembered only the emotion, but she could still hum the melody. Shivering on a steep trail as she looked down along a mountainside to see a line of people like ants on the march; some were frightened children like her and the rest were frightening soldiers.

She did not remember marching into the Hundred among that crowd of prisoners; nor had she any real memory of what she had left behind in the land from which she had been taken. She did not remember coming for the first time through the gates of their home although she had been told the story often enough, that Papa arrived home one late afternoon from a carting job and announced, "Look, I found our lost daughter," and carried her in.

Thus had it been from that day on. She was Alon's and Denas's sister. She was cousin to Nanni, Ailia, Nonit, and Darit, never one word otherwise from the family or anyone who knew them.

So she made the only plan that would work.

She would offer herself for the work gang in Papa's place.

15

In the first market town Dannarah and her reeves visited, on the southern edge of the Weldur Forest where the River Ili met the River Istri, they were told that no one made or sold redheart wreaths anymore because the Beltak priests had forbidden the practice as superstition. They flew north up the River Ili to a market village, friendly enough but cautious. The people in the tiny market were reluctant to speak to reeves until Reyad blithely lied and told folk he needed a wreath for his own upcoming wedding. An old woman charmed by his smile informed him that redheart was only harvested at the full moon and then only made to order; they would have to come back and, no, she'd sold no redheart wreaths last month at all because it was not the season for marrying, not in these parts anyway. They might have better luck at River's Bend, she added; it was a large town at the meeting place of five trade roads.

They flew north, sweeping over the forest so Reyad could get a good look at a place he should have seen during his training. Seeing the beauty and complexity of the land from this vantage never failed to make Dannarah's spirit swell with amazement and joy.

The forest had layers: birds fluttering above the canopy, the topmost layer of leaves and reaching branches, the dense canopy zone and the emptier mid-tree regions, and beneath all flashes of ground cover or bare earth. As with people, it was hard to see what lay underneath.

Weldur the Heart.

Somewhere in a faded chronicle buried away in a temple

dedicated to the Hundred goddess Sapanasu the Lantern, King Anjihosh had discovered references to the vast forest using this appellation. There was even a line in one of the tales of the Hundred: *Weldur the heart that has fallen silent.* The heart of what? How can a living, breathing forest be silent?

The phrase had the feel of a dusty remnant from an older time when the temples to the seven gods were newly built, a time memorialized in ancient tales. Her father and her brother had let the Hundred's customs continue untouched, and their respective queens, Zayrah and Yevah, who had both been born and raised in the empire, had kept their Beltak worship private.

Under Jehosh and Chorannah that time was over.

Recent logging cut into the forest like gouges into flesh. Circles of ash marred the ground where wood had been piled and burned to make charcoal. The ugly sights disturbed Dannarah as much as if she were looking down on a wounded body. It hadn't been like this before.

She spotted the distinctive reddish-tinged columns of a redheart grove not too far from a clearing slashed out of the trees. Although reeves could fly over the Wild, the eagles always refused to fly directly over redheart. Leaving the other two aloft she landed, unhitched, then walked the edge of the clearing looking for a trail that would allow her to approach the redheart grove.

At the clearing's edge grew wild sweet-thorn, lovely when trimmed in a garden and so fearsomely thick here she doubted a machete could hack through it. The impenetrable sweet-thorn blocked her way, and the people living in the Wild killed trespassers. Yet for redheart wreaths to make their way to the doors of newlyweds, there had to be some communication among people who in the ancient stories were considered siblings born from the Four Mothers. The wildings were one of the eight children of the Hundred, as the old teaching song said: *These are the eight children, the dragonlings, the firelings, the delvings, the wildings, the lendings, the merlings, the demon-hearts, and the blind-hearts.*

Blind-hearts was the ancient name for humans, and today she felt she wasn't seeing something that ought to be obvious to her.

She strode back to Terror, who was clawing at the dirt with her talons, perhaps disturbed by their proximity to the red-heart. Every instinct told her this was a place to avoid, and yet she wanted so badly to explore. This was not the time.

She hooked in and whistled the raptor up.

Eagles could fly in a morning what took soldiers days to march.

Soon they reached the spot where the River Ili flowed in a bow curve around the town of River's Bend. In the shadow of the forest a huge Beltak shrine was going up, swarmed by labor-ers, but what drew her eye was a flight of eagles circling the town. One broke away from the flight and descended toward the ban-ners that marked the town's assizes court. To her amazement the eagle wore the gold-painted harness of Chief Marshal Auri.

Why in the hells had Auri left Farihosh to come to this out-of-the-way place?

Every town assizes was fitted with an open space with perches, a loft sufficient for a few raptors, and a shelter with a raised floor for reeves to overnight. As Terror circled in, Dan-narah saw that an assizes was in session in the judge's amphithe-ater. Folk spilled out from under the roofed area as more people crowded in to hear the proceedings than the amphitheater could hold. The assizes was surrounded by soldiers wearing the red-and-white tabards of the Spears.

Terror braked, wings wide and talons extended, and thumped onto a perch. Reyad followed her down while Tarnit stayed aloft. Dannarah meant to wait for Reyad to unbuckle his own harness before she went into the amphitheater but Auri was actually struggling to get out of his gear like a fledgling reeve who has never hooked in before.

Seeing her, he peremptorily beckoned her over. As if she were a fawkner whose job was to serve him!

Auri's eagle had a soft golden-brown color, a perfectly formed head and hooked beak, and eyes so gold they gleamed. Slip had a gentle nature; she'd known the man who had been harnessed to Slip before Auri, a skilled reeve who had died of a fever. The eagle had flown away, as eagles did after the death of their reeve. It had always griped her when Slip had shown up later in harness to such an asswipe.

The arrival of the bigger and more aggressive Terror caused Slip to lower his head defensively. Dannarah paused outside his strike range and with her baton gestured the signal for *at-rest*. Slip bobbed restlessly, then settled his feathers.

Auri finally got the hooks undone and dropped to the ground. He stepped out from under Slip's shadow and raised a hand to gesture to Dannarah to hood the bird. Just then he saw Reyad. The young reeve had already hooded Surly and stepped away to wait, but the way Reyad stood so tensely with gaze fixed on the ground and hands in fists was a signal.

Auri's smirk on seeing the young man really disturbed her.

"I'm surprised to see you here, Reeve Reyad," called the chief marshal. "How is your pretty wife?"

Dannarah needed only one look at Reyad's whitened lips. "Reyad, go to the loft and see if there's any harness oil."

He stalked away toward the loft. Terror and Surly settled under their hoods.

"What's he doing here?" Auri sauntered over, leaving Slip unhooded.

Did he truly not know better after eighteen years as a reeve than to leave an unhooded bird amid such commotion?

She pitched her voice louder than necessary so as many soldiers and people in the crowd as possible could hear. "Greetings, Chief Marshal. You need help hooding your bird?"

The double-pronged insult made him flush, and he turned back. His eagle shifted huge feet nervously but accepted the hood meekly enough, however hastily the man pulled it over the raptor's head and scooted out of reach of the talons.

Before Auri could say anything else, Dannarah struck again, offering her blandest smile like the last rice cake on a platter. "I've seconded Reyad to my wing, Chief Marshal. With your permission."

Auri gave way just as she knew he would. "Much good you'll have in him. I have discovered him to be troublesome and incompetent."

"Incompetents are the worst sort, I've always found. But I'll be glad to have him transferred to Horn Hall, for I am short on reeves what with all the unexpected and unannounced transfers going on from one hall to another these days. That's settled then."

Auri changed color, realizing she had just boxed him in.

What a useless ass he was! A man as lazy as he was never had time to do the work that needed doing.

"Why are you here in River's Bend, Marshal Dannarah?"

"Scouting out demons, Chief Marshal, just as you ordered. Why are you here? I thought you were accompanying Prince Farihosh to the dedication in Olo'osson."

"No, I was just taking his young lordship a message from his mother. I'm here to accompany Prince Tavahosh. As part of his training in the priesthood he has come here to pass judgment on cases brought before the court for blasphemy and for rebellion against the god's edicts. Queen Chorannah always requests that I escort one or the other of the princes when they leave the palace."

"You are Chief Marshal of the Reeve Halls. Not a bodyguard."

"I serve the palace," he said stiffly.

"Odd, for I was sure the chief marshal serves the reeve halls first before anything."

"You are a naive old woman, lost in the past." He relished the words as they dripped off his tongue. "But we will not have to tolerate your kind of reeve much longer."

"My kind of reeve? What in the hells does that mean?"

Auri practically bounced on his toes, so eager was he to tell her. But then, more ominously, he controlled himself. "You're not worth my notice, as you'll soon discover."

He turned toward the amphitheater. The tone of the crowd altered as a new case started. People murmured angrily. She didn't like the crack of tension any more than she liked Auri's threatening demeanor.

She followed Auri through the ranks of the soldiers who surrounded the amphitheater. She often regretted her lost youth but she was glad to be old enough that the palace soldiers hesitated to interfere as she passed from sun into blessed shade. In the docket below stood a man in ordinary laborer's clothing: a faded kilt and a mended jacket. Nine local judges sat in attendance, hands folded in the sign for total obedience, mouths shut. A young man preened at the center with all eyes on his elaborately embroidered priest's robe and the peaked gold cap worn by Sirniakan nobility. Prince Tavahosh had a loud voice and a hectoring tone. He spoke the language of the Hundred so awkwardly that she guessed he had learned it in the schoolroom.

"The man gives his name as Geron of Five Roads Clan. By trade he is a carter. Witnesses see him blaspheme against the god's holy law. He is commanded to dispose of criminals but he disobeys. He illegally constructs a death ladder. This savagery is forbidden by the edicts of Beltak, the Shining One Who Rules Alone."

Whispers raced like wasps through the watching crowd.

Satisfaction gleamed in the prince's expression as he pronounced the sentence. "In the case of Geron the Carter the god is merciful and does not demand death in exchange for grievous error. The prisoner owes seven years' labor serving the god."

The mood spiked as people nudged each other. The angriest shook fists toward the judges.

Dannarah hurried down the last steps but, before she reached Tavahosh, a tall young woman shoved out of the crowd and planted herself before the judges. The young person was an outlander. Instead of brown skin, hers was black. Dannarah paused at the edge of the open semicircle where the prisoner waited and the judges sat. The crowd went dead silent.

The girl stamped a foot on the ground in the traditional way, three times to announce that she had words to say. Her hands gestured with the hand-talk Dannarah had only learned imperfectly; the girl's fluent gestures marked her as a child of the Hundred.

Shame. Shame. Shame. She emphasized the gesture, palm out and back of the hand shading the face. She had a bold voice.

"This hardworking man Geron the Carter pays his tithes in coin and labor, yet you persecute him! Is there a law that prevents those who still give offerings at the temples to lay out their dead in the traditional manner?"

Prince Tavahosh quivered, flourishing his priest's staff as prelude to striking her. "Slaves do not have the right to speak!"

As the girl opened her mouth to retort, the criminal Geron broke in. "Lifka is my daughter, and daughter of my clan. She is not a slave."

"She cannot be your daughter," said the prince. "Anyone with eyes can see this."

Geron had the simple directness of countryfolk. "She is our daughter by the old custom. By our saying so, it makes it so."

The prince slammed his staff twice on the stone pavement to quiet the calls of agreement from the crowd. "The god commands that the children of people our armies defeat must serve their masters. She is a captive from the north. Thus she is required to bear the mark of shame. By not inking her, you have broken another law! Three years more you must serve the god. Ten years together you will serve! The girl will be inked and taken away from your clan."

The crowd broke into cries of protest. Above, the soldiers tightened their ranks around the amphitheater.

With baton raised Dannarah strode across the floor. Her authoritative action cut through the crowd's seething; she had seen people break into violence, and she refused to let that happen today. Maybe her failure to capture the prisoners in Elsharat made her want a victory, however small.

She raised her voice. "Your Holiness, I object. What the god left undone to this child cannot be done now. Anyway you cannot prove she came from the north with the captives King Jehosh brought many years ago."

"Who are you to speak so disrespectfully, old woman?" demanded the prince, as if she weren't holding a reeve's baton and wearing reeve's leathers inscribed with a marshal's wings. "Inside the shrine, women are forbidden from speaking before the god and the law."

Two could sing that song.

"We are in the assizes, not the shrine. By the law of the Hundred reeves have the right and indeed the duty to speak at the assizes. Furthermore I am your great-aunt, Lady Dannarah, daughter of Anjihosh the Glorious Unifier, sister of Atani the Law-Giver, aunt of your father King Jehosh. Have you some objection to my presence, grand-nephew? Must I fly to the palace and mention to your father the king that I have been treated with disrespect by his son?"

The girl snorted, not bothering to hide her amusement. When Dannarah glanced at her to remind her to hold her tongue, the young woman sketched the hand gesture of respect that was properly offered by the young to the old.

Prince Tavahosh glared, no doubt calculating the damage Dannarah could do him in the complicated politics of the palace. His silence gave her a chance to examine the young outlander.

On his final major military expedition into the north fourteen years ago, when he had at last completely conquered the kingdom of Ithik Eldim, Jehosh had brought back thousands of prisoners to be sold into servitude and thus help finance his expedition. Most of the northerners had pale skin and brown hair. But Ithik Eldim was also famous for its thriving ports, bustling with outlanders in all their varied clothing, customs, and looks.

Still, it was jarring that a girl so obviously foreign-looking as this one bore the Mothers' inked bands on her right forearm and left calf to mark her as fire-born, just like any ordinary Hundred girl.

"I am not a slave," the girl said in a clear voice. "Therefore it is my right to offer myself in my father's place, to serve out his sentence as a laborer."

"Lifka! You must not!" cried Geron, but it was too late; the offer had been made before witnesses.

Prince Tavahosh slammed his staff onto the ground. "A woman's service is worth half that of a man's. You are offering to indenture yourself for twenty years."

"By Hundred law a woman's service is worth exactly the same as a man's," she objected.

Dannarah admired her boldness.

"I make the ruling under the auspices of the Glorious Beltak, the Shining One Who Rules Alone. Twenty years."

"Fourteen, which is twice seven," said the girl at once, as if she were bargaining in the marketplace!

By the way Tavahosh's jaw was clenched Dannarah guessed he was getting cursed angry at the girl's defiance.

"I beg you, Your Holiness, the fault is mine, not hers," said the father. "She is young. Let her stay with the clan and I will go peacefully."

"She cannot stay. She is a slave. You have defied not just the god but the king by pretending she is your daughter. Let her be arrested and inked with a slave's mark, as is required."

"She is the clan's daughter, not a slave, whatever you may say, you whose ancestors came from foreign lands to rule this one," said Geron the Carter with a scorn that agitated the crowd.

"I took you for an outlaw the instant I laid eyes on you." Prince Tavahosh's expression gritted into a rage-filled grin. "For defiance, a further two years of service to the shrine. Guards! Take them both away."

The local judges said nothing; they had no authority to countermand a prince.

Dannarah saw the young woman hoist her staff with the grim confidence of a person who knows how to fight. Trouble was coming, and it would be bloody.

"Prince Tavahosh!" Dannarah stepped between them. "By bargaining with the girl over the length of her indenture you have implicitly recognized her right to be treated as a daughter of the clan."

The crowd laughed, relaxing a little, but the girl was still as taut as a pulled bowstring.

"I am not to be trifled with and mocked in this way!" the prince said to Dannarah, switching to Sirni even though it was both rude and stupid to speak in a language the crowd could not understand. He turned to the nearest guard. "Call Chief

Marshal Auri to silence this reeve. Tell the soldiers to silence the crowd! Such disrespect is unacceptable."

"Is this what you call an expedition to hear the voices of the common people?" she prodded. "That you expect everyone to acquiesce to you trampling on their old customs?"

"Are you turned outlaw, too? Defying the palace with such rebellious words? The priests have argued for years that women are not fit to be reeves, and now I see the truth of it!"

"Who do you think chooses reeves? The eagles choose us."

"Then they choose wrong."

A scream rent the air, followed by shouts of alarm. Terror chuffed a warning even though blinded by the hood. On the plaza above a weight whumped down, its impact shuddering through the ground. People shrieked and scattered. Shoving broke out as the frightened crowd stampeded down onto the floor of the amphitheater, trying to get away from something horrible.

The press of bodies staggered Dannarah, and she stumbled. Abruptly a hand braced her up; the girl stepped in beside her. Together, Dannarah with her baton and the girl with her staff, they carved a path up the steps to see what disturbance roiled the courtyard.

Just as they reached the top the crowd bled away, leaving them alone with the eagles.

Slip had lost his hood and broken his jess. He had launched off the perch and landed on top of a soldier, pinning the man to the dirt with his talons. The man was still alive, foot twitching, gulping down screams of pain as he tried to play dead. Stink and a wet stain spread around him.

Slip's fierce gaze burned the air. He was clearly agitated by the crowd's anger, and when the hood had slipped off he must have struck in a panic.

What if he attacked Terror and Surly, who were blinded by their hoods?

Curse it! She looked around but could not see Auri, the fucking coward.

The girl gasped. "No! Runt! Stay back!"

A silver-gray dog about knee-high came racing through the open gates of the assizes enclosure as if late to the party. It spotted the girl and ran with all the oblivious excitement of a youngster who believes it has been left behind. Too late it ran in under the shadow of the eagle; too late it felt the monstrous beast fix its golden glare on this tidy morsel. Cowering to a stop it began to bark furiously as Slip lowered his massive head to confront the noisy intruder.

In her youth Dannarah could have grabbed the girl and stopped her, but now she was too cursed slow, for the girl was already past her, running toward the dog. Dannarah coldly hoped the girl's father was still stuck down in the docket so he would not witness the ugly death about to come.

"Hush, you runt!" snapped the girl, striding in under the eagle's shadow and scooping up the dog, which was of a size to fit along her forearm. It ceased barking at once, ears down, quivering.

Slip released the injured guard and raised a talon, poised clumsily on one foot. The guard moaned as he tried to drag himself away; one of his legs was twisted at an awful angle, broken almost in two. The girl stood her ground, not moving, not ducking, not shouting. With the dog tucked under one arm and her staff clutched in the other, the girl stared down the eagle.

In a calm voice Dannarah said, "Take one very slow step back. Don't move fast."

The eagle lowered his raised talon and lowered his head even farther, then gave the girl a look from each eye, examining her with the uncanny stare that brought more criminals to justice than any reeve's training or experience. The girl responded by dropping her staff and clamping a hand over the dog's muzzle as if she feared the dog might try to bite the huge raptor!

Dannarah finally spotted Auri backing away, mouth white with fear.

"May the Shining Lord act to show His righteousness," the prince exclaimed, coming up beside her with his priest's staff. He had more courage than Auri; she had to give him that.

"The eagles have lived in the Hundred long before our family came, Prince Tavahosh," she said, irritated by his pious excitement.

"It shall be as the god wills. The slave was rude and rebellious! The god will judge her!"

"A quieter voice serves best not to draw the raptor's attention," added Dannarah, and Tavahosh took a prudent step back.

Yet Slip settled his feathers, calming, and the young woman took a cautious step forward and grasped the harness, exactly the right thing to do. Only then did she look toward Dannarah, meeting her gaze across the gap between them as she wordlessly asked for advice.

"The hells," Dannarah muttered. "She might join the reeve halls as a fawkner. That would count for her service, would it not, Prince Tavahosh?"

"Can't you control your eagle?" he demanded.

"That's not my eagle. That is your chief marshal's eagle. There he is!" She pointed with her elbow to where Auri had slunk behind the front rank of soldiers, trying to keep out of sight. Over by Surly, Reyad moved into view holding a spare jess, gaze fixed on Slip and the girl just as if he meant to go in and help secure the raptor. Good lad!

"Chief Marshal Auri!" The prince's voice carried easily. "This is outrageous. Control your eagle at once or I will command you be stripped of your position!"

Reyad's gaze met Dannarah's. Cursed if the nice young man didn't smile like a knife, so busy enjoying the chief marshal's humiliation that he ignored the soldier trying to drag himself out of reach of the eagle. She gestured. Reyad saw the injured man and his expression darkened to a look of horror. He eased in on the eagle's blind side, grabbed the wounded man's wrists, and at a steady but not hasty speed dragged him back. But Reyad's gaze flicked up to watch as, stung by the prince's scolding words, Auri strode forward to Slip.

Flushed and perspiring, the chief marshal cringed as he came into the eagle's shadow. His hunched shoulders made him look like a rat caught out in the open. Movement rippled along Slip's wings; his talons shifted. Dannarah shoved Tavahosh out of the way.

Slip ripped the harness out of the girl's hands and pounced.

Auri screamed as talons unfurled and Slip pinned him to the earth. His chest and right arm were caught. He waved his left arm frantically, shrieking.

Thank all the gods the girl was too stunned to move, staring in shock.

Slip tumbled Auri over in his talons and squeezed again. The chief marshal's head lolled back as his body went limp.

It happened so fast.

Auri's face was scuffed with dirt from the tumble. Blood spattered the ground. The crushing grip of Slip's talons had killed the reeve more mercifully than many a criminal condemned to be whipped and then hog-tied to a pole to die of thirst and suppurating wounds. That had been her father's favored punishment for those he considered irredeemable criminals.

Behind her the prince hissed, "Why did you not stop the eagle from attacking?"

She wanted to smack him in the face with her baton but she murmured instead, "Every reeve lives with the knowledge that their eagle can at any time kill them."

The raptor shook the corpse loose.

Reyad had pulled the wounded soldier out of reach. His grimace flashed into a grin of ugly triumph, quickly erased.

Slip raised his head and examined the silent onlookers as if deciding whom to kill next.

The prince cried, "Captain! Have your men shoot to kill."

Just like that, the young woman stepped up and grasped the harness again as boldly as if Auri did not lie dead on the dirt. Slip lowered his head and stared at her for the longest time, not one person in the courtyard moving or speaking. Dannarah held her breath.

Slip nudged the girl with his beak, then relaxed as abruptly as if he had not just killed a man.

"Hold your weapons!" cried Dannarah. "You have been answered, Prince Tavahosh. Her service is no longer yours to claim. She's a reeve now. The eagle has jessed her."

16

It wasn't the eagle's attention fixed on her that rooted Lifka to the ground. Nor was it the Runt's quivering fear or the bloody body of the man that held her steady, for she knew better than to look at the dead man. The cursed raptor loomed monstrously over her. Common sense told her that if she ran, it would pounce.

She met its golden-amber gaze.

A feather-light touch tickled down her spine. Pain burned in her bones. Yet when she opened her mouth to exhale, a shiver sprouted like icy feathers in the heart of her being.

The courtyard faded from her sight. Around her, seen as

through glass, lay the clear air of a cloudless sky. Everywhere within view rose steep mountains patched with white growths that she had once had a name for. *Snow.* She glided above. She had been here before, up on this frigid wind, alive in the heavens, flying.

Then her thoughts cleared, and she found herself back standing in the assizes courtyard in front of a huge and deadly eagle. With the first intake of breath she knew she was not the same person who had stood here a moment before.

A leash had tangled in her gut and heart and throat. She could not have stepped away from the eagle if she'd wanted to, and in truth she no longer wanted to although she could not have said why. The eagle had a stunning head, fierce and proud. Its beautiful feathers settled in a way she hoped meant calm.

The Runt whined low in his throat, and the eagle shifted closer to get a better look at the shaking dog. The bird made a funny chirp, odd coming from such a massive creature. Lifka tightened a hand over the Runt's muzzle before he could begin barking in sheer terror.

"Hush, you two," she said sternly. "I expect you to get along."

She tugged down on the dangling harness. There were leashes and buckles. Was that its own reeve it had just killed? Best not to think.

A whistling scald of notes surprised her. The eagle folded its wings. She glanced around and saw the older reeve approach. It was the bravest thing she had ever seen anyone do except the day when Aunt Ediko had confronted the soldiers. The day Ediko had died.

"Lifka, stay holding the harness," said the woman in a tone that made Lifka realize how easy it would be for the raptor to puncture her flesh with its vicious talons as it had the two men. "The hood is caught in the harness. Pull it out and drag it over the eagle's head."

"I can't," said Lifka. "I've not got a free hand."

"You have to put down the dog."

"I can't put down the dog. What if the eagle kills him?"

Papa appeared, curse him. He walked right up beside the old reeve, too close. He should have run and gotten away during the trouble. "Lifka, put down the dog. I'll call him over."

"If he runs the eagle will strike, thinking he's prey!"

"Daughter! Do as I say!"

On the rare occasions Papa snapped, no one disobeyed him. Before she knew she meant to she set the Runt on the ground. Papa whistled, but the Runt cowered on top of her feet, trembling so hard that her heart melted.

She winkled the hood loose. The old reeve whistled an odd and repetitive melody and by the grace of all the seven gods the eagle waited patiently while she figured out how to pull the cloth over its head. The moment its eyes were covered the eagle went quiescent.

"Stay back, ver." The reeve strode in. "Reeve Lifka, I am Marshal Dannarah. You will have to come with me."

Lifka gaped at her. The light was so bright all of a sudden. Everything seemed sharper, stronger: her vision more clear, her hearing more keen.

"Come along."

Lifka allowed the woman to lead her away from the eagle. The Runt crowded her steps, unwilling to let even a handbreadth separate them so that she kept stumbling over him.

Papa grabbed her in a tight embrace as she began to shake. "I thought you'd be killed."

The reeve turned to the prince. "Release Geron the Carter from his sentence."

"So will I, Lady Dannarah." The prince spoke poorly, as if he were a foreigner even though he had been born and raised in the Hundred. "This girl's labor will serve the sentence against blasphemy. The man must still serve three years' labor for not having the slave inked."

Papa released her. He turned on the priest.

"Papa, don't—" Lifka began.

"Your words insult Five Roads Clan as well as my daughter!"

"She must be given the slave mark."

Marshal Dannarah stepped between the two men. Older than Papa, she had a brisk authority that Lifka admired even as her thoughts stumbled in confusion.

"Prince Tavahosh, any fledgling reeve chosen by an eagle must immediately begin training. She has no time to recover from being inked, not even a few days. The eagle's needs preclude anything else. If you do not believe me, you may ask the chief marshal..." Was the woman gloating over a man's death? "But you can't ask him, can you? Because his eagle has killed him due to his own incompetence. So you must take the truth from me. This young woman cannot be a slave because she is a reeve."

The prince gave the old woman a long look that might as well have shouted his disdain. Then he stamped away for all the world like a boy who cannot accept a rightful scolding.

"As the gods speak, so do we hear." Papa grasped Lifka's hand. "I pray you, Marshal, may she at least come home to gather a few things and say a private good-bye to those who cherish her?"

For the first time Lifka saw Mum and Uncle and two of her girl cousins—Darit and Nonit—pushing up against the soldiers who held back the crowd of gawking and horrified onlookers. Alon and Denas and Nanni had not been able to come to the assizes because they needed work; the clan needed coin that badly. Uncle was teary and Mum looked ready to slap every soldier in her way.

"Of course you may," said Marshal Dannarah, her expression

softening. "It is traditional for a newly jessed reeve to take leave of her clan. But I fear the exalted prince has not been satisfied in the matter of the slave mark. You will need to go to court to make sure there is no further trouble for your clan, ver."

"We can't afford to go to court, verea," Papa said. "Anyone who wishes to bring a case to the assizes must pay fees."

"The reeve halls pay a clan for the loss of the new reeve's labor and prospects. I will personally take responsibility to see a fair sum is brought to you as soon as can be. With your permission I would like to accompany you and your daughter to your clan's compound so I can speak to your family of what she can expect. It is a hard thing to give a child to the reeves, but I promise you, you will be proud of her."

"We are already proud of her," said Papa in a voice husky with emotion.

The marshal walked away to where the other reeve waited between the two hooded eagles. They were so big.

"Oh, Papa, I don't want to leave home." She burst into tears.

"Here now, Lifka. Are you sure you have to go? We can find a way to take it to the assizes."

She sucked down the tears, wiping her cheeks with the back of a hand. "I couldn't walk away from that eagle if I tried, Papa. It's like a hook in me, whatever I might want. I can't explain it."

"The Runt will miss you." He rubbed the dog's back as the Runt's quavering growl faded. "But if you're a reeve surely you can come and see us now and again."

"I'll have to, to make sure that awful prince doesn't plague you and the family."

"Not so loud, girl. Best you work a little harder to keep your voice down."

"Folk see me even if I'm quiet."

"True enough. They take you for someone you're not just

because they think they can judge you. Well, then, Lifka. Do what is right. That's all I can say."

"Papa." For the first time in years she examined how different they were: she long and powerfully built, taller now than he was, and he short and stocky. The pecan-brown color of his skin had an entirely different tone from her black complexion. He kept his black hair shorn short; her coils would never go straight like his.

He frowned, waiting as if he knew what she meant to say, and probably he did.

"Should I have had the slave ink?"

"The gods brought you, Lifka. The moment I saw you, and you saw me, I knew you were meant to come home to us. You are our child and you always will be."

She wiped her streaming eyes, too choked up to speak.

Papa touched her elbow. "Be strong so your mother does not cry."

He looked at the sky, eyes going wide. Guards and onlookers scattered as another eagle plummeted recklessly down only to brake with wings spread and come to land on the last empty perch. Her mouth dropped open. How splendid and exciting!

She thought, *I will learn how to do that. I will fly.*

She kept a strong face all the way home and through a meal of rice porridge and radish, the best they could put on for their visitor.

She kept a strong face as Mum tucked the silk length of her own wedding taloos into an embroidered pouch made by Aunt Ediko.

"You must take the cloth, Lifka," Mum said in her scolding voice. "You will not go to a distant place and have them thinking your clan hasn't even a decent length of silk to its name."

The necessities the clan could spare were sparse enough to

break her heart: her sandals, a work kilt, and an extra sleeveless vest; a spoon, a metal cup, a wooden bowl, a knife, and a hatchet so she wouldn't have to beg such implements from strangers; a broad-toothed comb specially carved for her by Uncle. Such things the family could scarcely afford to let go, but they insisted.

She kept a strong face as she made farewells and made Nonit and Darit promise a hundred times to get word to Ailia. She kissed Darit's baby and Nonit's two little ones. The young men came running home, having heard the news, and she had to make farewells all over again.

At last she walked away with the reeve while the family sang from the gate the traditional song for children leaving home to make their way in the world:

The road runs to the hills, to the city, to the sea,
but when you pause to look back
your tracks in the dirt lead your eye to home.

Her feet thudded on the path like rocks. Voices drifted after her; she could not look back because her neck got so stiff it wouldn't turn. A cold blindness seized her as the dry rice fields and the crowns of the forest seemed to fade into mist.

Shards of memory burst like sparks in the haze.

All she could see was that terrible march through the mountains when she was a child. The bitter cold ached in her bones, stiffened her tiny hands, and stung her cracked lips and pus-encrusted eyes. The lash of a whip fell on her narrow back. Her belly ached with hunger. She stumbled along on her stick-thin legs trying to keep up with the other children for she was the smallest left after so many captives had died on the road. The soldiers had called her the Runt.

Out of this skein of twisted misery arose Papa's gentle face, but he was younger, less lined, no white in his hair. He had the eyes of a man who saw her when for an endless time no one had seen her. She remembered seeing Papa like she had seen the eagle, knowing an unseen leash bound her to him. She had seen him, and he had seen her, and he had taken her home.

A frantic yapping bark-bark-bark tugged her back to the earth.

The reeve was speaking as if she had no idea Lifka had been gone. "Once you've completed your training and are safe to care for your eagle on your own, you'll be granted leave to come home. I give my reeves a three-day pass home once a month although a few marshals only allow leave twice a year. Which if you ask me…" She glanced back, a frown flickering across her face.

The Runt was racing after them with that funny hitched run he had, back legs pushing in tandem. Lifka knelt, and he barreled into her and licked her on the nose.

They were out of sight of the compound, nothing but fields and orchard. Birds sought bugs in the rice field. Alon and Denas and Nanni appeared on the path, on the Runt's trail.

She waved. They halted. The clan didn't need the Runt. They had better-natured dogs, and enough mouths to feed.

"Can I bring him along?" she asked the reeve.

The woman took a long look at the Runt. He put down his ears.

"Slip might eat him. A tidy morsel like that will be sorely tempting."

"Slip?"

"That's your eagle's name."

"Will the eagle kill me?"

She shrugged. "It's rare for an eagle to kill its reeve, and anyway Slip is a particularly sweet-natured eagle. I can't say I blame him for killing that prick Auri, though I do feel bad for the soldier. It's not his fault Auri was too lazy-handed to tether the eagle properly."

Lifka blinked about ten times at this blunt speaking. But the truth was, the two kills had happened so fast and she had been so fixed on the eagle and the Runt that she hadn't really examined the bodies nor fully absorbed their wounds. It was more like a story someone had told her. She hadn't the leisure to dwell on it and be afraid of what could not be changed.

"Are you saying I can take the dog?" she asked instead.

"On your head, then. No business of mine."

Marshal Dannarah started walking again, stride clipping away the distance. Lifka gathered up the dog. Denas and Alon and Nanni waved again and danced luck to her; she heard their voices as from an impossible distance, and she knew that if she lingered she would cry. Then Mum would ask, and the lads could never lie to Mum, and so Lifka had to put on her strong face.

She waved a last farewell and hurried onward with the pouch bouncing on her back and the Runt clutched to her chest. He panted in contentment.

"What's it like, being a reeve?" Lifka asked when she caught up.

Marshal Dannarah cast her a look. "I'm not sure I know any longer what it is like. But for you, Lifka, I promise you, it will not be easy."

17

Dannarah knew she had avoided the palace for too many years. If she was honest with herself, it wasn't just her complicated relationship with King Jehosh that had kept her away. Walking alone where she had once walked with the people she loved best had become too painful, and she had let the pain win. Auri's death offered the perfect opportunity to test the waters of the palace again, and maybe see if she could pound a little sense into Jehosh.

The spectacular approach made her smile with the same pure joy she had felt in her first months as a reeve: Simple astonishment at seeing the world in a wholly new way. The city stood on a spur of ground at the confluence of the River Istri with its tributary, the Lesser Istri. Law Rock's high promontory rose at the prow of the city where the rivers met. Below it, the darker waters of the Istri blended with the faster, lighter Lesser Istri in a constant ecstatic union.

When humans had carved a thousand steps up the landward cliffside of Law Rock, they had promptly constructed four complexes on top set around an open space called Justice Square: council hall, Assizes Tower, storehouses, and reeve hall. Her father had turned the council hall and storehouses into a palace, and Atani hadn't altered much. Now, scanning Law Rock from above, she was struck dumb by how Justice Square had been filled in with stately buildings and tiny courtyards crowded around a huge square Beltak shrine. The shrine her father had built for her mother had been small, placed out of the way. This architectural monstrosity stood at the center.

She and the other three eagles circled down to Palace Hall, the reeve enclosure with its open yard and big wooden perches. The chief marshal administered the six reeve halls from here, although in the last five years Auri had split his time between Palace Hall and Argent Hall.

On-duty fawkners hurried to take care of the eagles while off-duty reeves and fawkners gathered in the shade to stare. They studied Lifka especially. She looked dazed as she gaped at the view. She had rigged a sling to hold the anxious little dog against her chest like a snarling baby.

"Reyad, you and Lifka stay here in the hall. I want you to go over all the parts of the harness with Lifka again. Oil and repair all four harnesses. It's the best way to get acquainted with the gear."

Reyad frowned.

"Next time you can tour the rock," added Dannarah, seeing his disappointment.

"Yes, Marshal," he said, acquiescing.

Dannarah walked with Tarnit to the gate.

"You never command him to show me all the parts of my harness," said Tarnit.

"I'm pretty sure you already know where all your parts are."

"That dog is a little monster." Tarnit held up her left hand to display the reddened marks where the dog had nipped her last night. "I was just trying to pet it."

"Go easy, Tar. Not everyone melts immediately beneath your irrepressible charm."

"You say that as if it's a good thing."

"Try it on this sour face I see ahead of us."

At the gate a man wearing the tabard of a palace steward confronted them. He carried a reeve's baton although he was clearly no reeve.

Tarnit greeted him with her sunniest smile. "Well met, ver. A fine day, is it not?"

"By whose order are you come to Law Rock?" he said curtly.

"It's *Marshal* to you, ver," replied Tarnit, letting her smile widen aggressively.

His stance grew more belligerent as he tried to use his greater height to intimidate. "By whose order are you come? What is your purpose here?"

Dannarah had had enough. "By my own order, as marshal of Horn Hall. I am come to see the king."

The man's gaze skipped along their shaved-down hair and

sleeveless vests. "Reeves must stay in the reeve enclosure. I will assign a person to take your message to the king's clerks. You can wait for a reply."

Dannarah tapped him on the chest with her baton. "What is your name?"

He blinked, startled by the way she had assertively stepped in on him. Around the forecourt, people were turning to stare. "Steward Toughid," he said tightly.

Dannarah nodded. "An honorable name to honor a soldier who died in the service of King Anjihosh the Glorious Unifier. Anjihosh being, I will now mention politely, my father. So you can get out of my way or I will crack you over the head with my baton on charges of obstructing a marshal about her duty. I am here to see my nephew the king."

He retreated. Dannarah led Tarnit onto the plateau of Law Rock. There were soldiers everywhere wearing tabards embroidered with crossed spears. Every path was paved with swept stone. She quickly lost her way in an unfamiliar maze of colonnaded porticoes, walled and gated paths, and buildings crammed one up against the next. The fittings on every gate and door were polished to a brilliant gleam. Palace stewards garbed in red and gold stared disapprovingly at the two women. The shrine walls gleamed whitely in the sun. Beyond the walls rose ranks of noble-lance trees native to the empire, and above their spearlike crowns shone the gilded dome of the inner shrine precinct dedicated to Beltak.

Dannarah recognized a portico with a shaded passage painted with grand herons on the hunt and hapless frogs trying to hide beneath lilies. "Ver, isn't that the way to the palace barracks?" she called to a passing steward.

He cast an anxious glance over his shoulder. "That is now the priests' living quarters, verea. Not permitted for women to walk there."

"How do I reach the King's Audience Hall? At this time of day the king must be holding the court assizes."

He hesitated, as if he felt he ought to refuse, but instead he pointed down another narrow walled street. It led to a portico she recognized as the entrance to the King's Audience Hall although last time she had been here this entire area had been a gracious courtyard fitted with shaded benches so supplicants had a place to wait in comfort. No petitioners waited today to beg justice from the king, not as they had in her father's and brother's day.

Soldiers blocked the main doors. Tarnit's brow lowered into an entirely unfamiliar broodiness as she eyed their hostile stances. Dannarah pushed past them into the hall.

The walls were still painted in gold and silver patterns as she remembered them. But where a tapestry depicting lions and gazelles had once hung there now sprawled a mural depicting the triumph of the young King Jehosh over the northern kingdom of Ithik Eldim, when he had toppled the Eldim king from power after a war that had lasted seven years. In the painting Jehosh towered above his generals, soldiers, and courtiers. Beneath his outstretched sword knelt captured prisoners, conspicuously not including the king's daughter he had seized and married to become his second wife. Tiny figures of enslaved children lined up in ranks at his feet, foreign children as young as five and six brought south to be sold to Hundred clans eager to expand their workforce with captives who need not be paid except in food and shelter and who had no family to redeem their debt. She scanned the ranks for children who looked something like Lifka and found a few; the features of the children were as varied as those of sailors in any port.

As a girl Dannarah had been allowed to sit behind a lattice-work screen and observe the proceedings when her father pre-

sided over an afternoon assizes court during which he passed
judgment on cases brought before him. When Atani ruled she
had sat directly beside him, when she wasn't out on reeve business. Now the room was filled with men seated at low desks,
busy writing in ledgers and account books. On a raised dais
Jehosh lounged on a brocade couch draped with cushions and
gold fringe. A square gaming table rested before him, another
man seated at each side, two in profile and one with his back
to her.

Courtiers and underlings gathered about them, an audience
eagerly attending to a game of four-sided castles. They were
actually taking wagers; strings of coin changed hands in the
most inappropriate fashion as the four players traded jocular
insults and moved pieces.

When her father had sat in stern judgment, his Qin bodyguards had stood behind him like the silent promise of justice.
Atani had presided with a sad compassion that often reduced
criminals to tears. Today a priest of Beltak wearing the beaded
headdress and veiled face covering of a high exalted observed
the gaming men with a vulture's patience.

A weight like stone tightened in the pit of her stomach at the
sight of a Beltak priest standing above the king.

As she strode forward men fell away from her path because
they did not quite know how to respond to an older woman
who demanded space for herself in this all-male company.

Jehosh looked up and, seeing her, stood. "Aunt Dannarah!"

Everyone leaped to their feet, for no one could sit when the
king stood. They stared as she took the steps up to the dais
without so much as asking permission to approach. The hall fell
quiet. She glanced again at the priest. She had a hunch he did
not speak the language of the Hundred, while Jehosh and his
cronies had grown up using both languages.

So she spoke in the Hundred-speech, not in Sirni.

"Nephew, I am come with an urgent message. Chief Marshal Auri is dead. He was killed by his own eagle."

Jehosh glanced at the priest, whose narrowed eyes suggested exactly the annoyance she had hoped for. The king's mouth quirked with amusement.

"Let me get us privacy," he answered in the same language.

He gestured. As the men cleared out, she examined him. Jehosh was now a man in his midforties, dressed in the simple military fashion his grandfather Anjihosh had favored. He wore his long hair neatly pulled back into an elaborate topknot and kept his strong chin clean-shaven. Three rings commemorated his three signal victories in the Ithik Eldim wars in the early years of his reign.

At length she found herself alone with Jehosh, his three gaming companions, and the lurking priest. If she had ever seen this particular priest before she could not know, as she could only see his eyes. One of Jehosh's companions was Supreme Captain Ulyar. Another was his childhood friend Lord Vanas, who had married Jehosh's younger sister. The third wore a general's tabard. He looked familiar but she could not place him. Like Jehosh, they all appeared assuredly aware of their authority and status.

"The sad news about Auri we have already heard," Jehosh said, still in the Hundred-speech. "His wing flew in with his corpse, which has been taken to the shrine."

"May he find peace in the Shining One's embrace," she said. The priest fairly radiated sanctimonious disapproval with his rigid stance. "There will have to be a reeve convocation to elect a new chief marshal."

Jehosh's gaze flicked down to the board. He would win, she saw, as the others likely hadn't noticed yet that his army was arrayed in a manner to tear theirs apart in good time. He always won games.

"You must wish to clean up and have some refreshment, Aunt Dannarah," he said. "Lord Vanas will see you and your attendant suitably settled. Place them in the cliff room of my personal audience suite, Vanas. We need to finish our game and then I am pledged to meet with the guild heads to enjoy a theatrical performance this afternoon."

The hells! Jehosh had just returned to the palace after months away. She wanted to inform him that King Anjihosh would never have sat playing a game before he had thoroughly examined all the books and records and interviewed all his administrators, but for once she held her tongue.

"My lord king," said Ulyar, "the god-fearing priests of Beltak who guide us in our daily lives would find it inappropriate for you to lodge women in any of your chambers."

"Of course they would," said Jehosh without looking up, "but Aunt Dannarah isn't a woman. She is my aunt."

Dannarah barely choked down a snort of amusement, and then realized she had in fact chuckled out loud when Jehosh flashed a warning look at her.

She was not ready to let Ulyar get away with such snide interference so easily. "Supreme Captain Ulyar, I'm sorry to inform you there has been trouble on the roads, prisoners escaping and roaming the countryside at will. That kind of thing never used to be a problem."

Ulyar had a fierce frown. "Chief Marshal Auri and I have been in constant communication about these recent disturbances, I assure you."

"That's good to hear." She looked the priest right in the eye. "Do you need a translation, Your Holiness?" she asked in Sirni.

The offended flare of his eyes revealed that he did, but he wasn't about to ask her for one.

"If you would allow me to guide you, Marshal Dannarah," said Lord Vanas blandly.

She, Tarnit, and Vanas walked to the iron-banded door that led into the inner palace. Once they were in the corridor a retinue of stewards and courtiers dogged their heels as if expecting a bone to be thrown over which they could squabble. Vanas escorted her and Tarnit down a curtain-swagged corridor she did not recognize. He was the same age as Jehosh, a good-looking and somewhat portly man with the confidence that comes from knowing you have the king's ear.

"Lord Vanas, I haven't seen you for years. I remember you and Jehosh were great friends as children. You made a charming pair with your antics. As I recall, you served in the Black Wolves in your youth."

"Injured in the second Eldim campaign, Marshal," he said with admirable politeness, "and unable to serve as a soldier afterward, so I found a way to serve the king at court."

"That's right. You married Jehosh's younger sister and became head of the treasury. I remember hearing rumors that you married her in order to get your hands on the treasury."

"Do you trust rumors, Lady Dannarah?" he asked without turning a hair.

"I also remember hearing stories that you endured the brutal training to make the cut as a Black Wolf in order to prove yourself worthy of her."

"I like that rumor better."

She noted how he smiled as at a fond memory, then frowned as at a gloomy one.

"I recall her as a quiet girl, like her mother, exceedingly shy," reflected Dannarah, thinking back to the many happy days she had spent with Atani and his household. "Atani made it clear she wasn't to be sent south to the empire to marry, as three of our younger sisters were. A fate I escaped myself, I should note. I hope you have been a good husband to her, Lord Vanas."

His step faltered as his shoulders stiffened. He increased his stride to force her to trot along after. "Why would you doubt that I had? You never approved of Jehosh and his friends, did you?"

"Some of the reckless mischief you got up to when you were young might have caused me to doubt your common sense. Certainly Jehosh has made some unwise decisions over the years. I'm not the only person who has mentioned it. In fact, I recall people wondering why Jehosh would have agreed to marry his sister to you, considering that your elder brother Seras murdered King Atani."

"Demons got their claws into many people at that time. Seras died that day, too, didn't he? The demons made sure of that. His death is one act I can honestly thank demons for!"

"I don't blame you for your brother's treachery, but I've never understood why you stood back and allowed Seras's innocent sons to be punished with castration for their father's crime. They were children. Your own nephews!"

He gave her a sharp look. "Did you never hear the full story? Seras thought that if he killed King Atani while Jehosh was still young—just twenty-one that year!—then Seras—being older and established as a strong military man—could overthrow an unready Jehosh and make himself king. You were among those who thought Jehosh was unready, weren't you, Lady Dannarah? Sometimes I think you thought Jehosh would never be ready, never be able to fill the boots of his grandfather and father."

She said nothing, taken aback by the fierceness of his speech.

"That's why Seras's sons had to be punished. It made a statement to everyone who had secretly supported Seras: Move against the king and you'll get your balls cut off."

Tarnit's eyes had gotten very wide, though she knew better than to voice an opinion. Dannarah found herself grudgingly impressed by Vanas's defense of the man he served. Yet she could not keep the skepticism from her tone.

"How large do you imagine this conspiracy to have been? My investigations after the fact led me to believe that Seras was acting alone with fifty loyal retainers and thirty-odd hired killers. It was generally agreed he was acting under the command of a demon, who appeared briefly at the scene and vanished again after ascertaining that both Atani and Seras were dead. The Black Wolves weren't able to kill the demon."

He glanced sidelong at her. "If you ask me, Captain Kellas got off easy."

A thrill of disquiet thrummed in her bones to hear that name after all these years. "Kellas would never have betrayed Atani."

"So everyone kept saying."

She yanked him to a halt. "Do you know something I don't?"

He looked ready to shake off her arm, so she tightened her fingers. Old she might be, but forty years as a reeve had kept her tough.

He looked down at her hand, then back up. Anger wrinkled his eyes, but his tone remained cool. "We could never prove the captain was demon-ridden and involved in the plot even though half the army witnessed him speaking to a demon."

"So they claimed at the time."

"*Claimed?* Jehosh was the one who chased the demon off. Captain Kellas should have been executed for his part in the plot."

"I was in charge of my brother's security just as much as Captain Kellas was. Do you think I was in on the plot?"

"It is my opinion that all those who did not sufficiently protect King Atani had a hand in his death, even those who did not intend it."

"Is that meant to chastise me, Lord Vanas?"

"I believe King Jehosh recommended you retire."

Tarnit's cough caused Dannarah to glance down. Without realizing, she had clenched her right hand to a fist. The hells! She knew better than to let this pup goad her into losing her temper.

"Yes, well, I believe you will find I rarely listen to people who know nothing about how reeves and eagles actually function. But since I did not have Jehosh's confidence, I stepped down as chief marshal. I don't like to be a person who stays in high office just because of my connections."

He leaned just a little too far into her space. "I don't like to be such a person, either, Lady Dannarah. That is why the king's treasury is far richer today than it was twenty years ago. You don't know as much as you think you do. My brother Seras's children haven't stayed so very innocent as they have grown up, have they? Supreme Captain Ulyar recently discovered that the whole scheming household has negotiated a marriage alliance with Silvers. Seras's children are gaining a fortune in exchange for placing a Ri Amarah daughter at court. Do you not find that odd?"

"The hells." She realized she had been told of the marriage at the Ri Amarah estate in Elsharat and let it pass without question. "But I don't understand what the Ri Amarah have to do with Seras's ambitions. They were never implicated in Atani's death . . ." She got that prickling feeling on her neck, her instincts telling her to stop and look at what she had overlooked. "Except that one of their women was found with the wagon drivers who were part of the ambush."

"The king will speak to you after you have refreshed yourself," Vanas said in the tone of a man who has decided he has said too much. "This way, Lady Dannarah."

The corridor opened onto a colonnade that overlooked a lovely garden. The whitewashed height of the old Assizes Tower loomed above the far wall of the garden. At one end rose a round pavilion with trellis walls that had been constructed in the tent-like manner of the Qin, nomads who lived far away on the vast plains of the interior herding horses and sheep and conquering their neighbors. Her father had often spoken of how much he had treasured the simplicity and purity of that life, which he had been forced by dynastic politics to leave far behind.

Past the pavilion stood a humble portico in a building she rec-ognized from her youth, little changed from those days. Vanas escorted her past the guarded doors into a chamber empty but for a neat pile of cushions in the center of a plank floor. This sparsely furnished chamber had rice-paper-screened walls on two sides. One screen was open and through the gap Dannarah saw a room floored with mats in the Hundred style, its storage cupboards closed, and not a single scrap of furnishing or deco-ration. The third wall was solid and inset with a foreign door, the kind with hinges so that instead of sliding like a proper door it swung open.

The hinged door let onto a spacious chamber furnished with gold brocade couches, a room meant for conversation. The walls were painted with vines and flowers surrounding figures dressed in long wrapped kilts who might be male or female. The gold filigree surrounding the painted figures made her wonder if they were meant to be holy acolytes, but they looked nothing like Beltak priests or even the holy men and women who served the seven gods of the Hundred.

On one side the chamber opened onto a balcony whose rail-ing ran along the cliff face. She walked out onto the balcony, enamored of its view south across the river overlooking the low-land rice fields and orchards of the province of Istria. The cliff face plunged straight down from the railing to the mighty river below. With its solid walls and solidly hinged door, the room was as good as a prison.

"Stewards will bring wash-water and refreshments," said Lord Vanas. He left.

With a whistle of astonishment, Tarnit walked onto the balcony and leaned right over the railing to examine the cliff face below. "There are rooms carved into the rock beneath us!"

Dannarah joined her. "While you were propositioning Reyad did you glean any information about his time at Argent Hall? Or Auri's possible relationship to Reyad's wife?"

Tarnit pulled a hand through her short hair, spiking it up. "No. Should I have? Do you think Reyad's wife was abused in some manner at Argent Hall?"

"In River's Bend I witnessed a brief but ugly exchange between Reyad and Auri. For a pleasant and charming young man Reyad looked cursedly happy when Auri died."

"I hope for her sake nothing awful happened to her. Reyad is hells happy to be out of there, though. Now what, Marshal?"

"Now we shall see if I still have any influence with Jehosh. When he was a youth he liked me because of the shocking things I said out loud."

Voices rumbled in the outer chamber. Stewards processed in bearing basins, towels, numerous pitchers of water, and folded garments. They set down platters of food and departed, closing the door behind them. Everything looked so inviting, and the food smelled delicious: spicy lamb in coconut milk, a slip-fry of bitter melon and bean curd, and a clear soup swimming with onion and noodle.

Before either reeve could wash a click resounded from the wall, and one of the painted figures slid sideways and back to reveal a narrow opening. A tall beardless man wearing striped trousers, a braided sash, and a harness of knives stepped out of the secret door. Tarnit drew her long knife but Dannarah stayed her with a hand.

"Why does Jehosh hide a eunuch from the Sirniakan Empire

in his suite?" she demanded, but the mysterious eunuch did not answer as he stationed himself at the outer door.

"My servant does not belong to Jehosh." A woman appeared in the opening. She wore flowing robes and a shawl over her hair, its trailing edge pulled up to conceal all but her eyes. "Well, Dannarah, you have grown old, have you not? You look like a Hundred woman now, except you will always have Father's nose, more's the pity for you. Then on top of all else you dress like a man."

The voice was harsh as if raddled by too much smoke. Dannarah did not recognize it; nor did the woman's dark eyes look familiar. "Who are you?"

"I suppose I should not have expected you to remember me. Not like Atani. He always had time for us little girls. And now he is dead. Jehosh tells me he was killed by traitors in thrall to a demon. His own Black Wolves failed him. Such a thing would never have happened under our father's rule. Atani was too kind."

Dannarah's thoughts fell into spinning confusion. "Three of my sisters were sent south to marry men in the empire," she murmured. "Sukiyah. Gedassah. And..." Her second-youngest sister had been five when Dannarah had been chosen by an eagle and left the women's wing without once looking back.

The woman nodded although she still did not reveal her face. "Yes. I am Sadah."

Sadah! Dannarah fished back through her memories although it was brutally difficult to recall anything about the sisters who had been sent south to a fate she had herself rejected.

"That's right! You were Mama's greatest triumph. The other girls were married to highly placed lords. But you she managed to marry to her own nephew, Emperor Faruchalihosh."

"I was the emperor's fourth wife but never his senior or his favored queen. Mama did not make that alliance for my sake. Before I went she reminded me over and over I was to be her eyes and ears in the royal household to make sure there was no trouble for Atani."

"Trouble for Atani?"

"Do not be stupid, Dannarah! Atani had a claim to the Sirniakan throne through both Father and Mother. Mother sent me to be an ambassador into the imperial household to assure them Atani would never make such a claim. Keeping him safe as king in the Hundred was all she cared about."

"That's true," agreed Dannarah. "So why are you here?"

"Emperor Faruchalihosh has died."

"The hells he has! I've heard nothing of this!" She looked at Tarnit, who shook her head.

"Faruchalihosh died unexpectedly. I have outraced rumor in my haste to reach our nephew. I am come to beg Jehosh to support *my* son's bid to become emperor."

18

"Impossible!" cried Dannarah as the shock of the words hit home.

"Of course it is not impossible," said Sadah. "Do you think my son unworthy or incompetent?"

She saw her mistake at once. "I meant it is impossible for me to absorb such stunning news until after I have washed off the dirt of travel and eaten. You may of course join us."

Sadah reclined on one of the couches as the two reeves cleaned up and then sat down to eat together at the table the stewards had laid. "Is this woman not your servant, to wait upon you?" she exclaimed with exaggerated astonishment.

"Tarnit is a reeve, as I am. Reeves wash and eat together, sharing what we have and never holding extra for ourselves. We only survive and flourish in the reeve halls if all are cared for."

"How frightful for you to have fallen so low, Dannarah." Her tone dripped disdain.

"What in the hells is she saying to you, Marshal?" Tarnit whispered in the Hundred-speech.

"Nothing important, Tar. I'll fill you in later."

"Can I speak freely before the woman, Dannarah?"

"I trust her with my life. And she doesn't speak Sirni."

"Very well." Sadah lowered the shawl. She had the pallid complexion of a woman who rarely feels the force of the sun. Her imperial court diction made her sound like a condescending teacher imparting knowledge to a recalcitrant pupil. "May Emperor Faruchalihosh stand in both mercy and justice before the throne of the Shining One. He left behind six sons, four adult and two underage. Only one man can sit on the imperial throne."

"Even I know that!"

"That is a relief. Perhaps I need not explain how factions arise as a war for succession begins."

Dannarah was so surprised the little girl she only vaguely recalled could release such needling words that she waved away the scathing comment. "It would help me to understand the situation."

"Emperor Faruchalihosh took four wives. His senior queen is Janassah. Her son Ovadihosh was the eldest of the princes, and she also has a much younger son who is still underage. Ounah is the second queen, a woman of great cunning and brutality. Her son Ahituhosh is beloved by the army. The third queen, Kessiah, is dead but her son Edesihosh is a competent man who has support from kin in the northern districts."

"I'll never remember all these names," muttered Dannarah to Tarnit.

"I myself bore the emperor *three* sons, more than any of the others! But because I was his fourth and least wife, my boys never gained support from the powerful barons, the palace officials, the army, or the priesthood." Her gaze drilled into Dannarah, bleak and angry. "My two younger sons are already dead, murdered in the palace school by Queen Ounah's servants."

A bath of cold water thrown over her head could not have shocked her more. She winced. "You have my sympathies—"

"Your sympathies! What do you know of what it means to lose a beloved child? I am given to understand you never had children."

"I do not regret my childless condition if that's of any matter to you. Our mother's heartfelt speeches about how her children were her sole fortune fell on deaf ears when it came to me. But how can you know anything about my life here in the Hundred, trapped as you were in the women's palace in the empire?"

"How ignorant you are! In the women's palace, we live and die by what we know. Have you the slightest inkling what happened to our other sisters?"

"Of course I know! Sukiyah and Gedassah and you were married into the empire. Little Anah shocked everyone by marrying an actor, of all things, a traveling player. At the time I thought Mama would take to her bed and die but Atani coaxed her through the shock. I'm glad to say Mother lived long enough to see Atani become king and fortunately died before his murder. As for Meenah, she was too frail to marry so Atani kept her in his household, and indeed she and Atani's queen became good friends."

"What of Atani's queen, Yevah? Where did she go after Atani's death?"

Dannarah puzzled through this question. "I'm not sure."

Sadah went on. "Did you ever bother to ask what happened to the three of us who were married into the empire?"

Her sister's grief bled so raw that an unfamiliar pain nudged Dannarah up under the ribs: shame that she had never bothered to ask about, much less keep track of them. She had left all that to Atani while he was alive, and after he died she had buried herself in reeve business. She stayed active on patrol when other older marshals ran their halls from their desks and let younger reeves take policing duties, but flying was her solace and her delight.

"I did not ask," she admitted, accepting the blame.

"Let me tell you of your sisters, for it is proper you should know what befell them when they took on the responsibility you refused. Sukiyah lived far to the south in a disease-ridden province. Her husband spent most of his time at court, away from her. She and I corresponded faithfully. She died fifteen years ago of a wasting illness. Her daughter I was able to bring to me to raise with my own girls but her sons I lost track of after their father married again. Gedassah was married to the noble Lord of the Five Chambers and Courtesy Master of the Fourth Portico, a humble man who treated her well. I hope she has gone into hiding for otherwise my son's rivals will kill her just because of her connection to me."

Dannarah glanced at Tarnit, who sat with brow furrowed as she desperately tried to pick out words in the conversation. "Sadah, do you honestly believe your son could become emperor?"

"Yes, I do. The field is open. Janassah grabbed hold of the reins at court as Faruchalihosh was dying. Some say she poisoned him herself. She coerced the priests to anoint her elder son Ovadihosh as emperor. To put it plainly, Emperor Farova-dihosh, as he is now called, is feeble in the head and given to seizures. His position is so weak he can never leave the imperial city and must cower where his mother's robes can shelter him."

"How can she possibly hope to keep him in power, if he is not a full man?"

"Because she intends to keep him in power only until her younger son comes of age."

"She can't act as regent for the younger boy?"

"By imperial law an underage boy cannot rule, and by holy law no woman may sit upon the throne even as regent." Sadah leaned forward to pluck at Dannarah's hand like a vulture sensing the final throes. "Don't you see? No one is going to wait ten years for a child to grow up. In three months the empire will be in complete turmoil."

"Lady Sadah." The eunuch spoke from the door in warning.

Sadah rose and retreated to the balcony.

The door opened. Jehosh swept in and slammed the door shut in the faces of the men attending him so none could follow him in. He surveyed the armed eunuch, the empty platters, and the woman on the balcony.

"I see you and Aunt Sadah have made what I hope is a happy reunion," he said to Dannarah with a sarcastic quirk of the lips.

"What in the hells are you up to, Jehosh? First you go running off to the north to put down a rebellion in Ithik Eldim that any one of your generals could have quelled without your help. Now you are hiding the mother of one of the rivals for the Sirniakan imperial throne in your private chambers."

"I want your reeve out, Aunt Dannarah."

She nodded, and Tarnit left, although the eunuch stayed. Jehosh moved to the balcony, looked to either side, then up and down the cliff exactly like a man looking for spies clinging to the rock wall.

When he returned inside, Sadah knelt at his feet and pressed her forehead to his hands. "Nephew, I beg you, do not reject my plea. The dreaded red hounds already race on the trail of my son Irsamahosh. They will murder him and carry his severed head to the imperial palace."

"Where is he?" asked Jehosh too quickly.

She sat back on her heels. "When I have your assurances, and the coin and army we need, then we can talk further."

He walked back to the balcony and stared for the longest time at the splendid view across the fields and orchards beyond the river. His shoulders were taut but at length they dropped, and he turned and came back in. "I must put the welfare of the Hundred above the life of one man."

"He is your kinsman!"

"So are the other claimants my kinsmen. If I involve myself and your son does not succeed, then whichever prince becomes emperor will have an excuse to punish or annex the Hundred."

"With your help my son will not fail! His supporters in the empire cannot proclaim themselves if he has no army behind him."

"How do you think the barons and lords and generals of the empire will receive an army from the Hundred? I have a claim to the imperial throne, too, however distant it may be. The nobles may believe I am moving in on my own behalf."

She laughed. "No claimant from the scrap of land that is the Hundred could ever hope to conquer the empire."

"True enough, which is why I cannot embroil myself in the empire's troubles. It is too risky."

His argument seemed prudent to Dannarah. Just as she opened her mouth to agree with him, Sadah spoke.

"Has your wife Chorannah already chosen the claimant she intends you to support, Jehosh?"

He looked away.

"Chorannah?" Dannarah murmured. "That cow-witted girl?"

"Cow-witted?" Sadah grasped the couch and pushed up to

her feet, grunting with the effort. "Queen Chorannah has a better grasp of the situation than you do, Dannarah. She certainly knows more than you do."

Jehosh turned back. "I cannot help you, Aunt Sadah. My hands are tied."

"You are ruled by a woman!"

"I am ruled by necessity."

Sadah gave him a scornful look, and this time he did not look away. "Do you mean to send me to my death by throwing me back into the empire? The red hounds will tear me limb from limb after they have forced me to watch my son die."

"You need not return to the empire. I am not ungenerous. Coin can be secretly delivered to you if you need it. But you and your son must leave the Hundred, Aunt Sadah, and make a new life in a foreign land. If my agents discover you are still here in a month's time I will have no choice but to hand you over to the red hounds. I must protect the Hundred."

"The hells," murmured Dannarah, but neither of them looked at her. They were engaged in their own struggle, Sadah stiff with desperation and Jehosh intransigent.

Sadah reached under her shawl and wiped tears from her cheeks. "So you have spoken, King Jehosh. Or perhaps it is not you who have spoken. Perhaps you speak the words Chorannah has set on your tongue."

He said nothing.

"Where do you mean to go?" asked Dannarah.

Sadah waved her away. "You left my life years ago, Dannarah. Do not think I need you now."

Jehosh took a step toward her. "Aunt Sadah, what of my offer to aid you in making your way to a refuge in another land, far from here?"

"I am not a beggar. I will depart as I arrived, without your help."

She walked to the secret door and opened it by a mechanism

Dannarah could not see. Seen from behind she appeared only as cloth, a stranger concealed by the weight of the years they had lived apart. The gloomy stairwell swallowed her, the guardsman treading behind. The wall closed.

"What does she mean about Chorannah? Are you ruled by her? What happened to the king's daughter from Ithik Eldim you kidnapped? I always suspected you started the first Eldim war because of that girl. When you hear of four Sirniakan queens fighting over whose son will claim the Sirniakan throne, do you pause to ask yourself if your two queens also see themselves at odds over whose son will succeed you in the Hundred?"

Jehosh gave her a hard, measuring look, then deliberately turned his back and walked out onto the balcony, now half in shadow as the sun sank toward the western horizon with its clouds and misty haze. He placed himself in a band of sun. Strands of white streaked his hair. Impossible to think of the boy she had seen take his first toddling steps become a man beginning the long descent into old age. When she had been his age she had felt old, yet he looked young to her now.

"What news, Aunt Dannarah?" he asked without moving. "What brings you to visit me after so many years?"

"So you mean not to answer my questions?"

"I have questions of my own. Come see the sunset."

She walked out to him. Above she saw the Assizes Tower still painted with light, but the barred windows and a few broken tiles on the roof gave the lie to its bright promise: It was abandoned, for a demon's coil lay at its heart, and demons, above all things in this land, must always be sealed away.

"You have always been my favorite relative, Aunt Dannarah."

"Not your grandfather Anjihosh? Or your grandmother Zayrah?"

He shrugged. "I barely remember him. And I found her rather

boring, if you want to know the truth. I always knew it was my father she cared for most in all the world."

"And you wanted it to be *you* that people cared for most?"

He clapped hands to his chest as if he'd been struck. "I've missed you, Aunt Dannarah. You and your little daggers of insinuation."

"Obviously you missed me so much you could never be bothered to request my presence at the palace. Or even visit me as you could easily do if you had bothered to travel about the Hundred visiting the assizes and meeting with local town councils as your father and grandfather did. Instead you keep running off to the north time and again at every chance of a skirmish to fight in."

"I'm a good leader." He lifted his chin to give himself a noble profile, resembling the portrait of Jehosh the Triumphant in the audience hall.

"A good leader at war. I am not so sure you have been a good leader in peace. Consider Sadah. A king who concerned himself intimately with the news from the empire might have heard of Emperor Faruchalihosh's death before his sequestered aunt brought him the news."

"Are you rebuking me?" He seemed amused more than annoyed. They had fallen easily back into the teasing relationship they'd enjoyed when he was a lad.

"I am merely remarking in the course of the conversation. You are wise to refuse to get involved in civil war in the empire. What will happen to Sadah now?"

"I expect she and her attendants will go to the harbor, there to return to the vessel that brought them."

"Which is?"

"No one is quite sure as her arrival was entirely unanticipated. Ulyar's agents will track her when she leaves."

"And then what? Will you betray her for a price? Did you reject her plea because of some plot your meek little wife has in hand?"

He snorted. "You labor under a misapprehension. Chorannah is not meek. Furthermore what she knows she assuredly does not confide in me. Surely you recall that Queen Janassah is Chorannah's elder sister."

"I had forgotten, if you must know."

He braced himself on the railing, tapped restlessly with his fingers, then turned to regard her with a frown. "You are correct, Aunt Dannarah."

The unexpected comment made her laugh. "Not that I doubt you, but how do you mean?"

"I *have* spent too much time in the north. I have allowed myself to be seduced away by border skirmishes and minor rebellions that my military governor in Ithik Eldim could easily have handled without my intervention. It's just…"

His sigh might have moved mountains to tears.

"It's just… what?" she prompted.

"I feel more at home with the army out in the field than I ever have in the palace, among the officials and clerks. I like Ithik Eldim. I like winning, and we have won there time and time again."

"Maybe so, but consider how much of the Hundred's coin you must have spent across three wars and twenty-two years with our forces acting as foreign military governors over a hostile population. Has it been worth it?"

"I suspect you have no idea how much money we gather through taxes, tithes, and licenses imposed on the people of Ithik Eldim at a higher rate than we impose here in the Hundred. Taxes collected at the main port alone, Gyre Port, finance our entire military administration there."

When she thought of Lord Vanas's glossy confidence, it all made sense.

"Ithik Eldim remains important to us," Jehosh said, looking into the distance with the expression of a man who expects his garden of flowers to bloom all at once. "The north is meant to be my gift to Kasad, but Dia refuses to send Kasad there to become the military governor even though he is twenty-one, old enough to take on such a responsibility. She even refuses to go back herself no matter how many times I offer to accompany her. I think…"

She waited out his silence, sensing the opening of a door long closed between them.

He was not quite yet ready to confide his inner heart. With a shake of the head, like a horse shaking off flies, he turned to face her. "I have neglected the Hundred. Now I am home and I mean to stick here until I have visited every assizes court and town council in the land." He had always had a sweet smile when he chose to use it. Age had not dampened its dry touch. "I will become what my father and you wished for me, Aunt. A more prudent and cautious man than in my youth. Which is why I am the most fortunate of men, having you here to consult."

He led her to the far end of the balcony, a wedge of planking like a dock thrust out over the air. Wind skirled around them, and she smiled into its heady currents as she leaned on the railing to look down upon the boats, as small as toys, passing on the river below.

He stayed one step back, not as comfortable with the height. "Out here I am sure no one can overhear me."

"Thus causing immediate suspicion when you stand here with anyone."

"I bring every honored guest and supplicant to this place."

"The better to throw them over if they displease you?"

"To be sure it's been a tempting thought on more than one occasion, but then I think of what my father would have done and I stay my hand. Aunt Dannarah, I need your advice."

"My advice?" She laughed. "My advice is that you name me immediately as chief marshal, so I can undo the damage done under Auri's mismanagement. You were a fool to remove me in the first place, just because you didn't enjoy hearing the truths I told you."

"I would think the less of you if you did not scald me in this way. But alas, it is no joking matter."

"I never said it was!"

"I need your help, Aunt Dannarah. I fear I am losing control of the palace."

"What do you mean?"

"Chorannah hated Dia from the moment I brought Dia to the palace twenty-two years ago."

"Were you that naive, Jehosh? Did you think Chorannah would be like your mother, Yevah, becoming best of friends with the lover your father kept close all those years? You are not your father to keep two women..."

"Satisfied? I can keep more than two women satisfied!"

"Do not try to impress me with your manful exploits. Men are never more tiresome than when they are boasting about sex. Your father kept both a wife and a lover happy because he treated them with equal respect and affection. That he was handsome did not hurt, I imagine."

"I am handsome!"

"Yes, but you have to say so and he never did."

To her surprise he laughed.

It was one of those moments that made her like him so much. She patted him on the elbow, even if it felt a little awkward, and when she rested the hand on his arm he accepted the touch.

"Yet I can understand why you might have believed Chorannah would acquiesce quietly. She always seemed like such a mouse."

"A mouse with two sons. She fears I favor Dia's son Kasad over Farihosh and Tavahosh."

"The woman you were required to marry and never loved compared with the woman you grabbed for yourself and adored? Why ever would she fear that?"

"I so appreciate your sarcasm. It is true I made a few missteps that I now regret."

"Kidnapping Dia?"

"Never that! But I might have handled it better when I brought her here. Mock Chorannah all you wish, for I know you never liked her. But she tried to poison Dia and her children."

The shock of such an accusation was like having her tongue bitten out for hypocrisy.

She groped for words. "Have you proof?"

"Nothing I can use. Dia lives most of the year at her estate in the country. I had to build a lower palace, down in the city, to house her when she comes to court to keep the two queens apart. Chorannah controls the upper palace entirely, except for this paltry set of chambers and my garden."

"Why does Queen Dia come to court at all? If her son Kasad is third-born of your sons, and she the junior queen, she can't believe he is likely to inherit."

"Dia is not a mouse."

"But Farihosh is your heir, is he not? I met him on the road just a few days ago. I liked him."

"High praise from you!"

She wondered if that sulky look was meant as humor or if he was irritated by her praise of his son. "I met Tavahosh, too, at River's Bend when Auri died. I wasn't as taken with him."

"He listens too much to the priests. Farihosh is level-headed and intelligent but Chorannah has made sure he does not trust me. Never forget that Chorannah is empire-born and empire-bred. She favors Sirniakan ways and scorns the customs of the Hundred. She has raised her sons to do likewise despite my efforts to steer a course down the middle of the road."

"Are you telling me you *do* favor Kasad and would like to make him your heir over his older brothers?"

"I have reason to believe an attempt to discredit and possibly murder Kasad was made two nights ago by people who believe I favor him too much."

"What incident might that be?"

"The murder of a Silver coachman that the conspirators meant to pin on him. If someone is willing to murder an innocent bystander in order to destroy Kasad, then surely the next step is to murder me. Why should Farihosh wait for the father to falter and be put out to pasture? Why not just take what he wants now, if he has the support?"

"The hells, Jehosh. This is a serious charge."

How hard his voice fell. "I am perfectly serious. If I don't know who was behind the attempt on Kasad, then how can I know who to trust?"

"Do you no longer trust your closest friends? Auri? Ulyar? Vanas? The men who have been your companions and councilors throughout your reign?"

"What person can I trust, Aunt Dannarah?"

She removed her hand from his arm and looked skyward, tracking an eagle gliding in a high spiral far above, coming down as the last light waned. The irony of his question made her smile and shake her head.

"Strange you should ask me that," she remarked drily as old memories surfaced, the ones she least wanted to recollect.

"What do you mean?"

She shook the past firmly away. "Never mind. What about your own mother, Queen Yevah?"

"She never forgave me for my brothers' deaths in the Eldim wars. Nor was she happy about Vanas taking away her only daughter. I no longer see her."

She sighed. "Well, then, who else did your father trust?"

"You, first and above all."

"Thank you for that."

"I mean no flattery. It is the truth. He trusted his bodyguards. Most of them died trying to save him. But Captain Kellas survived."

Her heart began pounding, and she flushed. "He resigned his captaincy and left the palace as soon as he recovered from his wound."

"Yes. He was disgraced and dishonored. He said so to me himself. Many considered him complicit in the ambush."

She let out a long breath, surprised at how anxiously her mind raced. "Do you suppose he is still alive? He would be seventy-four now."

"He is alive, hale and vigorous still."

The words jolted her more than Sadah's earlier declaration. Kellas! Still alive! "You know where he is?"

"I do. He has kinsfolk here in Toskala. He grew up here."

"He left the palace but remained here in Toskala all this time?"

"No. He does not live in Toskala. He visits his clan once a year when he travels here as representative for the merchant clan he now calls home."

"Kellas is a merchant? That is difficult to believe."

"I doubt if the legendary Captain Kellas hawks wares in the marketplace. I suspect he uses his skills to discover information that helps the household trade to their best benefit. They are a prosperous clan with ties all along the coast and even across the ocean."

Dannarah had taken and discarded lovers over the years; she

did not like anyone to stay for too long because they always and eventually got on her nerves. After a childhood growing up in a suite with six little sisters and numerous girls and women in attendance, she cherished having an intimate space that was hers alone, not to be shared with a companion. After all these years she had kept tokens from three lovers only: The man she had cared for most. The man who had died before she had tired of him. And Kellas, who had once brought her a wood bracelet, a humble enough gift in its way but better than gold to an infatuated seventeen-year-old who pretended that he slept with her because he couldn't resist her and not because he couldn't refuse. She turned the bracelet several times, feeling the twining bitter-leaf vine carved into the wood. Something he had picked up in the province of Mar on one of his missions there, he had told her. Bitter-leaf was so tough that its vines could be used to make rope, while its sharp-flavored leaves spiced the distinctive local grain called barsh. Something like you, Dannarah, he had said, resilient and unforgettable.

"Where is he?" she asked, and was surprised how her voice quavered.

"Mar. In the port city of Salya."

"Mar!" She let go of the bracelet as a blade of unease sliced through her. Atani had gone to Mar, all those years ago when he was sixteen. She wasn't going to confide in Jehosh about an incident Atani had never spoken of afterward, not even to her. That Kellas lived there now likely didn't mean anything anyway. Just a coincidence. "What makes you mention Captain Kellas?"

The sun set, and lamplight glimmered awake on the city's avenues and squares far below. It was balmy, the wind rolling along the height with the promise of rain soon to come.

"If any man can kill a target in the Hundred, it is Kellas. If any man can uncover a plot, it is Kellas. If any man can secure my son Kasad's safety, it is Kellas. He served my grandfather and father with absolute loyalty, but he walked away from *me*."

"He walked away from Atani's murder."

"Bring him back to serve me. Do that, and I will appoint you chief marshal."

19

Out on Messalia Bay the water seemed to go on forever. Kellas had come out fishing with his three granddaughters but he kept getting distracted by the view. To the east, the barrier islands were too far away to be seen, but their presence was marked by clouds piled into brooding massifs that caught on the islands before they spilled over the huge bay.

"Let's go in," said the eldest, Ranit. "We've got enough fish. I'm leaking."

She was already mother to three children including a thriving one-year-old.

"I'm going to take a dip first," said the youngest, Treya, the brash one. She threw a playful smile at Kellas. "You want to race me to the islands, Grandpa?"

"Don't tempt him," said Fohiono, who sat in the stern with the steering blade. "You know he'll do it like he did twelve years ago to get the lads to stop boasting."

With a laugh Treya somersaulted out of the canoe and splashed into the clear water, but Fo frowned as she studied the horizon and the swells, her feet pressed firmly onto the belly of the canoe so she could listen to what the boat told her.

"Get back in, Trey! A storm is coming." At twenty, Fo was already an experienced steerswoman with a keen understanding of the sea, the strength to handle weather, and the ability to stay calm no matter the waves they hit.

She was born to be a wolf. But the moment he thought it, he frowned, irritated at himself for wishing such a life on anyone.

"What is it, Grandpa?" Fo asked, reading him as easily as the water.

"Just thinking of the first time I swam this bay when I was not much older than you, Fo."

"As if we don't know the story by heart! *I swam the bay battling against the monstrous tide and eight-tentacled beasts that tried to drag me to my death beneath the waves, and then afterward I saw the woman I would love forever.*"

"One of those three things is not true," he said with a smile. "Treya! We're leaving."

Treya pushed up and over the gunnel into the canoe. They set paddles to water, Treya setting the pace with Ranit and Kellas behind her. Fo caught a few bumps, swells giving the canoe and its float a lift. The wind ran at their backs.

The port town of Salya rose in tiers up the low hills just south of the mouth of the River Messali. Four eagles circled, and one plummeted toward the town. The canoe approached Gull Pier with its pilings encrusted with barnacles to the high-tide mark and its banner-posts topped with beautifully carved gulls at rest. Past Gull Pier lay Gull Beach. Six young men came running to help them carry the canoe up under a thatched roof. Fo and Treya weren't married yet, and the clan was prosperous enough that everyone in town knew the marriage status of its young people. It didn't hurt the lads' interest that Treya's vest and kilt were plastered to her body, and she flaunted it. Let youth enjoy its blossoming while it may, that was Kellas's philosophy.

But the lads also greeted him respectfully, or shyly, or jokingly, depending on their nature. He knew better than to pretend their attention didn't flatter him.

He and the girls carried their baskets along the shore to the Grand Pier and headed inland up the wide avenue known locally as Drunk's Lane. Lined with inns and drinking houses frequented by sailors, it was quiet at this time of day. One scruffy fellow was throwing up at the foot of the stairs that led up to the Inn of Fortune's Star. It was just here—without the accompaniment of a vomiting man—that on his very first mission as a Black Wolf he had seen Mai for the first time fifty-two years ago: Standing on the street in a simple cotton taloos that on her looked like best-quality silk, a woman so striking he had forgotten all his training at going unnoticed and instead had blatantly stared.

That kind of beauty is dangerous to chase, his companion at the time—Esisha—had said, reminding him that he mustn't get distracted. He had been so eager to prove himself tough enough to become one of the king's most valued soldiers.

Fo slipped a hand into the crook of his elbow. "You need some help, old man?"

He chuckled and they kept walking. Ranit had the impatient stride of a nursing woman getting uncomfortable with full breasts who sees relief ahead. Treya peered onto every inn veranda, looking for someone more interesting than her current companions.

Fo slipped her hand off his arm with a grin. "Don't think you can get me to carry your share of the fish. You're still strong enough that you have to work for your food."

"I heard a rumor there's trouble at Bronze Hall," said Treya suddenly. "The new marshal is telling all the reeves they have to worship at the Beltak shrine. There's talk of pushing him into the ocean because everyone knows he can't swim and is afraid of the water."

Kellas whistled. "Such talk is not for the street," he said in a low voice.

Ranit gave Treya a side-eye while Fo sketched the hand gesture for keeping one's mouth shut, adding a rude flourish at the end.

"I heard it from someone who knows," Treya muttered stubbornly.

"Heya! That reeve you've been keeping company with, eh?" said Ranit. "He's trouble, mark my words."

"He knows so much good gossip, especially about pirates in the Turian Sea! As traders we need not scorn any way of scooping up rumor. Don't scold me for hearing things before the rest of you do."

"Did you know already, Grandpa?" asked Fo.

He scratched his cheek.

Fo crowed. "You did know! You always know everything first."

Treya shook her head with the admiring grin she had: He would have to talk to her about her habit of being too uncritical of people she thought possessed a quality she wanted for herself. "I don't think anything can surprise you, Grandpa."

"I'll be surprised the day you stop to think before jumping into the ocean," he remarked, and they all laughed.

How he loved these girls.

They turned off onto the slope of Roaring Hill and up the yellow stairs to their own street. An elderly neighbor greeted them as they passed. The hells! Elderly! The woman was younger than he was: She'd been born in the Year of the White Goat whereas he was a Brown Ibex. Here in Mar people still cared about things like what year you were born in, as folk had in his youth. Here in Mar people still gave their children the Mother inks like those he had on his forearm and calf, marking him as child of the Fire Mother. Fo was Earth-born, Treya Fire, and Ranit Water. In the palace the old customs had fallen out of favor. Here in Salya, each of the seven gods and goddesses still had a temple where people left offerings and dedicated each of their children while the small Beltak shrine sat on the outskirts of town and the only people who went there were sailors, soldiers, and clerks in the service of ships put into harbor.

"When do you think we'll get another letter from Uncle Mori?" Treya asked. "I want to become a sailor like him and sail away east over the ocean."

"And be gone for five years at a stretch?" asked Ranit.

"Just because you never want to go anywhere doesn't mean the rest of us don't wish for adventure," retorted Treya. "Grandpa, didn't you start sending Uncle Mori off to gather information for our trading ventures when we decided to expand to ports over the ocean?"

"Mori wanted to sail far afield, so I trained him to write in code and send reports home. But it was his choice to go. Playing with other people's lives is no game, Treya. Not when they die."

Fo nudged him. "Is that Father out in front? Who's he with?"

They came into sight of their home, hung with banners painted with stylized plum blossoms. The spacious front veranda ran the length of the compound, offering a spectacular view of the harbor and the bay. Shaded by a roof, it was a splendid outdoor space for entertaining visitors and discussing trade preliminaries. The setting was so lovely and comfortable that it was impossible to complain of any lack of hospitality when you were seated on quilted cushions and served tea and rice cakes on a lacquered tray. But if you didn't get inside the house into the visitors' hall, then you knew you were not going into business with Plum Blossom Clan.

The girls' father, Hari, stood on the veranda talking to a white-haired woman wearing reeve leathers. Kellas had watched

Hari grow from a scrawny, cheerful, content eight-year-old child into a stout, cheerful, content man of fifty-two with six children and already eight grandchildren.

However, at this moment Hari was standing arms-crossed and grim-faced to block the doors. One of the guard dogs bristled on alert behind him. When Hari saw them coming, he spoke to the visitor.

She turned.

The shock of seeing Lady Dannarah's face after so many years caused Kellas to miss a step. Fo grabbed his arm and Treya whisked the basket he was carrying out of his arms.

"I don't need help," he said more curtly than he intended.

What in the hells did this mean? Lady Dannarah looked him over in that scorching way he remembered so well. No doubt she intended to again inform him, as she had the last time he had seen her twenty-two years ago, that it was his fault Atani had died.

But he already knew that.

The girls clustered behind him as if expecting to catch him when he toppled over.

"It has been a hells long time since we last met, Captain Kellas," Dannarah said, more air than voice, as if she too had been punched in the gut.

"Do I look that old? The years have treated you kindly, Lady Dannarah."

The years *had* treated her kindly. Age had burnished her, and she looked straight and strong and utterly confident.

Then she spoiled it by blushing as awkwardly as a shy girl. "My thanks, Captain. But that's not what I meant. You look hale and vigorous, as I was told."

Treya giggled, Ranit guffawed, and even Fo snickered.

Hari said, "Girls, take the fish to the kitchen," and because his habitual smile had vanished, they obeyed without any questions.

Kellas clambered past his surprise and sought something intelligent to say. "You have made the acquaintance of my son, Hari."

She glanced between the two of them. "He isn't really your son."

"Did my seed sire him? No. Has he been as a son to me over the years, and I as a father to him, and a grandfather to his children, like those three young women? I hope so."

"I call him Father, which should be enough for anyone," said Hari, a sting in his gently spoken words.

"I'd like to know why he looks so cursed much like Anjihosh. And like my sister Sadah, for that matter. The bump in the nose is distinctive." She brushed a finger along the bridge of her own distinctive nose.

Even at his angriest Hari could never resist smiling when life gave him the least opportunity. "Around here they call it the eagle's beak. I have explained many times it is a sign of intelligence and good fortune."

She swept her penetrating gaze along the exterior of the house and out toward the bay, which was chopping up as clouds rolled in from the east. "I think I never knew you at all, Captain. You were the most devoted of my father's servants. Did you keep a secret family all the time I thought you were serving my father?" She indicated Hari. "Or perhaps this man was part of an arrangement my father made that he commanded you to oversee."

Kellas could see her making a tale in her mind in which Hari was Anjihosh's son by a lover, a child to be kept safe but far away from the palace and the succession, guarded over by his most loyal captain. Let her think that. It was almost true, and anyway it was for the best. "Why are you here, Lady Dannarah? Your visit has taken us quite by surprise."

Her eyes met his, dark with secrets and accusations. "Jehosh wants you to return to the palace, Captain."

He felt his heart congealing to stone. "Why?"

She glanced at Hari and then back at him, a question in her shrug.

"There is nothing you can say to me that you can't say in front of my son," snapped Kellas. Hari rested a hand on his shoulder, and he was shocked to find himself trembling. "Why does Jehosh want me?"

"He is afraid a succession battle is about to break out among his three sons and two queens."

"Is he ill, that they feel they must move now?"

Her smile had the same caustic slant he remembered from her days as chief marshal. "No, his health seems good. He no longer trusts Queen Chorannah, her sons, his council, or his companions."

"An ironic turn of events, do you not think?"

A flash of understanding passed between them, the memory of their secret alliance in the last days of Atani's life.

"I was surprised when he of all people asked for my help, yes." She looked again at Hari, brow wrinkling. "If Hari is Anjihosh's son, could *he* claim the throne?"

Hari said nothing but looked as out of sorts as Kellas had ever seen him.

"It would be deeply unwise of you to think of Hari as anything but a merchant living in Salya, Lady Dannarah." Kellas hoped his brutally impassive tone made an impression on her. "Do not for a moment consider throwing him into whatever storm is brewing in the palace. Does anyone else know of this errand you run for Jehosh?"

"No one else in the palace knows, except perhaps Lord Vanas."

She gestured skyward. "I am accompanied by three reeves, although none knows the true reason we have come."

"I need to wash the stink of fish off me. We will sit down for tea in the proper manner befitting visitors. With this storm coming in, you and your people will have to sleep over, Lady Dannarah. I don't recommend you fly into that storm to try to get to Bronze Hall unless you know the wind patterns out on the islands very well."

"I'll have my wing land at Salya's assizes court, then. I presume there is still a loft there."

"There is, but more conveniently there is a small loft available for eagles and reeves in a field just at the top of this hill."

"There is a loft built so close to your house? That's a little odd, isn't it?"

Hari stuck fists to hips. With a rare, reckless show of pique, he broke in. "My mother has been a good friend to the reeves of Bronze Hall. They visit her often."

She folded her arms. "Who is your mother, ver? Heir to a prosperous house, I can see."

Kellas nudged Hari's foot with his own but it was too late.

"She built this clan with my aunt and uncle from nothing!"

"May I meet her?"

Kellas broke in before Hari said something they would regret. "That won't be possible. She happens to be away at the moment, visiting Hari's wife's sister. Hari, go fetch Fo. She can show Marshal Dannarah up to the field to flag down the other reeves before it starts to rain. We'll get wash-water heated and a meal ready."

Hari cast him a sharp gaze but sketched a brief *excuse me* with a hand and went into the house.

"Who is his mother, truly? Some lover or concubine my father discarded? He wasn't a man to throw things away carelessly. Perhaps he decided to make sure her retirement was secure by commanding you, his most obedient soldier, to marry her."

Kellas whistled the dog over and rubbed its ears until the roar of anger in his heart passed. When he was sure he could speak in a level voice and with a calm face, he straightened.

"Understand me, Lady Dannarah. I do not mean this as an insult, but you and Jehosh have no claim on me. I broke with the palace when Atani died and I'm not going back."

20

Getting jessed, leaving home, seeing Law Rock, and flying so far south that the air became thick and hot: Lifka could not steady herself. Half the time the days passed like a dream.

"Everything has been so bewildering," she said to Fohiono and Treya, the sisters who had taken charge of her when they had reached the house. They were relaxing with her in a small stone pool that overlooked a garden. Rain could not dampen the garden's lush beauty.

"Did you never travel far from home? Didn't you say your clan are carters?" Fohiono didn't say the word in a scornful way, simply as a question.

"Carters on my father's side. Caravan guards on my mother's. I could have gone with my cousin Ailia when she took employment as an apprentice caravan guard last year, but I didn't want to..." She hesitated, afraid they would say the words strangers always said to her: *Where did you really come from? Where is your real home?*

Fo said, "Being a caravan guard isn't the life for everyone, I imagine. What about the carter's trade, though?"

Lifka exhaled in relief. "My father and his sister Ediko traveled a great deal hauling along the roads, but that was when I was too little to go along. A few years ago the law changed and now you have to buy a license from the archon for permission to cart loads between towns. We can't afford it so we cut and haul wood for coin. I've never seen the River Istri or a city so large like Toskala. To see Law Rock itself after hearing about it in all the tales! That was something! Afterward we flew here. It's so different! It's hot! Everything smells of the sea. I knew there was a port called Salya because I know my Hundred Count of all the towns, but...it all happened so fast."

"What about that reeve Reyad?" The younger one, Treya, had what Papa would call a mischief eye, ready to get into trouble just for the fun of it. "Too bad he decided to stay at the loft and mind the eagles, neh?"

Lifka shrugged. "He only ever talks about reeve business or his wife. He was born in the Year of the Brown Rat. Sentimental, hardworking, and dull."

Fohiono stroked an arm through the water like the pull of a thought. "I'm a Crane, and Treya of course is a flighty Ibex. What are you, Lifka?"

In Lifka's experience people asked that question to get her to admit she wasn't born in the Hundred, but Fohiono had a curious gleam in her eye, Cranes being the sort of people who were always trying to understand things. After the utter confusion of the last few days, the girls reminded her comfortably of her cousins.

"Mum says I must be an Ox because I'm dauntless and stubborn. Aunt Ediko was certain I am a Snake, and of course a Red Snake at that. Passionate. Self-reliant. Ready to strike my enemies a deadly blow."

Fo giggled charmingly.

Over behind the curtained entrance, the Runt barked once to remind her that she had tied him up outside. She'd have left him in the company of the household's three watchdogs but he'd already almost gotten into a fight with them.

"We should take you down to the harbor," said Treya. "There are sailors there from all over, some as black as you. They might know something about where you really come from."

Fo kicked her under the water. "Can you never think before you let words fly off your tongue? Lifka's already told us she's a daughter of Five Roads Clan near River's Bend."

Somehow in this soaking bath in a well-to-do household half the Hundred away from the humble compound where she had grown up, with two young women she did not know, she could say words she had never shared with anyone else.

"I once saw a man who looked something like me. He had a slave inking on his cheek. He was a guard for a merchant caravan that came through River's Bend on its way north to Herelia. When he saw me his whole expression changed. He said something to me in words I couldn't understand. I ran away because it scared me."

"It scared you to see him?" asked Fo gently.

"Because to my eyes he looked like an outlander. That was the first time I truly realized people thought of *me* as an outlander." She wasn't shy about being naked but she drew her knees up to her chest now as if they could hide her from the memory. "It was the first time I wondered if someone had made a mistake and was going to come back and take me away from my family."

"You aren't even a little curious?" asked Treya.

"I don't know." She could not say the words aloud: *I'm afraid if I'm too curious the gods will tear me away from my family. I couldn't bear that to happen twice.*

Fo studied her warily but Treya prattled blithely on.

"Because I'm curious! There's probably a Tandi ship in port. They go everywhere and see everything, and I bet they would know. Maybe you're one of them. They're very good-looking, and I can't say that for all outlanders. I slept with one of the men once. He was so sweet. I'd've sailed off with him in a heartbeat but they don't marry like we do."

"Could you just shut up, Trey!" Fo slapped a hand over her eyes.

"Who are Tandi?" Lifka asked, caught by the name as if it had plucked a string knotted deep in her bones.

Fo scratched her left cheek in the same way her grandfather did, obviously copied from his behavior. "The Tandi are a consortium of merchant houses out of the east, from over the ocean. We've been trading with Tandi ships for about ten years. They sell cunning little lockboxes, fine metal tools for goldsmiths—"

"The most beautiful glass and porcelain you've ever seen," broke in Treya. "But the one thing they never bring is slaves. The Tandi consortium does not traffic in people. The men have wings inked on their faces to mark their lineage affiliation, and the women wear the ink of their lineage on their back. Something like that scar you have."

Suddenly uneasy, Lifka brushed a hand over the raised scar on the back of her neck, crude lines that had been carved up each shoulder and partway down her spine. "It's just a scar."

"That's not *just* a scar, like you would get from a knife fight or an accident—"

"Aui! Trey, you're such an ass. My sister doesn't mean anything by it, Lifka. My apologies."

"Why should it be wrong to mention it?" said Treya with an impatient wave of her hand. "I thought you might be interested in the Tandi, Lifka. If we hurry we can go down to the harbor and get back before supper."

"It's raining too hard to go down to the harbor," said Fo, elbowing her cousin.

They soaked for a bit in awkward silence as rain fell with

a soothingly relentless patter. The wind was picking up, making branches sway. On the other side of the curtain the Runt snuffled at the canvas, then grunted in that way he had when he lay down full of grinding disappointment that he wasn't getting what he wanted. Lifka asked about the plants, and Fo named them: Muzz. Proudhorn. Musk vine. Stardrops.

"That's a Devourer's garden," said Lifka, for she had spent many a lazy hour in the temple of Ushara the Merciless One, Goddess of Love, Death, and Desire, whose garden was a meeting place for lovers.

"It's a Devouring garden because our grandmother has the most amazing love story ever told in all the tales of the Hundred," said Treya eagerly. "She was forbidden by the jealous king from ever taking a man as her lover. Yet she found a way for years and years while the king was still alive to secretly meet her true love! Because she was more clever than the king ever could be, and her lover was the boldest man in the Hundred, and the king had no cause or right to stop her anyway!"

"Hush!" Fo snapped. "Can you never think?"

The girl's lips whitened. "I'm sorry."

Splashing up, she dripped away to a bench, grabbed a faded cotton taloos, and wrapped it around her without even drying herself off. Then she pushed past the curtain, briefly revealing a startled Runt. Her footsteps slapped away.

The Runt barked twice.

Lifka hesitated, embarrassed but so curious she thought her head would burst.

Fo pulled her wet hair back and wrung water out of it. "Just say it. Whatever it is."

"I couldn't help but notice that your father, Hari, looks a bit like Marshal Dannarah. There's only one king you could be talking about by reason of their age, and that would be King

Anjihosh the Glorious Unifier. He was the outlander who saved us from a terrible darkness that almost swallowed the Hundred into its monstrous belly. He was rewarded with the love of a woman as beautiful as plum blossoms shimmering dew-laden at dawn. But then she was stolen from him by a jealous lilu and he could never give his heart to another woman afterward. So the tale goes."

Fo watched her in silence.

"I heard a different version from a troupe of Hasibal's players who came through town a few years ago. A king captures a beautiful woman and locks her in a cage so only he can admire her, and she escapes using her wits and intelligence and by praying to Hasibal the Merciful One. Your house is called Plum Blossom Clan. The plum blossom is your badge."

Fohiono sighed. "You will make a good reeve, for reeves must be observant above all else."

"Is your father, Hari, the son of King Anjihosh by the plum blossom lover?"

"No, he isn't. My dad doesn't belong to the palace." Fo twisted her wet hair up on top of her head and fixed it there with a pair of lacquered hairsticks. The hairsticks were lovely work far too expensive for the likes of Lifka's family. Everything she had seen since she had been ushered inside the compound of Plum Blossom House revealed a clan as prosperous as hers was poor.

Lifka hugged her knees. "I shouldn't have asked. You've been so hospitable."

"You have a duty to ask because you're a reeve. But honestly, Lifka, you are so naive. You can't just trust people because they are hospitable."

Lifka stared at her. "Like you?"

"Like me. I know it's your duty to tell the marshal what

you've learned, but it would be a kindness if you would never tell anyone else except her. Now we better go before they eat all the food without us."

Lifka thought it best to wear Mum's wedding taloos. Fo complimented her on its yellowish-orange color but Lifka was horribly aware of how casually the other women of the household wore shimmering silk of finest quality while hers had the coarse weave of least-quality cloth. The marshal and Tarnit had washed before her; they wore their reeve leathers.

The opulence of the compound made her afraid to touch anything. The audience hall was floored with best-quality reed mats. The chamber was decorated with a beautiful heron painting and an alcove altar drenched with flowers in offering to Hasibal the Merciful One, here depicted with a lovely painting of Hasibal's Tears: a branch of a plum tree laden with seven blossoms, one for each of the gods. Lifka felt comforted that the old religion was followed here, that it hadn't been crowded out by the outlanders' god.

Captain Kellas was an upright and vigorous old man with a face that had pleasant lineaments, but he did not smile once during the meal. His granddaughters served the guests. She had never been served in her life. When her grandmother had been alive it had been her and Ailia's duty as the youngest girls to make sure Grandmother had everything she needed before they ate.

Since it was terribly rude to discuss business while eating, the older people traded poetic lines from the old tales although Lifka could not help but notice that Marshal Dannarah's choices were always the most obvious ones from the most well-known tales, as if she hadn't learned a hundred tales by heart as everyone else had. Maybe she hadn't, growing up in the palace above the city where people spoke an outlander language. The thought of always being accounted an outsider made her think longingly of River's Bend and home.

When they had finished the marshal told Lifka to take a covered basket of food out to Reyad before it got too dark to see. It was an obvious ploy to get her out of the chamber while the elders conferred. Lifka changed back into her kilt and vest, and Fo offered to go with her.

"Treya's still sulking in the back but don't feel sorry for her. She loves the attention. Are you going to bring your dog?"

"He hates the rain so much. But I'm afraid to leave him here alone."

Ears pinned back and looking morose, the Runt followed them into the weather.

"What a big baby!" said Fo, watching him.

They laughed together as they splashed through water pouring along the street. On the hillward side of the street beyond Plum Blossom Clan, two large compounds kept closed gates and darkened verandas, as if their inhabitants were already asleep although it wasn't late. At the end of the street, stairs led up through bushes into a grassy clearing where a loft had been built. The eagles were hooded. Reyad sat cross-legged beneath a hanging lamp, whittling on a piece of wood. His eyes got very wide as they trotted up, and Lifka glanced down to realize that both she and Fo were halfway to being naked, wet cloth adhering to their bodies. Fo knew it, too, and they both laughed unrestrainedly as he blushed. The Runt shook himself, spraying water all over.

"You're a horrid dog," said Reyad.

"What a thing to say!" cried Fo.

He showed Fo the scabbed puncture at his knuckle where the Runt had snapped. The Runt shivered, looking miserable, caught between the rain and the hooded eagles. To make up for it, he showed his teeth to Reyad.

"Do you want company tonight?" Lifka asked even though she wanted to go back to the house with Fo.

His mouth tightened. "No. I'm content to be alone. I'm not looking for—"

"I didn't mean that kind of company. I have brothers and cousins, you know. That's all I meant. I was just being polite!"

Fo snorted, trying not to laugh. "Come back with me, Lifka. Mama has promised to sing from the Tale of Beginning, the episode of how the Four Mothers gave birth to the land. That's if we're very good and all the children have eaten their rice."

"Bring the lamp closer," said Reyad abruptly. He had the lid off the rice basket and was prodding at the rice with an eating stick.

Fo stiffened. "It's properly washed and cooked. I hope you don't think there are bugs in it!"

Reyad plucked a single grain out of the bowl and held it close to the flame. It was a reddish color, flecked with darker spots. "Where does this rice come from?"

"It's grown all around here. It's what everyone eats in Salya. You sound Mar-bred. Haven't you had red-nut before? It's the best flavor."

"I'm from the Suvash Hills but I've never seen this variety before." He glanced at Fohiono as if expecting her to sprout a lilu's writhing hair. "Lifka, let Marshal Dannarah know I have something to tell her."

Fo grabbed Lifka's hand. "The rain is slackening. Leave him the lamp and let's get back before it starts up again."

Lifka followed without protest. The rain had indeed slackened to spatters, although the wind still moaned.

"He's so full of himself," said Fo when they were out of earshot. "He just assumed you were propositioning him!"

Lifka snickered. "Don't tell anyone I said this, but the marshal adores him. I think he's tiresome."

"They show a different face to their elders, don't they?" agreed Fo.

"Yes. There was a funny thing about my eagle's harness..."
She hesitated. Reyad hadn't known how well she knew harnesses and tack, and she had not enlightened him when he went over the eagle's harness with her that first night at the marshal's order. The broken jess that had allowed Slip to pull free and kill his reeve at River's Bend had a funny look, as if it had been sliced partway through and then ripped the rest of the way. Reyad had confiscated the ruined jess, and she'd never seen it again.

But this wasn't home, where she could tell anything to anyone in her family. As much as Lifka liked Fo, reeve business had to stay reeve business.

"Are you all right?" Fo asked. "What about your eagle's harness?"

"Just that he was assigned to teach me about it and he never bothered to ask if I might know anything before he explained it all to me. It was funny when the Runt bit him. He was so indignant!"

"The dog, or Reyad?"

Lifka laughed again. "The Runt is very fearful. We've been training him not to snap at anything that gets in his face..." She faltered. The clouds had torn apart, turning the heavens into an ocean of stars streaked with scraps of mist. Descending out of the night toward the roof of Plum Blossom House rode a woman on a winged horse.

Lifka blinked, sure she was seeing an illusion brought on by mist and moonlight.

But there she was: a woman on a winged horse. A cloak like lamplight flowed off her shoulders, lifted by the wind.

A demon! Just like in the tales!

Fo whistled so sharply that Lifka winced, and the Runt barked in surprise, and Fo reached right into his face and of course he snapped. Lifka grabbed him, and by the time she had apologized to Fo and calmed the dog, the sky was just the sky.

"He didn't break the skin," said Fo. "Here comes the rain, up from the bay! We'd better hurry in."

"Did you see . . . ?"

"I did!" Fo exclaimed, still rubbing her hand. "The moon dazzled me. The way the light chases through the mist almost makes it seem like tales are being woven in the sky. But then the clouds came back in."

Lifka rubbed her eyes, overwhelmed by the turn her life had taken. "It's funny what you see when you're tired."

"It is," agreed Fo.

Rain swept up the hill, chasing them inside.

21

Dannarah had forgotten that Captain Kellas was a man so reserved you might as well pound on a stone wall as try to figure out what he was really thinking. She watched him pour tea: Although his white hair and lined face marked him as an old man, his hands had strength and steadiness.

Everyone else had gone to bed. She and the captain sat alone on the veranda by the light of a small oil lamp. Night settled a damp hush over the town now that the worst of the storm had blown through. Water dripped off eaves at random intervals. Now and again she heard the clacking sticks of the fire watch walking through town, although the chance of a conflagration catching in air as sodden as this struck Dannarah as unlikely.

He pushed a cup across the tray to her. Steam rose from the cup.

"Does Jehosh know about Hari?" She watched him closely, hoping to identify the words that could pierce his armor.

His gaze met hers, clear and strong. "Is that meant as a threat?"

"Do you fear I will tell him?"

The captain said nothing and by doing so gave up nothing.

"Jehosh stripped me of the chief marshalate twenty years ago. I was fortunate to be given Horn Hall to command as a sop to my pride and a nod to my exalted birth. But there is one thing I haven't told you yet."

"There always is." His smile flared and vanished. She missed it when it was gone. "Treya spoke rashly about Hari before your young reeve, and Lifka surely told you what she learned."

"Your granddaughter didn't reveal anything I couldn't have figured out for myself by looking at Hari. After almost sixty years thinking Atani is my only brother, it is odd to discover that my father sired a son by another woman. What else are you hiding, Captain?"

"If I'm hiding it, then I'm unlikely to tell you."

"We found rice in the outlaws' encampment in the Westhal Hills just like the red-nut we ate here for our supper."

He waited.

"This is how you got people to betray themselves, isn't it? By letting them talk. Very well. I am going to be brutally honest."

This time when he smiled, the expression held longer and she felt herself smile in return. "I would expect nothing less, Lady Dannarah."

"Chief Marshal Auri was killed by his eagle a few days ago."

He blinked. "That is unexpected."

"I'm relieved you don't magically know all about it already. More unexpected was that instead of flying away to the mountains and then returning a year or five years later to leash a new reeve, the eagle jessed Lifka right there on the spot."

He nodded as encouragement for her to go on.

"Lifka's situation is not of any particular importance, it's just unusual. What matters is that the reeve halls are without a chief marshal. Auri has done a terrible job."

"So we hear from the reeves we know at Bronze Hall. Their new marshal, appointed by Auri, is a blustering tyrant. I hope he is not the one expected to become the next chief marshal."

"Jehosh has promised to make me chief marshal if I bring you back. Will you come for my sake, Captain?"

"No."

"For the reeves, then? After fifteen years of Auri's mismanagement and incompetence, the reeve halls need a strong hand to restore them. Think of the Hundred, Captain. Jehosh made Auri chief marshal because Auri was one of his old friends, not because Auri was a good reeve or a good marshal. It is bad for the Hundred if the reeves are poorly commanded."

"No."

"What of your duty to serve the kings of the Hundred all your life, Captain? You gave an oath to my father the day he spared you from execution. I remember the day clearly although I was only seven years old. Do you mean to dishonor your own word and your own duty? All the years you served Anjihosh, tracking down his enemies and crushing any and all rebels and troublemakers who disturbed the peace of the land. Are those years nothing to you now?"

She put a hand around the bracelet. His gaze followed the movement, and an expression pinched his face: not anger but a fleeting ghost of something lost and wistful.

"I saw you had kept that trifle," he said in a low voice.

"Not a trifle to me at the time," she snapped. "I wear it to remind myself to carefully consider what it is I ask of people and if it might mean something different to them than it means to me."

He glanced down at the cup and its wisps of steam. Briefly he appeared shy, even coy.

"Have I offended, Lady Dannarah?" he asked, looking up just as she glanced at the ceiling, irritated with her own juvenile fancies.

"Yes! You have offended me by refusing to even consider the situation. Think of what I told you about my sister Sadah's situation! If Queen Chorannah has some feckless plan in regard to supporting her sister's incompetent son as emperor, and if he is killed as we must suppose he will be, then the prince who ends up becoming emperor may look north and decide to punish the Hundred for Chorannah's interference."

He sipped his tea.

She went on, sensing a vulnerable spot. "My sister Sadah reached the palace without being detected. Surely it disturbs you that Supreme Captain Ulyar's spies knew nothing until she arrived! That would never have happened when my father was king."

He set down the cup. His gaze flicked toward the closed doors as if he was waiting for a signal that hadn't come.

She pressed on. "Seeing Sadah after all these years reminded me of the one time Atani ran away from the palace. When he returned he never told me what drove him to leave, but there was something different about him. He was the same gentle, kind, compassionate person, but there was a steel in him that had been lacking before. All he told me was that he had seen something that made him understand what his task was meant to be as king of the Hundred. I know you recall the incident, Captain. You were sent to track him down and bring him back, which you did. Is there anything you can tell me about that time?"

His gaze held steady. "No."

"He brought back with him a necklace that he wore ever after. Years later I began to see such necklaces, called Hasibal's Tears. We found several at the outlaws' encampment. It's an odd thing to wear for a man who was raised in the palace with Beltak priests."

"It is a common thing to wear if you pray to the seven. If you favor the teaching of the Merciful One, whose compassion alleviates sorrow."

Dannarah studied his bland expression. It was cursed hard to imagine Anjihosh's most loyal soldier in league with demons. Whatever Lord Vanas might insinuate, she simply could not envision any scenario in which Kellas was involved in Atani's death.

"You and I both know how stubborn Jehosh is," she said. "Say no to me if you wish but he will keep sending people down here until you say yes. I cannot believe you want the king's gaze fixed on the people here whom you obviously care for."

"Is that a threat?"

An exasperated sigh escaped her. "I am not the one threatening you. Jehosh means you to come whether you will or no. He is reminding you that he knows where your kinsfolk live. I am just the messenger he chose. It should give you pause to note that he sent me instead of Supreme Captain Ulyar or Lord Vanas. Why me, and not them?"

"You have been bought by a promise. That is how Jehosh always has operated."

"I have been bought by duty, not by a promise. You and I remember how it was. My father brought peace and prosperity to the Hundred. You were one of his sharpest weapons in the war against injustice. Atani in his own way watched over the land with me by his side. Back in the day you and I both realized Jehosh wasn't the right heir. He does not have the temperament to be a strong and just king. But we missed our chance to change the fate of the Hundred. Didn't we, Captain?"

His eyes narrowed as if he were staring through a slit into the darkest day of their past, twenty-two years ago.

22

The encampment with its tents and soldiers wears a mantle of bright promise, the sun shining, men checking over their weapons and horses as they make ready to march. They are an arrow being brought to the string, soon to be loosed across rugged mountains and into the northern kingdom of Ithik Eldim.

"We will regret the war set in motion today." King Atani surveys the camp as Kellas waits beside him. The king's court clothes, a silk kilt that covers his legs to the ankles and a short sleeveless tunic sewn with ornamental pearls over it, contrast sharply with the martial air. "Its consequences will wound us in ways we cannot yet foresee."

"Have you some fear this expedition will end in failure, my lord?"

"Quite the contrary. I fear it will end in success. Jehosh hasn't the maturity to accept victory gracefully. Ruthlessness must be tempered by mercy, not allowed to trample where it wishes."

"The northern barbarians raided first."

Atani frowns rarely and when he does it is as if the blue sky has turned gray and will soon weep. "It's never been proven to my satisfaction that they did raid first. Regardless, we have strengthened the border, doubled and tripled the watch, fortified outlying villages, and moved the most vulnerable to new pastures and towns. Why does this not content my sister and my son?"

"Why do you not simply command the expedition be called off, my lord?"

Atani glances toward the cloth-of-gold tent as guards straighten to attention. A retinue approaches the tent, led by soldiers in red and gold tabards whose flash and swagger clash with the somber

Black Wolves who attend the king. Twenty-year-old Prince Jehosh strides among his retinue with easy laughter. The group vanishes inside the tent.

"If I do, the generals will be forced to side openly with my son."

"You cannot think...!"

"I cannot think the generals would feel obliged to depose me in favor of Jehosh? I dare not give them the excuse they need to do it. They want this war as much as he does."

"Do you actually think one of the generals might be plotting against you?"

From the sash wrapped around his waist Atani draws the commander's whip that once belonged to his father. Its leather gleams, lovingly tended and oiled. "If it is only the lash of the whip that brings peace, Captain, then there will always be someone who seeks to tear the whip out of the hand that wields it."

"You are not your father, my lord."

"No, I am not, but I am as trapped by my ambitions as he was by his. I need time to accomplish my plans. Thus I acquiesce to their war because it will keep them busy elsewhere, and I do it with eyes open to its consequences, the innocent lives it will take, the disruption it will cause. Captain, you will accompany the expedition and keep Jehosh from doing things he will regret later."

Kellas always travels with his full kit but even so the sudden change rocks him. "My lord, I have heard whispers, nothing I can put a finger on, but I prefer to stay close to you. I think it would be better to keep me here and send another of your Wolves."

"No. You know why I trust you more than anyone."

He does know. He places his right fist against his heart. "I am yours to command."

Atani's smile brings the soothing elegance of his features into full flower. His beauty is like the vault of the heavens: a bit intimidating. Then he raises an eyebrow as at a dry joke. "Whose you are to command I am never quite sure."

Kellas glances away, trying not to smile.

Atani looks skyward. "At last comes the chief marshal, just late enough to make an impressive entrance."

A triad of reeves circles overhead but only one descends in a showy plummet. Lady Dannarah's eagle has as demanding and flamboyant a temperament as she does. At the most precipitous moment the giant eagle brakes with wings high and taloned feet thrust forward as it thumps to earth. It is a magnificent bird, its wingspan truly impressive. Kellas grew up seeing eagles and reeves every day of his life, yet a thrill of fear always shoots through him to be so close to one of the huge raptors. Its brown-gold feathers fluff out, then settle as it peers around the encampment. A keen gaze touches him as a thorn might just before it jabs. The eagle's name is Terror because as a juvenile it killed its first two reeves within weeks of being jessed. Kellas holds still, and the eagle looks elsewhere.

She hoods the raptor without the least sign of nervousness and afterward stalks straight to her brother. As an adult, tempered by life, she radiates the intensity and ambition and natural air of command that so effortlessly marked King Anjihosh.

"Captain Kellas!" she exclaims in a fierce tone that causes him to tap his chest with his right fist. She slaps her brother's shoulder. "You do not like this at all, do you, Atani?"

"I cannot like Jehosh's eagerness, as if war is a festival at which he wishes to celebrate."

"Listen to me." She grabs her brother's wrists. They are of equal height, close in build. "A clear victory over the Eldim kings is the only way we will have peace on the northern frontier."

"It is never so simple. Anger and grief fester. What we do to them, they will wish to do to us in return."

"Crush the northerners now and it will take years for them to recover. As for Jehosh, he will learn wisdom, or he will die."

Her blunt speaking makes Kellas wince but Atani looks as if he already knew what she meant to say. Maybe he did. "I am not so certain he will learn wisdom, Dannarah."

"You are too hard on him, just as Father was too hard on you. For that is the seed of the matter, is it not? Jehosh is not you, Atani, just as you are not and never were our father."

"Indeed I am not," he agrees without the slightest hint of resentment. "You have always been far more like Father than I am."

"It's true." They speak easily together, two people who know and like each other. "No matter how many times I argued that village and town councils in the Hundred include women, Father was too bound by his own upbringing to name me as his heir even though I am better suited to rule."

"You've forgotten one thing, Dannarah," he answers with a wisp of a smile. "I do not agree with your assessment that you are better suited to rule. Which is why I am king and you are not."

She laughs with genuine amusement. "Your claws are so sharp because you so rarely unsheathe them."

She glances at Kellas to see what he makes of their exchange but he has long since perfected the art of suppressing emotion.

Turning back to her brother, she goes on. "Let Jehosh become the man he is meant to be, Atani. Once he rides north, then you and I will have peace to deal with the other matters that need our attention rather than what we do now, which is leaping from hearth to hearth putting out the fires Jehosh has started with his cockwitted escapades."

"Do you know what else I have heard?" Atani asks with a breath of impatience. "That in the first raid Jehosh led across the border he fell in love with—lust, more like—a beautiful young woman. She did not just refuse him. She scorned him. 'I am a king's daughter, not for the likes of a bandit like you.' The troops say he is leading this army to capture the girl and force her to marry him because she tarnished his honor."

Dannarah chuckles. "That sounds like Jehosh."

"It is no jest! What troubles me most is they all think it a hunt worth pursuing, to kidnap a girl because she rejected him. I cannot like it."

She shakes her head. "While Jehosh and the army are gone you can have a hundred pillars of law erected along the major roads. You've made a pet of that law pillar project. I've never understood why Father's reorganization of the assizes courts isn't enough for you."

"Law is a better shield than a sword." The king fixes a stern gaze on her. "Why do you believe a war with the northerners will unbind the knot that tangles me and my son? Jehosh despises me."

"You are a fool if you believe that. He loves you. He envies the ease with which you understand people and he does not. He is afraid you can see through his lies."

"He thinks me weak because I am not reckless and violent. He thinks I am a broken-down horse that needs to be put out to pasture to chew over my foolish bits of piecemeal wisdom."

"You must let him go, Atani."

He does not reply. After a moment he walks toward the tent.

She calls after him, "I'll be there in a moment. I need to adjust Terror's straps."

He shrugs and goes in.

Kellas watches her gaze measure the neat rows of tents, the horse lines, the ranks of wagons, and the cook fires where soldiers stand awaiting a meal of rice gruel and lentils. As a girl, her thick curling black hair had, with her intensely dark eyes, been her most striking feature, but a few years after becoming a reeve she had shaved her head. The bristling black cap of hair is now shot through with bits of gray, and her sun-weathered skin makes her look older than her thirty-seven years. But no one will ever mistake her for a woman in decline. She is handsome in a way she had never been as a girl. She has become the person she needs to be.

"You've never forgiven me, have you?" Her eyes have a lustrous gleam, shaded by long lashes.

"My lady, there is nothing for me to forgive."

"I'm trying to say that I am sorry for what I asked of you. I was too young then to think of it as taking advantage, but I understand now you could not say no."

He holds her gaze with a look that a proud young prince like Jehosh would see as defiance and have him punished for. "I kept your secret, Lady Dannarah. King Atani does not know."

"My father knew."

Kellas glances down at his clenched right hand. It is true he could not have said no, for so many reasons he dares not account them. Fixing his expression to dispassion, he nods. "Considering everything, I'm surprised your father did not kill me many times over."

"Maybe the night my father made you a Black Wolf he foresaw all the many uses to which you could be harnessed."

Dannarah has always valued plain speaking, and a crude joke.

"Harnessed? Is that meant to compare me to an ox?"

She laughs so delightedly that guards look their way. "No ox, Captain. Not as I recall it. A very satisfactory bull for the year you put up with my whims."

To his horror he flushes, for the conversation makes him feel all over again all the different ways in which their clandestine relationship had been an awful idea. Not that she demanded that particular service of him after the one year. In a way it wasn't really her fault. The seventeen-year-old Dannarah couldn't have understood the ramifications when she demanded that Kellas become her first lover.

"We all have our secrets, do we not?" she says with the quirk of the lips she uses to hide her mockery.

He is cursed sure there are things about his life she will never learn. "Why bring this old history up now, Lady Dannarah? What devious plan have you already set in motion?"

Her brown eyes have depths as black as tar and just as murky. Then she drops the hammer.

"Yes, loyal Captain Kellas, I do have a task for you. A few weeks ago I put it into Atani's mind that it would be a wise idea to send you north with the army to keep Jehosh safe from his own reckless idiocy. But I didn't tell my brother the real reason I want you to go." She presses callused fingers to his wrist with the pressure of a reeve accustomed to fearlessly guiding an eagle so huge that it can easily kill her should it decide it has had enough of her companionship. "Jehosh is too reckless and irresponsible to become king after Atani. Any of his younger siblings would be better suited to be heir. So he must not return from this war in the north. I count on you to make sure he does not."

23

Dannarah noticed the moment Kellas stopped paying attention to her, his gaze drawn inward to memory. She took the chance to study him. In her mind he remained the image of a mature man at the height of his power, as she had last seen him.

The jolt that came from seeing his familiar face grown old as if overnight jangled her.

Then, as quickly as his thoughts had drifted away, he came back. He pushed the cup around with unexpected restlessness, exhaled, and considered her. "Do you ever wonder why I agreed to obey your orders that day?"

"Because I ordered it done."

"You never asked yourself if I would follow your orders when it would seem likely to anyone that King Atani would have given different ones?"

"I knew you agreed with me about Jehosh. Sometimes we have to make the hard choices."

"Do you ever wonder if Atani suspected you had ordered me to kill Jehosh? If he acquiesced to the murder of his son by saying nothing and allowing me to go?"

The words hit like an ambush. She couldn't find a clever retort. "Atani loved his children!"

His tone grew a hard sheen, bright and unforgiving. "You can love someone very much and still make a decision that makes them grieve. You can harm that which you love most because you believe duty outweighs affection."

"I don't think he had it in him."

"You thought him soft, Lady Dannarah. But he wasn't. He was more ruthless than you ever understood."

She grasped the teacup and it was only her reluctance to shatter such a fine piece of workmanship that stopped her from throwing it right at his head for his disrespect. But she took in several calming breaths instead because she was no longer young and brash. She relaxed her hand and let go of the cup.

"Now I know I am old, to see you rein yourself in," remarked Kellas.

The anger poured away as quickly as if she had tipped the tea onto the dirt. "Old, indeed. I shudder to think how difficult it will be to stand up, and my hip is already hurting from sitting on this cushion for so long. We can speculate all we want but meanwhile Atani is dead."

"Yes, he is dead."

A warmly moist wind curled through the porch. The moon spread its silvery light along the rooftops and caught in shallow puddles on the street. He said nothing more, and she sensed a vulnerability in this line of argument, so she went on.

"Atani wasn't the only one my father commanded his Wolves to guard and serve. I am also Anjihosh's child."

"You are indeed. None more so, in some ways."

"Yes, and I take my duty to my father's legacy seriously. Jehosh has spent so much time having adventures in the north that he has likely lost hold of the palace, which is exactly the kind of problem I would have predicted for him back then. But he asked for my advice. He is desperate for help. We can insinuate ourselves in his good graces—"

"And run the kingdom as his advisers?"

"Incompetent and greedy people are advising him now and making a hash of things. Maybe he has learned humility now that he realizes how easily control has slipped away from him. What if we can work with him, help him become the strong king the Hundred needs? And if he cannot be that king, then we choose among his sons."

"Are you instigating a palace takeover, Lady Dannarah?"

"We must not let the land fall into disorder and chaos. You were a boy before my father rode into the Hundred. You remember when the demon war almost destroyed the Hundred. You remember when my father killed the demons and brought peace."

"I do remember."

"Think of Anjihosh and Atani, and what you promised them. The new laws Jehosh has set in motion are not what my father and brother intended for the Hundred. Artisans and laborers need to purchase licenses to carry on their trade when once they needed only to pay a yearly tithe. Massive building projects are fostering discontent as more men are arrested and sent off on work gangs. Meanwhile factions have begun to fight within the palace, which will only make things worse. One way or the other—with Jehosh or without him—we can change things, Captain. This is our opportunity to restore the Hundred that we knew in our youth."

One of the rice-paper-screened doors that led into the house slid aside and Hari appeared, lampless. She hadn't even heard him approach and she suddenly wondered if he had been standing there listening all along.

"Father? A quick word, if you will. I'll sit with the marshal."

Kellas absorbed these words without the slightest indication of surprise. He got to his feet with his usual uncanny grace, scarcely hobbled by the aching knees and sore hip that burdened her. With a nod at her, he went inside.

After carefully closing the door Hari took his place opposite her. "More tea, Marshal?"

"A quick word with whom?"

"You know how households are. There is always one crisis or another."

She liked this cheerful man and did not want to see him harmed but she knew better than to be ruled by sentiment. "In all the years I have known Captain Kellas he served the Hundred as its most exceptionally devoted soldier. I had not the least inkling he had kept a secret family all this while."

Hari's friendly expression might fool most but she saw how the smile deflected suspicion. "People are often surprising, are they not? Will you have more tea?"

"The tea is a fine brew, I assure you. But I would rather have more answers."

"Ah, well, answers are like fish, hard to catch if you don't have lines and nets."

"You are a slippery customer."

"All the better at the bargaining table, Marshal. I am a good merchant, and I intend to stay a merchant. I've no ambition to leave home or take up a new profession."

Brisk footfalls broke into their little sparring match, and Kellas returned. Hari rose to let Kellas have the cushion, but rather than sitting, Kellas remained at attention. He nodded at Hari, and the man sketched a brief *good night* and went inside.

After a silence Kellas spoke with obvious reluctance, like a man who has accepted orders he cannot refuse.

"I travel once or twice a year to Toskala for business and stay with my kinsfolk there. I can move up the visit, go now instead of later."

His crisp words sucked the air right out of her mouth.

"Not to serve King Jehosh but merely to speak to him, mind you. I will tell him you convinced me to come. I ask one favor of you in return. Hari wants nothing to do with the palace. Do you understand me?"

She crossed her arms. "Did King Anjihosh know of Hari's existence?"

"Of course he knew." For once he sounded impatient and a little angry. "You have guessed correctly that Hari is his child. It will only cause trouble if anyone in the palace discovers his existence. Let him and his family live here in peace, please."

"Did Atani know of Hari's existence?"

This time he said nothing.

"Atani knew and never told me?"

His gaze was grave and unyielding. "Yes, he discovered the truth when he was sixteen, when he ran away from the palace."

For several shaky breaths she was actually too upset to speak, but at length the tremors calmed. "It probably should come as no surprise to me that my father sired a child on another woman. He had lovers but he was always discreet and so careful never to complicate matters. He hated complications. He hated anything he could not control."

Kellas's lips moved but no sound came out. She waited, but he made no further attempt to speak. Rather, he stood at attention with hands at soldier's rest behind his back, just as he had for all the years he had served the palace. The grandfatherly man walking up the street with his granddaughters had vanished back into the soldier accepting his orders.

Then, breaking the moment, he looked past her, alerted by a movement in the darkened audience hall. "Come out," he said sharply.

One of the girls paced out of the interior with head bowed and eyes cast down but a steely defiance in her unbowed shoulders. Her gaze flashed up. "Take me, please, Grandpa. You promised me."

"Not this time, Fo," said Kellas.

"You said I'm ready! Melisa went out when she was younger than me!"

"Don't argue with me, Fohiono."

"We can fly out tomorrow," said Dannarah as the girl turned away, shoulders heaving. "It's no trouble to take both of you."

The girl turned back eagerly.

"I absolutely refuse it, Fohiono," said Kellas. "As for me, I am not being slung like a sack from one of those cursed eagles. I will make my own way."

"It will take at least twenty days for you to travel overland!" Dannarah protested.

"My arrival will seem less suspicious if I come on my own. Fo, go to bed."

It was the voice Dannarah had heard him use on soldiers.

The young woman obeyed instantly, wiping away tears as she left.

Hari reappeared. He smiled with the most amiable manner imaginable, not a shadow in his face except that cast by lamplight bruised by night. "I'm to escort Lady Dannarah to the loft."

Kellas nodded. "Good night, Lady Dannarah. Will I see you in Toskala?"

"That is up to King Jehosh, is it not? I will return to Horn Hall and await a summons."

They made polite farewells.

Hari escorted Dannarah all the way to the loft in the clearing, deflecting her attempt to question him about his mysterious mother by telling her amusing stories about his childhood that made her laugh. The ordinary tales of a mischievous child who liked to play cheerful pranks were, she thought, his way of letting her know he was a successful merchant with connections, wealth, a large and affectionate family, and hirelings whom he spoke of as if he considered them family, too.

"I am sorry not to have the opportunity to meet your mother," she said as they reached the clearing.

"So you have said five times already," he retorted with a smile.

"And heard the same reply five times over," she replied, wondering what it would have been like to grow up with a cheerful, joking brother like this man. But if he'd grown up in the palace, under her father's eye, he'd not have been so easygoing.

He halted halfway across the clearing, as if to make clear she had to walk the last part on her own. "We are not weapons to be used in your war."

"My war? We all want what is best for the Hundred, do we not?"

"Indeed we do."

"Why is Captain Kellas here?"

"Because he married my mother."

"How long ago?"

"Why do you care? Good night, Lady Dannarah." He left her with the lamp, walking home without it because he was sure of himself in a place he knew so well.

Why *did* she care? It was none of her business. The infatuation she had nursed as an adolescent had long since faded. In all her years as a reeve she had not pined over Kellas. But now she wondered if he had already been involved with this mysterious woman when young Dannarah had demanded he become her lover. Had he met her when he'd tracked Atani to Mar? Imagine how a man might feel, commanded to have sex with one woman when he loved another.

The hells! He'd as good as told her tonight, hadn't he?

You can love someone very much and still make a decision that makes them grieve. You can harm that which you love most because you believe duty outweighs affection.

She had always gotten what she wanted: independence, a reeve's status, lovers as she wanted them, respect, skill, and eventually co-ruler of sorts with her brother. Atani's death had shattered all she had worked for. But afterward she had made a decent life at Horn Hall, taken care of her people, done her duty. Coming here cut a fissure in the world she thought she knew, one that revealed unseen patterns beneath like a broken vessel teeming with maggots aswarm over meat you never knew was rotten.

Reyad was on watch, whittling to pass the time. Tarnit and Lifka slept on bunks built into a back corner. The eagles were settled and quiet. Odd how little she'd had to do with Bronze Hall over the years. Odder still that a loft had been built specifically to facilitate communication between Bronze Hall and Plum Blossom Clan.

"Marshal, did they say anything about the rice?" Reyad asked as she walked up.

"A man like Captain Kellas is not to be caught out easily. We'll have to find out if this variety is grown anywhere else." She studied him. He was carving one part of a leafy branch that resembled the spiky leaves of redheart. "Reyad, do you wish to enlighten me about that little exchange between you and Auri at River's Bend?"

His knife-hand paused. He glanced at her and then away. "No."

"No?"

"No, Marshal, I do not."

She knew exactly how far to push the reeves under her command, so switched tactics. "We can fly out over the Suvash Hills if you'd like. There's no reason we can't stop at your clan's holding on our way back to Horn Hall."

Trembling, he set knife and wood on the dark shavings. "If it would be no trouble... Yes." He pressed a hand to his mouth, lowered it, raised it again to cover his eyes.

"I'll take watch, Reeve."

"Yes, Marshal." He put everything away in his pouch and made his way to the bunks.

She leaned against one of the support pillars; it was too uncomfortable to stand for long periods because her back would hurt. The grass in the clearing glimmered, still wet from the storm. Her bare feet were cold and her heart was stunned.

Atani knew about Hari. That her father had concealed the truth she could understand because he was a private man who never shared his intimate life with anyone, not even her mother, his queen, whom he had never loved nor respected. But for Atani to learn of it and never tell her confounded her. She had shared everything with him, all her hopes and dreams and her ugliest thoughts. Everything!

Every report she had heard about Atani's death mentioned a demon who had spoken familiarly to Atani, who had called him "brother," perhaps in mockery, and then guided Lord Seras's hand in throwing the spear that had killed him. That's how the story was told ever afterward. She had thought it mere embroidery to give Seras's vile act more drama, to make sense of how any person who knew Atani could be driven to kill a man everyone loved and respected.

Atani's disappearance and return at sixteen took on a more ominous cast. It seemed likely he had discovered the truth about Hari, and still he had not shared what he had learned with her. She should have asked Hari if he had ever met Atani, if Atani had visited here more than once. If they had become acquainted as brothers. Fishing back through her memories she recalled bitterly how, the evening before he was killed, Atani had said some strange things to her about demons that she hadn't understood at the time. Had a demon stalked him and he'd been afraid to confess his fear? What if he had been trying to confide in her and she hadn't listened?

Wings fluttered across her sight, and she jerked back, banging her shoulders against the wall. But it was only a nightjar that vanished away above the roofs of the town. Following its flight drew her gaze to a break in the clearing.

A figure stood in the shadows, wrapped in cloth. After a moment its shoulders tensed with determination and the creature strode forward, swishing through the grass to reveal itself as a granddaughter, wearing a long shawl wrapped around her body.

"Fohiono," said Dannarah by way of making sure she remembered the name correctly.

"Marshal Dannarah, take me with you to the palace when you leave at dawn."

Dannarah studied the girl's shining face and fierce gaze. "I am not in the habit of carrying off a young person when their elders have already forbidden it."

"He doesn't understand!" said Fohiono with passionate intensity. "I have trained since I was seven to be skilled at all the things he is skilled at. Why won't he let me go with him?"

"He's protecting you."

She pressed a fist to her forehead, then lowered it. "No one protected him."

"That your grandfather cares for you enough to protect you is the burden you carry. If you sneak away with us and harm comes to you, he will mourn you for the rest of his life. Do you want to be responsible for his grief?"

She looked away.

"Love can cut as well as nurture," Dannarah added.

"No one is ever weakened by love," she retorted. "That's what Grandmama says."

"Your mysterious grandmother, of whom I had never heard before today and cannot meet because she is not here. Who seems to have given birth to a son sired by my father, a child I had never heard the least whisper of before today. What else can you tell me?"

The girl met her gaze squarely. "You won't take me no matter what. But I had to ask."

"You remind me of Kellas," said Dannarah wryly, already liking the girl. "Tight-lipped. Disciplined. Hard to take by surprise."

"My thanks. I take that as the highest praise."

"As you should, for it is meant that way." This was the girl Lifka had been friendly with, something to consider for later. There was more than one way to worm into a close-knit clan's confidence. "I was seven years old when I saw Captain Kellas for the first time, did you know that?"

"When he was brought into King Anjihosh's service because

he climbed Law Rock even though it was forbidden? Yes, he's told us that story."

"There must be some story I can tell you about your grand-father that you haven't heard." A vicious little voice woke, prod-ding her to shock the poor girl, but she ventured into safer waters. "Like the time he saved King Anjihosh from getting an arrow in the back."

"That's his shoulder scar," said the girl, unperturbed in a way that allowed Dannarah to see how much of Kellas's aplomb she had absorbed. "When he threw himself between the king and the enemy."

"Marshal?" Tarnit's voice called softly from the bunks. "Is all well?"

"Just visiting with one of the clan. All's well. Go back to sleep."

"I'd better go." Fohiono lingered, making no move to leave. "What is King Jehosh like? Is he as brilliant and ruthless as King Anjihosh? As wise and compassionate as King Atani?"

"Jehosh is his own man," Dannarah temporized.

A gust of air made the grass shiver. Mist swirled up where the path met the clearing, only to resolve into a woman watching them. What Dannarah had taken for mist was in fact a cloak white as bone that stirred mistlike in the blowsy wind. With absolute certainty Dannarah knew she was facing a demon.

Fohiono huffed out a breath, then made a curt fare-thee-well and stomped down through the clearing. Meeting the demon as if it were an ordinary woman, she ducked her head like a scolded child, said something with a defiant twitch of her shoul-ders, and vanished down the path, headed for home. She was no more surprised to meet a demon in the clearing than she would have been surprised to see an owl swoop past.

The girl was gone but the demon remained.

Dannarah had never in her long life shrunk from a confrontation. She pushed away from the wall and headed down. The darkness made it hard to see but the demon did indeed look like an ordinary woman, one somewhat younger than Tarnit. She was even dressed like a reeve, with an attractive face and a confident stance. Nothing frightening about her at all. Across the gap their gazes met.

A vision of the past blossomed so vividly in her head that it slammed Dannarah to a halt.

The wind buffets her and Jehosh where they stand on his balcony. Far below the boats on the river look like toys. "I need your help, Aunt Dannarah; I am losing control of the palace," he says as memory skips forward through their conversation. "What person can I trust?"

"Captain Kellas survived."

Yet all through their discussion she thinks of how ironic it is that she had once ordered Kellas to kill Jehosh.

As if a gale has torn tiles off a roof, her recent meeting with Jehosh scatters and an older memory emerges: She unhooks herself from Terror and runs across a clearing to where Atani lies unmoving on the cold earth, his long black hair fanned out around him and blood seeping from the wound in his back.

Her entire being, all of her mind, winces away from the dreadful memory and the piercing grief. Anything is better than remembering his death.

The demon claws her yet farther back into memories of her youth.

"Captain Kellas, does my father know you are here?" says the girl she was a long time ago.

"He does, Lady Dannarah," he answers.

Too restless to sit, seventeen-year-old Dannarah paces along a balcony overlooking the ocean at the estate where her mother retreats when she needs a break from the endless intrigues of the palace. The man she admires above all others stands by the door with hands clasped behind his back, watching her with an impassive expression. She is all quivering emotion: joy, anger, demands, ambition, everything on the surface. He never shows the least sign of fear or alarm or pain or anger. He is all the things she wants to be: brave, accomplished, strong, smart, observant, and calm. Except she also wants to be king. She wants a lot of things. She wants a man like him to be in love with her in part because she's not meant to have a lover at all and it will shock both her mother and her father, but mostly because she is furiously, ridiculously infatuated with him. She has made a story that he secretly pines for her although a princess like her is utterly forbidden to a humble soldier like him. She pretends she is beautiful even though she knows she isn't. But strength of mind is alluring. Youth is alluring. Power is alluring.

If she gives him a direct order he cannot say no.

"Curse it," Dannarah said aloud, brushing a hand over her eyes to break the gaze that had hooked her into the past. "I am too cursed old for this. I was reckless and a fool and selfish, and I never thought about anyone's desires but my own. Are you content, demon? Do you want me to be ashamed? Or have you some other scheme in mind?"

The crinkling crow's-feet at the demon's eyes gave her a look of weary resignation, rather like Dannarah herself when she was disappointed in one of the reeves under her command. "I do not expect you to trust me. But I did want to see for myself if we can trust you."

"Of course you can't trust me! Steel can't kill you, but it will stop you for long enough that I can tear off your poisonous skin."

"That's how Captain Anji taught his soldiers to hunt down and kill demons."

"King Anjihosh is his proper name."

"He was called Captain Anji when he came to the Hundred, before you were born, Lady Dannarah. He took what did not belong to him."

"He didn't take anything. He saved the Hundred from destruction and war. He brought stability and prosperity. Do not trouble me with your lies and lures."

"My lies and lures? Isn't that a line from the Tale of the Young Carpenter and the Three Lilu?" The demon chuckled as might a comrade when friendly companions are drinking at an inn. The laugh made Dannarah want to trust her, for she wore the aspect of a woman of intelligence and humor. "I am not trying to seduce you."

"Of course you are! Seduction is about changing people's hearts and convincing them to act against what they know is right for them. As I did, when I was seventeen and tried to seduce Captain Kellas. When I failed, I used my position to demand he become my lover. I'm not proud of what I did, and it was a long time ago. But you did not answer my question, demon. What do you want from me?"

"I wanted to discover if King Jehosh's summons is an honest one. It seems that as far as you know, it is."

"Why do you care about Jehosh's honesty? What can demons know of honesty or loyalty? Are the accusations true? Did you and the other demons plot Atani's murder?"

"Atani was the last person we would have wanted dead. Did he trust you so little that he never told you anything? Or did he know you were too much your father's daughter to be trusted?"

The earth swayed under Dannarah like a ship in stormy seas. Staggering, she fell to hands and knees. Only after sucking in deep breaths could she steady her dizzied vision. When she at last raised her head, the demon was gone.

Wind stirred in the foliage, then abruptly died. The whole world seemed to cup around her like she was a seed in a bowl of ill fortune, about to be ground down by the hammer of truth.

Atani hadn't trusted her.

24

For the first stage of her journey to meet the man she had demanded to marry, Sarai traveled in a closed carriage down-stream alongside the River Elshar to where it met the east-flowing Lesser Istri. At the town of Eleford Wash she and her uncle and cousin transferred to a barge.

From the vantage point of a screened and roofed balcony built atop the main cabin she reveled in her freedom as the days went by and she watched the shoreline pass. Villages sprouted in picturesque clusters on the banks. Men tended rice fields wearing nothing more than a linen kilt tied around their waists, their brown skin damp with sweat and rain. Women walked about at all manner of work, usually wearing the wrapped dress called a taloos but sometimes wearing no more than the men.

Every night when they tied up she interrogated Uncle Abrisho and Cousin Beniel.

"I read in one of Uncle Makel's books that in Sirniaka women live and work separately from men? Do women in the palace live entirely apart? Do they cover their hair? What do I need to know? I should not like to make a bad impression."

Her uncle pressed his hands together, preparatory to a lecture. "King Jehosh has two queens. Queen Chorannah is a noble princess from the Sirniakan Empire. She lives in the upper palace atop Law Rock according to Sirniakan custom, as you say, women separated from men. They dress modestly and rarely appear in public but when they do they cover their hair. Queen Dia is from Ithik Eldim. Some say the northerners are barbarians but by all accounts she is a savvy businesswoman. However she worships neither Beltak nor the seven Hundred gods but a northern god, and she has few allies at court except the king. He built the lower palace for her."

Beniel topped off his cup, his moon face already shining with the kiss of rice wine. "Lord Gilaras is a favorite companion of Prince Kasad, Queen Dia's only son. I'm part of their circle, too. I have been invited to five of the drinking parties hosted by Lord Tyras of Clan White Leaf. I was allowed to be one of the party when there was a horse race across Old Camp between Lord Gilaras and Prince Kasad. Lord Gilaras won, of course." He had the breathless excitement of a pampered puppy scampering after feral dogs. "King Jehosh favors Queen Dia. So that will be good for you, Sarai."

"I cannot like these irresponsible adventures and the disrespectful way of speaking you have picked up from the young lords." Abrisho patted his forehead with a linen cloth, for it was hot and humid, awaiting rain. "The king favors Queen Dia's bed. That is not the same thing as Dia having power within the palace administration. You must tread carefully, Sarai. Lord Gilaras's brothers have served loyally in the army and restored some of the family's honor although not their fortune. But Gilaras's uncle, Lord Vanas, still bears a grudge toward that branch of the clan because gossip says he has never forgiven his older brother for vilely murdering King Atani and thus tarnishing the memory of their noble progenitor, the famous General Sengel—"

"Who was one of the most trusted officers of King Anjihosh. Yes, I remember, Uncle. Are you saying Lord Vanas will try to undermine any attempts by Lord Gilaras to make a place for himself at court? Does Vanas have the influence to do so?"

"He controls the treasury."

"Then why marry me to Lord Gilaras, if Lord Vanas hates his branch of the family?"

"No one else is desperate enough to marry a Ri Amarah girl. It is worth the risk, Sarai. Even if they never get farther in than the fringe of court circles they still give us access to clans with whom we would like to set up trade arrangements."

Abrisho nursed his sweet tea as if it were the last cup he would ever see, even though on the river he downed four cups every day to settle his stomach because water travel did not agree with him. Nothing agreed with him, Sarai thought, watching the way he turned the cup, sipped at one side, then turned it to sip at the other, always turning and always restless.

"You have to make a life in the palace, Sarai. You can visit our clan as a guest but never again with the intimacy of a Ri Amarah woman."

"How am I to manage with no support or advice from the women of my own people?"

"Of course you will consult with me frequently! You have a Book of Accounts. Record everything in it in our usual code, and we will go over it weekly."

"I have no woman's mirror," she said, to see how they would react.

Beniel flinched.

Abrisho slapped a hand down on the table so hard the teacup spilled. "You must never speak of that which we keep secret. Our lives depend on our silence and our adherence to the law!"

"Of course, Uncle." Her hand trembled as she set out brush and ink and paper. Fear fluttered through her breast. What if the women found out what she'd done? But she refused to regret it. Her mother would have wanted her to have the mirror.

Recording her day's observations in the letter she was writing for Great-Aunt Tsania calmed her. As she wrote, Abrisho scolded Beniel for drinking too much wine, the words flowing past her in much the same way as the sound of the river rolled along as background noise. Out on the barge the rivermen smoked pipes and chatted among themselves. Their accent had an intonation different from the speech of Yava and Elit. It reminded her of gardener Zilli's; Yava had said he was a newcomer to the area, and apparently he and Elit were allies in some smoky business to do with escaped prisoners being hunted by the King's Spears.

She had to believe Elit was not involved in any criminal acts. Anyway she could not help but think sympathetically toward people being hunted down by the king's soldiers, considering her mother had been ruthlessly slaughtered by Black Wolves. That detail was all she knew; it was all anyone in the family knew, really. Her mother had married the richest Ri Amarah man in the Hundred, given birth to a boy and then, later, to Sarai, and afterward fled her home, leaving the boy behind but taking the infant girl with her. Just because Nadai had fled with a wagon driver who was later involved in the murder of King Atani did not mean her mother had been part of the conspiracy, but how could Sarai ever know what the truth was? Proximity equaled guilt. Her mother had been there.

The river widened. They passed towns with houses strung like beads along cobbled streets. Here the banks of the rice fields were feathered with mulberry trees. Cows and sheep grazed in grassy clearings. Necklaces of flowers draped doors and gates. It was a different world, brilliant with color and life. Every bend in the river brought new sights, which she compared with descriptions she had read in books.

One late afternoon the cook fires of dusk hazed the air with a thicker veil than usual. In every direction lamps glittered and fires gleamed. As full night fell, a golden smear brushing the eastern horizon resolved into a beast with a hundred hundred lit eyes: They had reached Toskala.

When the barge was tied up to the dock Beniel left to fetch a carriage. The water that lapped around the barge reeked of rubbish and urine. Voices drifted over the water, their speech as abrupt as hammering rain. Her stomach felt queasy from the heat and the stink and the knowledge that she had come too far to turn back. She grabbed the washbasin just in time to throw up the rice porridge and leek chicken she had eaten earlier.

Uncle Abrisho slid the cabin door aside. "What is that smell?"

"My apologies, Uncle, I am not feeling well."

"This is a sorry note! I hope you are not sickening. We have arrived just in time. The marriage procession and feast will take place tomorrow!"

"Why so soon?"

"The Hundred-folk take auguries—"

"That's right," she broke in, feeling a spurt of interest that took her mind off her nervousness. "They take auguries for the most beneficent days for weddings and funerals and any fresh enterprise, according to their calendar in which each day of the year is designated by one of twelve animals and one of three states, resting, wakened, and transcendent. So, for example, each new year and new month always begin on the day called Resting Eagle. Tomorrow is—"

"Evidently considered a prosperous day for a wedding," he broke in impatiently. "Which is just as well, since it is best we get it done quickly."

He did not say *before they change their minds* but she could almost hear his thought.

"Also Beniel has returned with excellent news," he added. "A suite of rooms awaits you in the lower palace. This is a promising start."

She clasped her hands together, unable to shake her anxiety. "Am I not even to be allowed to spend one night in the family compound among familiar things?"

He shook his head decisively. "You can no longer enter the women's compound, Sarai."

"Never?" Her voice quavered.

"You never have been truly a daughter of the Ri Amarah. Surely you have always understood that your mother's shame makes that impossible."

He spoke so calmly that the words hurt worse for his indifference. She pressed a hand to her throat, wondering if she could even count herself as a living, breathing person if she had no kin to call her own, but her heart beat stubbornly and her breath slipped in and out just as always.

Abrisho gave a grimace. "You understood the bargain when you made it, Sarai. You will sleep tonight in the place where you will live henceforth. Now come along."

As the carriage rolled through the streets Abrisho said no kindly words to reassure her that all would be well, so in her mind she composed a letter to Tsania about the evening smells and sounds of Toskala. By identifying and cataloging them, she found it was easy to forget the dreary dark passage. Of course her family did not want her and were happy to be rid of her stained and shameful presence. But now she was free to explore outside the confines of the estate's walls.

At length the carriage came to a stop. Guardsmen demanded a pass for entrance. The wheels rattled on a graveled surface, then on a smooth one, then ceased their turning. She emerged from the carriage with her lower face covered by her shawl to find two women standing beside an open gate. The high wooden doors were carved with scenes the lamplight was not strong enough to illuminate. Everything was half seen and imperfectly understood.

"Verea, greetings of the evening," said the older of the women. "We are hirelings brought in to help you get settled until you can arrange for your own people. I am Welo. This is my niece Iadit. My two nephews are downstairs but will stay out of your way. For indoor servants we have myself, Iadit, and two girls to clean. If you approve, verea."

"My thanks, verea."

The woman had the solid, amiable features of a Hundred-born woman, and although she was short and stocky instead of tall and portly she reminded Sarai of Yava. The niece was about Sarai's age, thin, with her thick black hair braided into a decorative knot at the back of her head. When Iadit caught Sarai's gaze she winked, a bold gesture that made Sarai flush for she had no idea how she might properly respond. Not that they could see anything but her eyes.

"I'll leave you here. We will come tomorrow for the sealing of the contract and the wedding feast." Abrisho abandoned her without even asking to inspect the interior.

"Here now, be welcome, verea," said Welo with a thought-ful frown as she escorted Sarai across the threshold and into a courtyard barely large enough to receive visitors on a narrow veranda. On this raised porch they took off their shoes. Welo led her up a flight of stairs to a second veranda and into a square room fitted with lamps, woven mats for flooring, a painted screen depicting cranes and flowers, and cushions arranged for seating.

Iadit opened sliding doors to reveal a balcony looking over an expansive garden from which singing and laughter floated up. Welo herded her past the overlook and into a private chamber with doors slid aside to reveal shelves on one side and a small lattice-screened balcony on another.

"There are refreshments on the balcony, verea. Iadit can unroll your bed and make you comfortable for the night. You have traveled a long way."

Sarai felt like a rat caught in lamplight. The shawl she still held across her face gave her the courage to speak. "My thanks, verea. If Iadit would show me how to arrange the bedding I would be grateful. We use a different manner of bed and I do not mean by that to suggest I am displeased, not at all, it's just that I don't know how to make this one into a place to sleep. Afterward, if you please, might I perhaps be alone and we can take up this conversation in the morning for I am indeed very tired from my journey."

She silently chided herself for how breathless and rude she sounded. And she had forgotten to ask how she might wash and relieve herself! She had a sudden urge to laugh, imagining herself jiggling all night unable to sleep lest she wet herself for not having found a toilet.

"It is understandable things seem strange in a new place, verea." At a signal from her aunt, Iadit tugged a large rolled-up mattress from the shelves, unrolled it, and briskly dressed it with linen as Welo continued speaking. "Private stairs behind this screen lead down to a washroom and a sand toilet that a man rakes clean every day. If you need us, Iadit and I will be down the stairs in the kitchen wing. Do not hesitate to disturb us, verea."

"My thanks."

They left. She set down the bag and cast the shawl onto the

bed. Barefoot she crept down the back steps, so narrow her shoulders almost brushed either wall, and at the base discovered sandals woven from reeds for her to slip on so she could relieve herself. Afterward she washed in a separate chamber with a brass washtub and cold water piped through bamboo. She pulled on a gauzy nightshift conveniently left beside the towels.

Upstairs, she ventured onto the private enclosed balcony, where she discovered rice wine, pear juice enlivened with ginger, and a tray of food: sweetened bean curd wrapped in a woven latticework of noodles, thin slices of beef, grilled fish, melon carved into the shape of a bird.

The sound of a stark gasp jolted her.

She raised the lamp to reveal a young man seated in the shadowed corner.

"I have servants here," she said as calmly as she could manage past her racing heart. "I can scream. I will throw the lamp at you. Hot oil scalds."

A shallow saucer-like wine cup rested in his upraised palm. His eyes were wide with astonishment.

"How in the hells did you get that scar?" he asked in the friendly tone of a man who is happily drunk and therefore not yet maudlin or cruel. He had an attractive face, long black hair bound up in the topknot worn by military men, and the look of a person not at all concerned that he is sitting where he ought not be.

"I will consider telling you the answer to your boringly obvious question if you will tell me who you are...No. Wait. Perhaps I would rather not know."

He grinned, egging her on.

She raised her free hand to brush her left cheek. "Is it that frightful?"

"Not at all. It's a striking white curve, as delicate as the most perfect brushwork on a masterfully glazed bowl. It has the flare of a crescent moon, as if you were kissed by the old goddess Atiratu the Huntress, not that I mean any insult since I know you have your own gods and my people worship at the shrine of Beltak but that's really only for political reasons if you see what I mean. But what kind of cut would leave such a scar as that? That's what I can't figure."

Her anger had drained away at the mention of moons and flares and kisses and perfection, and she was growing increasingly more curious. "Are you drunk or do you always talk like this?"

He saluted her with the cup. "Drunk with your beauty."

She stifled a giggle, for the gesture was both theatrical and somehow sweet. "Yet I note you have not yet drunk from the cup, not in my seeing. So I must conclude you are a criminal about some complicated fraud. Or a reckless ne'er-do-well with more hair than wit sneaking about where he is not wanted. Or you are Gilaras Herelian."

He gestured again with the cup to acknowledge her accuracy but by his tone he sounded a trifle disappointed. "Can I not be all three?"

"I forgot the fourth possibility."

His grin flashed with such brilliance that it hit her like a blow. She caught in her breath.

He leaned forward. "Please do tell me."

"A reeve warned me I would be a swan among feral dogs."

"She must have seen your beautiful face."

She shook her head to warn him off his nonsense. "Do you honestly expect me to believe you think my face is beautiful?"

"It is beautiful to me."

She wanted to make him smile again, and wanting anything from him made her speak tartly. "My face? Or my treasury?"

He rocked back, spilling a few drops of wine. "My dearest...
May I call you Sarai-ya? I have been at some pains to ascertain
what the correct form might be and no one seems to know."

Sarai-ya was the form of her name used as an endearment.
For a moment she could not speak and could scarcely breathe,
not knowing what the bright laughter in his eyes meant.

He had already gone on, taking her silence for assent. "Treasury used in that way is a poet's allusion to a woman's..." He
essayed a tight oval with his cupless hand.

Perhaps she ought to have blushed but instead she laughed.
"Do you really think my face is beautiful and hope my treasury
may be likewise, or are you most struck by the beauty of my
abundant chests of coin, which are meant to restore your family's fortunes and, it appears, your own? For if the story I hear
is accurate, then you are an irresponsible troublemaker whose
only value to your clan is that you are the last man among them
who carries a treasury of his own."

"No, no, a man doesn't have a treasury." There blazed the
smile again. "He has eggs or sacks and a...Do I need to go on?"

She raised the lamp. "Are you blushing?"

"No more than you are!"

He set down the cup on a side table whose wood was inlaid
with a mosaic of flowers and vines, astonishing work that distracted her briefly. The steadiness of his hand gave him away.

"You're just pretending to be drunk to give yourself an excuse
to have crept up here where you are not meant to be. In case I
objected, or someone caught you."

He studied her in silence for long enough that she quirked an
eyebrow.

He shrugged. "We are meant to meet tomorrow when the
contract is sealed and your abundant chests of coin handed over
into my family's coffers. I wanted to see and speak to you before
the rest get their claws in. They're lilu, all of them."

"Lilu are demons who suck the juice and life out of their prey. I'm surprised you would compare your family to demons."

"You won't be once you meet them. Never trust them, no matter how pleasantly they greet you. They connived over what hirelings to insinuate into the household so they could spy on us. I arranged for these hirelings myself. Welo and I are old friends from back when she cooked at the wrestling guild I briefly attended. Iadit was my first lover although that was some years ago . . ." He paused, taking in the expression that pinched her face.

It seemed odd for him to so casually remark on the fact. She wondered if he thought it such a commonplace admission that she would find it of no significance. "Your first lover?"

"Yes, we were both sixteen and eager to try it out. It was enjoyable enough but she isn't really my type. She's not got enough flesh on her. Anyway she was already sure she preferred women. She needed a trusted friend to see if men held any interest."

She spoke more sharply than she intended. "If you were her only male lover how could she know if it was men in the entirety or just you she found unexciting?"

"A point I long worried over as a dog worries over a bone, you can be sure! But I tell you all this so you know I trust Iadit more than I trust my own sister, which I admit is not saying much. Iadit is the one who kicks me when I'm an idiot and an ass."

"Are you often an idiot and ass?"

"As often as possible. I hate my life."

"Does she trust you?"

He slapped a hand to his gut as at a hit. "There's the blade wielded against me. I like to think she does but I'm not sure I can be trusted. I like you, and you being a sensible, calm, attractive, and clever woman is far more than I expected."

"Is that what you came to tell me?"

At last he took the cup, sipped, and offered it to her as if sharing a cup of warm rice wine between them meant something to him that she did not understand, a pledge or an oath. Cautiously she took it and sipped in turn. The wine had a soft flavor, not too sweet or too dry.

"I don't know what I meant to say when I first saw you come in," he admitted, watching her set down the cup beside the lacquered tray of food as if the shape of her hand fascinated him. "It's the scar. Not that it's ugly, not at all. It's just so visible and large and unexpected that it startled me. Having said such a rude thing to start I suppose I feel I can say anything and it won't offend you."

"You haven't tried very hard to offend me."

His gaze brushed up to her uncovered hair. "Do you have horns?"

She threw the wine into his face.

The dimpling smile and merry wit vanished as wine dribbled down his skin. Bitterness creased his eyes, a glimpse into the feral dog. "I saw horns on a dead Silver man. No longer than my thumb."

Shaking, she stood. "Please stop. I liked you until just now."

He rose and retreated to the balcony's lattice screen. "My apologies, Sarai-ya. I'm accustomed to saying whatever I want, and the more crass the better."

"To speak of such matters is forbidden." All the years the taboo had been hammered in fell like a bolt on her tongue: Men may never witness women's magic. No woman may speak of men's horns. If she could have scoured out her ears and unheard his words, she would have.

He wiped wine from his cheeks like tears. "I truly did not hope to offend. Best if I go."

"Why did you say it if you didn't hope to offend?"

He watched her cautiously. "Because I'm curious. Wouldn't you be?"

If he was angry at her for throwing the wine she saw no sign of it. "I would be curious, too. You shouldn't have said it. But I'm sorry about the wine."

"No, it was the right thing to do. I thought it was charming."

"*Charming?* To toss wine in your face?"

He smiled. "I truly am sorry. Please forgive my rudeness. I will see you tomorrow."

He unlatched a section of the lattice although to her eyes it looked like a single piece.

"Are there hidden hooks? A secret ladder?"

"There are hooks but no ladder. The vines are strong enough to hold my weight if you know where to put your hands and feet. Do you want me to show you?"

"In my nightshift?"

"I had noticed you've nothing on beneath it, because the fabric is thin and the light is behind you. Not that there's any reason you should have anything on beneath. I usually sleep naked. Which is something you may discover for yourself. If you wish."

She ought to have been embarrassed but she was going to marry this man tomorrow.

She took the chance to look him over: The way his mouth could smile or sulk. The scuffed and worn knees of his leather trousers, cut like those worn by reeves and meant for climbing and running. His dimple peeping out as he watched her peruse him from top to bottom and up again as if he guessed she was measuring what he might look like without clothes.

He came here to be honest, she thought. *He came here to defy them.*

"It's a sword cut," she said.

He whistled, taken aback. "The scar is a sword cut. How did you survive it?"

She touched the scar on her cheek. "My mother was cut down by soldiers while she was holding me. The sword cut peeled away a flap of skin on my cheek. Exposed down to the bone, I am told. My clan calls it the mark of my shame."

"The hells!" Unexpectedly he took her hand in his and kissed the tips of her fingers, each one in turn. His lips were cool and dry. "We will make you the prize of court, Sarai-ya. Women will paint scars on their faces and hope to look like you."

Lamplight made his skin glow. His nose was slightly crooked as if it had been broken. It was charming. He was charming.

Perhaps she leaned closer or perhaps he did. His breath misted her scarred cheek. Lifting her chin brought her mouth up. They kissed lightly the first time like a brush testing paper, then a second time more deeply with a thrill that flowed down her skin and into her genitals.

A shrill whistle penetrated the quiet of the space. Breaking off, they both blinked. It took her a moment to remember where she was and why she was here.

"The hells," he said, releasing her hand. "That's the watch. I have to go before the gates close at midnight. Tomorrow then, Sarai-ya."

He swung open the secret door and climbed down into the dark pool of the garden. The scratch and creak of his passage on the vines made a kind of music as she breathed through the pounding of her heart. When he was gone, she paced herself back to stillness.

But the calm was a lie.

Years ago she had made a journey in the back of a wagon through no volition of her own, an abandoned infant born in shame, irrevocably tainted. For so long she had believed she had no choice but to make herself content with scraps. Now she had fetched up on a new shore at her own choosing. The curse of longing she had spent all her life crushing into silence burst so hard in her heart that it hurt, but this time the pain made her smile.

25

Gil found his friends in a riverside tavern called the Drunken Fish.

"What took you so long?" Tyras made an effort to get up and decided against it when he couldn't keep his legs under him. "Did you get into the lower palace?"

"I told you he couldn't." For once Kasad looked less drunk than Ty.

"Did you see your betrothed? Does she have horns?"

"I'm tired," Gil snapped, suddenly bored. "I'm going home."

Kasad began to sing "He Climbed Up to Her Open Window."

Something about Kasad's smirk spiked the mellow pleasure Gil had taken in his secret expedition. His temper had been sleeping but it all went sour before Kasad got to the lewd chorus.

His hands went to fists.

Tyras passed out, slumping over the table.

Kasad broke off the tune, and for an instant Gil thought he meant to apologize.

"My father the king knows about your betrothal, Gil. Beware. He's going to ask to have her brought to his audience hall to make her obeisance before him."

He drawled out the word *obeisance*. Gil hauled Kasad to his feet, jostling the low table. Rice wine spilled in streams. Tyras sprawled limply, an arm flopping to the floor.

"I will put my fist in your face or possibly up your fucking ass. Shut the hells up."

Kasad was drunk enough to laugh. Seeing how many people in the tavern had turned to look, Gil dropped him. Kasad sat heavily.

Everyone knew them here. Over in one corner a group of young men who nipped at his and Kas's and Ty's heels like hopeful suitors were watching. A young Silver man who was trying to graze his way into the inner court circles sat with a number of younger sons and junior military captains. Curse it! Wasn't this fawning Silver a cousin to Sarai-ya?

Gil righted the table, picked up all the fallen cups, adjusted Tyras's head so that if he threw up he wouldn't choke on his own vomit, and tossed a pair of leya to the man tending the counter to pay for the mess.

"I was just joking!" said Kasad as he rubbed a smear of blood from his bleeding nose.

Gil did not even recall punching him.

"You should be the last one to joke about your father the king lusting after women. One of my brothers died because of a war your father fought so he could kidnap your mother."

Kasad boiled up and punched Gil so hard in the chest that he staggered back, coughing, and slammed into the men seated behind them.

The men nervously righted him and shoved him back toward Kasad.

The prince faced him, both fists raised. "The king fought the war to save the Hundred from outlaws, bandits, and raiders, you ass. Your brothers lost their balls because of your father's treachery. Don't blame the king for that."

The entire tavern had gone quiet.

Gil was still trying to catch his breath from the force of Kasad's punch.

Kasad closed the gap between them as the men they had disturbed scrambled to get out of the way. He leaned close, his wine-soaked breath flying like a lover's chance-met promise along Gil's cheek. "Leave my mother out of this or any public dispute."

Gil sucked in air. "Leave my wife out of this or any public dispute. I'll kill your father if he tries to touch her just to add her as a prize curiosity to his warehouse of conquests."

Kasad laughed and, putting an arm around Gil, whispered into his ear. "If you do kill him, give me warning so I can hide before Farihosh becomes king and Queen Chorannah finally succeeds in having me murdered the way they do in the empire to less powerful sons."

The words froze Gil to the bone. "Fuck your brothers and their mother, too! I'll not let anyone murder you. Unless I kill you."

Kasad broke off the embrace with a kiss and shook free. "My loyal Gilaras! You did sneak into the lower palace, didn't you? You saw her. That's what's put you in this raw felting."

When in the hells had Kasad gotten so observant? Gil turned away before Kasad could scrutinize his expression. "I have to go. Take Ty home, will you? Before he chokes on himself."

From across the room the young Silver was gazing at him as though hopeful of gaining his notice, so Gil made the gesture called *hail, my friend* commonly used in the staged plays adapted from the talking stories: When two characters first met, the audience would know without needing any further explanation that the two people already knew and trusted each other. The lad brightened as if a hundred lamps had just been lit around him. His companions slapped his back.

Chatter started up again as Gil went out onto the porch and squinted for his sandals. Weariness dragged at his limbs. He hailed a pair of men in charge of a drab litter and let them convey him through Flag Quarter to the large compound facing Banner Square that was Clan Herelia. The gate guards paid the litter-bearers. It was still early enough that the family audience hall and the evening parlor were lit, many voices rising as the family celebrated their triumph. He hugged the shadows and made it to the tiny cubicle where he rarely slept. No one had replenished the water in the washing pitcher, curse them. They never bothered to take care of him or notice where he was or what he was doing unless he got into trouble. After he pulled the lumpy bedding out of the closest and unrolled it, he took the pitcher to the well in the back courtyard, did his business, and went to sleep.

Waking in the morning with a sour mouth, he blinked at the way light filtered in a strange pattern across the mats until he realized he was seeing the angles of an early-morning sun.

During the night his mind had come unmoored. It took all his concentration to rise, dress in his threadbare jacket and faded trousers, and wander the compound staring at the convulsions of activity. The guest kitchen—closed for years due to lack of funds—was being cleaned and furnished for the expected banquets and entertaining that would follow on his marriage. The Ivory Audience Hall and the Jasmine Morning Parlor were being re-roofed and new mats and screens brought in. A wagon trundled into the courtyard, piled high with embroidered silk cushions.

In the family eating hall his older sister Sinara made him sit beside her over a tray of rice soaked in tea, pickled cucumber and radish, bream stewed with walnut and pepper, and roasted eggs.

"How soon can you get me a line of credit on Silk Street?" she demanded. "I am ashamed that I must appear today at the banquet and the marriage sealing in such faded silks."

"Whatever you wish, my darling Sinara. I will be as generous to you as you have ever been ungenerous to me. But if you are unkind to the woman I am marrying or if I ever hear any least whisper of gossip or sneering about her and can trace it to your nasty jealous tongue, I will have your name struck out at every shop where you might ever wish to buy silks and baubles."

Sinara was a pretty woman and she knew it, but the flicker of ugliness that flashed when she forced a frown into a smile revealed the truth of her. "Why do you hate me so, Gil? What have I ever done to you?"

"What have you ever not done? Got me arrested the first time."

"Don't fault me! Fault your stupid prank and your more stupid friends. I was just protecting my prospects. It wasn't easy for me to get the Black Petals Clan to agree to allow Lati to court me."

"You offered me up on a platter so his clan could get the reward."

"I'm not the one who stole the planks out of Guardian Bridge! Why do you insist on blaming me, Gil? Why do you never blame yourself? Our brothers lost everything."

"It's not my fault our mother was still pregnant with me when the command came down to castrate all the household sons of this traitorous branch. That's one thing you can't lay at my feet!"

She had eaten most of the food off the tray but he snagged the last egg before she put her grasping fingers on it. He hadn't had an egg for months. The family could not afford them.

"You're such an ass, Gil."

"Everyone says so," he agreed before he remembered how Sarai-ya had laughed. The memory of her throwing the wine into his face made him smile. There was one person in his rotten life who might judge him not for his reputation but for what he actually said. He was glad of the marriage now, and he wasn't just thinking that because the thin shift had done nothing to conceal her full breasts and belly and her round thighs and the dark mat of hair nestled between them. Even so it was the easy way they had conversed that stayed with him.

He popped the egg in his mouth and savored the smear of the yolk. After this he could have an egg every day and not waste a moment's thought over the luxury.

"You have such a smirk, thinking you've done so well for yourself." She dug her fingernails into his forearm. "She's probably ugly. Don't you ever wonder why the Silvers would give up one of their women when you know they never marry outside their own people? There's something wrong with her, I'm sure of it. Some reason none of their own men will have her."

He bent an affectionately false smile on her, catching one of her arms behind her back so she could not pull away as she instinctively tried to do. "My darling Sinara, do me one favor. Do not visit me or my wife in our new rooms in the lower palace for any reason except the required family wedding visit. Marry your unctuous toad-licker and I wish you well of him and his nasty ass-nuzzling clan. But remember through whose offices the money has come to this family. If you want your children to receive a single vey of spending coin you will stay away from me and my wife."

He released her.

She straightened her sleeves. "You are so contemptible."

"As for your line of credit on Silk Street, you may apply to Shevad. Don't ask me again."

Her upper lip trembled. She dabbed at an eye.

"Your tears don't work on me."

Gil threaded his way out of the eating hall. He was stopped at least ten times by cousins and hangers-on congratulating him but escaped at last only to have his brother Usi cut him off on the porch.

"Shevad desires the pleasure of your company." Usi was the youngest of the boys who had survived the cutting. He had been five. While Shevad and Yofar had gone into the military to prove their loyalty, Usi had taken to writing plays and poems for Bell Quarter entertainers. He had become so well known that palace courtiers who had pretensions to be lauded as singers and actors commissioned him to write flattering love songs and poetic sketches for them to perform.

"What does he want to see me for?" Gil studied Usi's face looking for some twitch that might reveal Shevad's intentions.

Usi shook his head wearily. "I don't know, Gil. Maybe he wants to make sure you intend to go through with it and not leave us hanging from the rafters with our mouths gaping open and our cocks stuffed in them so we are made to look fools in front of the entire court just at our moment of triumph."

Gil raised both hands palms up, placed them on his chest, and bowed as younger to older. "I am yours to command, older brother."

"Let the sarcasm sink to the muddy bottom of the well, my brother. Confine yourself to sulking fury and unmuzzled biting."

"I have to go to the market. I'll come see Shev afterward."

"To the market? Why?"

"I thought I should buy a trifling wedding gift for my betrothed."

Usi's brows wrinkled. "What an odd notion for you to get. You can send one of the hirelings out to do that, can you not?"

"No."

"Come see Shev first and then I'll go with you. I know all the best places."

"I want to do this alone."

"Usually you hate being alone. You're always flying around with that restless flock that hovers under the shade of Prince Kasad's tender wings."

"I like to think I am the one who shades them, since it's me they fly after."

Usi chuckled. "I would mock your conceit but it is true you're the instigator of most of their idiotic pranks, if we can believe everything we hear."

"Since you hear it all from Supreme Captain Ulyar, we must surely believe it is all true. Why would that fine, honest man lie?"

"Hush, you leaking puppy. Come along."

Gil went along rather than fight. As head of household Shevad had a separate chamber all to himself where he kept the clan records, met with creditors he was trying to appease, and entertained military comrades when he could afford rice wine and bean cakes. Gil settled on a pillow so cleverly mended that the stitches looked like part of the decoration.

"I had arranged for trusted hirelings to serve at your palace apartments, Gilaras." Shevad's use of Gil's full name was inauspicious. "Yet now I hear you have replaced them with an insufficient staff whose experience is not at all up to the rigors of court etiquette."

"So I have. In three days after all the banqueting and visiting have ceased, my wife will make some determination about what she wishes for our establishment. I would think you would be more respectful to me, Shev, now that I have repaired the family fortunes."

"Do not take that tone with me, Gilaras. I sent the hirelings I chose over there this morning to take over but the Silver woman turned them away! I expect my people to be put in place."

Gil's hands tightened on his bent knees, but for once he kept his tongue in his mouth even though he wanted nothing more than to laugh in Shevad's face. "Very well. I'll make no objection. Can I go now? I have an errand to run before noon."

"Strange it is to see your bright face in morning's light," said Usi. "I think it has been a year or more since you've been awake before midday."

"A man does not get married every day, does he?"

He took his leave without waiting for Usi. The shops of Silk Street and Ribbon Lane produced nothing that struck him, but in a peddlers' market on Canal Street he stumbled upon a woman selling inexpensive medallions. Among the trifles lay a brass brooch patterned in a cunning maze-work of interlace with a single turquoise bead inlaid at the center. He knew at once it was the right thing. He did not bargain; the woman looked insulted by his acquiescence to her outrageous opening price.

Tucked in a tiny silk pouch, the brooch got him through the tedious dressing ceremony at home when he had to stand in the middle of the parlor with brothers and cousins and retainers in attendance while a fussy tailor dressed him in court finery acquired from a shop that had for years refused to serve the family because of nonpayment. Hung around his neck and concealed beneath his embroidered marriage jacket, the brooch in its pouch carried him through the procession to the lower palace in which he was required to sit stone-faced in an open carriage as drums beat and horns cried attention. City folk gathered to stare and call out congratulations or lewd suggestions. It seemed every soap seller and fishmonger and giggling child knew his business.

All the important contracts had been written days ago in the privacy of household offices, detailing how much coin was to be transferred and at what intervals and how much Clan Herelia would control and how much would be subject to Sarai Ri Amarah's oversight. Conduct, access to court, clothing allowances for Gilaras: All this and more was packed into densely brushed lines and sealed by Abrisho Elder, the secondary head of the Fourth Branch clan of the Ri Amarah, and by certain unnamed Ri Amarah women who acted as guardians on behalf of the unmarried girl. It had been further witnessed by the male and female heads of Clan Herelia on behalf of Gilaras, by an exalted priest of Beltak, and by a contingent of clerks from the city's Sapanasu House, which had once been a temple to the goddess of record keeping and was now a government clearing-house for contracts, trade agreements and manifests, and court chronicles.

The lower palace took up an entire neighborhood of Bell Quarter near Guardian Bridge. The original houses and com-pounds had been demolished to make room for the vast com-pound with its "thousand chambers" packed into two stories. Gilaras was led by his kinsfolk onto the Grand Portico whose gilded pillars and silk drapery made a dramatic backdrop.

He had not given a thought to Sarai's situation, and he raked himself for his thoughtlessness as he sought her out. She stood flanked by a contingent of Ri Amarah men whose hair was con-cealed beneath cloth. He hugged the knowledge of their hidden horns behind closed lips.

At least her people had bothered to bring her best-quality silk to wear, although elaborate embroidery would have been more proper for court than unadorned silk no matter its qual-ity. The style of Ri Amarah women was to cover all limbs in a loose tunic that fell to midcalf; beneath it belled trousers tied tightly at the ankle, and her feet were ornamented by beaded slippers. Compared with the women of the upper palace wear-ing elaborately folded jackets in vivid colors and crownlike hats decorated with gold, she looked drab. With her hair covered by a shawl and cloth drawn across her face to hide all but her eyes, she looked doubly out of place, a true outlander.

Gil caught her eye down the length of the hall and smiled without smiling, nodded without nodding. By the tilt of her head he knew she acknowledged what he offered.

Whatever the hells that was.

They would spit in the face of everyone who intended to use them as stepping-stones to long-thwarted ambitions.

The ceremony of meeting and the sealing of contract he endured, kneeling on the opposite side of a screen from her, the barrier a sop to upper palace custom where men and women never met in public. They were seated at separate tables at the banquet in the Silent Hall, a name chosen ironically since all lower palace festivals took place here with music and poetry contests. Usi had written an adaptation of the Tale of the Silk Slippers to enliven the proceedings and had hired the best singers with their talking hands to lure the audience in and draw them along as inexorably as a boat down a flooding river.

King Jehosh did not appear, nor either of his queens. The princes Farihosh and Tavahosh were likewise absent, as Gil had expected. But Kasad sat at the royal table. This mark of royal approval meant that attendance at the banquet was ten times as large as might otherwise have been expected for an event involving the junior son of a disgraced clan.

Ri Amarah coin paid for it all.

Everyone drank too much. Gil pretended to.

At last day walked through dusk into night. All the celebrants and singers and hirelings rose to make the traditional path of lamps from the entry porch of Silent Hall. The parallel line of glowing flame ran out of sight down a path toward the residential wing. Lamps hissed, heat billowing outward. In the first rank stood Kasad, and beyond him high-ranking clans, and beyond them courtiers and military men and officials and hangers-on. Even hirelings and servants were allowed to hold lamps.

He took Sarai's hand in his, publicly choosing the older custom of his Hundred grandmother in whose household men and women lived together rather than the formal separation between men and women observed in the palace.

Her fingers tightened on his. "Gil, what if I do it now? Let them all see my scar. Show I'm not ashamed. That I am my own person now."

"Whatever you wish, I will support you. We will build our household free of their interference."

She gave a strangled laugh. "Do you believe we can be free of their interference?"

"No. They will never let us be, and they have some claim on us, it is true. But what matters is what you and I pledge to each other. Let this be our pledge, if that suits you."

What courage it took for her he did not know, for she had grown up in isolation and he had lived with public scrutiny since childhood. She hooked down the shawl and brushed the fabric over her shoulders. Her hair remained covered but her round face shone full into the light.

A murmur like wind rushed down along the two columns as he paced forward with her beside him. All the faces wavered in and out of sight in the blazing light. This was better than all the pointless escapades and japes that had filled up his last few wine-soaked years. This was the best of all: that people stared, stunned and shocked, outraged and envious, approving and curious.

By the path of lamps he and she at last reached the entry portico of their apartment where Welo, Iadit, and Welo's stocky twin nephews—Parad and Nobi—waited. Sarai acknowledged each of the four. Gil made the traditional gesture of festive leave-taking to the procession. Then they escaped inside. Welo and Iadit helped them remove the heavy outer layers of formal clothing, leaving Gil in cotton trousers and undervest and Sarai in a silk robe.

Upstairs they collapsed onto cushions in the parlor. Alone at last.

"People from your house came around this morning with new hirelings but I sent them away," she said. "I hope you do not mind. I like Welo and her people."

He leaned into her. She was alert, not sure of what was about to come, but she did not pull away. "I promised my brother that I will not object when he replaces Welo with his own flunkies. I did not mention that you would object and that I will not countermand your decision."

She chuckled. "Cleverly spoken! Parad and Nobi look like experienced fighters."

"They compete in the wrestling circuit. I got to know Welo and her clan when I wanted to train, not that I was good enough for the circuit. Nobi broke my nose when I was trying to throw him." He brushed a forefinger along the curve of her scar. "You were magnificent."

Their faces were so close he could have kissed her, but he waited.

"Do we have sex now?" she asked.

Her voice sounded calm, but he could feel the waves of heat boiling off her blushing skin.

"Whatever you are comfortable with, Sarai-ya."

She chewed on her lower lip, obviously working herself up to speak. The silk slipped over the curve of her breasts; beneath the cloth her nipples were erect. A scent of jasmine perfume wafted from her person. She smelled so good.

He insinuated his fingers between hers. "You can say whatever you need to me."

All her breath came out. "Don't we have to have sex to say we are married? Among my people the act of consummation makes the marriage, the man . . . coming into the woman."

He blinked. "I thought it was the sealing of the contract that made the marriage, which is between our clans. You and I are just the vessels. Anyone can have sex. What does that have to do with marriage?"

"You are expected to sire children on me."

"You might as well say you are expected to germinate children from the rain of my seed."

Her smile heartened him. But she said nothing.

"Here. I brought something for you. Close your eyes."

That she closed her eyes trustingly cheered him. He thought of pressing a kiss on her lips while her eyes were shut but decided against it. When he pressed the brooch into her hand, she opened her eyes.

Her lips parted. Her eyes flew wide.

"Gil!" she said, on a gasp, and he was suddenly aroused, thinking what it would be like to hear that tone from her in the midst of lovemaking. "Do you know what this is?"

He studied the six-sided spiral wrapped around the blue stone. "It's a brooch to hold fabric together. It's meant for the shoulder drape on a taloos."

The intensity of her dark gaze made him wonder if she was about to punch him.

"It's a demon's coil!"

"Demon's coils are forbidden for people to walk on or even to talk about. Why would anyone make brooches of them?"

"Maybe because people like dangerous things." She turned it so the lamplight gleamed on its loops and angles. "I would want to know who fashioned this, if you could find the person you bought it from."

"How can you know it is patterned after a demon's coil?"

She looked down.

"Sarai-ya?" He tugged on her sleeve. "How do you know? Is it something you read...?" A blush deepened the color of her cheeks. "The hells! You've seen one, haven't you?"

He broke out laughing.

"Why do you find that so funny?" Her gaze flashed up to meet his with wary scrutiny.

"I thought I was a reckless troublemaker. I am the least of rule breakers compared with you!"

"My aunt—" She broke off, considered something, then went

on. "There is a demon's coil on one of the hills by the estate. For some years I have been making a study of it. From afar, of course! No person can walk on one although I would like to test that assertion."

"Sarai!"

"Of course I could never speak to anyone about what I'm doing. Nor have I ever had an opportunity to observe any other demon's coil to compare one with the other."

He released her hand and reclined on his back, hands cupped behind his head. "I know where a demon's coil lies shut away here in Toskala. Not that I've ever tried to reach it."

She lay down alongside him. Her lips teased his ear. "Could we, Gil? There must be a way to just look on it without anyone knowing."

He hummed, pretending to consider.

She kissed him lightly on the lips.

With immense difficulty he did not move. "You're not trying to seduce me into defying all custom and law and taking you to a demon's coil, are you?"

She hitched her body up over his, breasts brushing over his chest, thighs sliding over his hips. Every part of his body became much more alert and responsive.

"I'm not quite sure what would please you. I've only had... You don't mind, do you? That I had sex with a woman before this? You did, too. You told me about Iadit."

"You're full of surprises tonight," he said encouragingly, keeping his hands folded behind his head. "Tell me more."

She unlaced his vest. "I've never touched a man before you, Gilaras. A Ri Amarah woman is only meant to touch the man she marries, no other. But my great-aunt has a trusted hireling named Yava, a local woman, not Ri Amarah. Yava has a daughter named Elit. Elit and I grew up together. We were lovers before Elit was called away to serve Hasibal the Merciful One.

I am happy for her calling, but I miss her in so many ways." She rested more of her weight on him. "Can I touch everything?"

"Please." He grunted faintly, eyes fluttering. "Touch anything you want."

She ran her tongue around his nipples with a practiced surety. Despite what everyone believed, it had been months since Gil had had sex with anyone besides his own hand. He did not have coin to pay flower girls and would not have paid for the pleasure regardless, not when his grandmother had raised him on stories of how when she was a girl she and her friends had visited Devouring temples where people went to worship the goddess as a form of holy offering. Coin cheapened a blessed and reverent act, she had said most emphatically, and once coin began changing hands, an act that should be a shared offering merely became a transaction that a rich person could force upon a desperate poor one.

Remembering his grandmother's words he had to chuckle, hoping his own situation did not cut too close to something she would have disapproved of.

She drew back slightly, brow wrinkling. "Is something wrong?"

"I'm not going to last long," he said on a broken catch of a breath, reflecting that honesty was the best gift he could give her. "Let me do what you want done to you first because usually the first time a woman has a man in her it is not always the most pleasurable thing for her, not like it will be later."

"Will it?" she asked, fingers stroking up his erection in a way that made him glad there was cloth between her skin and his skin lest he embarrass himself right this instant. "Be pleasurable later?"

His voice was hoarse. "I like to think it will."

"The best way to go about it is to try it and see." She wiggled against him, the silk of her shift slippery against his bare chest. "I'll show you some of the things Elit did that I liked."

Since many of these involved his mouth on her breasts or his fingers inside her he was very much in charity with Elit by the time he worked through several interesting variations that Sarai suggested. Was this what it had been like back in days long since, when two people shared each other under the protection of Ushara the Merciless One, the All-Consuming Devourer? Under lamplight he enjoyed her and she enjoyed him.

When it came to the actual penetration he did not last long but she liked it better than he could have hoped, being well oiled. Afterward she cuddled up against him. He traced her scar. He really loved that scar because it seemed the talisman of their trust, the surprise that had cut into their reserve and allowed them to speak frankly and as friends right from the beginning.

She said, "Women don't have horns."

"What?" After a moment of confusion he realized what she was talking about. "I'm sorry I ever said anything about it. I wasn't stroking your hair for that reason!"

"I never thought you were. I would like to try all that again, Gil."

"Now? Or after we sleep?"

"Maybe after." She yawned. "I barely slept last night, I was so nervous."

He found the indoor robes set aside for them. Wrapped in the knee-length silk jackets, they stood on the screened balcony and looked over the palace garden with its lamplit pathways. He draped an arm around her shoulders. She fit perfectly, tucked against him.

The lower palace was wrapped around expansive inner gardens in whose elaborate landscape backstabbing, deal making, kisses, gossip, threats, and slander could be accomplished both in plain sight or behind a vine-draped trellis. He had not spent much time in the lower palace, preferring the freedom of drinking in the city with his friends, and he had never actually stood on one of the apartment balconies at night to look over the whole in a moment of peace.

He hadn't experienced a moment of peace in years, not like this.

She opened her hand to reveal the brooch. Lamplight glinted along its lines; shadows brewed in its angles. Intensity scored her expression, making it very like the one she had worn in the midst of sex. "Is there really a demon's coil in Toskala?"

Disquiet stirred in his gut. "It's walled off and boarded away in the Assizes Tower in the upper palace. No one can get inside."

"Can't you get inside, Gil?" Her teasing voice was as provocative as the way her hand slid down his back. "Think of what we could discover if we could examine one up close!"

He chuckled, aroused again. "There's nothing I can't do. Let me show you, and we'll talk about the demon's coil and how to unlock a forbidden tower...tomorrow."

26

Dannarah led her wing southwest out of Salya. She found it valuable to learn as much as she could about the home circumstances of each reeve under her command, and so she observed with interest as Reyad guided them to a valley amid the green Suvash Hills. Scattered herds of goats grazed on the hillsides, tended by youths who stared as the eagles swept low. She signaled Tarnit to stay aloft on watch and with the other two came down in open ground near a village. Its steep-roofed houses were set below terraced rice fields and mounded fields of bitter-leaf.

People left their work; children came running. By the time the three reeves had hooded their eagles and Dannarah had checked Slip's jesses and hood to make sure Lifka had done everything correctly—which she had—several hundred people had gathered at a respectful distance.

"Stay with the eagles, Lifka," she said. "Use the whistle if you need to get my attention or if Tarnit flags an alert. Don't let anyone come close."

A stout woman about her own age sang a greeting, everyone in the crowd gesturing along with the words: *Be welcome, guest. Be welcome, child who returns.* The greeting was so old-fashioned that Dannarah did not recognize some of the words. A woman offered rice wine and rice cake to Dannarah. Several older women and men embraced Reyad, and then he was completely surrounded by children all gabbling at once. He bent to whisper in one lad's ear, and the boy took off running, headed out of the village with a younger girl at his heels.

In procession the villagers led her to the village's tiny assizes court, nothing more than a thatch-roofed shelter with benches set between two temples, one dedicated to Taru the Witherer, the god of growing things, and the other dedicated to Atiratu the Lady of Beasts. The temples were little more than open-sided sheds. A large, flat rock heaped with flowers lay off to one side, a typical altar to Hasibal the Merciful One who built no temples, not like the other gods. That was why Hasibal's pilgrims always wandered: All of the Hundred was traditionally said to be their home.

At the thought of Hasibal's players the memory of a woman's face tickled at the edge of her mind, but when the archon invited her to sit she let go of the thought. Bowls of wash-water were brought, then trays with a murky soup, pickled radish, and slip-fried sprouts. By this time Dannarah had figured out that Reyad was the grandson of the archon. After asking for permission, his relatives swept him away to the largest house in the village.

"We have two stubbornly unresolved legal cases in our valley, Marshal," said the archon, who remained behind. "Perhaps you would preside over a hearing."

"Do no judges come this way once a year, as is mandated under the law?" Dannarah asked.

The woman sat in silence for a while, a custom Dannarah at length realized meant that she had nothing good to say about the local judges and thus would prefer not to criticize them in front of a person who was also an enforcer of the king's law.

Dannarah coughed politely. "What are the cases?"

The archon nodded. "One is a boundary dispute."

Dannarah smiled. "Of course. There is always a boundary dispute."

"It has been a point of contention since my grandmother's time. Fortunately my family is not involved."

"The other case?"

The archon glanced toward her clan's home with a flicker of irritation. Reyad was standing on the porch staring at the hills while his elders gesticulated in the manner of people trying to convince him of what he did not want to hear.

"A divorce case that has dragged on for two years."

"A dispute over the settlement?"

"No. One of the parties refuses to return his half of the betrothal ribbons. But perhaps you may assist us, Marshal. Reyad is under your command now."

"I don't understand."

"The girl was always unsuitable. Goatherders. Hill people. But he defied the family's wishes and of course that sort of girl would leap at a respectable and wealthy clan like ours."

Wealth? Dannarah glanced around the humble village. Compared with the palace, of course, they had nothing to remark on, but the people looked well fed, decently clothed, and the rice wine was good. In her years as a reeve Dannarah had learned that wealth could often be measured as lack of hunger.

"You want him to divorce her, and she is refusing?"

"No, she wants the divorce, and he is refusing. Can you not order him to obey his elders?"

Dannarah smiled wryly. "Verea, this is not a matter in which I can involve myself."

The archon sighed. "Aui! Then perhaps you will consider the matter of the boundary dispute."

"Yes, of course. If you will acquaint me with the case I can investigate it now. I have a new reeve who can observe and learn."

"The young one? When I saw her I thought she must be a for- eigner, maybe one of those Tandi merchants we see at Nia Port or a sailor's daughter from Kost. But she is obviously a Hundred girl for she replied in the correct manner to the greeting. Exactly like my own children. You, however, are clearly outlander-born, Marshal. I mean no offense. It is just an observation."

"None taken. I am born in the Hundred but don't consider myself Hundred-born, as you are, verea. I'm of Sirniakan and Qin descent. I was raised in the palace and learned the customs of the Hundred only after I became a reeve."

She spent a pleasant afternoon teaching Lifka about bound- ary disputes, pasturage rights, rockfalls on hillsides, streams that gouge new beds over the course of a heavy rainy season, and the stubborn intransigence of people who keep a dispute going mostly because they have little else to make themselves feel important. The two clans accepted her judgment, she sus- pected, mostly because no reeve marshal had ever before set foot in their village.

They spent the night, feasted by the entire village. Lifka sang and signed a version of the Tale of the Carter and his Barking

Dog that no one here had heard before, enlivened by the Runt sulking jealously on a cushion.

Tarnit whispered, "She has good hands. I can't tell a tale that well."

Dannarah insisted they sleep under the assizes shelter because it was important for reeves to take nothing but food and necessary repairs in exchange for their services. That was a rule she strictly held. Her father had taught her that the greatest danger to anyone who gains the least scrap of power is the rot of corruption. Lifka took the first watch over the hooded eagles.

For herself, she slept restlessly, an unpleasant habit she had fallen into after her monthly courses had ceased. Thus she woke in the middle of the night with Tarnit asleep beside her and voices murmuring conspiratorially nearby.

She grasped her baton and eased up, letting her eyes adjust to the darkness. Moonlight revealed figures pacing inside the Witherer's Temple. She crept to the edge of the assizes porch and across the shadows to the thin wall. There, she crouched to listen.

It was a lovers' quarrel.

"I thought you weren't going to come."

"I haven't changed my mind, Reyad. Just give me the divorce and stop being selfish."

"Please, Hetta. Listen to me."

"Why should I? You are all cowards."

"I'm not a coward."

"All of you just let Auri and his favorites do what they did to women and you did nothing about it because you were all afraid you would be next."

Dannarah blinked to get the sleep haze out of her eyes.

"I would never have let them hurt *you*!" Reyad's indignation sounded genuine, if a bit whiny.

"We like to tell ourselves that story, don't we? I left and came home because I was a coward, too. I should have stayed and fought. Those women had no chance to leave, not like me."

"You are just one person, Hetta. Not even a reeve. What could you have done?"

"If everyone had stood against him it would have stopped. But none of you did."

"I did."

"You did not! Stop telling yourself that. Do you ever ask yourself how you got your eagle? I hate more than anything the way you lie to yourself."

"I did nothing wrong! Anyway, the chief marshal is dead. I killed him."

Dannarah woke straight up with a rush of head-clearing alarm. The hells!

Tarnit snorted in her sleep and turned over, still dreaming.

"What do you mean?" Hetta's anger broke on the words.

"I sliced his eagle's jess partway through while no one was looking. Then I loosened the hood. I knew Slip would get agitated because there was a big crowd and lots of angry voices. He's a good raptor although not as steady like my Surly. Any decent reeve could calm that bird. But I knew Auri would get his harness all a-tangle for fear of looking an ass before so many people, including Marshal Dannarah and a prince! All he ever talks about is how the palace knows who he is, him an ordinary farmer's son elevated so high because of his loyalty. He would never want to look bad in front of folk like them. I knew he'd rile the bird, and he did."

"What do you mean, he did?"

"Slip killed him." A rooster crowing would have sounded less cocky. "I saw a chance and I took it. Now he can't do what he did to any more women. Isn't that what you wanted?"

Dannarah put a hand over her mouth to muffle her unsteady breathing.

Hetta said, in a flat tone, "You're a murderer."

"You can't possibly feel sorry for him."

"Do you expect me to thank you?"

"I did it for you! You're the one who said you wished he was dead!"

"Hush! What if you wake people up? The hells! How could you...? I want no part of this."

"But Hetta—!"

"I won't tell anyone if that's what you're worried about. Merciful One protect us! Just leave me alone, Reyad. Leave me alone."

A figure hurried from the mouth of the temple, fleeing through the silent village. Inside, Reyad paced for long enough that Dannarah's bad hip began to really hurt. She was too cursed old for surveillance. At last he stumbled like a grieving man from the temple and headed in the direction the young woman had gone.

With a soft groan Dannarah kneaded the worst of the ache out of her flesh, then staggered back to her sleeping mat. But she could not sleep. She turned the conversation around and around, like turning her tea bowl to study every side of its painted decoration.

As soon as the earliest risers began moving about hauling water and grinding grain, she nudged Tarnit awake. They walked to the village latrines.

"Still no sign of the wife, did you notice?" said Tarnit. "I think he's too cursed proud to admit she doesn't want him."

"His grandmother believes he married beneath him, to a goatherder's daughter."

Tarnit's laugh was so bright in the dawn quiet that a man hunting rats along the edge of a rice field paused to give them a warning stare. "After the stories we've heard from women who came to us from Argent Hall, I've sympathy for the young woman."

"Auri's dead now. We'll change things." A clever system of pipes brought a stream of water to a roofed washing area with blinds that could be drawn down for privacy. Dannarah rinsed her face and combed through her short hair with her fingers.

"Heya!" Tarnit nudged her. "Look there! Do you suppose that is the girl?"

Too far away to hear them but close enough to make out faces stood Reyad and a young woman. They were still arguing but standing close enough to touch. Dannarah had an idea that Hetta wasn't ready to forgive him, not yet. But as the shock wore off it might be hard for her not to succumb to the idea that ridding the world of a poisonous man on her behalf was a form of flattery.

Tarnit whistled. "Whsst! They look good together, don't they? She's gorgeous."

Standing together they were indeed exceptionally young and handsome.

"I remember being seventeen and wishing I looked like that," said Dannarah as she dried her face. "I didn't envy the girls who did as much as I despaired that I'd never be like them."

"Now that I've peed I can cry for my lost youth and the beauty I never had," said Tarnit with another laugh, sounding not one bit sorrowful. "Never stopped me from getting what I wanted. To tell the truth, nothing is funnier than to discover Reyad is the spoiled grandson of the archon of a farming village pining after a poor clan's pretty daughter who scolds him. It explains a lot."

Dannarah watched the way Reyad grasped Hetta's hand but let go the moment she pulled away. "Coming here has given me a better measure of the kind of man Reyad is and how he can be of use to me."

Tarnit cast her a sharp glance, alert to every nuance of Dannarah's mood. "How so?"

"I'll know when the moment is upon me."

As much as she wanted to congratulate Reyad for murdering that ass Auri, it was important he not know she knew. As her father had once said, *Never forget that a king wields many weapons, and some of them are men.*

They flew north to Horn Hall.

Guiding two reeves to their first landing at Horn Hall was not a task for the faint of heart. Wind always buffeted the escarpment landing ground. On a ridgetop the shifts in the prevailing winds, the thermals altering direction from morning to night, and the interaction of air currents with the surrounding hills and the day's weather all had to be taken into account as a reeve and her eagle approached the landing terraces.

Dannarah sent Tarnit down first onto the parade ground atop the ridge and flagged Reyad to follow. His eagle, Surly, made two passes before she decided she wanted to land. He managed a creditable job of coaxing her down but it was clear that at Argent Hall's less challenging landing ground he'd not been given the strict training regimen Dannarah required of her novices.

Terror wanted to dance along the updrafts, and indeed there were a few eagles playing high up in the wind, but she circled the raptor back to watch Lifka's approach.

The girl had an exceptional hand with the jesses; her experience with driving mules made the basics of handling a large raptor come easily to her. She had a lot to learn about eagles and air, but her sense of her surroundings and her ability to adjust to Slip's intelligence were already good. She had the instinct to be prudently nervous and enough natural confidence not to be fearful. Fortunately Slip remembered Horn Hall well enough that he did not balk at coming in with an inexperienced reeve at harness. After Lifka was safely down, Dannarah landed.

It was good to see familiar faces, like the big fawkner Ruri, who headed in to sort out Terror as Dannarah unbuckled her harness. "Heya! Marshal, good to have you back!"

"What news? What trouble did you get into while I was gone?"

In twenty years as a fawkner Ruri had never been badly injured thanks to his astonishing knack for settling the birds and a certain measure of luck. "Neh, Marshal. I only get in trouble when you're here so you can fish me out."

She thumped his meaty upper arm as greeting and left Terror to his ministrations. A young steward came running up to take her harness away to be cleaned and repaired, although she would check it thoroughly later. Her chief steward, an easy-tempered man about her age, had drawn Tarnit off to one side and was already interrogating her for news.

Dannarah went over to them. "Nesard, show Reyad to the men's barracks. He's joining us from Argent Hall, so assign someone to give him the tour and see him settled in."

"Of course, Marshal." He shifted his crutch and limped over to the young man. "I'm Nesard. How much gear did you leave behind at Argent Hall?"

Reyad was staring around the ridge with a look of the greatest delight, like a hungry man thrown into a pot of ginger-sesame fish. "Nothing that matters. If I never see that place again I'll not cry. Are those gardens and an orchard down at the other end of the ridge, Marshal?"

She nodded, so accustomed to the neat ranks of greenery that she scarcely noticed them now. "It is. We supply most of our own food."

"Where do we live?"

"In chambers carved into the rock. This is an ancient place, most likely made by delvings."

"Delving tunnels! Up so high and in the light? Isn't that unusual? One time Hetta and I walked partway down the entrance steps into an abandoned delving-home at the edge of the Suvash Hills, but then our candle began to flicker so we had to go back up. She's not afraid of anything! Are there private rooms here for married people?"

Tarnit waggled her baton like an erection, thankfully where Reyad couldn't see as Nesard led him off.

"Thank you for that enlightening demonstration of your knowledge of anatomy."

"You'd be disappointed if I didn't do it, Marshal."

"I'd be pretty certain you were unconscious, or dead. Show Lifka where she'll be sleeping, introduce her to a few people, and take her down to get measured for gear. Then bring her to my office. You'll take a week's leave after, at my order."

"Curse you, Marshal, you know how I despise having to visit my family!" Tarnit twirled the baton and sheathed it with a flourish. "Come along, Leaf. You'll love it. There are decent baths."

"How do you get the water up here?" the girl asked.

"There's a mechanism used to pump water up from a spring trapped deep within the rock."

"This is where I'm going to live now?"

Dannarah had to laugh at the way Lifka gaped at the spectacular view of sacred Mount Aua rising in splendor fifteen mey west.

"Yes. Come along." Tarnit tucked a hand in Lifka's elbow and led her away.

Dannarah descended steps cut into the cliff face that led to a wide terrace below. As she reached the terrace and its entrance into the cavernous eating hall, her hall officials hastened up, passing through bars of light from the shafts that lit and aerated the big chamber. Her chief reeve instructor and deputy Feder was a reeve no longer able to patrol after losing an arm below the elbow although he could still fly his eagle, Bright. The chief fawkner, Goro, had lost an eye years ago. Chief steward Nesard used a crutch to compensate for a twisted leg. Their experience and knowledge made them perfect to manage administrative tasks and oversee the hall, thus giving her freedom to patrol.

"Marshal!" Feder was always first to speak, having known her longer than anyone; they had trained together over forty years ago. "You're later than we expected. Iyar returned yesterday from Sardia with the reeves you left to hunt the escaped prisoners."

"Any news?"

"They found no one. He thought you would already be here. I must say you look pregnant with news."

"I am! Chief Marshal Auri is dead." She cut through their exclamations. "King Jehosh has promised to appoint me."

Feder slapped her on the back, as old comrades did.

Nesard grinned. "About time!"

Goro shook his head. "Does that mean we have to move to Palace Hall?"

"As much as this will surprise you, I'm thinking it might be wisest to follow Auri's example." She waited for their laughter to die down before going on. "Keep my administration here, and use Palace Hall as an auxiliary office I'll visit once or twice a week. That way Jehosh and I won't have to clash on a daily basis. It will work better for both of us. Meanwhile we'll wait for the summons. I have reason to believe the king won't act precipitously but will wait twenty days or so before he calls for the election."

She paused long enough to set down her gear in the marshal's cote, the traditional name for her study, then descended by a set of back stairs to the baths on the level below. After washing, she soaked in the nearby hot pool as her people filled her in on the patrols conducted in her absence and on cases her reeves had adjudicated at village assizes courts in the areas that fell under Horn Hall's patrol territory. Finally. Finally! She would get to set the reeve halls back in order.

Afterward she stretched out on a mat and for a measure of blessed silence a steward massaged the aches and pains of travel out of her muscles.

Back in the marshal's cote, seated at her desk, she sipped tea and discussed redheart wreaths and red-nut rice with her staff. "Auri refused to share information between halls, which is the first thing I will change. If demons are beginning to act this boldly all over the Hundred, we need to know and to coordinate our efforts to track them down. Send two reeves back to River's Bend to see if they can find who cut and who purchased redheart wreaths in the last month."

Tarnit entered the chamber with Lifka. They both had bathed and wore freshly laundered kilts and vests. A few examined Lifka, interested by her looks, but quickly got back to business.

"Nesard, as soon as I'm chief marshal you'll collect incident reports from all the reeve halls involving escaped prisoners and outlaws in the last three years. I also want you to begin to record and track the movements of all troupes of Hasibal's players throughout the Hundred."

"There was a troupe of Hasibal pilgrims up in Elsharat," said Tarnit thoughtfully.

"Exactly. I am particularly curious to know if Hasibal's players are carrying redheart wreaths or red-nut rice. Or harboring escapees."

"I'll have a clerk keep an account just as a merchant would," said Nesard. "Insofar as we can track their movements. It won't be easy."

"Did you see something in particular that makes you want to track Hasibal's players, Marshal?" Tarnit asked, watching her with a guarded expression.

Dannarah rubbed the bridge of her nose, trying to blink away the mild ache pressing right around her eyes. "Just an instinct. Feder, Reyad will need additional instruction in the basics that he missed at Argent Hall. I want him assigned to my flight. Also, I want you to personally supervise Lifka's reeve training. She'll be assigned to my flight as well."

"As a fledgling reeve she should be assigned to the fledgling flight, shouldn't she, Marshal?"

"I'm expecting trouble with Prince Tavahosh over her, so it's best I keep her close. As for that, I'll want dress tabards and gear ready for when King Jehosh calls the reeve convocation."

The bell for dinner rang in the distance. People shifted on their cushions. She wasn't the only one who was hungry, and she had kept them talking half the afternoon.

"It's good to be home," she added, then sketched the gesture for *mouth prudently closed*. "What we speak in this chamber goes nowhere else. I know each of you puts the security of the reeve halls above all else. That will be our task as we move forward."

Dannarah gestured for Tarnit to stay as the rest filed out. "One last thing, Tar. This is for you alone. Atani left a widow, Queen Yevah, and a lover, Eiko. My younger sister Meenah also lived with them. They left the palace after Atani died. Find them."

"Find them? Where do I start?"

"Queen Yevah had an estate close to Toskala. Possibly she retired there after his death."

"Does this have to do with our visit to Salya and the man Hari, whom I'm meant to keep secret? Now that your father is dead, maybe there are some questions it's better not to ask."

"There are never questions it's better not to ask. I'm going to find out everything my father and brother never told me."

Part Three

27

Late one afternoon Kellas walked through the city gates of Toskala. The guardsmen barely glanced at another old man trudging along with a battered sack slung over his back.

Because he visited Toskala every year he had no trouble navigating the changed streets of Stone Quarter, where he had grown up. The temple dedicated to Ilu the Herald where Kellas had served as a novice sixty years ago had been closed down in the last years of the reign of King Anjihosh. At that time the temple grounds had been turned into a carpentry yard. During the reign of Atani it had been built up into cheap row houses where families lived crammed together as rents rose elsewhere in the city. After the ascension of Jehosh a similar fate had met all the other temples within the city dedicated to the seven gods. In Toskala, at least, Beltak had truly become the Shining One Who Rules Alone.

The old temple gate still stood, flanked by stone guardians each wielding an envoy's staff. Inside lay a tiny courtyard, the last scrap of open ground from the expansive temple yard where once novices and envoys had paced out each day's devotions in his distant youth. Dusk was falling as Kellas slipped into the courtyard unobtrusively. A handful of others mumbled evening prayers amid the fraying silk banners and withered offerings of cut flowers. A restless child fidgeted while holding the hand of an old man. A trio of young women nervously plowed through a prayer as if they had laboriously memorized the whole rather than singing it every day of their young lives.

Horses trotted past beyond the gate. Hearing them, everyone in the courtyard stiffened. Sometimes guards arrested worshippers on order of the supreme exalted master of the Beltak shrine, but these guards rode on. Kellas said his prayers and left an offering of rice balls wrapped in nai leaves for the crippled old woman who swept the courtyard and intoned the full daily devotion. She had been an envoy once—she had Ilu's staff and key tattooed on her arm—but she was no one he recognized from his own novitiate.

After that he walked to the compound where he had grown up, still the home of Twelve Dogs Clan. The last of his sisters had died last year, but as he had been the youngest of that generation her death had come as no surprise.

His nephew Belon was closing the gates when he caught sight of Kel walking out of the twilight. "Uncle Kellas! Good tidings to you! What a surprise this is! We did not expect you until next season."

"I hope it is no trouble." He glanced toward a man loitering on the street. When the man saw Kellas looking, he ambled away.

Belon hadn't even noticed. "You're always welcome, Uncle. I'll have your room aired and bedding brought in. If you'd like, I can send a boy to your clerk's office to alert him you've arrived."

"I would like that, Belon. Thank you."

"Not at all! You've come just in time, like in the Tale of the Welcome Guest. We have a feast tonight. Your grand-niece Hedo—"

"She's the daughter of your sister Jadara."

"That's right. Hedo's just become betrothed to a Fifth Quarter man. Plenty of rice wine and fish and spicy bean curd!"

Belon escorted him to the porch, where he took off his sandals and settled on a pillow of honor on the matted veranda.

The main courtyard of the compound was bustling with the extended family all awake and merry. A gaggle of boys and girls brought him a tray with pickled plum and vegetables and a cup of warmed wine. They giggled when he counted down their names, because names were the sort of thing he never forgot.

"Uncle Kellas! How long are you going to stay? Will you tell us the story of how you climbed Law Rock?"

Gods, they were so young and so bright, their interest so flattering. After he related the well-worn story of his climb up Law Rock, they wanted another. It was tempting to let pour a few of the secrets stored away in his mind. He contented himself with telling how in the dead of night he had swum to shore from a ship anchored in Messalia Bay to sneak into the household of the woman he had fallen in love with but was forbidden to ever see, and swum back with no one the wiser.

"Another story!" the children clamored, and he smiled wryly.

Too many of the stories he had to tell weren't right for these sweet children.

Everyone rose to sing the traditional songs to celebrate the betrothal. The betrothed girl was lively and attractive, and had such good manners that she served him supper with her own hands, a platter of fish baked in coriander and pepper and garnished with mango, and a stew of turnips and greens ladled on rice. Probably he drank too much.

He woke disoriented in the early morning upon finding himself in the room he had slept in as a boy. Melancholy swamped him as he creaked to his feet and stood with a hand on the open window, looking over the courtyard. Women chatted by the open hearth as they prepared rice porridge. Children were raking and sweeping. If he blinked, he almost expected to see his sisters and cousins and mother and aunts walking into the compound through the open gate with buckets filled to the brim with water from the neighborhood well.

Back then he had chafed, thinking the simple chores not just tedious but pointless. He had wanted excitement, adventure, a purpose. The palace had swept him away and the clan had gone on without him, although he was pretty sure he had broken his mother's heart regardless of how many times he had come to visit her over the years before she died.

A stick rapped the wall alongside the curtained door. "Uncle Kellas? Are you awake?"

He pulled on his vest. "I'm awake," he said, stepping outside.

Belon's smile quivered with an unexpected pinch of nervousness. "It's just that the boy we sent yesterday to your office with the message never returned."

The last traces of bleary-eyed sleep vanished. "Which boy?"

"Not one of our own boys. As you may recall, to make ends meet we've had to rent out rooms to country laborers come in to find work."

"That's right. When I was here last year you had begun housing a few in the second workshop."

"Yes, away from the main courtyard. We prefer them not to mix with the family."

"How did this sad turn of fortune's wheel come about, Belon? The clan's carving is still first-rate. Circles used to be the most popular game in Toskala because King Anjihosh played it."

"That was quite some time ago. No one in the palace plays Circles now. They play games brought from the empire. We were fortunate that when Queen Dia first came here she took a fancy to our carving and had us fashion hair ornaments and curtain pulls. That kept us prosperous for many years. But suddenly last year Queen Chorannah let it be known that anyone who wanted her favor should not follow any of Queen Dia's fashions. Now people are afraid to purchase our wares."

"I'm sorry to hear it."

"We'll come about, Uncle. We're trying out some new carv-

ings for decorative brooches and door amulets, things not tied
to palace favor. The thing is that taxes have been raised again,
so we need the extra coin from boarders just to pay our quar-
terly license fee."

Kellas looked around to make sure no one could overhear. "Is
there some specific reason you didn't send one of your own boys
with the message?"

Belon glanced away with a shame-filled flicker of his eyes. "I
sent the lad, Karladas, because he is always happy to run errands
and deliveries to make a few extra vey. But the truth is, the city
isn't as safe as it used to be. Wolf Quarter is especially bad."

Kellas scratched his head. "More crime?"

"Maybe a bit but it isn't crime we worry about. Young men
get arrested right off the streets by Beltak priests. The priests
will claim a lad has broken some holy law and next thing you
know he's sent off on a work gang. Our neighbor's son vanished six months ago when he was out carousing one night in
Wolf Quarter. They've never heard where he was sent." His eyes
flared. "Not that I'm complaining, mind you..."

"No, of course not." Kellas hated the fear in his nephew's usually placid face. Belon was a good man who was proud to call
Kel his uncle and went out of his way to treat him with proper
familial obligation. "I'm aware of the activities of the Beltak
priests, but surely they only take criminals to the work gangs."

"They can take who they want if there's no one to say they
didn't catch the lad doing something wrong. Anyone who
argues against them is charged with blasphemy and ends up in
a work gang as well."

Kellas frowned. "That's troubling news. We've not had that
problem in Mar."

Belon dropped his voice to a whisper, as if he was afraid the
priests could overhear through magic. "People say they are
cracking down in the cities first and then they mean to spread

their Beltak law. They're using the prisoners to build new shrines all over."

"Nothing I can do about that," said Kellas, careful to keep his tone bland as he filed the information away to send back to Salya in his first dispatch. "But maybe I can find the boy. Describe Karladas."

"North country boy, from the high valley of Amat. A sweet lad, everyone's favorite. He came here with his older brother. Adiki is hot-tempered, a real brawler and constantly in fights, but he's devoted to his brother, which is the only reason we let him stay."

Memory sifted to reveal faces and names. "I recall Karladas. A good-looking boy. Born in the Year of the Blue Lion. The two lads had come in from the country about the time I left last year."

"Heya!" Belon chuckled as his expression eased. "You never forget a thing, do you, Uncle?"

Kellas trawled deeper into the memory. "I remember because I met young Karladas at the compound gate the night before I returned to Salya. The boy saw my novice's ink and told me he had wished to dedicate himself to Ilu's service but his clan could not afford the dedicatory offering. That's why he and his brother came to the city. They planned to earn enough money so Adiki can raise a marriage portion and Karladas can take his envoy's oath."

"How can you recall all that, from a year ago, from one conversation?"

Kellas shrugged. "Merchants need a good memory to sort through inventory. I'm sure I've mentioned that my mother dedicated me to the temple of Ilu when I was fourteen. I spent all my days there wanting nothing more than to escape. So you can imagine how struck I was when the boy confided that he wanted the very thing I had so desperately wished to escape at his age."

"Can you find him?"

"I'll ask around."

Belon let out a troubled sigh. "Be careful, Uncle. Sheh! That things have come to this! Young folk abducted off the streets for no more crime than having no work and being angry about it. Eiya! Meanwhile, let us sit down to porridge and redberry juice and be grateful for our own good fortune."

Although Kellas smiled and chatted with the family as he shared the morning meal, he left as soon as politeness allowed. The young man named Adiki followed him out the compound gate, his north country accent marking him every time he opened his mouth.

"What comes of my brother? Where has he fallen to? Can you find him? Was it the outlander priests who stole him?" His words rattled down on Kellas like stone, drawing attention from passersby.

Kellas had never had trouble stopping young men with his gaze alone. "I have no authority here except age. Get yourself into trouble by speaking disrespectfully of the Beltak priests and you will find yourself in a work gang far from here. Do you understand me? Because you had better understand me and let me know right now that you do."

Adiki was not much older than Fohiono, a tall, broad-shouldered man with a scarred chin and a badly healed broken nose. He had a scrapper's belligerent stance, and brilliant eyes, and no ability to back down gracefully. "I promised the family I should look out for the boy! They feared at his coming here. He has too friendly a heart, ver. Please."

Kellas did not let his expression soften. "I will ask around. You must be patient."

The young man paced two steps back and one forward and finally turned his right hand palm up in the gesture of acquiescence. Kellas answered with the hand gesture *it will be what it will be*. Adiki's shoulders tensed with impatience.

Kellas gnawed on the problem all the way to Wolf Quarter and was still chewing through his options as he walked up to a modest storefront situated on Withering Square. Once a temple dedicated to Taru the Witherer had run along one entire side of the square but it had been replaced by a grain, vegetable, and herb market. The comings and goings of traders made the square a fruitful exchange point to pick up gossip and rumor in the city. That was why Plum Blossom Clan kept a clerk stationed here year-round behind a door banner marked with a five-petaled blossom. The clerk and his family who lived here sold from an inventory of unusual goods from overseas, but really they worked as scouts feeding information back to Kellas.

He stepped off the street onto the raised porch. The small gate that opened into the side courtyard was closed, odd at this time of the morning. On the upper story, the bamboo blinds were drawn down to conceal the balcony. Usually the family would be awake and about but he heard silence instead of the usual daily chatter and clatter. Something was wrong.

He took off his sandals so anyone on the street would not see him doing anything out of the ordinary. Hand hovering by his sheathed knife, he took a cautious step past the entry banners and onto the mats that floored the public customers' room. To his left the doors that opened onto the side porch, courtyard, hearth, and stairs were still closed although normally at this time of day they would be open. The door into the private office was partially open when it ought to be closed. A soldier stood in the center of the small room, his features obscured by the dimness.

"Oyard?" He slid his knife half out of its sheath. "What in the hells means this lurking?"

"Is that any way to greet me, Captain Kellas?"

Kellas went utterly still, absorbing the surprise. King Jehosh was wearing soldier's garb, not palace finery. A leather helmet with cheek guards sat on the mat at his feet.

"King Jehosh, this is an unexpected honor."

"I have surprised you. I confess that pleases me. I sent your factor for a pot of tea. Wasn't he cashiered out of the Wolves at the same time you were, for failing to protect my father?"

"Chief Oyard is a loyal man who was found blameless in the matter. He is also a good soldier who took a severe injury that day in defense of King Atani. He has been in my private employ ever since, as you surely know."

Uneasiness crawled through his flesh. What if the convoluted safeguards with which Plum Blossom Clan guarded their privacy had broken down?

He took a turn around the office but there was nothing out of place: ledgers stacked neatly on shelves, two lockboxes, writing paraphernalia, his city clothes packed away in paper, four cases of inventory, and a stack of cushions embroidered with ibexes leaping and running. Jehosh turned a slow circle, never letting Kellas get behind his back.

"I haven't stolen anything," Jehosh remarked, sounding amused.

"Old habit, my lord. I always scout my territory."

"Before you move in for the kill?"

Cursed if he was going to let Jehosh rile him over Atani's death. "Killing is usually the last and worst solution to a problem. Did you set an agent to watch my clan's compound? You and I made an agreement that if I retired quietly, you would leave my people alone."

"I have left your people alone, Captain. Now I want you to come back."

He halted before the king. "I no longer serve the palace, my lord."

"If you serve the Hundred, then you serve me, as its king."

"You personally disbanded the Black Wolves, my lord. There was no reason for you to trust me after such a devastating blow. I would have done the same in your situation. Had I been you, I would have appointed new people, ones I hoped would serve me better."

"I thought I had done so but now I realize I was mistaken."

The side door to the public room slid open. Kellas hurried to take the tea tray. Oyard swayed back, surprised to see Kellas, then recovered himself, retreated, and closed the door.

Kellas carried the tray into his office. Oyard had brought a teapot, a platter of sliced cucumber and ginger, fried shaved coconut, and several boiled eggs still in the shell. There was only a single cup. Kellas poured tea and offered Jehosh the cup, but the king waved it away.

"I need a man I trust inside the palace," said the king.

"That is what the Spears are for, Your Highness."

"I believe Chorannah has emptied her treasury by bribing the senior officers in my Spears to her cause."

"That is a strong claim."

"She would have corrupted the entire upper palace but she ran out of coin. However, the officials know Farihosh will succeed me. Now they are just waiting for me to die, at which point my son will control the Hundred's finances."

"That's taking a very long view, if I may say so, my lord. You are only forty-three. You can expect to live many more years, if fortune favors you."

Jehosh's right hand clenched into a fist. "As long as I do not interfere with Chorannah and her plans. To think I despised her as a weakling all these years. She means to steal the kingship from me in all but title, and she'll take that, too, if I do not go along with what she wants."

The words fell out before he knew it. "Can you not kill her, Your Highness?"

Four steps brought the king right up to Kellas, chest-to-chest. They were of a height, but Jehosh was a hale man in his prime while Kellas, though still fit and solid, was old. Twenty years ago he could have taken Jehosh in a direct fight, but only stealth and cunning would save him now if they came to blows.

"Have her killed? How like you to suggest it, Captain. I suppose it is exactly what King Anjihosh had done to anyone who crossed him. If you think of a way to manage it that will not drop the priests, my senior officials, and her sons on my head, then I urge you to act swiftly."

"That is a harsh indictment of Queen Chorannah, my lord."

"Perhaps if I had treated Chorannah with more affection she might not have raised her sons as my rivals."

It is you who sees everyone as a rival, Kellas thought, but he merely nodded.

Jehosh nodded in reply. "I want to make you supreme captain of the King's Spears."

Kellas wanted to say, *That is impossible, Your Highness.* He wanted to go home and go fishing with his granddaughters and sit quietly in the garden with his beloved wife, but that very beloved wife had given him his orders and so he held his tongue and waited as Jehosh went on.

"I need a man who can protect Dia's son, Kasad. I need a man who can discover what conspiracies are being whispered against me in the upper palace and expose them. I also need a competent man to find out what happened to my aunt Sadah. Aunt Dannarah will have told you the situation with the empire's succession dispute."

"She mentioned it."

"Sadah and her guardsmen embarked on a merchant's barge headed for Nessumara. Two days later agents boarded the barge at the Ili Toll Station but no trace of her could be found. Agents backtracked along the river but discovered nothing."

"It seems unlikely she could have left the barge without being traced. Not if your agents are thorough and know what they are doing."

"I've long suspected Ulyar is incompetent. The other possibility is that Chorannah found out about her and had her killed in order to support this ill-considered alliance with her sister to maintain her sister's feeble son on a throne he cannot possibly hope to hold on to."

Kellas decided to be rude and, still standing, drained the cup of tea by now too cool to be savored. "May I make a suggestion, Your Highness?"

Jehosh's mocking smile flashed and faded. "That is why I sent for you, is it not?"

"Do not alter the arrangements in the upper palace. Appoint me as your chief of security in the lower palace. If people believe Queen Chorannah remains hostile to Queen Dia, placing me in charge of lower palace security would be an obvious gesture on your part. It allows people to believe you are solely concerned about Dia and Kasad's safety."

"That will do." Uncannily Jehosh had barely moved for the entire conversation. Kellas remembered him as a restless young man, always pacing or shifting or stamping. "Which leaves me with one question, Captain. I dismissed you most brutally, after my father's death. I blamed you, and I let the palace and the army blame you. Why serve me now?"

In his years as a Black Wolf running clandestine missions, Kellas had learned an important lesson about working undercover: Always tell the truth when you can. Even if not the whole truth.

"My duty to your father still rules me. He commanded me to guard the Hundred, and so I will."

The gate rattled. In the silence Kellas heard Oyard's distinctive limp as he went over to open it. Men entered the side courtyard, one whistling a tune Kellas did not recognize.

"Here he is," said the king, stepping away from Kellas.

Oyard's voice lifted. "My lord Vanas. This is an unexpected honor."

Kellas slid the office screen open. Lord Vanas crossed the mats of the audience chamber. The same age as Jehosh, he had a vigorous stride and, so it was rumored, an eye quick to identify anyone who might be offered a privilege or honor he hadn't yet obtained.

Jehosh said, "Vanas, delegate men to assist the captain in moving into the gatehouse of the lower palace. Captain Kellas will be taking over as chief of security."

Vanas took in a breath, let it out, then nodded. "The lower palace. I will leave a cadre to escort you, Captain Kellas."

Jehosh fitted the helmet over his head and, just another ordinary soldier in a lord's household, departed with Vanas's entourage.

The hells! How often had Jehosh and Vanas played that game?

He wondered if Jehosh ran off to fight the Eldim rebels so he could pretend to be an ordinary soldier instead of a king.

He went out to the side courtyard. Eight soldiers stood at attention, waiting for orders under the stern eye of Oyard.

A woman came out of the kitchen, wiping her hands on a cloth. Moon-faced Yero with the red lips and the wary eyes was twenty-five years younger than Oyard. He had found her one night in Wolf Quarter, starving and holding on to a sickly baby who had died soon after. After nursing her back to health, Oyard had, with Kellas's permission, married her. A safe home and regular meals had allowed her to bloom. She had proven capable and trustworthy, an excellent cook and housekeeper, and startlingly effective at sorting useful marketplace rumor from idle gossip.

"If we are moving house I have a few questions, Captain," she said as calmly as if the king had not just sneaked in and out of her humble residence.

"Of course you do, verea," he said in the formal manner he used with her in front of strangers. "You will have to learn the protocol of the lower palace, where you can walk and where you're not allowed, whom to bow to and whom you may pass with only a greeting. People will offer you coin and preferment to spy on me."

She had a habit when considering unpleasant thoughts of brushing a fingertip over a burn scar on her chin, an injury she never discussed. Her gaze passed scornfully down the soldiers' ranks as if trying to decide which fool was hoping to bribe her to sell secrets she would never reveal for any price. "A person who offers to pay for my favor has already lost it," she said for their ears, then looked back at him. "Is there a palace school for the children of servants? Have they a chance to train for the civil service examinations? Or to apprentice out when the time comes?"

"What will be best for your children I can't yet say, if you will be patient."

"Of course. Let me just fetch the tea things." Passing him on the porch, she lowered her voice. "Hasibal's Tears. What of those?"

He glanced into the dim confines of the inner office. That the king had just stood there seemed like a dream, or a nightmare. "Soon they may begin to fall."

While Oyard and Yero sorted out the packing, he drank tea and ate, then wrote a note to the Beltak priest in charge of the South Gate shrine.

To the exalted sentinel of the shrine at South Gate, greetings and blessings in the name of Beltak, the Shining One Who Rules Alone. As Captain Kellas, chief captain of security for the lower palace, I address you, Exalted One. Business of my calling brings me to inquire if you have come into possession yesterday or today of a boy named Karladas, born in the Year of the Blue Lion. In the course of performing my duty in the name of King Jehosh I request the boy's presence in my new office at the guardhouse to the lower palace where I have been installed at the king's express command. My thanks for your attention to this matter. Sent according to the gracious power of the Lord of Lords and King of Kings, Shining Beltak to whom all are obedient, at the king's service, Captain Kellas.

He brushed the rice paper with sand and blew it dry, then found a neighborhood child to deliver the letter. Oyard called for a chair to convey him and at first he meant to refuse but the chief looked him in the eye and said, "For your consequence, Captain. You need to make a good impression if we're to hold on to any advantage. We'll follow with a wagon and the escort, to make you look important."

Kellas laughed, but he could not deny that Oyard was right.

So it was that Kellas sat all the way from Wolf Quarter to the lower palace gate in Bell Quarter, dozing a little because it was hot and he was tired. The sway of the curtained chair woke him every time the bearers turned a sharp enough corner to jolt his back. At length he gave up trying to nap and drew the curtain aside.

He remembered Bell Quarter as it had been fifty years ago, a warren of row houses, clan compounds, and markets stuffed with combs, cosmetics, perfumes, jewelers, apothecaries, and every kind of trinket and trifle to please a person who wanted to be entertained. The quarter was famous for its theaters, acrobats, singers, and the expansive Devouring temple, home to Ushara the Merciless One, where he had had sex for the first time like so many of the city lads and lasses back in those days.

The theaters and entertainment houses remained but Ushara's temple had long since been closed. Even the warehouses whose roofs he crossed on the night when he had made his infamous climb up Law Rock were gone. The lower palace with its sprawling wings and garden courtyards covered that ground now, overlooking the locks and Guardian Bridge.

They passed the palace's huge King's Gate, the monumental entrance used for the king, the lords, processions and festival parades, and other notable arrivals and departures. Instead, turning a corner past the guard tower, their little procession halted at a more modest gateway, the lintels framed as a sea serpent grappling with a sinuous dragonling. A bored guard stood on either side of the gate, yawning as servants and officials and residents passed in and out. As security, it was a disgrace.

Kellas went into the guardhouse. The young clerk on duty stammered, then fetched his supervisor.

This official had the florid face of a man who drinks too much. "Captain Kellas? The Kellas who climbed Law Rock?"

"The same. Although I wasn't a captain then. Just a young man about your clerk's age."

The young clerk had eyes like a fish. "I thought that was only a tale people sang."

The supervisor swatted him. "Show respect to your elders. My apologies, Captain Kellas. I thought you were dead."

Palace security was indeed ripe for change. "Not yet. I'm taking over this gatehouse from you, ver."

The man swatted the clerk again, as if it gave him something to do with his hands. "Lord Vanas sent a man to say you would be arriving. I will show you to your suite of rooms myself, if you will wait just a moment."

He vanished into the back and Kellas heard him peeing into a pot.

He went onto the porch to wait. The architect had designed

the approach so the gate guards could easily see who was coming. The lower palace was not a single building but rather an elaborate compound whose wings and additions surrounded a huge interior courtyard. Everything was built in wood and plastered white, high walls with no windows, only doors to each of the apartments where courtiers and officials lived who wished to dwell close to the upper palace or the junior queen.

He walked back inside. "What's your name?" he asked the young clerk.

"Sefi, Captain." The lad hunched his shoulders as if expecting a blow just for speaking.

"Does this gatehouse have a kitchen and living quarters?"

"Yes, Captain. The barracks sleeps one hundred and twenty but we're only forty now."

Kellas grunted. "From now on you and other clerks will sit on the porch and take a record of every person who enters and leaves the lower palace. Day and night, using the bells to mark time. Arrange duty rosters so this gatehouse maintains a complete and constant record of movement in and out of the palace."

The young man stared, too stunned to respond.

The supervisor returned. "Where is the tea?" He slapped the clerk on the head again. "Sefi, you should have already run to the kitchen to tell the cook. Now, Captain—"

"I no longer need your services, ver. You may pack up your household and leave."

"But—"

"I want you and your people out by the next bell."

He left Yero and Oyard to manage the changeover while he stepped back out onto the porch to study the gate. Once proper security was in place folk would grumble, and when those complaints reached high enough he would see who tried to interfere.

A pair of Spears came trotting up. "We seek Captain Kellas," they said to him as if he were just an old man loitering on a porch. "He has been summoned by Supreme Captain Ulyar."

"That was fast," remarked Kellas, and the two soldiers looked at each other as if not sure whether to answer. "Sefi!"

"Captain?" The lad bumbled out onto the porch carrying a ledger and brushes and ink. "I've got everything as you requested."

"Indeed you do. Tell Chief Oyard I've gone to see Supreme Captain Ulyar."

He walked over to the men with the chair, who were eating and drinking as they waited to be dismissed. "You will carry me to the upper palace."

The younger chair-carriers grimaced.

He gave them a hard stare. "If you are not fit for the task I can hire another chair."

Their headman hastily bowed. "My apologies, my lord. There will be no trouble."

The two Spears stared as he got into the chair, but they hurried along after. It was such a long and uncomfortable climb up the thousand steps to the top of Law Rock that he had plenty of time to recall climbing the cliff face fifty-two years ago.

The moonlight had cast its glow over the face of the rock all night long as he had felt his way from bump to knob to lip. It wasn't the climbing that was hard. It was the height, and the chance of a fatal fall. The abyss chasing at his heels made every grain of stone and breath of wind keenly experienced. For years afterward he had chased danger so as to live as vividly as on that night. Once when he had stopped to rest, a tremor had stirred along his skin where it was pressed against the rock. A faint sound of tapping had brushed his ear, probably exhaustion causing him to imagine buried creatures seeking a way out as he had been seeking a way out of the tedium of his boring life. Death was a way out. Death would be easy. But he did not fall, not then and not after. In time he had discovered in the most unexpected place a better reason to live than forever pursuing the knife's edge of disaster.

The chair came to a halt and he got down.

The floor of the supreme captain's office was laid with fresh mats. The open doors in back overlooked a courtyard adorned with flowers in the foreground and a wide training field behind. Men were skirmishing with wooden practice weapons, swinging, ducking, grunting, waiting their turn.

Kellas remembered Ulyar just as he remembered all of the Black Wolves who had been present on that awful day. Like many military men these days Ulyar had the looks of a man with a Qin grandfather. The supreme captain of the King's Loyal Spears regarded Kellas with such suspicion that Kellas wondered for an instant if King Jehosh had set him up for a fall.

But Ulyar did not intimidate him. With a calm smile Kellas sat on a cushion. An attendant brought tea. Ulyar spoke a blessing in the palace speech, mostly Sirni but with occasional words wandering in from the common language of the Hundred. They sipped politely, serenaded by the sparring of the soldiers in the courtyard.

Ulyar observed through half-lowered eyelids, as if he were about to fall asleep. A sick dislike crawled up Kellas's throat. Here sat an untrustworthy man.

"Captain Kellas, I have been given to understand you have been called in to take charge of security in the lower palace."

He gave in to the urge to wrestle for dominance. "Security has gotten lax. I agreed to step in and correct matters."

"Yes, indeed, many criminal incidents have arisen that would have been stopped a few years ago. A Silver coachman was murdered while in the hire of drunken palace lads." Ulyar pushed his teacup to the right and then back to the left. "Do you know about that?"

"A brief mention has reached my ears. I've also been asked to make inquires regarding the disappearance of a woman who was meant to be followed along the river. That kind of thing would never have happened under King Anjihosh's watch."

Ulyar stiffened at this reference to Lady Sadah. "Do not think I have forgotten the day you deserted your post guarding Prince Jehosh and came running back to King Atani's retinue to make sure the king was dead."

If Ulyar meant to play that game, then Kellas would indulge him. "If King Atani's retinue had protected him properly that day, I would not have been needed. As I recall, I found you in the rear guard, unscathed by the ambush. Unlike my factor, Chief Oyard, who almost died in the first attack."

"Are you calling me a coward?"

"I beg your pardon." Kellas affected a raised eyebrow. "I was merely observing that the ambush was planned with such dispatch and speed that the rear guard had not time to engage before I arrived. It was fortunate there were uninjured men I could rally to give chase."

Ulyar's forehead wrinkled as he sifted through Kellas's comment for a threat or an insult. "Yet still we failed. Do you know what I recall, Captain Kellas? I recall that you are a traitor."

The urge to leap up and punch him in the face surged so hard that Kellas had to grind his hands against the floor until it passed.

His soft smile was inappropriate for the occasion, and usually he had better control of his expression, but he had no other way to let the anger leak out without it flooding in a storm. "Now that we have that out of the way, Supreme Captain, is there anything else you wish to say to me?"

Ulyar folded his hands on his lap, looking content at his little victory. "So many curious coincidences, are there not? There was quite a fuss five days ago with the Herelian wedding. Did you see the Silver woman whose people paid Clan Herelia to marry her to their last son?"

"I was not in Toskala five days ago."

"At the beginning of the lamp procession she pulled her scarf right away from her face. No one had ever seen a Silver woman's face before. They scar their women, did you know? Everyone saw it, a tremendous scar that curved along her cheek. I find it shocking that the Silvers mutilate their women like that, don't you? Savage, even."

Memory jolted through Kellas. His hand began to tremble, and he set down his cup and rested the hand on a leg before Ulyar noticed. "Gilaras Herelian must be about twenty-two years of age. Is his bride the same age?"

"How are we to know? They are a secretive people. But what interests me is that Lord Gilaras's bride comes from the same clan as that of the Silver woman we saw that day, the one who was with the wagon drivers. Is Clan Herelia up to its old tricks? Have they a plot in mind to insinuate their way into the palace and then kill King Jehosh as they did King Atani?"

"A question that had not occurred to me, I admit," said Kellas, too jarred by this information to spar with Ulyar.

"No matter. Even if Lord Vanas were to support his nephews, which he claims not to do, Clan Herelia is too disgraced to have a chance of regaining past luster no matter how many warehouses full of coin the deal brings them."

How had such a gloating, petty, backstabbing man become the commander of the king's most elite fighting force? Did no one respect the need for competence any longer?

"As for palace security, that is why I have called you here today, Captain Kellas. Queen Chorannah holds an audience once a month. It is always her gracious wish to be acquainted with those who dwell under her wings. You will be expected to attend the next one, in three days."

"Of course, Supreme Captain. You may detail my responsibilities now or send me a note later, as you wish."

Ulyar looked past him and rose abruptly. Kel twisted to look behind. Two attendants swept past Ulyar's sentries. Behind them walked a young man who wore his hair in the complicated looped braids of men in training to become priests.

"Prince Tavahosh! This is an unexpected honor." Ulyar bent almost double.

Kellas got carefully to his feet spryly enough that he was pleased not to look slow. It never did to show them you were weakening. "Prince Tavahosh."

"So this is the infamous Captain Kellas, the man responsible for King Atani's death. I can't imagine why my father would give you responsibility for lower palace security. He must not love Queen Dia and my half brother Kasad as much as rumor says he does, ha ha."

The insult bothered him no more than a gnat's bite. What mattered was that everyone in the upper palace already seemed to know he was here and why.

The prince had a way of taking up room, like he wasn't sure there was enough air for everyone. "Ulyar, I wish to move up the reeve convocation so it takes place in three days."

"At the same time as the queen's formal audience?"

"Yes."

"But not all the marshals may be here by then, Your Highness."

"They will be here. I want soldiers in place."

"May I be of assistance with any of the security measures, Your Highness?" said Kellas, using age as his excuse for sliding into a conversation to which he had not been invited.

The young man's gaze lit on him, surprised to find him still there. He opened his mouth with the pleased expression of a man about to snap out a cutting retort, but abruptly dropped tense shoulders as he changed his mind about what he had been going to say. "My thanks for your offer, Captain. Your assistance is not needed. One of Ulyar's stewards will show you out."

A steward hurried forward and ushered Kellas out onto the entry porch, where he hovered as Kellas pulled on his sandals.

"It must be gratifying to Queen Chorannah to see her son so interested in administrative matters," Kellas remarked to the waiting steward.

"This way," said the man, showing him back to his chair.

Dusk was coming on when he at last climbed out of the chair at the gatehouse to find lamps lit and the outer hall set with an eating tray. He was stiff and sore from the day's exertions, but all that slipped away in the face of a very pleasant fish soup with leeks and ginger together with pickled vegetables and Yero's excellent savory rice stew. When he was done Oyard brought him wine.

"A young man has come by name of Adiki."

"Show him in."

The young man's shoulders were slumped.

"What did you discover, Adiki?" he asked as his heart plunged.

"I asked around at all the city gates and finally found a guardsman who said he'd seen a lad picked up last night that could have been Karladas. Taken into custody for the crime of loitering without a laborer's token."

"A laborer's token? What's that?"

"I only received notice of the new law this afternoon while you were in the upper palace, Captain," said Oyard. "Every resident of Toskala must apply for a token to show they reside in the city. Any person not a permanent resident must carry a token in order to labor. It's the way things are done in the Sirniakan Empire, the palace officials are saying. Every person carries a token to show where that person belongs."

"How can the lad have carried a token if he did not know he needed one and if there was none to be had?" demanded Kellas, aware that he was tired and still angry.

"That's what I asked!" Adiki raised both fists like he wanted to hammer someone's face in. "They said a new work gang was marched out this morning, at dawn. They said if I didn't want to be arrested for tomorrow's levy, I should take myself home."

A stab of frustration made Kellas's vision blur, and he realized he was truly exhausted. "Do you know where the work gang went?" he asked, forcing his tone to be even and calm.

"Some go to River's Bend, some to High Haldia, but I hear most of them head south."

"Certainly there is a lot of building going on in the south."

Adiki stared daggers at Kellas. "Please say there is something I can do! Because I'll do anything. The people sent off in those work gangs never come home."

Kellas met Oyard's gaze. The chief's arm had never fully recovered, and he limped badly, but he was a Black Wolf through and through, the real thing, not these jumped-up newcomers under the command of conniving Ulyar.

"It may be that the only way we can find out is to find a man willing to be arrested and inked."

"Put a spy in the work gang?" Adiki considered. "That's a cruel sentence because the ink can never perfectly be removed, and thus an innocent man will always be marked as guilty. But I would volunteer if it meant I could get my brother back."

"Think it over carefully. Meanwhile don't return to this office. I'll visit my clan tomorrow and speak to you then. Also, if you know anyone who can truly be trusted not to be swayed by bribes, send them to me. I need guards, and I'll pay a good wage to people who can meet my exacting specifications. Go on, then." He chased the lad out.

"You look grim," said Oyard when it was only the two of them in the flickering lamplight.

"Meeting Ulyar reminded me that several of the young Wolves I commandeered the day of Atani's death rose to become important men in Jehosh's court, yet I am not sure they all support him now," Kellas mused. "This is going to be a long and dirty business. Jehosh's position may be even weaker than I first estimated, which puts us at greater risk. Oyard, you have young children. If you cannot bring yourself to walk this path with me, let me know now, and you and your family may leave without question and with your honor intact."

Oyard stiffened to attention. "My children would be better dead than to live with their father's cowardice."

Kellas pressed a hand to the necklace of Hasibal's Tears hanging at his neck and considered how he had refused to allow Fohiono to come with him even though she was capable. "Maybe so. If we are too cowardly to act then assuredly we will always be ruled by fear. We still serve King Atani. We will not let him down this time."

28

After seven days of receiving visitors and having sex, not at the same time, Sarai began to feel restless.

"Are you bored of me already?" said Gil, watching as Sarai set out her writing desk, brushes, and ink. They had just shared a dawn meal of chicken rice soup and sweetened ginger tea on the balcony overlooking the dew-freshened garden. "Is the sex dull? We could invite a woman to our bed and share her."

"Why do you try to be outrageous? You do it all the time, even when there's no reason to."

He glanced at her sidelong. "I didn't think the suggestion was outrageous."

She laughed as she rolled up the bamboo blinds. It was a lovely early morning, still cool, the sky a soft blue not yet burnished to its daytime shine. "But you were hoping I would. Or more likely that I wouldn't. I'm not your family. You don't have to outrage me."

He sipped at his tea, looking sulky in the way he had whenever his family was mentioned.

"I like your brothers. Usi is very entertaining. General Shevad is sensible and intelligent. I admit Sinara is a trifle... demanding."

"It won't last."

"They have to be polite to me because I can cut the strings of the coin they spend. Even if they didn't, they might choose to treat me differently than they do you."

His sulky frown deepened. She found the expression amusing now but guessed she would lose patience for it soon.

"You don't understand..." He pared off a slice of mango but set it on the platter as his hands began to shake. She found herself tensing. Suddenly it seemed to her a monstrous presence inhabited the shadow creasing his frown.

"My mother was forced to watch as her five sons were castrated," he said in a low voice, "while being told that had she only alerted the palace to her lord husband's traitorous plot the boys might have been spared. So of course she blamed herself. The two youngest died despite her desperate nursing. Afterward, she was eaten up by the black dog of despair. She took her own life not long after I was born."

"Oh, Gil," she said. "I'm sorry. But it's not your fault she couldn't bear the pain."

"My family kept me ignorant of the truth for years. Welo is the one who told me, when I was sixteen. I think my family meant never to tell me how she died. They think she was weak, that she chose a shameful death, so they made sure to scold me as often as possible on my duty to the clan. They told me she wept every time she looked at me."

"Oh, Gil." She knelt beside him, but because he would not look at her she felt it prudent not to touch him. "It's not your fault that you lived and your brothers died."

He stared at her for a long time, then speared the slice of mango with a twisted, self-mocking grin. "How wise you are, my beautiful Sarai-ya. I suppose I do despise myself for having done nothing but be born more auspiciously than they were."

"Your mother wasn't weak, Gil. She was killed by accusations and by violence done to her children. I know this is no comfort, but she could have killed herself while she was still pregnant. She wanted you to live."

An angry blush heightened the color in his cheeks. "I wonder sometimes if she did know my father intended to kill the king. What if she was the one who goaded him into it? She was from a distinguished family, too, you know. Her father was one of King Anjihosh's other favorite Qin generals and her mother was from a wealthy Hundred clan. She and my father might have decided together that they were more worthy to rule than King Atani and his heirs."

It made her so angry to see him beaten down like this.

She grasped his hand. "What if they had a good reason to want the king dead?"

"Sarai!" He pulled away. "How can you even think that?"

"What kind of king trains Wolves who attack women and children?"

Arrested, he examined her in silence, then leaned closer as if he heard the wrath that smoldered in her heart. "My brothers are soldiers. They're honorable men. Anyway the Black Wolves were disbanded."

"Do you know what Sarai means, in the language of my people? It means 'sorrow.' My mother's name, Nadai, means 'joy.' Out of Joy came Sorrow. My mother took me and ran away from her husband and son. As I mentioned, I'm told she ran away with a lover. What I didn't tell you is that the lover was a wagon driver, one of the outlaws who were part of the ambush that killed King Atani. She was killed that same ambush. The Black Wolves cut down a woman who was carrying an infant in her arms!"

He whistled, eyes going wide, and clasped one of her hands between his warm ones. "We have more in common even than anyone could have guessed when they arranged the alliance."

"Perhaps. My uncles know about Clan Herelia's history. But they didn't expect I would be the one to marry you."

"Then fortune has kissed me after all," he murmured, giving her a quick kiss.

He released her hand to nibble distractedly on the mango. After the last of it was gone a tremor passed through his frame. If a man could take his anger and pain and neatly pack it away into compartments, he might look as Gil did now: uncurling fists to open hands, dropped hunched shoulders, smoothing out the tight press of his mouth, exhaling as if to expel the dregs of a long-buried anguish.

"The hells. That's all old news, isn't it? Is anything as boring as my brooding? My apologies. Do you want mango?" He sat up with a defiant shake of his shoulder and sliced off another wedge.

Instead of answering she crossed to the cupboard to fetch her Book of Accounts and paper from her lockbox. Its key hung from the same chain as her bronze mirror, which she always wore unless she was in bed.

"I like that silk robe," he remarked as she walked to the writing desk. "I can see right through the fabric to you."

Since Gil had obviously forgotten that his disliked brother Usi had gifted her the robe as "appropriate for amorous excursions," she merely smiled, sat on a cushion at the desk, and opened her Book of Accounts to where she had left off.

"I am so glad today is the last day of the marriage visits. Yesterday alone we received ninety-four people who arrived in eighteen different groups."

"The hells! Did you count them all?" He tossed a cushion down beside her and draped himself across her lap, getting in her way. He did have such lovely eyes, the kind you could stare into forever. "Do you keep track of everything?"

She kissed his cheek. "Not quite."

"That's a relief! I can imagine you recording your amount of satisfaction with each..."

"I shall have to ask Great-Aunt Tsania if she would like me to send a more detailed report than 'all parts of new husband are in working order.'"

"Please don't!" But he was laughing now.

"If you don't mind, Gil, I would like to write to my aunt. I want to finish up a set of bound pages so I can send it off with the family's courier."

He pushed up to stare at the ledger's open page, tracing a finger down the columns of writing in a way no Ri Amarah man ever would because of the custom that men's and women's knowledge must not mingle. Of course he couldn't read any of it; no outsider was allowed to learn.

"Everyone who wishes any kind of connection to us must offer greetings and a gift so it is just as well you are keeping track although I know Welo is also. Those who don't come are officially snubbing us, or letting us know they are too important to visit us."

"Like the two queens?"

"We aren't important enough to hear from them. Anyway, starting tomorrow we must return the visits."

She groaned, paging randomly back through the Book of Accounts, reminding herself of the deluge of items that had come into the household. "Every single one?"

"Yes. That's why each household leaves a token and a gift. We have a year to return the token with a reciprocal gift. It's a perfect way to let people in court know how well we value them by how long they have to wait to receive a visit from us."

"That seems...ruthless and petty."

"Now you understand why I hate the palace."

She studied his tousled hair and the silk robe he wore askew and with the silk sash from a different robe wrapping it closed. He dressed carelessly but he could get away with it because he looked good in that affected I-don't-care-for-your-rules style. She smoothed her hands down the front of her robe just to watch his gaze follow her touch along her breasts and belly. It was so entertaining to watch his penis stir and begin to rouse.

He leaned closer, breath sweet on her lips. "I think you're getting a little warm."

Just as she kissed him he jerked away and jumped to his feet. "Do you hear that?"

She listened: A beat of silence, then male voices in the courtyard.

"That's Ty. The hells! He's brought Kas with him." He hurried indoors to the cupboard where Welo had set away all the gift silk, wrapped in paper. The way he pawed through the neat ranks betrayed that he had never had to fold and put away cloth so it would be fit to wear later. "This orange...who brought that?"

She studied the ledger. "Their servants wore a badge with three roses?"

"Look for the White Leaf Clan. Ty's mother brought you silk with an orange pattern."

From downstairs voices rumbled as greetings were made.

"Ah, yes. The shelf below. To your left. That one." She locked away the Book of Accounts and her unfinished letter before she unfolded the silk. It was best-quality silk in a sophisticated floral pattern of light orange, dark orange, and brown. "Is there some way to interpret each gift and what its giver wants?"

"Ty's mother? Hard to say. I like her even though I would never admit that to him. I wouldn't think of her as one trying to take advantage. She has a Qin father and a mother who was one of Queen Zayrah's Sirniakan attendants, so Tyras is even more well connected than I am."

Elit had taught her the various ways of wrapping a length of cloth into a taloos. Iadit trotted upstairs to help Sarai fasten bracelets and anklets.

"I love all the ways you have to wrap scarves around your hair," said Iadit, fingering the elaborate knot Sarai had used to finish off the hair covering. "I didn't know whether to bow or scrape to Prince Kasad so I'm hiding up here."

"If other courtiers are watching who visits us, is a visit from Prince Kasad good or bad for our reputation?" Sarai asked.

Gil changed in front of Iadit, having not the least concern about her seeing him naked. "Hard to say. Probably Queen Dia wishes to show her approval for my loyal friendship. Others will see it as her wanting to see if we will take her side against Queen Chorannah."

Iadit set up a screen to divide the chamber into two in case Sarai wanted to sit concealed from the men. Welo brought the visitors in along with tea and fresh hot buns.

Gil slapped the two men on the shoulder. "I didn't know you could get up this early, Ty. Kas, that color looks terrible on you. Who dresses you? Oh, this is Sarai."

"I don't know how you got so cursed fortunate," said Tyras, eyeing her and blushing when Gil caught him at it. "I'll let my mother know you wore her silk, Lady Sarai."

"The fabric is quite beautiful, Lord Tyras. Please convey my particular appreciation."

"I will tell her you said so. It may soften her thorny heart. She's quite enamored of how rich Gil is and wishes to know if you have any sisters or cousins willing to shower their favor upon me."

Sarai dropped her gaze, not wanting to appear shy but knowing *No, I'm the only one they were willing to discard* was the wrong thing to say.

Kasad cleared his throat. He nodded at Welo by the stairs and Iadit by the screen, and they immediately went downstairs. When they were gone he held out a tiny silk pouch.

"My most honored mother, Queen Dia, has sent a small gift and a token in the hope you will return her visit when you are able."

Gil grabbed the object out of his friend's hand. "What's this about, Kas? We don't want to be involved in palace backstabbing and gut knifing."

"Our most humble thanks for the honor shown to us, Your Highness." Sarai plucked the pouch out of Gil's fingers. Inside she found an ivory disk carved with a two-masted ship. Beside it was nestled a large ivory clasp of the kind meant to decoratively hold aside door curtains, shaped like a head with two faces. "How lovely! If I am not mistaken this is a representation of a northern god called Enne with Two Faces."

"Enne Who Looks Both Ways," the prince corrected.

"Kas, you ass, Sarai worships her people's god so you shouldn't be giving her a present of yours. And what are you doing with an outlander god anyway? You worship at the Beltak shrine like everyone else in the palace."

"Is it required for people who live in the palace to worship there?" Sarai asked. "Because I cannot pray at the Beltak shrine."

"To rise in the ranks in the army or gain favor at court, a man must attend the ceremonies at the Shining One's shrine, Lady Sarai." Tyras clearly relished the role of the levelheaded friend. "I've heard the reeves may worship as they wish, since Beltak priests can't manage the reeves the same way they can manage the army. Out in the countryside people do as they did in the old days, I suppose."

"Not for long," broke in Kasad. "My brothers have taken upon themselves a project to build shrines to Beltak across the entire Hundred, not just in the cities. I hope you are not displeased by the gift, Lady Sarai." He had a nervous habit of rolling the hem of his sleeve between finger and thumb.

"Not at all! The workmanship is exquisite."

Kasad smiled gratefully.

Gil took the clasp from her. "I am surprised to hear you know anything about northern gods, Sarai."

"I read every book in my uncle's library. I also learned all sorts of thing from my dear friend Elit. I know I have mentioned her to you more than once, Gil." She enjoyed the deepening of color in his cheeks before she turned back to the other men. "She became a pilgrim of Hasibal."

"How exciting!" said Tyras. "One of Hasibal's players, acting out the old tales across the Hundred! Is she rich like you?"

Sarai smiled. "She isn't Ri Amarah, if that's what you mean. Just a local Hundred girl. Pilgrims of Hasibal give away all their possessions. Your Highness, I will treasure this gift."

"I will tell my mother the queen you said so." Prince Kasad walked onto the screened balcony. As the others hastened to follow, he said in a low voice, "My mother the queen hopes you may agree to be introduced to my sister, Princess Kasarah."

Tyras's mouth dropped open, and Gil's eyebrows lifted.

"I would be honored to call her friend," said Sarai. "Perhaps you will tell me whether it would be most appropriate for her to visit me or me to ask to visit her."

Kasad pressed his palms together, considering his next words. "I must warn you that if you are seen to befriend my sister, it will bring Queen Chorannah's displeasure down upon you."

Gil took hold of the prince's elbow. "What's going on, Kas? I still think Supreme Captain Ulyar was trying to set you up for the murder of the coachman to get rid of you."

Sarai thought Kasad would try to shake off Gil's grip but instead he tightened a hand atop Gil's fingers. "I am too stupid to know anything about that," he said in a tone that betrayed he knew perfectly well. "There will be a great deal of fuss and clamor in the upper palace tomorrow. Queen Chorannah's monthly audience day is now going to coincide with the reeve convocation. The queen will have stewards carefully recording who comes to pay their respects to her and who only attends the convocation."

"What is a reeve convocation?" Sarai asked.

Kasad let go of Gil. "All the reeve marshals have been summoned to elect a new chief marshal now the old one is dead."

Tyras winced. "I hear he was torn apart by his own eagle! I don't know how anyone dares be a reeve."

"An eagle killing its own reeve must be a rare occurrence, Lord Tyras, else it wouldn't be possible to have the reeve halls maintained for so many generations." When the men all looked at her she shook her head impatiently. "Surely you see my point! If the eagles were randomly and frequently killing their reeves, the institution would not be stable. So the question is, was what happened to the chief marshal unusual or expected? And if unusual, then why?"

Kasad shrugged. "I don't know. All I know is that it isn't

really an election. The marshals meet and the king appoints a new chief marshal from their ranks. You should also know that Queen Chorannah is very annoyed about the new chief captain of security the king appointed for the lower palace without consulting her."

"What about him?" said Gil. "That's got nothing to do with me, thank all the gods."

"Aui!" Tyras gestured to the gracious painted screen and the silk hangings and the expensive clothing Gil and Sarai were wearing. "Haven't you heard? Rumor says your people arranged for a new palace security captain with Queen Dia's connivance, using Ri Amarah coin to bribe the king's favor."

Gil had a hot temper and Sarai saw by the way he took a clipped step forward that he was boiling now. She pressed a hand on his sleeve and eased in front of him.

"I am so very ignorant of the palace, Lord Tyras. Can you please enlighten me as to why people might believe Gilaras's family would champion this new captain?"

"Don't you recognize the name of Captain Kellas, Gil?" Tyras demanded in a sneering tone that made Gil clench his jaw. "He's the Black Wolf who was disgraced when he allowed your father to cast a spear into King Atani's back."

"The hells!" Gil staggered. Sarai gently guided him toward a cushion, where he sat with a thump. He pressed a hand to his forehead as if he had sprung a headache.

"You can see how that might look," Tyras added helpfully. "Your family contracts an advantageous marriage and worms its way back into the palace. A man forced to retire from the Wolves because it couldn't be proven he wasn't party to the conspiracy is appointed as gatekeeper."

"How kind of my brothers not to warn me about this." Gil rubbed his brow.

"If they knew of the arrival of the captain, which they might not," objected Sarai. "You cannot assume you see the whole of the beast when you have your face right up against its ass."

For the space of three breaths their shock was like a ringing in her ears. How had that fallen out of her lips? It could never be unsaid now they had all heard it.

Gil began to laugh.

A moment later so did Tyras and the prince.

"A fair point," said Tyras, wiping his eyes. "Just because it stinks doesn't make it shit."

"I do wonder why my father suddenly brings in a man suspected of being party to my grandfather's death to guard my mother," said Kasad.

"A mystery, indeed," said Sarai. "Please let me pour tea. Our factor Welo makes the best savory buns."

It went against her upbringing to eat with men but she sat and ate with them because that was what Gil was accustomed to and what she must learn to be comfortable with. She waited for them to comment on the teapot with its painting of spiky orange and yellow proudhorn, the flower traditionally associated with fertility among newlyweds. But they made no jokes.

The tea's sharp aroma tingled in her nostrils as she listened to them discuss Captain Kellas. He was an old man now but in his youth had climbed the face of Law Rock and almost been executed for the crime, spared because of the exceptional nature of the feat. Stories about his career as a Black Wolf were legion: He was supposed to have uncovered numerous vile conspiracies to disturb the orderly peace of the Hundred and assassinated hundreds of men and women, all at the behest of King Anjihosh the Glorious Unifier in order to stamp out corrupt resistance to his righteous rule.

If the captain had been present when King Atani was murdered, might he know something about her mother? Her hand strayed to her cheek, and when Gil saw her touching the scar he shifted just enough so his knee touched hers, a tiny act of support that brought a smile to her lips.

"You two get along well," said Tyras, who had not missed the gesture. "What odds on that? You're very fortunate, Gil."

Gil said nothing for so long that Sarai held her breath, wondering if Tyras's words had offended him. But then he looked at her and smiled, and she had to look away as a blush spread hotly across her cheeks. Tyras laughed and Kasad hid his mouth behind a hand.

"I am more fortunate than I could ever have dreamed," said Gil.

They chatted awhile longer.

The men's departure left the room quiet and the cushions scattered. Sarai ate the last bun.

Gil paced. "I'm so glad this is the last day. This feels like a cage!"

"I feel trapped, too. Once we're done with this ceremony can we travel everywhere, Gil? Out to the markets? To the countryside? Even maybe..." She chewed on her lower lip, struggling to get the words out. "My mother married the richest Ri Amarah man in the Hundred. His clan lives in Nessumara." She gazed over the garden so as not to see his expression when she said the words. "What I didn't tell you is that my mother's husband is not my father. She got pregnant by her lover. A man who wasn't Ri Amarah. Which anyone would know if they saw me standing amid a crowd of women of my own people."

"Oh." The sound was more exhaled breath than word. "That's why you look a fair bit like ordinary Hundred folk. Is that why they let you marry me? Because your father isn't one of them?"

She stared at her hands. "It isn't my scar that is the mark of my mother's shameful behavior."

He took her hands in his. "I understand that to some people it would be unforgivable. But I don't care. My grandmother married an outlander. By marrying General Sengel, Grandmama tied her family to King Anjihosh, and meanwhile Grandpapa got ties into the local council and her clan's wealth and influence. Her son was half Qin thereby, and as I mentioned my mother was also born to a Qin soldier and a local woman. That's why I look the way I do, not quite Hundred-born, not quite Qin. That's what people do, isn't it? Set roots wherever they find themselves."

"Not among my people."

He shrugged as if her words didn't make sense. "If your mother and her husband had some manner of contract that specified sexual exclusivity or his assurance that any children she gave birth to were sired by him, then that would have been a matter to be negotiated between the families, would it not? Nothing to blame you for! But why do you want to go to Nessumara if it is a place your mother ran away from?"

The shame had been thrown against her all her life. But *he didn't care*. It was like an infested wound draining away.

"I have an older brother named Aram whom I have never been allowed to see although we have corresponded all my life. Uncle Abrisho has made it clear I'll never be allowed into any Ri Amarah compound again. If we were able to go to Nessumara maybe Aram could visit us wherever we were staying."

He gathered her closer. "As it happens, my darling Sarai-ya, my grandmother's people are a well-to-do Nessumara clan. I can easily go visit my cousins, if they will accept a visit from the likes of me. Which they will because Grandmama did favor me before she died. And because they will be madly curious to meet you. So we can easily travel to Nessumara. There is one more thing."

"What?"

"I know where there is a demon's coil outside Nessumara just isolated enough for us to visit. Be patient and you shall soon have what you desire."

"Gil!" She embraced him.

Downstairs the bell was rung. The man who announced himself was a clerk from the upper palace: Queen Chorannah commanded their attendance in her audience hall tomorrow morning.

Gil frowned as he studied the plain token polished to a shine. "She knows Kas came."

A shiver of apprehension rushed through her. "What does this mean?"

"You and I are being thrown into the boiling pot and they will milk us for every dribble of influence they can get." He put an arm around her, and they held each other. This she trusted in: His heart beat surely and loyally. "It means we have had our seven nights of peace. Now my family and yours will get what they paid for."

29

The next day they rose before dawn. As they left the lower palace, Gil examined the porch overlooking the palace gatehouse for signs of an elderly soldier who might be the legendary Captain Kellas, but he only saw young men on guard. Law Rock was a vast bulk still in shadow as he and Sarai waited on Guardian Bridge to begin the ascent. The Thousand Steps were cut into the rock back and forth along the cliff face, making a jagged pattern all the way to the top. Each landing on the switchback was lit by lamps. Iadit and Parad carried a change of clothes, perfume, and a parasol. Gil had insisted they hide a stash of coin under their court clothes for "sweetening the path."

So many courtiers and officials and couriers were making the climb that Gil braced himself for boredom, knowing the climb would go at a tortoise's pace. But Sarai was so delighted by the way the light of the rising sun spun shifting patterns across the towering promontory that he began to enjoy her astonishment. Sun glinted on crystals embedded in the stone. Here and there sprays of flowers bloomed on ledges.

Under cover of a hand she whispered, "It does look as if it is a giant spear of stone broken off at the top, just as it says in the tale."

He squeezed her hand, too nervous to reply. Sarai had such an incisive way of drawing connections between things in ways he had never considered that it was easy to forget she was entirely unprepared for the palace. His brothers had tried to teach him, but he had thrown off their attention like discarded clothing. Mocking their tendentious lectures had made him feel strong but now he was beginning to fear it had made him weak.

At each landing they had to pause to get permission for the next ladder of stairs, smoothed by slipping coins to the guards. He started savoring the wait because everything interested her: Trying to plot the climbing route the infamous Captain Kellas might have taken up the cliff; admiring the scenes painted on parasols unfurled by people around them; recognizing people who had come on the visiting days. Making up stories about the people she had never before seen.

The city sprawled below offered endless fascination. The two wide rivers shone, brilliant and powerful, as their water streamed southeast. The many docks with ships and boats and barges tied up or sheltered in wharves revealed a city bustling with activity. The jumbled character of the buildings and streets in Wolf and Stone Quarters stood in stark contrast with the straight avenues and open squares of Bell and Flag Quarters. Sarai pointed out how, in the sprawl of the city into Fifth Quarter and on to the fields barely discernible in the distance, you could see how the city grew outward along the two main roads and then filled in between them.

He squinted up to the white gate shining above them, its lintel freshly painted with the empty throne of the god Beltak. A fire-wreathed crown surmounted the throne, and above it shone the sun, moon, and stars. The unseen god's throne was flanked by a pair of exalted priests with their elaborate headdresses and decorated capes and by the six officers of his court, who were depicted as a man with a fish tail, one with the body of a scorpion, an ape-headed man, a stocky short man with claws for digging and shovels for feet, a man half in and half out of a fire, and a man with the body of a winged serpent.

Sarai stared like a child too innocent to know to disguise its wonderment. "Doesn't it remind you a bit of the stories of the eight children of the Hundred? If you count the two priests as human and demon?"

He stepped on her foot. "Don't say that kind of thing where people can hear you!"

"I'll stop," she whispered behind her hand.

At the top of the steps a steward wearing the crossed-spears tabard of the palace beckoned them up the last flight of steps. Sarai tucked her scarf across her lower face. Past the gate the passageway divided into three corridors. Taking their token, a steward sent them on their way with an escort. They were led down a series of streets and thence through a section of roofed corridors and at last into a partitioned room. There they were given leave to change into the voluminous court clothes required in the upper palace. He had never had privacy growing up and didn't miss it but he didn't like the sneaking suspicion that they were being watched through hidden spy-holes. Parad opened the entry door a crack so he could keep an eye on the corridor. Iadit stood by the opposite door, which was latched closed from the other side.

Gil dredged into the unused depths of his memory to recall things Usi had told him. "We must absolutely follow every protocol to its tiniest instance. Queen Chorannah insists on the protocol she was raised with in Sirniaka. We will be ushered into the Queen's Audience Hall. We will be told where to stand, men on one side, women on the other. We are not allowed to speak. The queen remains seated behind a screen the entire time and never speaks. Our names are announced to what seems empty air and then we are escorted out. That's all. An audience is a means to prove she has the power to make us wait. I've only been called once. It was frightful, hot, and tedious."

"How near to the locked Assizes Tower is the Queen's Audience Hall?"

"The hells!" He stalked a circumference of the chamber, hoping no spy listened from the walls. Glowering, he halted in front of her. "You promised you wouldn't do anything reckless."

"I'm just curious. If the tower has been closed off, then who controls access to it?"

"I suppose the Spears guard it. They serve King Jehosh."

"Do they? Didn't their supreme captain demand a bribe in exchange for not arresting you? Does he serve the king or his own greed? Or someone else?"

He tangled his fingers through hers. "We don't want to get involved in this, Sarai."

"We already are involved. We have to figure out the architecture of the palace's factions if we want to use it to our advantage. Why are you frowning?"

"You're enjoying this."

A steward appeared. They were taken down a corridor and

up a flight of stairs to a large chamber where a balcony overlooked a garden.

Sarai walked onto the balcony and Gil followed. She leaned on the railing, checking to make sure no one lurked in the colonnade beneath, and gestured the sign *empty*. She had learned the hand-talk from her lover Elit. Yet another thing to thank the woman for if he ever met her.

The garden had an ornamental pool and lovely flower beds. At one end stood a round pavilion near a wall with a closed gate. Beyond the wall rose a white tower four stories high.

"That is the Assizes Tower," he whispered. "In the old days before the Hundred had a king, the assizes were the only courts of law. Reeves would bring in criminals to local assizes. The local archon or town council would pass judgment. Difficult cases were held for the Guardians or brought here."

"The Guardians?"

"The demons who wear the cloaks called demon's skin used to be called Guardians."

"There were nine of them, isn't that right?"

"Yes. They were judges who rode a circuit of the land. Each had a territory they would cover. They looked into the hearts of the accused to discover the truth. But in the end they were corrupted by their own magic and dragged the Hundred into a terrible war."

"Being able to see into the hearts of people would be a dreadful power." Sarai pressed a hand to her right hip where, he knew, she carried her mother's old mirror like a talisman. "How could you resist using what you learned to benefit yourself or your clan? How could you bear to be intimate with someone whose every thought was unfolded before you? And how could you ever trust someone who could tear aside all the secrets you keep and the unpleasant thoughts you never act on? Didn't King Anjihosh command that all the Guardians be put to death?"

"He commanded it but cloaked demons can take horrible injuries and survive. To kill a demon you have to cut off its skin."

She winced.

"His Wolves were never able to kill them all. Some still roam the Hundred eating out the hearts of the unwary, although mostly they hide."

She rubbed her forehead.

"Are you well, Sarai? Just a little longer and we'll be free to go back to our rooms."

"Just a slight headache. Do you ever recall snatches of dreams? People you never actually saw but who are so vivid in your mind you feel you must have met them?"

"No. Usually I'm too drunk to remember my dreams."

His bad joke made her smile, as he had hoped it would. "So is the demon's coil inside the tower? I thought the coil must be embedded in rock."

"Before the Thousand Steps were carved only reeves could reach the top of Law Rock, by flying. They found the coil already here, in the rock. After the Thousand Steps were carved, the Assizes Tower was built over the coil to protect it because everyone knows people cannot walk on the coil, only demons can."

"What do you think the coils do?" she asked. "Why do the demons need them?"

They both went still as a group of men emerged from a portico opposite them and strode across the garden. The men wore sumptuous fabrics appropriate to court, and they were laughing and talking together. A few glanced up, seeing them. Sarai checked to make sure she still had her scarf pulled across her face. Then the men vanished into the building to the right.

"That was the king," murmured Gil, gripping her hand. "And my uncle Lord Vanas. He hates me. Never trust him."

"Was there never any question of your uncle Vanas being involved with your father in the king's murder? Often family members conspire together."

The words spoken so baldly made him feel he was a demon, skin flayed, bleeding out. "Vanas was a Black Wolf then. He was actually there and saw it happen. He tried to stop my father—his own brother!—from throwing the spear that hit the king in the back. The way he tells the story, when he saw he'd been too late and that the king was dead, he killed his own brother in a rage. Everyone loved King Atani."

"Hush. Someone's coming."

To his horror a door opened and his cursed uncle walked in with King Jehosh beside him.

"Gilaras Herelian." Jehosh spoke in the Hundred-speech, not Sirni. "And the Ri Amarah girl."

"My wife, Your Highness," said Gil, then cursed himself for the snap in his voice.

Every man there heard its disrespect.

"Are you protecting her beauty or her coin?" said the king, walking right up to Sarai.

She held her ground, resting a hand on her hip where her mirror hung hidden beneath the outer layer of enveloping robe. The way the scarf draped made a mystery of her eyes, and she had beautiful eyes regardless, shining now as she struggled to decide whether to choose prudent Ri Amarah modesty or defiant pride. He already knew her that well.

"And a rotten heap of stinking coin it is, so the rumor goes," said Lord Vanas with a curl of lip that marked him as Gil's enemy, always and ever. The worst of it was, they looked enough alike that anyone would guess them to be related.

"I never fault people for wishing to improve their circumstances by one means or another," said the king, not taking his gaze from Sarai. She finally gave way, looking toward Gil rather than with humility toward the floor. "I have never seen the face of a Ri Amarah woman. Nor heard one of their women speak."

"My voice is like that of any other woman, Your Highness," she said, speaking the Hundred-speech with the north country lilt that made her sound like a farmer's daughter. "As for my face, in public among strangers I still prefer the custom of my people, which allows me my privacy. Had you wished to see me as I am, you might have attended the lamp procession the day our marriage was sealed."

Men gasped at her effrontery. Gil braced himself, not knowing what he would do when the storm broke.

"Oho! You have caught a spark for your candle, Lord Gilaras," said the king with a laugh that made his retinue laugh likewise.

Gil swallowed the urge to punch the man and even glanced down to make sure his hands weren't in fists. The humiliation of having to stand here and do nothing was like burning.

"Your Highness, forgive me, for I am raised in the country and perhaps I do not understand the language as I ought, but is *a spark for a candle* not a reference to sexual intercourse? For if it is, am I meant to pronounce a witticism in response that also refers to carnal activities? If I have offended, please forgive me. I am not conversant with the manners of the palace. Nor can I feel fully comfortable, I confess, when I am the only woman in a room of men while such banter is tossed about like game play."

Sharp intakes of breath among the king's retinue hit like hammers to nails. But Gil would have crowed if he could have. The calm flow of her words, the steady heat of her eyes. Her courage. The way she laughed when he amused her. The treasures of her body, which she shared with such delight. To the hells with them all! He gave her a nod to show her they would go down together, never apart.

"Aui! I am put in my place most deftly, Lady Sarai," remarked the king in the tone of a man who has just seen an opening in a game he means to win. "I am given to understand that you and Lord Gilaras have been asked to attend upon Queen Chorannah today."

"That is correct, Your Highness," she said. "Just yesterday we were given the summons. Then there will be a reeve convocation afterward. How exciting!"

"Yes, but as is the custom of the palace, only men enter the King's Audience Hall. Women watch from the balcony." He turned to Gil. "Have you seen Kasad of late? I know you and my son are often comrades about your entertainments."

"Prince Kasad favored us with a brief visit yesterday, Your Highness," said Gil.

"Yes, I believe he brought an invitation for Lady Sarai to visit Queen Dia." Seen close up, the king was a good-looking man with the posture of the soldier he still preferred to be. But it was the humor creasing his eyes that startled Gil. "Beware you do not become the bone the two queens fight over. I would recommend you choose your side quickly, Lady Sarai, so as not to be chewed into splinters. Vanas? Have you anything you wish to say to your nephew?"

That Vanas had nothing he wished to say was made obvious by the sour anger he could not be bothered to stifle. "My felicitations on the unexpected wealth and notice General Shevad has gained through his efforts, Gilaras."

"The fortune is all mine, Uncle Vanas," said Gil, barely managing not to throw in a rude gesture.

"If you call your balls your fortune, which I suppose you must. Is she pregnant yet?" said Vanas so rudely that even the king turned to glare at him.

"Not for want of trying," said Sarai sweetly. "Or is that one of the things we are not meant to speak of in public? Do forgive me. There is so much for me to learn. I do beg your patience for my missteps."

King Jehosh laughed, then looked at his entourage in a way that made them all stay silent. He indicated the far doors, the entry to the queen's suite. "Let me escort you to Queen Chorannah, Lady Sarai. It is a privilege I can ask for, as king. You must tell me more about your clan. They are merchants, of course, being Silvers."

"Ri Amarah, Your Highness. Among ourselves we do not use the word Silvers. We consider it an insult."

"I'll remember that. My curiosity is aroused for I am sure they are people of acumen who seek to expand their net of connections."

"As do we all, Your Highness," she said, obediently moving away with the king.

Vanas caught Gil's arm and pulled him to a halt as the other men swarmed after Jehosh. "What plot have Shevad and the rest of your wormy household hatched?"

Gil could not keep a sneer from curling his mouth. "What makes you think they share their plans with me? I am nothing more than the one with balls, as they have ever reminded me since the day I was old enough to wonder why my brothers didn't have the same equipment. If they gave me anything it was bitterness, not trust. You are barking up the wrong tree. I just want..."

The thought pulled him up short. What in the hells *did* he want?

He had never wanted anything except an end to the pointless boredom of his existence and the constant dripping resentment of a family who couldn't be bothered to give him any responsibility. He was like the trash fish no one wanted to eat yet couldn't discard in case hunger drove them to desperate measures.

"Don't think I've forgotten the altercation you forced on my son over that worthless flower girl," muttered Vanas, "even though you convinced the watch he was at fault. You are such a useless prick, aren't you?"

He released Gil's arm and, thank Beltak and all the Hundred gods, pursued the king.

"No complaints of my prick yet," said Gil to his back, and then rolled his eyes, embarrassed to have stooped to such a juvenile comment.

A cough startled him. The hells! One of the king's officials had not followed the king into the audience hall. He was an old man, very trim, very straight, with the kind of keen eyes that made Gil want to rip his own eyes out so he wouldn't have to endure that soul-eating gaze. He stood at the same sort of parade rest Shevad fell into when he meant to stand for a long while.

An old soldier, then.

"Gilaras Herelian. Is a healthy young man like you not wanted for your clan's work?" His voice seemed mild but beneath it was edged steel.

"They have what they want from me. As should be obvious to anyone."

"Does it content you? You are known for a series of often foolish and sometimes daring escapades in the city. Some of them exhibiting careful planning and actual physical risk and strength. You didn't finish your thought just then. What *do* you want?"

Gil hoped a mocking smile would drive the man off. "I want to climb Law Rock with no rope and no aid. Wouldn't that be something!"

"Your hands aren't callused in the way of a man who has climbed cliffs and roofs. You'd be well served to get some experience before you attempted such a feat."

"I'm not serious."

"Aren't you? A year from now what will you be doing, Lord Gilaras? Will you be satisfied with yourself?" His cool demeanor and imposing presence drew an odd yearning out of Gil's heart.

Sarai was wonderful. But she held the coin while he was the stallion meant to sire a child on her. Once she gave birth to a healthy child or three he was nothing, just a useless prick.

The stranger examined him from head to toe in the way of a man who is considering buying a sword. "Nothing in your short history of troublemaking suggests you are the sort of person who will be content standing around the court hoping for a feather's touch of royal favor. Nor do you seem the sort who will be happy to lounge on the cushions of coin your marriage has brought you. I have a feeling you are the kind of man I could make use of."

There was a comment that begged for a reply!

"Make use of for what? King Jehosh has no reason to trust my family as I am sure you are aware. So it is not clear to me why a man trusted by the king to walk in his personal retinue could want my services. My apologies, ver, for while you know who I am, I am afraid I cannot say I know who you are."

"I am Captain Kellas. I hear you have been a loyal friend to Prince Kasad. To my mind, a young man with all the qualities you exhibit is being wasted by being put out to stud."

With a nod to end the conversation he walked after the king.

Gil stared after him. That old man had climbed Law Rock? Yet fifty years ago he would have been young. He had the posture and the cool confidence of someone who has seen so much that nothing flusters him. It would be something to have that kind of self-assurance. To have lived a life so full of incident and action that people whispered about your exploits and forgave you even though you were rumored to be implicated in the death of a king.

Shaking himself out of his reverie he hurried into the Queen's Audience Hall, a spacious room draped with painted silk curtains. Carved wooden screens divided the chamber into two halves with an aisle down the center leading toward a farther set of doors, the entry to the queen's wing. But he arrived too late. The king and Sarai had already gone into the private rooms. Of course King Jehosh hadn't waited for Gil. Jehosh had barely taken any notice of him at all, preferring to fawn over Sarai.

Attendants ushered Gil over to the men's side where several hundred men loitered, far more than usual. Like him they seemed trapped as they waited for someone else to determine their fate. What in the hells was he to do with himself once he and Sarai traveled to Nessumara, if his family did not try to put a spoke even in that mildly adventurous wheel? Confined in the pointless hothouse of court rivalries it would be so easy for his and Sarai's boredom to decay into resentment, and resentment was a rot that ate away everything that made hearts strong and wholesome.

This outer chamber was furnished in the imperial style, with plank floors instead of mats. Low couches were set along the walls but no one was sitting in them. Lamps set on stands lit the murals painted on the walls: A hunt unfolded with the hunters chasing antelope and lions. One hunter had had his arm ripped off by a lion, and his body and severed arm were being carried off on separate stretchers.

As abruptly as if he had received a hidden signal, Lord Vanas gathered up the king's personal retinue and left the chamber back the way they had come, with Captain Kellas bringing up the rear. The old man's gaze shifted to meet Gil's, as if he'd known Gil would be looking for him. His right hand sketched *patience.* Gil casually touched his ear to acknowledge he had heard. The exchange passed with such speed and subtlety that Gil doubted anyone else had noticed.

His frustration burned away in an instant. While the other courtiers milled anxiously, Gil soaked in a flood of heated excitement. All he could think about was how and when the captain might call him in, and what astounding mission he might be called upon to perform.

So it took him quite by surprise when a cohort of Spears entered the hall, led by Supreme Captain Ulyar.

"Lord Gilaras Herelian?" Supreme Captain Ulyar sauntered over.

"You know who I am," said Gil.

Ulyar's face was flushed, and he licked his lips as if his mouth was dry. His voice rang flat, like the lying weasel knew perfectly well that he had taken Herelian coin and sold them out anyway. He made sure to speak loud enough that everyone could hear.

"You are under arrest for the murder of a Silver coachman, the theft of his coach and horse, and an attempt to sell his body on the black market."

30

The dim antechamber where Sarai and the king waited was dark, and the king stood so close that his sleeve brushed hers. She shifted just enough to put a gap between them without seeming rude. His familiarity struck her as unusual given that, unlike her relationship with Gil, there was no contract between them. Drifts of gossip had collected over the week she and

Gil had received visitors. The king was known as a man who sailed from lover to lover, while at the same time his devotion to Queen Dia was spoken of as an embarrassment and perhaps even a sign of frailty.

A harsh scent in the air tickled her nostrils. She wrinkled up her nose so as not to sneeze.

A bell chimed and a door slid open to reveal a lamplit corridor. A beardless man stood on the threshold, startling for being bald and for an elaborate pattern of vines embroidered on his ankle-length jacket. He pressed hands flat against his chest and bowed to the king.

Should she have bowed to the king? Ri Amarah never bowed their heads to any person except the Hidden One, and she was not about to start now.

The beardless man spoke in Sirni, words incomprehensible to her.

The king grunted softly with displeasure, then turned to her. "Queen Chorannah has requested your presence but not mine." There was just enough light for her to study the meaningful gaze the king gave her. "I do not enter where I am not invited."

The hells! The king was flirting with her.

How was this to be handled? In the servants' parlor Elit had often persuaded Sarai to join her in acting out tales for the entertainment of the other local women. In one breath she sifted through and discarded options: The Coy Seamstress. The Shy Shepherdess. The Brassy Blacksmith's Daughter Who Could Pound a Man Flat with Five Strokes.

Find what is truest for you and use that, Elit had coached her, although she had never had Elit's skill.

The king had already made it clear he admired her cleverness.

She was grateful the scarf concealed most of her face. "The architecture of the palace is not yet familiar to me. I cannot yet be sure where I may be welcome and what I should prudently avoid."

His smile flashed. "Always avoid that which does not give you pleasure. Look for me at the reeve convocation, Lady Sarai. I will hope your eyes rest favorably upon me from the balcony of your exalted regard."

He waved fingers to shepherd her into the care of the beardless man, who led her down the corridor. The air was thick with a smell like a burning rice field after harvest. She did sneeze, quite loudly, as she entered a tiny courtyard wreathed in smoky incense.

All the decoration was lions: pillars carved with winged lions, banners painted with bold lion faces, a tapestry that depicted lions hunting down and ripping apart deer and men. Queen Chorannah sat on a half-circle couch splendidly embroidered with lions who bore the heads of men. Her loose silk robe was sewn in layers at the shoulders to give the appearance of a lion's mane. A towering headdress unfurled like wings. She was a stout woman with a face darker than that of most Hundred people and a slight resemblance to her husband. After all, because of the convoluted intermarriages among the Sirni princely houses, they were distant cousins.

Next to the queen stood a young woman dressed in a long, loose dark-blue tunic over belled trousers, as drab as the queen was bright, and hatless, her hair cut short. The queen spoke in Sirni, after which the young woman translated.

"You are Lady Sarai. Her Most Exalted Majesty Queen Chorannah observes you have come according to her command."

"Forgive me if I in any way offend. I am not acquainted with the customs of the palace. May it please you that I may know your name, who so kindly translates our words?"

By no flicker of expression did the young woman react to this attempt to be polite to her. "Her Highness says you would already know the speech of civilized people if you had been properly brought up in the city instead of being raised in the countryside like a savage."

Not so dull after all!

"I hope someday to remedy my deficiencies, Your Highness." Sarai tried to remember the short lesson Gil had given her in etiquette. He had not told her what one says to a queen who exudes insults like incense.

"Your people are very wealthy," added the translator after the queen spoke.

"I do not sit among the elders of my people to know the details of such matters, Your Highness. I am but a young bride."

"I am informed you are twenty-two, quite old to be married for the first time. I was fifteen when I was sent north to marry my cousin. You have been held back for a long time but I suppose that is because yours are a cunning and secretive people. They hide a magic deep in their homes that gives them the sorcerous skill to force people to sell to them at a loss. Their men grow horns that burn from cool to hot depending on how many strings of coin their customer has, so they may calculate how much to overcharge them. Their women wash themselves in a blue fire that makes them irresistible to their menfolk, and they must do so, and also hide themselves the rest of the time, because they possess warped and grotesque faces."

Sarai took in a long, slow breath, counting up prime numbers until she could find a calm voice, then unhooked the scarf. "I will let you judge the last one for yourself."

It was difficult not to blink a hundred times while the queen examined her with an expressionless stare that made the woman look dull and bored. Finally the queen spoke, and the young woman translated. "The queen says the scar is a frightful blemish."

Sarai had heard this slur too many times to react to it now.

"Are all your women marked in this unpleasant way?"

"No, just me. Forgive me if I in any way offend, Your Highness. I am unacquainted with the customs of the palace. But I cannot let pass the other rumors you mention, all of which are lies."

"You must say so, of course, but your people are obviously hiding something. Jehosh's grandfather King Anjihosh made a secret pact with them. They gave him coin and information, and in exchange he allowed them to live in peace under his rule and fill their coffers with strings of silver and gold. What do you know of this?"

"King Anjihosh was a fair and honest ruler who dealt with my ancestors respectfully and allowed them to live as they wished."

"If everyone lived as they wished, Lady Sarai, then the land would be chaos. Order must be imposed if there will be peace."

"Of course, Your Highness."

"I have done a study into your people and their wealth. Eight generations ago Ri Amarah arrived on the shores of the Sirniakan Empire by ship from the east. When they disembarked they burned their ships so they could not be forced to leave. When their chief men were brought before the emperor, they begged for asylum, a place to build homes and live quietly according to their own customs. Two generations were born and grew old in Sirniaka, left alone by the emperor's mercy to build their treasuries. Then the exalted priests of Beltak walked among the exiles and revealed to them the true worship of the Shining One. The wise bowed their heads to acknowledge the holy rule of Beltak but the rest stubbornly refused. When the priests confiscated their wealth as punishment, they left their homes and traveled north to the Hundred. Here they grew wealthy again, with the aid of their magic."

Sarai knew better than to argue. She sat like stone.

"Never have your people married outside their own households. Yet here you are. A strange change of heart, is it not? To find a Ri Amarah woman married to a traitor's son?"

"My people are not traitors, Your Highness."

"The peculiar and vulnerable situation your people find themselves in as distrusted outsiders in a peaceful land means they would be foolish indeed to plot against the king. Yet I might wonder if the Herelian traitors are attempting once more to disrupt the stable continuity of the palace, and in doing so are making your people unwitting conspirators."

She twisted her fingers together, seeking a calm voice. "I know nothing of such matters, Your Highness. I am merely a dutiful daughter."

A different bald, beardless man appeared. He bent to whisper in the queen's ear, and whatever he told her caused her to nod with satisfaction. As he retreated, Chorannah lifted a languid hand. Gem-encrusted rings crowded her fingers, each one a different stone and color.

"Let me assure the dutiful daughter that her people will be given the access and influence they desire. You will move here to the upper palace, Lady Sarai, and join my court. Your clan shall place their treasury at my disposal. Tayum will take you to your new chamber."

"My new chamber?"

"Did you not hear me, Lady Sarai?"

The beardless man dressed in the vine-embroidered robes extended a hand, but she took a step back to evade his grasp.

"But where is Lord Gilaras?"

Chorannah fixed her with a gaze that was anything but bored or dull. "Lord Gilaras has been arrested for murder, Lady Sarai. He will be inked as a criminal and handed over to the work gangs. You are fortunate to be spared his disgrace, but I have intervened purely out of the goodness of my heart. Now go along, as I have commanded."

Sarai felt she had no choice but to follow Tayum down a servants' alley where he sat her on a bench and stood braced before her so she could not escape. An oppressive weight swelled to fill every nook and cranny of her being. She simply could not think, only sit stunned. She might as well have just had her arm chopped off and been left to watch the severed end leak blood onto the plank floor.

After an endless stifling interval, another servant appeared and beckoned. Tayum led her through a confusion of passageways and thence into a room with a matted floor. There, to her relief, Uncle Abrisho waited, his somber clothing in stark contrast to the giddy smile on his face. His appearance struck her like a sunny flower in the midst of withering hopes.

He rushed over to grab her hands. "This is splendid! You are to be congratulated. Even I did not think you could bring us to the attention of Queen Chorannah with such shrewd maneuvering."

"Congratulated!" She wriggled out of his grasp and looked to the door, but Tayum blocked it. "My husband has been arrested and condemned to the work gangs!"

Abrisho led Sarai onto a tiny screened balcony that overlooked the king's garden. He was actually humming to himself, almost floating with triumph. "The alliance with Clan Herelia was a means to get into the palace. Now that the queen herself has honored you, we are better off without them."

That he could speak so callously about Gil made Sarai think she did not know him at all, but his enthusiasm forced her to realize how carefully she had to tread. "Was this your plan all along?"

"I was satisfied with the marriage, for it gave us access we did not have. But I admit that, yes, in my heart I dreamed we might gain a better position and even be able to jettison the Herelians."

"Ah, yes, like wastewater off a becalmed ship whose sails have finally caught the wind."

"Ha! Ha! How droll you are, Sarai." He rubbed his hands

together as if polishing his carefully laid plans. Standing this close to him it was easy for her to see how neat he was in all his ways, his head scarf perfectly creased and tied, his silver bracelets untarnished by any least blot, his clothing in keeping with the somber custom of the men of a Ri Amarah house yet splashed with a few bright jewel clasps on his jacket and an emerald pin in the shape of a lion on his head scarf as if to remind people of his exalted new ally in the palace. "You shall see this is the best we could have wished for. No taint of Herelian disgrace adheres to us."

She grasped the lattice, fingers woven around the carved wood, for otherwise her legs would have given out. But her voice shook only a little. "Of course, Uncle. I see how wise you are. Are there any particular business propositions you wish me to raise with the queen right away?"

"No, no!" He glanced toward the other room, at the man watching them. "First ingratiate yourself. I've brought a chest of coin for you to sweeten a path, as they say in the palace. Everyone likes a little gift, do they not? Later you may ask for advice, for people love nothing better than to give advice. You may learn a great deal from what they tell you, for it is exactly when they are expounding that they may most reveal themselves."

"I understand completely. Is there anything else you recommend?"

"Be patient. You are a credit to the clan despite everything that was said about your mother."

Her hands tightened on the lattice as she wished she could wrench it from its moorings and batter him over the head with it. He seemed not to notice the fixed glower of her smile. "Of course, Uncle. Am I to be allowed to return to my apartments in the lower palace to fetch my things?"

"No. It is a measure of the queen's good opinion of you that it has already been arranged for your things to be brought here."

"Ah." She tasted bile as the enormity of the disaster weighed into her. "So I am to remain here, not even allowed to see Gil before he is taken away..."

"As for that, Sarai," he said, then paused to clear his throat with the self-conscious rigor of a man about to say something delicate. His gaze dropped to her abdomen. "Do you know yet if you are pregnant?"

At once she pressed a hand to her belly.

He looked again toward the door where Tayum waited in stolid silence, then lowered his voice to a whisper. "There are ways to rid oneself... Women's knowledge..."

"What do you mean?" she demanded even though she knew exactly what he meant.

"If you are pregnant with his child then we retain an obligation both to him and to his clan, according to the conditions of the contract. If you are not, the queen will find you a more suitable husband, perhaps even a high official."

"So it would behoove me to make sure I am not pregnant, is that what you are suggesting?" she said through gritted teeth.

He grasped her hand, lifting it off her belly. "Yes, you understand me exactly! You are very clever, Sarai, just as Makel and Rua said you were. You and Great-Aunt Tsania know all about the pharmacology of plants and how to regulate women's courses."

She tugged her hand out of his, and to her relief he let her go and took a step away, obviously eager to be done with their interview.

"I'm thirsty," she said, and then more loudly, letting despair and fury give strength to her voice, "I'm thirsty and hungry; is there nothing here for me to eat and drink?"

"I will not stay," said Abrisho as he handed her the key to the coin chest.

She could scarcely abide the way he kissed her on each cheek as he would one of his own daughters. She did not walk him to the door. As Abrisho left, Tayum admitted a woman dressed in drab dark-blue trousers and a long jacket. She helped Sarai out of the suffocating court jacket and brightly colored under-robes with their weight of pleats, then poured perfumed water into a basin so Sarai could wash. She scrubbed her skin as if to rub the touch of Abrisho's approval right off, but nothing would ease the sense that she had been befouled by his ambition. And her own ambition! She had walked into the contract with open eyes. She had been willing to endure marriage to a man she cared nothing for or might even despise because she wanted the freedom it would bring her. It was Gil who had surprised her.

The attendant presented her with cotton trousers, a gauzy shift that fell to her calves, and, as an overgarment, a patterned knee-length shirt that tied closed with a bright-yellow sash. A second woman entered bearing a tray of rice porridge, salty greens, and a cup of pear juice. Obliged to eat under their eyes, she consumed the meal quickly. Under Tayum's supervision the women arranged a sleeping mat, several cushions, and a cham-ber pot as for an extended stay. The two attendants looked so alike in their drab blue tunics, their black hair cut too short even to braid, that Sarai had trouble telling their faces apart, but one worked with brisk, impatient movements while the other, who was missing the little finger on her right hand, fussed to make everything perfect.

When they had finished she handed each woman a hand-some gold cheyt, which they accepted with downcast eyes. Then they left her alone.

To do nothing was insupportable. She pressed herself against the door to listen. As soon as she could no longer hear footfalls she tested the latch. But of course they had locked her in.

31

Dannarah brought a full flight of eighteen reeves to attend her at the reeves' convocation, according to her father's maxim: *Come well armed to a hostile gathering.* All the marshals had come, so the reeve compound atop Law Rock bustled with fawkners trying to tend too many eagles. She landed with Tarnit and Lifka, leaving the rest of her flight to repair to a landing ground outside the city. Lifka's presence would prove Auri was dead in case anyone had their doubts.

Hammering and sawing serenaded the three reeves as they walked to the gate. Scaffolding surrounded an old barracks and an abandoned loft. Lifka scratched her dog's head as the little monster growled softly, uncomfortable with all the activity.

"This building activity is new since we were here last month," Dannarah remarked.

"Looks like they're expanding the compound," said Tarnit.

"Jehosh needs to consult me before he acts. This is exactly the problem I had with him before, the way he would jump in and expect me to follow whatever hair-witted scheme he came up with."

"Marshal, just remember—"

"Remember that arguing with Jehosh is what made him take the chief marshalate away from me twenty years ago? I haven't forgotten, Tar. I'll be polite and reasonable in all my dealings with him. Sheh!" Tarnit had such a comical way of rolling her eyes that Dannarah elbowed her, wanting to laugh but knowing that here in public it was below her dignity. "I will deal with him differently this time around. I will!"

Tarnit's ability to draw a laugh out of any fraught situation was another reason Dannarah kept her close.

"I know I'm too blunt and abrupt. I just want to get things done!"

"And you will, Marshal," said Tarnit with that cursedly sunny smile that made a person feel like warmth and heart and brightness still existed in the world. "You know all of us at Horn Hall will follow you anywhere."

A palace steward escorted them to the King's Audience Hall. The way Lifka carried the cursed little dog everywhere got people staring. If nothing else surely the girl could train the hells-spawned creature to bite anyone who annoyed the new chief marshal.

Dannarah nudged Tarnit as they followed the steward along a shaded portico lined with soldiers, so many palace guards it seemed Jehosh was reminding everyone who was in charge now that he was back from the north. "You ever heard of a Silver getting chosen by an eagle?"

"As a reeve? Never."

"Don't you think that's strange? I knew a man who started life as a Qin soldier who became a reeve. A couple of northerners who came to the Hundred from Ithik Eldim after the war likewise. A Sirniakan priest's daughter, to her father's horror. But I've never seen a Silver in reeve leathers."

Tarnit scratched her chin. "The men's scarves would come off in the wind. Then we'd find out what sort of horns they really have."

Cracking a smile at Tarnit's predictable joke forced Dannarah to realize how tightly wound she had become, like wet cloth being wrung. A crowd of officials and high-ranking servants waited outside as if eager to be the first to hear the news. Entering the King's Audience Hall did nothing to dispel her nerves.

Instead of a convocation of reeves alone, in the traditional manner, King Jehosh had draped the proceedings in a full panoply of kingly majesty. The king's chair, currently empty, was placed on the dais and ornamented with silk banners. *Here I am*, it said.

On the step below the king's chair stood three chairs, one for each of his sons.

On the step below that, nine chairs for the judges, called Guardians, who oversaw the assizes. Each chair had a different-colored cushion to represent the nine provinces of the Hundred: green for Mar, heaven blue for Olo'osson, silver for Sardia, red for Herelia, gold for Teriayne, brown for Istria, purple for Haldia, black for Arro, and white for Ofria. Only five Judge Guardians were present today, three of whom Dannarah had never seen before and did not recognize. They looked cursed young; two had no gray in their hair at all. In Anjihosh's day the Judge Guardians had always been elders chosen because of an exceptional reputation for honesty and wisdom.

On the step below the judges, Supreme Captain Ulyar and three generals sat on camp stools, representing the army.

On the lowest step the six reeve marshals were allowed to sit on cushions. She was the last one to arrive, as she had planned.

Courtiers and officials waiting for the king and princes to arrive packed the hall, five or six hundred at least. Everyone who aspired to be anyone was here. The gathering seethed with the energy of men eager to claw their brothers' eyes out for a chance to climb one rung higher in court now the king was back. She strode right into the mass just to watch them see her and step back. It wasn't their deference that pleased her. People who embraced sycophancy were useless to her. All she needed was their recognition that they had to get out of her way.

Scanning the screened-off balconies she glimpsed the bright silks of palace women waiting for the event. It seemed a puzzling lot of fanfare for the election by reeves of their new chief marshal, especially when everyone knew it was really the king's decision.

But that was exactly it, wasn't it? Jehosh did not have Atani's generosity of spirit nor Anjihosh's astute judgment of character. But he had a finely honed sense of how to stage himself to best effect and reassert his power after his long absence.

The crowd quieted as everyone watched her take her place. She greeted each of the marshals by name: stolid Ivo of Iron Hall, even older than she was and rarely at court, a place he despised; quiet Goard of Gold Hall, who had been her lover many years ago, an affair they had regretted in its immediate aftermath and later come to laugh over; handsome Fuli of Copper Hall, a man always standoffish. Arrogant Toas of Argent Hall could barely be bothered to give her a nod. Bronze Hall's marshal was a fellow she did not know, cursed young and clearly of Sirniakan ancestry; he offered her a condescending smirk as she acknowledged him.

"Otham," he said, giving her his name but not asking hers. They all knew who she was.

As she sat, she hoped her knees wouldn't crack too loudly or her stiff hip seize up and make her look like an invalid, but she made it down without scrutiny because they were all staring at Lifka and the quivering little dog as the girl and Tarnit took a place among reeves standing off to the side. To her disgust no other female reeves were in attendance. The last woman besides her who had been marshal had died ten years ago and been replaced by a man. It hadn't been like this before. Other than consolidating the reeves into military operations, her father had left the halls alone to administer themselves in the old way. When Anjihosh had died, the reeve halls had prudently elected her chief marshal in her father's place. It was her inheritance from him, as he had planned.

Jehosh had wasted the lives of too many reeves in the Eldim wars and afterward rewarded those who had supported him with offices and authority they didn't deserve, turning out experienced administrators and generals in favor of men who told him what he wanted to hear.

Let it go.

That water had long since flowed under the bridge. She and Jehosh needed each other now. This time they could work together.

The doors in the back opened. Guards filed in, followed by Prince Tavahosh draped in the white robes of the priesthood and Prince Kasad wearing a long jacket and loose trousers in sober purple like a courtier in the palace who does not want to draw too much attention to himself. Tavahosh could barely disguise a triumphant sneer, while Kasad had the look of a kicked dog trying to creep out of sight to safety. Farihosh had not yet returned from the south.

After the princes seated themselves, rustling occurred in the balconies: the unseen entrance of the queens to sit among the women already at their places.

Last, King Jehosh strode in with such a thunderously ominous frown that a murmur ran through the crowd.

He sat.

Yet after all he was not the last to enter. True servants should already have been waiting in obedience for the arrival of the king. In utter defiance of tradition, three priests entered in his wake. The eldest was fitted out in a towering headdress, embroidered veil, and voluminous vestments whose panoply marked him as the supreme exalted priest under whose holy authority the benighted peoples of the Hundred sheltered.

"Here we assemble," said Jehosh at once, as if he had tired of a charade she wasn't aware they were playing. His tone was sour, and shadows darkened his eyes. "Let the priests sing a prayer of mourning in praise of Chief Marshal Auri whose spirit has so recently departed the mortal land and returned to the embrace of Beltak the Shining One."

The priest who sang the prayer had a pleasant voice that spun a praise to grief and exaltation into a soaring melody that her mother would have loved. But even as lovely and heartfelt as the man's voice was, Dannarah could not relax. She surveyed the crowd, seeking the rats biding their time among the mice. Off to one side she saw Captain Kellas standing so still he seemed part of the mural commemorating Jehosh's great military victory. Catching her glance, he dipped his chin in acknowledgment. She tilted her head as a question but he had already looked away.

The priest finished the prayer. People murmured the correct response. Her lips moved in the phrases she had memorized as a girl, although she had long ago given up making any but required offerings. Her mother's compassionately simple belief in a shining god who brought happiness and good fortune into the hearts of believers seemed a far sight removed from the elaborate hierarchy of the priests Chorannah favored.

Jehosh stood. "In the honored tradition of the land, it is time to elect a chief marshal who will oversee the administration, training, and well-being of the reeve halls. The reeves are the eyes of the land. They are the messages flowing among us, the voice that speaks here atop Law Rock and then can fly to every border station in the Hundred within a few days. Our victories in Ithik Eldim came about because of the reeves. Peace in the land rests on their vigilant patrol."

"Peace in our hearts and our spirits rests on the vigilant patrol of Beltak's appointed holy leaders, Your Highness," said the high exalted priest. "As it is said, *Let the servants of the Shining One see into your hearts so all darkness may be cleansed from the world*."

The shock of this impudent man interrupting the king jolted Dannarah out of her complacency.

Jehosh went red. His gaze flew to the screen behind which Queen Chorannah was seated, then dropped as Tavahosh abruptly got to his feet. Without being invited to do so, the prince took a step up to his father's side.

"My thanks, Father," he said in a voice that carried to the corners of the hall. "You will not regret the responsibility you grant to me today. Your wisdom in passing the reeve halls out of the supervision of the army and in under the sheltering hand of the shrine will serve the land well in the years to come. The reeves will be trained by priests to see with a righteous heart. Hand in hand with the shrines they will serve the god's justice at the assizes." He placed both hands against his chest in the manner of priests bowing with hand to heart before the god. "I will serve as chief marshal at your command with an eye only for purity and a heart only for the god's justice."

The hells!

Jehosh's blindsided expression would have made her laugh except that the attack came at her expense. It was exquisitely done: the interruption, the claim made via the king's authority before the king had a chance to make his own appointment. Jehosh looked weak for allowing the interruption and would look weaker if he denied the whole and tried to bluster his way back into control of the assembly.

Frustration and humiliation seared through the king's face but he turned it into a smile as he fought for a last piece of ground in this rout. "As you are not yourself a reeve, I appoint Marshal Dannarah to act as your second and adviser in all matters."

She strode up through the generals and the Guardians to join Jehosh, embracing the disaster even as she was spittingly furious. "Naturally I am at your disposal, nephew," she said to Jehosh, then whispered, "Call an end to the assembly now, while you still can."

Jehosh grasped Tavahosh's arm as he addressed the hall. "All has now been revealed. Everyone shall go at once to the West Portico where a troupe of singers and players under the direction of the Honorable Lord Usi of Clan Herelia will entertain with a series of tales."

Not waiting for a response, he dragged Tavahosh out the back door of the hall. Supreme Captain Ulyar bolted after him, and Tarnit and Lifka hustled after Dannarah quickly enough that the three of them got through the door before Ulyar closed and barred it so no one else could follow.

In a private inner corridor King Jehosh tightened his grip on his son's arm as the young man gritted his teeth. "Tomorrow morning we will announce there has been a change of plans and you have decided to resume your studies with the priesthood. You know perfectly well I intend Dannarah to become chief marshal."

Tavahosh carried his pride like a mighty banner. "I will do no such thing. It has already been arranged and settled. Under the oversight of the supreme exalted priest and the shrine hierarchy, the reeve halls will finally make needed changes."

"Already arranged and settled!" Jehosh released his son with a shout. "This is nothing more than a naked gambit by your mother to increase the power of the shrine hierarchy and thus wrench control of the Hundred away from me!"

"We are not plotting against you, Father. We are saving the Hundred. You have spent your coin chasing women and pretending to be a soldier in the north when you should have been here administering your kingdom. You take the advice of outlanders and consort with people who do not worship at the shrine. We are the ones doing what is best for the Hundred."

Jehosh raised a hand as if to slap his son, then laughed harshly as he caught himself and lowered it.

Dannarah broke in although she knew she ought to wait for Jehosh to speak. "You can't transfer control of the reeve halls to the priests."

"Of course we can transfer control to the priests," said Tavahosh. He wasn't even crowing with victory. He was convinced he was right. "It should have been done years ago."

"The priests know nothing about reeves and eagles!"

"The priests know it is long past time to make changes."

"What sort of changes?" she demanded, for his words struck her in a most ominous way.

"For one thing, it is absurd that women serve in such dangerous and violent positions. Women are too subject to emotion to make rigorous decisions. Pregnancies interrupt their duties. They can be more easily hurt than men and therefore put other reeves at risk. They aren't strong and forceful enough to apprehend criminals. The women currently in service will be allowed to retire honorably—"

"Your ignorance stuns me, Tavahosh. Besides the evident fact that women have served capably as reeves for generations, reeves don't *retire*."

"Why not? Their eagles can simply be issued to new reeves."

Such words spewing from his lips made her go blind with anger for one heart-hammering moment.

"Aunt Dannarah, calm down," said Jehosh in a commanding tone.

"Calm down? Are you afraid I will whistle Terror down from the heavens to rip you all apart in order to end this travesty now? Because I give my oath that it is a cursed tempting idea. As for you, Tavahosh..." Her contempt was too roused to calm now. "Either you and your priests are stupid, or you are all as bloated with arrogance as a full bladder is with urine. Eagles jess reeves. We humans have nothing to do with it."

"So everyone claims, but King Anjihosh arranged for you to become a reeve!"

She laughed wildly. "Is that what you believe?"

"Here you stand! He even arranged for you to become chief marshal. Is that not proof?"

The beauty of such ignorant words sprayed by a voice so sure of its knowledge and authority never failed to impress Dannarah. "Arranging for me to be properly trained to act as chief marshal is not the same as arranging for me to become a reeve. When Terror jessed me it was as much a surprise to my father as it was to me."

"The reeves all say that, but we have only their word for it. People follow custom blindly until they are shown a better path. Under the shrine's supervision, things will change. For now, those women who do not choose to retire will be allowed to carry on serving, separated from men. It isn't fitting for women to roam about the roads and be asked to arrest and confront men."

"Even though they have always done it and without any trouble?"

"So you must claim. Those women who remain in the halls will be remanded to a new service, as couriers."

"What in the hells are you talking about?"

Jehosh had gone utterly still, his body tensed as for battle although he did not even twitch. Back by the wall, Ulyar watched.

Tavahosh was well wound up and happy to keep talking, secure in his triumph. "We will institute a service for any reeves deemed unsuitable for military service and patrol. They will fly as couriers for the palace and the shrine, and as hired couriers for merchants and other people who can pay for a message to be taken at speed from one place to another."

"Reeves have never been paid for their service or hired out.

We are paid in kind. We serve the land, not ourselves. Hiring out reeves like hiring wagoners is a sure road to corruption."

He tugged at an ear as if to make sure everyone knew what a clever lad he was to think so fast. "Since you are so concerned with the matter I will grant you this honor to your great age. You may oversee the new courier patrol. It will be based here atop Law Rock. The reeve compound is being refurbished even now so it can house more reeves."

With abrupt decision, Jehosh turned. "Captain Ulyar, arrest my son."

The man pressed a hand to his heart. "Your Highness! Do not demand a rash action that you will regret!"

Jehosh put a hand on the hilt of the jeweled dagger he wore as part of his formal garb. "Then you are dismissed, Ulyar."

"He is not dismissed!" blurted out Tavahosh. "Supreme Captain Ulyar has served loyally for years. With great distinction and efficiency, I must add."

The contrast between the son's youthful vigor and confidence and the father's weathered face and frayed tension became stark. One was coming into his own with every expectation of victory and the other had already started down the slope into oblivion. Yet for all that Jehosh had spent his youth making one reckless and idiotic decision after the next, he had enough wisdom now to lower his hand from the dagger.

When his gaze crossed with Ulyar's, it was the captain who looked away. "It seems you no longer serve me, Ulyar. As for you, Tavahosh, is there anything else you care to reveal?"

Tavahosh hesitated as if unsure whether he had just made a blunder. Although Dannarah would gladly have let him know he had, she kept her mouth shut this time. Let Jehosh scrape a sliver of satisfaction from the fray.

To her disquiet Prince Tavahosh's gaze flashed to Lifka.

What simmered in his expression disturbed her because he was a man who did not like to be thwarted.

"All who live in the Hundred owe their loyalty to the god and to the king," said Tavahosh tendentiously. "All must serve god and king first rather than their own plots and plans. I have seen with my own eyes a slave girl steal the eagle of the chief marshal. Yet my aunt stands aside and lets it happen, perhaps even approves it. After what I witnessed in River's Bend, Lady Dannarah, how can you convince me that eagles are not merely tools in the hands of ambitious people?"

"With your own words you speak of yourself," she said.

"Enough!" The king stepped between them. "You may go, Tavahosh. Take Ulyar with you since apparently you already have."

Ulyar bowed in the proper fashion, caught the prince's eye, and nodded. They left together, not bothering to hide their alliance now it was revealed.

Captain Kellas stepped out of the shadows. "That went well."

Jehosh was rubbing his forehead. "They ambushed me."

"It was well played on their part," agreed Kellas blandly. "It certainly caught everyone by surprise, even me."

"Chorannah means to render me superfluous at my own court!"

"Yes, you are stuck in the ditch they dug for you, Your Highness, while Lady Dannarah has lost her temper in such a way that Prince Tavahosh may be excused for cutting her off entirely."

"You're wrong about that," said Dannarah as her rage abated and she could think again. "I recognize his sort of folly. He'll decide he has to prove me wrong in such a way that he can gloat over my fall. To do that he has to keep me close, as he already means to do since he has just assigned me to be head of this courier service. In truth, Jehosh, this works to your benefit."

"To my benefit? How can you possibly say so?" The king began to pace.

"Be patient, Jehosh. They will overreach, and when they do, you'll find your opening."

"My opening!" he said bitterly. "They treat me as if I am no longer king. Why doesn't Chorannah just have me murdered and get it over with?"

Kellas chuckled in a way that made the king stop dead and stare at him, alarmed. "No, Your Highness, I'm not saying I have proof that she plans to do so. But it is a question worth pondering. If she intended merely for Farihosh to take over as soon as possible, murdering you would be the wiser move." His gaze met Dannarah's in private acknowledgment of their long-ago pact that had come to nothing, then returned to the king. "Why grab hold of the reeve halls so boldly and publicly now, while leaving you alive?"

"The hells," muttered Jehosh. "Auri must have been working with them all along, too."

Kellas nodded. "I think they did not intend to act publicly yet. Mostly likely they were forced to act precipitously upon Auri's death to protect an asset they can't afford to lose control over."

"The reeve halls." Dannarah turned to her nephew. "Do you still control the treasury?"

"Yes, I control the treasury and all taxes and tolls and other such imposts and income."

"So Chorannah's treasury is dependent on whatever allowance you give her?"

Jehosh stared down the empty corridor to a sun-washed garden where a fountain splashed merrily. The sheer toil it took to feed, water, and maintain people atop Law Rock was one of the reasons Anjihosh had kept his palace small and housed most of his administration in the city below. But people who had no concern for the amount of labor and inconvenience needed to keep them in their own personal luxuries would never stop to consider such incidentals.

"Yes. Chorannah is always after me for coin. How much control I retain over the assizes I am no longer sure, now that the shrine demands the right to arrest people for blasphemy. As for the rest, Ulyar controls the army although I believe I retain the loyalty of certain of the generals, like Shevad, and the military governor and forces stationed in Ithik Eldim. Lord Vanas also supervises the granaries and my personal guards."

"Are you sure you can trust Vanas?" Dannarah asked.

"Oh, yes, I am sure of him," said Jehosh so carelessly that she might as well have asked if the sky was blue. "I believe you are right, Captain. I appointed Vanas, Auri, and Ulyar to protect my interests so I could come and go as I needed. But clearly over the last few years Chorannah turned Auri and Ulyar against me. It's so obvious now! If Auri were alive she'd have left things as they were because I was still oblivious to her maneuvering."

He began pacing again, five steps up and five steps back as he talked. "I was left completely ignorant about the situation in Sirniaka because Ulyar and Auri control the information I receive. That's why Aunt Sadah's visit and the news she told me about the strife between the imperial princes took me by surprise! Now I must wonder if Chorannah had Aunt Sadah murdered."

The captain nodded. "I shall see if I can offer you better intelligence, my lord."

The king went on as if he hadn't heard, his words as clipped as his restless stride. "I have held Kasad at arm's length so as not to seem like I favor him more than the older boys. If Chorannah truly believes I intend to disinherit her sons and put Kasad on the throne, then she will feel she must have a powerful ally to protect her sons."

"The priests," said Dannarah drily.

"Yes, but the priests here in the Hundred only have as much power as she can create for them. To really back her up she needs someone like a queen mother of the Sirniakan emperor. How convenient that her older sister now fills that position! But Chorannah knows I will never involve the Hundred in a Sirniakan civil war, so she has hidden her involvement from me."

"She must have had this in mind for some years," said Kellas, "what with Emperor Faruchalihosh getting older, especially if Farovadihosh is truly an incapable heir."

"Yes, yes," murmured Jehosh, still pacing.

"That's why Auri moved the base of his operations to Argent Hall in the south!" exclaimed Dannarah as the cunning complexity of the plan unfurled in her mind's eye like wings lifted for flight. "If Auri and Ulyar have been in on Chorannah's plan for years, then it makes perfect sense to move the reeve administration to where they can best control any news from the empire."

Jehosh slammed to a halt as suddenly as if he'd hit an invisible wall. "They think they've kicked me but all they've done is forced me to see the truth. My troops still love me. Maybe I can't strip Ulyar of his position openly, not yet, but we'll see how long he lasts as supreme captain when I rally the soldiers to my side. Are you with me, Aunt Dannarah? Captain Kellas?"

32

Lifka had never expected to find herself pressed against a wall forced to listen while the king argued with his son the prince in a language she couldn't understand. A pleasant woodcutting journey into the skirts of the Wild with Papa seemed like the best thing in the world right now, the mules plodding in their patient way, the dogs eager with their happy faces, and she and Papa talking about anything that came into their thoughts. She didn't want or need palaces.

The Runt whined. She clamped a hand over his muzzle as movement along the wall caught her eye. A boy slithered along the shadows behind the colonnade, trying to approach without alerting the arguing nobles. The long formal robe he wore looked strange on a lad that age who, as Mum would say, ought to be running about freely in a kilt like an ordinary child. The extraordinary shimmering shine of the silk impressed her, as did the spray of freckles on his pale cheeks.

Old Captain Kellas of Plum Blossom Clan stood in the shadows, obscured by a pillar. When he had arrived in Toskala she did not know. He caught the boy's sleeve, pried the child's hand open to look at the object the boy was clutching, then released him. The boy wriggled along the wall and pressed this object into Lifka's hand: It was flat and round.

Beside her, Tarnit stiffened. Lifka looked over to see the king had placed a hand on his jeweled dagger, about to draw a blade on his own son. The hells! She had a dog muzzled with one hand and a mysterious object clutched in the other when what she really needed was to unsling her staff to protect herself and, perhaps, the king.

But the king did not unsheathe the knife even though Prince Tavahosh spouted mocking words, a strutting cock crowing in all its finery of self-regard. When the king abruptly dismissed the prince, the young man stalked off in such a temper that Lifka could practically smell the fumes of his anger—but not before he stared directly at Lifka to remind her he'd not forgotten her defiance.

Captain Kellas whispered in the mysterious boy's ear and the child ghosted after the prince like a tiny spy. Evidently the boy was a servant to be ordered around despite being dressed in silk her clan could not afford even if it saved every string of vey earned for ten years.

That's what it meant to be rich.

The Runt wiggled impatiently in the harness she had rigged for him at her chest. Her hand was starting to ache from gripping his muzzle, so she let go. Immediately he barked in protest, as if to say *Why do you treat me so discourteously?*

Startled by the sound, the king turned.

"What are these two reeves doing here?" he demanded in the Hundred language.

He noted Tarnit with a brief nod, as if he recognized her, but he took his time examining Lifka. Indeed, his gaze jumped from her face down to her tightly laced vest. The Runt growled.

"Does the dog bite?" he asked with a smile so charming that her mouth twitched, and then she gave in and smiled back as she again clamped a hand around the Runt's muzzle.

"Nerves make anyone bite, as it says in the tale."

The king laughed. "I won't bite. I'm just curious. Where are you from, Reeve?"

"Near River's Bend, Your Highness. Across the river from the Weldur Forest."

"I would have thought you a girl from Nessumara where all sorts of sailors and travelers come to harbor. Your parents must be outlanders."

Captain Kellas stepped forward to interrupt. "What did the boy give you, Lifka?"

"What boy?" asked Marshal Dannarah.

All looked at Lifka expectantly. The Runt heaved a great sigh of displeasure and resignation, a sure sign that he would be obedient for a little while. She released his muzzle and opened the other hand. In it lay a round ivory token, engraved with a loom on one side and a tree leafed with stars on the other.

"Dia!" The king snatched the token rudely right out of Lifka's fingers. "This is for me!"

"Best we ask Queen Dia, since the messenger evidently gave it to my reeve, not to you, Jehosh," said the marshal crisply.

A blush curdled the king's cheek like that of a lovelorn youth. He pulled a face and, uncurling his fingers from their desperate clutch of the token, gave it back to Lifka. "Had it been meant for me, it would have been given to me," he agreed.

"What do you mean, my lord?" asked Captain Kellas.

"Dia has no reason to trust anyone at court and especially not people who might be in league with Chorannah. Therefore she only admits people to her presence if they are carrying one of these tokens. That way only people she has personally summoned can see her, thus thwarting spies and murderers."

"Anyone can carve ivory," objected Dannarah.

"The tokens are imbued with magic. It burns the hand of anyone who wishes her harm. The magic smells like pepper."

"Pepper!" The marshal plucked the token out of Lifka's fingers and sniffed at it. "The hells! It does smell of pepper!"

The king's wry smile imperfectly concealed the anger and frustration that had boiled over in the ugly confrontation with his son. "Dia knows how to protect herself. Although what she wants with this young reeve I cannot imagine. As for you, Aunt Dannarah, my apologies. I meant to offer you a better welcome back to the palace."

"Had you left me as chief marshal none of this would be happening."

"I earned that barb," he said, and Lifka was amazed to watch him calmly absorb such blunt criticism. He turned to the old man. "Captain, what do you advise? I'm inclined to leave Aunt Dannarah as Tavahosh's second, if she'll agree."

Captain Kellas glanced at the marshal with a wry smile that he then transferred to the king. Although the servant, he spoke with a dignity that made him seem in charge. "Your Highness, I advise you to make an immediate inventory of your officials, your army, your clerks, and the various tasks they administer. You must discover which you control and which have been undermined from within. You are right to focus on the army first. I suggest you begin by assessing your support within the city militia. If they will not back you, then prudence dictates you flee the city."

The king muttered words Lifka could not understand but it sounded like a string of angry curses. Then he nodded, his hot, hostile gaze fixed not on anyone here but on the situation that had just collapsed around him.

"Come along, Captain. We'd best start planning our campaign."

He and Kellas walked out into the sun-drenched garden, leaving the women in the shadowed corridor.

"That was illuminating," said the marshal with a curt and unamused laugh. "Let us go discover what in the hells Queen Dia wants from you, Lifka."

She handed the token back to Lifka and set off with a brisk stride. Lifka tucked it under her vest down along the side of her breast where, she hoped, no one would feel they had the right to simply insert their fingers without permission. She didn't care about Queen Dia's favor; she was just not used to such grabby manners. At home everyone shared everything but you asked before you took what someone else was handling.

"I thought Queen Dia lived in the lower palace," said Tarnit as they crossed a shaded colonnade that ringed the garden.

"She does," said the marshal. "But if I am judging matters rightly, Dia will have shown her support for Jehosh by attending the reeve convocation, sequestered on the women's balcony of course. As well, she cannot possibly trust Chorannah. Therefore she will surely remain in the upper palace until Prince Kasad is safely under her wing. Jehosh has private chambers here, and I only recently discovered it has a hidden room that is linked by a secret passageway to the Thousand Steps. A clever way for a king to bring people in and out whom he doesn't want others to know about."

Her somber tone and bitter frown caused Tarnit to look alarmed.

The marshal glanced at Tarnit and said, "No, I don't want to talk about my father."

They walked on in an awkward silence. Besides the fountain and a decorative shelter, the space bloomed with flowers and hedges.

"What a lovely garden this is," said Tarnit with a nod at Lifka as if tossing her a dropped ring in a game of hooks-and-ropes.

Lifka said the first thing that came into her head. "How do they water all this?"

"Spoken like a country girl," said the marshal with a laugh as Tarnit cast Lifka a grateful look.

"I've hauled enough water from the local well to know how much work gardening takes."

"By no means am I criticizing you, Lifka," said the marshal, with a meaningful glance at Tarnit. "I like my reeves to be smart and observant. Do you realize that the upper palace, situated as it is atop Law Rock, is a bad place to get stuck in a siege unless you control the eagles? By placing me in charge of the reeves here Tavahosh and the shrine haven't the least idea of how much power they've just put in my hands. I'll be party to all palace and shrine messages."

"Trust you to find a way to work the situation to your advantage, Marshal," said Tarnit.

A steward wearing the king's badge of crossed spears spotted them heading for the king's private chambers and raced in pursuit, but they reached a portico before he caught them. The guards recognized Marshal Dannarah and slid a door aside.

The women took off their sandals and stepped up onto a matted floor in a chamber furnished only with seating cushions. Two outlanders stood guard by a closed door, one armed with a staff and the other with two swords crossed in a harness at her back. Like the boy they were a pale brown, cheeks dusted with freckles. One bore the slave mark prominently inked onto a cheek although she carried her weapon with the same easy confidence as the other, unmarked woman. Lifka tried not to stare at the mark she had escaped. Like a bell ringing softly in her head a buried resonance filled her with a certainty that long ago she had walked among people with their coloring and looks.

"The token," said the marshal.

Lifka handed it to the woman with the staff, who held it to her cheek, nodded, and went over to tap a rhythm of knocks on the door at the back of the room. They were let through. In the room beyond, the walls were painted with golden figures floating amid vines and flowers so cunningly rendered they seemed alive. The fourth wall was a balcony looking over fields far below.

Even unversed in the ways of a palace, Lifka recognized the queen at once because she was beautiful despite her pallor. Her skin had the color of the milled rice that wealthy people ate for dessert. She sat amid a flock of women, not separated from them by decorated chairs or elaborate screens but all crowded familiarly onto low couches arranged for conversation. Some had a similar coloring to the queen while the rest had such diverse features they might have been at home in any port, and about half bore the slave mark although the ones so branded did not act in any way different from the others. Every woman had handwork under way: embroidery, knitting, mending, netting. They all looked up expectantly as the reeves halted inside the chamber and the door was shut.

The queen set down her needles and yarn and, to Lifka's horror, looked at her with an expression of the greatest curiosity. She spoke words in a foreign language whose sounds meant nothing but whose timbre and rhythm burrowed into her flesh until it almost seemed they could fall off her tongue. Snatches pecked at her: *Mothers? Ship?*

The figures painted on the wall dizzily faded and brightened like her thoughts blinking in and out, but that was only the light and shadow in the room.

The Runt sneezed.

All the women laughed.

"What an adorable little dog," said the queen in pleasantly accented Hundred-speech. "May I pet it?"

Lifka still felt dizzied, and to her relief the marshal answered for her. "I think it is safer not, Your Highness. He snaps. I fear you have startled my reeve by speaking in a language none of us know. I am Marshal Dannarah, as you may recall. I believe you and I only met when you first came to the Hundred. I have not been much in the favor of the palace these last twenty years."

Queen Dia's smile had an enigmatic curl. "Nor have I been in favor of the palace, truth be told, Lady Dannarah. Since the unusual circumstances that brought me to the Hundred, I have preferred to remain on my country estate with my trusted people around me."

"Yet the king built the lower palace so you might bide more often at court."

Queen Dia set her handwork to one side. "So he did, as he intends to spend most of his time here in Toskala administering the Hundred from now on."

"So we may hope. What words did you say to my reeve just now?"

Shapes rose in Lifka's mind. She spoke aloud as if bidden by a spell. "By what names are your mothers known? In what ship does your soul know its home?" She wiped a tear from her eye, for her heart had wakened the memory of a five-year-old's fear and grief. "I thought I had forgotten all that."

The queen rose and with measured dignity and a slight limp crossed the mats.

"May I?" She indicated Lifka's neck.

Lifka wanted to step out of reach but she was pretty sure it would be insulting to do so. Suddenly she knew what the queen wanted. So she tucked the Runt's nose in the crook of an elbow and sucked in a breath, bracing herself.

The queen felt along the back of Lifka's neck and examined the scar although Dia could only see the part of it on her neck, not the part on her back hidden beneath her reeve's vest.

"Do you remember getting this scar, child?"

"No," Lifka lied.

The queen nodded as if she knew perfectly well that Lifka was lying. "It must be difficult to speak of something that would have happened so long ago and surely in tragic and frightening circumstances. But its distinctive pattern suggests it was deliberately carved there by a person who wanted to mark you as with an inking but had no needles or ink, only a knife."

She spoke an order in a language Lifka did not know. An attendant opened a hidden door in the wall and vanished down a flight of steps.

"Do you truly not know who you are?" The queen examined Lifka with an expression of astonishment.

It got tiring to be treated like a curiosity. "Of course I know who I am, Your Highness. I realize it must be obvious to everyone here that my parents did not themselves seed me and birth me. I am one of the children brought south from Ithik Eldim thirteen years ago. Even though I was born somewhere else, Five Roads Clan are my father and mother, my uncle and aunt, my brothers and cousins. I wear the Fire Mother's tattoos, just like any other Hundred girl. That's all."

"Oh, no," said the queen with a portentous shake of the head, "that is not all."

Footsteps thumped on the stairs and two women about the same age as the queen entered the room. Armed with long knives, both carried themselves as soldiers and were dressed in loose trousers and sleeveless vests. One had a northern complexion, a patch covering her left eye, and a slave's mark. The other bore no ink; she was as black as Lifka, a tall woman with a gruesome knotted scar on her left shoulder and a nick in her chin as if a blade had scored a wedge out of it. This woman stopped dead, staring.

The Runt barked five or six times, caught up in the tension now permeating the room.

"She bears the mark of the Phoenix, Odoriga," said the queen, still in the Hundred-speech.

"It cannot be," said the scarred soldier without any of the bowing or courtesy common to servants. "The last heiresses of that lineage died in the attack on Gyre Port thirteen years ago."

"The one led by Jehosh," said the marshal with a glance at the queen.

"That's right," said Dia in an unfathomable tone. "The one led by Jehosh."

The soldier spoke in a singsong lilt like the refrain to a tale: "So many sisters and brothers, mothers and uncles, died that day. All the Phoenix ships burned, their children lost to fire and sea."

"This child survived," said the queen.

"What are you talking about?" Lifka demanded, forgetting that she was talking to a queen.

The queen's look felt more like threat than comfort. "It means you are heiress to a fortune."

Odoriga sheathed her knife and crossed her muscular arms. "Anyone with coin can claim a fortune. Money is the least of her value, if this is true. If this is true, she would be the last sur-viving born-daughter of the Phoenix Lineage."

"What is the Phoenix Lineage?" Marshal Dannarah asked.

"Long ago, across the ocean, the Tandi people became famous seafarers and then merchants. They organized themselves into a consortium, and within that into lineages, each named after a bird. Until the massacre at Gyre Port, the Phoenix Lineage commanded the largest fleet and most powerful reputation within the Tandi consortium, like to that of queens and their brother kings flying above their lesser subjects. If she is who she seems to be, every Tandi lineage will want to get their hands on her in order to sell her back to the remnants of the Phoenix Lineage or to marry her to one of their own women—as is their custom—in the hope she will give birth to daughters who can rebuild the lost ships." Her hard gaze fixed on Lifka. The Runt quivered under Lifka's muzzling hand. "You'll need protection against the greed of your lineage's rivals."

Lifka was too stunned to form words. Fortunately the mar-shal was not.

"Are you yourself of Tandi lineage, verea? To make this claim?"

The soldier said, "I am not. My people come originally from the land of Kost. But my people have for many generations hired out as guards on Tandi ships. That's why I know their language and some of their lore. This knowledge I have shared with Dia."

"Which is why we are willing to offer you protection, child," said the queen. "You would be wise to accept our offer. You will be well rewarded if you do."

This was really too much! Lifka released the Runt's muzzle, and his growl made everyone go still. Still not knowing what to say, she cast a desperate glance at the marshal.

Sure enough, the old woman slipped her baton from its loop and tapped it twice against a thigh. No queen intimidated her!

"If Lifka wishes to speak to you later on her own account, I will not get in her way. If she does not, then you will leave her alone. Do you understand me?"

Queen Dia exchanged a glance with Odoriga, yet her acquiescent shrug did not reassure Lifka. Nor did her words. "The girl may believe it is better to hide from her past, but it will engulf her regardless of what she thinks she wants. Others will come for the girl once the news gets out. They will not be as accommodating as I am willing to be."

33

Kellas admired the masterful way Jehosh held the rapt attention of the young militiamen in the Flag Quarter barracks as he told them a story from the first Eldim war.

"Just when our escape route had been cut off and we were sure to be slaughtered by superior numbers, the eagles arrived. Each reeve was carrying a Wolf."

"A wolf, Your Highness?" exclaimed one of the young men in a tone of honest surprise. "Wouldn't the wolves bite the reeves? How could they carry them?"

Several of the soldiers guffawed at his ignorance, and another young bantam puffed his chest up and said, "My uncle was a Black Wolf. In our grandfathers' time they were the Hundred's most elite soldiers, you ass. Eiya! Begging your pardon, Your Highness. They disgraced themselves when they did not protect your honored father and it was ill done of me to praise them."

"It's never a disgrace to remember our elders kindly, as you do your uncle. It was once a great honor to serve the king as a Black

Wolf." Jehosh glanced at Kellas, hesitated, then went on without mentioning Kellas's history. "Anyway, there we were, outnumbered and trapped, a cliff on one side and our enemy on the other. The reeves flew in Wolves and dropped them at the rear of their army. We crushed them from two directions. Later we called it the nutcracker."

Jehosh wore a glowing smile as his audience laughed appreciatively at this predictable joke, then soaked up their approbation as he briefly spoke to each one in turn before he and Kellas went on their way.

Out on the street, he said, "I really have let the administration slip out of my hands. What if I begin to make rounds regularly of the militia stations here in the city, Captain?"

"You are good with soldiers, Your Highness."

"All the best times of my life have been in the field. When I'm not living out of a camp tent and waiting for the next skirmish, I miss the knife's edge. Here in the palace I feel I become a clerk, counting coins. Perhaps I should institute a new custom. I could ride a circuit of the assizes courts, hear the people's grievances, make myself known."

"King Anjihosh did just that, Your Highness. He made his presence known throughout the Hundred by attending assizes courts in every region in the company of the Judge Guardians. Your father continued the circuit."

"Yes, I remember how it annoyed me when he required me to ride with him when I was a boy. Sitting and listening to court cases seemed the most tedious thing in the world. Let dutiful men do that work, I told him!"

"As I recall you wanted to join the Black Wolves. Lord Vanas already had."

"I passed every test for the Black Wolves, Captain."

"Did you? I never knew that."

"Even you didn't know everything, Captain. I convinced my father it would be proper and fitting for his son to join."

"But you never did."

"I just wanted to prove I could. The truth is, I wanted my own company, not to be one of his. I wanted to fight the northern raiders on my own terms and with my own people."

Kellas glanced toward Lord Vanas, who waited patiently at the head of the company of mounted soldiers accompanying the king. These guardsmen, and indeed all the city militia, wore badges whose embroidery cleverly displayed the crossed spears indicating their loyalty to the palace interwoven with a wreath of green ribbons, the mark of Vanas's personal household.

"On to the Wolf Quarter, Vanas!" called the king.

"Wolf Quarter is restless at night, Your Highness." Vanas indicated the starry sky. Their impromptu tour of the militia barracks and posts in each quarter of the city had taken the whole of the afternoon after the fiasco of the reeves' convocation, something for the king to do to make him feel he still had control. Now darkness cast an ominous shadow on Vanas's words.

"All the better I should inspect these troubled neighborhoods for myself, is it not?" demanded Jehosh with an edge of challenge.

Vanas glanced at Kellas. "What does your chief of security say?"

Kellas had been given a quiet gelding, and he rested hands on the pommel, enjoying the restful feeling of a solid horse beneath him. "The king's chief of security feels that if any quarter of this city is so dangerous that the king cannot safely ride there, then we have greater problems even than court officials eager to ally with his heirs in expectation of his death. If you cannot establish control over one city, Your Highness, then how can you expect to be respected and obeyed as king?"

Vanas's glare had the bite of lightning.

Jehosh's smile was sunny. "Wolf Quarter it is. I have not forgotten how to command men, eh, Captain Kellas?"

"By all accounts you have always conducted yourself gloriously as a field general, Your Highness."

Jehosh raised a hand with a flourish, as in answer, and they moved forward with foot soldiers advancing before and behind carrying lanterns on poles. On the main avenues folk had come out to light threshold lamps, as required by a law enacted in the first year of Anjihosh's reign. People stared and, as they belatedly recognized the king, tapped fists to chest in the old-fashioned way. Jehosh blazed, his good mood gaining strength. But Kellas wasn't so sure every gaze was a friendly one, and he noted how Vanas subtly altered the order of the march to make sure the king was surrounded by soldiers on every side so a cast spear or loosed arrow would strike one of them instead of the king.

Kellas's instincts did not give him any sense they were walking into an ambush, nor did he see ugly hatred in people's gazes, just discontent and frustration. Yet a stormy murmuring became audible as they neared South Gate, where arrested men were held in the shrine prison before being marched out on work gangs.

"Let me ride ahead," said Vanas.

"No! If I fear those I rule, I might as well hand the reins to Chorannah and let her do the driving."

Jehosh drove his horse forward, outpacing everyone. Vanas blocked Kellas's horse as soldiers surged after the king.

"Captain Kellas, are you trying to get him killed? It was never proven to my satisfaction that you weren't involved in

King Atani's death. You might wish to see Jehosh suffer the same ugly fate."

Kellas glanced at Vanas's sword, still sheathed, and let his gaze rest on Vanas for long enough that the other man shifted nervously in the saddle. No need to raise his voice. He could make a quiet tone snap harder than a whip just by telling a truth no one dared admit. "If you encourage King Jehosh to hide in his chambers then I can assure you, Lord Vanas, you will kill his kingship as readily as if you cast the spear yourself. I mean no offense, but Jehosh has a streak of laziness and self-indulgence that we all observed when he was young. Has anyone checked him in all these years? I wonder, for it appears several of his once trusted companions have changed allegiance. Have you, Lord Vanas? Now, if you don't mind, as his chief of security I would like to make sure his person is secure."

He clipped his mount forward quickly enough that he entered South Gate Square at the king's side. The Beltak shrine rose on one side of the main gate, and the prison on the other. Although all the gates were closed for the night, lines of soldiers braced themselves behind big, rectangular shields in front of the prison gate, and soldiers had moved into position atop the walls with crossbows cranked and ready to release.

Despite this show of force a crowd of several hundred people stood shoulder-to-shoulder in front of South Gate, singing lustily and in a ragged unison the ancient story of the dragonling who had rescued her sweetheart from the prison of a tyrant. Their voices faded to silence as Jehosh rode into the square with soldiers behind him and all the weight of kingship on his brow.

He still knew how to make an entrance.

That the assembly was surprised to see the king was evident by the buzz of whispers. Torches and lanterns burned, illuminating faces: rough-looking men ready for a fight; older women draped in anguish, no doubt the mothers and aunts of young men condemned to the work gangs; women hiding their faces beneath scarves so they couldn't be recognized; men of all ages shifting with determined anger.

His face reddened from anger, Vanas reined his horse up beside the king's. "I will order them to disperse, Your Highness. If they do not, then we will arrest them."

Jehosh studied the people, for all their faces were turned to him. "No. Bring me a shield and four strong men."

"But Jehosh..." Vanas muttered in a tone so direct, without the usual distance of hierarchy, that it set Kellas's ears humming.

"I know what I am doing, Van," replied Jehosh in a similar voice, like the argument of brothers. "If we cannot quiet a restless gathering, then think what a party our enemies will make of our incompetence. Let the choices we made years ago not end in our spears cutting down old women armed with baskets of food."

With obvious reluctance Vanas called forward four soldiers from those guarding the prison gate. They came with haste, stepping on toes, shoving several people aside too brusquely. People stamped feet to make thunder. The air charged as in the moment before lightning strikes. The pulse of danger flooded through Kellas in warning, and he slipped his sword halfway out of its sheath.

"Enough!" shouted the king. "I will have silence!"

To people who had only glimpsed the king in passing and never heard his voice, the sound struck like a hammer's blow. They subsided, making way, and the four soldiers set down their shields. Jehosh stepped onto one and they hoisted it up to their shoulders. Now he seemed a figure out of a tale, floating upon the air with the sky as a cloak. The players of Hasibal used this trick to elevate characters meant to have a towering presence.

"On law, the land is built." Jehosh had a clear, loud voice, and his command of the Hundred-speech made him seem one of the people. "So spoke my grandfather King Anjihosh the Glorious Unifier, he who brought peace. Law is a better shield than a sword! So spoke my father, King Atani the Law-Giver, who believed that every road in the Hundred should be marked with a law pillar. That way every person who walks out the door of their household can see that the law reaches from the north to the south, from the Eagles' Claws to the Spires, from the east to the west, from the ocean to Heaven's Ridge. In every town stands an assizes where judges make their rulings. The nine Judge Guardians—the highest judges in the land—oversee these courts."

"Sheh!" cried a woman's voice out of the crowd. "My son committed no crime, Your Highness. He was swept up off the street for no reason."

"My brother, too!" shouted a man closer to the front, emboldened by the woman's interruption. "He was inked and marched out without ever standing before any assizes."

Jehosh cast a startled glance at Vanas, who shook his head in the manner of a man who cannot answer the question. But the king did not retreat.

"Let no person say justice is not served in the Hundred! All people arrested must first have a hearing before the assizes. Only then, if they are found guilty, will they be remanded to the work gangs. I will send extra clerks to every quarter's assizes to assist in recording all claims brought forward. The king's assizes atop Law Rock shall be the final arbiter. Let it be known, by my word as king, spoken this night."

The burning torches lit him but he burned with a fire of a different kind: his grandfather's steely presence, his father's quiet determination. *Where had this Jehosh come from?* Kellas wondered as he studied the crowd and the soldiers whose faces turned like flowers toward a life-giving sun. Maybe the years had matured him. Had Jehosh become a man who could be worked with, influenced, and perhaps even persuaded to a different path?

"I will tour the prison tonight!" cried Jehosh. "Those whose cases have been properly adjudicated at the assizes will be marched out tomorrow. Those who have not been seen will be retained for judgment. Now I ask you to disperse peaceably to your homes so that we may make an orderly beginning tomorrow."

Remarkably, the expectation of a storm about to hit faded. The king waited, still elevated on the shield, as first a few people slipped away into the side streets, heading home, then others followed in larger groups. Only people carrying sacks of provisions for condemned kinsmen remained, unwilling to depart.

When the square had cleared the four soldiers holding up the shield eased it down and Jehosh stepped gracefully onto solid ground looking as smug as if he had just come from Queen Dia's bedchamber. Only then, when the danger had passed, did the prison gates open and a familiar man venture out with the sort of swagger a man wears when he isn't sure of his welcome.

"Your Highness! What brings you to South Gate?"

"News of trouble that I have quelled," retorted Jehosh, looking the other man up and down. "And what brings you here, Supreme Captain Ulyar? What has the commander of my Spears to do with a shrine prison that houses criminals about to be sent out on work gangs? Last I saw you earlier today, you were shit-nosing my son Tavahosh as he usurped a post that should not belong to him."

Ulyar had the look of a spooked horse trying to shy away from a ravening bear, but he made a business of signaling his attendants to bring up his horse as he recovered his self-possession. "I work in concert with the priests to keep the Hundred safe, Your Highness. I could not help but hear your ringing words, and it would go against my promise to safeguard the land if I did not speak up. Every man in this prison is a criminal. The shrines simply have expedited the process of condemning criminals so as not to clog up the assizes from practical and necessary matters. It will take days to clear the work gang in the prison now, and that will mean everyone must wait and the prison will become clogged with yet more people awaiting their hearing."

"Then it might behoove the priests to stop arresting young men merely for loitering and for not having work tokens," remarked Kellas.

Ulyar shot him a glare meant to wither his pretensions. Kellas sighed. This sort of posturing got so dull so fast.

Jehosh hadn't even noticed. "Ulyar, I will appoint more judges, and the assizes can simply double its number of hearings. Is this going to be a problem?"

"How are we to keep order? We'll need more guards. The city militia does not have enough men."

"You requested the city militia be doubled two years ago. Where are all those men? What happened to the coin spent to train and arm them?"

"They...ah...were sent to High Haldia due to the recent disturbances there, Your Highness."

Jehosh rubbed at his eyes as if Ulyar's words, like dust thrown in his face, were obscuring his vision. "What of the elite soldiers you are meant to command? Temporarily call in the Fourth Company of the Spears. Now that I recollect, I thought they were sent to High Haldia to deal with the riots there, not the city militia."

A craven grimace flashed across Ulyar's face, like that of a child caught out in a lie, and Kellas knew at once that Ulyar was hiding something important from the king. "It's not... They aren't...Yes, of course, I will take care of it all at once, Your Highness."

"Just to make sure there is no further trouble I want these same conditions put into place in Nessumara, High Haldia, Horn, Olossi, and any other major towns where you have heard report of disturbance. It would be best to impose a curfew until people's confidence is restored." He beckoned to Vanas. "Do it quietly, not with a heavy hand. Double night patrols so people become accustomed to seeing guards on the streets. Let them feel uneasy about sneaking about and assembling wherever they please."

"Yes, Your Highness," said Vanas with a triumphant sneer directed at Ulyar.

The other man said, "But Your Highness—"

"That is an order, Supreme Captain Ulyar. Do I need to repeat it?"

"I am yours to command, Your Highness."

"It is a relief to me to hear you say so. I was afraid I might have to appoint Captain Kellas in your place." As Jehosh turned away, Ulyar could not restrain an expression of such raw fury that Kellas tensed, wondering if he would have to stop the man from stabbing Jehosh in the back, but Ulyar retreated to the horse being held ready for him. Vanas watched him go with a gloating smile.

"Kill him, Captain Kellas," said the king. "I want to be rid of that traitor."

"I recommend against it at this time, Your Highness. Consolidate your position before you force Chorannah into open war. Ulyar is easy to deal with because you know where he stands."

Jehosh looked at Kellas. "Do you disapprove of my actions this evening?"

"Not at all, Your Highness. Your decisiveness with the crowd was exactly the measure needed. I am sure there would have been bloodshed had you not seen to the situation yourself. Naturally I approve of your solution."

Jehosh squared his shoulders, preening a little. "Do you, Captain? And why is that?"

"Law is a better shield than the sword, as King Atani always said and as he believed."

Jehosh snorted. "Those idiotic law pillars my father insisted on raising. As if people have time to stop and read them, if they can even read."

"Yet of those pillars erected on the Istri Walk between Nessumara and Toskala, you have taken none down."

"Have you counted them all? No harm in being left as they are. I recollect that my father presided over the assizes on alternate afternoons. He always said people like to see justice out in the open. I shall do as he did. For I assure you, Captain, I see how I have allowed Chorannah to get the jump on me. It seems so obvious now! She's far more clever than I realized. She's offered the priests supervision of the assizes and the reeve halls in exchange for their support. That ends now."

Ulyar paused by his mount, turning back as if realizing he ought to listen in.

Jehosh called, "Ulyar! You may return to the upper palace, since you have made your bed there."

"Be careful, Your Highness," said Kellas.

Jehosh barked a laugh. He seemed almost giddy. "We all know where we stand. Vanas, remain on guard outside so I am not disturbed. Let the people carrying provisions be admitted one by one through the night to give their gifts to their kinsmen. Captain Kellas, accompany me."

Kellas had to hurry to keep up with the king's brisk stride as he approached the prison gate.

"Your Highness!" A priest hurried forward, his white robes

shimmering in the lamplight and his lower lip smeared with what looked like red bean paste from a pastry. He was not high ranking enough to veil his face. "I am the holy sentinel in charge of the prison. My name is—"

"Open the gates. I am inspecting the prison."

"Your Highness, you cannot wish to endure the stink and misery of—"

"I require a clerk to show me which men have been properly adjudicated at the assizes and so can be marched out tomorrow at dawn, and which must be held back for a proper hearing."

"Your Highness, the priests have already ruled the men are criminals according to holy statutes."

"Do not argue with me, Your Holiness. Fetch me a clerk to show me around."

The priest bowed. "Please allow me to take on that honor myself, Your Highness."

Jehosh's tight shoulders dropped a little in response to the priest's respectful manner. "Very well. Lead on, Your Holiness."

In Kellas's youth the large compound had been the main city temple dedicated to Kotaru the Thunderer. At the outset of Jehosh's reign it had been converted into a barracks and stables for the army, and indeed its wide inner courtyard was lined with empty water troughs and hitching rails. However, within the last five years the priests had taken it over for a holding prison. Now guards stood at every closed gate that led into the interior buildings. Lamps burned on all sides, illuminating the king's confident stride as he crossed the dusty yard. Out of the shadows a man approached.

"Your Highness! A word, if you will."

Jehosh halted, and Kellas stepped in front of him, then relaxed, seeing General Shevad emerge from the gloom with a belligerent stride but a desperate expression.

"What do you want?" Jehosh said curtly, measuring the man with hostility.

The general knelt with unexpected humility. "Your Highness, I have served you faithfully, have I not?"

"You have served honorably in Ithik Eldim, it's true." Jehosh's tone was grudging. "Even if your father served me very ill by murdering my beloved father."

"My brother Yofar died in your service, Your Highness, with never a disloyal word."

"I remember him," remarked Jehosh with less rancor. "He was a good soldier."

"My thanks, Your Highness. I come to you with a plea for help. My brother Gilaras has been arrested by Supreme Captain Ulyar for a murder he did not commit. He has been condemned to the work gangs. They mean to march him out tomorrow without even the courtesy of a hearing at the assizes. His hair has already been shorn and his face scarred with a criminal's marking!"

"Gilaras...Ah, the one who married the Ri Amarah woman."

Shevad reared back, eyes narrowing. "Yes. You know of the match?"

"Everyone has heard of the alliance, General Shevad. How your impoverished and disgraced clan managed to convince the Ri Amarah to part with one of their mysterious women no one knows. But she is very rich, and very clever."

"You have met her?"

Jehosh tilted his head to one side, touching a thoughtful finger to his lips.

At the sight General Shevad lost his temper. "Are you behind his arrest? Do you want her for yourself?"

Kellas again stepped between the two men, gesturing to the priest and guards to move away.

The king gripped his sword hilt, knuckles white. "Do not threaten me, General. I have been patient for years with you and your foul clan."

Shevad had the look of a soldier who has survived too many battles to be easily intimidated. "Do you not find it suspicious that Prince Kasad's best companions are disgraced and removed from the court at the same time Prince Tavahosh is elevated to the office of chief marshal, under the oversight of the priests?"

Jehosh's hesitation was so marked that Kellas glanced between the two men, then scanned the courtyard, but they were alone, the priest and guards now standing at a distance.

"Gilaras has been a loyal friend to my son," murmured Jehosh.

Seeing the king soften, Shevad went on. "I just received orders from Supreme Captain Ulyar to travel north to Ithik Eldim, to take command of the garrison at Gyre Port."

"I have not ordered a change of command in Ithik Eldim!" cried Jehosh, anger boiling back up. "By what right does Ulyar do so, unless to show he can countermand my arrangements?"

Kellas raised a hand. "If I may, Your Highness, I think we speak at cross purposes here. King Jehosh, did you order General Shevad to Eldim?"

"As I just said, I did not."

"General Shevad, I was with the king in the upper palace this morning. I can assure you he knew nothing of this scheme. Who actually arrested your brother?"

"Supreme Captain Ulyar, as I said! He gave me my new orders himself. I assumed you had a hand in it, Your Highness."

Jehosh took a step back, turned to one side and then the other as if looking for a way to pace out his fury. "General Shevad, I will personally see your brother released at once."

"Wait," said Kellas, the hand still raised and his tone peremptory. Age gave him an authority he was happy to abuse. "Give me a moment to think."

Both men stared at him, but they did not speak.

Opportunity must be seized, just as a person in the midst of a fight senses an opening before his eye quite registers it. He kept his arms extended as if keeping the two men apart before they came to blows, while he spoke in a low voice.

"Let me be blunt. Lord Gilaras is a restless and bored young man left to stew too long in his own juices. Meanwhile I have questions about the recent expansion of work gangs. I suggest we recruit young Gilaras to your service, Your Highness. Let him spy in a work gang."

"But he could die!" objected Shevad.

Kellas shook his head, tipping his hand to indicate that the priest waited just out of hearing. "If Ulyar has had him arrested, it means the queen wants him out of the way."

"That's exactly how it is!" broke in Shevad with a lack of control that betrayed anguish. "As soon as I heard the news I went to Lady Sarai's uncle, a man named Abrisho. The cursed Silver scolded me as if I were a hapless lad! He said the queen has already taken Lady Sarai into her court."

"She wants their coin," muttered Jehosh. "She has outwitted me again."

"Has she, Your Highness?" interposed Kellas in his calmest voice as he saw the advantage unfold. "For it seems to me Queen Chorannah has signaled her next move too soon. General Shevad, if the king releases your brother, he will be in greater danger, don't you see?"

"You think Chorannah will have him killed," said Shevad.

"People kill for far less than a treasure chest of coin."

"He can leave the city. Go to his kinsfolk in Nessumara."

"Ulyar has control of the Spears and their spies and assassins. You may recall that I was once such a man, sent out to rid the king of his enemies. I have seen too many dead in my time, General Shevad, and you have as well. If your brother will serve the king as a spy, then afterward, should he survive, he will be pardoned."

"Yes," murmured Jehosh, "it is a neat and plausible solution she will never suspect."

Kellas nodded, relieved that the two men were both smart enough to acquiesce without argument. "If you agree, Your Highness, I wish you to castigate General Shevad as an untrustworthy soldier in a loud voice that everyone can hear. Make sure to mention that his brother is a murdering criminal who deserves the sentence he has received. Once we leave, General, you will make a final visit to your brother and recruit him. Lord Gilaras may consider me his commanding officer."

"I like this plan." Jehosh smiled.

"You are a heartless man, Captain Kellas," said the general. He pressed a palm against his forehead, then dropped it as if the hand, like hope, was too heavy to hold up.

Kellas nodded. He had lived too long and seen too much to toss around pointless reassurances. "Yes. It is my duty to be heartless."

34

Wearied by fear and anxiety as the afternoon dragged on, Sarai tried to rest on the cushions, but that only reminded her of the way Gil would entertain her with light prattle while she wrote up her account of each day. He liked to sit on a cushion embroidered with virile roosters because, he had said with the laugh that delighted her, the strutting cocks reminded him of his duty. Her mind lurched through a mental accounting of the events that had landed her here. The queen had caught them out so thoroughly it had not occurred to Gil or any member of his family to beware. If she could think it through with a cool head she would find a means to action.

At length, unable to sit still any longer, she drifted out to the balcony with its lattice screen, yet another barrier fencing her in. Twisting her shawl in her hands, she studied the king's garden as shadows lengthened over its paths and flower beds. From this balcony she could not see the Assizes Tower. However, she could still see the pavilion in the center of the garden and, beyond it, the portico out of which the king had emerged when she and Gil had stood on a different balcony earlier in the day.

Oh, Gil. On a tiny balcony very like this one in their apartments, she and Gil had met for the first time because he had climbed the vines and sneaked in through the lattice...

She glanced back into the chamber. With dusk settling over the world the balcony lay in shadows, and it would therefore be difficult for someone spying on her through a hole in the wall to see what she was doing.

She traced the lattice from top to bottom and side to side, as Gil had shown her. Just as she was ready to give up, she found a hook nestled in the back of a carved flower. With a click it gave way, and a narrow segment of the lattice swung back. Never an agile climber like Elit, she still had clambered up enough trees with her lover to attempt these sturdy vines. The mirror pressed against her thigh as she scraped her way down, using her knees to brace herself. The little pouch of coin Gil had insisted she bring bumped at her hip. Now and again she had to ruck up the long shift as it tangled in the stems. Twice she paused, hooking her arm over a thick stem to catch her breath. Was this how her mother had fled, in desperation, with her baby girl tied to her back?

Her slippered feet brushed the ground. She scanned the king's garden for any opening or escape. There were four portals—two lamplit gates and two lamplit doors—one on each wall. Soldiers guarded all four. Since this was the king's garden, were these guards loyal to the king? If so, would the king turn her over to Chorannah anyway? Had he been part of the plot?

A young man strode out from one of the arched gateways and paused, face gilded by light from the bright lamps on either side of the opening. It was Prince Kasad, wearing the elaborately voluminous court jacket. He pressed a hand to his face in the manner of a man so overcome by bad news that he is stricken.

She grasped the chance, propelled herself out of the vines and onto a path that led most directly to where he stood. Guards stiffened, catching sight of her before Kasad did and seeing a potential threat, but perhaps her womanly figure puzzled them for not one left his station to intercept her. Kasad, however, ran to meet her, the skirts of his long jacket flapping.

"Lady Sarai!"

Out of breath, she staggered to a halt as soon as he was close. "Your Highness, I beg you…Lord Gilaras has been arrested—!"

"I just heard. Why are you still here, Lady Sarai?"

"Queen Chorannah commanded me to join her court."

His expression went rigid. "Do you mean to divorce Gil and fish for a better catch?"

"I will thank you not to judge me by the palace's standards!"

He winced.

Boldly she grabbed one of his hands. "Of course I don't want to divorce him. I have to get him out of prison. Please help me."

A shout rang out from the chamber she had just escaped. Light flashed behind the lattice-screened balcony as they searched for her.

Prince Kasad's expression creased with startled revelation.

He grasped her wrist and tugged recklessly. "Run! Or they'll see you."

But she had recovered her breath and her ability to think without panic. "We mustn't run. It's dark enough they can't see my face. Let us walk as if we are companions with nothing to flee from. Then they won't be sure it's me."

She began walking at a casual pace toward the gateway from which he had emerged. After a moment he followed, indicating she should head toward a lamplit portico where four soldiers stood guard. She hooked her shawl up to cover the lower half of her face. Fear made her throat ache, but she had to trust him; she had no one else.

"This would not have happened if Gil hadn't decided to be loyal to me against all good sense," he said in a hot, furious tone.

"Do you think Gil was arrested because of his ties to you?"

"Of course."

She remembered her uncle's words. "Is it possible Queen Chorannah engineered his arrest as a way to get access to my fortune?"

He murmured, "Thus felling three birds with one arrow. It fits her devious mind. Hurry."

They climbed steps to the portico.

"Your Highness!" A captain stepped forward with a courteous bow. "We received no word you were coming."

"I need to see my father at once." He had lost the diffidence and stammer that made him seem foolish. Even his posture changed, shoulders back and spine stiff.

"The king has gone down into the city, Your Highness. Queen Dia left earlier—"

"I know where my mother is." Kasad slid open the door himself rather than allow them to refuse him entry. Sarai almost trod on his heels in her haste to get out of view. The soldiers watched in disapproval but Kasad was a prince and not theirs to command.

Inside Sarai was startled to find an unremarkable chamber, furnished with a single writing desk, its implements carefully put away, and an alcove decorated with flowers, nothing luxurious and no expensive ornamentation. A steward greeted Kasad and gave her a frowning look because her face was hidden; she liked that the man could not know precisely who she was, even if he would guess later.

"When is King Jehosh expected back?" the prince said.

"My lord, I do not expect him to return to the upper palace tonight."

Kasad gestured with a hand as if flicking off an insect that he wished was not annoying him. His grimace gave him an aura of impatience quite unlike the diffident way he engaged with Gil and Tyras. "I will make my own way out."

"My lord, I have not been given permission by the king to allow you to enter…"

"I don't need permission. I have a key."

"But only the king has a key…"

He stepped past the protesting man. "Do you imagine my father leaves me unprotected in the upper palace? Come along," he added over his shoulder to Sarai.

She hastened after him through a second door. A single lit lamp illuminated glimmering golden figures painted on the walls, their serene faces those of holy personages rapt in prayer. Only when the hinged door closed behind them did she relax a little, knowing two doors and multiple guards now separated her from her pursuers. He did not relax but strode across the dim chamber to a balcony carved into the rock.

There he turned to face her. "I can't get Gil released from prison."

"Can the king do so?"

"If we can find the king before the prisoners are marched out at dawn. But I fear he is unlikely to expend any effort on Gilaras Herelian, with his own authority under attack. He will say that if he publicly goes against his own laws, then rebels and outlaws will claim the same privilege."

"What if I offer him coin?" She thought of the chest abandoned in the palace.

He laughed curtly. "My father is rich, Lady Sarai. He doesn't need your coin."

"What does he need?"

"Loyal officials who won't stab him in the back."

She discarded that idea and considered the next. "Would Gil's jailers, or the priests, take a bribe to release him?"

"They'll take the coin and then arrest you for offering a bribe."

"But if they arrested me then I would be with Gil, wouldn't I?"

He pondered this question where he stood on the brink of a balcony. It was too dark for her to see how great the leap would be but the distant murmur of a flowing river, the gusty bouts of wind, and glimmers of tiny lights revealed how very high up they stood. A person who leaped into the gulf of air would plunge to her death, and no matter how desperate her situation Sarai was bitterly determined not to fall prey to despair. She owed her brave mother the fight for life and freedom.

"It won't work," he said at last. "Women go in separate work gangs."

She dropped the scarf so he could see her expression as she raised her chin defiantly. "I can't just give up and abandon him."

He nodded. "Come."

A door was hidden in the wall. Lamp in hand he led her down a tight, steep stairwell. The passage opened into a chamber carved out of the rock and aerated by slit windows. The scent of sweet incense flavored the air, tickling her nostrils. The lamplight cast shadows upon shadows, the shapes of furnishings barely seen as they crossed to the far side of the room where another hinged door stood, this one barred and chained with a lock.

He slipped a key from his clothing and, with trembling hands, took several tries to fit it to the lock. Footsteps slapped the steps, and she flattened herself against the wall, hoping the shadows would hide her, but it was only the steward come in pursuit.

The man said, "I will close up after you, Prince Kasad."

Kasad pulled the chain and bar away and opened the door. Sarai followed him down a narrow stone corridor tunneled into the rock. The emotions that piled up in her heart threatened to crush her as she breathed the musty air. Could she hire people to cut Gil loose while he was on the road? Suddenly the rumors of escaped prisoners in the hills about her clan's estate made sense: Maybe they, too, had been unjustly arrested, and their loved ones had done everything they could to free them. What if Uncle Makel was actually involved with outlaws?

The thought made her pulse race and her eyes sting. Could Makel help her? Would her brother Aram aid her? If she fled to him in Nessumara, would he hand her back to Uncle Abrisho?

She had to fix her mind on the business at hand. "What is this passageway, Your Highness? Is it meant to be kept secret?"

He replied in a low voice almost drowned out by the scuff of their footsteps. "It's a lovers' passage, Lady Sarai. The story goes that my great-grandfather King Anjihosh did not want his concubines known within the palace, lest courtiers try to bribe them to assassinate him. So he brought them to and from the palace by means of this passage. For the period when they were his lovers—never any one for more than a month, so the story goes—they were locked into that lower chamber to await his pleasure."

"That sounds unpleasant," she whispered, shuddering.

"It was necessity, not cruelty. He was protecting himself, and the women. I've never heard any family story that he mistreated his lovers. When my father first married my mother, he kept her out of sight of Queen Chorannah by bringing her here. Later he had the lower palace built for her. Now he brings his other lovers to this chamber to keep them out of my mother's sight."

"Does the king keep many lovers?" she asked, remembering the way Jehosh had flirted with her. With the part of her mind braced in an icy clarity, she wondered if she might manipulate the king's interest in her as a means to help Gil. She began to make a mental inventory of the tools she had. Her clan's coin wasn't really hers. She had to find other means.

"He keeps as many lovers as he wishes, I am sure," replied Kasad with apparent indifference. "His loyalty to my mother has never wavered. And here we are."

He carefully opened a locked door that let into the dusty confines of a storage room, and closed it after them. Lantern light revealed storerooms carved out of rock and clustered along curving passages, hard to make sense of in the dark. Instead of taking her to the Thousand Steps he led her to a wide court-yard, flanked by warehouses, where guards stood watch over a pair of mighty winches, neatly coiled rope, and a collection of huge, sturdy baskets. A curl of wind chased around the court-yard through air thick with unshed moisture.

"Queen Chorannah won't think to look here right away," he said as the men hooked a basket to a winch.

"These men will surely tell her what they've done."

"We just have to stay ahead of her. Now, we sit in a basket and they lower us down. Don't worry. It's not as frightening as it may seem. You can't really see anything at night."

"I'm not afraid of heights," she said, wishing she could examine the mechanism, but instead she had to seat herself in the tight confines of a basket fitted with a woven bench on which Kasad sat gingerly beside her. The way he tried not to touch any part of her amused her briefly. Then her thoughts scattered as the basket rocked, lifted by the rope cable, and swayed out as it was swung over the cliff. The oddly still night magnified every noise: Kasad's breathing and his feet shifting on the floor each time the basket tipped slightly to one side or the other as he braced himself so as not to bump into her; the clack of the winch, fading as they sank lower; the creak of rope; the river's voice growing louder.

The walls of the basket were too high for her to see over. Above, high clouds imperfectly concealed the stars.

From below a man called out orders. Hooked poles caught the rope with jerking tugs, and they set down with a bump against a raised platform lit by a pair of lanterns. Kasad clambered out and helped her. Soon he had them seated in a hired carriage driven by two Ri Amarah men, a father and son. She looked enough like a Hundred woman that they did not remark on her at all.

As the carriage rattled through the streets she slid the window panel open a crack and peeked onto darkened buildings. "Our steward Welo mentioned a night market. May we stop there?"

"Why?"

"Because it's best to plan for every possible outcome. I'll be quick."

"I can't walk unguarded in public," he said.

"I don't need your escort in the market, Your Highness. No one will recognize me."

So it was that she ventured into a bewildering maze of rows and aisles, many fragrant with herbs or freshly cooked slip-fry. No one took any notice of her as she asked directions and chose what she needed, except for a few curious glances at her scar. When she returned to the carriage, people had gathered to watch the two Ri Amarah men walking the horses. They paid no attention to Sarai as she wove a path through the crowd to the carriage.

"Those cursed Silvers should have stayed where they came from. Did you hear the news? They got that lord who married one of their daughters arrested just so they can be rid of him and climb one step closer to the queen."

Kasad had a tight smile on his face, hard to interpret, when she climbed into the carriage carrying an old leather sack. He tapped on the roof, and they rolled away. Although he did not ask her about the market he fretted silently, too restless to sit still.

"I know your actions tonight expose you to danger," she said. "My thanks for your help."

Daringly he took her hand in the darkness of the carriage. She held herself very still, not sure what to expect, but his tone was solemn. "Whatever happens tonight I will not see you for some time, Lady Sarai. Perhaps never again. My mother is sending me to her country estate to get me away from court now this trouble has broken out. Gil has been a loyal friend to me. I will not forget it. But I can't be seen here. I'm sorry."

"I understand."

Soldiers manned the prison's entrance armed with swords and stolid expressions. A small clot of people stood outside the high wall, all clutching sacks that they begged the guards to take in to prisoners waiting to be marched out at dawn. Misery and fear washed the scene, succeeded by silence and then whispers as she emerged from the carriage. At the gates, an older woman surrounded by a substantial retinue was arguing with a priest whose stolid, if sympathetic, expression was that of a man who has been hearing the same complaints all night.

"They cut off my son's hair!" she was crying. "His face has been mutilated as if he is a common criminal!"

"Yes, all the prisoners have their hair shorn off and their faces inked the night before they are marched out. It marks their shame, and makes it difficult for them to escape and take up a new life without questions being asked. You know the law, Lady Palo."

"But my Tyras was never tried before the assizes! He had nothing to do with the Silver's death. It was the fault of his troublemaking friends, the sort of bad influences you'd not wish upon your own dear children. If only Tyras had learned to be as obedient as you, Your Holiness. I can reward you to the measure of your true worth if you would but see your way to making sure he stays behind when the condemned are marched out tomorrow." The praise sat awkwardly as an attempt at a bribe but it was the cloth pouch she held out that drew his gaze.

"I know you are frightened for your son, verea, so I will pretend I do not see the coin." As the hope in her face died, she tucked the pouch back into her sleeve and blinked back tears. The priest added, in a kindly but firm manner, "The king himself put his seal upon the judgment of guilt earlier this evening, verea. He came here to the prison."

Sarai halted, stunned by this information. How was Jehosh involved?

"But I heard the king promised every arrested man a proper hearing!" Lady Palo's grimace twisted to a meaner visage. "The Silvers probably paid plenty of coin to the king to get him to exile those innocent lads. How can we know the Silver coachman was really dead? They have evil sorcery that protects them. How can you take the side of people who worship a false god, Your Holiness?"

"I honor my vows to Beltak by striving to take the side of justice, verea."

At that instant the small pedestrian door set within the double gates opened, and Gil's older brother walked out. "Lady Palo, I just saw you inside. I wanted to say—"

"General Shevad, how dare you speak to me as if we are acquainted! I knew Gilaras's antics would end in disaster for his friends! What do you have to say in his defense?"

"Nothing, Lady Palo." General Shevad's grim expression turned dire as he spotted Sarai in the shadows. "We have washed our hands of Gilaras."

Sarai's mouth dropped open as the bitter words hit home.

But Shevad nodded at her as if nothing was wrong! Then he turned to the priest. "Your Holiness, may I take my brother's wife in to bid him farewell and repudiate him if she so wishes?"

Seeing Sarai, Lady Palo turned her back and stalked off.

The priest looked uncomfortable, whether at Sarai's presence or Lady Palo's insult she could not be sure. "The relatives of criminals are only allowed to see them if they bring provisions."

"And as you see, Lady Sarai carries a sack. I believe Lady Palo just delivered a similar gift to her son, Lord Tyras."

"So she did. Very well. Make haste. It will be dawn soon."

"I'm sorry, Lady Palo," Sarai said, but the other woman kept walking.

Abashed, Sarai followed the general inside, trotting to keep up as they crossed a wide inner courtyard. Thirteen years older than Gil, Shevad had a hardened look that she had once or twice thought would suit Gil should he grow up a little and not seem quite so weightless and lacking in depth. Now the idea that Gil would suffer nauseated her. How could she ever wish misery and pain on anyone, thinking it would make them more attractive? Wasn't happiness attractive?

"I have been ordered north to take over command of a garrison in Ithik Eldim," Shevad said in a low voice, indicating with his gaze that she too must speak softly so guards could not overhear.

"Thus neatly removing you from court."

He nodded approvingly. "Yes, you see how the matter stands. It appears as an honor but separates me from my clan. If I refuse, I will be arrested as a rebel. I have a single question, Lady Sarai. I request you speak truthfully. I have been wounded before and can take the injury."

With an effort she did not drop her gaze to the level of his genitals or what was presumably left of them.

He smiled wryly, as if he guessed her thoughts. "Do you mean to end our alliance?"

"No, I do not. Maybe it seems strange to you but Gil gave me the gift of not caring about the very thing my own clan called my shame. For that alone I owe him my loyalty. I also don't believe he killed any Ri Amarah. And anyway, I like him."

"No one has been more surprised than me by how well you two fell together." He stopped in front of the farthest gate and, quite unexpectedly, bent to kiss her lightly on the cheek, his scent of musk vine and stardrops as heady as desire. "We have been more fortunate than we could have hoped for in gaining you, Sarai." He stepped back and, while she was still too breathless to speak, added, "Are you pregnant?"

"I don't yet know."

"We must hope you are. This is the prison for the men who will be marched out tomorrow."

He led her into a building that Sarai guessed had once been a vast stable. Each stall had been converted into a small wooden cage. Each cage contained multiple men with shorn hair scattered at their bare feet. Every man's scalp had been raggedly and messily shaved. A party of guards and priests was working their way along the cages with bowls of water, needles, and ink. In the dim light the reddened skin of men shone with crossed spears inked into their cheeks, the mark of the work gang. The stench of voided bowels and an atmosphere of futility made her eyes water as Shevad led her to the darkest end of the barracks.

They reached a barred door. Shevad lifted the bar as Sarai grabbed a lamp from a nearby hook. Behind the door lay a lightless storage closet that stank of urine and sweat. It was long and low-ceilinged, the wall set with wooden hooks for hanging harness. Gil and Tyras sat side by side on a cot, braced and wary. Both had shaved heads, with inked spears still red and raw on their cheeks.

"Haven't you scolded me enough that you have to come back for more, Shev?" said Gil wearily. "I'll do what you asked me to do, I promise."

She stepped past Shevad and hung the lamp from a hook.

"Sarai-ya!" Gil leaped to his feet as she dumped the sack onto the cot and pulled out a folded taloos. "I didn't think I would see you again... What in the hells are you doing?"

She shook out a folded taloos and tied it to hooks to make a screen between cot and open door. "Lord Tyras, General Shevad, please stand at the door and make some manner of noise. I need to be alone with Gil."

"What?" Tyras looked stupefied as Shevad, cracking a smile, dragged him out past the cloth.

Gil's gaze met hers, his surprise turning to curiosity as he waited.

Probably her tone came out too crisp and flat. "Lie down, Gil. This is our last chance."

He gaped at her. "You want to...! Here...!"

She pushed him down on the cot and pressed her mouth on his. Fortunately his elaborate court clothes had been stripped from him and he'd been given a laborer's kilt to replace it; nothing easier to lift to get at the business end of him.

"What's going on?" said Tyras from the other side of the cloth.

Shevad leaped into battle. "Let me sing a lament for my lost kinsman, appropriate to a parting of ways." His bellow filled the space, his voice more pleasing than might be expected at such volume. "*The road runs to the sea, to the city, to the hills! But when you pause to look back, your tracks in the dirt lead your eye to home. Farewell to you, dearest ones. Your faces will ever walk in my heart. Let there be one more tender embrace.*"

She ran a hand down Gil's chest and belly to his penis. That part had no trouble grasping the plan as she curled her fingers around it. "If I'm not pregnant they will dissolve the marriage and try to force me to marry someone else."

"There's a useful thought," he murmured as she rubbed him. "I'm glad it occurred to you, Sarai-ya, because now that I think about it I've always rather dreamed of having sex with someone while people were trying to look, or maybe while they were looking."

The way he could dance fecklessly right across even this frantic disaster aroused her. "Do you want me to pull down the cloth then? And let everyone look?"

He squirmed, smiling at her in that way that made her want to laugh even in such straits as this. "I only want what you want, my peach."

Shevad boomed an extensive and melodic description of a kiss of nectar dampening the beak of the honey-seeking flutter-bird. Faltering at first, then gaining strength, Tyras joined in on the refrain.

Sarai kept working. "What did you mean by telling Shevad you would do what he asked?"

"He wants me to be a spy for Captain Kellas."

"Captain Kellas...?"

"*The sweet rose is filled with scent.*" Tyras launched into a new song with its catalog of the beauties of flowers blooming beneath fresh rains.

"The king's new chief of security. The king does not trust Queen Chorannah, because she is usurping his officials. Meanwhile the captain finds the number and movement of work gangs to be suspicious, especially as in the last year so many are being sent south."

"Something is definitely moving in the south," murmured Sarai.

"I can feel what is going on." He loosened her sash, slid his hands up beneath her shift, and found the drawstring of her trousers. "It's a good idea. I can pretend to be a spy instead of languishing as a sad helpless doomed prisoner. How do you like that?"

"I like it if you like it." She straddled Gil. No time for niceties! She applied herself to the task.

Of course he was laughing low in his throat as if it were all a game, and his hands found the places to touch her that she loved best.

Tyras arrived at length to the end of the flowers and rains and with Shevad singing a descant they flowed easily back to the refrain of parting, joined by defiant voices among the other prisoners. "*I shall stand at the gate and watch the road, waiting for the return of the one I nurtured and cast out into the land, waiting for them to return from—*"

"The hells!" gasped Gil as his eyes closed and his head tilted back.

"That's not in the verse," remarked Tyras as the prisoners kept the song going, voices gaining strength while the general's voice ceased.

"*The road runs to the sea, to the city, to the hills!*"

Sarai collapsed onto Gil as the familiar wash of pleasure flooded through her. What fleeting triumph! As his chest heaved against hers she savored the knowledge they'd had this bold chance to thwart those who were trying to separate them.

"You'll need a watchword, to distinguish friend from foe," she whispered as, eyes closed, he sighed with heady satisfaction. "Gil, are you paying attention to me?"

He nuzzled her ear. "Sheh! You injure me with your doubt. I was paying full attention as you certainly felt my awareness rise."

She tweaked his ear harder than she needed to as he grinned. "*Let my lament crown the heavens!*" the prisoners thundered.

He whispered, "I already chose a watchword and told it to Shevad. I will know my allies if they speak this: *the flare of the crescent moon*. The reply is, *It shines like a swan among feral dogs*."

Her heart burned to hear him speak of their first meeting, or maybe that was just the heat of lovemaking dissipating as they held each other close. "Oh, Gil. I will find a way to get you back. I will!"

"My treasure." He kissed her hard on the mouth. His breath was sour, but sweet to her regardless as he embraced her. A trace of moisture from the fresh ink stippled into his skin smeared her cheek, reminding her of the other things she had brought for him.

"Keep the wound clean until it heals. In the pouch you'll find soldier's friend, with the edged leaves. It is best for cuts, but the weed called red-bell if steeped in hot water makes an infusion to soothe wounds also. There is also ironseed that can be ground to a paste for strengthening the blood, and bark of purple thorn if your lungs sicken. Keep the cloth to use as a shelter or ground cloth. I bought sandals, too. Keep your feet healthy. Stay alive!"

"Take that cloth down!" shouted a loud male voice. The singing ceased abruptly.

Gil rolled her off the cot and they had both just tugged their garments into place when the priest ripped down the cloth and with lamp in hand glared at them with all the offended hauteur of a man who believes his god is the only true master.

To her surprise he burst out laughing. "Get out! But the hells if I wouldn't have tried it, too, at your age."

She stood with as much dignity as she could drape around herself. To serenade her departure Gil began singing a cheerfully lewd song called "The Fisherman's Hook." Actually she thought there was something a little wrong with Gil that made him find pleasure only when there was risk involved. But it didn't matter. Great-Aunt Tsania often said each person carried both a gift and a burden within themselves and sometimes they were the same thing.

The priest hustled Tyras back into the cell, shoved the door shut, and barred it. She didn't see General Shevad. He had vanished. The prisoners huddled at the back of their cells like whipped dogs, no longer bold enough to sing. A prickling of fear washed her skin as she looked toward the open gates.

The eunuch who was her guard at the palace, Tayum, strode toward her down the length of the stable like an executioner in haste to get the job done. Guards flanked him. He said nothing; he did not need to say anything.

If she had fled to the river first maybe she would have gotten away, or maybe they would have caught her anyway at the wharf. The prayer her people sang every morning must now be her guide: *Let us not cease working, let us not lose heart, for as we walk backward into a future we can never see, our eyes remain on the responsibility that has been given into our hands.*

Facing Tayum, she sorted through Elit's favorite roles and put on The Slightly Impatient Innkeeper with Too Much to Do.

"Ah, Tayum, there you are. I've been waiting for you. I am ready to return to the palace. We will need to pass by my apartments in the lower palace to pick up my things."

He gazed at her as if he could not understand her words and then, with a shrug, gestured for her to precede him. Outside, Prince Kasad and the Silver carriage were gone. Had both Kasad and Shevad abandoned her? But as she climbed into a new carriage she knew it wasn't true: Neither man could afford to let Tayum see her with him lest the eunuch tell Queen Chorannah.

They did not stop at the lower palace, and she was transferred from the carriage to a curtained chair for the ascent up the stairs. After much jostling and weaving the chair was set down and the curtains parted. Instead of the spacious chamber and balcony where she had been confined before, she was ushered by Tayum into a tiny closet of a room crammed in a row of others along a guarded corridor. It reminded her of the stalls in which the prisoners were kept, only her tiny room was furnished with shelves for her mattress and bedding, basin and pitcher on a table for washing, and her chest, which had been brought up already. The hasp of the lock had been broken. With a spurt of dread, fearing they had stolen her Book of Accounts, she knelt and opened the lid. The book lay atop folded cloth, her box of writing tools tucked beside it. She gripped the chest and breathed until her heart ceased its erratic gallop. By then they had slid shut the door, leaving her alone in darkness.

She slept a little, but was woken by a series of thuds and quiet chatter as people began moving about. The gray light of dawn leaked through the rice paper covering the door.

The door slid open and the two silent attendants who had served her before entered with a tray of chicken rice soup for breakfast and a pitcher of scented water to wash in. As soon as she had finished her dawn ablutions, Tayum beckoned peremptorily. She grabbed her book, determined not to leave it or her mirror behind as long as there was the faintest hope she might have a chance to escape. In silence he led her to a screened balcony overlooking a shrine in which veiled priests intoned prayers to Beltak the Shining One. He held aside a drapery and indicated she should enter to sit with the queen and her women. But here she balked.

"I am Ri Amarah. I do not bow my head to any god, and I cannot pray to this one."

He gestured more insistently. She held her ground, refusing to enter as the prayers droned on. She was exhausted, but as long as they waited for her to yield she would not show weakness. For a wild instant she thrilled to the idea the queen would cast her out.

Instead, after the prayers crescendoed and the women murmured a final response, she was swept up in their exit like a stick jostled into the wake of the queen. Tayum shepherded her along. In a chamber painted with vines and flowers the queen took a seat on an ebony stool. The ladies observed in chattering good humor as servants divested Chorannah of her prayer robes, perfumed and combed her, and draped her in fresh garments dyed in jewel-bright shades.

After this they processed to a spacious porch overlooking a lovely garden, not the king's. From this vantage Sarai saw the white Assizes Tower with its shuttered windows. Certain women were picked out to sit close to the queen and others relegated to corners in a scheme clearly meant to indicate favor. Tayum brought Sarai forward last of all, every gaze watching, and seated her on a cushion at the queen's left hand.

The queen declaimed a long speech as every woman listened with rapt attention. Sarai hadn't the faintest idea of what she was talking about because she spoke, of course, in Sirni. When she at length finished, the women brought out embroidery, crewelwork, miniature painting, and sewing. Sarai's legs were beginning to go numb from sitting still for so long, but she did not know what else to do except open her Book of Accounts and read over her old entries since her ink and brush were packed away in her writing box.

The translator sank down beside her with a harried look, her dark-blue skirts puddling around her legs. "Lady Sarai, it is not the custom for women to possess books. Contracts and religious tracts are men's work. Women are the keepers of poetry and song, all that is spoken. If you will give me the item, I can see it properly destroyed."

Sarai slapped the book shut and clasped it against her chest. "Among my people every married woman keeps a Book of Accounts. I can no more give this up than I can pray to your god."

The queen spoke in a low voice to one of her eunuchs, the translator was called away, and then nothing happened except that as the women worked they glanced now and again with curiosity at Sarai. She sensed no particular hostility, only calculation.

Later tea and cakes were brought by servingwomen all garbed in drab blue, easy to distinguish next to the bright colors of the court women. Over these delicacies the ladies stood up in turn, declaiming poems to applause and commentary. Last of all went the queen, who had quite the most prodigious memory. She spoke verses at such sonorous length that Sarai had to keep pinching herself to keep from falling asleep in the heavy heat of late afternoon.

How gratefully she rose when the queen finished. Her feet tingled, all pins and needles, making it painful to walk. Tayum showed her back to her narrow room where her boxes of gifts and fabrics had arrived and been unpacked onto the shelves. The curtain clasp given her by Queen Dia was the only thing not sorted away; it had been left on top of the covered chamber pot.

In this tiny cell she was now to live. She unrolled her mattress and lay with eyes shut, afraid to let go of the book lest they steal it from her while she slept. Weariness conquered her and she drifted off, only to wake with a jolt at the clanging of a bell.

Dusk had overtaken the world while she slept. All along the corridor doors scraped open, women talked in lively voices, and the glow of lamps oozed along the rice paper walls as people moved past. A light came to rest before her door. It slid open to reveal Tayum.

Supper was taken in a chamber decorated with tapestries. The meat-ridden barley stew came so strongly spiced she could only pick at it. Afterward they took their places in the Queen's Audience Hall where Sarai had last seen Gil. The ladies competed to show how many verses of poetry they could declaim. A singer from Bell Quarter was brought in to sing tragic death songs—the only thing Sarai understood—after which the women talked until very late while sipping wine, all in Sirni, like so much babble. At last the ordeal ended and they retired, each to her own cubicle.

The two women who had served her were kneeling outside her tiny room, but as she tried to wave them away, wanting to be alone, a commotion stirred at the end of the corridor. The queen sailed down the passage and came to rest by Sarai's door. Chorannah pulled a whip from her belt and handed it to Tayum. The two servants knelt, heads bowed, and the translator crept forward on her knees.

"What is this?" Sarai demanded, so alarmed at the sight of the whip and the groveling women that she forgot the queen's title.

Hands raised to her face, the translator spoke into her palms. "Her sublime highness, Queen Chorannah, desires an orderly existence. You have troubled her four times today, Lady Sarai. First you rudely departed the guest chamber most generously given to you, and compounded the offense by entering the men's courtyard when women and men are enjoined to serve the Shining One in separation."

Sarai said nothing because she had certainly done that.

"You refused to enter the shrine. You refused to surrender the book. And you follow the offensive custom of your people, in which women hide their faces when only the most exalted of priests are allowed that privilege. As it is said, *Those closest to the Shining One cradle some of His light in their faces, and thus betoken their holiness through what they are enjoined to conceal.*"

Sarai grabbed her book off the table. "I am Ri Amarah. I follow the customs of my own people. I did not ask to be brought here. Send me away, if I displease you." She thought of Gil and how the queen might still find a way to harm him, and so forced out the words, "Your Highness."

"Her exalted and honorable highness, Queen Chorannah, comprehends that the proper ways of the palace are new to you, Lady Sarai," said the translator, peeking through splayed fingers. Her dark eyes had something of the look of Gil's eyes, a slight fold that spoke of Qin ancestry, but the queen's court had so many people of a foreign look that Sarai could not sort out who might have come from where. Up here in the queen's wing no one looked Hundred-born like Elit or Yava. "Queen Chorannah is merciful. You may keep the book and not attend at the shrine, according to the ways of your people. But for the offense against hospitality your servingwomen must be punished for not stopping you from disgracing the queen's court by your disgraceful actions."

"My servingwomen? I brought no servants with me..."

The other two women were unbuttoning their jackets to bare their shoulders. Tayum weighed the whip in his hand. He had the muscled shoulders to really hurt them, and as the cloth slipped down their backs she saw how smooth and unblemished their brown skin was. Because of her they would feel the whip's bite.

"The queen will retract the punishment if you surrender the book and attend at the shrine," said the translator.

Sarai shuddered as her hands tightened on her precious book in a death grip. Her mouth burned with rage-fed words.

"No! If you must whip someone, whip me, because I am the one who acted, not them. Whipping them in my place falls on your head, not on mine! Do not think you can coerce me by making me believe I am obliged to protect them by denying who I am."

Her ragged breathing and frenzied pulse throbbed in her ears. All down the corridor the women of the court stared raptly at the tableau playing out in their midst like one of Elit's stories, all high emotion and furious threats.

Queen Chorannah raised an eyebrow and, with a shrug, signaled to Tayum. The two servingwomen bent over, bracing themselves on their hands, their expressions devoid of any spark of protest, not even a plea for mercy.

She forced herself to watch. Tayum applied the whip with precise rhythm: four lashes to one girl, four to the other, the sound so crisp and potent it filled Sarai's ears until she could hear nothing else. He might have been digging a ditch, work that needed to be done and must be gotten through. The girl who had worked impatiently whimpered as her skin reddened. The other girl gave only a faint grunt as each lash raised a welt on her shoulders.

Four passes he made, sixteen strokes to each young woman. Then he stepped away and held out the whip. Queen Chorannah took it, gathered up her particular attendants, and processed away down the corridor as the women who lived in the other cubicles bent double like stalks of grain bowed down by a passing wind. The translator rose to follow, and as she scurried away she murmured words in the language of the Hundred so Sarai would be sure to understand, "Thus is the selfishness of Silvers exposed."

Sarai's face burned with the heat of fury but she refused to answer.

The other court women retreated to their cubicles with their own blue-garbed servingwomen in attendance. One by one, lamps were extinguished for the night.

The two girls pulled their jackets back on. Moving slowly, postures made awkward by their efforts to keep cloth from rubbing against welted skin, they made clear through gestures that they were now to help Sarai make ready for bed.

She could not even force out a word. Instead, she fumbled in her pouch and pressed a gold cheyt into each girl's hand. With downcast eyes they accepted the coin wordlessly. She waved them away, then slid the door shut, desperate to be alone.

The queen had caged her and afterward in the most deliberate way possible marked her out as an outsider who could not be trusted. In its way it was a brilliant piece of maneuvering.

For a long time she sat with head sunk in her hands, too upset to sleep. When all was quiet, she eased open the door. At the end of the corridor a single lamp burned and a eunuch stood guard. Almost she lost her courage: She was a ship adrift without sail or oars, ballasted only by a dead mother, a frail aunt, a departed lover, and a wrongfully arrested husband. Almost the old whispers from her childhood strangled her: *She bears the mark of her mother's shame, and that is why her mother named her Sorrow.*

But sorrow is what you feel. It may be interwoven with your spirit because of the griefs you have suffered but it is not sewn into your flesh; it is not who you are. Her mother had left wealth, status, and a son behind, and although everyone said Nadai had selfishly chosen an outlaw lover over her responsibilities to her husband's respectable clan, Sarai was sure there was more to the story.

People hide what they don't wish you to know.

Why was the queen so desperate for her money? Where were Gil and the other arrested men being sent? Even confined by their walls she could play a part in this tale just as if she, like Gil, had been recruited as a spy, and just as if she, like Elit, had joined Hasibal's pilgrims.

35

Although the guards rousted them out at dawn, the prisoners waited under guard in the courtyard for half the morning.

"I'm hells thirsty," muttered Tyras. "This bag is so cursed heavy. How long do we have to wait? I wish they would just get on with it."

"Shut up," whispered Gil as a guard turned to look at them.

Perhaps spurred by Ty's complaint, a nearby prisoner called out, "How long do we have to wait here? If you're not going to march us out, why not let us go home to our clans?"

A guard pushed through the prisoners and whipped the man across the face, the tip drawing blood. With a scream the man dropped to his knees, hand pressed to his face. "My eye! My eye!"

"Shut up," said the guard, looking around at the nervous, sweating men. "No talking."

As the man whimpered, trying to gulp down his pain so he wouldn't get whipped again, Gil counted the prisoners: fifty-eight men, not one of them old enough to have more than a touch of gray in his hair. The mature men had the builds and muscle of laborers while the younger men came in all sorts. There was one big, broken-nosed, thuggish-looking fellow and several men with mean eyes and sour mouths who looked as if they might actually have been properly arrested criminals. The rest, like he and Ty, had the aggrieved stance of unfortunates caught in a street sweep and now too terrified to protest. Many carried a sack, the hopeful dregs of their lost life.

Two wagons piled with full grain sacks trundled in, accompanied by a swaggering chief, twenty-four guards armed with spears, long knives, crossbows, and a whole lot of rope. With the prison guards atop the wall-walk aiming crossbows down, no prisoner dared resist as they were roped together into two columns. Gil got caught several people ahead of Tyras, and so as they were marched—or better to say shuffled—out, he had no one to lean on, no one to feel stalwart beside. The men were tied so tightly together he smelled the stink of his neighbors, although he doubted he smelled any better wearing an unwashed short kilt and the miasma of the prison as his perfume.

Out South Gate they trudged. Loitering kinsfolk of the prisoners tried to call out farewells or offer a final embrace but the hells if they weren't shoved back by the guards. After that people gave them a wide berth except for a few stubborn mothers and aunts and sisters and wives and female sweethearts pacing them in silent grief; no men dared hang around, fearing they might get arrested, too. He held on to his memory of Sarai's visit, but mostly his thoughts circled around Shevad's astounding command that he play spy, as if he were joining the fabled Black Wolves of old.

What a joke! Yet he kept thinking of what Captain Kellas had said up in the palace.

Down to the Lesser Istri they made their slow way. There a barge took them across to the southern shore. Out on the water a few men tried to pee into the river to the curses of those they hit with their stream instead. Gil felt nauseated by the pitch and sway of the barge as the winch hauled it across the river, so though he hated being driven off the barge truly knowing he was leaving behind the city he had grown up in, he was at the same time relieved.

"Praise to the god, to the Shining One, save us," whispered the man walking beside him. "Do you pray to the Shining One, brother?"

"I am not your fucking brother," muttered Gil, not liking the unctuous tone of the man, then caught a guard scanning the column to see who was speaking.

On they walked without rest or food or anything to drink. They were kept on the verge of the main road as it ran through fields and orchards and past neat villages whose inhabitants pretended not to see them. A man in front of him pissed down his own leg, and no one laughed because as the afternoon wore on more and more men could not hold their bladders and soon the column stank of urine.

As the sun touched the horizon the wagons came to rest in a pasture. The grass was pounded down almost to dirt as if many had camped here before. The big stump of an ancient felled tree offered a place for the chief to supervise the cook setting out a big pot of cold millet.

"Now you men, if you can call yourselves that, listen up." The chief scratched his balls as he climbed up on the stump the better to look disappointed in his charges. "You call me Chief Roni. My task is to get you pathetic lot to our final destination..."

Here he paused and surveyed them as if daring anyone to speak. No one did.

"Very good," he agreed, as if to a heartfelt response. "Your task is to be no trouble to me and my men. Be peaceable, and you and I will get along. Because I'm a generous man who is paid for the number of men who make it to where we're going, I want you to stay healthy. So starting tonight you'll be taken out of the ropes and allowed a handful of millet as your supper and a dipper of wine to drink. In the morning those who have caused me no trouble will get the same. At midday those who have caused me no trouble will get the same. You see?"

Everyone wanted out of the ropes so they said nothing.

"Those who please me will get additional privileges, like a chance to wash and a ration of rice or even, if you're very good, fish or mutton. But not tonight. Tonight I just want to see that you can be obedient."

Released from the ropes, Gil rubbed his rope-burned ankles and wrists as he nudged up next to Tyras in the line that quickly formed for food. It was a sullen group that took their cold millet and a draught of the wine, gone to foul-tasting vinegar. Afterward as night came the prisoners settled down to rest. Gil dragged Tyras close to the fire where the cook was boiling up tomorrow's rations.

"What are you doing?" Tyras whispered, clutching the sack his mother had brought him against his belly. "Better to stay at the edge where we won't be noticed."

"I have a plan to make the cook friendly to us." Gil sat cross-legged and settled his sack on his lap. "Doesn't your face hurt?"

"Of course it hurts. There are men here still bleeding from the ink. What if the scars get inflamed? We could die!"

"Hsst! Quiet! What's this?"

Just out of sight in the shadows a man cursed, "That's mine!"

A whip snapped, the sound so resonant at night that every man visible in firelight flinched. The chief swaggered into view carrying a leather sack. He placed a lit lantern on the stump and dumped out the contents of the sack next to it.

"Let me see here. That's a nice silver bracelet but nothing you'll need on the work gang."

"My sister gave that to me!" cried the man, still unseen at the edge of the group. "You can't steal it—"

The whip cracked, and his yelp of pain crafted a pool of stillness over the prisoners. No one looked at each other. Gil grabbed Ty's hand.

"Here's a knife. Can't have that." The chief set it aside next to the bracelet. "And a nice loaf of bread. That you can keep, though I hope you don't have to fight with your comrades over it now they know you have it. And this old vest you can keep, though you're not allowed to wear it on the march. We need to be able to whip your bare back if you disobey, as you did just now."

He tossed the sack to a guard, who returned it to its now-mute owner. Then he turned, looked right at Gil and Tyras, and beckoned.

"Fuck," breathed Tyras.

Gil grabbed both sacks, kicked Tyras to keep him seated, and walked out to place them on the stump. He clasped both hands behind his back the way his brother Yofar had taught him back when Yofar was alive and drilling Gil in the skills a soldier needed: before Yofar died in a skirmish in the north, before Shevad had cruelly informed him that he was too valuable for his testicles and would never be allowed to go off to war like his courageous brothers.

Looking him over, the chief grunted a soft laugh. "Don't mock me, ver. You're no soldier."

"No offense intended, Chief. I have soldiers in the family. It's how we were taught."

"Eiya! You've a mouth on you, lad." The chief flicked his gaze past him toward Tyras—nothing escaped his notice, evidently—then opened up the beautifully embossed leather bag Lady Palo had given her son. It was hard not to gasp aloud when the chief emptied a pouch of coin onto the stump. Silver leya and a few gold cheyt glittered under the lamp.

"A nice bonus for my men," remarked the chief. He spun a fine knife with an ivory handle through his fingers with the skill of a man who likes playing with weapons. "Sheh! This is a pretty thing but it won't butcher a sheep, will it? No use to me. We'll sell it for beer at the next town."

Gil wanted to look over his shoulder at Ty to warn him not to protest but he knew better than to look away from the chief, who was enjoying his rapt audience as he picked through the ridiculously luxurious contents and one by one set them aside for his own purposes until nothing was left, not even the gorgeous leather sack, which itself was worth good money in any market. Tyras made no peep but Gil could have sworn he heard his friend's breathing grow loud and ragged. Finally Chief Roni picked through the worn leather sack Sarai had given Gil.

"By my balls, this is a sorry treasure chest! Dried herbs, an old copper ladle, a spoon and bowl my respected mother wouldn't deign to use, and a length of second-best cotton. Who gave you this rubbish?"

"My wife, Chief." *My exceedingly clever wife.*

"Aui! Here, have it back." He called forward another man, and Gil walked back to Tyras and sank down with a grunt of relief as the chief pawed through the next bag of provisions.

"Everything my mother brought me! Taken!" Tyras buried his face in hand.

"It was all useless to us, Ty. Your mother was thinking like a palace-born lady."

"We could have used that coin when we escape."

"Escape?"

"There are twice as many of us as there are of them."

"Did you somehow manage not to see their weapons? Anyway, we have a job to do. Don't you remember?"

"I never agreed to be a cursed spy—"

"Hush!"

A commotion at the roadside brought the chief's head around. A pair of guards dragged in a man Gil recognized as one of the sour-mouthed criminal-looking fellows he had noted earlier. The man struggled a little, more for show than anything, Gil thought, then went limp and said in a beseeching voice, "Just needed to take a shit, Chief."

The chief calmly picked up Ty's ivory-handled knife and tested its sharpness with a cut right across the man's throat.

Blood spurted. The prisoners cried out in surprise and dismay as the doomed man thrashed, choking and gurgling.

"Hold him tighter, you asswits," said the chief. This time he grabbed the man by the hair and held his head back. As blood pumped from a half-opened vein, the chief sawed so hard as the man flopped and struggled that Gil had to close his eyes lest he vomit. Even so he heard the thuds of the man's feet as he kicked and kicked against the ground, the liquid throttle, the sigh of his passing.

"May the Shining One protect us," prayed Tyras, and when Gil opened his eyes he saw that Ty was staring at the remains: the dead man cast onto the earth, the two guards shaking blood from their hands, the chief frowning at the pretty knife.

"As I said, this knife is useless for butchering. Nothing but an ornament for a man with more coin than balls. What a waste of steel." He handed it to one of the guards. "You can split the coin from selling it, you two. Drag this rubbish out of here."

Every gaze followed the path of the dead man, dumped out of sight in the brush.

"Now, before I continue with my inspection, let that be a lesson to you all," said the chief, his expression conveying dissatisfaction more than anger. "If you try to escape, you immediately become an outlaw and we have the right by law to kill you on the spot. Obedient men can live to see the end of their sentence. Who is next? I'll need to inspect all your sacks."

Many of the guards laughed at the crude joke. Men crowded forward as if afraid anyone found too far away from the cook fire and wagons would be deemed an escapee. Gil used the commotion to sidle up to the fire where the cook went about washing the millet as if he hadn't even noticed the execution.

"Is it against the rules to ask for a dip of water, ver?" he said to the cook. "To brew a bit of soldier's friend for our scars? I have a few herbs I'd be willing to share for the privilege. Make your food more tasty."

"Ask tomorrow," said the cook without looking up.

36

A rap on the door of his sleeping room woke Kellas. He roused by rolling to his knees and grabbing his short sword.

"It's Oyard, Captain."

"Come in." The way the shadows blotted the chamber told him it was not quite yet dawn.

The door slid aside to reveal Oyard kneeling, still wearing his sleeping robe. "A token from Queen Dia was just delivered to the sentry." He pushed it across the mats.

The ivory held a chill that tingled against Kellas's skin, and it smelled faintly of pepper. "Will you go at once?" Oyard looked as bleary-eyed as Kellas felt.

"No. I'll let her wait. I need to make clear to her that I am Jehosh's official, not hers."

After Oyard left Kellas dressed and went out to the back to wash. Then, as always, he oversaw the dawn practice with his usual attention to detail. It was important to push new recruits and see who began flagging first, who gave up, who pressed on, who kept their attention focused. So far he had forty potential Wolves, each one the sort of person palace officials would overlook: a roofer's son, a banner maker's daughter, siblings who spoke with almost incomprehensible accents because they hailed from an obscure northern port. All were restless, eager young people looking for adventure. He had been the same, at their age. He knew what qualities to look for.

As practice finished, Yero let in a vendor selling roasted eggs. When the old woman came around to Kellas and dropped a warm egg into his palm she whispered, "The new work gang took the road south."

Yero paid her, and she departed, her basket empty.

Kellas added the egg to his breakfast of rice gruel and fish steamed in a wrap of nai leaves, wondering if his newest, rawest recruits would survive the work gang.

After everyone had eaten, Kellas took recruits into his office in groups of eight for basic memory drills. He placed twelve objects on the floor and covered them with a cloth. After lifting the cloth, he gave them a span to look, then covered the objects. "Write down what you saw, arranged as you saw it."

Four of the eight set brushes to ink while the other four folded hands in laps, heads bowed as in shame.

"Why do you not write?" Kellas asked.

The roofer's son looked up. "My clan can't afford the school fees, Captain. I don't know how."

The banner maker's daughter nodded. "I don't, either. The

Beltak shrine schools all charge a fee, Captain. And they don't take girls at all."

"All the temple schools, the ones that used to be run by the clerks serving Sapanasu the Lantern...are they *all* closed?" he demanded. A spurt of anger welled up so strongly it made him light-headed. He'd thought his Toskala clan hired a tutor to educate their children as a mark of status, but now he wondered. "*All of them?*"

"My parents attended Lantern schools, but that was a long time ago," said the banner maker's daughter. The way she hunched her shoulders as his burst of temper frightened her made him reel himself in.

"What about you?" he said more evenly to the four who could write.

It turned out they were all from country villages and isolated towns where the seven gods still held sway and Sapanasu the Lantern lit the flame of knowledge in the hearts of the young.

"In my day," he muttered, aware of how old the peevish words made him sound, "every child was educated at the Lantern's temples without a fee except the tithe all clans pay to the gods."

"The Beltak priests say the seven gods are an evil superstition that the Shining One drove out," said the roofer's son, glancing toward the alcove where a painting depicted a beautiful woman with a compassionate face sitting in a shower of plum blossoms. "But you wear Hasibal's Tears, Captain, and you don't hide this altar to the Merciful One in your office even though the priests closed all the temples in Toskala years ago."

"I am an old man, and no one is surprised when an old man stubbornly clings to the beliefs common in his youth." Hands clasped behind his back, he considered the eight young people as they bowed their heads and grew still. He considered the forces arrayed against them all. He could not fight the Beltak priests. Not yet. "Those who do not know their letters will take extra training until they can read and write. Now, we'll begin again, and this time—"

The door slid open and Oyard beckoned. "Lord Vanas is here, Captain."

"The hells! I'm popular today." He chased the recruits out and remained standing as Lord Vanas entered. The man had a penchant for costly silk, that was certain. Years of living with a wife who loved silk had taught Kellas to distinguish the costliest weaves, and this yellow-orange fabric with embroidered leaves was definitely expensive.

"Had I known you wished to see me I would have waited upon you, my lord."

"Strange to think that when I was a young soldier, you and Chief Oyard commanded me, and yet now I can command you." Vanas settled on a cushion and gestured for Kellas to sit. "But I have my own reasons for coming to you."

"That is your prerogative as the legendary General Sengel's son and the current king's brother-in-law, my lord." Vanity was a sign of weakness, and it was odd of Vanas to display his so crudely, as if years feeding from the trough of wealth and preference had left him hungrier than before. "Shall I send for tea?"

"No. My question is blunt. How quickly can you undermine Ulyar and take over the Spears and in particular the spies and assassins who are currently under Ulyar's purview?"

"That depends on how Ulyar's loyalty was coaxed away from King Jehosh, how important he is to Queen Chorannah's plans, and what her plans may be."

"Have I not surprised you with my request, Captain?"

"Not really. Once Jehosh recalled me it was just a matter of time, was it not? To rule, Jehosh must control not only the generals and the army but especially those who work in the shadows to root out treason and plots against him. Such networks can be turned against him, either to harm him or to hide from him things people don't want him to know. That's what puzzles me about Ulyar. I recall when he, Auri, and you were young Black Wolves in the same cohort."

Vanas's smile twitched as if he had tasted something sour. "Yes, I'm disappointed in Ulyar. I thought he was our ally, but he was always one to suckle at the warmest teat."

"He wasn't from the palace, was he? He was recruited into the Wolves out of the army, in the usual way."

"I wasn't shown preference, I earned my way into the Wolves just like any other soldier," snapped Vanas.

Kellas nodded, because with the comment he had been scouting out the boundaries of Vanas's vanity. "So you did, Lord Vanas. I did not mean to suggest otherwise, because you can be sure that no man, or woman, could bribe their way into the Wolves. Not in my day."

"Auri also didn't grow up with Jehosh as I did," Vanas added, "but Jehosh came to trust him when he needed reliable officials after his father's death."

"Yet it seems clear that Auri defected to Chorannah's camp as well."

"I am fairly certain he must have. I can't otherwise explain why he moved his center of operations so far to the south five years ago."

"To keep a close eye on the Sirni Empire on behalf of Queen Chorannah and her sister."

Vanas leaned forward, one hand in a fist on his knee. "We must always expect trouble from the empire, Captain. Jehosh destroyed the Eldim kingdom twenty years ago when their kings tried to raid us. Even when this trouble with Queen Chorannah is sorted out, we still have two enemies who truly threaten us: the Sirniakan Empire, and the demons who continue to seek to destroy our peace and prosperity. That is why

Jehosh brought you back. Despite the suspicious way you left his service on the day his father was foully murdered."

Even after twenty-two years Kellas could not think of that day without his pulse racing so hard as to deluge his hearing.

It always starts with the memory of walking downhill on a rugged trail as the newly launched army marches north through the mountains, on its way to make a surprise attack on the Eldim kingdoms. The worst thing about the descent is the way his knees and hips ache from the constant jarring impact. That day he feels every step like a hammer in his bones as he strides alongside men half his age: The hells if he will let them take him for an old man! He is only fifty-two!

Because of the difficult terrain the soldiers move at a deliberate pace, forced into a column of four men abreast. Young Prince Jehosh walks at the center of a company of the Hundred's most experienced Wolves. Kellas has attached himself to the rear guard. It gives him time to consider the order he has been given by Lady Dannarah.

In his years as a Black Wolf, Kellas has killed fewer men and women than people generally believe. He lets people think the worst because it makes them cautious around him. Usually he found other ways to accomplish his missions including exile, a bargain too good to refuse, or such less violent but often equally calamitous expedients as holding a family member hostage for good behavior or ruining a clan financially. Bandits are another matter; to them he never gives mercy.

How might a man kill a prince?

Poison in his food? A sword in battle, blamed on the enemy? A wire to the throat late at night?

The men in front of him halt. Farther down the trail, soldiers are shouting.

He reins in his thoughts and glances up. A reeve circles, flagging "Alert." He pushes past the men in front of him. Jehosh's bodyguards part to let him through. The prince has his head tilted back, not looking at Kellas at all.

How easy it is to kill a man who trusts you.

"The hells!" cries Jehosh. "It's a cursed demon come to plague us!"

The scent of pine sap and crushed spruce needles settles over Kellas so sharply he knows he will never forget the smell that marks a sight he has long dreaded. Vast wings beating, a white horse flies into view over the trees. On its back rides a demon garbed in a cloak the color of bone. His thoughts dissolve into a cacophony of wordless buzzing. Heat flushing his face is succeeded instantly by a wash of cold. The shouts and murmurs of the soldiers die as they stare in astonishment.

Hesitation means death. He wrenches himself out of his paralysis and pushes out of the line of march so he stands, separate and away from the others. So she can see him.

In answer, the demon draws her sword. Then she and her horse dip down out of sight, alighting on a distant patch of open ground half glimpsed through the trees.

"All of you! You know the drill!" cries Prince Jehosh, his gaze as whitely wild as that of a spooked horse—and yet he is also bouncing on his toes in excitement. "No steel or arrow can kill the demon. You have to tear off its poisonous skin—"

"No, Your Highness," says Kellas. "It must be a trap. I have dealt with demons before. I will kill or drive it off." He turns to Chief Denni, who commands the cohort of Wolves surrounding the prince. "Stay where you are!"

Fear that something terrible has happened to the one he loves most fuels his scramble over the rocky ground and through tangled stands of juniper and scrub pine. At length the slope flattens into a clearing ringed with flowering late-cup bushes. At its center lies a grassy mire. On the mire waits the demon. A real horse would have sunk into the soft ground, but this creature does not. When the ground begins to squish beneath his boots, he halts lest he get stuck.

"What in the hells are you doing here, Marit, showing yourself like this?" He prides himself on his even temper and his absolute command of any kind of violent impact or sudden blindside, so it is a shock to find himself on the brink of rage.

"I had to find you."

A chill prickles his skin like icy water cast over him. "Is it Mai? Has something happened to her?"

"She is fine, as always. It's Atani. Tell me he's with you, Captain."

"No, he's not with us. You can see by our banners that he's not with us. He turned back two days ago and is riding back to the town of Neve Vayal on the lake. He couldn't have campaigned with the army anyway; you know that as well as I do. What's happened?"

"Arasit has uncovered a plot against his life."

"Arasit has uncovered a plot against Atani?"

"Yes. By pure chance in a tavern on the Istri Walk, Arasit stumbled across a young wagon driver hastening to meet up with a group of his fellows. He'd missed their rendezvous in Nessumara. Lord Seras is plotting to kill Atani."

"Lord Seras? General Sengel's son? Why would he want to kill Atani? He and Atani grew up together. Lord Seras is part of Atani's trusted escort…" The earth seems to sway under him, or maybe that is just his boots shifting in the soft mire.

"Exactly. From what Arasit saw of the young wagoner's mind, Lord Seras has hired wagon drivers pretending to be traveling with their families to bring supplies to upcountry villages, but really they are bringing armed men to ambush the king on the road to Neve Vayal."

"The road down from the mountains to Neve Vayal runs

through isolated country with only a few villages," he murmurs. "There are plenty of empty stretches perfect for an ambush."

"Arasit got word to me and I've been looking for you. Why aren't you with him? You promised to guard him! All our plans center on him!"

Kellas staggers as the ground tilts beneath him. A push from behind propels him to his knees. An arrow whistles past his ear. Marit grunts, jolted back as the arrow buries itself into the meat of her shoulder. A javelin catches in sunlight as it arcs overhead. Jehosh dashes past, sword in hand, and Kellas barely manages to grab the prince before they both flounder into the worst of the mire.

The horse's wings fan out. Soldiers duck as it gallops into the air and right over them, hooves almost clipping Jehosh's head. The horse's passage falls as a staccato series of blows. Wolves take aim but she sweeps them with a gaze that causes every man whose eyes she touches to flinch as from a slap. By the time they recover, the pale horse and Marit in her cloak of bone have vanished into the heavens.

"Captain!" Jehosh helps him to his feet as if he is an elderly uncle too drunk to stand. "The demon had you in thrall! It could have killed you."

Kellas wipes sweat from his brow as his mind races ahead with stark clarity. "King Atani is in danger. Call down an eagle to transport me. I have to find him now."

"My father? What are you talking about? What lies has the creature fed you? The demons must guess that the auspicious day for war against Eldim has come. They fear we will gain strength when we win a victory over the enemy and fill our treasury with Eldim trade and taxes." Then Jehosh's expression breaks apart as Kellas's words sink in. "Is my father truly in danger? Has the demon come to taunt us that we can do nothing to stop his murder? What must I do, Captain? Turn back, or go on?"

The irony of advising the man he has been ordered to kill flits across his thoughts like the sweep of a dark wing. But he has to push everything aside except action. Already one of the soldiers has flags out, signaling to the reeves overhead.

"You and the army are at least four days away from the king by now. It's too late for you to reach him."

"I could come with you, transported by eagle."

"Then you'll be vulnerable. That might be their plan, to make you act rashly and put you in danger, too. Any attack on King Atani is an attack on his sons as well. No, you must stay with the army. Everything is in place for the attack on Ithik Eldim, as you say. Furthermore there are forward troops depending on the timely arrival of this army. Don't forget King Atani has loyal Wolves with him, men he and I handpicked to serve as his personal guard. You know no man can lie to him."

"Men can lie if they are never forced to tell the truth," says the prince with a flash of anger. "How can you demand I continue the campaign when my father is in danger?"

"We never know what has become of those who are out of our sight, Your Highness. We only pretend we do. We are all hostage to chance. The king is my responsibility. I've sworn my life to protect his. I'll send word of what I find."

Jehosh cups a hand over his face while his shoulders heave and he struggles to contain his breathing. When he straightens he has not bothered to wipe the tears off his cheeks because tears are a man's pride, the sign of honest grief and affection. "I will hold you to it. *Go!*"

"Captain? Are you ill?"

Kellas's heart was still pounding, but he found a random thought drifting within reach of his tongue. "Just reflecting on how a man of thirty sees fifty as old, while a man of my age sees it as young. You realize Queen Chorannah must already be suspicious of the king's motives for bringing me in."

"Yes."

"I'll need more men."

Vanas patted the back of his sweating neck with a linen kerchief. "How many?"

"At least a hundred but I would prefer two hundred."

"Two hundred!"

"That's to start. With the trouble in the city I should be doubling the patrols and increasing the sentry presence for the lower palace." That he would eventually take his own people off these duties he did not mention. "Any upkeep for men you send to me will come out of my expenses."

"Where is the coin coming from to manage all this?" Vanas looked around the sparsely furnished chamber as if seeking Kellas's hidden riches.

"By arrangement with the king." No one but the king would ever know that the coin came directly from Plum Blossom Clan's ample coffers, coin stocked up over the years for exactly this chance. "Indeed, your comment makes me wonder if Ulyar's loyalty was coaxed away by something as crude as greed. A man who can be bribed merely with coin is best cut loose, don't you agree?"

Vanas had the grace to look ashamed as he hastily took his leave.

Oyard came in to report that Queen Dia had sent another token. "What do you suppose she wants so urgently, Captain?"

"I will go and find out." Kellas fought back a yawn. "The scourge of age is that I cannot rise before my usual hour and make it through an entire day as I once easily could. Waiting in comfort in the queen's antechambers for an audience will give me an opportunity to nap."

He took four young guards as an entourage. Their clothing

was mismatched, not yet a uniform: Yero was scouting Flag Quarter for a good source of matching cloth in bulk, always hard to come by.

The token admitted him to the queen's antechambers while the guards waited outside. He found a cushion, grateful that Dia's notorious paranoia made him feel safe enough to let his mind drift. Flashes of memory swam, always breaching when he relaxed: The way Mai pressed two fingers to his lips to caution him not to make a sound. When he had first become her secret lover, half the thrill had been knowing his life was forfeit if their trysts were discovered.

"Captain Kellas? You have such a smile on your face."

His eyes snapped open. For a dizzying moment he had no idea where he was, only that his back was up against a wall, the chamber was drenched in a golden haze of late-afternoon sunlight, and an old woman was looking down on him with an expression of amused puzzlement.

"You seem a little befuddled, Captain. Did I wake you from a pleasant dream? Did you come here with Jehosh?"

The hells! Banishing the cobwebs, he got to his feet. "Lady Dannarah! No, I am not with the king. I am here at the queen's summons."

"I just arrived."

"Were you also summoned?"

"No, I came on my own business. I have just been brusquely informed that the queen is entertaining the king and thus I must wait my turn."

"Entertaining the king?" he asked.

"I believe it a euphemism for afternoon sex, often the most gratifying, in my experience. I find it astounding that after all these years and all the lovers he has taken, his fascination for her has not dimmed."

"Do you?"

"I hope I am not embarrassing you, Captain. I meant no hidden reference to our own past."

Kellas had never encouraged the young Dannarah, and she had been wrong to use her rank to command him to sleep with her, but in the end he had used her naive infatuation to cover the tracks of his forbidden affair with Mai. Sleeping with Anjihosh's daughter had seemed a clever way of throwing the king off the scent. For that reason Kellas had put up no resistance to Dannarah's youthful offer. Even at the time it had made him feel a villain.

He inclined his head. "No, indeed, Lady Dannarah. One of the great pleasures of your company is that you never do feel obliged to hide your meaning. Had you meant to refer to our long association in all its varied stages, I am sure you would have said so quite bluntly."

She laughed so delightedly that all the guards looked at them.

Voices rose from farther in, Jehosh's distinctive laugh in reply to a teasing comment. Doors slid open and the king walked out with face and hands still moist from washing. He wore the smug look of a man who has just managed a satisfactory sexual performance. "Aunt Dannarah, greetings of the day. It's a surprise to see you here! Captain Kellas? Are you looking for me?"

"I have summoned the captain for my own purposes." Queen Dia paused at the threshold, and Jehosh turned back to kiss her right in front of everyone. It wasn't even possessive or flaunting. It seemed impulsive and genuine.

"I will return tonight with your permission, beloved. You can tell me the whole then. Captain, come to my audience hall in the lower palace tomorrow at the midday bell, if you will."

"I am at your command, Your Highness."

"Aunt Dannarah, has Tavahosh been causing you trouble?"

"He's not yet had time. The compound on Law Rock is insufficient for the number of eagles he has imprudently decided must now be housed there. I have some ideas I will present to him and his advisers."

"I am sure you will cut them down with your hard-won experience and your brutal tongue." He went out whistling.

"You may as well both come in," said Queen Dia. Her cheeks had a lot of color in them, by which Kellas presumed she had enjoyed herself as well. The king's daughter kidnapped by the handsome prince: What a tale! He wondered what the truth of it was.

Her spacious apartments were decorated in Eldim style: a plank floor instead of woven reed mats, and four couches on legs instead of cushions on the floor. Doors stood open to a neighboring room where several women were tidying up a mattress and taking away wash-water. Armed women guarded the other two doors. That women marked with slave inks and those without worked together like equals fascinated him; he had no idea what to make of Dia's household being populated by so many women who had once been captives of war.

"Please sit, Lady Dannarah," the queen was saying. "My kitchen is bringing a tray of delicacies that I hope may tempt you, for you look a little thin."

"Alas, reeves must always suffer in this way. We cannot overburden the eagles."

"Then I would think women best suited to be reeves, since on the whole they tend to be smaller and lighter than men."

"You will hear no argument from me, Dia. May I call you Dia? For I think of you like a niece and hope we may come to share a kinswomen's informality."

With some effort Kellas kept a straight face. Watching Dannarah assert her rank always amused him.

The queen raised a hand with an ambivalent wave, unable to refuse and apparently unwilling to acquiesce. She turned to Kellas. "You may remain standing, Captain. I am displeased with you although Jehosh assures me you are fit for the duty he has placed in your hands."

This ambush impressed him. He had to stand at parade rest and watch, mouth watering, while the women ate little cakes made from wheat instead of rice, stewed mango slices showered in fried coconut shavings, and small egg pancakes stuffed with a spicy vegetable mash.

"Do you think this business of reorganizing the reeve halls a good idea, Lady Dannarah?" Dia asked politely.

"It is a disastrous idea that cannot possibly work. I hope you are not wondering why I am here, Queen Dia." Ah. Dannarah was irritated. He recognized the bite in her amity.

Dia cut one of the tiny rectangular cakes into two. "Why are you here?"

"You sent another token to my reeve, Lifka."

"It was not a direct summons, just a reminder that she may come to see me at any time if she wishes."

"There lies the heart of the matter, Dia. You must go through me, not contact her without my knowledge. The girl properly brought your token to me. I am afraid she felt bullied by her initial encounter with you. You and your people lectured her on things she could not understand."

"Her ignorance surprises me. What manner of people have harmed her in this way?"

"Jehosh harmed her! She was brought to the Hundred as a captive after his third war in the north, after the burning of Gyre Port."

An expression of anger flashed across Dia's face before she controlled it by eating the cake.

What had set that off? The reference to captives? Or the three wars that had devastated the country of her birth?

Dannarah kept going like a sparring partner pressing the advantage. "In fact Lifka has been fortunate. Instead of being branded with a slave's mark, she was taken into a clan of carters who raised her as their own."

"Carters!" breathed Dia with a wince.

"The day Lifka was jessed I went by the clan's compound to explain her new situation to them. They had scarcely a string of vey to rub together, they're that poor, but they insisted on feeding me what I expect was the last of their rice. She's as fine a Hundred girl as I've ever met."

"She's not a Hundred girl."

"She is also a reeve under my command. Have I made myself clear?"

Dia folded her hands prettily in her lap. She wore no rings, an odd affectation. "Some matters are in the hands of the gods, Aunt Dannarah."

"It is my experience that the more people talk of the will of the gods, the more they mean their own wants and desires. My mother prayed to the Shining One all the years I knew her. Do you know what she asked for? Peace in the heart. Health for her children. Respect from those she dealt with, which I am sorry to say she rarely received and which I did not understand she deserved until too late. That is piety to me, not shrines built with taxes raked from the fields of struggling farmers and the shops of hardworking artisans, nor the service of a young person threatened with the will of the gods as if that means more than whatever it is she may want."

"Yet when an eagle is jessed, the reeve has no choice. Am I not right, Lady Dannarah?"

"Yes, yes, and when a pregnant woman goes into labor she has no choice but to go forward. There is necessity, and then there is the creation of what is afterward called necessity."

"If she is what we think she is, you will find she has less choice than you believe. The Tandi lineages will not leave this alone once they discover her."

"Why should they discover her if you do not tell them?"

"People have eyes, Lady Dannarah. Regardless, I will respect your wishes and not send another token to the girl." She rose. "We are finished here."

"I do not mean to quarrel with you, Dia. But never again try to go around me when it comes to the reeves under my command."

"I understand," said Dia curtly. "My people will show you out."

Dannarah walked to the door, then paused. "Let us not be enemies, Queen Dia. It is a difficult time for us both. I hope Prince Kasad is weathering the disgrace of his two loyal friends."

Dia's expression was stone. "I will be escorting him to my country estate where I can be sure he bides safely. Princess Kasarah will come to the palace to represent my interests in the meantime."

"If Prince Kasad is at risk then surely his twin sister may be in danger as well."

Dia glanced at her guards, so Kellas did, too, shifting his hands forward in case he had to grab his knives. Yes, there was a blowing tube mostly concealed in one woman's hand, the nub of a knife's hilt glimpsed up the sleeve of another, and an inner door open a crack behind which someone knelt, listening.

"According to the custom established by King Anjihosh, a woman cannot inherit the kingship, so Kasarah is no threat to Chorannah's sons. Anyway, Chorannah understands that Kasarah is not to be trifled with as she is Jehosh's only surviving daughter."

"Good fortune to her in this nest of vultures," said Dannarah, and she left with the brisk stride of a person close to losing her temper although, in truth, Dannarah had walked in that assertive way for her entire life.

"As for you, Captain, my business with you is swiftly said." The severity of Dia's clipped tone wrenched Kellas's attention back to her cold, pale face. "Never again under any circumstances ask a child of my household to spy for you and by doing so put their life at risk. Never."

Aui! It took him a moment to remember the child he'd sent after Tavahosh and Ulyar. He offered a slight bow. "It was an act of opportunity, Your Highness. May I ask if the child overheard anything?"

"No."

Through the slightly opened inner door a voice piped up. "Please, Aunt Dia. Please let me say. For I did a very good job spying. You even said so afterward. Wouldn't you hate if something bad happened and it could have been prevented?"

"What a rascal," muttered the queen with affection. One of the armed women smiled as fondly as if it were her own child, and maybe he was. "Come in and repeat what you heard."

The child slipped into the room. No longer enveloped in court clothes, he was revealed as a handsome boy with a slight build and a bit of a strut as he braced himself like a soldier reporting for duty. The words poured out as smoothly as if he had repeated them over and over to himself lest he forget. "Prince Tavahosh spoke of trouble at a river's bend. A crossroads of five roads must be swept clean and burned down so no trace remains because it has caused offense to the prince and there is a rebellion of people living there. He told Supreme Captain Ulyar to send men right away to kill anyone who resists and brand all the rest for the work gangs."

"Well done, ver," said Kellas with a solemn nod. The lad giggled and was promptly chased out of the chamber and the door shut behind him. Kellas measured the queen for whatever her reaction might betray. "Have you any idea what it means, Queen Dia?"

Her shrug told him nothing. "Is there a crossroads where five roads meet at a river's bend?"

He reviewed the elaborate map of the Hundred that he carried in his mind's eye, considering and dismissing possibilities. "Horn isn't close enough to a river. Nessumara is on a delta. The city of Olossi lies on a bend on a river but has the wrong number of roads…"

"What do you think it means, Captain Kellas?"

"I will let you know as soon as I am sure." He heard Dannarah's voice on the porch as she spoke to one of the guards. "Your Highness, as chief of security I must ask when your household is departing."

"Under the circumstances, and to protect my son, we are leaving tomorrow. I will leave a trusted group of retainers to guard my daughter when she arrives. In the meanwhile they will make sure no unwanted feet tread in these chambers."

"I comprehend you perfectly, Your Highness. I will work with them to make sure nothing is disturbed and that Princess Kasarah remains safe." He cocked his head, no longer hearing Dannarah. "If that is all, may I go?"

"I can see you are eager to depart. Do not fail Jehosh, Captain."

"It is not my intention to fail the king."

He hastened out to find Dannarah still on the porch, one boot on and the other in hand.

She caught Kellas with a look of mischief. "If we are going to keep meeting, Captain, we may wish to do so with more secrecy. Perhaps we can use the old watchword. Do you remember?"

He glanced away, disconcerted by her smile. "I do."

"That's not what I meant. Everyone guesses we are allied in supporting Jehosh. Yet they also wonder if we are enemies because of Atani's death. Let them wonder."

"Good advice. May I escort you to the Thousand Steps, Lady Dannarah?"

"You may escort me to the gatehouse where a coach awaits. I have an assignation arranged with an old acquaintance at the House of the Dagger, where I hope to spend the night in some comfort." Whatever expression marked his face he did not disguise well enough, for she laughed again. "I assure you I am not too old to have given up my pleasures, Captain."

"No, indeed, Lady Dannarah. Nor should you or anyone feel the need to do so."

She was not inclined to speak as they walked through the narrow-walled streets of the palace, and he wanted more privacy before he confided in her. Smoke curled from kitchens as they passed the apartments of courtiers and officials, its threads washed to shadows by the dusk. The four guards walked behind, half lost in the gloom.

A lighter set of steps underlay their own. Thank the gods he still had decent hearing! He used the age-old trick of raising a hand to halt their party and then listening to the pat of feet, which abruptly ceased. He glanced at Dannarah, but she hadn't heard.

By the lanterns of the gatehouse he examined the coach before she got in. The coachman was Ri Amarah, with a younger kinsman seated beside him holding a club across his knees.

"Take care," he said to the driver, "for I know one of your people was brutally killed some weeks ago."

"My thanks, Captain. You're the new head of security for the lower palace."

"I am. A piece of advice: Be cautious with your valuables in your households. Hide them, or move them elsewhere. Better to be overprotective than not vigilant enough."

"May you have blessings. Still, the old contract my people made with King Anjihosh holds. King Jehosh hasn't forgotten how we helped his grandfather. He has ordered extra patrols in

Bell and Wolf Quarter although I admit we are still pestered by angry slurs and thrown rocks. You see I've brought my son with me when he might be driving a separate coach."

"It's not my purview to command the city militia, but if you hear anything you think the militia aren't paying attention to, let me know."

Dannarah leaned out the still-open door. "Always on duty, aren't you, Captain?"

He touched a finger to his forehead as to acknowledge a hit, then leaned farther in, speaking softly so the coachmen could not overhear. "You may be interested in what I just heard, Lady Dannarah. On the day of the reeve convocation, Prince Tavahosh ordered Ulyar to send soldiers to burn homes and kill or indenture people involved in a rebellion at a crossroads where five roads meet, where a river bends. Have you any idea where that might be?"

"The hells! The Ili Cutoff, the Weldur Path, the Haya Track, and the Thread all pass through the town of River's Bend."

"That's four."

"The fifth is a secret trail through the center of the Wild, which reeves can see from the air and some of the local clans know about if they have business in the forest. But it runs close to no redheart groves, more's the pity."

"Redheart groves?"

"Just a random thought I had. My thanks for the information, Captain."

"Do the prince's words mean something to you?"

"They mean my night off is interrupted." She pressed a coin into the startled Silver's hand for his trouble, clambered down, and headed for Guardian Bridge and the Thousand Steps.

He returned to the gatehouse, where Oyard greeted him on the porch in a pretty glow of lamplight. "What was that about, Captain?"

"I'm not yet sure but I'd like to get more information about the Tandi consortium," he said as he took off his sandals and rinsed his feet. "Also, run an extra patrol through the lower palace and set a doubled sentry here. I may have heard someone following us."

"Yes, Captain. Yero left a tray of cold food in your office. I'll bring a lamp." He went off to fetch one.

Kellas thought of mangoes half drowned in fried coconut as, with a foot, he pushed aside the door to his darkened office. A waft of air blew at his ear. An object thunked into the door next to his head. He leaped back, whistling sharp and loud, and slammed the door shut as a second spike tore through the rice paper screen. Oyard appeared, burning lamp in hand, looking startled.

"Down." Kellas grabbed the lamp, shoved the door open, and tossed it in. Its trailing flare illuminated a person standing in the corner next to the altar. For one eye-blink the lamp distracted the killer. Kellas threw a dagger, drew his sword, and grabbed a reeve's baton from the rack of wooden practice weapons in the outer chamber as he shouted "Ya! Ya! Ya!" to break the enemy's concentration.

The lamp thudded onto the mats, oil spilling and fire hissing along its thread.

The dagger had missed but forced the man to dodge, giving Kellas time to advance, not really a sprint. Already people were converging on the office, yelling and rattling weapons. The man came up with Kellas's own dagger glinting in his gloved hand but by the time he flung it Kellas had gauged his angle of motion and the speed of his throw. He batted the knife aside with the baton. In silence the man leaped, thrusting with a slim short sword perfect for closed spaces.

Kellas meant to parry with his sword and knock the man unconscious with the baton but the twist of the man's blade caught a glint of fire right into Kellas's eyes. The body acted, no conscious thought, just survival. A step to the right, a jab with the baton to the chest to knock the enemy back, and his own blade thrust up under the ribs.

Oyard and multiple recruits slammed the doors aside, lamps and staffs and swords in hand, as the man slumped at Kellas's feet, grunted, and rolled onto the flames, putting them out.

"Find where he came in," snapped Kellas. "Does anyone recognize him?"

He had an ordinary face, any man one might see on the street. Several recruits vomited. They were the ones he had roll the body up in a length of cloth and lay it out in the courtyard. No one could find where the man had come in until Kellas himself walked a circuit and showed them two loose tiles in the kitchen roof. He had then to wake up Yero without disturbing her children.

"Heard you anything, Yero?"

"No, Captain." She was white-lipped, clutching one of her cooking knives.

"It may not be safe for you and your children to stay here, Yero."

She glanced at Oyard. "Captain, I have nowhere else to go, no kinsfolk, no village. Who is to say I would not be murdered if I took the children elsewhere in the city? We are still safer here."

"I am at fault," said Oyard.

"We have all been complacent. Chief, had I been killed, what would you have done?"

"Closed up everything tight, hunkered down, and waited until morning to alert the king."

"Let's do that. We'll send a messenger at dawn to the king's chambers, and see what rats crawl out from beneath the floor."

37

Lifka and Tarnit sat beside the open doors of the tack room, harness draped over their laps, the Runt dozing on his back with legs splayed. Lifka always felt most relaxed working in tandem with others. She found it easy to confide in Tarnit as they oiled and inspected the leather, hooks, and buckles. "Queen Dia can say what she wants about me, just like in the Tale of Fortune where the farmer passes off a rooster as a hen."

"You look like a hen to me," said Tarnit.

"It's just a scar, not ink." She displayed the inkings on her forearm, the flames that marked her as born into the lineage of the Fire Mother. Tarnit, of course, wore the inked waves of the Water Mother. "If there wasn't a fortune involved do you suppose anyone would care?"

"Don't you wonder?"

"To be honest, mostly I'm wondering if there *is* a fortune involved, because my family is poor. But Papa and Mum would never want coin gotten under false pretenses."

"Too proud, neh?"

"They would say it was wrong."

"Do you think you could be a Tandi child?"

"I only remember snatches, like dreams, from my life before. I just don't know."

Tarnit hung up the harness, lit a pair of lamps, and hung them to either side of the door so they could go through the signal flags for rips and worn spots. Outside the carpenters ceased hammering and sawing for the day. The extension to the loft hulked like a skeleton behind them.

"Heya!" Reyad trotted up to the tack room's little porch. "When is Marshal Dannarah coming back? There's a priest at the marshal's cote claiming he has urgent messages to be flown south right away. At least that's what the steward said he said. The priest only speaks Sirni."

"Did the steward tell the priest that eagles generally don't fly at night?" asked Tarnit.

"I don't know. I got out of there. How can you live in a place for years and not bother to learn how to talk to people?"

Reyad had a way of slouching against the wall that amused Lifka because it reminded her of her second lover, a friend of Denas's, who for months had hung around her family's compound with pretended casualness hoping she would notice. Now that Reyad felt his boundaries around the women were clear—that he wouldn't sleep with any of them, as if that was the foremost thing on women's minds!—he had relaxed enough to reveal himself as a person who hated being alone.

"What do you know about Tandi merchants?" she asked him.

"They sail to the Hundred from a land overseas. Twice a year we cart our surplus bitter-leaf and sweetwort—the best in Mar!—to Port Rossia on the Turian Sea. I've seen Tandi ships there."

"Did you ever see or talk to one of them?"

"The last time I went, right before I got jessed, a young Tandi woman invited me to come see her cabin aboard her clan's ship."

Tarnit winked at Lifka. "I've used that line myself."

"If I hadn't been courting Hetta at the time I would have taken her up on it just to see if it is true." He gave up his slouch against the wall to kick a cushion into place beside them and sit.

"If what is true?" asked Lifka.

Like any well-brought-up child he pulled a flag onto his lap, joining the work. "They say Tandi ships have the souls of birds

spelled into their hulls. That's why they are said to be so seawor-
thy that they never sink."

"No stranger than being jessed to an eagle," said Tarnit. "But
I thought you had to jess a living spirit to a living spirit. It seems
cruel to harness a living spirit to dead wood."

"Do you know anything else?" Lifka wrung the flag she was
holding.

"Each ship is a family, not just sailors. You always see children
onboard. The story goes that the Tandi do not have fathers, that
sea foam impregnates the women. But that's got to be just a
story. Every person knows who their father is."

"Lifka doesn't," said Tarnit.

Her head snapped around. "I know who my father is."

Tarnit paused in the act of rolling up a flag. "My apologies,
Lifka. Of course you know. I meant to say that where I grew
up there was a saying. *A man knows the woman he has gone into
but a woman knows the child who comes out of her.* The man my
sons believe is their father certainly seeded the older boy but
there's a chance with the younger that another man's seed might
have…" She frowned. "Never mind. It was a long time ago and
it doesn't matter."

"You have children? You never talk about them. Where are
they?"

"My spouse Errard and I grew up in neighboring villages in
the region of Sund. He went for the Black Wolves and as it happened I ended up jessed by an eagle. We have two boys. It was
easy enough for our sons, with two families to raise them even
though he and I were usually gone."

"Where is Errard now?"

The shadow in her face reminded Lifka of her uncle's grief.
"He died fourteen years ago. Huh. Now that I think about it, he
must have died in the same campaign where you were captured."

"Eiya! You must miss him." Yet Lifka did not like to think that a man Tarnit loved had been part of the war that had killed her original people, whoever they might be.

Perhaps Tarnit understood her discomfort because she rested a hand on her arm. "There are a lot of reasons Marshal Dannarah is a good marshal. She may seem harsh but she knows when to rein a reeve in and when to allow slack. I see my sons every month."

Reyad whistled. "At Argent Hall, under Auri, we were only allowed leave twice in a year, and then only if we hadn't displeased the chief marshal or broken some pissy regulation."

"Auri was not just an ass but a cursed useless marshal." Tarnit flexed her hands like remembering a punch she'd once thrown. "I hope Prince Tavahosh deigns to expand this humble tack room as well. And doesn't make us double-shift in these inadequate barracks because this place doesn't have enough bunks for all the reeves he expects to live here! Heya!"

The sound of footsteps outside brought them to their feet. Marshal Dannarah walked in looking blown and flushed. She wiped her brow with a cloth. "Here you are."

Tarnit said, "I thought you were going to the House of the Dagger for some well-deserved—"

"I forgot something." One measure of how long the marshal and Tarnit had known each other was that, if you looked for it, you could see them communicate without words. Tarnit's gaze flicked to Reyad and back to the marshal; the marshal lifted her chin slightly, then added a quick sidelong glance that took in Lifka.

Apparently oblivious to this interplay, Reyad said, "Marshal, there's a priest—"

"So I have been informed by at least ten anxious people eager to be rid of his bleating. Where does he want messages sent?"

"South to Olossi. To Shrine Hall."

"Shrine Hall? What in the hells is that?"

"Chief Marshal Auri set up a special reeve hall near the new shrine they're building near the Kandaran Pass and the mountains. I was assigned to patrol territory that never included the area so I never went there. Only certain reeves were assigned there. New reeves, mostly."

"Excellent!" The marshal walked along the hooks, inspecting the harness. "You'll take this courier mission, Reyad. Tell them you're a Shrine Hall reeve. They'll see your Argent Hall green tabard and won't know the difference. I want a full report of everything you see when you return."

"Oh." He glanced into the night, and then they all did, looking to see if anyone could be out there listening, but no one was. "You think—"

"I do, and the less said the better. You have your orders. Go on."

His shoulders snapped back and chin lifted. "Yes, Marshal!" He trotted off eagerly.

The marshal's intense gaze shifted to Lifka. The expectation that people would obey her was simply part of the marshal's presence, like sun and rain to the sky. The palace had never meant much to Lifka. It dwelled as far outside her life as the gold coins called cheyt, which she knew existed but had never so much as glimpsed. For Marshal Dannarah, daughter of King Anjihosh the Glorious Unifier, to accept her clan's humble meal of rice and stewed dandelions as if it were a perfectly respectable feast had impressed her deeply.

"You're harnessing exceptionally fast but you are still a fledgling, Lifka. Because of the way everything has been upended you're going to have to be trained on the fly, as we used to say."

"Yes, Marshal."

"Are you sure you're not tempted by Queen Dia's talk of fortunes?"

"It's like the Tale of the Barge where the man dreamed that water was gold but it kept pouring through his fingers. Of course I am curious about what they said. But I'd rather be under your command, Marshal. Anyway, I can't just desert my family."

"Five Roads Clan."

The marshal's tone stirred an instinct in her gut. "Is there trouble?"

Dannarah walked a circuit of the tack room, opened a shutter to look into the neighboring loft where four hooded eagles slumbered, and circled back around. "Tar, on your way back from your leave you went by the estate owned by Atani's queen, as ordered."

"Yes, I found the estate being run in an orderly manner, as I reported."

"But her steward told you that Queen Yevah was away from the estate and not expected back anytime soon."

"That's right. Do you want Lifka to hear this?"

"Lifka already knows of the situation at Plum Blossom Clan."

"I'm sure King Atani's widowed queen hadn't lived there in years, if that's what you mean," said Tarnit. "The steward had such a cursed closed mouth that I was suspicious of his motives. Let this lie, Marshal..."

"No, I don't think so. My mother, Queen Zayrah, had an estate on the Beacon Coast south of Nessumara. On her death my mother willed the estate to Atani. It's isolated. Maybe his widow lives there now. I want you to scout it out. Take Lifka with you. It'll be good training. There's one other thing before I go."

The Runt shifted an ear, hearing a change in tone, and rolled up to his feet, shaking himself. Lifka tensed, for it seemed to her an incoming storm felt like this: a whiff of changed air, and then the gale.

"Words were overheard in the palace two days ago. Prince

Tavahosh told Supreme Captain Ulyar to send men to take care of trouble in River's Bend. A place with five roads that needs to be swept clean so no trace remains, because of an offense it caused to the prince. Just thought I would mention it as a curiosity. I'm going now, back to my interrupted pleasures in the city. I won't return here until midday tomorrow."

"The hells!" Lifka cried, forgetting how softly the others were speaking. "If they sent a reeve, my family could be dead already!"

Tarnit grabbed Lifka by the elbow as the marshal strode off. "Keep your mouth shut."

"I can't abandon my clan!"

"Hush. Of course the marshal doesn't expect you to. Officially we are headed to the Beacon Coast on an errand for Marshal Dannarah but the route we take to get there can be any sort of roundabout way. Do you understand?"

"May the gods protect them." She who never cried burst into tears while the Runt pressed against her legs and growled at Tarnit.

Soon after dawn Supreme Captain Ulyar stamped up onto the porch of the closed gatehouse and demanded to see the man in charge. Kellas liked to think of himself as a man above petty emotion but the shocked look on Ulyar's face when Kellas himself met him at the door was so very gratifying.

"Ah, Supreme Captain Ulyar. How convenient that you stopped by just now. I'm wondering if you can identify this bit of rubbish that came into our possession last night most unexpectedly." He rolled the wrapped corpse out onto the porch.

"I don't know what you're talking about," said Ulyar with unconvincing bluster.

"Aui! So be it. It shall have to remain a mystery. I was just sitting down to my morning gruel and fish if you wish to join me."

"I'm only passing by on my way elsewhere." The sniveling coward took a step back, without even the courage to admit the attempt!

"What of this?" Kellas again indicated the corpse.

"It's not mine!" He as good as fled although he pretended to walk away in a huff.

Oyard moved up beside him to watch the man go. "Will he try again?"

"It's an awkward move at an odd time. I am grateful it was directed at me but we can't assume they won't target the rest of the household now."

"Do you think Ulyar acted alone? Fearful that the king will promote you over him?"

"It's possible, but Ulyar doesn't strike me as bold or independent. I think Queen Chorannah put him up to it. We have sorely underestimated her, Chief. Think about it. What if she is the one who conspired with Lord Seras to commit murder?"

"I did not know King Atani as you did, Captain. Did Queen Chorannah have a reason to want her husband's father dead?"

Kellas shook his head. "I can't imagine what it would be. He treated her as kindly as he did everyone, and more kindly than most who thought her meek and dull and of no account. And how he loved little Farihosh. The little boy looked like him, you know. He used to joke about it. I remember that particularly. Atani loved children. His first grandchild was a delight to him. Obviously he never lived to see Tavahosh, or Dia's children."

"If he loved Chorannah's eldest child then it is difficult to see how it would benefit the queen if he died. Unless the baby wasn't Jehosh's and she feared people would discover it. That could be a reason, Captain. If Lord Seras was the real father she would want to rid herself of both her father-in-law and her husband so she could act as regent for the baby."

"I hadn't even considered such a scenario." Kellas paced to the end of the porch, surveying the gate, then returned to where Oyard stood over the corpse. "How could Farihosh look like King Atani if he was Lord Seras's son instead of Jehosh's? Still, we can't rule out her involvement now we see how she has bribed Ulyar and almost certainly Auri to march under her banner. Maybe that was her plan all along: Kill everyone who stood between the kingship and her sons."

"Might Ulyar and Auri have been already in her pay at the time of Atani's death?"

"She was fifteen when she was sent here. She spoke only Sirni and knew nothing about the Hundred. How could she have made contact with two rank-and-file soldiers with no palace connections when she had nothing to do with the military and never saw any man except her husband, her eunuchs, and King Atani? Still, it's a sobering thought that I might have overlooked her culpability because all I saw was a meek girl."

Oyard nudged the body with the toe of his boot, frowning. "What now, Captain?"

"We sharpen our swords. As for this flesh, hire a carter to take it to the Beltak shrine."

In the office the burned mat had been replaced and the blood scrubbed away. With the doors open to the inner courtyard he ate his gruel and fish while he watched the recruits drilling with renewed purpose and grim expressions. Yero and Oyard's son took a stick and joined the drill at the very back. The boy was so cursed young, just sixteen like Treya, and so cursed eager. Once Kellas had been the young person loosed into the wind to fly or fall, not knowing whether he would survive each mission. Then, he had believed that he would be both archer and arrow, but age had brought him around to be the archer instead of the arrow. So often the young are nothing more than tools to be wielded by those who have power.

Such thoughts always brought him back to Fohiono, the child in whom he believed he had found a worthy heir, if heirship meant anything when you were a disgraced soldier. Was he going to turn into one of those cowards who allowed other people's children to die while protecting his own?

A skirling and harsh melody broke into his thoughts. Pipes sang out a tune so alien and strange that the drillmaster faltered and all the novices at their training looked up as if the sky had commenced singing an outlandish tune.

He whistled. "Everyone outside. Now!"

The speed at which they moved pleased him. Thus, when Queen Dia rode through the gate with her precious son on a fine horse beside her, Kellas's people had already formed up as an honor guard on either side of the roadway. He noted the discipline of Dia's troops and the bladed pole weapons her women carried. A good choice, since reach offered certain advantages over close combat for lighter opponents. Dia had archers, too, and pack mules instead of wagons: They were traveling cursed light, like they thought they would be pursued. The music whirled through the air, high, shrill, and frantic, nothing like the resonant songs of the Hundred. No one looking at Queen Dia and her entourage would see her as anything but an outlander, except for her frowning son who had his father's looks and wore the curious blend of clothing popular among men at court: long jackets cut for riding, Qin trousers, and silk sashes and sleeves.

Was Dia admitting defeat and retreating from the battleground? Or was this just the beginning of a new phase of what he now understood as a war between the queens?

Seeing Kellas, Dia offered a proud nod to acknowledge their earlier conversation, a reminder that he must watch over her daughter. He answered with a fist set against his chest, the salute of a dutiful soldier. Just then Yero hurried out on the porch and shook out the banner she had been making for the troops under Kellas's command. It unfurled in the morning breeze to ornament their ranks: a length of iron-gray silk painted with the stylized head of a black wolf.

38

Knowing that in one morning the eagles could cover ground that took carters days did not comfort Lifka when Tarnit insisted they depart in the opposite direction, pretending to head south for Horn Hall. Indeed an unknown reeve and eagle paced them half the morning before finally swinging away. Only then could they turn back and fly north toward River's Bend.

Normally the view dazzled her, slung as she was beneath the eagle with the world laid out below her feet, every tree and roof and goat visible. Yet all that endless afternoon as they backtracked across the fields of Istria and then followed the River Ili upstream, she could not draw a decent draught of air. She was out of breath and aching with fear by the time the curve of River's Bend, the scarred forest, and massive building site finally came into view. By now it was late afternoon, folk trudging home from fields and labor, the work camps packed with men standing in lines for their meager ration of food.

Her family lived two mey west of the city just off the road commonly called the Thread, because it threaded the province of Haldia from top to bottom. So when she spotted soldiers on the road at the one-mey stone, marching west, her breath seized in her throat and terror muddied the world.

The soldiers waved at the eagles. A flag waved, calling them down, and she was at first surprised when Tarnit flagged a response and began to circle as if she meant to land. The soldiers halted to wait for her, and Lifka was grateful for any pause that gave her more time.

She flew on, leaving Tarnit circling behind. The ground slid away beneath the gliding eagle so quickly that she overshot her clan's compound and in a frantic haste tugged Slip three different wrong ways before coming down with a thump in a neighbor's rice field. She fumbled with the hooks of her harness and was shaking with frustration before she unclipped and got her staff unbuckled. Trapped in his little harness at her chest, the Runt began to wriggle and whine, seeing home.

Goblin and Yap started barking from the gate. The Runt began yipping so loud it hurt her ears and she saw Mum and the lads and Uncle appear, all staring in surprise and none too eager to approach. Slip cocked his head, trying to figure out what she wanted.

"Leaf? What in the hells are you doing back?" Alon's shout carried across the gap.

By now everyone in the compound crowded at the gate: Mum, Papa, Uncle, Grandfather leaning on his cane, the three young men, her two female cousins and the husband they were both sleeping with, her cousin Nanni's pregnant wife Saloa, six children, and to her shock her cousin Ailia who was supposed to be working as a caravan guard. By the evidence of her thickening middle, Ailia was pregnant. When had that happened? A young man stepped up beside Ailia escorting old Eda, a crippled woman Papa had taken in rather than see her beg on the streets of River's Bend.

At last the Runt stopped barking for long enough that she

remembered the correct reeve signal. She pulled her reeve's whistle from around her neck and blew the pattern that meant her eagle should fly and wait. He thrust upward, the downdraft from his wings rustling the rice stubble. The moment she unhooked the Runt and set him down he dashed for the gate. Goblin and Yap raced to greet her with a frenzy of whimpering and waggling, but she barely patted their heads.

Probably it was the look on her face that quieted them as she ran up. "Soldiers are coming from River's Bend to arrest or kill everyone and burn down our compound, courtesy of Prince Tavahosh who was at the assizes, just because his pride was bruised. Grab only what you must. We've got to flee."

Denas climbed up the wall and, shading his eyes, stared westward.

"I mean it. Move!"

"I see dust," called Denas. "And another eagle up high."

Tarnit had never landed, just pretended to. If the soldiers never got close enough to see her face then they could never definitively identify her.

Papa said, "Aui! So be it. Ailia, gather everyone who can't fight. You'll drive the wagon."

"No, you drive it, Geron," said Mum. "The mules listen to you best. They'll balk for anyone else. Children, attention!" She gave the older children specific directions: collect rice, kitchen and wood-chopping gear, and cloth. Then she turned to the young man standing with Ailia. "You'll go with the wagon, Jonon. Don't argue with me. You'll just get in the way."

"I see them!" shouted Denas from the wall as the other young adults grabbed all the clan's staffs and knives, their legacy from Mum's people. "Eighteen . . . no, twenty."

Mum shouted, "Do you see crossbows?"

"Can't tell yet. Hope not. Shrine guards don't usually carry them."

Lifka ran to the stalls to help harness the mules, just returned from a day's work and at their feed and none too happy at being rousted out again. Courageous tried to kick but Papa knew all the mule's tricks and together he and Lifka got the pair hitched up. The children shoved rice and belongings into the bed of the wagon.

Mum trotted up carrying her staff. "They're too close. If we try to run, they'll catch us strung out in the fields."

"If you don't run, you'll end up dead or in the work gangs," cried Lifka.

"We all know what we can expect, Lifka. So we fight." Mum gave a look to each person in turn, and each one nodded, even the littlest sensing the gravity of the situation. "Here's what we do. We let them enter the compound. We make them squeeze in through the gate. I'll go outside to weed the garden so they think they've taken us unawares."

Uncle stepped forward. "No, let me do that part. If they kill me it doesn't matter."

"That isn't true!" His daughter Nonit grabbed at Uncle's hand.

"Hush, that's not what I mean. I'm not the best fighter and my leg is half crippled anyway. This gives the rest of you a chance." He stared down Mum until she let out a harsh exhalation and nodded.

"Very well. You're the lure. Geron, be ready to go when the gate is clear. Big kids, under the cart. When the wagon rolls, you run alongside." The two elders and the littlest children lay down in the bed of the cart amid the sacks. Saloa stuck by the tenuous safety offered by the wagon; she was too gentle a soul to hurt anyone. Ailia grabbed a staff and took up a position beside Papa, the final line of defense to protect the wagon and mules. Lifka felt a moment of pity for Ailia's bewildered young man who had not been raised by a mother who had grown up in a clan of guards-for-hire. The dogs stood on either side of Papa, the Runt bristling from behind him.

Uncle took a long, curved brush knife. After giving each of his children and grandchildren a kiss he went out the gate to the garden by the road.

Mum handed Papa his ax, her expression so cold that Lifka shivered to see it. No kisses from her! She tapped Lifka on the shoulder. "You have reach so I want you behind me."

The other adults were rolling barrels into a line alongside the gate. Nanni dragged the table out to make an obstacle at the gate that would force the soldiers into two narrow files. By now they could all hear the tramp of feet. Lifka whispered a prayer to Kotaru the Thunderer that these soldiers hadn't seen her land outside the compound. Denas whistled. From inside the house her cousin Nonit braced herself in the open window with the family's only crossbow, once Aunt Ediko's.

"Heya! Is this Five Roads Clan?" called a brusque voice from the road.

Uncle took his time answering. "Sheh! Doesn't it say so right above the gate? Didn't you lads learn to read and write at Sapanasu's temple? Aui! A sad day when a man can carry a weapon and not even a little bit of knowledge in his head."

Death struck with an ordinary grunt: a blade's impact into flesh, a man's surprised gasp at the blow. Cloth rended. A spray of liquid spattering the earth. A thud as a body's weight hit dirt.

Inside the compound no one moved or spoke as they accepted the desperate struggle that must follow on this emphatic statement. Lifka knew she had been right to come: No mercy today.

Two soldiers trotted in through the open gate, clearly expecting no resistance.

A quarrel took one in the throat, and Mum used the turn of her hips to power her staff into the neck of the second. They both dropped like stone.

"Two," she said, dropping down behind a barrel as the next group of soldiers shouted from the gate and pushed forward. Again the two in the lead had to split apart because of the table and again Nonit shot. This time the bolt slammed into the man's shoulder. Lifka thrust the tip of her staff into his midsection, doubling him over, as Alon tripped the soldier beside him with a sweep of his staff and with a quick loop cracked the shaft down over the man's head.

Swords came out in a hiss. Shouts poured off the path as a shadow swept down from the heavens over the men crowded outside the gates. A man screamed, thrashing as Slip lifted from a strike carrying the man like prey, talons digging into human flesh.

Mum said, "Five."

But now a press of soldiers kicked down the upended table and pushed into the compound, yelling with the fury of men whose blood has been roused. Using the barrels to dodge around, giving her reach against their swords, Lifka used her staff as a pole, jabbing bellies and chests to send men stumbling so the others could hit them while they were unable to parry.

Nanni staggered back as a sword slashed across his leg. Lifka poked the swordsman in the eye. There was cousin Darit, hidden behind their little granary, leaping out to clobber a man on the head with her staff and jumping back out of sight.

Grunting, twisting side to side, Lifka parried blows, hit a blow across the man's knees, then torqued back to crush his throat.

Soldiers broke past the barrels to run for the shed where the wagon waited. Papa wasn't much of a fighter and Lifka was stuck with Alon and Nanni still defending the gate, but there went Mum, raining down blows as she worked the staff down their ranks, each time spinning away before their swords could touch her.

Swords had cutting edges but staffs had reach. Stay out of reach, and you stay alive.

Lifka lost count of who had gone down and how many remained. Three barged through the gate and right at her. A shadow shivered over them. Slip plummeted, thudding at a dive into two of the men so hard that everyone heard their bones break and their horrific shrieks. The tip of the third man's sword raked past her nose as she threw herself back. The metal stank of death, and blood flicked from its edge to spatter her lips. Uncle's blood.

Denas cut in front of her and pounded the man into the dirt with a series of hammering blows from the sledgehammer that shattered the man's skull and spewed gray tissue and blood everywhere.

She spun, staff extended and ready, sucking in air as she struggled to catch her breath. No one attacked. A footstep scraped along the ground and she whirled to confront, but it was Nanni dragging his injured leg. A man moaned, and a child cried fearfully. A voice panted in pain. Ailia darted out from the wagon and slashed the throat of a man trying to rise from the ground.

Silence fell horribly over the compound, its dusty courtyard and wood house with three rooms and a roofed shelter that served as a kitchen. The granary and the shed made up the rest of it, with the latrine outside the walls. Not much of a place, but it had been theirs, the only home Lifka remembered.

Slip chirped in that oddly soft voice he had. Alon stood frozen, close enough that the raptor could tear his head off. She stepped between her brother and the eagle.

"Alon..." Because she was still out of breath it was hard to talk, and he, too, was breathing shallow and fast. "Move back one slow step at a time. Nanni, how bad is it?"

Nanni had taken a deep wound in the thigh, and it was he

who was panting with the pain of it. Papa had an arm around Mum; he peeled back her torn vest to reveal a bloody cut scored along her ribs.

"It's shallow, thank the gods," he rasped.

"Eh, giving birth hurt the hells worse than this scratch," said Mum, but she winced when she moved. Blood oozed in trails down her torso.

Denas helped Nanni limp to the wagon, where his wife cut up lengths of a faded cotton taloos to bind wounds. Alon ventured out the gate and she followed to see four soldiers running back toward River's Bend.

"No use trying to catch them on foot," she said.

Alon grabbed her arm. "Let them go. You can't take them alone on the eagle. Let's wrap up Uncle."

Tarnit circled overhead, signaling a temporary "All Clear." Lifka and Alon cut apart tabards to make a shroud for Uncle and slung his wrapped corpse into the back of the wagon. Alon kept watch from the wall while Lifka counted off: Mum and Nanni injured; Denas had sprained an ankle and his right hand had gotten smashed. Saloa began cramping, never a good sign in a woman midway through pregnancy. Everyone was speechless. Nonit and Darit were frantically gathering pots and utensils from the kitchen, weeping for their father but moving fast.

In his raspy old voice Grandfather said to Papa, "We picked a good wife for you, Geron. Always good to have a woman in the house who can beat the brains out of thieves and bandits and train the children to do the same."

"Where can we go, Leaf?" Ailia's voice jolted Lifka. Beside her, the young man stood stunned, gray with fear. "Jonon and I left Iliyat because the archon there announced a new law that every clan owes a labor tax they must pay in coin or serve in labor. We didn't have the coin and we wouldn't give the labor."

Lifka turned to her parents. "The family got coin for my

reeve's service. Is there enough to travel to another region and set up a new compound?"

Mum said in a strained voice, "Two days after a reeve brought the coin, the archon here demanded coin as a fine for not having a license to cut wood. Then more coin as fees for your Papa having been brought before the assizes, not that it ever used to cost anything before. And he fined the family for not giving you the slave mark, but I don't want you for a moment to blame yourself for that, Lifka."

"You're saying all the coin from my reeve's portion is gone." The stink of blood was beginning to nauseate her, and she wanted to get Slip out of the way before he decided to tear into one of the corpses although she had been assured that eagles did not eat people. "It doesn't matter. We have to go. For now we can hide in the Weldur, at least until we figure out what to do."

Papa shook his head. "We may seek refuge in the Wild as it says in the tale—*under these trees let the innocent shelter*—but refugees have to move on after one passage of the moon or the wildings take a tithe. We'll run out of rice sooner than that anyway."

"We can eat for a week with what we've got in the wagon." Mum had her back to the rest of them, arms raised, while Nonit bound her ribs with cloth cut from a soldier's tabard. "Take all their weapons, their belts, what cloth you can easily cut away. We can sell that. Search them for coin and anything else useful."

"If we set up a drop point I can bring in supplies." Queen Dia's talk of fortunes danced in Lifka's mind as a lure but she dismissed it. She couldn't go back to the palace now. The Runt cowered by Slip's huge talons as if he trusted the raptor more than the frantic activity as everyone made ready to abandon their home. She and Alon shoved the barrels aside so the wagon could get out while her cousins and the older children looted the corpses and dragged them off to one side. She actually felt she had been ripped into two people: the calm reeve sorting out an escape, and a girl recoiling from the mayhem, mind racing as images from the skirmish piled through her head over and over again. They had torn lives from living people and chased their spirits through the spirit gate that led to the other side.

Finally they sprinkled oil on wood shavings in the shed and house and set them alight. The family set out across the rice track through neighboring fields, flames rising behind them. As it got dark they had to bring out their one lantern and its precious oil. Tarnit landed in a field so she could guard the eagles overnight while Lifka escorted her family to the north ferry. No one could sleep. Papa did not say a word, Alon talked nonstop in a low voice, and Lifka kept wiping her mouth thinking Uncle's blood was still on her lips.

They crossed the river at dawn, paying the charge with coin they had taken from the dead soldiers.

She kissed Mum and Papa last of all. "I'll come as soon as I can."

When she walked away the Runt ran after her, whining, and after all they did not need another mouth to feed so she scooped him up and he licked her face ecstatically.

Aloft, she and Tarnit circled until the ragged line of people and their mules and wagon and dogs vanished under the canopy of the great forest, heading for a towering redheart grove where they could hope to find water. A small clearing beyond the redheart grove would be their drop point.

In the distance smoke marked burning. She and Tarnit flew back the way they had come to find soldiers following the track through the fields along which the family had fled. The compound was still smoldering.

Tarnit flew north to the Ili Hills and brought them down in a tiny eyrie perched on the rocky crown of a thickly forested knoll.

After they hooded the eagles and the Runt went sniffing off to explore, Lifka scrambled up a slope of loose rock to the top. Wind buffeted her, and she wished she could turn into wind if only the transformation would obliterate the heart-crushing dread and confusion eating up her insides. Tarnit climbed up behind her, puffing.

"What if they run out of food? What if they can't find water? What if they're caught—"

"The sun sets and rises every day, Lifka. Every day we are alive is a day we can act. You and I were given two errands to run. One is accomplished."

"But they're not safe!"

"No, but for the moment they are alive." Tarnit wrapped strong fingers around her wrist. "Come down to the shelter with me; it's cold up here. We need to eat and rest before we go on tomorrow."

She led Lifka down and around to the less windy side of the hill where a crude rock wall turned an overhang into a shelter, with a hearth. The Runt was probing a stack of firewood for rodents, tail wagging madly, paying no attention to their return.

"We have a second task. As we fly I need you to pay particular attention to our route and the landmarks. Knowing the land as intimately as a lover's body is what gives reeves an expertise no one else has."

Lifka rubbed her eyes, by now so gritty with exhaustion and fear that they might as well have been coated with sand. "Last month I was happy. Now I'm a killer and my clan is outlaw. Why did I have to be chosen as a reeve? What if I walk away from the reeve halls?"

"Being jessed changes you in a way you can never leave behind. You'll always be a reeve, Leaf. Until the day you die. Nothing can alter that. Nothing."

"I can't believe it happened."

Tarnit sat right next to her, almost touching, her presence like balm. "Do you want to tell me about it?"

She did! She told her about the entire skirmish in detail as Tarnit listened, doing nothing but nodding and occasionally saying, "Ah!" or "Oh!" or "Eiya!"

That night Lifka slept in snatches, jolting awake and then, exhausted, falling asleep again.

In the morning they flew south, skimming the shore of the Weldur Forest before they reached the River Istri. The great river, lifeblood of the richest farmlands in the Hundred, flowed southeast into Istria Bay. On the way Tarnit pointed out eyries where a reeve could shelter for a night.

The delta of the River Istri sprawled in a network of water and islands and tremendous numbers of birds flocking. Fishermen poled back channels of muddy water. They did not land at Copper Hall, the reeve hall set within the island city of Nessumara. The city itself was a skein of bridges, boardwalks, canals, and houses perched on stilts, dazzling in its complexity, like a puzzle that needed solving. Even preoccupied as she was, Lifka was thrilled when Tarnit had them circle the city in a lazy glide so Lifka could pick out a few of the most prominent landmarks.

Turning south along the shore of Istria Bay, Tarnit brought them to the westernmost peak of the Ossuran Hills. An old hearth and stone shelter marked an eyrie. At the top of the hill stood a tower with firewood laid beneath a tile roof.

"It's a coastal beacon, to be lit in times of trouble," Tarnit explained after they'd released the eagles and gone up to explore the old tower with its cracked tiles and dusty corners.

Lifka poked at the wood with the tip of her baton and found spots decayed to rot beneath ancient spiderwebs. "This thing hasn't been touched in years. That cut on my cousin Nanni's thigh was deep. I hope it isn't festering."

"Turn around."

The cloudless day and the sinking sun washed the waters of the bay to a deep glossy shine.

"Oh," said Lifka.

"It's always beautiful if you stop to look, and it will be beautiful long after we are gone from here," said Tarnit. "Sometimes people ask me how I can stay so cheerful. But how can you not feel joy when you see so much beauty?"

"Last night I dreamed the forest turned to knives and hacked my family to death."

Tarnit took her hand, and Lifka found the gesture surprisingly comforting. "Does your clan follow the old traditions? Did you apprentice for a year with one of the seven gods?"

"Yes. Kotaru the Thunderer."

"I was an ordinand of Kotaru for a year, too. That makes us both daughters of the god, and thus sisters in His worship. We'll leave an offering to Kotaru to pray for their safety." She released Lifka's hand and pointed with her elbow toward a distant headland beneath which Lifka could just see a tiny cove tucked into the rocky shoreline. "That's where we're going tomorrow. Marshal Dannarah's mother, Queen Zayrah, kept an estate there. Can you see the fields? There should be a vineyard, too. And an extensive herb plantation. I don't know what we'll find there, but I do know that if I deem it safe I'm going to leave you there for a few days while I return to the palace to report. You haven't been sleeping, and you need to rest."

"Every time I close my eyes I can't stop thinking about them."

"About your family? Or the people you killed? As a reeve you need to find a way to make peace with the violence and the fear and the ugliness. It will never go away, not truly. Reeves who try to bury it find it keeps crawling back up their throats. It's part of who you are now."

"Partly it's knowing I have killed someone—that's horrible

enough, but really we had no choice. It's more that I can't stop thinking about everything my clan needs to survive. They only have enough rice for a week, and there are sixteen of them, and the dogs and the mules, and two goats, and the chickens—"

"I know where the drop point is. I'm going to fly back to the palace and let the marshal know. You have to stay away because you're so recognizable."

"If only I hadn't argued with Prince Tavahosh at the assizes. If I'd just let him put the slave mark on me and put me in the work gang this wouldn't have happened."

"No, the prince is the one who did the wrong thing. You mustn't be angry at yourself, Lifka. You did what was right."

"Wouldn't it be wiser for me and safer for you and Marshal Dannarah if I abandon the reeve halls? If I release Slip I could walk into the Weldur and no one would see me."

"You don't understand what it means for a reeve to desert the reeve halls. It does happen sometimes. A reeve will go rogue and vanish with their eagle. The thing is, you can never leave your eagle behind, and although you have learned the basics incredibly fast, you're still very inexperienced. Your eagle may well sicken and die, and then you'll die."

The words struck Lifka to silence.

Tarnit went on, her steady gaze the one thing Lifka could focus on. "Abandoning the discipline of the halls, not to mention your duty as a reeve, is not going to help your family."

"But I can't be a reeve if it means taking orders from Prince Tavahosh. Aui! I'm being selfish! What about you, Tarnit? I didn't mean for you to get caught up in this."

"Don't worry about me. They can't prove I was involved even if they suspect me. Marshal Dannarah has her own feud with Prince Tavahosh, so you can be sure she will protect her people. But you have to do your part and right now that means you must lay low and trust me. Heya!"

She shaded her eyes, to follow the glide of one of the eagles. Already Lifka could tell it was River, not Slip. Just then the bird pulled in her wings and stooped, plummeting so fast Lifka gasped out loud. A hill cut off their view.

"Why do eagles choose the people they do?" Lifka asked past a lump in her throat.

"No one knows."

The Runt thrashed out of a stand of high grass with a rat in his jaws.

Tarnit grinned. "That is our signal to make supper."

He paused, growling at her.

"No, you malevolent little dog," Tarnit retorted, chuckling. "We don't want your rat!"

In the morning they glided down to the cove, the end point of a small valley worn into the hills by a stream. The stream had been partially dammed to make a string of ponds whose water was channeled into irrigation canals that wove a network down through the gardens and fields of two separate villages, one high in the valley and the other down by the beach where boats were pulled up on the strand. They landed near a large one-story house built off by itself. Its wide terrace offered a splendid view over the glistening waters of the cove. Shuttered windows gave the house the look of a person with closed eyes, and the reception room was littered with dirty straw and goat manure.

At length a man walked up from the beach-side village, several youths trailing along behind with wide-eyed curiosity.

"How may I help you reeves?" he said. Lifka had a little trouble understanding his accent. "We would be honored to share a meal with you as the law instructs: *Let the people feed the reeves who guard the land.*"

"My thanks, ver," said Tarnit. "We will accept your hospitality gladly."

They released the eagles and walked with him back to the village. He soon made a friend of the Runt, although the dog snarled when the children tried to come too close.

Two reeves were a season's wonder, quite the most interesting event to happen for months, and they were happy to take in Lifka for as long as she needed to get over what Tarnit kept referring to as "her recent illness."

Lifka's looks did not astonish them; they sheltered the occasional sailor and traded with a few foreign merchants. A feast of rice and fish filled Lifka until she burped, and they insisted she taste each one of the four varieties of rice wine they brewed and the three varieties of liquor they distilled. The more she drank the better she liked them. They were an old-fashioned people isolated by sea and hills, and hadn't even heard of the new law about work gangs.

"Did the old queen not live here for a time?" Tarnit asked.

The man had assigned himself as their spokesman. "The gracious Queen Zayrah. Our elders recall her. The young prince— him who became King Atani—and his sisters used to come. There were merlings in the cove then. They would sing for him at night."

With a lift of her eyebrows at this unexpected detail, Tarnit glanced at Lifka. "Who inherited the estate after the queen died?"

"The prince, who then became King Atani. He visited here a few times, with his household."

"And when he died? Who now owns the estate?"

"Why, we do, verea. The labor and tithe we owed Queen Zayrah was gifted at King Atani's death to all the families who live here. Now we owe what is due to the seven gods and the assizes and you reeves. Also we maintain the nearby beacon, the one you can see there on the headland. We keep our portion of the Beacon Path that runs along this shore under repair. That is our tithe, just as it was in the old days, before there were kings."

"And King Atani's household? You never saw them again?"

"No, verea. We never saw them again."

39

As the days passed and the work gang crossed the Istri Plain and climbed to the Aua Gap, the frightened prisoners began to complain, in whispers, as they camped each night.

Tyras sat with forearms and head resting on his bent knees. "The hells, Gil. I'm so hungry I could puke."

"Do you know what I've noticed?" They sat close enough to touch. Some of the other men had taken to calling them lovers, which suited Gil because it meant they could whisper together. "Every morning there are more prisoners. It's like they sneak in under cover of night. They get fed from the other wagon, and they get rice, meat, and greens. Also, the new prisoners aren't marked. They just have ink brushed on their faces. You can see it wear off in patches and in the morning someone's drawn it on again."

Ty rolled his head to one side on his arms to glare at Gil. "Are you really taking this spying business seriously?"

"Of course I am!"

"It's a stupid idea."

"It's a cursed sight better than being stuck in the palace flattering courtiers just for the hope of a nod and a wink."

"You're such an ass, Gil. This isn't better."

"You hated the endless processions and audiences and kissing asses just as much as I did, Ty. Don't start claiming now that you miss it."

"What about your wife? I thought you liked her. I have to say that was hells bold of her, having sex with you in the prison. And she gave you useful things that don't look valuable. I can't believe my mother gave me enough coin to buy an estate, which anyone with one thought to rub together would know the guards would steal, like they did. It's because of the herbs Sarai-ya gave you that our faces aren't inflamed like half the other prisoners. And we have a cloth to sleep on at night."

Gil stroked the old leather sack, which was too worn to be worth stealing but strong enough to survive. She had chosen wisely. How like her to do so!

When he shut his eyes he thought of her silky skin and the sweet way her nipples tasted, then sighed. That was definitely not a road to walk down, not now. "I do miss her. But I don't know, Ty. If we had stayed on for years in the lower palace, wouldn't we have gotten bored with each other? Then started fighting? It's not that I wanted to be arrested and marched out in a work gang—"

"I sure as the hells did not want it!" Ty spat on the ground as if the taste of bad fortune stank in his mouth.

"—but you have to admit there's something thrilling about being a spy, just like in the tales! And maybe we're helping Kas."

"What does Kas have to do with this?"

"You can't need me to string this together. It makes sense that they wanted me gone to get at Sarai-ya's coin. You being arrested doesn't make sense unless they want to isolate Kas and make every man fear being seen as his friend. Who will go out drinking with him now?"

Tyras said nothing.

"You're not regretting it, are you?" Gil demanded. "Befriending Kas, I mean?"

"I still don't see how us being thrown into this cursed work gang *helps* him."

"If they think he's isolated enough, they might leave him alone. Queen Dia might send him back to her country estate and get him out of the cursed palace."

"Hush." Ty curled a hand around Gil's ankle. "That man's been watching us for days."

The young man Ty indicated had broad shoulders, rippling muscles, a scar along his ribs as from a knife wound, a badly healed broken nose, and the Water Mother's inks down his right arm and left leg. When he caught Gil looking, he narrowed his eyes as if he was deciding whether to engage in a staring contest, which Gil would certainly lose the moment the other man decided to punch him in the face. Gil offered his brightest smile, and the fellow paced away.

"I'd wager he was arrested for murder," muttered Tyras. "Probably slit the throat of a man he was robbing. You smiling at him is an invitation for a thug like that to come wandering back to bully us."

"I don't think so."

"You never do think, Gil." Tyras scratched a bug off his ear, leaving a welt.

"I noticed him at the prison with a few other criminal-looking men. One was killed the first night—"

"For trying to escape. I can't forget that."

"The second tried to get me to worship Beltak, and the third is now marching with the new prisoners, if you hadn't noticed."

"What?"

Gil glanced around. Men sat alone or huddled in nervous groups. One pack of three sulky-looking young men were muttering intimately together like old acquaintances, just as he and Ty were, and nodding toward the cook wagons. He wasn't the only one to have noticed that the new arrivals got fed more and received rice instead of millet. "You can count, Ty. There are now about equal numbers of those of us who marched out of the prison in Toskala and those who joined on the road."

"They're work gangs from other places."

"No. There's something else going on." His gaze crossed paths with that of one of the men sitting in the group of three. When the man gave him a hard stare, Gil stared hard back, not liking to give anyone here the idea he was frightened of them. There was something vaguely familiar about the other man's face—his high forehead, his cleft chin, the noticeable gap between his two front teeth—but he couldn't place where he'd seen him before.

The chief clapped his hands to get everyone's attention. "Any man who agrees to drill will get an extra ration. Line up in ranks."

"These asswits want us to drill after walking all day?" Gil exclaimed.

His words rose into the air just as everyone else quieted.

The chief looked around. "Who said that?"

Enough men glanced their way that there was no hiding. So Gil stood. "I did. It just seems like the walking is enough exercise given how little feed we get. Oxen aren't expected to drill at the end of a day's haul. You might at least offer us rice."

The chief strolled over. Prisoners drew back, isolating them.

"Fuck," Gil murmured. Instinct told him the chief was looking for an excuse to make another example. "Ty, back away with the others. Stay out of this."

"Don't ask me to be a coward." Tyras didn't shift.

Gil took a step forward, bracing himself. He just hoped it would be fast.

The chief stepped past him and grabbed Ty by the arm.

"Heya!" Gil lunged for them but guards blocked his way. One slapped a baton so hard across Gil's chest that the blow stopped him in his tracks. Searing pain spread outward from the impact.

The chief shoved Tyras toward a group of guards but his gaze stuck to Gil. "Don't fuck with us, you piece of shit. Don't think you're too good to get what is coming to you. I see you two and your good sandals even though every one of you cursed prisoners is meant to walk into the gang with nothing but the kilt you're issued. I see your soft hands. So you think you can mouth off whenever you please just because you're boys born into rich clans."

He surveyed the silent prisoners, most of whom were now staring at the ground hoping to avoid notice. "When I say you can get an extra ration if you drill, I mean a ration of rice gruel. If you don't drill, here's the extra ration you'll get."

When the guards threw Tyras facedown to the ground and yanked up his kilt in the most demeaning manner imaginable, Gil was for several stark breaths taken so unawares that he couldn't move or think. The guards blocking his way grabbed his arms just as he realized what was going to happen. He tried to break free but they held too tight.

"Fuck me, you fuckers!" Gil screamed as the chief rubbed his own cock until it stood erect and then got down on his knees between Ty's forcibly spread legs. "I'm the one who said it! Punish me! Fucking cowards! You pissing cowards!"

The hells Ty struggled, kicking as the guards held him down, cursing them and then grunting in coughing shrieks as he tried to choke down the pain of the man ripping into him. Gil elbowed, kicked, threw his weight against the men holding him, tried to bite the cursed hands of the cursed guards but he could not get free. But he could not stop fighting to try to reach

Ty because it was a betrayal to stand and watch. Around him a few men laughed nervously but mostly it was deadly silent.

After an agony of time the chief gasped and held still with the grimace of orgasm. *Oh gods*, Tyras tried not to whimper as the man pulled out of him and stood.

"So, who's next?" said the chief, Ty still pinned on the ground and the chief looking around at the guards.

Gil shoved and twisted, fighting and cursing, because he could see how the guards were deciding who was going to have the next go at Ty. Oh fuck what a nightmare. What an ass he was to think this was some grand adventure like in the tales.

The thug Tyras had noticed earlier sauntered out from the mass of prisoners, looking brutal and nasty and like he would do any cruel thing for an extra ration of gruel.

"You want a go at him, lad?" said the chief with a laugh. "That's the first time I've had a prisoner want to join in."

"A go at *him*?" The thug looked around as if surprised to see the whole appalled audience. "I thought you meant a go at being the one held down on the ground. I like it a bit rough." He cast a gaze around the guards. "I can give it or I can take it and I must say after ten days on the road I am cursed bored and hells hungry. So if we're not going to get on with the drilling so I can take an extra ration of gruel, I'll take whatever pony I can get now. Nothing like sex to take your thoughts off hunger, neh?" He glanced over his shoulder at Gil, then away.

Gil stopped fighting because there was no fathoming that look. Everyone else was watching the chief.

"Let him go," said the chief. "Line up in ranks of ten."

Of course every man there lined up for drill. Gil darted over to Ty but when he put a hand on Ty's shoulder his friend slapped him away.

"Fuck you, Gil. Fuck you and your fucking schemes." He

lurched to his feet, staggering. Tears dribbled down his cheeks and semen down the back of one leg. "And fuck your mother, too."

"My mother's dead, Ty. Get in line. We're drilling now."

"You fucker, don't touch me! Don't tell me what to do." He clawed tears from his face but he couldn't stand in a way that did not cause him pain.

"Do you want them to drag you off to fuck you some more, Ty? Is that what you want? Because that's what they want you to do. They want any excuse now they've started in on you. So you can tell me to go fuck myself and be fucked and fuck all but you are fucking getting in line for this drill because I am not going to fucking watch that again, do you hear me?"

Ty paused, an odd expression breaking through his pain. "The hells, Gil. You're crying."

"Heya! You two!" The chief shoved his baton in between them, then grinned to remind them of what else the baton could do. "You drilling or you hugging each other for later?"

"We're drilling," said Gil.

He whispered thanks to all his grandmother's seven gods that Tyras went meekly. It took more cursed courage than Gil had for Ty to jerkily stump through the drill. Gil had learned drill as a boy when he'd run around after Shevad and Yofar. The drill the chief ran them through was a basic drill for recruits to get them used to moving together and being aware of where the men on either side of you were. The prisoners lumbered around, some clumsy and some getting the hang of it. But the other men, the ones who sneaked into the work gang at night, drilled with precision. They were already soldiers.

Afterward the prisoners formed meekly into line for their extra rations, grateful for a splash of gruel. Gil waited until he saw where the thug sat down alone and dragged Tyras over. He plopped down without invitation.

"What in the hells did you do that for?" Gil asked in a low voice.

Instead of answering the young man watched Tyras shifting restlessly trying to find a comfortable way to sit.

"Lie on your side," said the thug. "It'll take a few days to feel better."

"Fuck you," said Tyras, but he rolled onto his side.

"Why did you do it?" Gil asked again.

The man jerked his chin sideways to indicate guards were patrolling close by. So Gil ate. The rice gruel was chewy, undercooked, cold, and tasteless and maybe the best meal he had ever had. Afterward darkness fell, stars blazing and a bright moon rising. People settled down to sleep. Gil lay beside Ty, who shifted away from him, and cursed if the thug didn't lie down on Tyras's other side.

"I told you to fuck off," said Tyras, voice rising.

The thug answered in a whisper. "Just protecting your ass. You don't think the guards don't see you as their toy now one's gotten his cock into you when you didn't want it? Why do you think they played out this game? As soon as they hear prisoners whispering complaints they set up another punishment to keep people in line."

"The chief said this was the first time a prisoner had offered to join in," murmured Gil. "Which means they've done exactly the same thing before."

"Exactly," agreed the thug. "What I can't figure is whether they picked on you two on purpose or if your fat mouth just gave them the excuse they've been looking for. Smart of them to punish your friend instead of you. I didn't see that coming."

"Shut up," said Ty.

"Why did you walk out there like that?" repeated Gil, too weary to be angered.

The man rolled onto his back to gaze up at the moon. "It's a lovely night, isn't it? I always admire the flare of a crescent moon."

The moon wasn't a crescent at all; it was a waxing Lamp moon, swelling with each day.

Then the words hit him.

He raised up onto an arm. On the other side of Ty the thug stretched out utterly relaxed, as if he were arrested, branded, shorn, and marched away from everything he knew every day. When his head turned, Gil knew the man was looking at him, awaiting an answer he expected.

"How in the hells is a handsome swan like you come to rest among feral dogs like us?" Gil said, almost laughing because it was so absurd.

"I've been circling around you for days, Lord Gilaras. It just seemed a good moment to make a move that would give us an excuse to form a pact. I'm called Adiki. I'm here at the behest of Captain Kellas. And with business of my own besides."

Tyras rolled onto his stomach. After a silence, he muttered, "My thanks, ver. You saved me from much worse."

"It wasn't your fault, Lord Tyras. It's hard not to feel shame at being treated like that but I hope you don't." Gil was surprised such a gentle tone could pass the lips of such a brute of a man. Then he ruined it. "I guessed they were going to go after one of you two cockwitted lords sooner or later. You stand out like beacons in this group."

Tyras buried his face in his arms and did not reply.

"Are there any others besides you?" Gil asked.

"Not that I know of but that doesn't mean a thing. We have to assume the guards have their own spies among the work gang."

"You mean besides the soldiers who are marching with us in disguise?"

Adiki had startlingly white teeth, a flash in the night when he grinned. "You noticed that, too?"

A guard paced into view out of the gloom, making his rounds. Gil sank back so they wouldn't be caught talking and for good measure settled on his back. The thought of being dragged away into the night to be assaulted made it impossible to sleep. The moon rose higher and then sank. Adiki breathed easily beside them. Very late, Gil woke from a doze to hear Tyras weeping with snuffling tears he tried to muffle in his arms. He didn't know how to comfort him, what to say, what to do. So he said nothing and pretended he was still asleep.

The worst thing in the middle of a long night with no hope of anything but more of the same on the morrow was that he could not stop thinking of Sarai, trapped in the upper palace with no one to guard her back. At least he and Tyras had each other and now this new ally.

Silently he prayed first to Beltak the Shining One as everyone must who steps foot within the palace. He chanted the offering prayers to the seven gods as his grandmother had taught him, although he had nothing to offer except his voice. He asked the Merciful One to watch over them, She in whose compassionate embrace all hurts and miseries fade into oblivion.

"Let her people's Hidden One keep Sarai-ya safe," he murmured to the heavens.

The lambent stars offered no hope and no answer.

40

Every morning Tayum opened the door of Sarai's cubicle at dawn to escort her to the shrine for the dawn worship service. Every morning Sarai drew her shawl across the lower half of her face to signify her refusal and her defiance. Every morning after the other women had filed into the shrine's balcony, she tested all the doors that led out of the queen's wing of the palace; they were always barred to her.

But even if her body was trapped and her wealth held hostage, her mind could range where it willed. Every morning during the long prayer service she walked in the queen's garden on the pretext of cataloging the plants and their pharmacological properties, which she shared as her contribution at the daily Recitation even though few of the women could understand the Hundred-speech. Meanwhile she recorded her observations of the queen's court in code while also devising a glossary and verb table for the Sirni language as she worked to learn it without anyone being the wiser.

Baby's delight flowers with the first rains. Its crumbled petals sweeten cordial and other dishes prepared for the new year festival.

Queen Chorannah presides over exactly thirty-two noble ladies; a woman was sent to her country estate to make room for me. Her household officials number sixteen. Probable that the servants number sixty-four. Eunuch guards likewise. Everything in multiples or divisions of eight: poems with sixteen stanzas; embroidery flowers with eight-sided blooms; twenty-four dishes brought in four courses for dinner.

Shrubs of purple thorn whose bark when ground up keeps away insects.

The hierarchy of the priesthood is a ladder with eight rungs. Priests known as exalted, that is on the seventh and eighth rungs, veil their faces. At the top of the ladder stands the exalted lord priest who lives in the holy parkland of the Grand Shrine which lies at the center of the Emperor's Palace. The Emperor's Palace is a city unto itself at the heart of the vast octagonal city that is really eight cities. These are called Riamru, Hassisadru, Salsali, Vassagri, Jolarno,

Magarno, Assaroei, Tirgatoei. The exalted lord priest is said to be so spiritually elevated that he is ageless and cannot die.

Bright Blue is best known for the powder made from its bulb that stems bleeding.

The holy parkland and shrine complex at the heart of the Emperor's Palace at the heart of the octagonal city at the heart of the empire is called Dalilasah. This is similar to a noble-woman's name, which always ends in -ah. The Beltak doctrine claims that every holy shrine is a feminine structure, being an inert form constructed by the efforts of men, named by men, and given spiritual life by men who go into and out of it with their prayers and enlightened knowledge.

The overpowering scent of muzz may conceal strong smells and is traditionally associated with the pleasure gardens dedicated to the Hundred goddess known as Ushara the Merciless One, Mistress of Love, Death, and Desire. This makes sense because muzz, brewed in a strong enough quantity, brings on a woman's bleeding.

The words for "woman" and "holy" come from the same root.

"Sunbright make my favorite garlands," said a husky voice. Sarai looked up, hand poised above the page.

Attended by a eunuch wearing a guard's tabard, a tall and lovely woman walked up the path between brilliantly intense sprays of yellow sunbright. "You are Lady Sarai. I have been commanded to give you particular greetings from Prince Kasad."

"Princess Kasarah? You look very like your brother."

"Most people do remark on how much my twin and I resemble each other."

Sarai thought the princess more striking and assured in manner, but she was not about to say so. The princess's robes draped loosely, the silk textured with leaves and vines woven into a gold-and-brown fabric. Where the prince wore only simple bead earrings, his sister wore four dangling confections on each ear that knocked into each other every time she moved her head. She had covered her hair in the palace style but wore no tiered hat as the other ladies did.

"I am honored to meet you, Princess Kasarah. I heard a rumor that Queen Dia left the palace and you were coming to stand guard over her territory."

"So I have."

"How are you come here? I have not seen you in Chorannah's chambers before."

"Chorannah does not control every gate," said Kasarah with a glance at Tayum, who had moved closer in order to listen. The princess's smile had the fragility of a fresh line of ink, easily smudged. "Are you writing in your book? What is that stick you use instead of a brush?"

Her brusque familiarity startled Sarai. "Ah. Well. This is a reed pen, easily cut from several varieties of bamboo."

Kasarah peered at the open pages. "Rumor whispers that you write in magical signs."

Sarai closed the book. "Among my people, women are taught to read and write and do the accounts. It is nothing unusual or magical for us."

"I have displeased you. My apologies."

"Of course it is natural to be inquisitive. I am inquisitive myself. That is why I am cataloging all the plants in the garden."

"Are you indeed?" The princess looked again at the guard hovering close, then at Tayum's frowning face, then back at Sarai. She shook out the embroidered hem of a voluminous sleeve, making rather an obvious business of it. "Gardening is my chief love and profession."

"How lovely!" Was this an awkward and rushed attempt to befriend her? Or a warning?

"My mother has a country estate where she has long spent most of her time. My brother and I spent our childhood there. As you know, my mother has built up a great weaving enterprise—"

"I did not know."

"Yes, she makes a great deal of coin selling inexpensive bulk cloth on the market. It's why she is so rich. She herself is an accomplished weaver. I became interested in dyes, thus I studied plants."

Kasarah began walking. Too curious to let the opportunity pass, Sarai followed her under an archway of flowering patience. The two eunuchs paced them. Because she and Kasarah were not speaking Sirni she wasn't sure if the men could understand.

"Do you not pray at the Shining One's shrine with the others, Princess Kasarah?"

Kasarah looked sidelong at her with a knowing smile, like sharing a silent laugh. Her lips, reddened by carmine, looked as soft and pliant as flower petals. "I place my offerings at the altar of the northern deity known as Enne Who Looks Both Ways. Enne is the seed that may wither, or flourish. Enne is the lover's offering that may be rejected, or accepted. Enne is the friendship that may fade, or prosper."

Sarai wasn't sure if this was an invitation, or just an explanation. Certainly Kasarah had a flair of attractiveness that her awkward brother lacked, and she wore a distinctive and appealing perfume distilled from the sweet-smelling flower called falling-star.

The princess halted in front of a gate flanked on either side by a eunuch guard standing in the shade of rice-grain-flower trees. The shuttered Assizes Tower rose like a blind man above the wall. Morning light cast the tower's shadow right over where they stood.

"Do you happen to know what this plant is?" Kasarah asked in an overly loud voice, as if she had abruptly discovered Sarai was deaf.

"This is the rice-grain-flower," said Sarai, wondering if the princess was being deliberately obtuse since the plant was common. "You might use its tiny flowers to ornament your hair, or scent tea or clothing. It won't flower again until the rains, next year."

"How many days has it been since you came to the upper palace, Lady Sarai?"

"Twenty-one days."

"You must hope for respite from these walls, then."

With a click and a scrape, a shutter was pulled away from a small square grille set into the center of the gate. Someone looked through and saw them. Then the gate opened and King Jehosh stepped into the garden to give a kiss of greeting to his daughter. He waved his fingers peremptorily at the eunuch guards. "I shall bring Lady Sarai back after we have had tea in the commander's pavilion."

"Your Highness, I have orders she must not leave the garden." Tayum bowed, and kept his body between her and the king. Sarai could not help but look at his strong hands and wonder if the girls would be whipped again.

King Jehosh had the smile of a man who finds the frustration of his opponents amusing. "I understand that is your duty. However you cannot refuse a direct order from me."

Tayum and the two guards watched in silent disapproval as Sarai hurried after the king. She was astounded at her good fortune and prayed, under her breath, that the girls wouldn't be touched. But she would not let that stop her.

Beyond the open gate lay a walled courtyard stripped clean of decoration. Here rose the Assizes Tower. A ramp sloped up to the main double doors, which were chained shut. As they crossed the courtyard, a tingling like the swarming of ants buzzed along her thigh where the mirror rested. But when they passed through a second gate and into the king's garden, the swarming and tickling ceased. Either she had experienced a trick of the nerves because she wanted to get into the Assizes Tower so badly, or something in the tower—perhaps the demon's coil—was casting off magical power that tangled in the mirror.

Anyway, right now none of that mattered. She finally had her opportunity to escape.

"My thanks, Your Highness!" she said breathlessly.

"You must wait to see how the tea suits you before you thank me for it." Instead of leading her away to safety, the king ushered her up steps into the central pavilion. Its walls were silk curtains tied back to let the breeze through.

She looked around a little desperately as he indicated she should settle herself on the cushions. Princess Kasarah shrugged in a way that might be understood as apology, or helplessness. "Did Prince Kasad not explain my situation, Your Highness?"

"You believe I am helping you flee Chorannah's vise. But I am not."

"Are you not the king, to make it possible?"

"Am I not the king?" He rubbed his chin. "A question I have come to ask myself more than once in recent months."

Over her life Sarai had been more inclined to despair than anger. But his air of self-pity irritated her. She took in several breaths to descend the ladder of anger before she replied as cautiously as she could manage. "Then why the invitation, Your Highness?"

His gaze skimmed down the length of her body before returning to her eyes. "To offer you a respite from the queen's court. I have heard you are off your food, and I thought to offer you delicacies that may be more to your liking."

He gestured. A soldier brought a tray with ginger tea, sweet rice cakes, fruit lightly dusted with ginger shavings, and rice porridge stewed in coconut milk. She considered an indignant and principled refusal but the aroma of the warm porridge assaulted her nostrils and, after a brief struggle, she sat down and let her shawl drop.

Kasarah's gaze flashed to Sarai's scarred cheek and away.

Jehosh started with obvious surprise, but once he had recovered he examined her with keen interest. "Your eyes gave me to expect something different, for in truth you look much like most ordinary Hundred folk. You honor me by allowing me to speak to you face-to-face, Lady Sarai."

"It is an intimacy that no other Ri Amarah woman will allow you, Your Highness. However, I must advise you that in the lower palace I had already adopted the local custom, so I offer you nothing I have not already given to the people who visited Lord Gilaras and me."

"So I am put in my place."

"How I act in the queen's court in protest of her desire to force me to worship at the shrine is another matter."

"Ah. I see. A justifiable cause, and I am pleased to hear you are refusing Chorannah what you have freely offered to me. Will you have porridge and a cake?"

"If you please."

The king himself served her. His hands were callused from riding and weapons training. His regard was disconcerting but he had a gift of seeming charming rather than intrusive, as if he was completely delighted by their meeting. "I hope this food is more to your taste than what is served out of Chorannah's kitchen. Ginger is soothing to the stomach. I have heard a rumor you have as yet shown no sign of a woman's bleeding. It is presumed you may be pregnant by the disgraced Lord Gilaras."

She set down her spoon. "You are a blunt speaker, Your Highness."

He cast a smile to the winds, swift and sure. "It is one of the privileges of being king, Lady Sarai."

"How am I to answer such an intimate question?"

"With the truth?"

"Why is it important to you to know, since you have already refused to help me find a way to rejoin my lost husband?"

"The situation in the palace is always complicated."

"Truly it is. Queen Chorannah and my uncle are scheming to annul the marriage with Lord Gilaras and ally my clan's wealth to one of her high officials."

"I have heard this rumor but it is good to hear you confirm it."

"Then you can see why I am desperate to escape."

"And you can surely see, Lady Sarai, that I need a better source of information in Queen Chorannah's court. More tea?"

When she nodded, he poured. Chimes hung at each of the four cardinal directions, singing as the wind stirred them and also, she supposed, tangling with their words so that guards listening from afar would have trouble hearing what was said, just in case not all of the king's guardsmen were loyal.

"Your Highness, do you hope to keep me in Queen Chorannah's company to spy on her? Because you know I don't want to be there and so that means you believe you can trust what I tell you?"

"You are a clever enough woman to work your way into Chorannah's good graces, Lady Sarai. Play upon the mystery and attraction you offer. The scar gives you a rather bandit air, does it not? How did you get it?"

"What if we strike a bargain? Release my husband from the work gang in exchange for my help."

"That I cannot do."

"He is innocent of the crime he was arrested and condemned for."

"No Herelian is innocent. Need I remind you that Lord Gilaras's father murdered my beloved father?"

"Gil did not kill your father. He wasn't even born yet. If you can't help me get him back, and you won't help me leave here, why should I help you?"

The king had lovely eyes, although not as lovely as Gil's longlashed deep-set orbs. But Gil never looked at her with such an odd mixture of interest and calculation. Gil was not a mystery to be solved, as this man was.

He picked up the teapot and, as he spoke, refilled all three cups.

"This place where we sit is called the commander's pavilion, after my grandfather, King Anjihosh. He was a military man from an early age. When I was a young man I desired to be like him. It is said he captured that which he desired most, first of all the heart of a beautiful maiden and afterward the war-ridden land of the Hundred, to which he brought peace."

"Did he bring peace to the heart of the beautiful maiden as well?"

He set down the teapot. "The story goes that she died, and broke his heart."

"An odd way to phrase it, as if she died in order to break his heart."

Kasarah plucked a cake off the tray, the first time she had moved since they had sat down. "My honored mother once said you always wanted a captured maiden of your own, Father, just as your grandfather had."

The king pressed fingers affectionately on his daughter's hand. "I can only imagine the snap of her eyes and the blistering heat of Dia's tongue as she said it. Fortunately your mother has not died and broken my heart." Having said the words lightly, he frowned, eyes dark. "Bad enough—"

Kasarah sucked in a warning breath.

He rose and took a turn around the pavilion, tapping each set of chimes to make them ring. Then he sat back down.

"Lady Sarai, when I am in the upper palace I take tea here in honor of my grandfather's memory. In this way I honor the work he did in bringing peace and stability to the Hundred. Do you not also want the Hundred to be at peace? For I am sure you have heard there is unrest in the city. Many people blame the Ri Amarah for the ills that afflict them, because they need someone to blame."

She gasped, and realized she had slapped an open hand to her chest like Elit playing a part in a scene of The Dreaded News, Just Heard.

The king said nothing. Kasarah pushed her uneaten cake around her platter, face composed and thus unreadable.

A terrible and reckless urge seized her. She had nothing left to lose, and no further appeals she could make. "I'll do it on one condition."

His satisfaction curled in the air like smoke. "I like a woman who bargains. What is that condition, Lady Sarai?"

"Two conditions. You protect my people."

"That's one. What is the second?"

"I want to see the inside of the Assizes Tower."

His body canted back, absorbing the unexpected words. "Impossible. Why?"

"As a matter of intellectual curiosity I want to see a demon's coil up close. I am given to understand there is one carved into the rock at the base of the tower."

"No one can walk on a demon's coil. They are inimical to humans. Are you in a demon's employ, Lady Sarai?"

"Would it matter to you if I was?" She glanced at Kasarah

as she said it, but the princess was staring at her clasped hands, biting her lower lip.

"I admit I am intrigued," murmured the king, drawing her attention back to him. "Demons were involved in my father's death but I've never understood how or why. Maybe…"

The catch in his voice, the way he studied her too closely, made her recoil not from any physical aversion but rather from realizing she was allowing herself to get caught up in the thrill of a chase. But this was not a game.

Yet the thought of that demon's coil lying so close, the tingling of her mirror, propelled her forward. "Only by study can we learn what a thing truly is."

"The tales say that demons feed in the coils. That they can speak to each other inside them. Most demons ride winged horses, but it's said some walk across vast distances by means of stepping from one coil onto another. Don't such things frighten you?"

Unthinkingly, Sarai rested fingers atop his fist. "Frighten me? It just makes me want to know more!"

He looked down at her hand but did not dislodge it. "To what purpose?"

Releasing him, she sat back, unable to disguise her frustration. "Have you never in your life wished to discover something just because it was a puzzle to you?"

"I'm not sure what you mean."

She knew better than to pour out her heart to this man as she had felt safe doing with Gil. Yet he was king, and she needed him to want to help her.

"A mind lives no matter where it resides. It is a gift we have with us always. For example, my great-aunt's life may seem trivial to many people but she never ceases thinking and wondering. She raised me to investigate, just as she does. You could cage me in the upper palace for the rest of my life and yet my mind would still fly, and it would still ask questions, and it would still desire answers. A demon's coil is there to be seen and wondered at. Which means it can also be explained."

"Demons are dangerous." He picked up a spoon and rolled it along his fingers as if he were playing her words along his skin all the better to absorb them.

"But you want to know if demons were involved in your father's death, don't you?"

A bell rang in the queen's wing to mark the end of morning prayer.

Was that a look of relief that flashed across his face? Or was he annoyed that their conversation had been interrupted? The truth was, she did not know him at all, and it was foolish for her to pretend that she could.

"You must attend the queen now, Lady Sarai."

She rose, shaking down her long jacket impatiently, angry at having made the impulsive demand and knowing she had lost anyway. Just as she grasped the end of her scarf to pull it up, Kasarah looked up.

"I can get Lady Sarai into the Assizes Tower, Father. Back when we were young and still friendly, Farihosh showed me and Kasad a secret way in."

"Farihosh! I can't tell whether to embrace him for having the intelligence and ambition to be a proper heir, or to await his knife in my back. I know the secret way, too, but I never showed him."

What thoughts chased behind the king's dark eyes Sarai could not guess, because she was no demon to reach into a person's mind and fish out their innermost heart. All she knew was that a door had opened to reveal a question that gnawed at him.

"Very well, Lady Sarai. You spy for me. I get you into the Assizes Tower."

The triple tap woke Kellas out of a dreamless sleep. As a younger man he would have been on his feet with a weapon in hand before the second set of triple taps. Now he had to content himself with sitting up too fast and hoping he hadn't pulled something as he grabbed the sword he always placed on the mat beside his mattress. "Report."

"Captain, it's Sefi," said the young man through the closed screen. Lamplight turned his slender body into a bulky shadow against the rice paper. "A person is here with a private message for you."

"Has Chief Oyard been woken?"

The thump of a person stumbling into a wall in the dark answered him. "The hells! Sefi, hold that light over here. I stubbed my toe, curse it."

Every night before he slept Kellas laid out clothing so he could dress in the dark if need be. He pulled on a light under-robe with sleeves, then a formal sleeveless ankle-length vest. When Oyard opened the door, looking disheveled in only an under-robe, Kellas was calmly tying his sash. Sefi held a lamp and a folded piece of paper.

With a dagger Oyard skewered the paper and lifted it out of Sefi's fingers. "Have you not attended to lessons? People mix poison into ink and kill people with letters and reports. Never accept letters, cloth, and food from strangers with your bare hands."

The young man licked his lips nervously. "She handed me this paper, and told me she brings a verbal message from the queen."

"Queen Dia?" A wave of alertness washed through Kellas. He rubbed the last bleary clots of sleep from his eyes. "Describe the woman."

"She is dressed in the fashion of servants from the upper palace. She's old."

"As old as I am?"

"Oh, no, Captain! Much younger than you, more like my blessed mother's age."

Kellas busied himself lighting a lamp to hide his smile as the lad went on obliviously.

"She arrived in a curtained chair carried by four eunuchs who serve Queen Chorannah."

"How can you be sure they are Chorannah's palace men?"

"They must be hers. All four are Sirniakan. The Beltak priests do not admit cut men to their ranks. These have slave collars around their necks, as her eunuchs do."

"Well observed."

The young man beamed.

Kellas unhooked a mesh of wires he hung every night from the ceiling to discourage prowlers. In the office he sat on his usual cushion at his desk. Oyard deposited the letter on a tray of sand and Kellas prised it open with a pair of sticks. Inside, in the blocky Sirni script, was written: *Why do you hate my sons?*

"This arouses my curiosity. Show in the person, Sefi."

"Captain, are you sure that is wise?" objected Oyard.

"If it is another attempt to murder me then I am intrigued by its novelty."

The woman wore the calf-length embroidered jacket and patterned belled trousers typical of palace women, all of whom dressed in the Sirniakan style. Very hot to be covered in so much cloth, but he knew better than to say so. A brass collar of interlocking leaves hid her neck, and a polished metal net made of many tiny brass coils weighed down her hair. She had the stout vigor of a woman in good health, and almost imperceptible calluses on her fingers. Embroidery, perhaps; some kind of handwork.

She looked around the room to make sure there was no one else present. "Is there no couch on which to sit?" she asked in Sirni.

"There are two cushions." He indicated them where they sat right out in plain sight on the other side of his desk. Her distaste showed itself by a twist of her lips but, with some difficulty, she sat.

When she did not speak he ventured to do so. "I am Captain Kellas. You bring a message from Queen Chorannah."

"You think Jehosh is the injured party. You think the queen ambitious and greedy."

The attack took him off guard.

"Do you ever wonder why Chorannah has only two children?" she added.

He had his suspicions but before he could answer she went on.

"The day he brought the northern woman home is the day he stopped coming to Chorannah's bed. Everyone thinks Dia the victim and yet Dia is the one who holds Jehosh in contempt, leading him on a leash, telling him when he can visit her conjugally so that after twenty years he still pants after her like a youth after a teasing lover. Dia is the one who has amassed a fortune while Chorannah is left destitute, begging for funds from his grudging treasury. And yet he believes Chorannah and her sons plot against him. Given his preference for the other woman it is far more likely he seeks to kill Chorannah's sons to make way for Dia's boy. It's what he does, you know. He kills those who stand in his way."

"Does he?" Kellas was by now wide awake, drenched in the flood of her pent-up anger.

"He forced his sister to marry his best friend."

"I heard it was a love match."

"Of course that's what you heard. He rid himself of his brothers!"

"They went into the army."

"At his urging and against his mother's wishes. After they both died Queen Yevah broke with him and left the palace. Have you never asked yourself why Lord Seras killed King Atani?"

"Given that I am said to have had a hand in it, I admit I have asked myself that question more than once."

"I never believed the story of how the demons used you as their weapon, Captain."

"My thanks."

"I know the truth."

"Do you? After all these years I am skeptical that anyone knows the truth."

Her ability to keep her hands folded quietly in her lap despite her impassioned words impressed him. "Jehosh promised his friend Vanas that he would get Vanas's older brother out of the way so Vanas could take all his holdings. Seras got wind of the plot but mistakenly believed it had originated with King Atani."

"This is a tale I've not heard sung before. It has a certain pleasant neatness to it. Seras kills Atani to stop the king from elevating his younger brother over him. The problem is, no one who knew King Atani would believe that was how he went about things. Seras knew Atani."

She shifted as if sitting cross-legged on the floor was uncomfortable, and maybe it was but he was not inclined to do anything about it. "Lord Seras believed King Atani was not strong enough to keep the Hundred safe. Perhaps the truth, Captain, is that it was necessary to kill King Atani before he lost the inheritance his father Anjihosh gave him."

Almost he slammed a fist onto his writing table. Almost he leaped to his feet to scream at her. What stupid, selfish stories people told themselves! Poison leaked into their hearts as they smiled with condescension, thinking their view of the world to be the only right one.

She smiled, observing his struggle although not one word passed between them. Cold anger washed away the heat. He reined in his fury, adjusted his sleeves, and caught his breath.

Then he struck.

"What actually brings you here in the middle of the night, Your Highness?"

"I wondered how long it would take you." She did not look at all worried. Instead she leaned toward him as toward a confidante. "Farihosh and Tavahosh are good boys, healthy, smart, and vigorous, just as Jehosh himself was at that age. I need you to convince Jehosh I am not his enemy. I am his ally."

"Since we are speaking bluntly, Your Highness, I will venture to humbly remind you that you tried to poison Prince Kasad eight years ago."

"That was not my doing."

How blandly she spoke the words! Either she was a convincing liar or she was telling the truth, but he was no demon to hook her thoughts out of her mind.

"Whose doing was the poison, then?" he asked.

"Dia poisoned him herself with just enough of a dose to make him ill but not to kill him. She did it to gain Jehosh's sympathy, for at that time Farihosh was showing himself to be such a fine and promising heir that Dia feared Jehosh would turn away from her and back to me."

"Has the king ever tried to strip Prince Farihosh of his heirship?" Yet he thought of the unkind thing Jehosh had said about the young man—*rancid cunning*—and of how startlingly flattering Dannarah's description of Farihosh had been.

"Jehosh is biding his time until the right moment to strike. The palace officials and the high army officers and all of the priests support me and my sons because we are the righteous ones. Jehosh knows his elder sons are his only rightful heirs, yet his cock rules his mind."

Whatever idea he had ever had that Chorannah was a meek, shy creature was by now rubbed into oblivion like sand scraping ink from a page.

She went on. "Jehosh is angling for the attention of the Silver girl now. Probably he wants her money but more likely it is just to thwart me."

"Thwart you, Your Highness? What has the Silver girl to do with you?"

Her expression turned sly. "I could offer her to you, Captain. A wealthy young bride. She's no beauty, and the frightful scar can never be unseen, but coin gilds a hopeful lover's eyes, does it not?"

"She is married, Your Highness."

Her gaze flicked around the chamber as if she had seen a ghost. "So she is, if Lord Gilaras still lives. But contracts that have produced no children can be easily annulled."

For a drawn-out while she studied the objects on his desk: a burning lamp, an unlit lamp, the tray of sand with her note and the dagger, a dry ink block, a closed brush box, and a polished river stone the size of his fist.

"You are a tidy man, Captain."

"I find it beneficial to be so. I can find anything, even in the dark."

"All I ask is that you support my sons. King Atani loved Farihosh."

"He did, Your Highness. I recall it well. He thought the sun rose and set upon that little boy."

"Everything would be different if Atani had not died. He would have approved of the man Farihosh has become. If you are loyal to Atani, then follow his wishes. Support my son. Do not throw away your loyalty by giving it to Jehosh. He has none to give to you in return, not as a true lord ought. Look at my sons, and learn."

She wiped a tear from her face or pretended to. "There, Captain. I have thrown myself on your mercy. Consider your duty to the kings who came before. Were you not King Anjihosh's most loyal soldier? Did you not serve King Atani afterward more faithfully than any other?"

"My duty to them resides in my thoughts day and night, I assure you. But I have one question. If the palace officials, the army officers, and the priests support you, then what need do you have of me? I am nothing, a mere captain of security."

"I appreciate your wit, Captain. You and I both know you were King Anjihosh's most trusted and experienced Wolf. Do not try to pretend to be something else now." She got to her feet, went to the door, and there she paused in shadow. "People see only the king's charm and not the monster beneath. All Jehosh cares about is himself."

41

At dawn Sarai knelt by the door of her tiny cubicle, listening to the chatter of the other women rising and going about their morning ablutions in the washroom everyone shared. She held her mother's mirror against her chest. Would Kasarah come today? Would King Jehosh show her the secret way into the Assizes Tower? As the soft footsteps of the women filed away toward the shrine, she traced the lines engraved on the back to soothe her racing heart.

The engraving on the back was a six-sided spiral cut through with diagonal lines. As had become her habit she counted numbers along the spiral, assigned the number 1 to the center-point, and then 2, 3, 4, and on around at even intervals. That the prime numbers fell along certain of the diagonal lines carved through the spiral she had realized quickly although she could not explain it. Often she imagined that everything was built on numbers, that the Hidden One was not the Creator of All but a vast, clean, beautiful pattern underlying everything. Maybe the pattern itself was the handprint of divinity. Hard to say but surely possible to measure.

The last footfalls faded. She tied the mirror under her outer skirt, tucked her book, ink, and writing box into a leather satchel, arranged her shawl to conceal her face, and slid open the door, eager to get to the garden.

Tayum blocked the corridor. "Lady Sarai. Come with me."

Sirni had no word for "please," only forms of verbs that meant either "it is commanded" or "it is requested." He commanded her to come, in his capacity as the queen's representative. Gripped by a sense of stalking dread, she followed him through the corridors and then down a servants' alley.

She clutched the book more tightly as he slid open a door into the very chamber in which she and Uncle Abrisho had met weeks ago. The queen walked only on carpets; the matted floor of this chamber made her feel she was being allowed to set foot back into the familiar world of the Hundred. By the opening that led onto the small balcony waited Uncle Abrisho and Cousin Beniel, their familiar faces like sunny flowers.

"Sarai!" They greeted her with a formal kinsman's kiss on each cheek. It was the first time anyone had touched her in so many days that she wanted to throw her arms around them, even though her uncle had betrayed her. Tayum watched from the door.

Abrisho rubbed his hands together in excitement as he led Sarai onto the balcony that overlooked the king's garden like a spy's nest. She pushed her face up against the lattice screen. A figure sat in the commander's pavilion. The king was waiting for her, and she was stuck here.

"Sit here, Sarai." Abrisho pointed to a cushion resting behind a painted folding screen.

Obediently she sat although the folding screen cut off her view outside and left her only the walls to observe: They were painted with scenes of women luxuriating in baths while men peeped through lattices to spy on their naked forms.

The hells! as Gil would have said. How had she not noticed these last time? Was this a chamber meant for an assignation?

A door slid open and she heard someone enter as Abrisho hurried to greet them.

"Exalted Prince, it is an honor, an honor indeed that you receive us with such honor." Her uncle's robes sighed and fluttered as he bowed perhaps a hundred times.

"All honor goes to my mother the queen," said a voice Sarai did not recognize, but it was young and proud and male and it spoke the Hundred-speech with an awkward lurch, like trotting out memorized phrases. Since Farihosh was in the south, this must be Tavahosh. "It is with her permission, it is on her urging and command, that this meeting takes place. Tayum!" The prince switched to Sirni, giving a command for tea.

"Your Highness, may I make known to you my son Beniel?"

"All respect and honor to you, Your Highness. Your notice honors me, Your Highness."

Sarai stared at the ceiling's painted vines and flowers, wondering if she could more fruitfully pass the time by counting how often the men used the word *honor*.

Her uncle was still extolling the beauty of the garden when servants returned with the tea. A tray was placed on her side of the screen so she could pour without any part of her visible except her hands. The custom of Sirniakan women tattooing their hands suddenly made sense to her as the men settled on the other side of the screen and silently watched her fill three cups, one for each of them and none for herself.

The scent of the tea curled up her nose and her stomach growled softly.

"A lovely morning!" exclaimed Beniel.

"As the Shining One wills," said the prince.

"The light shines brightly upon the sunbright in the garden!" Beniel added.

"In flowers we see the beauty of the Shining One's mercy and kindness," said the prince.

They went on in this way for far too long, Sarai's part to listen and to pour. Elit would have spouted mellifluous poetry that shamed their paltry verses. Gil would have made outrageous jokes until she convulsed in laughter. Had the king left the pavilion yet?

At length, the prince took his leave, by no word or gesture indicating he knew she was in the chamber although he had accepted tea from her very hands.

As soon as the door slid closed Abrisho clapped his hands in glee and folded back the screen. "A triumph, Sarai! With what courtesy he spoke to us!"

"Yes, one tendentious phrase after the next, all memorized, I should imagine. I've never been so bored! Enough of the prince! Is there a letter from Tsania? I have some pages of news for her if I may entrust you with them."

"I have no letter from Tsania."

"If you care for me at all, Uncle, if you have any concern for Tsania, you will do as you promised and make sure she and I remain in contact!"

He hesitated, then said, "I will see your letter is delivered."

She had a trimming knife for cutting reed pens, and she used this now to slice off two pages from the back of the book on which she had been writing a letter to Tsania with a message embedded in code: *I am trapped here.* She folded the paper up in an elaborate pattern that, if they unfolded it to read, they could not duplicate; so Tsania would know their own relatives were spying on them. But she smiled prettily as she handed it over. "What gossip from home, Uncle? Is there news about Lord Gilaras?"

"Forget about Lord Gilaras! We are having a new contract drawn up to sever the old one."

"But I don't want to sever the old one!" She pressed a hand to her belly.

"Are you pregnant?"

"I believe I am, having missed my regular courses and feeling mild nausea in the mornings. A child born of his seed and mine means we retain an obligation both to him and to his clan."

Hooking fingers over his sash, Abrisho paced into the main room, muttering to himself, then trod as heavily back as if weighted by necessity. Beniel looked alarmed.

"There are ways to rid yourself of such a burden, Sarai." He grasped her fingers too tightly. "I know your Aunt Rua is wise in these matters..."

She pulled her hands out of his grip. "What do you mean?"

"Did you not understand what just transpired? Queen Chorannah has given Prince Tavahosh permission to marry you."

She staggered back and bumped into the wall. Confusion muddied her thoughts. "Prince Tavahosh? Why would I want to marry him?"

"You foolish girl! Have you not heard of the attack on a Ri Amarah clan house in High Haldia? Our fellow Ri Amarah forced to walk about in groups, bearing clubs? Households having to hire local men to guard our gates? A bounty on Ri

Amarah corpses? Lord Gilaras was arrested for the murder of a Ri Amarah coachman whose body he tried to sell—"

"He didn't do it!"

"You have the means to secure the safety of your people by acquiescing to this brilliant marriage."

The words knifed her in the heart. When she glanced outside, the commander's pavilion was empty. The king had left, and her chance with him. The queen's bell rang to signal the end of the prayer service.

"I must go at once," she said, to be rid of them, and they saw her off with smiles and bright, happy words.

Once back among the women, she begged illness so as not to face the rigors of the day. It was easier to hide in her cubicle, caged up like a chicken at market, than to sit at the queen's side knowing the queen expected her gratitude. Servants brought food but she was so queasy from waves of hopeless frustration that she refused everything except plain rice and water. All her yearning for Elit, all her fear for Gil, rushed to fill every crease and joint of her body. Her lips crackled with it; her eyes went dry. She tried to sleep but every creak woke her out of troubled dreams in which she lost everyone she loved.

They meant to steal from her every scrap of who she was until she was reduced to a mute, acquiescent shadow.

Was this how her mother had felt all those years ago? Little better than a cornered rat?

The walls surrounding her were so high and for the first time in her life she was alone.

The dawn whistle jolted Gil awake from the kind of dream he'd have preferred not to wake from. He opened his eyes with a sigh, still feeling the bruises from the fight Ty had gotten him and Adiki into a few days ago. Cautiously he looked around in the sleepy dawn light.

An older man named Natas stirred to his right. The man had taken to following the three of them around without asking for anything in return. Since he didn't cause any trouble and could talk easily and knowledgeably about his life as a pipefitter in Toskala before he was arrested for the crime of walking home drunk from a tavern, Gil warily let him stay. Safety in numbers, after all.

Tyras lay to Gil's left, on his side, face buried in a bent elbow. Fading contusions ornamented his bare back. On the other side of Ty, Adiki sat up, combing bits and pieces of grass out of his month's growth of beard and hair. The only reason Gil and Ty hadn't gotten badly beaten up by their opponents was because Adiki was a brutal and experienced brawler, the kind of man who runs toward a fight rather than prudently away.

The big man glanced at the contours of Gil's kilt where it was rucked up a bit. "Dreaming of me again, lover?"

Gil grinned. "Of my wife. You're not enticing enough to get a rise out of me."

He got to his feet and brushed grass and dirt off the kilt as his erection subsided. The linen crackled with grime because they marched, drilled, and slept in the same piece of clothing.

Natas gave him a weary smile. "Maybe they'll let us bathe tonight."

"Yes, to go along with a banquet of chicken dumplings, chili beef, and fried coconut pastries adorned with slices of pearl-kiss and starfruit."

Natas groaned, and Adiki said, "You forget rice boiled in moro milk and sweetened with cane."

"Poor man's banquet," retorted Gil.

"Thus my favorite because it can be enjoyed by any poor village son at festival time."

A second whistle shrilled across the stretch of ground where the work gang had bedded down for the night. Already the men who were actually soldiers had formed up ranks and were getting fed rice gruel heaped onto rounds of flat bread while the real prisoners were still pissing and moaning.

He knelt to shake Ty's shoulder. "Heya! Fuckwit. Wake up!"

"Fuck you," said Ty into his arm.

"Every man in line before the third whistle gets a morning ration."

Tyras didn't shift. All around them the other prisoners were rubbing sleep out of their eyes and staring around at a landscape that looked very different from the river plain, with its plentiful fields and lush orchards, that surrounded the city of Toskala.

After passing the city of Horn they had marched for days on the West Track alongside the River Hayi. The guards used the river's promise to mock them every night as the false prisoners were allowed to cavort in its cool water. He surely stank, and he certainly itched. A bath had become as much of a dream as his nightly excursions into Sarai's bed.

To the east the ground sloped upward to become a shimmering grassland, called the Lend, that flowed ever higher like cloth unrolled from an unseen table far away. Despite the nearby river, the dry air and flecks of dead grass floating on the wind gave his tongue the feel of sandpaper. Thirst dogged him, yet his mouth was so dry that even the sight of the guards passing around a water jar to the men already at muster couldn't raise any saliva.

With a sigh he nodded to Adiki, who shrugged and headed off to muster with Natas trailing a step behind.

Gil sank down beside Tyras, whose bruised face was finally healing from the second-to-last fight he'd gotten into. "I'll just sit here with you. I don't need to eat or drink. I don't mind another whipping. That one I had when you refused to get up the day after what the chief did to you? It wasn't too bad. Only one of the stripes bled."

"Shut up."

"It's interesting how they play you and me off each other, isn't it? Punish one for what the other did."

"Fuck you, Gil."

"That's the problem, isn't it? No one will. Who knew these pricks would be more interested in how well we can drill than with how well we can be fucked? We're already pretty fucked over, don't you think? Two men have tried to escape so far, and both have been executed. By now we're too cursed far from home to have a hope of running back there before we starve, even if we could run. But I'll just try an escape now—maybe out onto the Lend as it looks pretty wild and uninhabited— if that's what it will take to get you moving. Because I would rather die than know I let you die after it's my fault you got sucked into this business just because I had to be a reckless asshole for no better reason than to piss off my family."

"Fuck you," said Ty, but he got up, then peed in a stream of strong-smelling urine so close to Gil's feet that he skipped back with a yelp of laughter.

A column of false prisoners was heading out to take a place in the vanguard. Several glanced over. Recognizing Ty, one called, "Heya, peaches, where's my kiss?"

Ty lunged for him, and Gil yanked him to a halt as the men laughed mockingly. "Get in line, Ty. Don't be an ass. They'll just beat you up again. Ignore them."

Without another word Ty trudged over to take a place in the ranks beside Adiki. Gil slipped into line behind them, forming up with the man with the cleft chin and gap-toothed grin and his two buddies just as the third whistle blew. Chief Roni strutted out from his tent as two guards pulled it swiftly down behind him.

Guards moved down the line, giving each man a gulp of water and a fist-size hank of coarse barley bread smeared with a coating of warm rice gruel. Gods, it tasted good, and even though the water was laced with rice vinegar he could have swallowed ten times more. They were allowed a brief space in which to eat. Meanwhile more guards walked along the ranks handing out the frail sticks—nothing stout enough to serve as a weapon—they marched with every day. The sticks stood in for spears to allow them to drill as they walked.

Adiki glanced over his shoulder. "I just heard a rumor two men went missing last night."

"The hells," Gil muttered. "We'll all get whipped, no doubt."

Gap Tooth said, "Think they got away? Hard to find a man out on the grass, don't you think?"

Gil was licking his fingers, wishing there was another drop of gruel. "If you don't die of thirst because you can't find water, you'll get dismembered by the lendings for trespassing on their territory."

Gap Tooth and his friends exchanged mocking grins. "Lendings? You mean like in the tales? I thought they were all gone long ago."

Adiki signaled to warn them to lower their voices. "I know the tales but I've never seen any of the other children of the Hundred, not even a demon."

"I think they're all just stories, even demons," said Gap Tooth as his friends nodded wisely. "Meant to scare us and keep us in our place while our foreign rulers rake in all our coin and our land claiming it's for our own good."

"My grandfather met the lendings," said Gil.

Gap Tooth snorted a laugh. "Did he now?"

"He did." The man's ignorance irritated Gil, who vividly recalled the solemn, stately grandfather, General Sengel, who had inspired so much awe in so many people. "He negotiated with them. They agreed on boundaries around the grasslands past which no human folk would pass."

Gap Tooth's amusement hardened into a stare so stone-like that Gil was suddenly sure he had seen it before. "You don't remember us, do you? Street rats like us must all look alike to a rich, spoiled lordling like you."

"Rich?" Gil laughed.

Tyras actually looked around as if he meant to offer a sarcastic rejoinder.

The *shwee-shwee-shwee!* whistle that always started the day's march broke over their conversation. A drummer picked up the patterns that commanded their steps, the same soldiers' drill Gil had learned as a child.

Attention! Eyes forward! Spears at ready!

Gil tapped the stick on the ground once, twice, and thrice, in unison with the others. The one thing that could make him forget his hunger was the discipline of the drill, even if it was just chanting martial songs and tales as they walked along.

March! beat the drummer.

The false prisoners always marched in two groups, one before and one behind the work gang. Once the vanguard got going, the work gang stepped out. In brisk unison they crossed the uneven ground toward the wide road called West Track that linked the city of Horn to the city of Olossi far to the south. Chief Roni counted off the work gang as they passed in rows of six.

The chief's sudden bark of command brought the drummer to a stuttering halt.

"Two men missing!" yelled Chief Roni.

From the road, men shouted in consternation, and this swirl of confusion within the vanguard caught the chief's attention.

Everyone looked that way. Men broke from the front lines to stumble onto the grassy verge and throw up. All Gil could think was what a waste of food it was.

The chief jogged away to the vanguard to investigate.

Adiki muttered, "Shit, this can't be good."

"Move up, move up," said the guards, chivvying them forward.

The vanguard parted, spilling off the road away from whatever had frightened them. Gil saw a strange jumble of rubbish scattered across the West Track's stone surface. Seated with his back to the debris was a man trussed in rope and blindfolded.

Chief Roni stopped dead where the remains of the vanguard quivered, each one trying to back away. A man retched. A bird's staccato call drifted from out on the grass: weet weet weet weet weet. Flies buzzed.

The chief grabbed the trussed man and dragged him roughly back over the ground as the fellow twisted, trying to get his feet under him. Throwing him down in front of the work gang, the chief ripped off the blindfold to reveal one of the older men, a quiet person who had never given any trouble that Gil recalled, only slogged along each day with head bowed.

"Tell me what happened!" growled Chief Roni.

The man wriggled in his bonds but did not answer.

"Tell me!"

The prisoner rolled on his side, his fingers twitching within the tight coil of rope.

"Oh fuck," murmured Gap Tooth, nudging Gil as if the gesture passed on a message.

Chief Roni had the look of a man pushed too far. He began screaming. "Tell me, you stupid fuck! How did this happen? What does it mean? Use your pissing mouth or I will..."

The man was still squirming, trying to get his hands free, and yet he said nothing.

With a roar more like panic than anger, the chief yelled at the nearest soldiers. "Piss in his pissing mouth until he talks! Do it! Do it!"

"I know him from Wolf Quarter; he's mute," whispered Gap Tooth.

"Mute?" Gil said.

"Unlike you, he can't talk or even make a noise. Probably got arrested in the first place for not answering when the cursed priests spoke to him."

Two men began peeing on the trussed-up man's head as two others kicked him every time he tried to roll over to hide his face.

"Back me up," said Gil as he finally made sense of the debris on the road and the swarm of insects hovering over it. A shudder rolled through his body. Bile scorched his throat. But the hells if he would let some hapless person be abused. "Ty. Adiki. Stay here."

He strode forward and had almost reached the chief before anyone noticed.

"Heya! Chief Roni! I can explain why he won't talk, and what happened to our friend on the road."

The way the chief and the nearby soldiers flinched at the sound of his voice would have made him laugh if he wasn't now getting an even closer look at the grotesque display strewn across the road. Gap Tooth had, in fact, followed, and Gil heard the other man grunt and choke as he realized that the debris was the dismembered remains of a person. Nausea churned through Gil's stomach but he managed to speak without spewing.

"This man is a mute. He can't answer your questions with his mouth."

The chief turned on them, eyes wild with what Gil could now identify as terror.

"His name is Avimon," added Gap Tooth in more of a mumble than a voice. "He's a shoemaker in Wolf Quarter. Story goes that he's never been able to make any kind of sound. He's trying to talk to you with his hands, Chief."

"Stop," said the chief to the soldiers, and they tucked themselves up tight and backed away. He gave Gap Tooth a nod of permission, and the man hurried forward to untie Avimon.

Men huddled in groups, trying not to look at the arms and legs and feet and hands, the head, the internal organs dug out of the eviscerated torso, the entrails covered by flies. The wind blew out of the east, mercifully carrying the smell away from them.

"Tell me what you know," said the chief to Gil.

No sense in giving up too much about his illustrious ancestry. "I am sure you can tell by looking at me that both of my grandfathers were Qin soldiers who rode into the Hundred with King Anjihosh. I heard a few stories straight from their lips, before they died. One of the things my father's father told me was that a few of the Qin soldiers got to pushing into the grasslands, thinking to carve out a herding life like the one they had come from back on the steppe. They grew up with flocks, movable houses, that sort of thing. In response the lendings would kill a man in this fashion as a warning not to cross the boundaries that had been agreed upon between them and the king."

"We are right here by the road," cried the chief hoarsely, "so how are we to know where the boundaries are? This never happened before on any of my runs!"

"How many runs have you made?" Gil asked, congratulating himself for his cleverness in probing with more questions while the chief was rattled. "On any of the other runs did men attempt to escape into the Lend?"

Chief Roni scratched at the back of his neck, thinking it over. But just as Gil thought the chief might actually reply, Gap Tooth set Avimon on his feet.

"Tell him to answer my question!" shouted the chief.

"He's mute, not deaf," mumbled Gap Tooth.

The mute man rubbed his wrists. Because he still had his back to the road he had not seen the horrific remains. The sketch he made of words was so simple and innocent that Gil wondered if he even had a full basket of wits.

"He went out to take a shit, Chief; says he got permission from the sentry," said Gap Tooth, reading the truncated hand-talk. "Then he stumbled around, heard something, got scared, got hit over the head, and when he woke up he was tied up and blindfolded. I'd believe him. Avimon the shoemaker was known as an honest man in Wolf Quarter, and there aren't many of them. I can't even call myself one."

He caught Gil's eye as he spoke and gave a wink. Gil couldn't help but grin.

"And what's your name?" the chief asked, studying Gap Tooth as if trying to decide if he had an ax hidden about his bare torso with which he meant to chop up the rest of them.

"Menon, Chief. I'm just a common street rat, a terrible disappointment to my hardworking parents. I mean no offense. Please don't hurt me."

"Let's get moving," said the chief, keeping his back stalwartly turned to the road.

The men moved out in staggered ranks, swinging wide to avoid the awful sight. Only when they left the night's campsite far behind did the columns tighten back up into military precision, feet slapping on the stone of the road. Men glanced frequently toward the grasslands rising to the east as if expecting lendings to charge out of the grass and slaughter them, not that a single one of them had the slightest idea of what a lending even looked like.

Why would the lendings strike now? Gil wondered. Was it a warning no one knew how to read? People had mostly forgotten the old covenants set up in ancient days, even the ones recently reinforced during the reigns of King Anjihosh and King Atani.

Beside him, Menon said, "That took guts for you to intervene like that."

"I don't like pissing on people who can't defend themselves. How do I know you?"

"You still don't remember us, do you, you prick? We fought over that Silver's coach. We tried to steal it from you."

Gil laughed until his stomach hurt, and for the first time in days even Ty cracked a smile.

"I'm Menon, as I said. This asshole who farts all the time is Kurard, and this tiny dick here is Posenas but don't bother to listen to anything he has to say because it is all shit."

Tyras looked over his shoulder at Gil, his glance a question, which was the most Gil had gotten out of him for days. Adiki raised an eyebrow.

Gil said, "No law against us forming our own little cohort, is there? I like to think I can trust a man who tried to steal what I had already stolen. Aui! The gods have a strange sense of humor."

In the vanguard a man began to chant the Tale of the Demon Hunter, the splendid story of a reeve who tracks a demon across the Hundred, although the story was actually a detailed tour of the location of all the known demon's coils. Even the weariest of men walked straighter as they called out the responses and thumped their useless sticks for emphasis as they strode along. Chief Roni paced the line, and after a while he fetched up walking alongside Gil.

"Don't think you've impressed me with your big talk," said the chief. "I crush lads like you because you think you know so much just because you have Qin grandfathers. Those men are all dead now, aren't they? But I'm alive and I'm right here watching for you to do one wrong thing. Do you understand me?"

Tyras, Adiki, Natas, Menon, Kurard, Posenas, and even piss-soaked Avimon all looked at him, waiting to see how he would answer. Yet for the first time in days, perversely, Gil felt a lightening in his heart. Maybe this was what it was like to climb Law Rock.

He ventured a falsely placating smile, the one he learned to use as a boy to worm his way out of mischief. "I won't give you any trouble, Chief Roni. I've learned my lesson seeing that poor man cut up like a cow at the butcher's shop. For all we know, you did it yourself to teach us all a lesson. One we will never forget."

"Don't get cocky, boy. You're laying it on too thick."

Gil braced himself for a fist or a knife, but instead the chief called for his horse.

"I've got my eye on you," he added before he rode away to the head of the line while they marched in the vanguard's dust. South, to points unknown. For the first time Gil really began to wonder where in the hells they were going, and why.

42

Awake before dawn Sarai lay curled on the mattress, chewing on her nails, until at last the sun came up. She dressed and carried her book out to the queen's garden, Tayum ten paces behind her. This was how it would be from now on.

She sank onto a bench and scrubbed her eyes until the tears stopped trying to flow. What if she never heard from Great-Aunt Tsania? Abrisho could withhold all communication if she did not submit. If she married Prince Tavahosh surely she would have some control over her own finances, some freedom of movement...

No. She wouldn't do it.

A screek-screek noise scraped at her ears. Beyond the wall the flag with crossed spears was being drawn up the pole of the commander's pavilion, cloth drooping shapelessly on this windless morning. She ran to the gate and slammed a fist against it as a startled Tayum hurried after.

"I wish to visit the commander's pavilion," she said into the closed grille.

The locks and latches clicked and the gate was opened just as Tayum reached her. She slipped through before he could grab her. There stood King Jehosh on the other side, smiling.

"I waited for you yesterday, Lady Sarai, but you never came...You've been crying." A frown tightened his eyes as Tayum appeared in the gap. The king spoke harshly in Sirni, and Sarai caught the gist of his anger: Had Queen Chorannah mistreated Lady Sarai because of the king's command that she take tea with him?

A woman walked out from behind the curve of the Assizes Tower and waved merrily at Sarai. With Jehosh still lecturing Tayum, Sarai hurried over to her. Kasarah's bright smile flattened to a look of concern, and she extended a hand.

Sarai grasped it. "Please...I..." She was out of breath, overcome by relief and fear.

Kasarah led her around to the back of the tower, where a small terrace overlooked the Istri Plain. Stray leaves swept its stones, and a single redbeak fluttered away as they walked closer. The view over a patchwork of fields and tidy villages would have captured Sarai's interest another time. Kasarah sat her on cushions at a low table where tea things and platters of food had been decoratively arranged. It would have been tempting if she had been hungry.

"You're shaking, Lady Sarai," she said, still holding Sarai's hand, her fingers cool and her grip comforting.

A flare of incandescent frustration flamed up inside her. "Can you get me out of here? Your brother showed me a secret passage that leads out of the king's chambers. You must know where it is, too. He had a key."

Kasarah's brows tightened. She glanced toward the sound of her father's voice, still berating Tayum. "I cannot move as freely in the upper palace as my brother can. You and I cannot walk through the palace or ask the aid of guards without being held for questioning. We might even be abused, if we met the wrong men, those drunk on power who don't fear the king. They might harm us as a means to insult him. I can't risk it."

Sarai scanned the tower from its roof down along its white-washed sides and shuttered windows marking rooms on each of its four floors to a narrow door. Unlike the formal entrance ramp at the front, this modest door was not chained and barred.

There was a more dangerous way to turn the queen against her, and it loped eagerly alongside her ever-present desire to investigate the hidden workings of the world. She stood, tugging Kasarah up with her.

"You said you would show me the demon's coil."

The princess hesitated, glancing again toward the unseen men, who were still arguing. Without a word she led Sarai to the door. It had no latch but rather a complicated lock whose mechanism was a puzzle. Kasarah hid its workings from Sarai's sight but Sarai listened to the pattern and tones of the clicks and their final clunk, trying to memorize the pattern.

Kasarah pushed the heavy door inward to reveal a corridor.

After the misery of the last few days it was not quite true that every thought fled Sarai's mind behind a brilliant flash of utter stark exhilaration, or that the expectation that she might actually see a demon's coil up close made the whole world light as with the blinding power of the rising sun. But it felt that way, all thoughts of Tavahosh obliterated.

A shadow fell on her neck. "Move quickly. A demon's haunts are forbidden even to a king."

Grinning like a mischievous child, Jehosh stepped past them into the dim corridor. They followed him into a musty hall lined with benches set in a semicircle facing a dais. Dust lay so heavy on the floor that each step left a print. Lines of light shone through gaps in age-warped shutters.

Kasarah released Sarai's hand to pick up an unlit lamp conveniently left beside the door.

"This way," said the king, taking the lamp from his daughter.

"What is this chamber?" Sarai asked.

"Back before my grandfather saved the Hundred, the land was ruled by demons. They called themselves Guardians, and pretended to act as judges. That is how assizes courts came to be set up in every region and town and village. People brought their conflicts, and the local assizes court settled the case. Difficult and important cases were brought to the attention of the so-called Guardians." He indicated the benches and the dais. "One or more demons would preside. Their word became law."

"If demons can see into the hearts of people, then they would always know the truth of any matter, would they not?"

"If you could see into the hearts of people, how would you be sure your own judgment was not compromised by your own selfish wishes?" he countered.

"I wonder the same thing. Yet how do we know which of our wishes are selfish, and which necessity? Isn't it always our duty to judge as righteously as we know how?"

He cocked his head to one side, examining her, then deftly sparked flint and lit the lamp. Oil hissed up its wick. The lamplight gave him an aura, shining golden on his face.

"Yet here we are, Lady Sarai, breaking the very law I, as king, swore to uphold. Selfish, or necessary? Do you want to go on?"

Her mirror tingled against her thigh. "Yes."

"Kasarah, you stay up here. Close the door, and keep watch."

The princess looked at Sarai and tilted her head as if asking Sarai's permission. But there was no time to reply because Sarai had to hurry after the impatient king. Kasarah could not help her, however sympathetic she seemed.

Beyond a stone archway, steps descended into the rock. He led the way quite boldly for a man who had just told her this journey was forbidden even for a king; a reckless rebel lived in him, too, she thought. Like Gil he was a man happy to be goaded into action. The stairs ended in a tiny anteroom with a single opening: a doorway whose lintel was carved with outstretched wings. Beyond lay a stygian hall without door or window whose dimensions she could not discern. By now the mirror prickled so harshly against her thigh that she set her book down on the last step and took the mirror from under her outer skirt, holding it up so its burnished surface faced the darkness.

To her shock, the floor of the hall started to gleam as if the polished surface of the mirror had woken it.

A demon's coil was indeed engraved into the rock like a ribbon of crystal. The king whistled softly as a delicate threadlike glamor intensified to trace a hexagonal spiral maze distorted with convoluted turns and reversals, so exactly like the one on Demon's Eye Peak that she wanted to measure it to compare. This massive spiral coiled around a center of writhing blue flame that looked and acted like the magical fire housed in the glass vessel in the tower of the estate where she had grown up, which only Ri Amarah women and girls were allowed to see.

She had been up in the flame tower the day she had decided to force her uncle to allow her to marry a man she had never met.

Breath fled. Her soul soared at the stunning mystery and beauty of the radiant path.

The mirror burned against her fingers. Blue light crawled along the lines incised onto the mirror's back. The engraving came very close to mirroring the demon's coil. Odd convolutions in the coil looked like the splintered remains of the diagonal lines cut across the spiral lines on the mirror's back.

The women of her people kept a magical blue flame trapped in glass vessels to protect themselves. Did the coils also cage magic, or were they some manner of lens or tool that channeled it?

Like strands blown astray from a spiderweb, threads of light chased from the mirror's face toward the entry point of the coil. When the thread touched the tip of the coil, light flared so strongly that she threw up her free arm to cover her eyes. Cold throbbed from the heart of the mirror, icing her face and freezing her hand until her bones ached.

"We should go back. This isn't safe." Each syllable of the king's whisper made pulses of light dance along the coil. He retreated to the arch. "Lady Sarai!"

Ri Amarah women carried mirrors not for vanity's sake. Magic, so Ri Amarah children were taught, was too dangerous for men. But girls had to be women before they were given a mirror of their own and taught these secrets. She hadn't married a Ri Amarah man but she was married and thus, by her people's custom, an adult woman. She had the right to know.

She eased forward across the floor right up to the entrance to the coil, its edge like glowing stone laid into the earth.

"Lady Sarai! Come back from there! It is death to touch a coil!"

She knelt and set the mirror down on the floor, faceup, then pushed it forward until the incised back slid fully onto the gleaming path although she still touched the handle.

A shivering force like the exhalation of a thousand whispers raced up her arm. At first, beneath the luminous blue pattern that shone through from the back, all she saw reflected in the mirror was her cheek with its scar making the flare of a crescent moon, her mouth open in awe, and her eyes dark with wonder.

Slowly, shadows churned up within the mirror's surface like a creature trying to break free of murky waters.

There shimmered into view a monstrous visage, a face whose single eye was a spiral coil grown into its flesh as a glittering scar. Threads of blue fire like burning veins shone on its face.

It spoke through a gash of a mouth.

"Don't wake them!"

She recoiled, dragging the mirror off the coil. With trembling hands she tucked it under her outer skirt.

The bright coil faded until its spiraling shape was nothing more than an afterimage swirling into oblivion, dwindling, and then vanished. She blinked perhaps ten times before she realized the solitary pinprick of light in the otherwise pitch-black chamber belonged to the lamp.

"Lady Sarai?" The lamp swayed as the king took several steps into the dark, brave man! Shadows hid his expression; lamplight pooled along the floor, revealing the steps behind him.

"Don't move, Your Highness. I'll walk toward you," she said.

"Are you injured?"

"No, Your Highness." She slid her feet along the stone floor, sure an abyss would yawn open at her feet and swallow her. Her pulse surged, heart thunderous in her ears. Words poured out as implications cascaded through her mind. "Are the coils natural outgrowths like the hexagonal patterns in a honeycomb or the seed spirals of sunflowers? Or are they magical constructions built according to an unknown principle of proportion that can safely house magic? Are the mirrors incised in imitation or are they also—"

She broke off, realizing she must not reveal Ri Amarah secrets. Stumbling in the dark, she pitched into the king hard enough that he staggered back and tripped on the steps. He went down with her on top. Her hand slipped down the silk of his kingly garb as she tried to steady herself against his body. He started laughing; she began laughing from the nervous energy rushing through her flesh and the hot urgent thoughts racing through her mind.

He leaned forward and kissed her on the mouth.

She scrambled off him, trying to catch her breath as she squeezed out words as if she had been running. "Your Highness, I beg your pardon and I am sure I do not mean to offend, but I hope I have not given you any reason to think I mean to bargain with such tools."

"The tools of seduction?" His dry tone calmed her a little. He made no further move, only studied her. "You might be a lilu sent to bewitch me, for I assure you I am utterly entranced not just by your attractive form but especially by the way you boldly and recklessly approached the demon's coil. What is the object you carry with you? It looks like a mirror, and thus it draws my gaze and reflects your beauty. Yet you hide it under your clothes."

The words teased her; he meant them to. He waited, gaze fixed on her.

All at once she remembered Kasarah's warning: *We might even be abused, if we met the wrong men.*

Something in her expression made him tip his head back as at a glimpse of rot beneath a shiny surface. He got to his feet.

"You are safe with me, Lady Sarai," he said curtly. "And frankly I prefer not to linger here knowing the coil could come back to life at any moment. Have the Ri Amarah woven demon magic into mirrors? Demons threaten the Hundred because they want to rule here again. They poisoned my father with their false promises and seductive words. Should I fear your people now, too?"

"No! We only want to be left in peace."

He cast her a disbelieving look and, after picking up the lamp, began to ascend. She grabbed her book and hurried after.

"Your people are infamous for their secretive nature and inscrutable machinations. Can I trust any of you? I don't think so."

She had to convince him. "You are king because of the provisions and coin my people gave to King Anjihosh years and years ago. If there is anyone you should not trust, it would be Queen Chorannah. That's why I was crying. I came to tell you..."

They reached the dusty, dim assizes court. He held the burning lamp between them as if he wasn't sure whether he would need to use it to fend her off. "To tell me what?"

After what he had seen, she had to make this proclamation scare him more than the woken coil did. "Queen Chorannah wants me to marry Prince Tavahosh. To fatten her treasury."

The words fell as into a pool of toxic silence. Kasarah appeared briefly at the edge of the light, over by the stairs rather than the corridor, and retreated into the darkness as if she didn't want her father to wonder how much she had seen and heard.

"Marry Tavahosh? Have you bewitched Chorannah? Is this the measure of Ri Amarah magic, that you can compel people to do your bidding and raise you to the heights of power?"

"I don't want to marry him. I want to retain my contract with Lord Gilaras."

"Curse that woman to all the hells. She's kept me looking in the wrong direction by feuding with Dia." He strode toward the corridor. "Come along. I've played about for too long."

"I don't want to marry Tavahosh," she repeated because she did not like the look on his face.

"Of course you will marry him." His tone frightened her more than had the inexplicable whisper of a mist-formed face. "Chorannah is using this upheaval as a decoy to conceal her real purpose. The coin. The work gangs. The building projects. All this talk of shrines is a disguise to hide their true plan to overthrow me. Men speak intimately with the women they are in bed with. How better than you in bed with Tavahosh to discover her plans? This will work very well."

43

"Captain?"

Kellas woke instantly and grabbed the knife tucked under his mattress. "Who are you?"

"Nevora, Captain."

"Ah, yes, the banner maker's daughter." He identified her form as an opaque block on the other side of the rice-paper-screened door. "What is the alarm?"

"A Silver has come begging for help, Captain. He claims you made him a promise. Should I turn him away?"

"No!" He sat up, shedding his quilt. "I'll come out."

Chief Oyard met him on the porch, where a Ri Amarah man paced with frantic energy, bracelets jangling. One end of the cloth that tightly wrapped his hair had come half untucked. Seeing Kellas, the distraught man knelt, grasped the captain's ankles, and touched his forehead to Kellas's sandaled feet. Kellas recognized him as the coachman he had spoken to weeks ago.

"Stand up, please, ver," Kellas said.

He remained kneeling. "I beg you, Captain. A mob has surrounded our compound in Wolf Quarter. They are beating at our gates and casting torches over the wall. The lane of row houses next to our wall has already caught fire. They mean to burn us out and kill us. There are soldiers there, but they are only watching, letting it happen!"

Kellas cocked his head. "I don't hear the fire drums."

"No one is coming!" The man broke into anguished sobs.

Kellas whistled the sharp high-low alarm. In answer a bell rang thrice, and thrice again, from the barracks. At his nod, Nevora ran across the square to alert the militia on loan from Lord Vanas. "Chief, I want you to go yourself to the fire watch in Wolf Quarter and see what is keeping them. Ver, you will show me the way to your compound."

"What can you and I do alone, Captain? I thought you might have the power to beg the king to aid us, just as it says in the old contract sealed between King Anjihosh and our forebears."

"There are four Ri Amarah compounds in Toskala, are there not? Are they all under attack?"

"I don't know. We are the only ones in Wolf Quarter. The others are richer and live in Flag Quarter."

"Thus more tempting targets, one might imagine."

"They have higher walls and the coin to hire guards," said the coachman. "We are just working people, like anyone. It was one of our men who was murdered some months ago. The mob is shouting that we made up the accusation of murder in order to get a young lord condemned to the work gang."

"So I have heard. It seems to me the Ri Amarah are taking the blame for the discontent and frustration people feel toward the palace. I'll do what I can."

At last the man clambered to his feet. He grasped one of Kellas's hands between his own, trembling. "My thanks, Captain. My thanks."

The first trainees were racing out to line up, still buckling boiled-leather coats and fumbling with staffs and knives. Chief

Oyard peeled off the first ten and headed out at a jog. Vanas's soldiers began to emerge from the warehouse in rambling confusion. Kellas went back inside and kitted himself out with the speed of long practice. Back on the porch he whistled the command to form into marching ranks. His company shifted with good discipline. All his people were ready while Vanas's soldiers were still milling around.

He beckoned to Nevora. "You're Toskalan born and bred. You know where the other Ri Amarah clans live?"

"Yes, Captain."

"Take Vanas's militiamen and split them into four groups. You take three groups, with a runner each, and set a guard at the other compounds. Send me word if there is any trouble."

"Yes, Captain!" Her face was shining with excitement. She was so cursed young.

He turned to young Sefi, now awake and standing at quivering attention. "Sefi, you will stay behind with the gate guards, using the fourth group of militia as reinforcement, and with a runner in case this is a diversion meant to pull us away from the lower palace."

"Yes, Captain!" In the weeks since Kellas's arrival the diffident, cringing young man had gained a brisk confidence that came from being trusted with responsibility.

Kellas led his recruits out at a trot. The coachman had the stamina of the desperate and at first kept up, although increasingly he stumbled and had to be supported. It was very late, only night lamps burning above the closed gates of dark compounds. As they entered Wolf Quarter, Kellas felt tension spark the air. He smelled smoke. Ash filtered through the glow of streetlamps.

Still he heard no fire drums, no alarm.

Fire could devastate Toskala. It was the greatest danger of all. The ugly growling of the beast called a mob grumbled through the air. They found a hundred or more in full prowl before the gates of a modest compound notable for the four-story tower at its center, which every Ri Amarah compound had. The agitated men shouted curses and taunted those inside to "show your faces" and "unbind your heads!" Unbelievably some reckless idiots had thrown torches and lit lanterns over the wall, and now smoke boiled up from inside. He heard horses snorting and stamping in fear, the coachmen's harness animals. A group of militiamen stood away from the mob, somewhat down the street. Kellas jogged over to them.

"Where's your captain?"

A man he did not recognize stepped forward. He was wearing an expensive brigandine coat of lacquered leather plate and had a sour face and one twitching eye. "Who are you?"

"I'm Captain Kellas, chief of security for the lower palace. Why haven't you driven away these troublemakers?"

"We have no orders."

"You can take initiative! Do you want the city to burn down?"

"We have no orders."

A roaring cheer rose from the mob as flames licked down the long tile roof of the compound's carriage house and stables.

"Let their sorcery put out the fire of justice!"

"Those Silvers murdered one of their own just to claw their way closer to the queen."

"Our blood feeds their treasury!"

With a shout, a group of men carrying a log slammed it into the gates as a battering ram. The gates shuddered, and the mob howled approvingly. Kellas gave up on the militia and ran back to his own people who had formed up as tight as a turtle in its shell.

A second hit on the gate by the log caused an audible crack and buckling.

The coachman grabbed Kellas's arm as soon as he stopped beside him. "We shall burn to death rather than allow our women and children be beaten and abused by the mob."

He nodded. "Get inside the wedge, ver, or you'll be picked off. Wolves! Attention! Use your shields as we trained. Punch through those who strike at you. Keep together. Ver, you must convince your people to let in mine so we can help you with an orderly evacuation."

Kellas whistled the command to advance, and his trainees pushed forward. Their determined shout of "Ya! Ya! Ya!" rang out over the belligerent cries of the crowd. People turned, trying to sort out what was happening. Men shoved and yelled, trying to block their path; his recruits were fewer in number but had the discipline of training. They shoved back with unity and thus better effectiveness, plowing toward the closed gates, shields locked to protect each other. Rocks slammed into their shields, their bodies, their headgear. Several stumbled, but they righted themselves as the press carried them along.

Horribly, fire leaped the wall and took hold on the shingled roofs of ordinary row houses along a lane that abutted the compound. Panicked people began running from the back lane into the crowd clutching children, dogs, and birdcages in their arms.

The chaos spread more quickly than the fire.

He himself cut sideways through the outermost layer of the throng. With his helmet tucked under an arm, his old face startled no one and in the confusion no one took a second look to realize he was armed. The turbulent churning of the crowd allowed him to get a better look at the loitering militiamen without them spotting him.

Smoke and hazy torchlight drenched the scene until shadow and shape were hard to tell apart, but he was cursed sure he saw Lord Vanas half hidden at the back, head turned to one side as he chatted to a soldier. The hells! Was that Jehosh?

What game was the king playing?

The fire drum finally began to beat, its rumble rolling through the air. Oyard had done his job. The shoving match between his people and the crowd slackened as the crowd gave way to superior discipline and his Wolves took up position to block the broken gate.

An unknown voice shouted, "It wasn't *these* Silvers who played the young lords false. It was them over in Flag Quarter!"

As the quarter's fire wagons laden with water and sand rumbled into view, the crowd melted away. When he turned to look again, Vanas and Jehosh and the militiamen were gone as if they had never been there.

It took most of the rest of the night to put out the fire; meanwhile he had his people stand guard over the scorched row houses and the battered compound. The Ri Amarah refused to leave their compound even when half its buildings were scorched and unsafe, nor was he allowed to enter to see what he could do to help. In the end all he could do was leave his weary, soot-stained Wolves on guard. Yet by their steady gazes he saw they were proud to be trusted with this duty.

He commandeered a horse. Wolf Quarter's streets lay quiet not with calm but with tension. Folk peeked out through shuttered windows. Men muttered in alleyways but did not confront him or the cohort that attended him. They rode to Flag Quarter to find the three Ri Amarah compounds untouched by the night's outburst. A few Ri Amarah men came out to hear his grim news.

"We had no trouble here tonight, but we have hired extra guards to protect ourselves," said a man named Abrisho. His confident manner contrasted with the coachman's anxious fear. Kellas thought him a man who was a little too sure of himself.

"Did you have warning of possible trouble, ver?"

"No warning, no. We are a cautious people, Captain. Our ancestors escaped worse persecution than this. Thus we always remain prepared. We removed most everything of value from our city households months ago, after the attacks in High Haldia."

"What of the marriage? It was your niece who was wed to Lord Gilaras Herelian, was it not? Why would people blame the Ri Amarah for his arrest?"

"Apologies, Captain. We do not speak of contracts and business to outsiders. This wave of violence will pass and all will be well again."

Kellas was not so sure. He left militia on guard for the rest of the night. Six of his young Wolves had taken injuries—three deep gashes, one broken arm, and two concussions—and he accompanied them back through the deserted streets to Guardian Bridge and the foot of Law Rock. The roofs and walls of the lower palace blocked his view of the base of the Thousand Steps but he saw lanterns ascending the face of the cliff; the steps were closed at night except in emergencies, or for the king.

Had he really seen Jehosh and Vanas? How did violence against the Ri Amarah benefit them? Why was the man Abrisho so sure this storm would soon be over? Either Jehosh wasn't telling Kellas something, or Jehosh didn't know all the currents washing down this stream.

After he stripped out of his armor and washed the ash off his hands and face, he sat for a long time in front of the altar with its flowers and lamp. The flame as beacon calmed his mind. The painting on the altar smiled on him with effortless compassion.

"Why do you love me?" he had asked her once. "My duty as a Black Wolf must come first. We will always live apart and love in secret as long as Anjihosh is alive. This could still end in disaster."

She had touched two fingers to his lips to silence him. "Never turn away a chance at joy, Kel. As for the other, no matter how tightly you harness those you mean to control, there is no way to know what will happen next. What matters is that we act when the moment demands action."

Jehosh was far more vulnerable than he had realized. Dia's goals and motives so far remained inscrutable, but if Chorannah's faction got its claws well hooked into the Hundred then the Beltak priests might impose any kind of stringent measures.

It had not been this way under King Anjihosh, who had allowed only the lower and thus most humble levels of the priesthood to attend on Queen Zayrah. Kellas realized now how much Chorannah and the priests needed each other: Chorannah needed their ability to act as intermediaries for her with the world outside the women's wing of the palace, and in return she offered their high exalted priests the foothold into the Hundred that Anjihosh had denied them.

Kellas needed trained people in place to back him up, not Vanas's slack troops and his own trainees, however much potential the recruits had showed in this brief but not at all deadly skirmish.

An arrow left in the quiver can make no impact, because it will never fly.

With a sigh he went to his desk. The letter took only a few strokes to brush although he felt each mark like it was being carved into his ribs. *There is no way to protect the ones you love.*

Granddaughter, you may join me.

In the morning he climbed Law Rock early and went to the reeve compound, threading his way through workmen whose hammering and sawing gave him a headache. An arrogant steward got in his way.

"No one is allowed in without authorization from the chief marshal." The steward was wearing princely red and white to mark his allegiance to Chorannah's sons.

He stepped right up into the man's officious face. "I am Captain

Kellas, chief of security at the lower palace. I am here to see Marshal Dannarah."

"You can't—"

"What did you say your name was?" No need to raise his voice. A hard stare usually took the piss out of them.

"Toughid."

"Toughid! Eiya! An honorable name is a high mark to live up to, is it not?"

"Yes, Captain," the man mumbled, by now sure that Kellas was mocking him.

"You will personally escort me to the marshal's cote, Steward Toughid."

The reeve hall was a large rectangular compound ringed by high walls except on the side overlooking the cliff. The compound had a wide front courtyard where eagles could land. Three large lofts faced the landing ground. The barracks, tack rooms, and storehouses were built into the outer walls, a lot of people crammed into a small space. At the back of the compound a small garden flourished, planted with troughs of sunburst and lazy-blue-blinks around a dry fountain. The marshal's cote had the malingering look of a structure that has gone unrepaired for years. Despite all the carpenters laboring around the lofts, he discerned not an oat's worth of work on the cracked tiles of the cote's roof or a porch made uneven by listing support posts.

Two soldiers in red-and-white tabards waited at the base of the steps that led up to the porch. The doors into the outer audience room were closed, but angry words spilled through them nevertheless.

"—you are hiding the girl from me!"

"What manner of child's tale are you telling yourself, Tavahosh?" The derision in Dannarah's tone was as rich and smooth as butter. "Now that you have assigned me to be marshal of your new courier service, I must send my reeves with messages. She is on courier duty."

"Then you don't even know what your own reeves are up to. I was warned that you would treat me with exactly this level of disrespect and incompetence. I should never have given in to my father's pleading and left you in charge."

"Since you are in charge, nephew, I need you to give me more carpenters. If I have to house four flights of courier reeves here instead of the current two, either we must expand both lofts and barracks or I will have to house most of my reeves and eagles outside Toskala. I can scarcely manage an efficient courier service if I have to send a courier to fetch a courier in order to send a courier out on courier duty."

"You defy me at your peril, Lady Dannarah. I told you the girl was to be branded as a slave. Slaves have no right to be reeves."

"That choice is not ours to make."

"So you erroneously claim. It turns out the slave was raised in a nest of outlaws. Sixteen soldiers were killed when the archon's soldiers went to arrest the family—"

"The hells!" Kellas muttered, and the two guards glanced at him suspiciously.

Inside the prince and his great-aunt went on quarreling.

"Why would her clan need arresting, Tavahosh? They are humble carters who sell firewood."

"You are such a fool, taken in by their lies. They made an unprovoked attack on the soldiers. When they are in my hands—and they will all come into my hands, I assure you, for the priests have a means to track those who have insulted the god—I will institute the old imperial punishment."

"Left to die of thirst in a cage by the road?"

"An example to all who pass!"

"You still have not explained to me what Lifka has to do with this regrettable incident."

"If you do not bring her to me, you will indeed regret it."

The door slammed aside. Prince Tavahosh stamped across the creaking porch and down the steps past Kellas without noticing him. To Kellas's amusement Steward Toughid scurried after the prince like a dog hoping for scraps, followed by the guards. Not a single steward, guard, or reeve remained in sight. He walked in on Lady Dannarah slicing a short scroll into jagged pieces.

"What in the hells do you want? Aui!" She set down the knife, put a hand over her eyes, let out a breath, and lowered the hand. "Captain Kellas. I did not expect you."

"Sixteen soldiers dead? Is this true?"

"If I knew, why would I tell you? I can keep secrets from you just as you have kept secrets from me."

He hooked his hands together behind his back. She rarely got into this high a temper, but when she did he knew better than to stoke the flames. "Well, then, Marshal, let me not keep you. I am come to ask if you will deliver a message to my home in Salya."

"My reeves are not your personal messenger service!"

"Nor do I believe they are. I ask this from my position as chief of security of the lower palace, under the king's authority. Last night there was a serious disturbance in the city—"

"I heard. I also heard your people were the first ones to bring order to the scene."

"The city militia had no orders to act, so I took action. If there is going to be more trouble in the city then I need a core of effective troops to really protect the lower palace."

"And you keep a core of effective troops in Salya?"

He hesitated for an instant too long.

She swept the cut-up pieces of scroll into an untidy pile,

but her gaze did not leave him. "Here's the thing that puzzles me still. The story goes that because Lord Seras was the son of my father's most brilliant general, he hoped to become king in Atani's place. To set himself on the throne while the army was in the north. But he didn't act alone. He had allies, men driving carts, their families, and hired soldiers. Several of these were later identified as men who had some time previously been whipped out of the Black Wolves for criminal activities and insubordination. That's why for the longest time I was sure you were party to the conspiracy, wittingly or unwittingly coerced by demons."

The accusation still stung, especially from her. "As easy to argue it was you behind the plot to kill him, Lady Dannarah."

"The hells! You don't really think I had anything to do with it."

"At the time, when I was convalescing, I could not help but think that if you hadn't assigned me to go with the army, I would have been with King Atani."

"You think your presence could have prevented his death? You were with him at the end, were you not?"

At the end.

He didn't want to remember, but he did.

44

Too late. Too late.

Fear hammers in Kellas's head as the eagle glides down the currents, following a road that is little more than a pair of wagon ruts winding through forest. Several isolated villages carve out their precarious existence here in the high foothills with the mountains towering at their backs. The goats and gardens and the sheds where pelts and fur are treated and stored for trade show no sign of trouble, seen from above. Tiny figures of people go about their business with scarcely a glance for the eagle and its reeve and passenger overhead.

He scans for any sign of the rear guard. When they skim over what appears to be the last night's campsite, now abandoned except for ashy fire pits and still-flattened grass, he finds himself so tense that the reeve speaks.

"No need to worry, Captain. The passenger harness is safe. River has never harmed a single person in all her years."

As if in answer, River squawks with the high-pitched and rather ridiculous noise that would be comical in other circumstances but he cannot laugh now. He cannot even speak. He doesn't care if the reeve thinks flying harnessed beneath the eagle frightens him; it does, and it doesn't matter that it does. All that matters is the threat to Atani.

"There!" cries the reeve, nudging him from behind with a knee and pointing with an elbow.

He stares at treetops and the tangled scar of the road, but he hasn't a reeve's skill at identifying the contours of the land from the air. The eagle banks to the left, shifting angle, and he sees it: bodies sprawled on the road, empty wagons with canvas covers flung every which way, an overturned cart with tent canvas rolled out over the ground, ten horses down. A kneeling man keeps himself upright by using a spear as a staff, then slowly pitches over as his wounds master him.

His throat closes as the fear slips its leash and opens its maw to devour him.

He is too late. The ambush has already happened.

His training kicks in, and his mind catalogs the sight as they fly over and bank around to find a landing place. The king and his entourage and carts were traveling south, down out of the foot-hills, and met a wagon train coming north up the track. Because the road has only one set of ruts, the wagoners split into two lines, one on each side of the road, to allow the king right-of-way.

If he had been in command he would never have allowed the king to keep riding and thus pass between the two rows of wagons.

But as the eagle descends with the speed that on another day would cause him to throw up from sheer terror, he sees children cowering behind the wagons and he knows how the ambush succeeded: The instigators used their families as cover to lull the king's Wolves into a false sense of security. Atani's reign has been peaceful except for the sporadic northern raids out of Ithik Eldim that Prince Jehosh has used as an excuse to instigate a war.

No one expected this.

They thump so hard on landing that he lurches forward and then slams back into the reeve, who curses and adds, sharply, "Quit twisting."

"You need to get back aloft to alert Marshal Dannarah. She was accompanying the king."

"The marshal is flying the advance scout for the king," says the young, female reeve, whose name Kellas does not even know. "Give me a moment to unhook us both, and the hells don't bolt or River will think you are prey. I'll find the marshal."

Bile rises in Kellas's throat and he has to swallow all of it: His fear, his anger, his grief, his raging sense of impotence. His hope, because he is cursed sure he does not see King Atani's body on the ground. Atani had been escorted by his six day-and-night bodyguards, eight stewards, and a cohort of thirty-six Black Wolves. Many people lie dead and wounded on the ground, many of them Wolves. Four of the day-and-night guards are dead and one is unconscious and by the blood bubbling from his parted lips he is likely dying. It is obvious from the angle and penetration of their wounds that they shielded the king with their own bodies. Two dead men wear the gold tabards marking them as soldiers under the command of Lord Seras in his capacity as governor of the province of Teriayne. The remaining men wear leather-scale armor and no identifying colors or symbols. A few are apparently unarmed workingmen and -women in laborers' clothes.

The moment the reeve walks him out from under the shadow of the eagle he runs toward the wagons. Chief Oyard limps out to meet him, leaning on a spear. The very young man he first met at the long-ago ambush when he uncovered a traitor within the Wolves has become an extremely fit and disciplined officer. Right now Oyard has blood on his trousers and scale coat, a seeping wound at his shoulder, and his left hand bound with a bloodstained cloth.

"What happened, Chief?"

"They said they were delivering salt and rice to the upland villages. They had children with them! A traveling clan of carters, it looked like. They courteously swung to either side—"

"Splitting their line and allowing the king's party to ride between them. Yes, I see the rest. Instead of rice and salt they were carrying armed men, hidden by the canvas covers."

Oyard rubs his eyes as if trying to smear away the soot of failure. Kellas can see he is fading, weakened by blood loss and pain.

"Where is the king?" he demands.

"We were trapped, easy prey for their first assault with arrows and spears, and our men hampered by not wanting to kill the children. Chief Tobuk broke the king out in search of defensible ground..." He gestures toward trampled undergrowth and broken branches marking a trail into the forest toward the ridgeline rising beyond. "Lord Seras followed in support—"

"Lord Seras is the man behind this attack!"

As the truth hits him Oyard sags, and Kellas catches him and eases him to the ground. Looking around, he spots several uninjured soldiers moving among the bodies and killing any of the injured among the enemy. A woman is sobbing over the body of an unarmed man but Kellas looks away. He cannot allow himself to be distracted. "Heya! Help me here!"

Six young Wolves trot over. "Why aren't you hurt?" he snaps, wishing it was Atani standing before him instead of them with their wary, tense faces.

"Captain Kellas!" All the young Wolves know of him but the one who answers, Vanas, is known to him because he has long been Jehosh's best friend…and Lord Seras's younger brother. "We were the rear guard. We just caught up."

"Very well. You!" He indicates Vanas, then changes his mind and indicates a different man. Best to keep Vanas close by him in case he is in on his brother's plot. "Stay here, and keep order and treat the wounded until Marshal Dannarah arrives to take charge. You five come with me."

He and the soldiers set off, following the trail of destruction, listening for sounds of fighting ahead. He asks names so he can more easily call orders: Ulyar, Auri, Tanard, Kedi.

Ulyar served under him briefly two years ago—nothing remarkable—and he does not know the other three. They find the body of an armed man—not a Wolf—twisted on the ground and then a second man slumped against a tree, both so close to death it isn't worth the trouble to kill them.

"Captain?" asks Vanas in a low voice. "Did the king's spies have no inkling of a plot?"

"Nothing." Kellas whacks the top off a sapling that is in his way, then another, but spares his sword the third blow although he really wants to fell every tree within sight with a burst of fury at his own incompetence and failure. He should have known something was brewing. "Be sure we will not rest until we have recovered him and brought all the conspirators to justice."

Branches rustle ahead. He gestures an order; they fan out, faces grim, swords ready.

Instead of enemies they discover a woman and two children huddling beneath a bushy milk-sap tree. The older child has an arrow in its hip, the shaft broken off. It stares at them with pain-filled eyes as the woman lifts begging hands.

"Please help us. We knew nothing. We ran when the fighting started."

Her plea scrapes at him but he nods at the soldiers and they move on without an answer. The day is cool and the sky clear. Except for their own footfalls and the creak of their leather-scale coats they hear no sign of fighting men but they know they are following the right trail when they find two more men, one dead gold tabard belonging to Lord Seras and one unmarked attacker trying to crawl away into the brush. Kellas signals, and Auri dispatches him as the rest push on. Birds warble songs he does not recognize, for he grew up in the city.

Abruptly Ulyar whispers. His drawn-out vowels and the slow roll of his words reveal a northern hill country origin. "That's the fourth time I've heard the spark's call, Captain. Don't you find that odd?"

"What is a spark?"

"It's a mountain bird. That high-pitched whistle that cracks..." He gives a creditable imitation, a distinctive call Kellas realizes he has heard without making note of it.

"We are in the mountains, are we not?"

Ulyar shakes his head. He has a scar on the back of his neck, an injury that just missed his spine. "I grew up in Amsharith. Sparks nest in the rock above the tree line. They don't fly in the forest. That's no spark."

"Make a wedge," says Kellas.

Without breaking stride they shift from double file to a wedge with three in front, two behind, and a single man at the back, able to shift quickly to face three men toward any threat. Fortunately the undergrowth is thinning as they climb the slope so it is possible to move without breaking formation. He studies the young Wolves. Jaws clenched, backs straight, weapons ready: They are ashamed of having lost the king, as they should be, and thus determined to make things right. Vanas looks as stunned as any of the others, but it can be hard to tell.

A bird calls with a falling lilt of notes, not the spark this time but a marsh chat that lives in the boggy sinks around Salya. No marsh chat would fly here.

A branch snaps in the trees behind them. At the rear Ulyar swings around to aim his crossbow toward the sound. A young woman with a baby in a sling staggers out of the trees, wide-eyed and shivering, gripping a walking staff as if it is the only thing keeping her upright. She looks foreign with the eye-fold and pale-golden-bronze skin Kellas associates with the Silvers, but no Ri Amarah woman uncovers her face in public. No Ri Amarah woman would be traveling with humble, treacherous carters out in this wilderness away from her secretive clan.

One of the young Wolves whistles under his breath and for a jarring instant Kellas sees past his mission to note her unexpectedly stunning loveliness. Irritated at his lapse of discipline, he examines her to see if she is concealing a weapon.

"Stay back, verea," calls Kellas. The baby stirs with a questioning, anxious babble, cut off by the mother giving the infant a finger to suckle on. "We mean you and the child no harm."

She stares without speaking in a way that makes him wonder if she is deaf or mute. Then she blurts out in perfectly ordinary Hundred-speech, "I can't lose my man. I have no one else. Please don't kill him, ver. He and his uncle needed the money.

They didn't know until it was too late to leave without the lord killing us. Please believe me."

"Where are they?" Kellas asks. "How many are left?"

"I don't know. It all happened so fast. I ran after them and fell behind."

Maybe she is telling the truth. Maybe she lies. She wears a taloos of ordinary cotton like any ordinary woman, the cloth grimy and rumpled. Her arms are not those of a fighter or even of someone who has engaged in hard physical labor. If she means to use the staff as a weapon she's not had much training, so he judges her a lesser threat.

A distant shout catches his ear, rolling on the wind down from the top of the ridge.

"Move!" he commands.

They scramble up an increasingly steep slope clumped with sedge grass and straggling vines. At the top of the ridge amid pine and juniper they discover a game trail. People passed this way recently, rockrose and broom trodden down, a scrap of fabric caught on a twig, a spray of blood. It is simple to tell which way the Wolves have gone: Upslope on the trail a man lies on his back, one eye open and sightless and the other a pool of blood where a blade flayed off half his face. The setting sun pours a shimmering golden gleam over the corpse. Beyond rises a knobby crown of rock rimmed with shrubs and twisted juniper, exactly the sort of defensible position a beleaguered cohort of Wolves would seek. Below, soft footfalls draw his attention: The young woman is following them, puffing as she climbs the steep slope with a look of fixed desperation.

"What do we do about her, Captain?" whispers one of the Wolves.

"Nothing."

Driven as by a whip, mind fixed to his purpose, Kellas runs for the tower of rock. With the five Wolves spread out around him he easily scales the height, which rises no more than the height of three men. They fetch up behind a convenient stand of mountain-blue swaying in the wind. Its scent fills his lungs as he crawls forward on elbows and knees to see what awaits them.

The crown has a flat plateau no more than a spear's toss in width and length, rimmed with twisted juniper, and on its east face a slab of higher rock creates several deep overhangs like shallow caves. Deep within one of the overhangs shines a metallic gleam. Has Atani led his men to a demon's coil, the strange artifacts that in Kellas's youth were known as Guardian altars?

He blinks and realizes the man he is looking for stands in plain view in the middle of the tiny plateau. The king's riding clothes are scuffed and untidy but he is alive, with his remaining bodyguard on his right and a grizzled veteran Wolf on his left. A circle of sixteen Wolves surround a group of kneeling men with hands on their heads in the traditional pose of surrender. These are evidently the last sixteen survivors from the unmarked ambushers, although four wear no scale coat and have the callused hands of carters. By drawing the fight out of the confined space between wagons, the Wolves have won their victory.

But the king isn't yet safe.

Six men wearing the gold tabards of Teriayne stand off to the south, guarding what seems to be a path up the back side of the knob of rock. Lord Seras waits beside them. He is a burly man of thirty-four. Seras and Vanas look quite a bit alike. Both have the broad cheekbones and stockier stature of the foreign-born Qin soldiers. Like most younger sons of the Qin soldiers who came to the Hundred with Anjihosh, Vanas went into the Wolves to prove himself.

Unlike his spear- and sword-wielding men, Lord Seras holds no weapon. One might think him at ease now the king is safe and the threat foiled, except he shifts from foot to foot as he watches the famously tranquil king rip into Chief Tobuk.

"Once they lay down their arms, as these have done, we do not execute them. The carters were not armed at all. They ran because they were afraid."

"But Your Highness, they tried to kill you. They were in on the plot."

"And they will stand trial for the offense. That is how the law works. Law is our shield. We do not govern by the sword. Furthermore we can only discover who hatched the plot if we have someone to question." He turns his gaze from Chief Tobuk, braced at attention to better absorb the reprimand, to the kneeling men. "Now let me ask again. Who hired you? Who do you work for?"

The light changes as the sun touches the horizon. Silence sinks like the weight of anguish as the wind abruptly stills. None of the defeated men looks up. It's as if they already know what Atani is, even though only ten people in the whole wide world have ever known who and what he truly is.

There are three kinds of demons in the Hundred.

There are ordinary demons, called demon-hearts in the old tales.

There are cloaked demons, once called Guardians, whose demon skin gives them terrible powers. Most people believe that ordinary demons and cloaked demons are the only kinds of demons. But Kellas knows better.

Atani and his hidden sister, the girl called Arasit, are also demons. Anjihosh sired both Atani and Arasit, it's true, but their genesis as demons is far stranger. In dark days years ago, Mai found refuge beside a pool of liquid blue fire. The very bones and flesh of the two children she gave birth to are saturated with the substance of mysterious creatures called firelings, one of the Eight Children of the Four Mothers who gave birth to the Hundred according to the ancient tale.

Arasit is scarcely human at all. Kellas has seen her struck by lightning and laugh as if the jolt merely tickled her. Like the nine who wear cloaks she can rip open a human mind and look into it as easily as a cook cracks open a crab's shell. But that isn't all she can do.

Atani is almost as human as any other person. He cannot see into the thoughts of others, but he senses emotions and can use his gaze and voice to influence people's actions. Like his sister he can blot out of a person's mind the last tangled skein of their most recent memory so it is erased as if it never was. Unlike Arasit, who has few compunctions, this last is a particularly cruel gift he has only used three times.

"Look at me," says the king in the voice no one dares disobey because it is a demon's voice, subtle and staggering and calm. "Do not lie for I will know if you are lying."

Lord Seras extends a hand to one of his soldiers to take the man's spear.

Kellas jumps up, whistling the alert that all Wolves know.

"Vanas, stay here as rear guard," he says.

He crashes out from the branches as Atani's Wolves spin around, weapons raised to confront this new threat. When they recognize their captain and five fellow Wolves, they relax infinitesimally. But Kellas sprints forward, seeing Seras's hand close around the shaft of a spear.

He cries, "Beware Lord Seras—"

"Captain Kellas is the traitor! The demons have their claws into him!" shouts Seras.

Their hesitation is all Seras needs. He flings the weapon toward the knot of men as if at Kellas. Suddenly everyone is shouting at once as Atani goes down beneath one of his bodyguards.

Seras's voice rings out. "The Wolves are in Kellas's power. Strike to save the king!"

At that instant Kellas must choose to go to the king or go after Seras.

His thoughts race, and the scene around him slows until he can mark every piece of it: the bodyguard with the spear in his back he has taken to save his king; Atani squirming to get out from under; the Wolves hesitating as their captain and brother Wolves race toward them like attackers; Vanas holding the rear guard as ordered; the gold tabards bolting forward with swords drawn; the surrendered men leaping up as they see their chance to escape.

He dodges left, headed toward Seras as Seras hefts another spear. A stumbling man blocks his path. Whatever he is, he is no Wolf, and he is in the way. Kellas cuts him down because he has to get to Seras before the spear is cast.

"Isar!" A woman darts up beside him, swinging a staff. Its blow catches him off guard and he staggers sideways. She flings herself down beside the fallen man, grabbing a knife from the man's boot. As Kellas rights himself, she slashes at him.

He catches the knife's edge on his blade, then cuts inside. Too late his eye registers the sling with the baby tucked inside. He pulls the blow.

In a desperate frenzy of defense she leaps in, jabbing at him with a blow that thumps up under the flap of his armored coat. He counterpunches with the hilt of his sword. The cross-hilt slams into her face, puncturing her eye. Liquid spatters. Her scream and the spasm with which she jerks away, her hand shoving off his chest, rock him. As he twists to gain balance, his blade comes down on the baby's head. Flesh parts beneath the edge.

But he is already moving, jumping over the woman as she collapses.

"Traitor!" The word sparks amid the clamor, and Kellas can't even tell who shouted it.

Atani rolls the wounded bodyguard off as the Wolves scatter to catch the fleeing ambushers.

"My lord! Stay down! Lord Seras is the traitor!" Kellas glances around but he has lost track of Seras. His vision blurs. A terrible pain blossoms in his side as he realizes the woman's knife penetrated his flesh.

Atani does not stay down. He stands, the cursed fool, and whistles in the way Kellas taught him years ago, the sound so shrill and penetrating it chokes the clamor and confusion. "Stand down! Everyone! Stand down!"

His voice has magic.

Soldiers pause, obedient to his will.

The baby is wailing. The king strides to where the woman has fallen on top of the man she ran to. One side of her face has become a ruin. The cotton pulled tight across her breasts has soaked through but not with blood: Her milk has let down. Its warm smell blends with the iron of blood and the stink of urine and voided bowels.

Her fall has dislodged the sling, spilling the baby onto the dirt. The infant's cheek lies opened to the bone, skin peeled up. Blood paints its eyes and hair, and it is screaming.

Atani kneels beside the young woman. Her taloos has unwound enough to reveal an unexpectedly fine silk undervest, garb only a very rich woman can afford. Seeing this, the king slices off strips of silk and binds the baby's face, then tucks the little body against his chest. Its squalls cease the moment he looks into its dark eyes.

"This woman is Ri Amarah," says the king. "How is she come to leave her people and fall in with this group?"

Too late Kellas sees Seras pushing forward through a screen of his own men, the king's back to him.

"Atani, beware!" He can place himself in the way. He can take the spear in his own heart.

He leaps forward, but instead he is so weak that he stumbles.

Atani staggers as if punched from behind. His eyebrows draw down in puzzlement. Still grasping the infant, the king pitches forward into Kellas's arms, the baby caught between them.

A spear sticks out of the king's back, its shaft tilted crazily like a grotesque ornament.

Another spear passes over Kellas's bent back and buries itself in Seras's chest. Vanas races into view and cuts his brother's throat as the man lies twitching on the ground.

"Curse you to the hells!" Vanas shrieks, choked with rage. "Curse you to all the hells, Seras!"

The fallen man has risen to his knees, sobbing: "Nadit! Stay with me, my darling!"

The Black Wolves stare in shock. An eagle and reeve appear in the heavens, circling down. The whole world eddies around this one point.

Blood trickles from Atani's nose. His gaze tracks to the overhang. A light shudders in the dimness, tracing a knotted pattern that sears into Kellas's throbbing vision. Through its hazy, intangible contours he can see only one thing: The generous, joyful boy who laughed as his little sister beat him at a child's game is dying in his arms.

"Arasit is coming," Atani whispers. "Don't let them kill her, Captain."

A faintly wry smile creases Kellas's lips. "As if they could kill one like her. Can the coil not heal you as it does the others, Atani? Let me carry you there."

He tries to rise but his legs give out from under him, and he finally realizes how deep is the wound in his side.

"Too late," whispers Atani. "I am weighted with too much flesh to be healed as they are. Captain, I rely on you ... on you to remain loyal..."

The light leaves his eyes. Flesh transforms to mere meat.

The baby begins screaming again.

There is no healing when the spirit departs the body. There is only emptiness.

The demon's coil flares so brightly that the entire scene is lit as by a thousand lamps. Deadly Arasit shines as she appears on the coil. She is the only demon who can walk through one coil across vast distances onto another, because her substance is more fireling than flesh. Her brilliance reflects off a scuffed bronze mirror tied by a leather cord to the belt of the dead Ri Amarah woman, mirrors reflecting mirrors until the world is nothing but glare.

Then darkness falls with a hammer, and he collapses beside the inconsolable baby and the corpse of the man he swore on his life and honor to protect.

"He still died, even though you were there, and everyone saw that you knew the demon, even though the creature escaped," Dannarah was saying.

Kellas climbed out of the hole of memory and recalled that he was seated in the marshal's cote, trying to convince Dannarah to take a message to Salya.

Oblivious to his silence, she had started piling the cut paper into an unsteady pillar as if to build a new memory out of sundered truths. "Let me tell you a thing I've never mentioned before, Captain. On his deathbed, my father told me that of all the people still living, the only one I could trust to be honest with me was *you*. All of his original Qin bodyguard were dead by then, of course. I couldn't help but notice that he did not say Atani."

Now he regretted letting emotion rule his words. He should have said nothing about ever having had any suspicions of her being involved in Atani's death.

She folded her hands beside the pile of torn paper and burned him with her glare. "Tell me how and why my supposed plot to murder my beloved brother would have unfolded."

"You separated me from Atani and told me to kill Jehosh. Had they both died, you would have been left to act as regent for the younger boys."

To his surprise she nodded. "A reasonable plan. But as I know you know, I had nothing to do with Atani's death. It hurt me more than anyone, in my heart and also in my life and ambition."

She struck flint and spark to light a lamp. One by one she fed scraps to the flame, letting the paper flare in her fingers and afterward dusting the ash to the table. The scrape of saws and adzes and the knocking of hammers gave the only sign of nearby life except for a pair of gold-feathered sun-wings chirping under the eaves.

"Then why did you ask me to go with the army and kill Jehosh?"

She looked up, the weathering of her many years evident on her face. The wind and rain and sky had kept her strong. "Because I didn't trust Jehosh not to ruin what my brilliant father accomplished. King Anjihosh the Glorious took a chaotic, strife-ridden land and made it peaceful, orderly, and prosperous. Atani was a good steward of that peace. Jehosh was too eager to go to war. It's true he has acquitted himself well in the field, but at home he puts his own desires and whims before the needs of the Hundred. I can't help but see what has become of the palace during Jehosh's reign and believe that I was right to ask you to kill him. The court has splintered into at least four factions because Jehosh is lazy and thus weak."

"Four? Jehosh, Chorannah, Dia."

"A person is a fool who doesn't see that Lord Vanas is looking out for his own interests. Are you a fool, Captain?"

"I try not to be."

"The Hundred became strong because my father made it strong. It is the duty of his heirs to rule with strength and wisdom. Jehosh is not a strong ruler and I am not convinced he ever can be. I certainly can't trust either queen. We are entering a dangerous time for King Anjihosh's legacy. You know it as well as I do."

"I do know it," he agreed. "Which is why I ask you to see this message taken to Salya."

She held out a hand. "Very well."

He handed her the folded and sealed paper.

She tapped the paper against her arm, then set her gaze on him in a way that made him understand he could not look away. "Where did Atani's household go, after he died?"

"Your question takes me by surprise. Have you had no contact with them since his death?"

"I saw Queen Yevah briefly in the palace after Atani's death when everyone was arguing over the funeral rites and how to punish the conspirators and Lord Seras's helpless sons. After that fiasco of castrating innocent boys I was too angry to stay. Then I was too busy with the administration of the reeve halls. Then Jehosh returned from his first war and threw me out as chief marshal. I busied myself as marshal of Horn Hall, and I knew I was not welcome at the palace...So, I haven't seen her for twenty years. Yet I feel I would have heard if Yevah had died. Surely Jehosh would mourn his mother's passing."

He hoped and prayed that the years they had been separated made him opaque to her. "Why do you care after all this time, if you have not sought contact with her before this?"

"It has come to my attention that there may have been things about his life that Atani never told me. I'm just trying to thread some broken chains together. Where did they go?"

"Queen Yevah has an estate outside Toskala."

"I have ascertained that she does not live there, Captain. Where else might she have gone?"

"Queen Zayrah on her deathbed willed her estate on the Beacon Coast to Atani. I always suspected she did it to give Lady Eiko some place to stay, for as you know Lady Eiko cared for Atani's mother as kindly as if she were the queen's own kinswoman and not just Atani's lover."

"Aui! Is that meant to put me in my place, Captain? That I did not care properly for my mother?"

"Nothing of the kind, Lady Dannarah," he retorted more sharply than he meant to. "It happened that way. That is all."

"That is never all. Anyway, I have ascertained they aren't there, either. Have you anything else to tell me?"

He had seen her angry many times but something deeper coiled in her words now, and he dreaded it. "I do not know what else you wish to know."

"Was my brother a demon?"

The words tumbled through his mind like avalanching rocks ripping a gouge into a mountainside. His throat closed over any reply, because this was the most dangerous ground of all.

She held the folded paper he had given her over the flame until the edges began to brown, then withdrew it before it caught on fire. "When I was in Salya at your clan's house I saw a cloaked demon, who called herself Marit. I saw your granddaughter Fohiono nod her head at this demon as if the creature was familiar and ordinary to her rather than a threat. Does Plum Blossom Clan consort with demons, Captain?"

"What do you mean, Lady Dannarah?" He kept his voice placid, but he felt as if his ears were in flames because he could see no way this conversation was not about to go wrong in a hundred different directions.

"The demon tried to seduce me with her lies and lures into believing that no demons ever wanted Atani dead. But my father taught me that demons hate the king. Demons want to keep the Hundred weak and fractured instead of strong and unified. Killing Atani brought a weak ruler like Jehosh to the throne, and now indeed the court is fracturing."

She glanced at the paper half crumpled in her hand, and let it drop. It dipped winglike before clapping onto the desk. Then she rose to confront him.

"Tell me the truth, Captain. Was Atani a demon?"

He bowed his head, ticking over the words, the deeds, the years. Finally he looked up, knowing he would rue the words he was about to say. "The things your brother did not choose to tell you, I cannot reveal. That is the oath I made to him."

A cold anger shut down her face, the look of a person who has just decided you cannot be trusted. Once he had seen the same expression cloud King Anjihosh's face: the day Anjihosh finally discovered that Kellas had defied him by becoming the secret lover of the woman forbidden to all men if Anji could not have her.

Kellas really had expected to die that day. That instant. Anjihosh's sword had already scraped out of its scabbard.

Atani had saved him by intervening in the only way possible: by making his father forget the damning piece of evidence that had betrayed Kellas. Half a year later Anjihosh was dead at sixty, felled by disease and entirely oblivious to the fact he had once briefly known Kellas was no longer his loyal soldier.

Yet secrets have a way of bending around to stab a person in the back when least expected. Kellas had flattered himself with the idea that Dannarah was still a little infatuated with him in exactly the way she had been when she was seventeen. But she had lived a long and fruitful life far beyond that one anomalous year. He had been a rung on her ladder, as she had surmounted one by one the strictures laid on her by the strict palace protocol that was a legacy of Sirniakan customs brought into the Hundred by her conquering father. He saw the truth of how very far past her youthful self she had grown. She studied him with a flat stare, exactly as her brilliant and ruthless father had done on that long-ago day.

"Very well, Captain. It suits my purpose to have your message delivered to Salya. So it will be done. You are dismissed."

"Lady Dannarah..."

"You are dismissed."

45

Sarai woke at dawn, tired but wide awake. She had used up her entire week's ration of lamp oil by staying up half the night to write down in code her every impression of the demon's coil and then making a separate copy for Tsania. Just as she made ready to leave for the garden, eager to share all her thoughts with Princess Kasarah and the king, the door slid open and Tayum beckoned. He escorted her to the chamber where she had last seen her uncle, and placed himself on guard.

The door opened. She peered around the screen, hoping she could convince her uncle to attach this page to the letter for Tsania she had already given him.

Prince Tavahosh entered the room, alone.

The hells! She jerked back out of sight. By Ri Amarah custom a man was never alone with any adult woman except his wife. A woman alone with a man was assumed to have had sexual relations with him. She clutched the mirror beneath her skirts, wondering if it was solid enough to bash the prince over the head without breaking.

Tavahosh sat on the other side of the screen, speaking in labored Hundred-speech sprinkled with Sirni words and phrases she was coming to understand. "A fine morning, Lady Sarai."

"It is a fine morning, Your Highness."

"The correct address is Your Exalted Highness, Lady Sarai. I am a prince and I am also a priest on the exalted ladder of service to the Shining One."

"Yes, Your Exalted Highness. It must be tiring to have to change from prince's clothing to priest's clothing every day."

"No work is tiring in the service of the Shining One. All that we do reflects the glory of the Shining One Who Rules Alone."

"Ah. Of course for a person with a holy calling such holy work would seem most pleasing."

"Yes, you understand me, Lady Sarai. I was informed that your understanding is superior. It is a shame you are so old to be wed for the first time. Please do not feel you need worry, for I do not find your condition shameful."

She opened her mouth and closed it. Fortunately the tea tray arrived. The prince waited politely while she poured a cup for him and one for herself. Cautiously she pushed his cup forward, and watched his hands embrace it. They were neatly manicured and ordinary, smudged on the right little finger and forefinger with faint ink marks; not the hands of a laborer but not those of a man who did nothing.

Their isolation was so complete that she heard him sip. She raised the cup to her lips but its powerfully sweet smell made her throat close and she set down the cup without drinking.

"You are about the same age I am, Your Exalted Highness. Are you already wed?"

"Of course. To Princess Ernisah, a cousin twice removed. She is born into the imperial family of Sirniaka."

"I have not met her in the queen's chambers. I would have thought such a woman would sit next to the queen."

"She dwells in the country according to my honored mother's wish, with our two young sons."

"You have two sons already!"

"Yes, they are healthy boys," he said with a young father's modest pride, "a three-year-old and an infant."

"You must have been very young when you married Princess Ernisah. Your older brother, His Highness Prince Farihosh—is he married, too?"

His hesitation imperfectly concealed an exhalation, but she could not interpret his feelings from the brief sound. "No, he is not."

"Then I hope and pray you are as generous in your brother's case as in mine and do not find his unmarried situation to be shameful, either. He is two years older than I am!"

"You jest with me, Lady Sarai. He will marry soon."

"Is he already betrothed? When he marries, will his new wife live here in the palace or out at a quiet country estate like yours?"

He cleared his throat and made a business of setting down his cup as if by these small gestures he was trying to make something known to her. "Too many questions in a woman make her bitter like rotten fruit. Now, as I was saying, it is to your credit that you display a natural reluctance to be seen leaping from one man to the next. Nor would I wish to bind myself to a woman stained by greedful lust."

She choked down a hysterical chuckle. What would he think if he could have seen her and Elit embracing their greedful lust back in Elsharat? Or her and Gil in the prison, for that matter. Or his father kissing her on the tower stairs!

"Furthermore I am obliged to remind you of your obligation to your people."

"What do you mean?" she broke in despite his rejoinder about questions.

"You must exert yourself to please the other ladies, Lady Sarai. The mood in the city is troubling. Many whisper against the Silvers, saying they have amassed wealth by stealing it."

"My people have stolen nothing, Your Exalted Highness."

"Why your people are continually accused of theft rather than frugal business practices remains a puzzle. I have chewed through this matter—that is a poetic way of phrasing it, you comprehend—at some length. Stubbornness causes people to become suspicious of you because you refuse to embrace the proper way of life and instead cling to foreign customs. By your own actions you Silvers make people wonder if you are trustworthy."

"We call ourselves Ri Amarah," she said wearily.

"Yes, so I am aware, but most people call you Silvers because of the bracelets your men wear."

"Oh! Do they? I never knew that, Your Exalted Highness!"

"Then I am pleased to have been the one to enlighten you."

She could either cast the tea at where she supposed his face to be or drink to stop herself from the gesture, so she drank. At once she coughed, for this was not the usual brew.

"Lady Sarai?"

Her tongue stung from the tea. "If you are suggesting that by marrying you I will protect my clan, I would remind you that the king of the Hundred already protects the Ri Amarah according to a covenant sealed between King Anjihosh the Glorious Unifier and my people."

"That was a long time ago, Lady Sarai. People forget. Now, let me inform you as to my schedule."

How quickly she had forgotten: the taste of the tea dissolving on her tongue was muzz. Flowering muzz decorated the gardens of lovers not because it instilled passion but because it brought on a woman's bleeding when she did not wish to be pregnant.

"...at my convocation at Horn Hall I will be ceremoniously invested with the bronze baton, gold sash, iron diadem, silver cape, copper chain, and horn whistle of the chief marshal's office..."

They wanted her to miscarry so no legal impediment stood in the way of a hasty marriage and access to her family's coin.

"...when I return from the convocation our marriage feast will be celebrated. Afterward you and I will consummate the contract and thus seal our flesh as one, never to be unbound..."

How much had she swallowed? She clasped her arms over her belly.

"...so we will be part of the greater unification. It is the will of the Shining One that the land of a hundred gods and quarrels be brought firmly under the sheltering sword of Beltak so every person's spirit may be granted the peace of His blessing bowl..."

The words jarred her out of her shock. She got her mouth to open. "Is that why so many shrines are being built? Will you require every person to visit the Beltak shrines? Or only those who wish to, as is the current practice?"

She could hear him frown as he gave a little huff of exasperation.

"I had not yet finished explaining the matter to you, Lady Sarai. In the future it would behoove you to wait until I am done."

What an ass! as Gil would say. Elit used words less; she would have acted it out with a cocky strut and a mimicry of rooster calling. Sarai choked down an inopportune giggle, which came out as a choked gurgle.

Fortunately he was still speaking. "That is why Queen Dia and her children are a pernicious presence within the court, worshipping as they do a bloodthirsty two-faced god. As it is said in the Poem of the Wanderer, fifth chapter, fourth stanza, second verse, *Two faces make a liar of a man*. How much more true of a god! My gracious and honored mother wishes to keep you close by her to protect you from their malign influence. Also she has become fond of you."

Fond of my coin!

"I know you will follow her wishes in all things. As it is written, *Dutiful obedience is a woman's glory...*"

As he droned on she trickled the tea all along the edge where the mats met the wall, hoping the darker stitching of the seam would hide the stain. Eventually he wore down and ceased.

"More tea, Your Exalted Highness?"

"When we are married we will share a second cup, Lady Sarai, as it says in the poem, *Share a second cup with your wife*. Now I have business, and must leave you."

She had broken out in a sweat. "May I humbly inquire as to when the convocation at Horn Hall will take place and how soon afterward you will return here?"

"The convocation will take place in ten or fourteen days at Horn Hall, according to which auspicious day the priests choose. I must then remain some days at Horn Hall to conduct reeve business, purging the halls of unsuitable reeves and beginning a new regimen of training. It should not take me more than five or ten days to cut out the worst of the rot. Do not fear. You will not have to wait long, not more than a month. Be at peace under the light of the Shining One, Lady Sarai. When I return all shall have been settled in the best possible way."

He left.

Padding obediently after Tayum she paged in her mind through Tsania's meticulous herbarium. How long before symptoms would start? What signs need she look for? Every twinge in her abdomen sent her into a frenzy of fear.

She begged leave to visit the latrine closet. Even knowing Tayum was standing outside and could hear, she stuck two fingers down her throat until she vomited up a thin spew of liquid.

She could not let them suspect she knew. *Be bold when you need to be bold, and soft when you need to be soft*, Elit always said.

She went to the morning audience and greeted everyone in awkward Sirni, which made them all exclaim and clap their hands. Horribly, at the midday meal Queen Chorannah insisted Sarai share a platter for food. The stew was so heavily spiced she feared she would not be able to taste an abortifacient. When the queen offered her tea, bile burned up her throat and she rushed out of the room to a latrine closet to vomit again.

Late that night, when people's moods were oiled by wine, she cunningly asked if Princess Kasarah ever paid her respects to Chorannah.

"I saw her in the garden the other day," she added, attempting an innocent smile.

"She is not welcome here because she is of evil mind and will falsely accuse Queen Chorannah of cruel acts," said the translator.

Like poison? Sarai wanted to say it but kept silent.

"You will not see her again. The queen has discovered about the gate, and how the princess walked in where she is not welcome or invited. The queen has sent a message to the king that the garden gate must now be blocked up, and he has agreed."

For half the night her belly cramped. Pale spots of blood stained her thighs. Very late the pain ceased. She slept, and woke before dawn ravenously hungry. The spotting had stopped. Most likely she hadn't miscarried, but she couldn't yet be sure.

She might void the pregnancy tomorrow or the next day. Anyway they would not stop trying until they were certain.

At sunrise when the other women filed away for prayers she fled to the queen's garden, hoping there might be a chance to beg for escape through the gate. Workmen were already laboring on the other side. The slap of mortar and bricks and their cheerful banter hit like a slap to the face. Retreating, she huddled on a bench in the cool dawn air. She had long ago given up trusting in a deity who had let her mother be killed, but her lips shaped the comforting prayers regardless.

"Let the hidden heart which is peace lift us above our troubles."

Calmed, she considered her options. She could try to climb the wall, but the king would just have her thrown back. She had to play Elit's part and choose her role in the unfolding story.

After the worship service ended she joined the other women and set herself to please Queen Chorannah. She stumblingly coughed up words and phrases of Sirni as the women laughed at her clumsy attempts even though she could already understand more than they knew. She asked about Prince Tavahosh and discovered he had already left for Horn Hall to prepare for the upcoming convocation. They confided, with some glee, that he had chosen to hold the convocation at Horn Hall partly because of its impressive site but mostly to put Lady Dannarah in her place.

She ate, and then went to the latrine and threw it all up. Afterward she complained of cramping and begged leave to go to the separate chamber, set beside the laundry and across from the kitchen, where menstruating women sat out their periods. The priests banned these women from prayer at the shrine and even from sharing platters of food cooked in the main kitchen, which was daily purified by prayer for the queen's health and spiritual blessing.

The tiny courtyard and rooms had plush and comfortable furnishings and an entire separate set of lovely clothing to be worn there, together with tools for handwork kept exclusively in those chambers. Two girls not yet of menstruating age cooked simple meals and cleaned. As they were not overseen by the ambitious eunuchs, they kept only a casual eye on Sarai. They allowed her to brew her own tea and to eat gruel and flat bread she cooked herself. She showed the others the sponges Ri Amarah women used to catch their menstrual flow and, careful to time her visits to the latrines when another woman had just gone to swap out her pungent rags, rubbed the sponges against the bloody discharge to make it seem she was bleeding, too.

As long as she had her wits she wasn't helpless but all too soon she would start to show. Even if she was forced to have sex with Tavahosh and could hope they would think she was pregnant by him, Chorannah would count the days and suspect the truth. A woman willing to poison children would be perfectly happy to murder a newborn.

46

Lifka and Tarnit approached Salya from the north over Messalia Bay. The swirl of currents fascinated Lifka. Shapes flashed beneath the surface; a school of fish too small to make out as individuals surged and darted as if a single shimmering beast. The swarm parted around a circle of brilliantly blue water, a hole into unknown depths wreathed by a tangle of brown seaweed. After a moment she realized people drifted lazily within the kelp. They had silvery torsos and fish tails instead of legs.

Eyes turned heavenward, they watched the eagles pass overhead as if a mirror of her staring down on them.

Their tails slapped the water. In a flurry of ripples they vanished as if they had never been, dragging the kelp down with them.

Had she just seen the fabled merfolk, or only imagined them?

The great tide was out, exposing sand. The harbor at Salya took advantage of the outflow of the River Messali, which cut a deep channel in the bay through the tidal flats. Several ships were anchored farther out in the deep waters, waiting for the tide.

Tarnit guided them to a landing on the hillside perch Lifka remembered from their last trip here.

"Why are we leaving River's harness on?" Lifka asked after Tarnit had supervised Lifka stripping the harness off Slip and checking his feathers.

"I'm returning to Toskala as soon as my business is completed. I don't like leaving the marshal unattended among vipers. She needs me to watch her back."

"What about me?"

"If the clan agrees, you'll stay here for now. It will take a long time before Prince Tavahosh thinks to look for you in Salya."

Down the hill Fohiono and Treya appeared, waved excitedly, and hurried up to embrace them like old friends. Walking with them to Plum Blossom Compound salved a bit of the fear in Lifka's heart. Tarnit took the message to the office, leaving Lifka to wash and then soak in the bath. She regaled them with the awful story of the fight, Uncle's death, and the escape. Fo had a way of listening that made it easy to talk.

"I shouldn't talk about it but I had to tell someone! I'm so scared for them."

"I think it's glamorous," said Treya. "On the run from the palace. Just like a tale."

"It's not funny, Trey." Fo splashed water at her. "Leaf, if you stayed with us we could hide you from the palace."

"That is Marshal Dannarah's plan, if your clan agrees."

Fo got a thoughtful look on her face. "Oh, I am sure Grandmama will think it a good idea."

"Will I get to meet your grandmother this time?"

Treya grinned but Fo pinched her before she could say anything.

"Let's see what happens" was all Fo would say.

Lifka helped Treya and some of the younger children set out the midday meal. But the family members who settled on cushions to eat did not include an elderly grandmother. The eldest people there were Hari and his reticent but not-at-all-meek wife, Naniko, who as Hari joked did the tidy accounts while he did the untidy negotiating.

Fo plopped down beside Lifka. "We're going to Toskala!" she confided, bumping shoulders with Lifka just as Ailia had used to when they were plotting some escapade.

"Who is *we*? Treya, too?"

Fo's gaze flicked to her father, Hari, who was chatting about crop yields to Tarnit in the cheerful tone of a man who can make anything interesting through the music of his voice. Watching two cheerful people talk cheerfully together made Lifka's throat tighten.

She missed her family so much.

"I've said all I can." Fo fingered a necklace of Hasibal's Tears with its silver branch and blossoms. "I've been waiting all my life for this. Don't you have something you've always dreamed of, Leaf? An adventure to embark on?"

Lifka touched the scar behind her ear. "I want my family to be safe, healthy, and together."

Tarnit said to Hari, "This red-nut rice is so tasty. I've never seen it anywhere else. Where do you buy it?"

"It's a variety from the Arash Peninsula, south of here. We happen to grow it ourselves."

"Not here in Salya."

"No, not in Salya. My mother bought up land southwest of here, on the lower reaches of the Suvash Hills." Hari smiled wistfully. "It's a favorite old family story having to do with how she and Captain Kellas met for the third time. I won't bore you with it. I know you're in a hurry to leave. We'll keep Lifka safe here, and release her to no reeve except you or Marshal Dannarah."

Tarnit rose, nodding around the family. "You have my thanks."

Lifka walked her up to the loft. Fo and the others were already bustling about, for it seemed that "going to Toskala" was a far more complicated enterprise than Lifka would have imagined. Several of the children had already been sent with messages into town.

They took the path cut through a stand of jabi bushes to the clearing on the hillside where the eagles' loft stood. Lifka would have grazed goats in this clearing but she supposed that would just be tempting eagles a bit too much. The tall grass went uncut, and stalks of crane-flower waved elongated white petals in the breeze.

"Do you think Prince Tavahosh will really try to track me down?" Lifka asked Tarnit.

"I do. He strikes me as the type who won't let go until he's gotten his way."

"How can I be a reeve if he is the chief marshal?"

"Marshal Dannarah will find a way. Be patient." Tarnit took her hand and turned to face her. "You're about the same age as my younger son. He's a smart, funny, clever, and hardworking lad, apprenticed to a roofer. Very responsible. Handsome, too, like his father. He'll make a good husband, if you're looking."

Lifka laughed. "Not yet, but my thanks."

Tarnit's sunny smile made even a difficult parting seem brighter. "The truth is, I would take you to Sund and leave you with my family. But they're ordinary villagers. If the prince found you, they'd have no way to protect you or themselves and he would destroy them."

"The last thing I want is to bring down on others what was brought down on my family!"

"I know. That's why you're here."

"Do you really think Plum Blossom Clan can protect me?"

"The marshal thinks they can. I don't know what game Captain Kellas is playing, but he has the king's ear, and that might be protection enough. I'm cursed curious to discover they eat the very same red-nut rice we found in the outlaw encampment in Elsharat. Maybe it's a coincidence, but the marshal believes it is not. If you can find out more, do so."

"Are you asking me to spy on the people who are sheltering me?"

Tarnit released her hand. "Lifka, you're a reeve under the command of Marshal Dannarah. She sent you to shelter here but also to do your duty. As reeves we scout out anything and anyone who is disrupting the Hundred. Outlaws and criminals disrupt the Hundred. If Plum Blossom Clan is involved with such people, we need to know."

"My clan is outlaw now."

"That's different—"

"Is it?" Lifka demanded. "If Prince Tavahosh can command they be arrested and killed on a whim, then isn't he the problem, and not them? Why should I support the reeve halls if he commands them? It's not just that I can't obey him as chief marshal because he'll have me arrested. It's because I won't."

Tarnit sighed, fingered her bone whistle as if trying to decide how to reply, then glanced up at the loft where the eagles waited.

It was early afternoon. A strong eagle could cover a long distance in what was left of the day, gliding on the high currents.

"I need to go, Lifka. We'll discuss this later."

As the older woman started walking up to the loft, Lifka grabbed her wrist. "I just... Take care, Tarnit. Be safe."

"Here now, don't cry, it'll turn out all right." Tarnit squeezed her in a friendly embrace.

But as Lifka walked alone back to the compound, she couldn't shake a terrible feeling that it would not.

That evening Lifka helped carry in platters of food for the family's supper, after which she coaxed the shy toddler onto her lap with baby games like "spider walking" and "where's your nose?" Lifka could not imagine owning so much oil that you could squander it on eating after dark, but she knew better than to say so. They dug into a wholesome meal of rice, fish brushed with sesame oil and turmeric, bean curd glazed with tamarind sauce, and slip-fried bamboo shoots. The toddler was so accustomed to plenty of food that he refused everything except the rice with its pretty red speckles. Was Plum Blossom Clan involved with outlaws? But when she thought about how close her father had come to being sentenced to the work gangs, it seemed like it was the palace and the Beltak priests that caused the trouble. After what she had seen of conditions at the work site at River's Bend, she could not blame people who wanted to escape the work gangs.

She'd have been bound to a grueling, cruel life if Papa hadn't found her.

Probably she'd be dead by now.

The clan's dogs weren't allowed into the house, and in fact the Runt, having accepted the supremacy of the other dogs, had been happy to explore the garden, so she allowed him to join the dogs on guard about the compound for the night. She slept on a pallet in the girls' chamber, the younger ones ecstatic to have a visitor sleep over. The furnishings were simple but everything of the highest quality. Lifka could not help but wonder what it would be like to build such a compound for her family, to know they were secure, well fed, maybe even have enough coin to dedicate Denas to the service of Sapanasu the Lantern as he had always wished. Ailia was having a baby. Alon wanted to get married, and now he could never court the young woman he'd had his eye on.

At dawn Fo nudged Lifka awake, whispering while the others slept. She was already dressed. "Heya! Leaf. Wake up. You want to come with me and my dad to the harbor? You said you've never seen a harbor up close before. Also, it's a lovely day."

Lifka was up and dressed before Fo finished speaking. Treya lay curled in a ball, one of her cousins rolled over against her back and another cousin sprawled off her mattress with a foot nudged up against the wall. They sneaked out, exchanging conspiratorial glances, and when they were safely on the front porch broke out in giggles.

"See, I knew you were the kind to want an adventure," Fo whispered.

"What are we going to do at the harbor?" Lifka picked through a basket of sandals to fish out her own.

"There are two ships bound for Nessumara. We have to see how much it will cost us to displace their cargo with people."

"How many people?"

"Two hundred."

"Are two hundred people going to Toskala at your grandfather's command?"

"Yes." On her right forefinger Fo wore a thick iron ring with a wolf's head. She twisted it around as she bit her lip. "There is one thing. You aren't keen to see the Tandi. But one of the ships we'll be negotiating with is a Tandi ship. If that bothers you, then don't come."

"I don't know how I feel about it." If she really was heiress to a fortune she could help her family, but as quickly as the thought occurred to her she shook it off as useless dreaming. "It's hard for me to see how anyone could know for sure after so many years."

"Most likely your family is dead anyway."

Lifka looked up sharply from where she was seated on the steps tying on her sandals. "My family is alive. They are refugees in Weldur Forest."

Fo pressed a hand to her lips. "I'm sorry," she said through her fingers.

The door slid aside and Hari came out carrying the household's youngest child in a sling. He resembled Marshal Dannarah a great deal, having a similar complexion and facial structure, but he reminded Lifka of her own papa in having a solicitous gaze and a kind smile.

"So pleasant to have a fresh face for company, Lifka."

"Would you like me to carry the baby, ver?" Lifka asked.

"That would be so kind of you as long as it is understood I will take the baby back once I begin negotiating. Winsome babies are a fine bargaining tool to distract the unsuspecting."

Like the infants in her own clan the little fellow was accustomed to being passed around to whichever hands were free. The comfort of holding a trusting child in her arms settled her anxious heart for the first time in days. To her surprise she savored the walk down to the harbor. As they descended Grand Avenue people called out greetings to her companions; it seemed everyone knew them. Shops lined the avenue, so many things for sale Lifka had never seen in River's Bend that she kept halting to stare: heaps of spices that didn't grow where she lived; wavy-bladed knives whose blades were etched with scenes from stories she did not recognize; every color of rice.

"I never got to go to the market in Toskala," she said.

Fo nudged her with an elbow. "We'll go shopping together in Toskala, I promise."

"I can't go back. Remember?"

"That's right. I'm sorry."

A youth pushing a wheelbarrow overloaded with bricks cut them off. Lifka skipped back to avoid a collision but couldn't help watching the wheelbarrow wobble on a precariously fast roll as it turned onto a side street. The youth swerved around a man frozen in the middle of the side street whose gaze was fixed on her. In the Hundred she was tall, but he stood a head taller. He was as black as she was. A silvery inked design like the wing of a gull flared from the corner of his right eye, past his ear, and halfway around his shaved head. The intent way he examined her made her nervous. She looked around and spotted Fohiono talking to a woman who was showing off the bright-gold fabric of her taloos.

"Fo?"

Fo excused herself and returned. "What is it?"

"I saw . . ." The man was gone. The baby reached for Fo, and once Lifka's arms were free she slipped her staff from its strap on her back, feeling better with a weapon to hand.

"Girls?" Hari beckoned from down the avenue, and they hurried after him.

As they entered the harbor district Lifka caught sight of the tall man. He kept his distance but never lost sight of them; nor did he make any effort to pretend he just happened to be moving in the same direction.

"That man is following us."

"That's odd," said Fo, shifting the baby to her other hip. "See the gull? That marks him as a born-son of the Gull. They're the only Tandi ship in the harbor right now."

"The ones we're going to see?"

"Yes."

A shiver like a foretaste of calamity rushed through her flesh. "It was a bad idea for me to come along."

"Do you want to go back to the house?" Fo asked with a look of concern.

Lifka rubbed a hand along the curve of her neck, sure his stare was fixed there. If she didn't usually keep her hair pulled back he'd never have seen the scar. Her skin prickled as if an invisible feather traced its lines. "No. My papa would say it's best to walk up and hit your fears over the head with an ax."

"Come along, girls," called Hari from the steps of a veranda that wrapped around an inn. He took the baby from Fo and climbed stairs that ascended to a second floor. A corridor divided the space into rooms on either side, which Fo explained were residences and offices for visiting merchants seeking an onshore venue to do business. A white-skinned woman with honey-colored hair coiled into a braid atop her head stood guard at a door. She smiled politely at Hari and made a creditable greeting in a strong accent as she slid open the door to allow him to enter.

Lifka balked on the threshold. Three Tandi merchants awaited them: two women and a man. The women's hair was covered by scarves, one sky blue and one sun yellow. They wore wrapped tops that left their shoulders bare, and both had elegant wings inked up over their shoulders from the back but no design on their faces. They had a look of such self-assurance that admiration stirred like a whisper of infatuation in her heart.

The man wore a knee-length tunic, and his calves were bare. Instead of a shaved head he had his hair in multiple small braids worn tight against his head in a boxy pattern. He also had a design unfurled from his right eye, but his was a wing that looked more like a seven-rayed flame. An itch of memory crawled in her mind, like faces she couldn't quite see through dense underbrush.

"You don't have to go in," whispered Fo from behind her.

"No, it's all right." To look at them excited her and yet it scared her, too. It was so hard to decide whether she had been wise to come or dreadfully wrong.

Footsteps tapped in the corridor, and the tall man who had been following them walked into the room. He exchanged a flurry of hand signs with the others, but the signs were nothing like the gestures of the Hundred so she couldn't understand them. Hari and the women exchanged greetings in the way of acquaintances who have dealt with each other before. To her surprise Hari spoke to them in a language that teased at the edge of her understanding, then faded as if lost to light.

More quickly than she had expected the Tandi women opened their hands as with regret, switching to the Hundred-speech. "Your cargo we cannot carry, ver, because we have changed our plans and need to sail east to our homeland, not to Nessumara after all," said the woman wearing the yellow scarf. "My apologies. When next we come to Salya I hope we can do business."

Hari turned a hand palm up in the sign of acceptance. "We are always open to do business with you, verea. We have had a prosperous relationship these last ten years."

"We have. Yet one question I have left."

Lifka tensed as all four Tandi looked at her. The woman asked a question directly to her in the other language. Words fluttered up like moths to light, something about her name and her mother and her ship.

"I am Lifka of Five Roads Clan. Who are you that you speak to me as if you think you know me?"

"Who stole you from your people that you dress in this way and do not answer the greeting with your mother's lineage and your guild ship? It seems you wear the mark of the Phoenix Lineage."

Lifka tightened her grip on the staff. "I am not one of you. I am Lifka of Five Roads Clan. By my name you hear that I am dedicated to the Fire Mother as my most ancient ancestor, and you can see my Fire ancestry by the fire inks on my arm and leg. I served Kotaru the Thunderer for my temple year. It's likely I was born in the Year of the Snake. My clan comes from River's Bend."

"You are no Hundred woman. Why do you claim so?"

"I am who I say I am!"

Hari's kindly aspect changed as he got to his feet with a nod at Fo, who strode over to open the door. "Verea, please do not disturb this young woman with your words, however well meant they are. She is a reeve, bound to the service of the reeve halls. She was raised in the Hundred. I think she is not your responsibility nor anyone you can lay claim to. You may bring a case before the assizes in the usual way, if that is your desire. For now I will tell you this young person is a guest at our house and so we feel responsible for her."

The yellow-scarf woman beckoned for the man with the seven-rayed wing inked on his face to step forward. The lines depicted a wing with far more sophistication and elegance than the crude scar cut into her back, and yet she could see how it might be said to resemble her scar more than the blade-like stylization of the gull's wing on the others.

"Do you not recognize your own brother, Lifka Five Roads?"

Brother?

Broad cheekbones, stocky build, narrow chin, not even as tall as she was: She saw no resemblance. Nothing about him raised any shred of memory out of the abyss that was her past.

"He is not my brother. My brothers are Alon and Denas. You have no right to intrude on my life in this way."

"This is really enough," said Hari to the merchants. Without raising his voice he throttled whatever words the others might have spoken. "I am disappointed in this bitter accusation. You have disturbed the peace of a young person who came here with no ill intent and indeed in obvious ignorance that you would speak so sternly to her. Fohiono. Lifka. We are leaving."

How the Tandi stared! But she thought their faces wore not surprise but calculation. Hari went out first, still holding the baby, and Fo stepped into place behind Lifka. Once they were down the steps of the inn and back out on the street, Hari spoke.

"My apologies, Lifka."

"It wasn't your fault!"

"Had you any notion they would confront you so directly? Have you seen them before?"

"No! I never knew Tandi existed until Treya mentioned it last time I was here. But when I was at the palace afterward one of Queen Dia's women claimed to recognize my scar as a guild mark. She said the Phoenix Lineage lost all its children in the Eldim war."

Fo said, "The tall man is waiting on the steps to see which way we go. Father, perhaps I should take Lifka back to the house instead of going on to the other shipmaster."

They all looked back. The man with the gull's wing was indeed poised on the steps as if to dash after them.

"Yes. You girls go home while I settle this."

With the baby in his arms he approached the man with such a bland expression on his face that Fo whistled. "Sheh! Pa's angry!"

"He is?"

"If Pa's not smiling it means he's furious. Let's go!"

They wove through the bustling harbor-side traffic toward Grand Avenue. Fo had a formidable way of using her elbows to ram through the passersby and carts and wagons. Unaccustomed to dodging traffic, Lifka fell back as a cohort of sailors jostled past. A man pushed a cart between her and Fo.

A hand came down on her shoulder from behind. The white guardswoman tugged Lifka roughly around to face the man the Tandi called her brother. His frown made him look concerned, even worried, as she might herself have been if Denas or Alon had started spouting nonsense about belonging to some other clan.

He touched the ink on his face. "You and me are sister and brother of the Phoenix."

She ducked out from the guardswoman's grip. "Leave me alone!"

"Leaf!" cried Fo as a wagon drawn by oxen rumbled past, cutting them apart from each other.

Lifka bolted, and slammed into a solid, muscular body. A glance at his height told her who it was. She elbowed him up under the ribs, gripped her staff, and swept low for his knees to jar him off his feet. With astonishing reflexes he jumped over the swing and came down with a chop to her elbow that broke her hold on her staff.

A cough of pain: her own.

"Leaf! Where are you?"

A net of silver lacework poured over her face like rain from a cloudburst. Its weight drove her to her knees even as its strands adhered to her skin and then began to dissolve.

Her body melted as if she, too, were rain pouring away through the sieve of her body into a new vessel. Everything became light, too opaque to see through, although her ears still worked. Words swam like fish through a weir, trapping more and more of them until they began to crowd her thoughts in flashing silvery waves. The ground heaved, then settled into a rocking sway that unsettled her stomach so much that she opened her eyes.

Nausea roiled her stomach. She swallowed, then regretted the burning in her throat as it turned to a gagging cough. Arms hauled her up and held her over the rim of a wagon as she heaved up everything in her stomach. The road beneath glittered and splashed. Shadows rippled across its flowing surface.

This was no wagon. They had thrown her in a boat. Oars beat on either side in perfect rhythm as they dipped in and out of the water. Her captor pulled her away from the gunnel and she realized her hands were tied behind her back and her ankles wrapped with rope so all she could do was squirm in an effort to get away from him. But the tall man had a powerful grasp and a sour frown because evidently flecks of her vomit had gotten on his fancy silk sleeve. She couldn't decide whether to laugh at him or to throw up all over his pretty tunic in the hope of pissing him off.

Find your calm space before you fight, Mum would say.

They had trained so often on this skill that Lifka could reach right down to the cool center behind her breastbone and quiet her nerves.

So here she was, kidnapped, in the stern of a narrow boat being rowed by eight people, including the three women and the other man. The speed at which they skimmed over the water astonished her. The port of Salya fell behind, buildings already small. Ahead they neared the deep-water anchorage where ships awaited the tide's turning.

Make no predictable move, Mum would say. Even though she had grown up swimming in the river, with her hands and feet tied she was not about to throw herself into the bay. Fo had explained earlier that the tide's turning was hours away. Plenty of time for the others to catch up.

Yet even as they pulled up alongside one of the ships, sailors already swarmed the rigging and ropes to unfurl canvas. With the greatest indignity she was trussed in a fishing net and lugged up, bumping against the hull like a sack of rice. Slung onto the deck, she wriggled to try to get out of the netting. People raced around her shouting orders in that language she knew and yet could not understand.

The tall man hoisted her to get her out of the way. With her stomach pressed into his shoulder she had the pleasure of spewing the last of her bile down the back of his tunic. Sometimes you had to take whatever petty revenge you could get. He dumped her onto a coil of rope wedged between heavy jars and a cage of pigeons, then cursed again as he tried to shake out his tunic.

"Asshole," she said, to relieve her ill humor. The rough netting scratched her lips.

He walked away with the easy pitch of a man accustomed to the way the deck didn't stay still. Her stomach clenched, made queasy again by the incessant movement. She tried to hook her chin to the leather cord twisted against her neck, worked her head forward against the netting. If she could just reach the bone whistle, she could call Slip.

"Sister." The stocky man knelt beside her. He patted his chest. "You are the sister. I am the brother. I am called Ilekovi."

"I am not your sister and you are not my brother."

He reached toward her face but when she drew back he did not touch her skin. "The scar was cut by a desperate person. This person knew you must not be lost to your people, so they made the mark to remind you. Who cut you?"

"I don't remember. I want to go home."

"We are taking you home."

"No, you're doing to me what soldiers did when I was a child."

"No. We are rescuing you. Word has already spread that a Phoenix daughter survived. If we had not found you, some worse person would take you to sell you to the Imperators."

"Is this how a rescue goes? My feet are going numb because they are tied too tightly."

"Ah. Too tight. He is worried and too eager for the prize, that one."

"The asshole?"

"The hole of the ass? Ah!" He laughed in a way that made her want to like him. "Yes. We call it a man with a rude nose."

"A rude nose?"

He began to peel her out of the netting. "Maybe *nose* is the wrong word. My speech is not so good. This is my first time to the western continent and I learn the language only as we sail. He is a man hard to like because he is a bitter food to the tongue. He pokes his nose in and says harsh words before he knows the truth."

Mum would say to keep them talking to relax and distract them. "That sounds right. Are you related to him?"

"No, we are not kinsmen. He is my spouse."

"Your *husband*?"

"*Husband?* I do not know that word. Clans arrange a marriage to tie two families together. We are spouse to each other. Is it not this way in all lands, that the elders choose what persons their children will marry?"

"Not if that means kidnapping people."

"This is not a kidnap. The elders of the Tandi Guild will pay a bounty to the Gull Lineage for bringing in the last borndaughter of the Phoenix Lineage. You are precious, of highest worth. The guild will find you a spouse in the proper way. Maybe a more likable one than mine!" He smiled just as if he and she were accustomed to jesting.

"You people stole me to get a reward?"

"It is other people who stole you, when you were a child."

A sail rumbled into place, but there was so little wind it hung slack. Surely they could not sail against the tide!

She smiled wanly in the hope of rousing his sympathy. "If I am precious I hope you do not damage me. My ankles are scraped raw. Look! Blood! Can you retie me so it doesn't hurt?"

Kotaru the Thunderer must have been watching over her because he untied her ankles while elsewhere on deck the grind of the anchor chain came to a thumping halt and a second sail was unfurled. She stood, steadying herself on one of the giant ceramic jars as she stamped feeling back into her feet. He offered her a sip from his flask. The harsh flavor of a bracing liquor slammed straight between her eyes and cleared her mind wonderfully.

"My apologies, sister. I must tie your feet again but I will not tie so tight."

"I can't feel my hands at all," she lied. "They've gone numb."

The third sail rolled open. A cry like a seabird's keening caught at the edge of her hearing. An uncanny force spilled through the ship like the breath of a giant creature shivering into wakefulness.

All three sails filled as if with a steady following wind, only it wasn't windy.

Shadows played across the canvas like sheared wings lifting on the breeze. She blinked to clear her vision.

He shaded a hand to look toward the cloudless sky. "To see the spirit waken is magnificent."

Masts threw shadows across the deck and onto the water. Sailors worked the ropes and scrambled about their business. The bay spread around them as a sheet of water with the green shore hulking in the distance. Overhead the sky had the cloudless blue sheen of a dawn-thrush's egg.

A massive shadow rippled across the decks as if clouds were passing the sun. Slip's shadow looked just this way as it flowed across the ground when she and the eagle flew aloft, only this shadow was larger even than Slip and it had narrow, bladed wings and a blunt tail.

The ship began to move as if the shadowy wings lifted wind out of another realm into this one.

As if the ship had a bird's shadow haunting it, just as Reyad had said.

It was frightening but also so incredible it made her want to try to touch that shadow and see if she could feel what a bound shadow felt like.

But not today. Not now, or anytime soon.

While he wasn't looking at her, she sat on the rope, tucked her unbound feet out of sight beneath the coiled rope, and twisted her bound hands up. "My hands are numb. You said you would loosen the rope. Is it really true a gull's spirit haunts this ship?"

The ruse worked, because he wanted her to trust him.

"The shadows of birds are bound into the hulls of our ships, yes," he said as he bent over to pick at the rope pinching her wrists.

"Don't you keep such powerful magic a secret?"

"How can we keep secret a thing people can see?"

"So it isn't only Tandi who see the shadow of the bird? Anyone might?"

"Any person might or might not see the shadow, regardless of who their mother is. But every person sees a ship sail where there is no wind, even if they do not see the shadow."

Over his shoulder, in the direction of land, two specks appeared in the sky within her field of view: two eagles.

"Ah! Why does the asshole bind the rope so tight?" Ilekovi muttered under his breath as he pried a finger under the wet cord.

The rope finally began to loosen enough to give her hands play.

She head-butted him, slamming her forehead into his nose so hard the pain almost cracked her head in half, but she was already pushing to her feet. He reeled back, blood pouring over his lips. She jumped for the railing shoulder-first, ramming a hapless sailor aside. His surprised cry was lost within the slap of the wind in the sails and the shouts of sailors. Ilekovi staggered into her. She kicked, and he reeled back, tripped, and hit the deck hard.

The rope burned as she scraped her left hand free where he had begun loosening it. Clambering up the rail, she swung her legs over.

The tall man loomed to her right, looking furious. He scooped up the discarded netting and flung it. She pushed off and cut right through the shadow of wings through air so cold her skin went instantly numb. Then she hit the sea. The force drove her down and down, water boiling up around her and the ends of the rope unraveling like a writhing snake. The netting tangled over her head but she was heavier and kept dropping into the depths as the water slowed the net's descent.

She had forgotten to take a breath.

She kicked back toward the hull, bumped into it, and came up gasping for air. The sailors weren't looking down; they pointed at the clump of netting as it brushed the surface. She inhaled, dove, and swam under the hull, popping up on the other side. After shedding the rope she dove again and swam underwater as far as she could manage away from the ship. The sandy bottom was stippled with rocky clumps like a hundred small outcroppings, fish teeming among them. She surfaced to take another gasp of air, then dove and swam, and surfaced again this time with eyes stinging and lungs throbbing. A glance toward the ship showed that no one was yet deliberately looking for her on this side, but the sailors in the rigging had already begun to survey the water on all sides. They would put rowboats in and come after her.

But what really made it hard to breathe was how the ship looked now, no longer just a ship with sails set. A vast gull's shadow glided within the masts, like mist intertwined with the wood and rope and canvas of the vessel.

Magic.

She dove again. Probably they could see right down into the clear waters with her a too-large fish swimming all clumsy where it should be sleek. But cursed if she was going to go without a fight. Slip was coming. The jess tugged on her soul.

Wasn't the bond between reeve and eagle also a kind of magic?

She burst again to the surface. Treading water, she turned a circle as she scanned the sky.

There!

"There!" cried a voice from the ship. They had spotted her.

An eagle's shadow spread over the water. A reeve she didn't recognize swooped low, a rope dangling from his harness. Lifka grabbed for the end of the rope but missed and had to watch helplessly as reeve and eagle banked up and looped to swing back around. Oars splashed the water as a rowboat appeared from around the hull and sped toward her.

Out of the sky Slip dove for the boat. His talons grazed a sailor but he didn't get a grip. The man screamed and slumped over the gunnel of the boat, his companions shouting. Slip flew sharply up and circled around for another strike.

She had to tear her gaze away and focus on the other eagle as it circled back around. The rope's tip skimmed the surface of the water, the reeve measuring his approach. Lifka lunged and grabbed it. Her weight jerked down the eagle but this one was a bigger, stronger eagle than Slip and lugged Lifka like a sack through the water. Lifka thought her arm would pull out of her shoulder even as she tried to wrap the end of the cord around her wrist so she wouldn't lose her grip.

The cord scored an abrasion across her fingers and she lost hold and sank back into the water. Her fingers burned painfully. The whole side of her back felt pulled out of line. Her mouth tasted of brine. Still, she was farther away than before, and the sailors had stopped rowing and raised their oars to protect their heads.

Slip circled for another dive. She wanted to cheer him on but she had to tread water.

The sails of the Tandi ship began luffing. The huge gull's shadow rose off the mast like steam off a boiling kettle. It shattered into so many smaller shadows she could not count them as each took the shape of a small gull. The shadow gulls split into two flocks and raced across the waters to mob the big eagles, diving and harassing until the eagles sheared off.

Lifka couldn't bear to watch. The agony of shifting her right arm made her grit her teeth, but she began a slow stroke anyway toward the green horizon. Swimming hurt, but the thought of her family starving in Weldur Forest with no one to look out for them and nowhere to go drove her past the pain. They had never done anything except work and garden so as to live a peaceable life. The shrine's work gangs, the archon's unfair licenses and demands for money, the prince's swollen pride, the Tandi merchants who had decided she must be some person they wanted her to be, and even the reeves carrying her away from home: What right had they to trample in and take whatever they wanted from people who couldn't fight back?

The splash of oars grew louder. She was exhausted and in pain but she kept swimming. They would have to haul her kicking and biting out of the water if they wanted her.

"Lifka!"

Fo's shout startled her so much she took on a mouthful of water. Fo came up in a canoe alongside her while she was still coughing and trying to keep her head above water rather than swallow more. Men hauled her over the gunnel, and she hung there hacking out seawater.

Fo stowed her paddle and raised a crossbow. The rowboat plowed closer, the tall man standing in the prow. The mob of shadows turned away from the retreating eagles and instead swooped and turned around the becalmed ship until they became a twisting sheet of darkness.

"There are ten more canoes coming from Salya," Fo called across the waves to the rowboat with the tall man. "You can see them right behind me. We don't take kindly to having our guests stolen. You want a fight, you've got one. But I recommend you go on your way and never come back."

The tall man raised a hand, and his sailors stopped rowing.

The two vessels floated in silence. Water sighed at the hull. Lifka craned her neck to see the two eagles flying in a wide sweep, cautious after the attack of the shadowy gulls. In the far distance several more specks appeared, reeves from Bronze Hall coming to investigate.

The tall man crossed his arms in disgust. "Did you and your brother Ilekovi arrange the escape between you?" he shouted. "So his clan's ship can get the prize money for bringing you in?"

Lifka coughed, then spat, trying not to throw up again.

He shook his head with an expression of offended scorn, and gave a curt command. The boat slewed around and headed back for the ship.

"You've made an enemy of that one," remarked Fo.

Blood dripped from the abrasion on Lifka's fingers. It hurt so much it made her dizzy. "He's not my enemy. He's just a man with a rude nose. These Tandi already knew about me, Fo. How could they have known? Do you think Treya told them?"

"No! Even she's not that stupid." Fohiono shaded her eyes, examining the ship. The shadow wings had vanished, but wisps of darkness chased along the ropes as the spirit awaited a new command to fly. "When there's coin involved, people's ears grow wings."

"Queen Dia and her people knew all about this vanished Phoenix Lineage. She must have sent out word. I can't trust anyone in the palace, can I?"

Fo gave her a long look, then whistled a signal. The paddlers dug to get the canoe up and moving. Lifka huddled with legs drawn up to her chest and her back pressed against Fo's knees. She couldn't help but notice that all the paddlers had weapons, and all wore a wolf's head ring.

When they reached the rest of the canoes the other boats turned to form up around them. In this comforting pack they headed back to shore.

"Do you want to go with the Tandi?" Fo asked in a low voice. "Lots of people would love to discover they are lost heirs to a legendary fortune."

Lifka thought of Ailia, pregnant and with her young man bewildered by the trouble into which he had fallen. She could still see Mum with gashes in her side and Denas's crushed hand and the gaping wound on Nanni's thigh. The normally rambunctious children had been scared into muteness. The dogs hadn't barked and through the night the mules had pulled eagerly at the wagon as if they knew perfectly well they would be slaughtered to assuage a prince's pride.

"The Gull Clan only wants me because I will bring them coin and prestige. Do you know how I came into my family? Thirteen years ago my father hired out to haul supplies for the army to High Haldia. He finished the job and got paid two leya for two weeks' work."

"Two leya? That's all?"

"You take what you can get when your clan only has enough rice for a week to feed itself. He was still in High Haldia when a company marched in from Ithik Eldim with several hundred captives, all children. People were eager to buy labor for so cheap. Only one leya for the runt!"

Fo gasped but said nothing.

"But no one wanted to buy the runt. A silver leya was too much for a worthless, starving, half-dead child not more than

five years old. Yet the moment he saw me he knew I needed
to come home where I belonged. He spent half the coin he'd
earned, when the whole clan was counting on that coin to buy
food. They are my family, Fo. This Phoenix Lineage means
nothing to me. Nothing."

Yet when she looked back at the ship growing smaller behind
them, she wondered if a fortune could keep her family safe
against a prince's prideful wrath.

"What are you going to do now?" Fo asked. "Prince Tavahosh seems to have it in for you and your clan."

"I don't know."

The canoe carved through the water, paddles flashing in and
out with trails of spray, salt heavy in the air. The wind was glorious as they flew along the water, but her heart sank like stone.

Fo changed her steering paddle over to the other side, angled
against the hull to slightly alter the canoe's path. "We can shelter your family. It won't be easy to move them without being
caught, but with your cooperation we can do it. But you will
have to leave the reeve halls and join us."

47

Drums beat pum-put-a-pum-put-a-pum like an army on the
march.

What in the hells Tavahosh was thinking to bring drums to
the convocation at Horn Hall Dannarah could not imagine, ril-
ing up eagles and disturbing everyone's peace. Yet here she was
with a shrine steward on either side of her as if the Beltak priests
now commanded Horn Hall. The men escorted her toward a

tier of benches. A self-congratulating assembly of about two hundred reeves, palace officials, courtiers, and exalted priests looked over the parade ground of Horn Hall in exactly the way people sat on terraced seats in a Bell Quarter theater awaiting a troupe of Hasibal's players putting on a show. Wind rumbled over the high ridge, tearing at everyone's clothes and hair.

She caught sight of Reyad standing with a clump of other Horn Hall reeves, watching as she was directed to the seats. Thank Beltak he was safe! She'd begun to think it a mistake to send him south. When she caught his eye he dipped his chin in acknowledgment, nothing showy. Her other loyal people marked her with nods as well, but she could not help but notice how they were made to stand in the back.

"This way, Marshal." A steward had the effrontery to attempt to direct her toward the back where she wouldn't be able to see.

She shoved past him and climbed to where Marshal Goard of Gold Hall sat.

"I don't like what's going on at all," he muttered as she plopped down beside him.

She was about to ask him what he meant when those cursed drums banged more loudly. Everyone jolted upright.

Prince Tavahosh processed in, accompanied by a cohort of red-and-white-clothed soldiers. A beautifully embroidered eagle decorated the silver cape he wore, wings wrapping his torso; a gold sash bound his robes. A horn whistle dangled from a copper chain, and he carried a bronze baton. His spiky headdress of iron-gray silk folded into intricate patterns, its scaffolding hung with bells. The drummers ceased—thank every god in existence!—but only so that four of his attendants could sing an imperial hymn to Beltak's magnificence. The loud wind mostly drowned out the words but she could hear those cursed tinkling bells nagging at the edge of her hearing.

"Very impressive for a company of fledgling actors," she

remarked to Marshal Goard. They were seated at the back of a section where marshals and notable reeves took a place of honor while the last of the old guard—she and Goard and a few other aged men—were separated out from the younger men like the outcasts they now were. "I see Ivo and his loyal reeves from Iron Hall haven't bothered to show up. Maybe he keeled over dead in disgust when he heard. What is this nonsense?"

"I wouldn't joke if I were you, Dannarah." Popular among his reeves at Gold Hall, Goard was a solid, responsible, and competent reeve a few years younger than she was. After their affair he had married an intelligent woman from a clan that made salves, balms, and medicinal oils, had sired numerous children, and both he and his wife had become her friends. There were few people she trusted more.

"Why not?"

"See that slope-browed fellow there? The young one? They are calling him marshal of Iron Hall. When I asked where Ivo was, they said he had retired and left the command to a younger, fitter man. They said Ivo's eagle has taken a new reeve."

She hissed in an inhalation as a tremor of foreboding passed through her chest. "The hells!"

The tedious hymn came to an end. Following the Sirni tradition the prince sang a short, poetic aria in a surprisingly tuneful and strong voice. After he finished praising the Shining One as "the vigorous Sun of our hearts" and "the spear of righteous anger wielded in a just Hand," he and his retinue filed up onto the terraced seats and took their places at the front.

"Do you think they've taken Auri's death and Lifka's unexpectedly swift jessing of Slip as an excuse to start murdering reeves they want to be rid of?" she muttered.

"Best not spoken of now," he said, so agitated his voice came out louder than a whisper.

From lower down, two young men wearing marshals' regalia

glanced over their shoulders with rebuking looks as if to scold their elders into silence. Puppies!

Eiya! The drummers rum-pum-pummed back to life, the rhythm making everyone sit up even straighter for it was certain something new was about to happen.

Every reeve hall had lofts to house its eagles. Of course there was a complicated scheme by which some eagles were on patrol, some hunting, others resting or injured, and a few flown away to breed in the mountains, so no reeve hall was ever "full." Besides that, generations of being jessed to people and living in proximity in the reeve halls had instilled a high degree of sociability among the raptors. Nevertheless every reeve hall kept isolated lofts for visiting eagles and for any individual eagles who needed separation and solitude.

The ridgetop here at Horn Hall had garden plots at one end and visiting lofts at the other. Today's tiered seats had been raised to face the most solitary of these lofts, one erected close to the prow of the ridge. The loft doors were closed; netting strung from its roof had been stretched out to fasten onto perches, thus making a rope cage. Net cages were sometimes used to confine young eagles new to the halls, and in the rare cases she had authorized such a netting cage she had kept it well away from the bustle and flow of the hall.

She glanced around to the area, off to the left, where her Horn Hall reeves, fawkners, and stewards clustered to watch. Steward Nesard was scanning the benches, and he raised a hand to indicate he'd seen her. He had the worst expression on his face; she couldn't imagine what would make him frown like that except news of an untimely death, probably Ivo's. Clearly he wanted to speak to her. She stood, meaning to climb back down and go over to him.

Goard grabbed her knee. "Sit down. Don't make any move now with Prince Tavahosh watching everything you do. Didn't it occur to you he's holding the convocation here at Horn Hall specifically to taunt you?"

"The hells." She should have seen it. Every lineament of this cursed day was clearly determined to remind her of how badly she had lost the battle for control of the reeve halls.

The drums roared into a loud whump whump whump whump whose emphatic clap made everyone crane their necks. Two columns of young men marched into view, shoulder-to-shoulder in perfect matched step. Although all wore reeve leathers, not one had a bone whistle on a leather cord around his neck as every reeve must. It was as if Tavahosh was mocking the reeves he now commanded by parading pretend reeves as an honor guard.

Each young man carried a reeve baton. With flash and precision they raised and lowered the batons, twirled them, tapped them on thighs and forearms, on each shoulder, in the kind of martial dance practiced in the old temples dedicated to Kotaru the Thunderer. They were very good, batons dancing to the beat of the drums. In fact, they were a pleasure to watch, very stirring and handsome in the way young men can carry strength and poise without thinking about it.

"Sit down! I can't see!" hissed a man behind her.

She had forgotten she was still standing. With a thump she sat, and leaned into Goard. "Is this some new style of reeve training?"

"Never seen it before," he whispered. "None of them have whistles, though."

The two columns peeled away from each other and the men lined up on either side of the netting cage. She had a good memory for faces, not that she'd seen any of these men before. There were twenty-four. Half looked Sirni to her, curly hair instead of straight, a tendency to bigger noses, complexion of a more reddish- than golden-brown shade. Eagerness quivered through them. It quite caught her up; she could feel their excitement and thus so could everyone else in the same way children anticipate a promised platter of sweet rice cakes at festival time.

The prince rose, arms stretched to either side so the drape of his clothing made him seem larger. The silver cape rippled as the air tore at it, fluttering the amber-threaded wings of the embroidered eagle. Dannarah admired the way his sonorous voice penetrated the wind.

"Let the candidates be praised! Let these young men be acclaimed as talons, for they have undergone tests of courage and endurance. They have proven themselves worthy for the honor of risking their lives today. But only one can claim the prize! Only one will walk away as a reeve."

"Talons?" Dannarah looked at Goard, but he shrugged.

Four stewards wearing Argent Hall green ran forward and rolled back the big doors of the loft to reveal a hooded eagle on an interior perch. Its feathers were ruffled, its talons opening and closing restlessly even though it was hooded and should thus be settled and calm.

Dannarah's hand closed on Goard's knee. "Isn't that Bright?"

His reply was drowned out by a rumbling gust of wind.

A masked fawkner used a pole to hook the hood off the raptor and then dashed into the safety of a tack room.

"The hells!" Her hand tightened until Goard grunted in discomfort. "Bright is Feder's eagle. You remember him. He trains all my fledglings... What in the hells?"

She stood despite the yelps of protest from the men whose view she blocked.

The young man at the head of the talon line ducked under the netting and stepped into the caged area. So proud he was, shoulders back, his long hair bound up in a soldier's looped topknot. Fledgling reeves began by learning the basic baton signals and whistles to control their eagles.

He slapped the baton diagonally across his chest: *Come to me.*

Bright launched.

Dannarah braced herself; she didn't bother to yell a warning.

Bright landed half on top of the young man, bowling him over. Then she hopped back. A sociable bird, she was trying to warn him off, and indeed, bleeding and with a dislocated shoulder, he took the hint and crawled out like a defeated marmot, looking ashamed. Unsettled, Bright fluttered at the netting, dropped back, flapped her wings, dipped her head. She wanted to fly.

Where was Feder?

Dannarah cast around and spotted Nesard signaling her. He gestured a cut across his own throat: *Dead.*

Feder was dead!

No wonder Bright was trying to leave. When their reeves died, eagles flew away and did not return for months or even years but always at a time of their choosing and always with a new young reeve already jessed to them.

Yet instead of pulling the netting aside to let Bright go, the stewards and fawkners stayed fixed in place. Drums rolled like distant thunder, then quieted. A second young man ducked under the netting to face the eagle. Bright hopped threateningly toward him and in response he thumped his chest with the baton.

Goard stood beside her, voice rising in anger. "What are they playing at? This is obscene."

She tapped his elbow. "Sit down, play along, and keep your distance from me, my friend. Don't be seen as my ally. You need to stay in command of Gold Hall."

Without waiting for a reply she shoved her way down the benches, whacking people's shoulders with her baton to get them to make room, treading on toes and clipping knees and hands. She ignored the furious words thrown at her. The little dance of Bright warning off that poor duped youth and the next lad trying to capture Bright's interest fixed Dannarah's attention far more than the bleats of asslickers who couldn't be bothered to call a halt to a crime.

She called, "Prince Tavahosh! End this now! I don't know what in the hells you think you are doing with this ridiculous display…"

Half the reeves leaped to their feet, but it was long since too late.

Goaded and trapped, unable to get peace, the eagle struck. Wickedly sharp talons punctured the man's torso. Yet the fellow did not scream, only shut his eyes, lips moving as in prayer. Bright squeezed, and mercifully the body went limp. Blood streaked the ground as the eagle dragged the limp body around before finally shaking it off her claws.

The drums rolled, and quieted.

As she reached him, Tavahosh pulled himself to his full height to try and make her feel small. "This is a proper ceremony. This is a true test of manhood."

"What in the hells are you talking about?"

"We must seek worthy candidates to become reeves. This is not a duty and an honor to be granted to your random farmer's child out weeding in the garden patch and chosen by chance as the wind blows a frantic eagle that way! Deserving men must be allowed to stand forth, ones we have raised up through discipline and training. If the Shining One rests His blessing upon a man, then he will be chosen as a reeve to serve at Beltak's will."

A third man crawled under the net. Folk murmured admiring words at the new talon's willingness to enter where the last had died.

"Bad enough to see men's lives thrown away because you've convinced them it's worth risking death as a mark of bravado. I cannot stand here and watch you people ruin a fine eagle!"

"You do not have my permission to intervene."

"I don't need your permission. The only way to put a stop to this travesty is to hood the eagle, settle her, and then let her go as has been the tradition since the beginning of the reeve halls."

"You believe in the old superstitions. There is nothing spiritual about reeves. The eagles want to be jessed. It is their obligation and duty as beasts to be hooded before their masters."

"We are not their masters. We are their partners."

"The eagles are animals, Lady Dannarah, not creatures of spirit as men are."

Bright flapped back to the perch, so disturbed that her confusion made Dannarah ache. The third young talon had the sense to approach the eagle at a creep while stewards got hold of the dead man's feet and dragged him out of the netting cage.

She grabbed the prince's arm. "This won't work. Eagles choose, not men."

"It has worked in Argent Hall for three years now," he crowed. "Of course a few men die during the Talon Ceremony. Not all of us are worthy! But in the end the eagles submit, according to the will of the Shining One. Eagles want to be jessed."

"Three years you've been doing this? You cage unjessed eagles and don't let them fly until they've chosen a new reeve..." The implication of the words hit as she realized that Feder had been alive and healthy the last time she had seen him. "How do you have unjessed eagles in cages?"

"Their reeves are dead. Now take your hand off my arm."

She abruptly recalled the conversation between Reyad and Hetta that night in the Suvash Hills. She had thought they were talking about women being mishandled and assaulted, and maybe they were, too, but a far more ominous explanation presented itself. "These talons you've trained up. You only allow men to become candidates."

"It is a duty fitted to men, as you and I have already discussed. The Talon Ceremony will become the tradition among all the reeve halls. Leaving reeveship to a chance meeting on the road is a disgrace. The reeve administrators should have implemented reforms long ago."

She released his arm as the full glory of his plan unfolded in her mind's eye. "You can't cage every unjessed eagle. Some will continue to fly on their way and jess as they please. But each time you manage to cage one more and force it to choose from a selection of male candidates you set before it, the reeve halls will change. Fewer and fewer women. The tradition of eagles jessing as they wish will be lost and eventually considered just another tale of the ancient past. When children who are now babies are old, they will think the Talon Ceremony is how it has always been done."

"And you will be dead, Lady Dannarah." He straightened his shoulders and shook out his magnificent sleeves. "Your time is over."

Bright sprang from the perch and knocked down the third candidate. Yet even so she pulled the rake of her talon. The man screamed as the claw slashed across his face. Staggering back, he fell, blood streaming. Bright retreated, huffing and chirping in distress. One young man toward the back of the line of hopeful talons stepped forward as if he felt the eagle's distress, but it wasn't his turn to go. The candidates were ranked in an order they were not allowed to break.

"I don't see you down there offering yourself to the eagle, Tavahosh. You are a coward willing to risk other people's lives but not your own."

No point in waiting for his outraged reply. She pushed rudely past him and clattered down the final few tiers to the ground. As she strode toward the netting cage she whistled. Nesard and Ruri pushed out from the crowd of onlookers and hurried over to her. Reyad trotted after them like a stick caught in their wake.

"What are those whip marks on your face?" she asked Ruri.

"We had trouble when the prince's people came. Feder fell from the cliff but we think he was pushed."

"The hells!"

"Then afterward they said a crippled man wasn't fit to be a reeve anyway, so it was best a whole man could now take command of his eagle. That's when I slugged them."

"Take that rebellious woman into custody!" Tavahosh shouted.

"Marshal," said Reyad. "I have important information."

"Not now."

She strode up to the netting and ducked under it, Ruri at her side holding a length of leash. Now that they were inside none of Tavahosh's strutting guards would dare follow. Nesard and Reyad helped the injured man out of the netting.

She whistled a calming tune; had they taught these candidates nothing about how to handle eagles?

Bright knew her and Ruri well enough to clumsily flap a pace backward but she was still big enough and angry enough to strike at a pigeon's worth of provocation. Knowing death could fall in a flash of wings always comforted Dannarah; a quick killing by eagle would be far better than the ugly illness that had eaten away her beloved father for half a year before his raving, painful death.

Ruri worked his way around one side of Bright, who knew the fawkner well and somewhat anxiously ignored his coaxing whistles and gestures. Dannarah eased forward with arms outstretched to make herself look bigger. She was a great whistler; eagles liked her for it. Yet the raptor was bewildered, thwarted of the instinct to fly away to the mountains and there mourn in whatever way eagles did; this was a mystery unknown to humankind. It wasn't right to make the raptors turn and turn about like beasts hitched to a wagon that they must pull until the day they dropped dead. No one really knew what eagles felt about their reeves but surely they, too, needed a period of rest and reflection, of freedom, to choose what to do next.

Some eagles never returned after the death of a reeve.

The right thing to do would be to pull up the netting and let Bright fly away. But she had a good idea of what carnage would happen if she tried to release Bright with them surrounded by Tavahosh's soldiers and by the priests and officials who stood to gain prestige and riches from whatever they planned to turn the reeve halls into. Through Ulyar and Tavahosh, Queen Chorannah would control the army and the reeves. Nothing Dannarah had seen so far convinced her Jehosh had the skill or temperament to fight a war within the palace.

Bright huffed, feathers settling a little as she started to calm. Her golden gaze flashed right, toward the talons, and then back to Ruri. The fawkner halted.

The drums remained silent. The wind rumbled, and no one spoke.

In the eerie silence and under the glaring sun, Dannarah remembered being young, the day she had daringly asked her father about the Devouring temples, the ones dedicated to the goddess Ushara, She Who Rules Over Love, Death, and Desire. Of course at sixteen Dannarah had wanted to know if it was true that beyond the palace walls young people could just go to Ushara's temple and meet with acolytes who might teach the shy and hesitant about sex, or rendezvous with their own chosen lovers in a safe place, not under their clan's eye. Of course she had been curious. In answer her father had closed Ushara's temples, first in Toskala and afterward in all the major cities. Children growing up in the cities now knew nothing of the Devourer except as an old superstition spoken of by their aged grandparents.

How had her father's actions been different from what Tavahosh intended?

Could anyone ever go back to the way things had been before, once they had changed that much? That which is lost can never fully be recovered.

Bright's golden eyes shifted again to the column of talons standing on the right side of the netting. While the other men stood in rigid lines, awaiting the prince's order, that one young man she had noticed before trembled as if he felt the eagle's distress. He had an ordinary face with a Sirni nose, he was fit and trim from training, and he had a scar on his shoulder. Broad hands. A shadow in his eye, like a cord of binding.

This mystery no one could explain. Some said there was only a single person fit for each individual eagle in every generation but Dannarah had never believed such a limiting tale. She believed there were people fitted for being reeves and somehow the eagles could find those people. Maybe it was similar to having a tuneful voice or a knack for embroidery, a space in your heart where the jess could hook.

She might be wrong about the young man, and she hated to the utter depths of her being to do anything that would make Tavahosh look good, but she was cursed if she would let Bright suffer.

The young man looked her way with an uneasy expression, as much plea as question. She nodded with the curt expectation of command. He ducked under the netting and murmured, "What must I do?" in Sirniakan.

"Copy the tune I am whistling. Do not signal the eagle to come. You must let her offer the jess. Wait for it."

The lad took a step toward Bright. She puffed her wings, and he halted.

A low rumble as of distant thunder rolled through the air, the cursed drums at it again.

"Glory to the Shining One!" gasped the young man.

Bright tilted her head in curiosity, as if asking the name of a new friend.

Jessed.

"Walk forward slowly and take hold of her harness," she said. "Ruri will show you how to hood the bird. Let Ruri teach you, lad. He knows Bright as well as any person alive."

With a look akin to awe on his face, the lad did as she told him. The drumroll faded as a murmur of voices rose from the men surrounding Prince Tavahosh.

She backed up to where Reyad held up the net, Nesard hovering behind him, and ducked out of the cage. The moment she was outside of the netting she blew three quick blasts on her bone whistle in the low tone that fell outside human range: the call of distress to her eagle.

"Nesard, those who can weather this storm will have to stay behind to manage what they can. But get out the ones who are at risk, especially the women here and in Toskala. Send a reeve immediately to alert Tarnit at Palace Hall. She must be back by now. Tell her to get all my people out of there at once."

"Where can we shelter so many eagles? Who can we trust?"

She hesitated. With Ivo missing and likely murdered, Iron Hall was no longer safe. She dared not burden Goard in Gold Hall. Argent, Horn, and Copper Halls were already under Tavahosh's thumb. That left Bronze Hall in Mar, with its odd relationship to Plum Blossom Clan in Salya. But even they had a new marshal they didn't like.

"We can't trust anyone. Fly west up the ridge of the Westhal Hills to Heaven's Ridge." She grasped for the first rendezvous point that came to mind in that vast wilderness. "There's a Ri Amarah estate in the Elsharat Valley next to Demon's Eye Peak. Send a reeve down there once a month. If I survive this I will drop a redheart wreath or basket of red-nut rice near the demon's coil where it will be visible only to reeves. Go!"

Nesard hurried away not a moment too soon, for Tavahosh approached the cage at the head of his soldiers. Judging by the furious sneer in his face, Dannarah guessed her intervention had given him the justification he needed to arrest her. That he would make an excuse to have her executed she did not doubt. Good luck to the poor lads who tried to jess Terror.

She grabbed Reyad's arm as if to detain him.

He spoke in a rush. "I found out two things. Hetta thought something terrible was happening to the women but I didn't really believe it. Now I know it's true. At Argent Hall they didn't transfer the last of the women reeves to other halls. They imprisoned them to save their eagles for Talon Ceremonies."

The terrible words did not even surprise her. She was already a blade in motion. "What's the other thing? Be quick."

"Most of the reeves are missing from Argent Hall and no one would tell me where they'd gone. Then they got suspicious of my questions. I crawled under the marshal's cote and I heard them plotting to arrest me. From what they were saying, I think they are part of a plot to overthrow the king. I got out only by a pinfeather."

An eagle's giant shadow glided over them. She did not glance up.

"You must pretend you are not my ally." She held Reyad's gaze, searching his face. He had such a pleasant visage it was difficult to imagine he had cold-bloodedly sliced Slip's jesses and Auri's harness. But people didn't necessarily show their deepest nature on the surface. Unlike demons, she could not see into his heart, only judge based on what she knew he had done. "Listen carefully, Reyad. Tavahosh will destroy the reeve halls if he is not stopped. Everything that went on at Argent Hall will happen in all the halls, if Tavahosh is not stopped. Do you understand me?"

He blinked. "Aui!"

"Take refuge with your clan afterward. I'll find you there."

Mouth tight, he said, "Yes, Marshal."

"I beg your pardon, I mean nothing by it, but this is the easiest story to make Tavahosh believe you dislike me." She pulled him close and kissed him on the mouth. He was so surprised he recoiled exactly as she would have wished. Taking her cue from Hasibal's players, she slapped him. As from down a long distance she heard men sniggering at the sight of an old woman pressing her suit on a handsome young man, just as she hoped. But it was the creak of a crossbow being wound back that grabbed her attention.

The shadow descended. Men shouted and scattered as Terror thumped down between her and the prince. Tavahosh was no coward but he hesitated as any prudent man would with Terror eyeing Tavahosh's cowering retinue as if deciding which one to snack on first.

"Arrest her!" cried Tavahosh.

Not one man moved in on the eagle. That wasn't cowardice; that was wisdom.

She scanned their numbers to see who had the crossbow. Men willing to kill Feder would delight in ridding the world of her but they would want to spare the eagle. She whistled. Terror walked forward with her swaying, awkward gait although there was nothing comic about the way the raptor loomed above Dannarah like the shadow of death. The expressions of enthralled panic on the arrogant faces of Tavahosh and his retinue diverted her for just long enough that she could not resist a final scratch.

"Prince Tavahosh. Nephew! Have you ever even been harnessed to an eagle? Been aloft? Show me your courage. Come with me now and see the land as reeves see it."

He wavered. Almost he leaped for the bait, seeing so many men around him watching him. Maybe he even dreamed of being offered an eagle's jess and the chance to prove himself as a reeve, as she had. Instead, he raised the bronze baton of his office as if to strike her with it.

"I strip you of your rank as marshal. You are nothing more than an old woman who should never have been allowed to be a reeve."

"Old I may be, but I am a reeve, Tavahosh, and you never will be one." She held out her hands in mocking supplication. "I invite you to arrest me with your own hands, right here with my eagle at my back."

His hesitation gave her the sliver of space she needed to step back under Terror. The harness slapped her shoulders. With the ease of long practice she swiftly hooked in, pressed the bone whistle to her lips, and blew the signal to fly.

48

When a woman returned from her sojourn in the menses court-yard, Queen Chorannah received her formally back into her court with a poem and a tray of sweet delicacies.

"You do not kneel and touch your head to the floor to show your gratitude to her sublime highness, Lady Sarai," remarked the translator with the false honey of a poisoned flower.

"Ri Amarah are enjoined to bow our heads before no one except our Creator, Your Highness." Sarai stood stubbornly, aware of how everyone seated in the queen's claustrophobic circle stared with interest. What their hopes were she could not tell: Did they plan to ingratiate themselves with Tavahosh's new bride or find ways to claw her until she bled?

Queen Chorannah said nothing.

The translator went on. "According to the report you took the book with you into the courtyard. Thus, it must now be burned."

She clutched the book in its leather case against her chest. "Burned? Why?"

"When a woman purifies herself through bleeding, all that she touches during that time is invested with a holy power dangerous to ordinary life."

"That is not the teaching of the Ri Amarah. A woman keeps a Book of Accounts throughout her life as her reckoning to the god, as her duty to the clan, and as a reminder of all the stages she makes on her own journey."

"But you are now betrothed to Prince Tavahosh."

"I am still Ri Amarah."

"Your people gave you to me in exchange for preferment," said Chorannah suddenly. "You are to become the wife of an exalted priest of Beltak who is also my son, a prince of kingly blood. His fate guides yours now. Your behavior is unseemly. Let the book be burned."

"No."

Every person in the hall leaned forward as the queen sucked in a sharp breath. Tension snapped. On an exhale, the queen drew the whip from her sash and handed it to Tayum.

Sarai trembled. She had grown up as a prisoner of shame imposed on her by others. Now she had become a vessel through which coin and connections might flow for the benefit of others. Physical pain had not been part of her life, and she did not know how well she could endure it; if she would scream, faint, beg, or otherwise humiliate herself. She feared that the trauma of a whipping might dislodge the pregnancy. But if she handed over her book she would become the shadow she feared above all else: mute flesh with a disgraced spirit too beaten down to dream.

She had not given in to shame and she would not give in to fear.

"Then whip me," she said in a calm voice. "I am sure Prince

Tavahosh will be pleased to know his mother feels free to discipline his wife rather than leaving such a decision to him. I will let him know that you have called his judgment and his manhood into question."

A flash of anger contorted the queen's face, quickly succeeded by a brief tease of a crooked smile like vexed respect. "You displease me, Lady Sarai. What this rebellious nature portends I cannot say, but you are correct that my son must have first crack at you."

The ominous phrase did not soothe Sarai's uneasy heart.

The queen went on. "You are forbidden the garden. Until Tavahosh's return you will stay in my sight, or be confined to your closet. That is all."

A servant withdrew the tray of delicacies without allowing Sarai a single one, but she didn't care. She had bought herself a few more days.

That evening after supper servants cleared away the tables and arranged all the couches at one end of the hall, leaving the other end open. Sarai tucked herself into the back corner by the servants' door, planning to stay still and silent and overlooked as she considered potential plans of attack. Tavahosh's arrogance was malleable. She had to convince him to allow her to correspond with Tsania. If she could do that then Tsania would figure out a way to help her.

The queen clapped her hands to draw their attention. "This evening comes a rare and exotic performance. King Jehosh has engaged a troupe of Hasibal's players to entertain the court. He has sent over the women players to play for us. I do not approve this childish manner of storytelling, but let us be polite."

Startled, Sarai looked up. Around her the court women whispered with delighted and possibly scandalized interest, then went still as a woman wearing a long robe and with a shawl wrapped over her hair appeared in an open door and paused there, awaiting their notice. She held a lamp in her hand to mark her as the "lantern" who would guide them through the story.

The queen nodded permission, and the woman entered the hall. Two musicians followed her, one with a seven-stringed zither and the other with a hand drum and rattle. The "lantern" sang the traditional melody, "*Let it be known, let it be told*," in an inviting voice. Sarai clasped her hands together. Her heart ached for remembering how paradisiacal those years with Elit had been, blossoming into shared womanhood, although she could only see that now.

The lantern bowed low before the queen and spoke in passable Sirni. "There can be no beauty except where the heavens smile. The torch tree saturated in fragrant oil does flame into light where your smile favors me."

The queen nodded her gracious permission to proceed.

"Tonight, O majestic one, we humbly offer a tale. Close your eyes but for a moment and imagine yourselves sailing along a river, with an eye on the bank where you glimpse the lives of people passing by." The zither player plucked a current of ripples out of her instrument, giving voice to the river and the passersby on the banks. "Let the current carry you into the Tale of Plenty. For on the road at that time there journeyed four travelers."

Other doors opened and to the beat of the drum players paraded in to transform into people on the road: Here an old person limping tiredly along. There a girl shepherding geese, the player acting both the part of the honking hissing geese and the goose-girl flicking her hands back from snapping beaks. Here then came the carter with his dog, another player barking so vociferously that women laughed, then covered their mouths as if unsure whether the queen would approve of this levity. Sarai leaned forward. She knew the tale well. It was one of her favorites. It was one of Elit's favorites.

Now sauntered in the central character of the first scene, the proud young scholar who would first cause so many complications and later fall in love with the goose-girl. He strutted like a man and he had a downy fuzz of a beard, but Sarai knew the broad-cheeked face and slender build, the perfect square chin and the laughing eyes: *Elit*.

Was she dreaming?

The first episode passed as Sarai stared, slack-jawed and too dazed to think.

Four characters meet on the road and set off a chain of reactions that will alter each of their lives forever. The geese scatter in fright from the barking dog. The elder stumbles and falls as the geese honk past. When the carter hurries to help the old person he unwittingly brushes against the proud young scholar. Taking offense, the young scholar punches him rather than heeding the pleas of the goose-girl to help her recover her geese, the gaggle on which her family depends for their livelihood. So it begins: unexpected meetings, chance kindnesses, and angry refusals.

Every story begins this way: at the instant when lives touch.

The narrator trilled a piercing ululation to mark a change of scene.

Four acrobats tumbled on for a comic interlude. They flipped into place, then pretended to be unruly children trying to be the first to reach a sweet rice cake by climbing up atop each other. How they made an unsteady tower of balancing people! The clamor was astounding. Even the eunuch guards crowded at open doors gaping as yet two more acrobats skipped in to climb the human architecture and grab for the imaginary treat while the women stuck holding up the base protested with such gusto that the audience laughed and laughed.

A person dressed in palace garb like Sarai's slid in beside her.

A hand brushed her arm from behind. A familiar voice whispered in her ear. "Change places and follow me."

Deftly the palace-garbed person switched places with Sarai. Elit took hold of her elbow and led her out the servants' door and down a corridor past the kitchen whose cooking Sarai smelled every day. They passed through two sets of sliding doors and entered a servants' antechamber where the other players were changing costume for the next scene. The far door was open a handbreadth. A man peeked in, nodding when he saw Elit and Sarai.

"Take off all your clothes," said Elit.

"I've heard that before," said Sarai with a shaky laugh, almost delirious with relief.

"Hurry!"

Sarai set down the leather case and untied her mirror. She was shaking so hard she could barely undo buttons but she stripped as Elit pulled a long strip of cloth from a basket.

"Push out all your air." Elit bound Sarai's breasts with tugs so hard that she could barely breathe.

Amused, the man said, "You'll never get men's roles with breasts like that."

Without looking at him Elit said, "You're just envious you won't get any roles with breasts like these, not like I have."

The man chuckled. "Victory to you, Elit."

Sarai blushed.

"Kneel," said Elit.

Sarai knelt. The other players tromped back toward the audience hall with shouts to announce their approach.

Elit bound Sarai's hair against her head and fixed a laborer's cap over the cloth. "Hold still."

How glorious Elit's eyes were as she perused Sarai's face, but her look was deadly serious. With a charcoal stick and paints she stippled a suggestion of stubble on Sarai's jaw, altered the look of her eye-folds, and shaded a new contour to her cheeks.

"How are you come here?"

"I can't change your face if you talk."

"Hush," said the man. "Do you hear that?"

As the women in the queen's hall stamped their feet in applause for the acrobats, a similar thunderous noise rose in the distance. "The performance in the king's hall is ending. My new comrade Sarri and I must go. You've got to go back on, El."

Elit kissed Sarai's lips, the touch so fleeting that by the time her lover had vanished back into the queen's wing Sarai only just brought a hand to her mouth, wondering if she had hallucinated the whole thing.

"Put on this man's tunic and trousers and this woman's robe over it," said the man, handing her clothing. The way he wasn't smiling as he looked her over made her wary.

When she finished dressing he handed her a token strung from a leather cord.

"Stay in the shadows and keep your head down. Don't respond to anyone or anything until we meet up with the others, and then stick to the middle. If someone questions you, cough as if you're ill. They'll take your token when we leave the Upper Gate. Don't lose it, or you can't get out."

"Whose token is it?"

"One of the men has joined the women and will go out with them when they leave. Come along. My name's Ani, by the way." She hurried to keep up as they walked down an exterior colonnade. He had the broad shoulders of a man who could wrestle an ox. "Take longer strides, not short quick ones. Be bold!"

Just as she was really getting out of breath they reached the grand entrance to the King's Audience Hall. Male players sang a robust tune as they paraded out of the hall, the audience stomping appreciatively behind them. Without seeming to notice Ani and Sarai the men absorbed them into their midst. Singing, they swaggered behind an escort of guards to the Upper Gate that opened onto the Thousand Steps. Here they surrendered their tokens.

A guard looked at her in her woman's robes. "What role do you play?" he said with a laugh.

Sarai coughed.

"Sarri's our Jolly Innkeeper, Coin-Fisted Mother-in-Law, and Hectoring Servant."

"Really?" Was the guard's curiosity feigned to stall them?

She pitched her voice to a false shrillness and mimicked Yava's speech. "Now is no good day to be getting into trouble, mistress."

The guards whooped. "Now there's a country accent if I ever heard one. Let's hear another!"

Another player jostled forward to declaim a speech as Ani pressed her under the archway. The players descended, keeping Sarai in the middle of the pack. Far below, the city spread like the night sky tipped over to become the bottom of a platter. Its pale stars were lamps set along streets or shining in courtyards. Here and there atop roofs glowed the red coals of braziers set out for cooking. Sound rose strangely into the air, snatches of yelling, a brazen laugh, the rumbling of wheels. The constant grind of anxiety made her unsteady on her feet. To distract herself she counted steps and was at 155 when a horn blared from the Upper Gate.

"Heya! Heya!"

"Keep going," said Ani.

Her throat grew thick with fear but she kept trudging even though she was sure they were about to drag her back, then arrest Elit and condemn her to the work gang, too, Elit and Gil lost forever. The rapid hammer of footsteps grew louder, a file of men chasing them down. Yet it was impossible for the troupe to run jammed together as they were on the stairs.

Out in the city light flared in a patch of darkness.

The soldiers caught up. "Move aside! Move aside!"

With the others Sarai pressed against the rock wall. A hundred guardsmen pounded past and kept going. When she could again get a view of the city, she realized the light was a bonfire. A pound of drums and a blast of horns announced the alarm for the fire brigades. Had a Ri Amarah compound been set on fire? She only vaguely understood the layout of the city and that was because Gil had sketched out a crude map, but this fire seemed too far out to be near the clan compound. Yet how could she really know? She'd never been a weeper, but she wept silently now, tears streaming down her cheeks.

"Let's go," said Ani as the last soldier clattered past.

By the time they reached the base of the steps her legs ached. She staggered across the wide square and over Guardian Bridge to discover guards at the far end of the span blocking their way.

"I remember you," their stout chief said. "You're the Hasibal players sent up to entertain. Not a good night for singing, is it? Where you headed?"

"The Rice Farmer's Beer."

"Don't know that place."

"It's an inn in Fifth Quarter. With your permission, ver, we'll wait for our women and walk together."

"Maybe you will and maybe you won't, for the king has imposed a curfew. All the gates are closed between the quarters from sunset to sunrise. You can't get to Fifth Quarter from here."

"We know about the curfew," said Ani. "We have a token that allows our party to return to our inn via South Gate."

"Neh, South Gate is the worst of it. There's been trouble there five nights running. Folk keep building a bonfire to block the gate. They don't want any more work gangs marched out. They say too many men have been arrested for nothing more than being drunk or getting in a fistfight. I'm thinking you'd be safer to go back to the upper palace. The city's on edge, especially what with all the rumors about those cursed Silvers and their coin."

"What rumors?" asked Sarai.

Ani trod on her foot in warning.

Well launched, the chief noticed nothing. "They've used their magic to ensnare Prince Tavahosh. He's to wed a Silver girl, that same one who first married the Herelian lad. When she saw bigger fish she got her first husband arrested and condemned to a work gang so she could seduce the prince."

Sarai hissed, trembling. Ani clamped an arm over her shoulders to crush back down her throat the words she wanted to spit in the guard's face.

One of the players poked Ani on the shoulder. "I told you this was a bad idea."

"What is a bad idea?" asked the chief.

"Coming to the city was a bad idea," Ani said. "In my grandmother's time the cities welcomed Hasibal's players but they are a sour place today."

A sentry whistled. "Chief! People coming down the steps!"

The chief loped away. The fire drums were beating rum pum rum pum rum rum rum pum. A smoky glare gleamed above the rooftops. From here Sarai could see the gatehouse of the lower palace, which lay about an arrow's shot away. When she and Gil had walked out that day all unsuspecting to attend Queen Chorannah's audience, a mere four guards had been on duty at the lower palace; now twenty manned the gate.

The man who had challenged Ani sidled up to her. "Is it true, what the chief says?"

After everything else this was really too much. She poked him hard in the chest. "I am escaping the prince, you ass. Not seducing him. Why else would I have to sneak out?"

"Because the king has forbidden the marriage and you mean to meet the prince elsewhere."

"Believe what you wish since you have already made up your mind. Elit can vouch for me."

"Yes." He leaned closer, breath hot on her ear. "You seduced Elit, too. She's always on about the mysterious lover she left behind."

"Heya!" Ani pushed between them. "Shut your nose, Vedar. We voted like we always do and even you agreed to the plan. Don't go weaseling out on it now."

Wsst! Wsst! shrilled one of the players.

The women clattered over the bridge in grim haste, and the men fell into step with them, the two groups effortlessly blending.

"My love." Elit slipped in beside her, catching her close with an arm around her back. "You look so weary and pale, and your cheeks so hollow. You're not well."

"I'm pregnant. I could only eat gruel and flat bread because they were trying to feed me muzz. How did this happen?"

"Aunt Tsania got word to the right people."

"I knew I could rely on her! But what *right people* does Aunt Tsania know?"

"I can't say more than that now. All will be well now we are together."

Elit kissed her on the cheek. Down Canal Street the players strode, singing the famous refrain from the Tale of Plenty: "*The only companion who follows even after death, is justice.*" The players flourished the props they used to tell their tales but in their hands she saw everyday objects become weapons: A pole used to simulate a horse being ridden became a fighting staff. An archon's ruling scepter had the weight of a club. An elder's cane hid a short steel lance. Elit had two stout sticks tucked in her belt; she swung them into her hands.

Smoke tainted the air. Canal Street remained empty of traffic. The Four Quarters Bridge where Bell, Flag, Stone, and Wolf Quarters joined was closed and barred. Out on the canal, boats bobbed, some lit by lamps.

Hooves clomped behind them. A column of soldiers rode past, led by King Jehosh himself. He looked dashing and at ease on horseback. Although he glanced up and down the troupe of players, he did not call his soldiers to a halt and she was certain he did not recognize her. His lead riders lit their way with lanterns bobbing on poles. A company of infantry marched behind. From deep in Wolf Quarter a militia horn blew as a call to arms. The riders cut into Wolf Quarter and vanished into the gloom.

Alarms clapped and clanged as people clamored in the distance as if fending off a roused beast. The troupe kept walking at that same steady pace down Canal Street. Sarai had no idea how far away Fifth Quarter lay or how the players could remain so calm.

At the next intersection, a lamp flared to life and was immediately snuffed out. Like leaves swirled into a meadow by a brusque blast of wind, twenty or thirty men loped out from alleys and side streets to block their way. The ambushers had knives, swords, and spears, so many edged blades that Sarai could taste their steel as if the edges were already awash in blood.

"Stay in the middle," said Elit.

At the front, big Ani pounded his staff three times on the ground. An old man and an older woman stepped up on either side of him and spoke in eerie unison.

"We are humble players dedicated to Hasibal the Merciful One. Let us make our way in peace as all shall be at peace within the merciful hands of compassion."

A flame snapped into life within the glass confines of a lantern. A man with a scarred chin walked up with lantern in hand to face them. "Rumor whispers that a troupe of players entertained in the upper palace this night. Folk must eat, so we don't begrudge you that. But the palace digs taxes out of our very flesh and leaves us hollow. We need our coin back. You can hand over whatever you earned tonight and we will be happy to let you go peacefully onward."

"We earn coin not for our own pockets but for the peace of the land. Let us pass."

The man whistled. The associates closed in to make a ring around them.

A spike of energy rushed through the troupe, breath pulled in. Together they exhaled in a shout: "Hoo! Hoo! Hah! Hah!"

The sound, so loud it echoed off the nearest buildings, cut right into her bones. The players stamped forward in perfect unison. "Hah! Hah! Ya! Ya! Ya!"

Ani leaped out and cracked the startled leader on the head. The man went down like a felled ox, his lamp shattering with a flash of oil and flame. A chaos of shrieks and howls rent the air as the other players leaped into action. Around Sarai the players splintered like a vessel split apart, flying in every direction as they attacked their assailants.

Elit grabbed her elbow. "Follow me."

They dodged between tangles and skirmishes, chased by the erratic rhythm of the thud of impacts onto flesh. She ran after Elit down a side street. The world bled darkness around them. As they turned a corner onto another street a door slapped shut. Gauzy lamplight shone through a rice paper door while a baby cried. They kept running, Elit tugging her along behind.

Elit paused at an intersection. Sarai panted, chest burning, already out of breath.

"Where . . . we . . . going?"

"I'm taking you to a safe house."

A dog barked.

Footsteps pounded behind them. A man called, "There! I see them."

They fled down a street of shop fronts closed up for the night. The men behind were gaining on them. Elit yanked her onto a smaller side street lined with darkened residences, then pivoted to pull her sideways into an alley scarcely wide enough for a delivery wagon and with a light burning at the end.

They ran right up against a wall, a dead end. There was no gate or door, only a shuttered window too high to reach from the ground and a lamp overhead.

Their pursuers emerged out of the night into the aura of lamplight. Two had knives and the third held a sword. Elit settled into a fighting stance, sticks at the ready.

They chuckled, low and mean. "We just want the king's coin, ver," said the one with the sword. "But if we can't get coin, we'll take a tithe in trade."

Sarai slipped her mirror from its sleeve and angled it to catch lamplight. The taller knife-man winced back as she caught its wink right into his gaze. Elit leaped forward and cracked him upside the jaw. He staggered back and fell on his side. She danced out of the way as the swordsman slashed at her.

"Behind me," said Elit.

The other knife-man fanned out to come at them from the side and thus split Elit's guard. Sarai backed into the wall, hands shaking so hard she almost dropped the mirror.

Above her, the shuttered window was flung open. An old man in soldier's gear appeared, poised on the sill and holding a small crossbow. With a thunk it released. A bolt slammed into the swordsman's gut. Elit sprang out to whack the other knife-man over the head; the blow didn't fell him but he grunted and swayed.

"Out of the way," said the old man.

Elit ducked back beside Sarai. A bolt thudded into the knife-man's shoulder, and more quickly than Sarai thought possible a third, a fourth, and a fifth, until all three men were down, groaning and thrashing as they tried to crawl away.

"Kill them," said the old man in the same tone he might have said *Here's your tea*.

Sarai's mouth opened and closed and opened and closed, yet no sound came out as Elit knelt, rolling the first one half over and bracing her weight so he couldn't struggle, then slit his throat with the same brisk efficiency as she had slaughtered sheep back in Elsharat. But this was not a sheep, and the blood that gushed not that of an animal but of a person.

Her gaze hazed, and her lips prickled as if she had eaten raw nettles.

A rope ladder unrolled down the wall and hit Sarai on the head. She flinched and got caught in the rungs. Footsteps pounded up out of the darkness, and panic made her thrash harder and get further tangled as a man raced into view.

Elit said, "Ani! I could have used your help sooner."

"Had to save that ass Vedar when he tripped."

"Ha! How like him. Here, you do the other two."

Elit trotted over to Sarai and roughly yanked her out of the entangling rungs.

"Climb, Sarai! Hurry!"

Sarai's hands had gone so numb she could barely feel the rope as she climbed. When she paused to catch her breath again, Elit shoved at her backside. Clambering across the sill she found herself in a storage room filled with chests. Elit swung easily up after her, followed by Ani, who had blood on his face and hands. Sarai braced herself on the wall; she was finding it hard to breathe, each inhalation more of a hoarse, whistling wheeze.

Once he had shuttered and barred the window, the old man indicated a corridor. "This way."

"Yes, Captain." Ani went out at once.

Sarai did not budge. The jumbling confusion of her thoughts, the dreadful image carved into her mind by blood pumping out of dying men, the tightness in her chest: All made words hard. "You killed them."

"Had we left them alive, they could later have identified you as coming here." The old man had a stare that cut words right off her tongue and left her speechless. He again indicated the corridor. "Wash off your disguises and change your clothes."

Elit stepped closer and caught Sarai's face between her hands. They had been apart for so long that Sarai had forgotten everything about Elit. The shape and heat of her lover poured over her with an immediacy that was almost painful.

Elit was taller than Sarai now, having been a little shorter for all of their childhood. A scar cut a stark white line across the back of her left hand where she had cut herself with pruning shears when they were both fourteen. Her shoulders were even broader than they had been before, sculpted with muscle from training, but the nape of her neck and the curve of her throat were exactly as Sarai recalled them: skin so sensitive to kisses.

She broke away. "What have you become, Elit?"

"I'm one of Hasibal's players," said Elit with a serious stare and a flutter of hands, as if she wanted to grasp Sarai's fingers and press them to her lips in the old familiar way. "We are soldiers now, Black Wolves fighting for the Hundred."

Sarai's pulse thundered in her ears. To hear her beloved name herself with that hated name pinned her to silence.

"We don't have time for this," said the captain.

A young woman of quite startling beauty poked her head in with a questioning look. "How much trouble?" she asked.

The captain spoke with brisk command. "Three dead men in the alley. Have them thrown into the river. Come along, you two!"

Sarai found herself moving even though she'd had no intention of following him. He led them down a corridor past small cubicles that reminded her of the palace's sleeping closets; the sounds of lovemaking drifted from behind closed doors. Stairs took them into a small courtyard, landscaped with herbs and flowers, that accommodated an outdoor washing area elevated on planks and amply supplied with water through bamboo pipes. A trellis heavily grown with muzz and proudhorn sheltered a heated bath for soaking. Four lanterns illuminated Ani standing on the planks and scrubbing dirt and blood from his body with a brush. As Elit stripped he merely handed her the brush. It meant nothing to them to stand out in plain view naked. He had scars on his left hip and powerfully muscled legs and arms with the girth of a very big man; Gil's shorter, slender frame was more to her taste. The tattoos down Ani's right arm marked him as a child of the Water Mother because they were the same as the inks Elit had on her right arm and left leg. Sarai stared at Elit's lean body, her firm ass and small breasts and the triangle of dark hair, but when she opened her mouth to speak all voice and emotion had fled.

Elit paused. "I forget you're not accustomed to this. I haven't bathed in private for three years." She showed Sarai a basin, where she washed the paint and pencil off her face. The captain had already gone inside. In an antechamber overlooking the courtyard they changed into cotton taloos.

"The captain is waiting for you." Elit indicated an adjoining room. "I'll stand as sentry outside so no one interrupts."

"Have you killed before that you can be so calm? You cut that man's throat like you were killing a sheep."

"It's not meant to be something you get used to. We pray, and give offerings, and chant to ask for forgiveness, to find a measure of peace. And we have nightmares, too."

"Is this what a merciful god asks you to do?"

Elit touched a finger to Sarai's lips, as she used to do when they were whispering secrets. "It is the path I've been called to. We fight for the Hundred. Talk to Captain Kellas."

Sarai walked stiffly to join the captain in a small audience room fitted with cushions and an altar set into an alcove in one wall. Illuminated by a tiny oil lamp, the alcove displayed a painting depicting the compassionate face of the Merciful One in her guise as a beautiful woman sitting in a shower of plum blossoms. The holy one did not resemble any of the women of the Hundred whom Sarai had ever seen, as if she were a foreigner who had wandered far before she found a home. Her dark eyes seemed to follow Sarai's hesitant tread with a kind, solicitous gaze.

Sarai let out a held breath and seated herself on a cushion, pushing the tea tray so it rested between her and the captain. His presence had such clarity and formality that it was easy for the mind to wipe away the shocking violence and just wait as she studied him. He had a pleasing face and the posture of a man still healthy and vigorous for all his years.

First he poured tea with efficient neatness and offered her the first cup, which she did not take. Then for an uncomfortable interlude he studied her face. Only by gripping the cloth of her taloos did she manage not to lift a hand to touch her scar.

"We live in a complicated time, Lady Sarai," he said.

"Elit cannot be a Black Wolf."

"Why not?"

"Because they are murderers!" She wanted to dash the contents of the cup into his face. "Anyway, they are all gone. They were disbanded after the death of King Atani."

"They lost their honor," he said softly.

To her surprise he reached across the tray with a hand seamed, callused, weathered, and worn with experience. His fingers traced her scar as with a feather's brush. With a faint sigh he withdrew his hand. "But they are not all gone."

"They should all have died! They killed my mother!"

"No, *they* did not," he said. "Only one man was responsible for your mother's death."

In his aged face she saw so many shadows she could not count them. She felt herself at the brink of a precipice yawning open at her unsuspecting feet. Almost she jumped up and ran. But she saw the truth in his expression, a cold burden that drenched all her hot anger.

Her voice cracked as she forced out words. "How did it happen? Why was she there?"

49

He knew who she was the moment he saw her, although he had begun to suspect the truth when he had seen Lord Gilaras with his veiled Ri Amarah wife, a girl of the right age from that specific clan, one whom the family was willing to marry out. The scar sealed it, but that wasn't all he had seen. Moments of great emotion sear into the mind. He could still recall her mother's face when she had approached them in the forest with her delicate and stubborn beauty. Sarai resembled her mother, although it was immediately obvious why her mother had fled a jealous husband with a baby who clearly had not been fathered by a Ri Amarah man.

"His name was Isar," he said.

"Isar?"

"The man your mother was with, the man she was defending. Possibly he was the man who sired you."

"We have a word for that in our language. A woman stained by lust who plants a false seed in her husband's garden."

He raised an eyebrow. "I confess I am old-fashioned enough to believe a baby matters more to a clan than which man fathered it."

She pressed a hand to her cheek as if the scar whispered a message to her. Her eyes were brilliant. He leaned back a little to give some distance from their intensity.

After several unsteady breaths she lowered the hand and spoke in a quavering voice. "Please do not spare me the details. I would rather know than remain ignorant as I have all these years."

He admired the way she did not waver, so he told her pieces of the truth: a rumored plot, his race after the king, the woman they'd met in the forest and how she had come after him with a staff on the ridgetop. Such altered retellings covered the worst wounds of the past.

"She stabbed me. I defended myself. I am trained to kill, Lady Sarai, and she had placed herself between me and the king."

"But when you realized I was strapped to her chest you tried not to kill me."

"I do not kill children."

"Don't you? If the adults who nurture them are dead, is that not a form of death for the children they cared for? As it was for me?" Her stare actually made him feel self-conscious, a feeling he had long thought scraped off by the rigors of his life. "Do you regret it, Captain?"

"I regret not saving King Atani. That before anything. As for her life, I think she was not my enemy but rather in that place at an ill time, for reasons of her own that had nothing to do with the king."

"That is a glib way to justify killing her."

"In times of crisis if you wait to act to be assured no one will suffer, then you will never act."

She set on her lap a bronze mirror whose incised back she stroked pensively as her eyes sought memories he could not see. Over the years he had learned to temper his impulsive, restless nature with patience. He sipped at his tea, enjoying its bitter aftertaste.

"Isar." She spoke the name precisely, as if committing it to memory. "Did he die, too?"

"Whether he died in the end I cannot say. When I fell unconscious he may have still been alive. I never saw or heard of him after that. I do remember he called out her name, Nadit."

"Her name was Nadai, but I suppose Nadit would have been the easiest way to make it sound like a Hundred name."

His gaze drifted to the altar with its painted image that people called the Merciful One but whom he called *beloved*.

He remarked, "When I was a boy, the god Hasibal was not called the Merciful One. Hasibal was known as the Formless One and could walk the world in any shape."

"Why do we change, Captain?" she asked in that slightly hoarse voice that made her utterances pleasing and warm and a little mysterious despite her thick hill country accent. "What causes a young woman to abandon wealth, status, and her own young son to die an outlaw in the wilderness?"

"Love?"

"Surely love rarely alters the trajectory of our motion to such an extreme."

"Does it not?"

"Ambition and a desire to learn to recite the old tales caused

Elit to dedicate herself to Hasibal, and yet now I discover she
has become a soldier. It was greed that got Gil arrested, but if I
recall rightly, you then used the opportunity to recruit him as a
spy. King Jehosh first wished to flirt with me no doubt because
as a Ri Amarah woman I seemed forbidden and thus alluring.
But as soon as the queen's plot was revealed to him he was willing to see me turned over to Prince Tavahosh because he wanted
to know what I could find out from his son about her plans.
Since you serve Jehosh, why not leave me where I was?"

"Do you want to go back?"

"No, I emphatically do not. What I want is Gil pardoned and
released."

"His work gang is out of my hands."

"Then what use are you, Captain?"

Her cool and rather sardonic interrogation delighted him. "A
fair question, Lady Sarai, but one that is not mine to answer. I
am merely a soldier under orders."

"Let me ask a different question then. What campaign are
you waging?"

"I am a traditionalist. I remember what the Hundred looked
like when I was a boy and I reflect on how many things have
changed."

"We cannot recover what is past, Captain. My mother stays
dead despite what I wish. The Hundred cannot return to
the days of righteous rule under King Anjihosh the Glorious
Unifier."

"No, indeed, it cannot."

"As you people set in motion your schemes and plots do you
think at all about those who will be caught in the conflict?
What will happen to the Ri Amarah, who are already being
attacked? What about me? I don't believe you rescued me out of
sympathy for my desperate situation. I think I am nothing more
than a piece in a game to all of you. So is Gil. So is Elit, even if

she believes otherwise. You shouldn't play games with people's lives!"

"Do not be naive, Lady Sarai. It does not suit you."

"Am I naive to think you use people as tools and weapons in a greater war? Regardless of the cost to them?"

"Many of the Ri Amarah have already left the city to take shelter at country estates. I am not unsympathetic to the difficult situation they find themselves in."

"My thanks," she said sardonically. "But you are right. It seems there is widespread unrest throughout the Hundred. Have I been roping the wrong horse? Is it demons you fear?"

Now he did chuckle. She had exactly the kind of incisive mind fitting for a Wolf. Those who only looked for martial prowess sorely mistook the matter. The more you narrowed your idea of who could be useful, the more rigid your blade and the easier it could snap.

"Why would you say so?" he temporized.

A mischievous smile softened her expression. He thought she would speak but instead the smile faded as she tucked the mirror into a cloth sleeve and placed it on top of the leather case she carried.

"Something King Jehosh said."

Fifty years as a soldier had honed his instinct for danger. A jolt of energy passed through his old frame, like the whisper of death breathing down his back. He leaned forward.

She said, "He told me that demons threaten the Hundred because they want to rule here again, as they did in the old days. He said they had poisoned his father, King Atani, with their false promises and seductive words."

The moment Sarai said the words, she saw how Captain Kellas went rigid, his eyes on her but no longer looking at her. She had lost him as thoroughly as if he had gotten up and left the room. If she had slammed Elit's sticks into the side of his head he couldn't have looked more stunned.

"Poisoned," he murmured. His gaze focused on her with a cold intensity that made her scoot away from him. "You are sure that is what he said. False promises and seductive words."

"Yes. I have an excellent memory. Anyway I wrote it down afterward."

From elsewhere in the building a loud hammering started. Voices raised in argument.

Elit slipped inside. "Supreme Captain Ulyar is here demanding to see you, Captain."

"Into the closet, Lady Sarai," he said without a pause. "Elit, you'll sit."

Sarai protested, "But—"

"Don't argue." Elit whisked her into a screened alcove lined with shelves on which were piled cushions and bedding. With the door shut a whisker's length from her knees, Sarai listened to the rustling of cloth as Elit arranged herself on a cushion.

A man who has just been told news he does not want to believe might look the way Captain Kellas had just looked. Yet he had cleared the expression so smoothly off his face, responding to the new crisis, that she might have been mistaken.

A person stomped into the chamber. "So, Captain Kellas, you are taking your ease at the House of the Dagger while the city burns."

"Is there a problem, Supreme Captain Ulyar? I came here to speak to one of my informants."

"A euphemism, I presume. She's young enough to be your granddaughter. I did not know you went in for that sort of thing."

"Why do you bore me with this manner of predictable insult? What do you want?"

"Prince Tavahosh's bride is missing. At first it was thought she had been taken ill but after all of the latrines and bathing rooms were searched, the queen realized the girl had been kidnapped. The queen sent me to track down the Habisal players who were in the palace earlier."

"Of course I am sorry to hear it but I have more pressing concerns, Ulyar. Perhaps you hadn't heard but there has been another fire at a Ri Amarah compound."

Sarai bit down on her lip but in her mind she spoke a prayer for mercy.

"The queen's enemies set that fire, no doubt at the king's instigation!"

"Odd that you should make such an accusation. Fortunately the fire brigade has isolated the blaze and gotten it under control. Also, a mob has raised a bonfire at South Gate, torn down the prison gates, and released the prisoners. The king himself has ridden to South Gate to impose order."

"How that man loves to strut!"

"He was always at his best in the field."

"A man cannot live on past glory forever."

"No, I suppose he cannot, Supreme Captain Ulyar, but at least he rode to confront the troubles at South Gate while you busy yourself haranguing me here. Why come to me at all? I am chief of security for the lower palace."

"The Hasibal players were invited into the palace by the king."

"Ah! You are saying the queen believes King Jehosh to be responsible for the Silver's disappearance and therefore think I may have had some knowledge of the deed beforehand. Aui! Ulyar, you know how Jehosh is. He loves the chase, and how much more forbidden and thus tempting a Ri Amarah bride. I cannot understand why Queen Chorannah would force through the marriage to her son now, when she might simply have waited for the king's passion to fade as it always does."

The pacing, impatient footsteps surely belonged to Ulyar, not Kellas. "Just as I thought, Captain Kellas! You do know where the girl is. I've sent a company to the Rice Farmer's Beer in Fifth Quarter to apprehend her. She was obviously smuggled out by the Hasibal players."

She cupped her hands over her nose and mouth, afraid he might hear her breathing.

"Ulyar, maybe this isn't about the young woman at all. Maybe the king sees an alliance between Ri Amarah wealth and Queen Chorannah's son as a threat to his rule and his person. Do you know anything about that?"

Ulyar broke off pacing. "If he believes his sons mean to betray him and put themselves on the throne in his place, that is only because he is looking into the mirror of his own face!"

"What do you mean?" Captain Kellas's voice sharpened.

Ulyar took in a hard, harsh breath. "I don't mean anything. I mean he's suspicious when he should be trusting! I know you are hiding the girl. An agent saw her run down the alley and never come out. I will have this establishment searched."

"Very well. May I finish my tea while you go about your business? Elit, can you freshen up this pot? It's gotten cold." Light steps departed into the interior of the house just as the door onto the courtyard slid open.

The door to the closet wasn't quite shut, leaving a narrow gap through which Sarai could peer. She caught a glimpse of Elit's back retreating. Then, as if changing places, the very beautiful woman they had seen briefly upstairs wafted into the chamber on a cloud of heady perfume.

"Ah, the Incomparable Melisayda. So pleased you could join us," said Captain Kellas. "Do you know Supreme Captain Ulyar?"

"I believe he and I have had the pleasure of meeting before," the woman said in a seductive voice as she passed out of Sarai's range of vision, undulating toward the two men in a way meant to draw attention to her hips.

The scrape of a sword drawn overlapped a sword drawn, one in response to the other. Sarai flinched back, banging her head against the shelves, but the noise did not matter because the ring of metal striking covered it. The hiss of cloth. A grunt almost of surprise.

"Curse it," remarked Captain Kellas.

The thud of a heavy weight dropping made the floor tremble.

Sarai eased the door open a tiny bit more. Ulyar sprawled on his back on the mat floor, his own sword spiked out at an angle where it had fallen from his hand. Blood seeped up through his tabard, moist and sluggish, but his slack face and empty eyes told the true tale.

"Are you hurt, Grandpa?" The beautiful young woman bent over the old man. He knelt, braced up on his bloody sword.

"It's nothing. I'm just getting old and slow." He fingered apart a sleeve, wincing as he examined his bleeding forearm.

The woman crouched beside him to run a finger along the wound. She had a lively face whose mobile expressions caught the eye. A tightly wrapped taloos of translucent violet silk did nothing to conceal the attractive curve of her ample breasts. "It's not too deep. You shouldn't have left Grandmama behind in Salya. She worries when you're gone about your expeditions, not that she would ever tell you."

Kellas chuckled through gritted teeth. "Of course she tells me. Aui! Don't poke at it. Are you trying to make it hurt more?"

The woman grinned. "Yes. Fortunately for you I have a store of wound-heal in the kitchen."

"We'll need the body transported elsewhere in the city . . . We could plant him by the fire at the Ri Amarah compound."

"No!" Sarai slammed the door open and crawled out, too shaken to stand. "Then people will blame my people for his murder and there will be more trouble for them!"

The woman cast her a skeptical glance, then shrugged. "Let me get the ointment and linen, Grandpa. Don't move."

"Make sure you clean the wound with boiled water or your strongest liquor," said Sarai to her back. "My aunt has conducted studies of injuries. A cleaned wound is less likely to suppurate. Silk should be used for the dressing—"

Melisayda raised beautifully trimmed eyebrows, like a challenge. "Did I ask for your advice, verea?"

"The Incomparable Melisayda," Sarai murmured, chasing down linked memories. "Gil told me about you. You're a—"

"Businesswoman and spy, and the beloved granddaughter of my wife," said the captain with a decided edge. "Melisa, send word to Arasit to come at once to Toskala. We await her and the Wolves from Salya."

As the Incomparable went out, Flit returned with a fresh pot of tea and took in the situation with a glance. "Captain, is he dead? Are you wounded?"

"Yes, he's dead. My own injury is shallow."

"What is going on?" demanded Sarai. "What are you not telling me?"

The captain rocked back from his knees to sit on his heels. Drawn and pale, he blew short breaths out through his lips to manage the pain. Sarai had a cursed good idea it wasn't physical agony that had felled him.

"I am looking into the mirror of my own face and realizing I mistook the matter this whole time, all these cursed years. As for you, Lady Sarai, the queen's agents are hunting you and there are far more of them than there are of us."

50

For so many years Dannarah had flown above the land, bound to its service and yet always a bit removed. Her memories of her childhood years when her father had shone as the sun in her sky with her brother as her constant companion had faded, because she had decided they needed to be put behind her. What mattered was carrying out the duty her father had charged her with those weeks she had sat with him as he died.

Never forget that chaos breeds illness and demons breed chaos. The reeves are the eyes of the king, Dannarah. You will become chief marshal of the reeve halls after me. Under your command you must make sure to root out corruption from the ranks wherever you see it, as I have done. There will always be someone who sees the reeves as a means to increase his power or enrich his purse. Some will come from within the reeves. Others will assail you from without. All will seek to turn the reeve halls to their own ends, but the reeves serve the king. A strong king keeps order because where people live in an orderly peace, they will prosper. People have already begun to take for granted the peace I built. They believe I defeated the demons, but we never defeat demons, only contain them. We must always be on our guard.

The contours of the land seen from on high tell a different story from what folk see who travel along the ground. Valleys hidden from the road are easy to spot from the air. A dense canopy of forest conceals a network of trails that an outlaw may use to escape. The main roads strike out across the land straight as spears, while the flat spirals of demon's coils wink from high peaks and isolated ledges, making one wonder: Why there? Why so hard to reach?

The precise pattern by which the coils were woven into the land could not be discerned, and yet a few reeves knew that the Hundred was named not after its "hundred" towns and villages but after the demon's coils. According to the most ancient lore passed down in the reeve halls, there were exactly one hundred demon's coils in the land and not a single one outside it.

Her father had a map on which he marked every known coil, and on his deathbed he had given it into her keeping. So far she had seventy-three. Every time she rolled out the map a sense tickled on the edge of her thoughts that an answer lay right in front of her eyes whose question she had not yet asked.

A pattern underlies the world. For so long she had kept her gaze on the rivers and the fields and the people walking about their business like ants on their busy trails that she had forgotten the other patterns that undergird lives: the spines of impassable mountains blocking painful memories, the sweet beauty of a flower-strewn meadow like the recollection of first love, the delta of secrets spreading from old lies.

After fleeing Horn Hall and the repulsive Talon Ceremony, she followed the West Track south with the river to the west and the grasslands called the Lend to the east. As the sun set she searched for a place to land for the night. On a stretch of road out of sight of any village and empty of traffic, she spotted an old Ladytree with its vast overhanging canopy. After landing, she released Terror to hunt.

The old tree hulked bigger on the ground than it had seemed from the air, with a cracked trunk and a hollow inside filled with dirt and debris from years of blowing winds. Once travelers would have spent the night under its gracious limbs, out of the rain, sheltered by the goddess Atiratu, the Lady of Beasts, in whose honor such trees were planted. But for years now such itinerancy had been forbidden by order of the Beltak priests, who demanded that travelers stay in licensed hostels where they paid a tithe to the priests for a mattress and a bowl of porridge.

Just beyond the outer branches of the Ladytree lay a scattering of boulders. One rock was set flush to the ground, flat as a bed. Withered wreaths lay there, given as offering to the old gods. She had to think a moment to recall that such rock altars were sacred to Hasibal the Merciful One, who grants peace, joy, and courage on the hard journey through life. It was the Merciful One who guided worshippers through the maze of grief one step at a time, never hurried and always compassionate.

For all his adult life Atani had worn one of the necklaces called Hasibal's Tears, but she had never seen him pray to any god except when required for palace ceremonies.

Alone in the dusk, birds silent, wind soft, she closed her eyes. Grief shut its vise onto her heart, a crushing weight that staggered her and brought tears.

Her old friends Feder and Ivo dead. Reeves whose names she would never know stuck in cages and killed like trash. Ceremonies that went against everything the reeves had always been.

That arrogant ass Tavahosh was going to destroy the reeve halls.

She loved the orderly land their father had passed on to her and Atani, which Anjihosh had so carefully cultivated by pulling out the weeds and tending the fields. Atani's quirks and odd schemes and those idiotic law pillars he erected on every major road had irritated her. She'd been jealous of the way he had retained Kellas's loyalty while she had felt pushed to arm's length. It wasn't that she pined over Kellas; she'd had far more enthusiastic lovers later, and from the distance of experience she knew he had done his duty without true passion, probably at her father's command.

Imagine how that scene might have gone!

Captain Kellas, my daughter is seventeen and does not wish to marry, but being a girl of exceptional spirit and intelligence, she will doubtless wish to experience sexual pleasure. I cannot trust her with just any random fellow who may wish to take advantage of the connection for personal gain. So I command you to safely guide her into these delicate waters.

Age gave her the wit to find it more amusing than humiliating. Of course her father had known. He had known everything, hadn't he?

Hadn't he?

But Captain Kellas's damning words, *The things your brother did not choose to tell you, I cannot reveal,* suggested otherwise.

She forced herself to consider that last night before Atani was killed.

As chief marshal she had accompanied the king and the army into the northwest into the foothills of Heaven's Ridge. When the army and Prince Jehosh had marched north to cross the border into Ithik Eldim she had turned back with Atani and his company, heading back into the Hundred.

They camp along the road beside a law pillar planted just four days earlier on the march up. Atani pretends to be his usual self, encouraging his men to talk, singing along to popular choruses, but she sees the lie in his eyes. As the encampment settles down she chases his bodyguards out of his tent and sits cross-legged on her bedroll while he lies on a cot with an arm flung over his brow. She cleans and oils her harness, glancing at him at intervals. He wears a sleeping kilt in the local style and no ornamentation except his wolf's head ring and his necklace of Hasibal's Tears with its tiny plum branch made of seven exquisitely lacquered blossoms.

The glow of a lamp hanging from the cross-poles bathes his face in light. His eyes remain open but he does not seem to be looking at anything.

When after a while he has still said nothing, she begins to talk. "Do you remember that time at Brushfire Cove when Mama took her embroidery and her attendants down to the strand while you and I played on the rocky beach? Merlings swam into the cove and whistled as if they were trying to talk to us. Atani, are you listening to me?"

He swings his legs over to sit on the edge of the cot. Grabbing her signal flags, he starts to comb through them looking for frays and tears. "There will be trouble with this 'king's daughter' Jehosh has been talking about, the one he ran into on one of his raids."

"You believe that story? That he saw a pretty girl in rich clothing in a town square and begged her for a kiss, and she looked down her nose at him and said that she was a king's daughter and thus far too high and mighty for the likes of him?"

"I do believe the story, unfortunately. He's going to bring her back and insist on installing her as a second wife like they do in the empire. I don't approve."

She snorts. "You have sat pretty all your life with your compliantly affectionate wife and your adoringly faithful lover—"

"Dannarah!"

"—so his running after the fruit forbidden to him is your own fault. You can't expect him to be content with that insipid girl you forced him to marry just because she has already pushed out one healthy boy and is pregnant again."

"Chorannah is a shy girl but not stupid. If Sirniakan lords do not allow their daughters to be educated in a wide range of disciplines then it is wrongheaded of the Beltak priests to claim women are unformed and ignorant."

She gestures, and he hands over the signal flags. "I wonder why you harnessed poor Jehosh to such an underwhelming brood mare if you object to the empire's customs regarding women."

"Father arranged the marriage before he died, as you know perfectly well."

She bundles up the flags. "Just as he arranged yours to Yevah. Why do we keep bringing their cowlike girls into our court rather than strengthening our ties by marrying into the most powerful local families here, as General Sengel and Father's other generals so wisely did?"

"Why do you ask when our mother of blessed memory was herself born and bred in the empire?"

"Father could scarcely refuse to marry Mama when his own mother brought her here and ordered him to marry her, could he?" She stoppers the vial of oil and tidies up before going over to the camp stand to wash her hands and face. "You were always Mama's champion."

"Someone had to be." The snap of his temper startles her.

She sits back down on her bedroll. "You were a good son to her, Atani. Better than I was a daughter. You treated her with respect while I resented her. I regret that now."

Atani leans forward to grasp her hand.

She says nothing, just lets him be.

After a while he releases her and curls his hand into a fist. "I just have a sense that Jehosh is in danger. I should have gone with him."

The hells? He's always had an uncanny ability to perceive emotion. Is he waiting for her to confess that she ordered Kellas to kill Jehosh?

The flame gutters as the wick sucks up the last of the oil. Darkness falls.

His voice emerges hushed and intense. "Do you think I should have marched north with the army?"

"Do you fear you are a coward? A man who chooses to negotiate rather than fight is not a coward. Sometimes he is bravest of all. But leaving Jehosh here to gain a taste of ruling while you prosecuted the war might have been a better choice. It would have answered the raids, stymied his desire for glory, and given him some tedious administration to oversee. Why did you not?"

The tent's canvas breathes in a soft mountain wind. A tightness grows in her chest. Her fingers dig into her own flesh as she leans forward, waiting as if for him to throw a knife at her.

His voice is that of a man buried beneath rock and heard through a slender pipe of bamboo. "For a long time now I have known that I am a demon, bound to the Hundred."

Is anxiety causing him to lose his mind? "You are no demon!"

"Am I not?" he says with a harsh laugh so unlike him that for an instant she wonders if a demon has truly risen up inside him to engulf his spirit.

"You're in a dark mood like you get sometimes, worried about events out of your control. It overwhelms you with fanciful nightmares."

He does not reply.

She gropes for and finds the neatly folded harness, for she needs something to hold. "It's natural to fear demons. In other lands people simply kill them. But for so long the people of the Hundred allowed demons to rule. Until Father put a stop to that and drove them into hiding."

He says nothing.

"Atani, what makes you say such a thing about yourself? What do you fear?"

The cot creaks as he lies down. "Never mind. I meant nothing by it."

A spike of anger drives pain straight up into her eyes. To spare him the troublesome ambition of his eldest son she has just arranged for that son to be killed. "How dare you shut me out after all the ways I've advised and supported you!"

His voice whispers in the blanketing night. "I'm sorry, Dannarah. There are some agitated thoughts it's better I keep to myself. I mean no reflection on you."

"You would have told Mama. Or Father."

"No, not even them. Go to sleep. Go to sleep."

The wind's tug at the tent flap and the voices of nearby sentries and the whistle of a snowy nightjar from the trees calm her like a lover combing through her hair. She yawns. Atani's is not a hoarding, jealous nature. If he has secrets that gnaw at him, then he will confide in her eventually. She just has to be patient.

But Dannarah knew now, years later, that she had been too preoccupied that night to truly listen. People often spoke in the manner of poets with phrases dramatic enough to catch your attention. She'd thought that was what Atani was doing. She hadn't wanted to hear what she didn't want to know.

For a long time I've known I am a demon, bound to the land.

She examined her campsite more closely and realized that chance had brought her from Horn Hall not merely to a Lady-tree and a Hasibal's Stone but to a place even more closely tied to her dead brother.

Between the offering rock and the empty road stood one of his law pillars, as wide as her shoulders and the height of a tall man. Yellow-green lichens fanned across its surface, obscuring the letters carved into the stone. Yet she knew them by heart even after all these years because she had listened to Atani go on and on about this project since the first year of his reign, back when she bothered to argue against it, before she had realized that he really did intend to erect pillars in every village and town and along every road, all of them carved with the same words.

With law shall the land be built.

The law shall not stand in only one precinct but it will stand beside all the roads and paths of the Hundred. Once a year it shall be read in full from every assizes court, in every reeve hall, by every town council.

No one shall murder. No one shall steal. No one shall move a boundary stone without permission or negotiation. No one shall defile a temple. When a person sells their labor into servitude in payment for a debt, that person will serve six years and in the seventh go free. No one shall take a slave as a prize in war. All contracts shall be witnessed by the temples and sealed by the assizes courts.

Generosity to the poor is the same as an offering to the gods. Offer refuge to the helpless and comfort to those who are ill, dying, or stricken by grief. Give respect and accept respect. Let kindness guide your heart.

May the rains come at the proper time. May the harvest be abundant.

The assizes shall serve justice. The reeves shall serve justice. May the world prosper and justice be served, because the only companion who follows even after death, is justice.

Each pillar carved with the same words, the same law, the same sentiments.

Only now as she traced incised letters with a finger did she finally realize what was missing: any mention of a king.

Where did outlaws find refuge and aid, who defied the rule of kings? She thought of the red-nut rice spilling through Reyad's fingers.

In the morning she flew east across the golden Lend, through the Suvo Gap, across swampy Mar, to Salya and Plum Blossom Clan.

51

With a cap pulled low to shadow her face, Sarai followed Elit through Wolf Quarter at dawn. They were pretending to be laborers hauling cloth banners, draped over a pole. Elit carried the front of a pole and Sarai the rear so the banners mostly concealed her. Militia wearing the red and white of the queen's men guarded the gate to the harbor district. Fear ate at her every step but Elit did not falter.

A soldier halted them. "Where are you bound, verea?"

"Upriver Dock with a delivery to a Three Ferries barge," said Elit in her flirting voice. "You look bored, ver. I'll come back and give you a kiss when I'm done, if you'll buy me a cup of cordial."

He laughed. "Less bored than I was. Go on."

While Wolf Quarter was run down and derelict, the harbor district had clean streets, night lamps oiled and polished, and soldiers at every corner. Dawn brought a bustle of merchants, laborers, beggars, and food sellers to the wharf-walk with its barges and cargo boats tied up to slips.

A man wearing a Three Ferries badge on his jacket fell into step beside them. "I'll take the banners from here. Step into the skiff with the orange moon banner."

Elit gave a night hatch's whistle, their old signal, and when the man stepped in midway along the pole and got his shoulder under it, Sarai let the banners slide away as he carried them off. She stood bare-faced in the bright sun for a shocking instant before Elit pulled her onto a wharf with several slips. A woman coiled rope in the stern of a skiff flying an orange moon banner. They hopped in, rocking the hull, and before Sarai quite realized what was about, the woman had poled out into the current. The boat bellied out and began to come around.

"The Lesser Istri has a pull like a woman's smile," said Elit with a lilt like sunrise.

"A woman can work while she's talking, just as the river does all night and all day," said the sailor, handing both women an oar before setting back to the rudder.

Sarai plopped down next to Elit and they began to row, although Sarai kept skipping her oar over the surface of the water.

"Keep your head down," Elit said. "The cap can only hide so much, and your scar is distinctive."

They slid downriver alongside the wharves and passed the rocky jumble of an old stone breakwater that divided the shore side of Wolf Quarter from that of Flag Quarter. The sun's stare warmed the back of Sarai's neck: Elit had clubbed up her hair to make it look less like curly Ri Amarah hair and more like straight Hundred hair. Too fast they came up behind a barge poling in toward Flag Quarter's narrow Fortune Wharf.

"My friends," said the woman, "as soon as we get this barge between us and the shore, you'll stow the oars. Jump in and swim to the boat with the orange flag between two green. Now is not the time to tell me you can't swim."

The barge's canvas walls cut off their view of the near shore.

"Keep close," said Elit, and stepped over the side smoothly. Sarai adjusted the strap of the oilcloth pouch she'd been given and sent a prayer to the Hidden One that the oilcloth was truly waterproof. Then she tumbled in. The water was sluggish for all its power, cold enough to constrict her chest. She kicked for the surface and breached sputtering. A rope ladder slapped her bare head. Curse it! She'd lost her cap.

"Grab my hand!"

With Elit tugging, she heaved herself over onto the deck of a single-masted cargo vessel. There were four other people in the boat, an awning at the stern for a cabin, and canvas tarps roped over cargo amidships. A man held up the bottom fold of a tarp, and Sarai followed Elit under.

The hold absolutely reeked of fish, and the planks were slippery with scales and grime. Even though there were no fish left she almost choked on a stink so thick it fouled her tongue and made her eyes water.

"Stay put until I say otherwise," said the man.

Trembling, Sarai untied and unrolled the oilcloth, and found the leather case and book dry within. She shut her eyes and breathed a soundless prayer. Abruptly, the boat lurched and its stern swung around. After a few terse commands were flung like a rope from one to another of the crew, the vessel swung back into line. A new strength gripped the hull; the boat almost seemed to startle forward as might a deer sensing a wolf.

"We've just hit the River Istri," remarked Elit.

"How do you know?"

"Every river is a journey with its own tale. Can't you feel how the waters changed? Here, rest your head on my shoulder."

She was too exhausted to be angry or horrified or indeed really to feel anything except relief, even with the stink. An oily skin of water coated her back as she listened to the mighty voice of the great river, the plop of wavelets against the hull, the murmurs of the boatmen. Elit began to chant in a low voice. She was not reciting an entire tale but working through a repetitive series of exercises meant to facilitate memorization. Her mellow golden tone soothed Sarai into sleep.

She blinked awake when the canvas was peeled away to let in a blast of fresh air.

"Look at you two, like pups curled up together." The boatman's face was obscured in the purple-rose hues of dusk, but his tone sounded distinctly more friendly than it had when they had come aboard.

"Blessed Tears! How far have we come?" Elit helped Sarai up.

Of Toskala they saw no sign. The river was so wide, and they nothing more than a stick cast upon it. There were other boats, some sailing upriver with the wind and others drifting downstream with the current. Along the northern shore a road ran parallel to the river, seen through gaps in the trees. Birds flashed along the bank, and skimmers swooped over the river on the hunt for bugs.

Sarai and Elit rinsed off with buckets of water drawn from

the river. Afterward they ate a meal of nai porridge so thick they scooped it with their fingers.

The shoreline faded as night fell. One of the boatmen hung a lamp from the prow and one at the stern. This late in the year and especially out on the water a chill kissed the night. The sailors kindly ignored them where they sat clasped together at the stern. Elit's arm curled around Sarai's waist, fingers brushing the curve of her breast with the remembered ache of shared pleasure.

Melancholy pervaded Sarai's flesh and spirit. She opened Elit's free hand on her lap and traced its lines. "What have you become, Elit?"

"I serve Hasibal, who shifts form to fit the trial and teaches us that all of life is contained within each least grain of sand and drop of blood. As Hasibal's players we walk the roads from village to village telling tales. Most people don't remember the old versions, so we remind them of how things once were. Then we tell them new versions to teach that things could be different if people ruled themselves with laws and councils as it is said was the tradition in the old days, before there was a king."

"But the Black Wolves serve the king. That is why my mother is dead."

Elit was silent, emotions chasing across her expressive face as lamplight winked over the restless waters. A fish splashed, and the noise jolted her into speech. "You know how sorry I am that your mother died before you had a chance to know her. But I can't undo the path I am on, Sarai-ya. Not even for you."

"I guess it was wrong of me to think you could walk out in the world for three years and not be changed by it. All the Ri Amarah chroniclers agree that war is butchery, however noble or necessary its cause. Is this a war?"

Elit pressed a finger to Sarai's lips. "I shouldn't have said as much as I have, and I hope you will not repeat it. Tell me about Lord Gilaras."

"Are you jealous?" She seized on the change of subject, although it was almost as uncomfortable.

"Yes. No. I don't know." She spread a hand over Sarai's belly as if to sound what grew within. "I'm the one who left you to walk Hasibal's path. I shouldn't begrudge you finding a path of your own. And good sex!" Elit nudged her shoulder with her own, then nipped her ear. Yet her attempt at humor fell sharp. "Was it good?"

"I taught him all the things you and I do together."

Elit laughed, ran her fingers down the length of Sarai's spine in a well-remembered caress that made her shiver, and kissed her.

"It's hard not knowing if he's well or if he's suffering. If I'll ever see him again." Thinking of Gil made her smile, and yet recalling his shorn hair and tattooed face made her frown, because it reminded her of how he had laughed when he'd told her he was going to become a spy.

"What's wrong, dearest?" Elit whispered. The tilt of her head made Sarai squeeze her tightly.

"You know I love you. You know I wanted you to follow Hasibal's calling. I knew you had to go because that is where your spirit calls you. But to become a Wolf, like the man who killed my mother!"

"It's just a name."

"Nothing is just a name. Gil, too. He's now a Wolf, too, isn't he? It's as if my fortune is that the ones I care for will be ripped from me by predators, and I will be a stone in a tomb, marking what is left behind."

"Don't say so!" Elit embraced her, her presence so familiar because they had always been like two souls destined from birth to twine together. "It will all be fine now. We'll reach Nessumara, take a ship to Salya, and you'll find refuge there until it's over. I'll come back for you then."

"What if I don't want to go to Salya?"

"Where else can you go?"

Out of the night rose the sound of hooves, easy to hear over the flowing river. On the road lamps bobbed into view from upriver and swept past to reveal a pair of riders headed downstream. Night couriers, traveling at speed.

They watched until the light vanished.

"The queen, the king, and your clan aren't going to stop looking for you," added Elit as gently as she might to a sick child. "Going to Salya is the best and safest course for you."

"Will you stay with me all the way to Nessumara?"

"Of course."

They sat in silence for a long time watching the dark river and the bright stars.

"Look there!" called the sailor who stood watch at the prow.

On the northern bank a lantern's light flashed three times, vanished, then flashed three times again. Out of the muzzy night a man's reedy voice floated in a melody: "*The sad girl and her happy lover, What a striking pair they made. One in shadow, and the other in light...*"

"That's the safe conduct signal," said the elder boatman. "We're landing."

The boat skimmed toward the bank, rocking against the current. In the shallows they scraped past a thick overhang of flowering bushes and nudged up against a line of pilings with planks fixed on top. A man caught their thrown rope and secured them to this makeshift pier.

The old boatman disembarked and followed the stranger into the brush. Elit grabbed her sticks, and Sarai slung her oilcloth pouch over her back in case they had to jump into the river and swim for it. But soon enough the boatman returned leading a woman dressed in what Sarai recognized as reeve leathers. She looked as much an outlander as the Ri Amarah in having similar eye-folds, but where Sarai's people had light complexions hers was black. The young reeve swung onto the boat and paced up and down it as if looking for spies and murderers, then paused in front of Elit and Sarai.

"Are you Elit?" Tracks of affliction had worn grooves into her weary, anxious voice, giving it a raspy scrape. "I'm called Lifka. I've received orders from the commander to fly you south, on my eagle. You have a new assignment."

"On your eagle?" Elit breathed, hand squeezing Sarai's fingers. "Hu! Is it safe?"

"Yes." The reeve gave Sarai a polite nod leavened by a distracted smile. "Verea. My apologies for ignoring you but we're in a hurry." She addressed Elit. "If you'll come with me then we can get everyone else aboard and the boat can go before any other soldiers pass on the road. Hurry."

The reeve jumped back onto the pier and hurried away in the brush. In silence Elit shifted from foot to foot like a child waiting for permission to bolt. What was the use of raking her over coals whose heat Sarai could not extinguish?

"Just go," whispered Sarai, feeling all the wind punched out of her.

Elit embraced her. "I love you."

She knew the words for truth. She murmured an echoing reply.

Yet when she let go of Elit and had to watch as her lover disembarked and slipped away into the night, Sarai tasted the dust of her mother's grave. She might herself become dust and allow the wind to blow her to the four corners of the Hundred, spread thin so no one and nothing had a hint of her passing.

More people than she expected emerged from the brush: several children including a baby in arms, an old man tottering and helped along by a girl, a young man carried by two other men. She counted them as the sailors handed them aboard: fifteen in all, weary, thin, ragged, and looking as out of place and

grief-stricken as the young reeve. They even coaxed two skeptical mules onboard, followed by two dogs, followed by two goats
whose bleating made Sarai stifle a giggle because after everything this was just one absurdity too much.

"Be well! Be well!" cried the young reeve from the shore to
the boarding family. With lantern light shimmering over her,
she sang with hands speaking in the old gestures. "*The road runs
to the hills, to the city, to the sea.*"

They cast off. The current caught the boat, drawing it onto
the waters. Sarai stared at the landing but night had already
swallowed the night-blooming white-thorn and the lonely dock.

Elit was gone.

A lamp hung on a bent pole out beyond the prow. The watch-
man scanned the river with a pole in hand to push off debris.
The new arrivals arranged themselves in the reeking hold, children snuffling and adults calming them in loving voices. They
murmured words of reassurance, settled back-to-back and
heart-to-heart.

A man groaned in stifled pain, "If only I had died instead of
Denas!"

"Don't say so, Nanni!" said another man. "His wound sick-
ened and yours did not. There's nothing anyone could have
done. Sometimes it is just in the hands of the gods. Your children and wife are glad to keep you here. So are we all. Now
close your eyes and drink this."

She pulled the sleeve off her mirror. The polished surface glistened under the flickering flame of the lantern hanging above the
stern. Blue threads chased within the engraved spiral, and she
rubbed her eyes to unhaze her vision. But still they glimmered
there like a spiderweb at dawn hung with fiery dew. Her face pale
with sorrow hovered like a chained bird in the misty reflection.

How badly she wanted what these people had: a sense of
comfort within a loving group. Many times she had begged

to be allowed to meet her brother Aram, but always her uncle refused.

Her face faded from the mirror's surface. In its place she saw like half-worn shadows a young Ri Amarah man seated in a courtyard with a laughing young Ri Amarah woman beside him. She had a baby on her knee while he was swinging a child around by the hands. He set down the child and touched the cloth that covered his hair. The woman spoke a question as he frowned with disquiet and, hand still on his head wrap, glanced around as if he felt he was being watched.

The same moon shone on them as on Sarai.

Stunned by this vision, she dropped the mirror and would have lost it to the river if she hadn't secured it with an extra cord to her belt. With a tug she fished it up and raised it, although her hand shook. Yet all she saw now was only her dull reflection.

One of the sailors laughed, and replied to an ongoing conversation that had nothing to do with her. In haste she tucked away the mirror.

A mule kicked, hoof impacting wood, and a man soothed, "Here now, here now, Steadfast."

"I'm hungry, Mother," whined a child.

A woman of an age to be Sarai's mother joined her at the railing. Her eyes were hollows filled with grief, and like Sarai her gaze remained fixed on what they had left behind. But she spoke in a kind way. "Greetings of the night, verea. What do you know of where they are taking us?"

"To Nessumara," said Sarai. "Thence by ship to Salya."

"What is in Salya besides a mysterious commander and whispers of revolt against the king?"

"You know as much as I do. How are you come into this, if I may ask?"

"My son is dead and laid on a Sorrowing Tower that we built in the forest. My daughter we have left behind now, too, for she has an eagle and thus she is valuable. Maybe more than we ever understood. Not that it matters. She came to us because the gods brought her to our hearts."

"That reeve was your daughter? But you're all Hundred-born people and she..." Sarai bit off the words and hung her head, thinking of how her mother's people had never counted her as fully theirs. "My apologies, verea. I spoke without thinking. May your gods bring you peace in all things. May your daughter remain well. I am sorry to hear about your son."

"My thanks for your kindness, verea. You are also bound for Salya, into the service of the Black Wolves?"

Sarai did not answer, nor did the woman press her further. For a long while they two stood companionably watching the boat leave a tail of consequence in the opaque waters. Every action leaves its wake. Even the slightest of people makes a whisper within the world, if only you pause to listen for a soft breath on your cheek.

When she touched the mirror hanging at her belt, when her fingers brushed her belly and her lips tingled with the memory of Elit's last kiss, when she recalled Tsania's final words to her, she understood at last that she had been running away to the wrong place all along.

She knew where she had to go.

52

The contours of the land seen from on high tell a different story from what folk see who travel along the ground. Plum Blossom Clan had built a loft for eagles in a clearing that lay at the end of their narrow dead-end street. Since there was also a small loft down at the assizes hall in Salya town proper, according to the normal custom, it was an odd quirk to have one here, too.

But the clearing with its loft wasn't what Dannarah took note of as she circled.

Plum Blossom Clan was the third compound from the end of the street. Two walled compounds lay between Kellas's household and the hillside clearing. From the ground, on the street, every large compound in Salya looked the same, with long entrance verandas used for entertaining and gates for deliveries. From above she saw what the outer walls hid.

The connections weren't as obvious as paths running up to one wall and resuming on the other side. Clearly whoever had landscaped the three compounds in recent years had considered that unfriendly reeves might fly over. Yet a suspicious reeve looking closely could identify interior gates and disguised walkways linking the three compounds.

In Plum Blossom Compound a woman and a child worked in the garden while dogs lolled in the shade. In the compound next door a gracious house covered half the area, with four courtyards tucked into pockets and a flower-and-herb garden ringed by mulberry trees. In one courtyard a man sat on a bench in the sun. He had no right arm below the elbow, no left hand, and wore a patch over his right eye. Two small children sat on the tile at his feet, playing a game with counters on a circular board. At once she recognized the playing pieces' zigzagging path: She and Atani had loved the game of Circles when they were that age, but these days people rarely played it.

A woman with silver-white hair stepped down off the porch, apparently calling to the man because he turned his head in the way of people who cannot see well, orienting himself to the direction of her voice. Then the woman glanced up, saw Terror, and vanished inside.

Inside the third compound evergreen blue-spear trees grew right around the walls to create a towering wall of dense branches reaching above the regular wall. This compound backed up directly against the hillside clearing with the eagle loft. A small gate screened by bushes opened onto a path that wound up the steep hillside onto the clearing, separate from the wider and quite obvious path that led from the street to the clearing. The instant she identified this hidden path she realized that the night she had seen the demon it had come not from the street but from the third compound.

Most of this compound was given over to a wide grassy space ringed by fruit trees. The only structure was a long and narrow warehouse with a wraparound porch and a stable at one end. In front of the building about fifty people drilled in formation with staffs and sticks, pacing in unison through the martial dance once observed by the ordinands of Kotaru the Thunderer before the Beltak priests had closed down Kotaru's temples in every city and major town.

Women and men drilled together, no distinction. Two horses grazed off in one corner, rumpled white blankets thrown over their backs.

Terror tilted her head, catching sight of something higher up in the hills, and veered away from the compound just as Dannarah realized the horses did not have blankets.

They had furled wings.

Terror abruptly headed south along the low ridge of hills, but once the compound was behind them the raptor began aimlessly circling on the updrafts. Dannarah spotted nothing of interest, no plump deer, no skulking demons, nothing to explain why Terror had so suddenly flown away. Reeve lore taught that the presence of demons often stupefied eagles. She swung Terror in a wide loop over Messalia Bay and this time guided her in directly to the loft.

Alone and suspicious, she left Terror unhooded on a perch. In dangerous situations she had a habit of rolling the leather cord that held her bone whistle through her fingers, testing its strength, and she caught herself doing it now as she walked down through the clearing toward the street. She drew her baton. Its weight in her hand always gave her confidence.

Instead of walking all the way to Plum Blossom Clan she mounted the steps onto the veranda of the middle compound, the one with the huge multiwinged house and the children playing Circles, and rang the visitors' bell. No one came to the door. Drifting over the wall from the neighboring compound came the sounds of feet stamping and the "hu! hah!" of collective voices.

She rang the bell again. Its melancholy tone shivered on the air longer than seemed normal.

The door of Plum Blossom Clan opened and Hari emerged. After a pause he left the veranda of Plum Blossom Clan and trotted over to the veranda she stood on.

She distrusted his cheerful smile at once.

"Marshal Dannarah, how may I help you?" he asked while he climbed up onto the veranda as if he had every right to guard the door of a house not his own.

"That is a question, is it not? Who is the man in the garden?"

His habitual smile faded.

"No answer, ver?"

He folded his hands and waited.

"Is it my brother? By some demon's magic did you revive Atani and bring him here to live broken and blind?"

"Marshal Dannarah, I beg you, calm yourself. Atani is dead." He extended his hands, palms up as in supplication. "He does not live hidden in a garden. He lives only in our hearts."

"You seem a reasonable man, ver, and yet you spout such rubbish. If he is dead he does not live in our hearts or anywhere else. If you knew him, then he must have known you although he never told me we had another brother. Someone hid you here who did not want you involved in the palace. Was it Atani? Was it my father?"

The door slid open. A woman stepped onto the veranda. Although much older than Dannarah, she had the straight posture and vigorous aspect of a much younger woman.

"Mother, I was going to take care of this," said Hari with all the exasperation of a son.

"This must be Lady Dannarah," said the woman in a voice so kind and sympathetic that Dannarah instantly took a step back. "I am Mai. Greetings of the day to you."

Youth flowers with beauty because it is fresh and new, but age unveils a longer story: Mai had a face marked with age spots and wrinkles but these were inconsequential, held within the bones and clarity of a woman at peace in herself. This old woman dressed in a taloos of ecstatic sky-blue silk had been beautiful once; she was beautiful still in the way stone can be worn down by wind and rain but hold strong and never lose its core. Dannarah's mother had not been a beauty. If a man made an arranged marriage to a bride he did not respect or love, then beauty like this might tempt him until he had to put her out of the way together with her son, who must never trouble the palace with misplaced ambition.

Dannarah tried to imagine her father in love with this woman. Had he smiled at her, a man whose smiles came rarely? Had he felt not just sexual passion but true affection?

"Please come in. We have tea to refresh you. A meal if you are hungry." She had the Mar accent with its slow *a*'s and sharp *s* but also the brush of an outlander's accent to match her outlander's looks with her eye-folds and round face.

"Red-nut rice, like that found in outlaw encampments?"

"Red-nut has such a rich and complex essence, does it not? It would be our honor to serve you."

"Who is the crippled man in the garden?"

Hari glanced at his mother but her smile gave away nothing, like a woman in the market who, as you pick through her wares looking for the choicest fruit, never changes expression so you can't gain any advantage in the coming negotiation.

"Why are you here, Marshal Dannarah?"

"Were you my father's lover? Did you give birth to his son?"

"If I say I was, and I did, will you please sit? If you will forgive me for being so bold as to remark on it, you look agitated and unsteady, as if you have sustained a shock. I can have tea brought out here on the veranda, if you prefer not to enter the house." She turned half around and gestured to someone unseen.

"When my father discarded you, did he order Captain Kellas to marry you? Is that how he took care of you? By handing you over to one of his loyal captains?"

Her smile did not waver, but Dannarah read pity in her gaze. "I fear you may not have known your father very well, Lady Dannarah."

"I knew him as well as anyone did! He raised me. He taught me. Everything I am comes from him."

"Yes, you saw the best in him."

"Is that what you are? The worst of him? Did you want something from my father that he wasn't willing to give you?"

Her pleasant expression did not change but a harder emotion flickered in the narrowing of her eyes. "I wanted my freedom and I took it."

A flutter of anger closed Dannarah's throat. "My father never enslaved anyone!"

"Only the Hundred."

"He saved the Hundred."

"Rescuing the Hundred from the conflicts and troubles of those days took the efforts of many working in concert. It was not the victory of one man alone."

"He had the vision. A wise king brings peace and order to a land. Under his steady and forceful hand, all can flourish."

"A peaceful land is built on law and justice, Lady Dannarah, not maintained at the point of a sword. Here is the tea. Will you sit?"

"Now you are mocking me."

A woman carrying a tea tray stepped onto the veranda. By the cut and color of her silver hair she was the woman who had spotted the eagle from the courtyard. Dannarah recoiled, stunned by seeing a woman she had at one stage in her life spoken to almost every day but who was now as old as herself. After all her efforts to track down Atani's household, they had been here all along.

"It has been many years since we last saw each other, Dannarah," said the woman.

"Eiko?"

How had Atani's lover gotten so old? Once the three of them had laughed in the palace garden, all so young with the whole world blossoming.

Eiko set down the tray and arranged the pot, a pretty celadon in the shape of a dragon whose mouth became its spout. Thirty years ago Dannarah had often sat down to tea poured from this exact pot into green cups glazed with stylized waves.

"Is Queen Yevah here, too?" she demanded.

"She is unwell today," Eiko said in the tranquil voice she had used to protect skittish, painfully shy Yevah from the buffets and storms of the palace. Dannarah had always marveled that Atani, Eiko, and Yevah lived together in the same household for over twenty years with never a whiff of burning.

She burned now, the memory gone to ash on her tongue. "This is where you originally come from, isn't it, Eiko? This house. Atani found you here in Salya when he was sixteen."

"I am part of what he found here." Eiko glanced at Mai—Kellas's wife!—who watched as from a lofty height like an eagle as it scans the ground with eyes sharper than human eyes. "I was very young when we met, only sixteen, like Atani. It was calf love. But he and I never got over our infatuation, as you know. How many years did we spend together? How often did you visit us, and we would swim in the ocean, or get drunk on plum blossom wine, or recite poetry although you never really had the patience for that because you always wanted to be up and doing something."

Dannarah clutched her bone whistle, for if there was one thing she could count on it was the jess that bound her to Terror. "Atani came to this place when he was sixteen. He found you, and he found our half brother Hari, and he found this woman, who was once our father's mistress. And Atani changed. Not in obvious ways but in subtle ways that most people could easily overlook. Even our father didn't see it. Especially our father didn't see it." She confronted Mai with a glare. "Did you make Atani become a demon?"

The old woman studied her, a faintly sad smile on her lips. "He was always a demon, Lady Dannarah. His demon-nature was a quiet one, hard to perceive and easy to hide. So he hid it because Anji could only see demons as threats to his power rather than as part of the land, as we each are part of the land."

"Demons are corrupt."

"Every person can become corrupt, Lady Dannarah, whether human or demon, blind-heart or demon-heart. You may be the humblest of fruit sellers in the market or the most powerful king, and still you may do harm to others or you may help them, or you may both harm and help at the same moment."

"I pray you, spare me your piecemeal bits of wisdom. I can only conclude you and your clan have allied with the demons who seek to overturn everything my father built and return the Hundred to chaos. Is it after all true that Captain Kellas betrayed the king and became part of the conspiracy that killed Atani?"

"You still do not understand, Lady Dannarah. Atani was part of the conspiracy."

She paused to let the words sink in, then went on as if she knew Dannarah would be too stunned to reply.

"Atani was part of the conspiracy. Demons did not kill him. They were his allies, his comrades, and therefore the last people who would have wanted him dead."

Dannarah braced herself on the railing and took several breaths to steady herself.

At length in a hoarse voice she said, "Yet he kept all his plans secret from me."

"You are your father's daughter, Lady Dannarah."

"Proud to be so!"

"Your loyalty was always to Anjihosh."

"It still is. The hells! What proof can you give me that Atani was a demon? The priests of Beltak tested him for the ghost-sight, as they did all of us in the palace school. He wore no demon's skin. Rode no winged horse. He could not look into a person's mind and see her thoughts."

"It's true he did not have the ghost-sight or any of the ordinary talents of demon-hearts. To become a Guardian—"

"A cloaked demon!"

Mai began again in a patient tone. "To become one of the nine Guardians, those whom your father also called demons, you must die in the pursuit of justice. Then the land restores you in the form of a Guardian with cloak and horse so you can continue to seek justice as a judge in the land."

"That's an old children's tale, all superstitions and lies."

"No, Lady Dannarah. The story that is a lie is the one told by Anjihosh and the Beltak priests. The story that is a lie is the one told by the foreigners who came from Sirniaka to impose their god and beliefs on the Hundred. Guardians are no more or less corrupt than anyone else."

"We both know Atani was not a Guardian, if you must insist on that word."

"He was not a Guardian but he was touched by the demon's coils nevertheless. His bones and flesh became permeated with the threads of living magic that live within the coils, the creatures we call firelings. He has been a demon from the day of his birth, when the firelings kissed him in welcome."

Dannarah laughed, although even to her own ears the sound had an edge of desperation. "How can you know this?"

Mai's soft smile made Dannarah flinch. "Because I was there."

"You attended Queen Zayrah at the birth?"

Her eyes like murky waters hid what lay beneath but for an instant Dannarah was sure she saw faint blue threads chasing through the dark pupils. "No. I gave birth to Atani in a cave beside a fireling's pool. Later, when I bargained for my freedom, Anji stole our baby from me and gave him to Zayrah to raise as her own. Later yet, in exchange he gave me the infant Hari to raise away from the palace. Hari is your full brother because Hari, like you, is a child of Anjihosh and Zayrah. You and Atani share only a sire. Zayrah loved Atani, and she was a good and loving and kind mother to him. But he came from my womb. Thus I know what transpired on the day of his birth and how he became the sort of demon he was."

The words tumbled like stones, grinding through Dannarah's mind.

After a bit she touched the nearest cup. Had they poisoned the tea so as to cause this nightmarish hallucination of accusations? She had not taken even the smallest sip. Deep in the pit of her belly she knew it as truth, however much she wanted to scream a denial, because it answered so much.

They studied her with calm expressions. None carried a weapon or at least no weapon she could see. But their soldiers drilled beyond the wall, and somewhere in these three compounds, two demons walked, having left their winged horses to graze. Their weapon was the secret they had concealed all these years.

"My father should have made me king instead of Atani," she said.

"Had he made you king, things would have turned out very differently. You would have kept the Hundred the way he wanted it to be." Mai nodded with a compassion that made Dannarah want to slam the baton into her serene face. "But Anjihosh could not learn the lessons the Hundred had to teach him. His mind ran deep but very narrow. In the world he knew, a king's heir is his son."

Sweet laughter broke into their stalemate. Up the street walked two young women. Lifka was impossible to mistake for anyone else. The other was an unusually pretty girl whose face seemed cursedly familiar. Then she had it: This was Reyad's estranged wife, Hetta, whom she had last seen in the Suvash Hills. She wore a taloos that looked as if it had been wrapped by four drunken children, and the way she had to keep tugging up its hem so as not to stumble kept the two young women in gales. What in the hells was this girl doing here?

"We are not your enemy, Lady Dannarah," said Mai. "Atani loved you. He admired and respected you."

"But he didn't trust me. Because I remained loyal to our father, he considered me his enemy, didn't he? You all plotted behind my back to destroy the Hundred that my father built. I think we know where you and I stand." She rudely turned her back and strode down the steps. "Reeve Lifka! Did Tarnit return to Toskala, as I ordered?"

The young reeve halted, glanced toward the people on the porch, and back at Dannarah. "Yes, Marshal. She left days ago for Toskala. Have you not seen her there?"

"We must leave at once." She took several steps toward the clearing before she realized Lifka had not moved to follow her.

In a shower of excited barking, the Runt barreled out of the open porch door of Plum Blossom Clan and raced to Lifka. She gathered him into her arms as he licked and whined. "I'm sorry, Marshal. I am no longer under your command."

"Has Tavahosh discovered you are here? Has he threatened you?"

"Prince Tavahosh does not command me. What I mean is, I no longer consider myself to be under the command of the reeve halls. My apologies." Lifka glanced toward Mai, who offered an encouraging nod in reply.

Demons needed no weapons except lies and lures. Her father had taught her that their power lay in being able to know what would tempt, or anger, or frighten you most. *Desire and vulnerability make you weak, Dannarah*, he had told her, and now when she looked at the woman called Mai she understood that her father had wanted a person who had rejected him and thus become his enemy.

"What did they offer you, Lifka?"

She was a good girl, well brought up, and honest enough that she scraped the toe of a sandal on the ground as she let out a troubled sigh. "Safety and security for my family."

Dannarah considered the report she had received from Tarnit right after the debacle of Lifka's clan being attacked by soldiers and burned to the ground. The injured, destitute family had been forced to take temporary shelter in the precarious and unpredictable shelter of the Weldur Forest among its mysterious and often hostile denizens. How clever of Plum Blossom Clan to figure out exactly the bargain Lifka could not bear to refuse.

An outlawed marshal had nothing better to offer the girl, not now.

Not yet.

Because she liked Lifka and anyway felt it prudent not to burn the bridge between them, she nodded. "I know you love your family. Very well. You have chosen, as we must all choose. So be it."

As she began to walk away the dog whined again. Lifka set him down. To Dannarah's surprise he ran after her, snuffled a circle around her ankles, and bolted back for Lifka.

From the porch they watched her go. No one said a word, not even *farewell.*

She flew to the Suvash Hills.

Reyad's eagle Surly was preening herself on a sunny hillside, out of her harness, so relaxed that she watched with only mild interest as Dannarah guided her raptor to the landing on the opposite side of the valley. She left Terror unhooded in case she was walking into an ambush. Folk were busy about their daily tasks, children at the temple school reciting their lessons in such loud voices she could hear them all the way up here. But word spreads fast. Reyad came pelting out of the archon's big house and raced up to meet her. He looked trim, clean, healthy, and brimful of news.

"Thanks to all the gods, Marshal! I was worried something had happened to you when I heard those rumors that all women reeves are to be arrested by the priests."

"Arrested by the priests?"

"Yes, Prince Tavahosh had an order ready to go."

"An order ready to go?"

The hells! Tavahosh was not only in the process of betraying the reeve halls; he had also deliberately lied to her, and to his own father, the better to ambush them later!

"What happened after I left Horn Hall? Did my people get away safely?"

"They did. Nesard got a messenger out immediately after your departure, sent to Toskala."

"If anyone can get my reeves out of Palace Hall before the priests take over, it will be Tarnit," she said, more to herself than to him.

"I have something to show you!"

He had the cocky grin of a good-looking lad accustomed to admiration. He led her out past the village washhouse where she and Tarnit had cleaned up that morning so many weeks ago, the very place from which they had overseen the meeting between Reyad and Hetta.

As they pushed up past terraced fields she asked, probing, "Have you had a happy reunion with your wife?"

His smile fell into a sulky frown. "She's left to get work in Salya. I wanted to go track her down, but I knew I had to wait here in case you came."

"Work" in Salya, indeed. Hetta was obviously up to her neck in the demons' rebellion, and it seemed equally clear Reyad hadn't the least idea of what was going on. Kellas was almost certainly training his own little army. Briefly she considered sending Reyad to Salya to infiltrate Plum Blossom Clan, but Hetta would prove too great a temptation.

"Here we are," he said, breaking into her thoughts.

Up on the hillside among scrub brush a disused trough likely used to water goats had fallen into disrepair. A rank odor made her squint as he pulled loose bricks off one end, reached into a hollow in the ground beneath the trough, and pulled out a damp, dirty cloth bag. Tipping it over he shook it, and a thing rolled out.

The smell hit her first as her eyes watered. But when her hazy vision cleared she had no trouble identifying the greasy tangles of hair, the pits where bugs had begun eating out the eyes, the ragged flesh and the white of the shattered spinal bones: Tava-hosh's head.

She blinked so many times her eyes got dry. The events of the past few days had stripped all emotion from her. Both outcast and outlaw, she had nothing left except her years of experience and the lessons her father had taught her. Yet for all that her father had loved her, he had still withheld from her the tools she needed to become what he was. So be it. She would forge her own tools and her own weapons.

She said, "How did you manage it and not get caught?"

He poked the head back into the bag with a stick. "That was easy. He heard what you said to me at the end and he wanted to know if it was true."

"That I had demanded sexual favors from you?" She laughed harshly. "Yes, he can't have known that my sexual interest in men your age is many years behind me, for which I am deeply grateful since mature men are quite more imaginative than callow youth."

His gaze flicked to the sky and he gave a little sigh, as of relief. As if he had been worried that she would importune him as Tarnit had!

He said, "That. Also you taunting him about not having the courage to fly as a reeve. He wanted to show he wasn't a coward. I suggested I would tell him the truth in private, which meant taking him up with me on a tour of the countryside. I said that about a tour to give a little time."

"Why did he trust you?"

"Because I told him what he wanted to hear. Anyway, I out-flew the reeves who were meant to escort us. Surly is fast and, honestly, they were inexperienced and not very well trained. He did talk a lot in the short time I knew him, insisting every-thing would be better now he was taking over and doing things in a proper way. It got to be so cursed annoying that I simply unhooked him and let him fall, then came back around to pick up his dead body."

"Where is his body?"

"I stripped the clothes and rings from it so it couldn't be identified, dropped it in the ocean, and brought the head here. Just as you ordered, Marshal."

She nodded as he shoved the bag back under the trough and replaced the bricks. "Good work, Reyad."

"How can it be good? You've become an exile and an outlaw. King Jehosh will not forgive you for murdering his son. What can we possibly do now, Marshal?"

The wind picked up, carving ripples through the tall grass. Over on another slope a pretty girl with her hair pulled back and her midriff showing stood watch over a munching tribe of goats. No doubt Reyad had first glimpsed Hetta when she was about such work, the poor goatherder's daughter who captured the interest of an archon's handsome grandson, who then defied his entire family to marry her. Reyad was far more ruthless than his congenial manners suggested.

A wave of exhaustion swept her as on a gust of wind. Unsteadily she sat on the edge of the trough, the scent of Tavahosh's murder tingling in her nostrils. It would be so easy to fly to the palace and get back into Jehosh's good graces by turning in Reyad as the murderer of his son. After all, Tavahosh, like Farihosh, stood between the throne and Kasad, who was clearly Jehosh's preferred heir. If she supported Kasad, Jehosh might finally name her chief marshal.

She slumped, bracing her head on her arms and her arms on her knees. How had it come to this, that she was trying to talk herself into another begging expedition to the very man she had once thought must be killed in order to save the Hundred?

"Marshal?"

Atani had lied to her for their entire adult lives. The boggling truth fit nowhere in the pattern she understood of her life and relationships. Atani had been the most honest and best of people. She preferred the idea that her father's discarded lover Mai was lying to her, but at every angle she turned the puzzle box of confessions and secrets they only made sense if Atani's last whispered intimacy had been him telling her the truth at last, and too late.

I am a demon.

Their childhood closeness, the illusion of trust, was gone forever. He had chosen a path she could not follow, and he had taken loyal Captain Kellas down that road with him.

"Are you all right, Marshal? I'd better take you to the house."

She lifted her head and took in a long inhalation of heady air. Sunlight gilded the slopes of hills. Everything was so bright it made her eyes water.

"I daresay I need to eat and sleep, rest for a day or two while I consider the terrible wrongs being done to the reeve halls. Also I have new information about a catastrophic conspiracy of demons that threatens the Hundred. I have to convince Prince Farihosh I am willing to help him overthrow his father and return peace to the land."

53

The flat waters of the salty Olo'o Sea shone under the hot sun. Dust coated Gil's face. Midday the work gang saw a pair of unfinished mud-brick towers rising in the distance. They marched into view of a compound with half-built walls. In the scant shade offered by the outer wall the work gang was allowed to rest while the chief vanished into the compound. The soldiers pretending not to be soldiers unrolled canvas between the wagons and sat beneath, sharing a midday ration that the work gang did not receive.

To avoid staring at the men eating, Gil studied the surroundings. A clot of ragged shelters was ringed by fields of drying bricks. Farther away stood a hill with a ruin atop it, an old fort; below a palisade ringed a much newer town. Along the shore people tended racks of drying fish.

"I'd sell my brother for one of those fish," said Menon.

"You don't have a brother," said Kurard, always the first to point out the obvious.

"He'd sell his sister for a fish," said Posenas with a glance around the others to see if they appreciated his edgy wit.

"Fuck you," said Menon genially. "What do you take me for? Three fish for my sister."

"What about *your* brother, Adiki?" said Posenas.

"You know better than to joke with me about my brother or say one unkind thing about him in my hearing, because I can beat the shit out of you and I will. So don't try my patience."

"Now, lads," said Natas. Old enough to be their uncle, he had taken on the part of peacemaker.

Adiki shaded his eyes to examine the men shaping bricks, laboring slowly in the heat. A few scrawny fellows wheeled carts stacked with bricks toward the gate, prodded along by guards with whips. "If this is the mighty Beltak shrine we've been headed for all along you'd think there'd be more laborers."

"The one they've been building for five years?" Gil looked toward the wide gate where bored soldiers stood guard in the shade. Over the top of the high wall all he could see was the ragged edges of the towers, not even that high. "I thought it would be mightier, and more finished. What do you think, Ty?"

Ty sat with head on knees, ignoring them. So cursed silent all the time.

"Heya!" Adiki lifted his chin toward the road. "Look there."

Dust rose from the road, kicked up by horsemen riding their way with banners flying. The chief's whistle brought them to their feet, all except Ty.

"Get up," Gil said, hooking Ty under the armpit.

Adiki moved back to help him. They dragged an unresisting Ty to his feet just as Chief Roni strode out of the gate in company with an elderly priest. The holy man's seamed face had a mean look Gil distrusted.

"All right." The chief paced down the line of the work gang. "Here we are at Shining Fort, soon to be a citadel of righteousness and holy worship. You lot have a choice. I can leave you here to make bricks and build walls. It's hot work but manageable for any simpleton. You get one ration a day. For nighttime you can build whatever shelter you can scrounge together. If that's your choice, go over to the brick building supervisor and get to work."

He paused to scan up and down the line, but no one spoke or moved.

"Alternatively I can sell your labor to his exalted holiness here." He indicated the old priest. "He'll be taking a work gang out to the naphtha fields west of here, in the Barrens. Working the fields is dangerous, but your ration will be increased to twice a day and you'll share barracks and be given boots as part of your work gear. Also, instead of seven years you'll only have to serve four."

Gil wanted to say, *And die twice as fast*, but he had learned his lesson and kept his mouth shut.

"What's the third choice?" asked Adiki in that way he had, like he couldn't decide whether to laugh at you or slap you.

The chief regarded him with the wary respect of a man facing a scorpion. "Those who are man enough will be allowed to choose glory and honor."

"How many rations a day and what gear does glory and honor come with?" Gil asked, because after all he just could not keep his mouth shut.

The chief smirked. "You've already been assigned to the naphtha fields. You and that one." He indicated Tyras.

"What if I don't want to go to the naphtha fields? What if I'd rather choose glory and honor?" Gil said.

Cursed if the man didn't close his beefy fingers around Tyras's upper arm. "I think you know what will happen if you say one more thing to me, Lord Gilaras. I'll have another hankering."

Tyras spat into the chief's face. The chief backhanded him so hard he staggered back, tripped, and fell on his ass. The other men—all except his own little squad—laughed nervously.

"Move," said the chief. "Go over to the exalted priest who is now your master."

"Fuck you, Gil," said Tyras under his breath as Gil tried to help him up. Shaking off Gil's grip he slouched over to the priest and stood there staring at the ground.

Adiki caught Gil's gaze and raised a brow as if to ask whether they should all go, but Gil shook his head and walked with head high to stand beside Tyras. No reason for their comrades to be fucked just because he and Ty were fucked. Likely the only reason he and Ty hadn't been murdered along the way was because the chief was paid for the number of prisoners he delivered.

As the chief strolled down the line the rest of the work gang tried to keep eyes forward, as they'd been trained. "Follow them if you're for the naphtha fields. As for the other, glory and honor come with a complete kit and three rations a day. You'll be treated as men instead of the worthless shit you are now. After three years' service you'll be released. Now's the one chance you have in your sorry lives to improve your lot."

No one moved.

"All for glory and honor, then. You won't regret it."

A bark of command broke over the feasting soldiers, shouted by one of their officers. They formed up into neat ranks, four by four. Having so little else to think about on the long journey, Gil had studied their organization. They marched, ate, and slept in squads of sixteen overseen by a subchief. Four squads constituted a cadre, commanded by a chief. Four chiefs and their 256 men came under the command of a captain and his three aides, with a support staff of twelve who arranged the cooking and supply although the soldiers themselves did all their own laundry and repair.

The riders Gil had noted before approached in an orderly formation. They wore field gear: scale armor, leather boots, spears in hand, and swords in practical sheaths rather than the jeweled cases beloved of courtiers in the palace. Most had rectangular banners affixed to their backs, white with a gold lion's head. They looked cursed impressive as they trotted up, wove a great circle, and came to a halt so the four men at the front of the company had a good view of the infantry in formation. The hungry work gang did their best to stand in a straight line and look glorious and honorable.

One man rode forward, his hair in a simple topknot, his clothing exactly like everyone else's. He surveyed the ranks of the soldiers. "The last company of Fourth Cohort. Excellent! You bring strength to our cause."

The soldiers bent to one knee as eager suppliants.

He trotted over to the work gang. "Chief Roni, here you are again, and just in time. How many of this work gang will serve?"

"All of them, Your Highness. It is a strong group, although they need fattening up. Just two for the naphtha fields..."

"Prince Farihosh?" said Gil, too loudly, because the shock of seeing a familiar face overwhelmed his hard-earned caution.

The prince looked their way, said something to the captain, and rode over.

"Lord Gilaras? Lord Tyras." His gaze flicked between the two of them, and he drew a whip from his belt and tapped it against his armored thigh speculatively. "How are you come here, bearing the work gang mark?"

Ty stepped on Gil's foot.

Gil elbowed him away. "Your Highness, I can explain everything. Either my uncle Lord Vanas still seeks revenge on my branch of the family because we still have more balls than him and his sons even after everything my brothers lost. Or your mother, the honored queen, wants my Ri Amarah bride's fortune and had to get rid of me. So here I am."

The sun in his eyes gave him a headache as he awaited the prince's answer. The chief stalked over with whip in hand, but the prince extended his own whip so its tip flicked the chief's chest lightly but in warning.

"I want these two cleaned up and sent to my camp."

"But Your Highness, I have particular orders—"

"And now you have *my* orders, Chief." The prince dangled the whip, swishing it just enough to get a whistling sound as it cut the air. "Is that a problem?"

During his three years engaged in endlessly pathetic attempts to roil the waters of the court with ridiculous pranks and stunts, Gil had never once seen Prince Farihosh lose his cool, not like Tavahosh whose pompous arrogance could so amusingly be riled into sputtering anger. Nor did Farihosh look the least discomposed now.

"I didn't hear you, Chief."

"As you command, Your Highness."

Given how irritated and worried the chief looked, why not press the advantage?

Gil stepped forward. "Your Highness, you have my deepest thanks and most profound gratitude for your intervention. May I ask that I be allowed to bring along my retinue as well?"

"Your retinue?"

"Every grandson of the legendary General Sengel must have a martial retinue, must he not?"

"Oh indeed I do believe he must. Which among these stalwart fellows do you count as your retinue, Lord Gilaras?"

Gil nodded at Adiki and the other five, then grinned. "Those six in particular. But I will welcome any who choose to stand with me, Your Highness."

"I think you more properly mean to say, any who choose to stand with me. You may choose one man to attend you now and the rest can join you tomorrow."

"Where am I going, Your Highness?"

"You and Lord Tyras will join me for supper in my tent. Given your clan's impoverished condition, I am curious to hear every detail about this unexpected Silver bride and her fortune, since it all seems to have played out after I left court."

He rejoined his horsemen. They rode past the brickworks onto a wide level ground where they began to drill on horseback despite the heat and chaff. The soldiers moved in the direction the riders had come from. When the chief snapped his whip the work gang hustled after the soldiers. As soon as they came around the corner of the shrine they saw a far larger walled compound in the distance, their destination.

Tyras stumped along in his usual bleak mood, but Gil assured each of his companions in turn that he would not forget them if good fortune fell his way. "Obviously if bad fortune falls my way, you'll do best to pretend you never knew me."

Last he walked beside Adiki. "You'll attend us. Try to be polite, and don't challenge anyone to a fight."

"Surely you're not afraid I'll lose?"

"No, I'm afraid you'll win."

Adiki angled his elbow to catch Gil in the ribs. "Can your good friend Prince Farihosh help me find my brother?"

"For all I know he's invited me to supper in order to poison me. Does it seem as strange to you as it does to me that yonder compound looks like an army camp and is vastly larger than the unfinished shrine?"

They entered a walled compound about three times the size of the shrine, with an annex that was obviously a reeve hall. A forge smoked in the distance, closer to the water. Inside the walls spun a hive of activity. Soldiers drilled with spears and swords on a parade ground, kicking dust up into a row of barred cages where about ten prisoners sat slumped on the ground including four women wearing reeve leathers.

In the shade of open storehouses, laborers built wagons while elsewhere folk laced together leather scales to make armored coats. The kitchens boiled with workers, and the smells made Gil's mouth hurt. Most of the work gang was driven off in one direction but the chief himself escorted Gil, Tyras, and Adiki to a back corner. Here, in a walled-off garden with only a few sapling trees, two troughs of sunbright, and a dry pool, stood the prince's tent flanked by guards. The chief turned them over to a steward.

"The prince wants them washed and dressed for supper."

"Is there anything else I need to know about these men?" asked the startled steward.

The chief had already lost interest. "They're no longer my business, ver."

The steward led them past the tent and its guards and

through an archway into a baths complex. Men with the long hair of soldiers wearing the loose trousers and jackets common to palace residents waited in line for their turn to bathe. Gil, Tyras, and Adiki were taken to the head of the line and handed over to the men who ran the baths.

They weren't proper baths, not like the ones in Toskala with ample water piped in and hot pools for relaxation after you were clean. Here, on planks raised up off the ground, they rinsed off the worst of the grime with salt water from the landlocked sea, then scrubbed their skin with sand, rinsed clean with scoops of water from a bucket, and last were given a razor and a mirror to shave. To Gil's relief Tyras didn't try to cut his own throat with the razor although he spent a disturbingly long time staring at the reflection of his thin face and sad cap of short hair.

"Your beautiful hair will grow back," Gil said.

Ty set down the mirror and turned his back on him.

"Do you know what I find strange?" Adiki said as he scraped the beard off his chin. Gil had forgotten the other man had an ugly scar along his jaw. "Besides those four caged reeves, and the women drying fish on the shoreline back where we camped, I haven't seen a single woman. Don't you find it a little odd to not have any women around? Like they've all vanished, or are in hiding?"

"Everything about this is a little odd," said Gil.

"Shut up, someone's coming," said Tyras.

A steward brought palace garb, trousers, jacket, sashes, and sandals, and a sachet of herbs to rub over their skin to freshen their scent. Gil felt quite born new as he sauntered past the curious guards and a pair of watchful reeves into Farihosh's spacious tent. Inside four military men stood chatting by a table covered with maps. An older man whose cheek bore the mark of the work gang sat cross-legged on a cushion, sewing up a rip in a tabard. Prince Farihosh stood at a basin washing his hands and face as a lad dressed in white and gold stood to one side holding a towel in readiness.

The prince glanced up with a smile that soothed rather than mocked. "Ah. Lord Gilaras. Lord Tyras. Too bad about your hair but otherwise you look much more like yourselves."

"Karladas!" Adiki shoved past Gil and was halfway across the space before Farihosh drew his sword and the four men leaped between him and the prince.

"Stop, you idiot." Gil darted forward to grab Adiki's arm. "Take a breath. If that is your brother then he looks whole and healthy to me."

Adiki was shaking, and Gil knew in another few breaths he would break free anyway and then a nasty fight would start, and end with Adiki's blood on the carpet and his own besides.

"Five against one, Adiki. They have blades. You don't. Take a breath."

The prince looked around at the lad. "Do you know this man, Karladas?"

The lad looked about fourteen, handsome in the way of youths who have never been laid low with the sting of rebukes or scorn. "It's my brother, Adiki. May I go to him, Your Highness?"

"You're not his slave to have to ask permission to come and go," snarled Adiki. Had he wanted to throw off Gil's hand he could easily have done so. At least he had the sense to rage in place. "Have you been harmed? Handled against your will? Abused? How are you come to be in the prince's tent? I should never have brought you to the city...Nor let you go off on your own that day just for a bit of coin to run a message..."

Farihosh gave an almost imperceptible nod.

The lad dashed over to his brother and embraced him. "Oh, no, it's nothing like that, Adiki. It was just bad fortune I got swept up into the work gang. But I've not been harmed and no one has touched me. You always think the worst of people!"

"You think too well of people," muttered Adiki. The other men stared to see a brute of a man like Adiki reduced to tears. Folk might find it surprising if they hadn't heard how he spoke of his brother and his clan.

"It's all worked out better than we could have hoped, Adiki. I serve Prince Farihosh now."

Adiki's gaze stabbed the prince, who returned his suspicion with a look of such calm that Gil truly could not tell if the prince found Adiki's distress and defiance risible, mutinous, dull, or exemplary. "As your guardian, I refuse to give you permission to stay here."

"But Adiki, you have a work gang mark. That means you were arrested, too. We have to follow the law."

"We do not serve people who make laws to hook coin into their own pockets and destroy the lives of men who have done nothing wrong."

Farihosh sheathed his sword and waved the other men to step away. "Let's eat. We'll make a better start with food in our stomachs and a cup of rice wine. Lord Gilaras, sit at my right, if you will. Lord Adiki, you may sit at my left hand."

"I am no lord of the palace."

"Call him Your Highness," whispered Karladas in a tone of outrage that made Farihosh's companions smile.

"You are a lord if I say you are one, Lord Adiki. I value your brother Karladas for his intelligence and diligence. My soldiers have come to see him as a token of our good fortune. I'll let him tell you the story later." He clapped his hands.

Stewards drew aside a curtain to reveal a table laden with food: It was no sophisticated palace feast but rather a sturdy collation of rice, grilled whitefish, and turnip stewed in sweetened rice wine and soybean brine. Tyras began by gulping down two cups of the flower wine set on the table. Gil wanted to bolt his food but he cautiously picked through both turnip and fish and filled up on rice, hoping not to upset a stomach too long accustomed to gruel.

Karladas stood at the prince's elbow holding a glass bottle with a smoky-colored liquid reserved for the prince. No matter how many dark looks Adiki threw at his younger brother, the lad looked proud and even protective.

Farihosh affected not to notice Adiki's glares and frowns. "I am curious to know what happened with you, Lord Gilaras. To find you and Lord Tyras in a work gang perplexes me."

"It perplexed me, too, Your Highness. But here we are. Are you saying you knew nothing of the scheme to destroy my clan's standing in court?"

"As I recall, I invited you to join my group of companions, but you refused me."

"My clan encouraged me to take your generous invitation, Your Highness. I had a habit of doing the opposite of what they wanted."

"So it wasn't me you wanted to insult? It was them?"

"Yes, that's right. My apologies. It really was nothing to do with you personally."

"It is a curious thing how often we act against wisdom simply because we feel driven to do so by the peculiar nature of our family relationships."

"Why did you invite me to become one of your companions here, Your Highness? My clan had nothing to offer you, as disgraced as it is."

"Several of your most elaborate pranks were not just criminal and impious but clever. I admire cleverness."

"I was not so clever as to escape this." Gil tapped the ink on his cheek.

"Yes, you were going to tell me about your bride."

"My clan arranged to marry me to a Ri Amarah woman and thus to her clan's distinguished fortune. Naturally I could not say no."

"Interesting. Yes, now and again a person finds themselves in a situation where they cannot say no." Unlike Tyras, now working on his fourth cup of wine, and the military men quaffing wine at almost the same pace, Farihosh drank sparingly and only from the bottle Karladas held. "Therefore I am delighted to welcome you and Lord Tyras and Lord Adiki to my enterprise."

"What if we don't wish to join your mysterious enterprise? What if we would rather work the naphtha fields?"

Karladas shifted from foot to foot as if he really desperately wanted to speak but had been trained to wait for permission.

Farihosh raised a hand, and a steward brought in jellied bean paste, which he offered first to all the other men before bringing the last piece to the prince. "That isn't an option. Now that you've seen all this, you can join me or I'll have to kill you. If you prefer death you'll spend the night in the cage and be executed at dawn with the other prisoners."

Gil laughed. He waited until the other men popped the jellied dessert into their mouths before trying it, just in case it was poisoned. In fact, it was delicious, little pieces of sweet potato layered in the jelly as a moist surprise.

"In that case, I find myself quite enthusiastic about your expedition, Your Highness. Are you intending to overthrow your father the king?"

Tyras said, "Oh the fuck you're an idiot, Gil. You don't just ask if people intend to commit treason."

The military men chortled.

Farihosh laughed with them. "I think it better to get straight to the point and not disguise words with honeyed innuendo. Why would I want to overthrow my father?"

"A young man can die almost as easily as an older man. Your father is healthy and vigorous. He could outlive you and then you'd never have a chance to be king."

"Or he could have plans that disinherit me," said Farihosh.

"You think your father wants to put Kas on the throne?"

"I think he wants to please Queen Dia. It would be an unnatural mother who did not want her son to become king over another woman's son."

"So it's Kas you want dead, then."

"You mistake me. I hold no grudge against Kasad. It's not his fault he was born, although I do find it puzzling he won't take over the military governorship of Ithik Eldim as our father clearly wants him to do. Regardless, I have to protect myself, Lord Gilaras."

"Thus this army?"

The prince frowned as a bell jangled at the tent's entrance. "Something like that."

The entrance flap was swept back. A reeve appeared, his face wind-chapped. He was chafing his hands as if they were still cold. "Your Highness, riders have been spotted, moving at speed. They fly the Banner of the Moon."

"Sooner than I expected! There must be trouble." Farihosh rose. "Captains, we depart at dawn. As for you, my friends, I am afraid I will have to place you under guard for the night. Please let me assure you that I intend you no harm as long as you cooperate."

Tyras had slumped over the table, too drunk to respond.

Adiki brooded, arms crossed on his chest as he studied his smiling brother. "How are you come to be so favored, Karladas? Why do soldiers consider you their good fortune?"

The lad ducked his head quite charmingly. "I accidentally saved the prince's life. You'll see, Adiki. This is the best thing that could have happened to us."

The captains went out and several guards entered to dismantle the chairs and bundle up the carpets. Farihosh himself began rolling up the maps and sliding them into leather map cases.

"Is there any chance I might send a letter to my wife, assuring her I am safe?" Gil asked, ambling over to take a look at the last map, an eight-sided city with eight main roads that cut the territory into sectors of alternating fields and habitations.

Farihosh set his left hand flat on the center of the map to hide something. He smiled in the cordial way he had that invited you in but cut you off before you got too close. "No communication. My apologies, Lord Gilaras. I hope you find the expedition to your taste, now that you are embarked upon it."

Gil took the hint and returned to the table, where Tyras had started snoring. He snagged the last jellied bean paste and popped it in his mouth as Farihosh sheathed the map and the guards started taking the table apart for transport. "We're not riding north to Toskala, are we? We're riding south into the empire. Queen Chorannah is taking sides in the succession war."

54

Sarai crept down an unlit lane in the city of Nessumara and halted by the servants' gate of the house where she had been born. Beside the latchless gate hung a cord. She tugged on it to release the muted thunk of a padded bell.

Silence greeted her. She glanced back the way she had come, but no one had followed her. Once they had transferred from the riverboat to an oceangoing ship bound for Salya, their new captain had told his fugitive passengers that the tide waited for no one. She had coordinated her departure so there wouldn't be opportunity to search for her before the ship had to sail.

Just as she thought she must tug the cord again, footsteps pattered up and a slit opened. A woman peered through, Hundred-born by her round eyes and dark skin, and examined Sarai's humble cotton taloos and the faded shawl draped over her hair.

"We have no deliveries engaged for this hour. What do you want?"

Sarai leaned closer to allow the lamplight to illuminate her face.

The woman recoiled, then swayed back into view. "Who are you?"

"I am here to see Master Aram."

"Aui! Aram Elder?"

Here came the crux of it. "Aram Elder still lives, does he not?"

The servant glanced over her shoulder, then back at Sarai. "Of course. He still rules this house."

"It is his son I seek, Aram Younger. I beg you, please tell him his sister is here."

"You are not his sister. His sisters are either married or still living at home. Are you a counterfeiter's daughter, with those eyes and that skin? It wouldn't surprise me. Come to extort coin from one of our men."

"Please, verea. That isn't my purpose here. If Aram Younger refuses then nothing changes."

"But I have to walk all the way and back again."

"You will have his thanks for it."

The servant shook her head in a way that made Sarai fear she was about to rebuff her. "No harm in telling him, I suppose, not that your wiles will have any luck with Aram Younger. He's a good man."

The shutter slammed closed. Footsteps pattered away. Sarai shifted from foot to foot. "A counterfeiter's daughter." The word *whore* did not exist in the language of the Hundred, the closest being *flower girl*. Among the Ri Amarah the description of a woman giving her husband false coin fit well enough.

The solidity of the land felt strange after days on the river. Nessumara had smoky, humid air and a reek that made her ill. She hid her face in her hands. Her palms were hot and her cheeks were hotter.

A cart turned down the street. She crept deeper into the shadows along the compound wall, but the man pushed the cart past her without a word or glance. It hadn't been easy to sneak off; the people of Five Roads Clan had been so kind on the river trip, treating her as an honored guest, even giving her a comb they could ill afford to lose. But she wasn't one of them, and anyway she was tired of having her future arranged by other people. If her brother refused to see her then she would try to get work as a clerk. People kept records going back many years. Somewhere in Nessumara's transport district she might find a trace of the failed conspiracy and the fate of a carter named Isar.

"Sarai?"

The sound of her name pronounced in the proper way jolted her. She pressed her hands against the door. Eyes she did not know stared at her through the narrow opening: long lashes, thick brows, a pale forehead.

"Aram? Are you my brother Aram?"

The shutter banged shut, the noise a slap to her heart.

Locked out.

Rejected again.

Bars scraped, and the door swung in. Because she was still leaning against it, she stumbled inside. The young man caught her arm and guided her to a bench. A young Ri Amarah woman closed and barred the door, then knelt before her. Her clothes had the starch of wealth but her face was relaxed and merry.

"Is this truly her, Aram? You look a bit alike. See, it is the scar they mention."

He stood with a hand on his chest as if stanching a wound to the heart.

"It is truly you, my sister," he said in a voice deeper than she expected, almost rumbling. He sat on the bench with a thump. How he stared! "I remember when you were born, not long before our mother ran away. Those first few months she used to let me hold you. She would say, 'Little colt, she is the most precious of your charges and you must protect her always' ..." He swallowed.

"Little colt?"

He wiped his eyes and went on. "Little colt was the pet name she called me. Like in the Tale of Trusted."

"I'll keep watch." The woman moved away into the shadows.

Sarai and Aram sat in an entry court that let onto a portico and, beyond it, a lane leading between storehouses. After the evening brightness of the upper palace where lamps burned incessantly, the courtyard had the dim aura of a frugal household held on a tight leash. Not even kitchen noises disturbed them, no levity, no evening laughter and singing.

"That's a children's story," Sarai said.

"It was my favorite story when I was a little boy. Mama told it to me every night at bedtime. It's my only real memory of her." He intoned the words. *"In the days of old, when the eldest of the ancestors were children your own age, there was a fine and splendid horse whose name was Trusted. He was the favorite steed of the Imperators of Gems and Knives, the ones who rule half the world. But one day Trusted discovered that the Imperators were cruel people."*

"No one ever told me this story at bedtime when I was a little girl."

"No one told you?"

"Great-Aunt Tsania told me stories of how flowers propagate and how we measure the passing of seasons by the position of the sun as it rises and sets. I was the only child actually raised at the estate even though the family always came up to spend the hottest month in the hills. So the tales I heard were the ones told by the local women who worked in the house. I grew up hearing the tales of the Hundred, not Ri Amarah tales. What did the Imperators do that was so cruel?" she asked, caught by the mystery of the tale and its quiet insight into the life her mother had fled.

"With magic the Imperators cut out the free heart of our people and turned them into slaves."

"How can magic cut out people's hearts? Wouldn't a scalpel be better?"

His smile brushed like balm over her heart. "I always asked that question, too, although not the part about the scalpel. Then she would say, 'Little colt, when you have taken a man's place in the hall you will hear the full tale.' Now shall I go on?"

"Yes," said Sarai, leaning toward him and, trustingly, he took her hand in his. It seemed to her he went on because once started he had to tell the whole story before he could stop, as if the ritual was itself the memory of a mother he had lost when he was only five.

"*Trusted went to his mother, the mare who gave birth to the world, and he told her of what he had learned. 'Little colt,' his mother the mare said to him, 'you are strong and bold and you must lead your people away from the Imperators and never return. You must steal the bridle of gold and the saddle of jewels with which the Imperators harness you so you can never be called back. But remember that once you have stolen the bridle and the saddle you can never put them on no matter how beautiful you look in them because if you do, the Imperators will know where you are and the magic will awaken and you will be dragged back to their stable.'*"

Again he wiped fingers across his eyes and let out a breath.

"She told me the story so many times we had made a game of it. After she mentioned being dragged back to the Imperators' stable, I would always ask, 'But what about you, Mother Mare? Will you not escape with me and the others to a safe place?'"

Again he paused, then sighed.

"Ai! It is so hard to say the words. She told me the story that night, that last night, because she wanted me to lie down and sleep. She said, 'Little colt, you are the trusted one whom the others will follow. I am the mare who birthed the world. I must stand astride the world and shelter all. We will part here and now, but know I am always with you, my dear son. My dear son. Know I am always with you.'

"But she was crying as she spoke. I asked her why she was crying and she said, 'These are not tears, they are starlight fallen to earth.'" He touched fingers to his lips as in imitation of the last time she had touched his. "'Starlight tastes salty, like the sea, because starlight is the path Trusted took across the wide ocean, he and all the herd who fled from the cruel Imperators.'"

He paused.

Sarai could not speak.

With a sigh, he went on in a quiet voice. "And that is the end of the story. She told me to close my eyes and sleep until morning."

For the longest time they looked at each other, strangers who had once been bound so closely, travelers out of the same womb. His confident air had the grace of a young man raised to expect he will one day be among the authoritative men of the house. But caution and a hint of fear brushed him with humility.

"You never saw her again?"

He glanced around as if seeking eavesdroppers. "I knew something was wrong. I pretended to be asleep and watched her. Instead of tucking you into your cradle as she usually did, she bundled you into a sling and grabbed a laden pouch and left our suite of rooms. I followed her."

"Where did she go?"

"Up the tower to where the holy flame lies hidden from the eyes of men. I should not have followed but I was so afraid. I saw a thing I ought never to have seen. Women's magic." He glanced in the direction his wife had walked, but the shadows hid her. Then he whispered, "She lifted the seal—the cap—off the vessel and laid the mirror across the mouth. The holy flame leaped up to catch in the surface of her mirror. The brilliance lit her face, and yours in her arms. She looked into its reflection. And then she was gone."

"Gone? Vanished?" She thought of the demon's coil.

"No. Whatever she saw in her mirror made her leave the house. I hid because I knew men aren't allowed in the tower and I didn't want her to see me and know I had broken our law. She never came back but my father returned unexpectedly later that night. He had been gone for six months on a trading mission. When he had left, you hadn't yet been born."

"He had never seen me?"

"No, you were born after he departed. It was many years before I understood she ran away because she didn't want him to see you, because if he did then he would know..."

He trailed off, a frown troubling his kind features.

"That I am a counterfeiter's daughter. It's no surprise to me what I am, Aram. You need not fear to say it."

He squeezed her hands. "If you had been his child they would have brought you back here instead of sending you to the country estate of our mother's clan. But you are another man's child, and that he would never, ever forgive."

Silence fell between them, yet she felt comforted by the ease with which they could reflect together on how they had been torn apart so many years ago. After a bit he said, "Why have you come, Sarai? We heard you are to marry Prince Tavahosh."

"That's why I ran away. I'm pregnant with Lord Gilaras's child. I don't want to marry Prince Tavahosh."

The young woman raced out of the shadows as if she had been listening all along. Again she knelt before Sarai. This time she grasped Sarai's hands. The pleasing features of her round face and the warm contours of her smile wormed their way right into Sarai's heart. "You'll live with us! We will be sisters. Our children will call you Aunt and your child will be their cousin."

"Hush, Jiara," Aram said with an affectionate touch to his wife's shoulder. "I would have had Sarai brought here years ago but it isn't safe for her."

"He's old and failing. By the grace of the Hidden One, he will die soon."

"Don't say so. It's ill luck upon all of us to wish death even upon the wicked."

"People do it all the time! Anyway it's true and you know it. Your father has been the ill wind that plagues the house. Five wives he has had, Aram! Three lie in the tomb, and your mother fled her own people and abandoned a son she loved to escape him. Even then death claimed her. It is only this last wife he does not beat and abuse, so we are told. The honest women will vote with me to demand the men's council cast lots on whether to keep him as headman of the house. But I can only call a vote once. If I do, you must back me up in the men's council. If enough men mark their tokens, then your father will no longer be headman. Sarai's arrival is the sign that now is the time to remove him. His hate and anger harm us all. You know it."

"Yes, yes, I know it, none better than me who lost my mother," he breathed.

"Do you have enough support on the men's council to unseat him?"

"The other men fear him."

"When will we stop fearing him and act?"

Sarai got to her feet. "I can't come here only to cause trouble for you. It's better if I go."

Jiara dragged her to a halt. "Where would you go? Who will keep you?"

"There's a ship," she lied, knowing the tide had already turned.

"Is there really a ship?" Aram touched a finger to her nose in a gesture that seemed so right and so familiar that she sagged into his embrace. "I used to touch your nose like that, and then you would laugh. You had the sweetest little chortle, like babies do. I never forgot it. Don't leave us, Sarai. Jiara is right. We have let things go on for too long. I've been too timid. My father is a terrible man. It is time he be retired to the elders' council so a more respectable and even-tempered man can stand in authority over the house."

"But what about the other people who live here? They need only look at my face to know me for what I am, a counterfeiter's daughter."

"Do not underestimate my influence." He raised his arms to display bracelets all the way to his elbow, like those of a much older man. "I am young but I have accomplished a great deal. I opened a new trade route over the ocean by negotiating with the Tandi consortium to convince them to establish a trading hall here in Nessumara. Please let me do what our mother charged me with. Let me protect you, as I should have had the courage to do long before this."

How her heart trembled.

"I'll take Sarai to the sacred flame where your father can't go," said Jiara. "We have to act quickly before he guesses you mean to unseat him."

Aram had a face as transparent as glass, easy to read as he worked from trepidation through consideration to compassion and conviction. "Yes. We'll do it now."

They walked past the empty kitchen and locked storerooms and along a portico. From there Aram directed her into the long atrium that in every Ri Amarah compound divided the men's wing from the women's wing, with the tower at the far end. No lights shone in the women's hall, not as they would have at home when all the cousins were visiting. How odd to think she missed the chatter, and had taken it for granted. In this house some of the men had stayed late at prayer, voices rising in somber melodies. The heavy sonority of their voices coursed through every part of her being, the comforting prayers of her childhood melding with apprehension to make each step seem poised over a chasm.

"Aram, I'll take her up while you go and speak to your allies." He hurried away to the men's wing. Jiara gave a stealthy glance around as they slipped into the tower. "Step where I step so you don't make the stairs creak."

They passed the first landing that let onto the room where women kept the accounts and ledgers. They paused for Sarai to catch her breath on the second landing that let onto the Master's Study. A vile taint drifted like bitter incense from behind the closed and locked door. Queasiness roiled her stomach, and she hurried after Jiara up the last flight to the top floor.

The last time she had stood in the women's tower she had overheard the argument between Makel and Abrisho that had catapulted her into a new life. Into this life. Every Ri Amarah tower held a sacred flame contained in a glass vessel. At their entrance the quiescent flames stirred, licking up the sides as if in response to their presence. Gouts of thready blue fire probed the sealed lid and fell back.

Her heart would not cease thumping.

"Sit now. You're out of breath." Jiara urged her onto a cushion and settled beside her. "Is it really true you were offered marriage to Prince Tavahosh? And rejected it?"

"It is."

"How was your other husband?"

"I like him."

Jiara hissed breath through pursed lips. "It's surprising you were allowed to marry out at all."

"Not really. They never thought of me as truly Ri Amarah."

"It's true anyone can see by looking at you that your mother shamed herself."

"Why is it shame for her if it would not be shame for a man to do the same thing? Why is it shame for her to find affection elsewhere if she was married to a man who abused her? You said yourself that Aram Elder has had five wives, and four of them are dead! He gets away with it because he is rich and powerful."

Jiara touched her gold hoop earrings. "Aram Elder gets away with it because all of us around him benefit from his wealth and power. It's easier to look the other way."

The top floor of the tower was open to the air just as at the estate. A railing and eaves ringed it. The life in the house below seemed muted, while from the tower she could see over the myriad lamps of Nessumara and its hundred islets and ships' masts like leafless trees along a distant wharf. The many-channeled waters and the crush of people all crammed together exuded a heavy odor laced with sewage and also the overpowering musk of vegetation caught between decay and flowering, between death and life.

"A Ri Amarah woman holds many responsibilities to her clan," Jiara went on. "The first and most important is that she must never give away any of its secrets. That's why women must be the most careful of all. That's what's shameful about what your mother did, not the sex."

"I don't understand."

"You need to understand, especially now you are married

and pregnant. When you married did they give you a Book of Accounts?"

Sarai indicated the leather case. "Yes."

"But they won't have given you a woman's mirror. That would be forbidden for someone going outside the clans." She kissed Sarai on the cheek in a spontaneous burst of sweetness. "Don't look so frightened! You're home now. We are really very kind, most of us. Well, a few of us are, and we'll protect you. It will be all right, Sarai. You'll see. Now wait here. I'm going to let my trusted friends know you're here so we can be ready to vote. I'll fetch you something to eat and drink."

"But what if someone comes up here?"

"No one comes up here this time of night. Aram Elder runs the household with such a tight fist no one dares use any lamp oil at night without his permission. I'll be back very soon."

The curve of the stairs cut off most sound from below. Although Sarai listened she could not hear Jiara's retreating footfalls. How strange it felt to have clan walls around her. She got up to pace, hugging the oilcloth pouch in which nestled the leather case with its book, writing implements, and comb. The mirror bumped against her thigh, hidden beneath cloth.

If she kept it hidden perhaps they would give her one of her own, and then it would never matter that she had stolen her mother's. Maybe at long last she would be taught the knowledge passed down through the women of her people.

As she paced she studied the sacred flame twisting and whispering under its seal within the vessel of glass. The blue fire seemed by all appearances to have a similar substance to the threads woven into demon's coils. The mirror's back was engraved with a maze similar in shape to that of the coils. It seemed unlikely to be mere coincidence. Were they related? She walked closer, paused to listen, but heard no footsteps on the stairs.

Never had she thought to touch the molded leather cap that covered the top of the glass. Its texture slipped smoothly under her fingers. When she pushed on it, the cap turned easily around the rim. She took out her mirror and then tipped off the seal, just as Aram had described their mother doing on the night she fled. Threads of blue fire snaked up the inside of the glass. Hastily she held the engraved side of the mirror over the top so the fire couldn't escape. The mirror was exactly the right size to cover the opening. Flame leaped up onto the bronze surface of the mirror, running molten through the engravings incised there.

"Where is she?" a man's harsh voice thundered from below, accompanied by the pound of feet on the steps.

She jerked the mirror off the opening and jammed the seal back down.

"Where you cannot reach her, Father. How did you know?"

"Who do you think pays the servants? Of course they tell me everything that happens. Where is she?" A door rattled, shaken on its hinges. "Is she hidden among the ledgers?"

"Stand down, Father. This is not your business anymore."

"Of course it is my business!" He stamped up the stairs, roaring as he came. "Her mother shamed me, passed me counterfeit coin. The girl is dirt. I'll kill her as I would have twenty-two years ago if I had been here when she was born. It is my right to rid the family of contamination!"

"You can't go in there!"

"Get out of my way!"

An old man burst into the tower, his face engorged with rage. With one hand he leaned on a cane but in the other he brandished a whip. He advanced like he was no longer human but a monstrous force of hate spewing from his eyes and his foul expression. To have such loathing flung at her choked her. She swung around side-to-side, desperate for an escape route. The shawl slithered off her shoulders and in agonizing slowness rippled toward the floor.

Fury made him quick.

The whip slapped down on her back. She staggered sideways, barely catching herself on the wall.

"Sarai!" screamed Jiara. "Aram, get the other women. Call them up here. Hurry! Hurry!"

The whip snapped down a second time, the blow landing on her head. Pain burst along her temple. The world turned a complete revolution around her. She heaved, coughing up bile.

Aram Elder raised his arm again. She thrust up to her feet and grabbed for whatever came closest to hand. Fabric caught in her fingers and she tugged. His head wrap tore free to expose his head.

Somehow she had kept hold of the mirror in her other hand.

Jiara stood in the door, eyes wide, mouth open, shouting words Sarai could not hear.

Threads of blue fire leaped from the mirror onto Aram Elder's arms and twisted around his silver bracelets. Silver absorbed the threads, hissing as the light whirled dizzily. His gaze fell to his arms and then up to the shining mirror as alarm suffused his face.

"Cover the mirror!" he cried.

A wire of blue flame caught a hook into the horns on his head where they peeped out from his thinning white hair. He blossomed in a net of fire that the silver bracelets could not neutralize. The mirror held the magic, and the horns amplified it until all Sarai could see was a man limned with violently glowing threads. The filaments wove together like a harness buckling itself around his body. A glittering ribbon of light traced a hexagonal spiral first in a wide circle around where he and she stood and thence tighter and tighter as it coiled around them both.

All this and she had yet to draw breath.

The magic had substance more like sound, like the humming

of bees about flowers, like the whistle of oil as it burns, like the song of the wind in eaves. A gale like claws blasted down the threads of magic and raked them into the maw of the demon's heart.

Mirror and horns made a gate. It opened with a clash of bells.

Aram Elder faded through it. She lunged, trying to get to Jiara at the door, but the tower and Jiara and everything she knew vanished into mist and smoke.

When the bright-blue light faded and her sight cleared, she stood clutching book and mirror at the center of a vast glassy lake. Its ice-white surface was scored with a huge hexagonal spiral as black as obsidian. Jagged mountains rose on all sides. Twin sentries hulked in the distance, standing so still that after she blinked several times she realized they were monumental statues. Beyond lay the rubble of more abandoned buildings than she could count. As the light dimmed not a single lantern or fire sparked. Wind keened across the dead city and frozen lake.

They stood in the center of a colossal demon's coil.

"What have you done, you stupid girl?" said Aram Elder. "Now the sleeping Imperators will wake, and find us. And it is all your fault."

55

With only Reyad in attendance Dannarah flew south along the West Track and past the city of Olossi and the salty inland Olo'o Sea, seeking signs of the monumental shrine everyone knew had been building here for five years. How hard could it be to talk a prince into rebelling against his father when he was likely already preparing for such an endeavor?

Flying in over the dusty town of Old Fort, she puzzled over a half-finished and unimpressive mud-brick shrine until she discovered, south of town, a brand-new reeve hall with lofts and barracks and landing ground. She ignored flags from the reeve hall demanding she and Reyad land and identify themselves, but circled for long enough to spot four eagles confined in big net cages as they waited for a new Talon Ceremony. A cold voice had taken charge in her head. If reeves had died to free those eagles then she would see them avenged. If Tarnit and the other women reeves in Toskala had been murdered...but her father had taught her never to allow the heat of anger to overmaster the calculations of intelligence.

There was a reasonable chance they had gotten word in time. She could not know.

There was so much she did not know.

Her own father hadn't told her the whole truth. His mind had run deep, but narrow. Mai's words hung in her memory: *Had he made you king, things would have turned out very differently. You would have kept the Hundred the way he wanted it to be.*

Beyond the reeve hall sprawled a huge walled army camp whose newly built grounds were strangely empty. If Farihosh was assembling an army to strike against his father, then where was it? She had seen no sign of its passage headed north on West Track. Had Jehosh actually been right? Was Queen Chorannah determined against all wisdom to support her sister's incompetent son in his bid to remain emperor?

They flew along the West Spur as it wound up into the foothills of the mighty Spires toward the Kandaran Pass. Only this one pass bridged these impassable mountains that for generations had kept the Hundred safe from the Sirniakan Empire.

Of course Terror spotted eagles before she did: at least two flights in wing formation. Two reeves swung back to pace her and Reyad. Late in the day she spotted the long border wall spanning the roadway ahead. She left Reyad circling aloft while she descended to a field beyond the border hill-town of Dast Korumbos.

An army camped in and around the town with its inns and taverns. Dast Korumbos figured in one of her father's stories about how he had first arrived in the Hundred. He had brought Dannarah and Atani here in the course of riding a circuit of the Hundred, as he had promised Dannarah that long-ago day when sixteen-year-old Atani was still missing. After Atani's return she and Atani always traveled with him when he journeyed through the Hundred sitting in judgment over assizes courts, inspecting reeve halls and army forts and border defenses, and meeting with town councils.

Dast Korumbos had grown during her father's reign as trade had increased with the empire. Now instead of ten houses it had ten inns, and a market hall, and new streets. With dusk settling hard, the last wagons of an army's field train trundled up. There were as many campfires in the surrounding fields and pastures as Jehosh's army had in the northern mountains twenty-two years ago on the eve of his invasion of Ithik Eldim. On the eve of Atani's murder.

Armies always brought death in their wake.

She hooded Terror and walked past a young man in reeve leathers who followed after her, saying, "Who are you? We have had no word from Shining Hall to expect a visiting reeve."

"Shining Hall? What kind of name is Shining Hall?" She fixed him with a glare and he stepped back. Gods, he was so young, bursting with youthful indignation.

"Are there really women who fly as reeves? The marshal says women are only allowed to fly as couriers."

"I am here to see Prince Farihosh on urgent business. You may escort me. What is your name?"

"Talon Wedum." He had enough wit to note the wings on her vest. "Marshal."

"Wedum. A Sirni name." He was speaking to her in Sirni. Before Tavahosh she had never spoken Sirni in the reeve halls. "Why are you called talon? Are you not a reeve?"

"I am to be allowed to stand as a candidate for reeve. When an eagle comes free." His pace quickened with excitement, and she had to push herself to keep up, curse his young legs. "It's a great honor, a true test of being a man!"

"Ah. My thanks for the explanation."

He led her up a central street so crowded with soldiers that they had to weave in and out between clusters of men. All the inns and taverns stood open, their forecourts and courtyards filled. Chimes tinkled from every eave. Ahead the famous inn called the Southmost shone with lamplight. The inn's shutters stood open under the peaked roof to air out the attic. Under an awning officers and lords attended Prince Farihosh, who sat on a humble cushion in their midst just as if he were an ordinary fellow.

She strode in, shedding the young talon. "Farihosh!"

He stared as if slow to recognize her, then shook himself and rose to greet her. "Aunt Dannarah! What brings you here?"

"Has Tavahosh sent word?" she asked, because she needed to know first of all if news of his brother's disappearance had reached him.

"I've heard nothing from Tavahosh since he left for his convocation as chief marshal. Do you come from that event, Aunt?"

"I do not. Have you any recent word from Toskala?"

"I have not but I left Shining Fort unexpectedly so it may take a day or two for messages to catch up. Please, share a taste of this excellent cordial." He gestured, and his companions moved away to leave her and the prince together with only a lad to attend them. The boy was perhaps fourteen, with an innocent face and an eager expression as he poured out a cup of cordial and offered it to her with more enthusiasm than precision.

Seated opposite Farihosh, she tasted the cordial to discover it sweet and smooth. She had already prepared a line of attack. "Your brother is a fool who wants to destroy the reeve halls all for the sake of winning praise from the Beltak priests."

Farihosh had a way of lowering his eyelashes as if he were flirting. "Kas plays a fool but I assume you mean Tav, who actually believes the things he says. There's no harm to him, Aunt Dannarah."

"No harm? I meant what I said about him destroying the reeve halls. These changes he means to institute will not only destroy the cohesion of the halls but with one dangerously foolhardy and shortsighted stroke will wipe out an entire generation of experienced and skilled reeves. That is not wisdom; it is ignorance and arrogance."

"Sometimes people have spent so long living in a familiar way they can't see it needs to be reformed."

"Destruction is not the same as change. If Tavahosh really wanted to institute reforms he would have called a council of reeves and set the question before them. But Tavahosh and those of the priests who are his allies are like a man who thinks he can make a dog obey by whipping it."

"A whipped dog will obey."

"Is that the sort of reeves you want when you are king, Farihosh? Whipped dogs who cringe instead of think?"

He studied her with hooded eyes. "Go on. I'm listening."

"Consider your situation right now. Reeves are an invaluable tool, not as fighters but as scouts. We are the eyes and the law. Very little escapes the gaze of a seasoned reeve. Would you rather have at your disposal flights filled with fledgling reeves who can barely harness their eagles, under the command of people who aren't jessed? Or would you rather have experienced, skilled reeves flying on your behalf, women as well as men?"

"The marshal of Shining Hall, in obedience to the directives of the priests, says it is inappropriate for men and women to work together in such intimate daily interactions."

"Then you need a different marshal, do you not? One who has the experience and energy to direct multiple wings of expert reeves on your behalf."

"Like you?" He sipped at a smoky-colored liquid. "Why are you here, Aunt Dannarah?"

"March your army back to Toskala, overthrow your father, and appoint me as chief marshal."

His crooked smile had a smug slant. "You mistake the matter. I am not at war with my father. I am perfectly happy to let him rule while he and my mother waste their energy dueling over that scrap of ground atop Law Rock they call a palace. A tenement of crammed-together rooms is not a palace!" He indicated a silk map painted with the eight-sided contours of the imperial city within a city that lay at the heart of the Sirniakan Empire. "As it says in the poem, *The emperor's palace is a city unto itself.*"

"You are a fool to involve yourself in the imperial succession on behalf of a man everyone knows is feeble-minded and weak. Even if he is your cousin."

"What makes you think I'm marching in support of the new emperor? Just because he is my mother's sister's only son does not mean I am required to support him."

She scrutinized his bland expression. "One of the other princes, then? I understand there are three other adult princes."

"Yes, there are three other adult princes, all of whom claim they are best suited to rule. But I will tell you something, Aunt. Emperor Faruchalihosh had a favorite child, one he took with him on his journeys all around the empire, one he taught the arcane details of the palace treasury, one who hunted at his side and who with him sailed *the foam-kissed waves of the Flower Shore.* As it says in the poem. The one in whose intelligence and ambition he saw himself."

He crossed his arms and leaned toward her. She wondered if he was a little drunk.

"I am bored in the Hundred, Aunt Dannarah. Aren't you? Don't you ask yourself if there is more to life than the irritating gossip of court and the false smiles of merchants seeking favor and the tedium of sitting through prayers twice a day only so you can be seen to have been there?"

"As a woman I need only attend prayers once a day, and as a reeve I need not attend at Beltak's shrine at all."

"I always wanted to be a reeve. Will you take me up on your eagle? I know reeves can harness a second person and carry them a distance."

"My eagle is as ill tempered as I am."

"All the better! The risk gives it piquancy." He *was* a little glassy-eyed.

The lad poured more of the smoky liquid into his cup and set the glass bottle aside before offering her more cordial from a ceramic pitcher. She flashed a hand up to decline.

"Are you fixed on this rash course of action, Farihosh?"

"You are mistaken in thinking it rash. I have carefully conceived and planned it out in coordination with my cousin."

"Your cousin?"

"Yes. My mother's sister's eldest child."

A ringing of bells as light as a summer's breeze rustled the night, a glissade with the searing beauty of a hymn. Voices rose out of the darkness, singing:

We are but arrows flying on the wind.
An unseen hand set us to fly,
The archer's thoughts unknown to us.

Whose heart we will pierce we cannot yet know.

Farihosh's head came up with the look of a deer surprised at the appearance of a lion. He climbed to his feet with more grace than she had expected and suddenly she doubted he was drunk at all. He waved toward the shadows. A trim young man in reeve leathers stepped into view.

"Marshal Armas! Am I mistaken—? You assured me they were not yet anywhere close to us. Four days' ride higher on the pass, you told me."

The marshal approached with a long side-eye at Dannarah. "I don't understand, Your Highness. The scouts saw the Banner of the Moon flying among a troop of several hundred riding at speed up the southern incline, and behind them in pursuit the banners of Prince Edesihosh with at least a thousand men."

"What other travelers did the reeves see on the pass?" Dannarah interrupted. "Did it not occur to the scouts that a larger group may act as decoy to protect a smaller one?"

"Can this be the case, Marshal Armas? Did that not occur to you?" A crease of displeasure clouded Farihosh's brow. He wiped his face and hands on a towel brought to him by the lad, then glanced in a mirror and flicked a strand of hair off his forehead just as a woman might who wanted to make sure she looked her best when meeting a lover. "Did you give your scouts no instruction to investigate other travelers?"

"I don't... We thought... There was one small party of decorated women, flower girls on their way to a new establishment, but no sign of any other imperial troupe..."

"That's exactly the kind of group you should be looking at most closely!" Dannarah said.

On the road soldiers fell back, parting to line up in disciplined ranks with a swiftness that her father would have approved. Out of the veil of night horses pranced into view, lanterns flaming around them. Flowing robes covered the riders from the top of the head to their knees. The hems and sleeves of their robes were sewn with tiny bells that made a music of their arrival. Even the knee-high boots they wore, painted with silvery vines and shining crescent moons, had bells affixed.

Farihosh clapped his hands three times, and his attendants, officers, and lords swarmed back from the neighboring rooms and courtyard to form up at his back with him centered among them. Dannarah noted a few familiar faces but she did not know his crowd, not as she knew her people.

"Marshal Dannarah, I hope you will stand beside me. Clearly you are the most experienced and canny of the reeves who attend me, as that little exchange just proved."

"Your brother tried to arrest me. The priests will not approve."

"Tavahosh's decisions do not rule mine. I am not interested in the priests' musty rectitude. I am interested in victory."

Two steps took her to his right hand, from which she watched as the horses executed a proud dip of heads in greeting.

One rider dismounted and walked forward, the bells sewn to her robes softly chiming like the whisper of ambition in the ears of unquiet youth who can be lured by a seductive proposition others cannot perceive. Farihosh walked forward to meet her, his hands extended palms up in greeting. Her hands were dark and slim, painted with moons flowering into bursts of flowers that vanished up beneath her long sleeves. Her eyes had all the mystery of forbidden secrets.

"Prince Farihosh, *we are met at last where the stars shine*," she said in a voice whose music was that of assurance.

"Princess Ruvikah." He trembled as on the cliff of elation. "*Under the lantern of the moon do we meet for the first time.*"

"Hu! I see it now," murmured Dannarah. She could not help but be caught by the night, and the lanterns, and the bells, and horses in their golden harness, and the ambitious prince who faced the dead emperor's favorite child, the one the emperor must have wished could inherit a throne that law and custom closed to her.

The princess withdrew her hands and stepped around him to study Dannarah with a look neither accusatory nor friendly. "Who are you?" she asked in the pure accent of the Sirniakan palace. "No woman of rank dresses in the coarse garb of a menial, yet I judge you no common woman."

Farihosh swept an arm like opening a door. "This is my new chief marshal, Lady Dannarah, who commands the reeves and thus will join and enhance our alliance with her years of experience and her caustic wisdom. Unless you have other plans, Aunt."

For the first time in days, months, even years, her heart unfurled from its guarded nest of diminishment and grief. In the release of a single breath a life can extinguish, or it can change and grow.

"Of course I am with you."

56

Kellas sat at his desk facing Chief Oyard, his granddaughters Fohiono and Melisa, and the woman he called daughter, Atani's sister, the demon Arasit. Oyard carefully did not look Arasit in the face, and she politely did not make him do so.

"All two hundred of the company that sailed with me from Salya to Nessumara have reported in," said Fohiono.

Oyard added, "They are housed in small groups in various workshops and clan compounds throughout Toskala as arranged by Yero."

"Very good."

"There is one other thing," said Fohiono with an eyelash-fluttering glance at her cousin Melisa, a signal of things they knew about each other that he didn't know about them. Seeing the two young women together made the accomplished businesswoman known in Toskala as the Incomparable Melisayda look younger and far more like the girl who used to stampede through the house with her cousins shrieking and laughing in voices loud enough to hurt the ears.

All the children of Plum Blossom Clan, raised in a multiple-household extended family, had a closeness that reminded him of his own childhood's bustling clan compound. For all that he had worked alone so much of his life, he understood now he'd always had the shelter of family to creep back to when needed, now as much as ever. In the end every person dies alone, it was true, but it made a cursed lot of difference knowing you had a chance of a hand holding your own when you crossed the spirit gate to the other side.

Fo rested a cupped hand on his desk. "Grandmama sent this for you. She said maybe it is time for you to put it on again."

She opened her hand to reveal a ring. His ring, the sigil of the Black Wolves.

He swayed back. "I'm not..."

I'm not ready. I'm not worthy. I failed him.

But he clamped down his mouth on the words. He would not burden his granddaughters with his fears. They mustn't ever feel responsible for those.

"I took it off after Atani died," he said, the only words he dared say.

Fo nudged Melisa, who drew a silver chain from around her neck and deftly strung the ring from it.

Fo held it out. "Grandmama said you wouldn't wear it at first, so Melisa and I thought you could wear it around your neck."

They both smiled at him like twin flowers, like sunbright so bold and vivid that it fixes in the heart forever. He had to prop his forehead on clasped hands for a moment to hide the smile of pure, giddy, fathomless love that washed through him for the children and grandchildren he had been so fortunate to raise as his own.

Honestly, it was impossible to refuse them.

"Grandpa? Are you well?"

He raised his head and snagged the chain from Fo's hand, then slipped it over his neck and tucked it beneath his inner tunic. The metal, although cool, seemed to burn straight to his heart.

With an exhale he rose. "It is time," he said as the others got to their feet with him.

Fohiono made to grasp his hand but remembered she was now a Black Wolf and clasped her hands behind her back instead. "Let me come with you, Grandpa."

"No. I must do this alone."

"Except for Arasit!" Fohiono blurted out with an indignation that made him smile.

"Let us know when you can walk on air, Fo," said Melisa with all the heady maturity of her two years serving in the field. "Or survive a hundred arrows drilled through your flesh."

Silent until now, Arasit brushed her gaze across Fo, more scold than threat. "You'll get your chance to die, Fo, no doubt sooner than you wish."

Kellas grabbed a practice sword and walked to the door but Fo and Melisa hurried after and hugged him. "Be careful, Grandpa," Melisa said.

Fo added, "I don't want to be the one to tell Grandmama that you aren't coming home."

He kissed their foreheads, nodded at the other two, and left the barracks and guardhouse, pausing briefly to contemplate— with some satisfaction—how he had built a tightly disciplined unit over the last few months.

The gods had granted him the mercy of a cool day with which to ascend the Thousand Steps, each stair-step another layer of memory building the story of his life: The restless and reckless young man offered the chance to serve King Anjihosh as one of his elite Black Wolves. The ambitious soldier who had chosen his profession over everything else. The loyal captain sent to track down a runaway sixteen-year-old prince. The man who had fallen in love with the one woman Anjihosh had ever loved, the woman who had forced the king to relinquish her. Anjihosh had done everything in his power to keep Mai from ever touching another man again. But Kellas had climbed cliffs, swum seas, endured physical hardship, and crept unseen into cities and isolated mountain valleys to hunt down outlaws who did not want to be found. The day Mai had invited Kellas to find a way to reach her, even knowing he would be executed were he caught, had been the day his life changed.

Had love made him a simpler man or a more complicated one?

No, even that was too incomplete an explanation.

He had respected and admired King Anjihosh the Glorious Unifier but he had loved Atani as the son he never had, however he had refused to admit it even to himself.

The ring hung heavily, like an itch that never goes away. Atani's death had scraped at him ever after because he could not understand how he had missed the signs, the warnings, and the instinct that should have told him to refuse Dannarah's order to kill Jehosh and stay with Atani instead. He had done everything else. How had he come to fail so disastrously that time?

The young guards standing on the porch of the king's apartments in the upper palace let him in at once, although as always he had to relinquish his sword to their care. Normally he would have left his sandals on the porch as well but he dangled them half hidden behind his back so he could sneak them inside. A steward greeted him in the audience chamber.

"The king has not yet returned from the assizes at South Gate, Captain. Did he ask you to meet with him here? He gave me no orders to prepare for your arrival."

"Stofi, is it not?"

"That's right, Captain. You always remember people's names."

"I do my best. The king has done a great deal to restore order and peace to Toskala in the twenty days since the riots. To preside over assizes down at South Gate, right in the center of the disturbances, was a graceful touch. If you don't mind, I'll await the king. It was a long climb."

"Yes, yes, of course, Captain. For an elderly man like yourself to still be able to ascend the Thousand Steps! By the will of the Shining One, I hope and pray to live to such a vigorous old age!"

Over the years Kellas had honed his stare into a potent weapon. "Yes, indeed, a man of my age needs a peaceful place to sit where he won't be interrupted until the king returns. A pot of tea would not go amiss."

Age gave a man the privilege of walking past the steward into the balcony room and then, ignoring Stofi's birdlike cries of protest, clicking the door in the wall and descending the stone steps to the chamber carved into the rock.

King Anjihosh's meek wife, Queen Zayrah, had birthed nine children, two sons and seven daughters, out of which six daughters had survived as well as the son he had sent away to be raised elsewhere. Anjihosh had never treated his queen as anything except a polite duty. Yet he also wasn't a man to flaunt in her face that he found pleasure elsewhere. So he had this chamber cut into the rock with its own private entrance, now chained and barred. As king, Atani had never come down here because it reminded him of the disrespect with which his father treated the woman he called Mother, the one who raised him and loved him.

Jehosh, of course, had found the hideaway charming and provocative. In the early days after the first northern war he had kept Dia here. Later, as Dia spent more and more time with her women and on her estate with her children and her weaving establishment, he brought lovers to these lush carpets and cushions. Like his grandfather he never kept any lover for long because there was only one woman he truly cared for in that way.

But whatever else Jehosh might be, he did not have his grandfather's brutal possessive streak, the will to prevent anyone else from tasting a nectar he wanted to keep for himself.

Jehosh loved the pursuit.

His grandfather desired control.

Atani had carved a different path for himself, cut short far too soon.

Hearing footsteps, Kellas turned as the steward brought in a tray of tea and a platter of warm flat bread with ewe's cheese sprinkled on top.

"My thanks, Stofi. I will indulge myself in a nap, if you can make certain I won't be disturbed by anyone except the king."

"Yes, Captain." The man paced once around the carpets and cushions, jangled the chains on the door to the secret passage, and went back up the other stairs. Kellas sat cross-legged on a cushion. He slowed his breathing and relaxed his body into a state of composed readiness, yet his mind would not fully fall quiet.

After establishing himself as king of the Hundred, Anjihosh had named the cloaked Guardians as demons and called them false and dangerous because a few had become corrupted. Under Anjihosh's command, the first thing his Wolves learned was how to kill a demon and cut away the cloak called a demon's skin so it could not rebirth itself into a new person. The Guardians had been forced to go into hiding, and with that the old customs had begun to die. Anjihosh had torn apart the fabric of the Hundred that had used to be, and remade it as an orderly, peaceful, prosperous land that thrived under his rule as long as no one challenged that rule. Those who tried to challenge him were hunted down and killed by the Black Wolves. It was for the best.

He had believed the lie for so long.

"Captain Kellas?"

Jehosh's voice seared across his clouded thoughts like a strike of lightning.

He was on his feet, weapon in hand, before the impulse to act formed as a thought in his head.

"What enemy are you expecting, Captain? You have your knife drawn."

His gaze caught the edge of the tray. "Just cutting this bread and cheese, Your Highness. Would you care for some?"

"I'm not hungry. Sitting in judgment over all those wrangling people and their endless complaints ruins my appetite." Weariness shadowed the king's eyes but he had the restless vigor of a man who does not like to stay still for long. He paced to one of the slit windows to look out over the view, a man elevated above the common run of life by an accident of birth. Light made a mask of his face. Jehosh seemed easy to read and yet he concealed so much.

So much that Kellas had never dreamed might be true.

"I have not seen you for some days, Captain. Not since the night of the riots, when Lady Sarai escaped the palace. Have you any news of Tavahosh? Chorannah is frantic and I must admit I am deeply concerned that he hasn't been seen since he was invested as chief marshal at Horn Hall. Can it possibly be true what the people at Horn Hall told me, that he decided to take a proper reeve's tour of the Hundred? He's always been such an obedient boy, I almost like to think he did choose to defy his mother. He's been gone a cursed long time with no word, though. It just seems odd, and worrisome."

"I admit I am as puzzled as you are, Your Highness," said Kellas truthfully. "I reflect that things would be very different today if you had appointed Lady Dannarah as chief marshal before Queen Chorannah snatched the initiative from you."

"Yes, I should never have let her get the jump on me. But Tavahosh has always let Chorannah push him around. Maybe he got tired of her demands and ran off with Lady Sarai to make a new life as rice farmers." His laugh grated.

Kellas said nothing. It took most of his concentration to keep his hands loose at his sides. He sank his focus into the ring lying lightly against his skin. He had been a loyal soldier. It was just he hadn't seen the ambush coming.

"This rash of disappearances troubles me like an itch I can't reach," Jehosh went on. "We've had days of seeming calm but I am certain there is a storm rising. Any news of Lady Sarai? And Ulyar, too! Chorannah has appointed his deputy as supreme captain but I intend to assert my power and place you in the position instead, Captain."

"That is why I came today, Your Highness. I have bad news. A body was fished out of the river downstream and identified as Ulyar."

"So Ulyar is dead." The king laughed again, running a nervous hand over his hair. "Under the circumstances I'm not sure that's bad news. Do you know what happened?"

"Yes. I killed him."

"What?"

Kellas did not repeat himself, just let the words hang there. Jehosh's gaze flicked toward Kellas's knife, then measured the distance to the steps and the angle of how Kellas was standing a little closer to the steps than he was. "Did you? Why?"

Kellas sheathed the knife and noted how Jehosh's shoulders relaxed. "We see our own face in the mirror. Don't we often look at the behavior of others only to see not them but what we know of ourselves?"

"What do you mean?"

"Of course you have always wondered why I left the palace after your father's death."

"You left in disgrace. Under suspicion."

"I failed in my duty to King Anjihosh. I did not protect Atani from the demons."

"It's true!" Like a man on fire Jehosh strode in the other direction, over to the chained door, and turned and strode all the way down the length of the chamber to the steps and then back to the chained door. "It was always true. My father told me himself that he had made a pact with demons!"

Years of experience had taught Kellas how to keep utterly still, to stay unnoticed, someone to be overlooked until he struck.

He spoke in a quiet voice. "So naturally I feared you also might be in league with demons, Your Highness. I feared the demons might have poisoned you with their false promises and seductive words in the same way they had poisoned King Atani. That's why I left the palace."

"I'm not in league with demons. It makes sense you would have feared I would succumb, if you knew for certain that demons had corrupted my father." He halted by the cupboard and tapped a hand against its side. "How did you find out? What proof convinced you?"

"Demons want to overthrow the king, do they not?"

"Yes, demons want to restore chaos in the land."

"It was right there in plain sight. King Atani raised law pillars calling for the restoration of the old custom of assizes courts and temple witnesses not under the oversight of a king. He meant to abolish the kingship."

"Yes, yes! You understand!" Jehosh clasped his hands together and touched them to his lips. A flush heightened the color in his cheeks. His eyes looked a little wild. "Such a foolish plan could never work. People called my father strong because he was calm and patient but in truth he was weak. He was really just a broken-down horse that needed to be put out to pasture to chew over his foolish bits of piecemeal wisdom. How I got tired of him lecturing me about justice and mercy!"

Rage may smolder where it lies buried, but when it catches dry tinder it flames. Kellas had to fix his trembling hands behind his back, standing in soldier's parade rest. He had to pretend to speak as with another man's voice, not his own; so might one of Hasibal's players take the part of the Loyal Captain Standing Before His Rightful Lord.

"It's just as well Lord Seras killed him, but I don't understand how Lord Seras discovered the truth about King Atani and the demons. How could the son of the revered and faithful General Sengel have thought to attack the chosen and named heir of King Anjihosh the Glorious Unifier?"

Jehosh shrugged as thoughtlessly as he might have swatted at a wandering fly. "I told him."

"You told Lord Seras?"

"Yes, after my father told me the truth about his law pillars and his pathetic plans. I realized he meant to disinherit me, and not even in favor of one of my younger brothers. I confess naming one of my brothers as heir over me would have angered me, but if I had been offered a generalship instead that might have been an acceptable bribe. Let them preside at assizes. But no! He meant to disinherit all three of us! He meant to dismantle the kingdom—everything!—his father built. He would have dragged down the Hundred with him."

"And you would never have become king."

"No one would have become king. He succumbed to the lies of the demons. That's what it means to be demon-ridden. I loved my father, Captain Kellas, but what can you do when someone becomes diseased? If they are suffering and there is no cure, isn't it better to kill them?"

"An act of mercy."

"No one loved him more than I did."

"And Lord Seras?"

"He understood the danger, too. He and I agreed that his daughter Sinara would marry Farihosh when they grew up. But Vanas wanted to inherit Lord Seras's place as head of the clan."

"Just as you wanted to rule."

"Vanas has a younger brother's sense of grievance. He felt he had to prove himself because Seras was not only older but so well loved and respected. My sole concern was for my grandfather's legacy. I have a duty to preserve it. You understand me. You served King Anjihosh."

"I was once his loyal captain," said Kellas, considering the distance between him and Jehosh, the king's greater height and speed and youth, and his own knife.

A tap brought Jehosh's head around to consider the chained door. "Who is there?" he demanded.

Silence answered.

"No one ever comes up that passageway if I have not arranged it beforehand. The far end of the corridor is secret, and anyway it is locked." The king walked to the door and set a hand against it as if by touch he could see through to the other side of the thick wood. "Who is there?"

"Your aunt," said a faint female voice.

"My aunt? Aunt Dannarah? I thought you went to the convocation."

"I am not Dannarah."

"Am I meant to guess? Lady Anah, who ran away with one of Hasibal's pilgrims when I was a boy? Sukiyah and Gedassah who went south to marry lords in the empire? I think you are not them, nor my Aunt Meenah who never spoke aloud in all the years I knew her." He glanced at Kellas as if to gauge whether the captain had moved but turned his attention back to the door like a fish snapping after bait. "Aunt Sadah, is it you? Are you returned with your son?"

She said, "I am your father's full sister, Your Highness, born to the same father and mother. You do know that your grandmother Queen Zayrah did not herself give birth to Atani, don't you? Did no one ever bother to tell you, Jehosh?"

Jehosh stared at the door for the longest time.

"Captain, is this incredible assertion true?"

Kellas took a step toward him, guessing that the best way to get Jehosh to do what he wanted was to tell him the opposite. "Don't open the door, Your Highness."

"Jehosh, let me in and I will tell you everything." Ghosts might tap with such soft insistence, seeking entry into your waking thoughts. "All the secrets they kept hidden from you."

The king touched a chain at his neck, fingering the key looped there.

Kellas took another step, again speaking to hold Jehosh's attention on the door and the person behind it and away from the man slowly closing in on him. "Don't open it, Your Highness. I fear it is a demon."

"What is your name?" the king asked.

"My name is Arasit, daughter of Anji and Mai. Mai was the woman Anjihosh truly loved, as much as he could love anything except his own ambition. She is the one who walked away from him because he wanted to keep her in a cage after he had used her wit and her strategy to conquer the Hundred, although conquest was never part of her plan. She just wanted to make a home. Atani was my older brother, their first child. Anji gave the baby to Zayrah to seal their marriage. He made Zayrah take an oath never to reveal that the boy did not come from her womb. I do not wish to diminish Zayrah's part in Atani's upbringing because by all accounts she truly loved him and treated him as her own son. Atani loved her and considered her his mother."

Kellas took another step.

"I don't believe it," said the king, pressing his cheek against the door. "Why would my father never have told me?"

"Why should Atani have confided in you, Jehosh? He knew you scorned the way he chose to rule."

"Did my mother know?"

"Queen Yevah obeyed her husband's wishes. After his death she didn't trust you. That's why she left the palace. Do you even know where she is now?"

Kellas took another step.

"Every month she sends me a letter by a courier and I reply. I am a dutiful son."

"Do you know why she never sees you, Your Highness?"

"She never liked the palace. She never wanted to stay, nor would I ever have kept her here."

"You gave her daughter to Lord Vanas although she was against the marriage. You sent both her other sons to die in your war although she begged you to leave one behind."

Another quiet step.

"They wanted to go!"

"They admired you, it is true, as younger brothers may admire an elder. They admired your Spears and your tales of glory and your beautiful prize, the king's daughter you brought back as a trophy. Your mother never forgave you for making your brothers believe they should want the same things you did."

"It isn't my fault they died. People die in war."

"A war whose pretext you created, Jehosh."

"A war my father allowed me to lead, because he wanted me out of the way so he could disinherit me and destroy the kingdom."

Kellas struck.

He plunged the knife into Jehosh's belly and up under his ribs, aiming for his heart. But he was slow, and not as strong as he had been in his prime. Jehosh slammed backward into the wall and with a shout broke away. The captain used the force of the push as a torque to spin himself around and attack again. Jehosh's elbow caught him under the chin, knocking his head back and throwing him against the door.

"Hai! Hai!" shouted the king, screaming for his guards. Blood soaked the front of his golden tabard.

Kellas flung his full weight into Jehosh to batter him back against the wall.

Jehosh got a hand around Kellas's neck and squeezed, trying to choke him, but Kellas dropped to his knees to loosen the hold. The king's fingers caught on the silver chain, pulling it loose. The ring skittered free to land behind them on the carpets, but no matter.

Kellas had the angle he needed to finish the job.

Again he stabbed Jehosh, right up under the ribs, and again, and when Jehosh sagged slackly between him and the wall, he stabbed him again and again and again. His rage coursed as bloody as the king's dying.

"Your Highness!" cried voices from the rooms above.

The words jolted him back to himself, where he knelt on a damp carpet over Jehosh's body. Footsteps pounded on the stairs. He yanked the key to the chained door from its chain around Jehosh's neck. His heart was racing and his mind had nothing in it except survival. Hands steady, he unlocked the pins.

As four guards clattered into the room and stared in astonished horror at the dead king, the chains slithered down in a hasp of sound. He shoved the bar out of place and turned the latch.

Arasit stepped into the room, dressed in reeve leathers—a good disguise—and with her curly hair loose over her shoulders. Although as old in years as Dannarah, she could have been mistaken as an age-mate of Fohiono or Melisa, one of the peculiar effects of her particular demon-nature.

She caught the soldiers in her demon's gaze. "You have seen nothing. You will go back upstairs and forget you ever came down here or that the king or Captain Kellas came down here. As far as you know, no one was down here."

They walked back up the stairs in silence.

"The way you can punch holes into minds never fails to disturb me," said Kellas, breathing calm back into his shattered heart. So he would bind fury into a smooth surface until the world again would see him as reasonable and wise. Many times before this he had climbed these thousand steps of coiling the rage into a tiny ball of shredded fragments that he could stow deep away and afterward pretend he was a whole man. Every person who lives suffers wounds. Some have a chance to repair them. Others live with them and pray to the gods that they be granted the strength to get through each day.

Arasit knelt beside Jehosh's inert body and held a palm above his face. For a moment she did not move; then she closed her hand around an object in the air invisible to Kellas, like a stray floating feather or a departing soul.

"The human spirit is so bright," she murmured. She opened her hand and he blinked, thinking he saw a spark of light. But it was only the sun angling through the narrow windows.

Jehosh's topknot had come partially undone in the struggle; she brushed wisps of hair off his forehead as tenderly as a loving child grooms an invalid elder.

"He doesn't remember meeting me," she said. "It was a long time ago. He must have been fifteen, and I looked fifteen at that time as well. He flirted with me, not knowing I was his aunt. I remember him being witty for his age. I know why Atani and my mother are veiled to my sight but I've never understood why all of Atani's children are also veiled. None show any other sign of demon kinship, but somehow they possess the mask that conceals them from demon-sight."

"Yet the rest of us are scrolls unrolled to their full length in your gaze," said Kellas.

She shrugged, still examining Jehosh as if looking for her lost humanity in his lifeless face. "Don't worry; you're safe from me peering into your mind, considering your relationship to my mother. I do think Jehosh loved Atani, though. Do you think Atani suspected that his son fomented the plot against him?"

"Love is the greatest veil of all. It's like looking into the sun when you should be looking at the shadow the light casts."

"We must get rid of the bloody rug." She stood, offering him a frown to go with a disapproving shake of her head. "I could have managed his death with much less fuss."

He, too, shook his head only to discover it throbbing. "It was my duty. My honor. My responsibility. Not anyone else's."

He had pulled a muscle in his back, but with teeth gritted he helped her roll Jehosh up in the carpet on which he had died. They dragged it into the narrow passageway, a dim corridor hacked into the rock and cut with air- and light holes at intervals. Then he went back into the carpeted chamber and, casting around, discovered the ring on the ground. With it clasped in a trembling hand he went back into the passageway. He stayed with the body as she closed, barred, chained, and locked the door from the inside, so she remained in the chamber while he waited in the lightless passageway. The ring dug into his palm.

In darkness he rested beside the cooling body.

Another aspect of Arasit's particular demon-nature was that she could walk on air, which meant she was perfectly placed to lock up from behind and exit the chamber through one of its rock-cut windows. Soon enough she squeezed through a light hole and dropped down beside him.

"Here's the key," she said, handing it over.

Her skin was cool; she had a pulse just like an ordinary person did, but she wasn't an ordinary person or even an ordinary demon. Probably he ought to fear what she was, but she was also Mai's daughter, and whenever her strange magic took him aback, he remembered the way he had met her atop a roof as she complained about the boy who had fallen in love with her dearest cousin and best friend just as any girl of fifteen might grumble.

They walked together down to the other end of the long passage up which untold women had made their way, some to meet the conqueror and others his grandson, each a part of the same chain. The other end opened into a dusty storeroom stacked with shelves of ledgers, the record room of the king's treasury. They locked and barred and chained this door, too. It would take a while for people to sort out what had happened to the king; Kellas knew of no other key, but probably Lord Vanas and Queen Dia each had one.

The only clue to the murderer of the king would be the sword Kellas had left behind at the entrance to the king's chambers, and he had made sure to bring along a student's training sword bought in the market and thus untraceable.

"I'm sorry, Uncle Kellas," Arasit said in a low voice as they paused in a storeroom, out of sight, so he could catch his breath and rub at the ache in his back. "I think you liked Jehosh."

"I did like him. But I loved Atani."

"Funny to think you were once King Anjihosh's loyal captain. I wonder if you are the only man who successfully betrayed him."

"No, he is the one who betrayed the Hundred by claiming

to save it and instead imprisoning it. The Hundred does not belong to its conquerors. It belongs to the people who live here. Yet I thought our plans would all be for nothing when Atani died."

"Mama didn't think so. She never gave up."

"It's your mother who has always been the patient one, able to take the long view even if that meant the struggle has to continue into the next generation. She is the strategist. I am only the sword."

He opened the door of the storeroom to peer through, and saw an empty corridor and, in a nearby room, clerks hunched over writing desks industriously filling in ledgers, all unaware of the chaos about to crash down over the palace.

At last he opened his hand and considered the ring.

He had obeyed Dannarah's order. But even as he thought it, he knew that today he had acted only for himself.

"Still," murmured Arasit, "even though my mother's secret network spans the Hundred, even though they think we have only four Guardians when we really have nine, even though they don't know about me, will it be enough? Jehosh's heirs and his queens and lords and courtiers and soldiers have the coin and the assizes and the administration. They will hang on to their power. I think you struck too soon."

"What matters is that we act when the moment demands action, not that we wait until we deem the time to be right."

"Compared with the army Jehosh's heirs can command, you don't even have that many Black Wolves trained and ready to go."

"That may be so," he said as he slipped the ring on his finger. The wolf's head gleamed. "But now we have one more."

Acknowledgments

Black Wolves became a tremendously difficult book to write because it got caught up in my beloved father's final illness and death. Therefore I have a long list of acknowledgments to people whose help proved more crucial than they could possibly know.

My thanks to: Alexander and David Rasmussen-Silverstein for long plot conversations and talking me off the ledge on multiple occasions. Rhiannon Rasmussen-Silverstein for listening when I needed to complain.

Jay Silverstein for sticking it out.

Delia Sherman, the Structure Whisperer, who talked me through my despair and into a plot/emotional structure that made sense.

Robin LaFevers and Malinda Lo for support at a pivotal time.

The participants in a Sirens Conference 2013 roundtable, led by Joy Kim, on "Women Political Leaders in Fantasy," whose comments about what they wanted to see in epic fantasy turned my head around in a way that made me reconsider the entire nature of the story.

Courtney Schafer and Alison Croggon for NaNoEpicMo, our tiny e-mail support group that helped us through November/December 2013 when we three were all struggling with recalcitrant manuscripts and other writing obstacles.

Paul Weimer for reading early drafts of the opening and giving me honest comments.

Karen Miller for heroically and generously reading an incomplete mess of a draft and reminding me that I was the only one who ultimately could decide whether the story was worth telling.

Bob Hole for the Twitter DM conversation that crystallized Tandi marriage customs.

Andrea Chandler and Cindy Pon for cheerleading.

Tricia Sullivan for an incredible boost at a vulnerable time.

Kari Sperring, Rochita Loenen-Ruiz, and Aliette de Bodard for the Rainy Writers Retreat in Brittany where we talked through so much.

Dani McKenzie and Justin Landon for close reading of the beta manuscript and extended discussions of plot and character afterward.

Jonah Sutton-Morse for incisive comments on the penultimate revision.

My Twitter support group, as we cheered each other on: You know who you are.

Devi Pillai, Jenni Hill, and Lindsey Hall for piling on the editorial comments without stinting; you wouldn't necessarily think that thirty pages of editorial comments make a writer's job easier, but they do. A particular special thank-you to Devi who kept me going when I wanted to give up.

Finally, my most heartfelt thanks to all of my readers. This wouldn't happen without you.

extras

www.orbitbooks.net

extras

about the author

Kate Elliott is the author of more than twenty novels, including the Spiritwalker Trilogy (*Cold Magic*), the Crossroads Trilogy (*Spirit Gate*), the Novels of the Jaran, and Young Adult fantasy *Court of Fives*. *King's Dragon*, the first novel in the Crown of Stars series, was a Nebula Award finalist; *The Golden Key* (with Melanie Rawn and Jennifer Roberson) was a World Fantasy Award finalist. Born in Iowa, she grew up in Oregon and now is ecstatic to be living in Hawaii.

For more information on Kate's writing and series, or to sign up for her new release/updates e-mail list, the author invites you to visit her website at KateElliott.com, to visit her Facebook page, or to follow her on Twitter @KateElliottSFF.

Find out more about Kate Elliott and other Orbit authors by registering for the free monthly newsletter at www.orbitbooks.net.

if you enjoyed

BLACK WOLVES

look out for

THIEF'S MAGIC

book one of Millennium's Rule

by

Trudi Canavan

CHAPTER 1

The corpse's shrivelled, unbending fingers surrendered the bundle reluctantly. Wrestling the object out of the dead man's grip seemed disrespectful so Tyen worked slowly, gently lifting a hand when a blackened fingernail snagged on the covering. He'd touched the ancient dead so often they didn't sicken or frighten him now. Their desiccated flesh had long ago stopped being a source of transferable sickness, and he did not believe in ghosts.

When the mysterious bundle came free Tyen straightened and smiled in triumph. He wasn't as ruthless at collecting ancient artefacts as his fellow students and his teacher, but bringing home nothing from these research trips would see him fail to graduate as a sorcerer-archaeologist. He willed his tiny magic-fuelled flame closer.

The object's covering, like the tomb's occupant, was dry and stiff having, by his estimate, lain undisturbed for six hundred years. Thick leather darkened with age, it had no markings – no adornment, no precious stones or metals. As he tried to open it the wrapping snapped apart and something inside began to slide out. His pulse quickened as he caught the object . . .

. . . and his heart sank a little. No treasure lay in his hands. Just a book. Not even a jewel-encrusted, gold-embellished book.

Not that a book didn't have potential historical value, but compared to the glittering treasures Professor Kilraker's other two students had unearthed for the Academy it was a disappointing find. After all the months of travel, research, digging and watching he had little to show for his own work. He had finally unearthed a tomb that hadn't already been ransacked by grave robbers and what did it contain? A plain stone coffin, an unadorned corpse and an old book.

Still, the old fossils at the Academy wouldn't regret sponsoring his journey if the book turned out to be significant. He examined it closely. Unlike the wrapping, the leather cover felt supple. The binding was in good condition. If he hadn't just broken apart the covering to get it out, he'd have guessed the book's age at no more than a hundred or so years. It had no title or text on the spine. Perhaps it had worn off. He opened it. No word marked the first page, so he turned it. The next was also blank and as he fanned through the rest of the pages he saw that they were as well.

He stared at it in disbelief. Why would anyone bury a blank book in a tomb, carefully wrapped and placed in the hands of the occupant? He looked at the corpse, but it offered no answer. Then something drew his eye back to the book, still open to one of the last pages. He looked closer.

A mark had appeared.

Next to it a dark patch formed, then dozens more. They spread and joined up.

Hello, they said. *My name is Vella.*

Tyen uttered a word his mother would have been shocked to hear if she had still been alive. Relief and wonder replaced disappointment. The book was magical. Though most sorcerous books used magic in minor and frivolous ways, they were so rare that the Academy would always take them for its collection. His trip hadn't been a waste.

So what did this book do? Why did text only appear when it was opened? Why did it have a name? More words formed on the page.

I've always had a name. I used to be a person. A living, breathing woman.

Tyen stared at the words. A chill ran down his spine, yet at the same time he felt a familiar thrill. Magic could sometimes be disturbing. It was often inexplicable. He liked that not everything about it was understood. It left room for new discoveries. Which was why he had chosen to study sorcery alongside history. In both fields there was an opportunity to make a name for himself.

He'd never heard of a person turning into a book before. *How is that possible?* he wondered.

I was made by a powerful sorcerer, replied the text. *He took my knowledge and flesh and transformed me.*

His skin tingled. The book had responded to the question he'd shaped in his mind. *Do you mean these pages are made of your flesh?* he asked.

Yes. My cover and pages are my skin. My binding is my hair, twisted together and sewn with needles fashioned from my bones and glue from tendons.

He shuddered. *And you're conscious?*

Yes.

You can hear my thoughts?

Yes, but only when you touch me. When not in contact with a living human, I am blind and deaf, trapped in the darkness with no sense of time passing. Not even sleeping. Not quite dead. The years of my life slipping past — wasted.

Tyen stared down at the book. The words remained, nearly filling a page now, dark against the creamy vellum. Which was her skin . . .

It was grotesque and yet . . . all vellum was made of skin. While these pages were human skin, they felt no different to that made of animals. They were soft and pleasant to touch. The book was not repulsive in the way an ancient, desiccated corpse was.

And it was so much more interesting. Conversing with it was akin to talking with the dead. If the book was as old as the tomb it knew about the time before it was laid there. Tyen smiled. He may not have found gold and jewels to help pay his way on this expedition, but the book could make up for that with historical information.

More text formed.

Contrary to appearances, I am not an "it".

Perhaps it was the effect of the light on the page, but the new words seemed a little larger and darker than the previous text. Tyen felt his face warm a little.

I'm sorry, Vella. It was bad mannered of me. I assure you, I meant no offence. It is not every day that a man addresses a talking book, and I am not entirely sure of the protocol.

She was a woman, he reminded himself. He ought to follow the etiquette he'd been raised to follow. Though talking to women could be fiendishly tricky, even when following all the rules about manners. It would be rude to begin their association by interrogating her about the past. Rules of conversation decreed he should ask after her wellbeing.

So . . . is it nice being a book?

When I am being held and read by someone nice, it is, she replied.

And when you are not, it is not? I can see that might be a disadvantage in your state, though one you must have anticipated before you became a book.

I would have, if I'd had foreknowledge of my fate.

So you did not choose to become a book. Why did your maker do that to you? Was it a punishment?

No, though perhaps it was natural justice for being too ambitious and vain. I sought his attention, and received more of it than I intended.

Why did you seek his attention?

He was famous. I wanted to impress him. I thought my friends would be envious.

And for that he turned you into a book. What manner of man could be so cruel?

He was the most powerful sorcerer of his time, Roporien the Clever.

Tyen caught his breath and a chill ran down his back. *Roporien! But he died over a thousand years ago!*

Indeed.

Then you are . . .

At least as old as that. Though in my time it wasn't polite to comment on a woman's age.

He smiled. *It still isn't — and I don't think it ever will be. I apologise again.*

You are a polite young man. I will enjoy being owned by you.

You want me to own you? Tyen suddenly felt uncomfortable. He realised he now thought of the book as a person, and owning a person was slavery — an immoral and uncivilised practice that had been illegal for over a hundred years.

Better that than spend my existence in oblivion. Books don't last for ever, not even magical ones. Keep me. Make use of me. I can give you a wealth of knowledge. All I ask is that you hold me as often as possible so that I can spend my lifespan awake and aware.

I don't know . . . The man who created you did many terrible things – as you experienced yourself. I don't want to follow in his shadow. Then something occurred to him that made his skin creep. *Forgive me for being blunt about it, but his book, or any of his tools, could be designed for evil purposes. Are you one such tool?*

I was not designed so, but that does not mean I could not be used so. A tool is only as evil as the hand that uses it.

The familiarity of the saying was startling and unexpectedly reassuring. It was one that Professor Weldan liked. The old historian had always been suspicious of magical things.

How do I know you're not lying about not being evil?

I cannot lie.

Really? But what if you're lying about not being able to lie?

You'll have to work that one out for yourself.

Tyen frowned as he considered how he might devise a test for her, then realised something was buzzing right beside his ear. He shied away from the sensation, then breathed a sigh of relief as he saw it was Beetle, his little mechanical creation. More than a toy, yet not quite what he'd describe as a pet, it had proven to be a useful companion on the expedition.

The palm-sized insectoid swooped down to land on his shoulder, folded its iridescent blue wings, then whistled three times. Which was a warning that . . .

"Tyen!"

. . . Miko, his friend and fellow archaeology student was approaching.

The voice echoed in the short passage leading from the outside world to the tomb. Tyen muttered a curse. He glanced down at the page. *Sorry, Vella. Have to go.* Footsteps neared the door of the tomb. With no time to slip her into his bag, he stuffed her down his shirt, where she settled against the waistband of his trousers. She was warm – which was a bit disturbing now that he knew she was a conscious thing created from human flesh – but he didn't have time to dwell on it. He turned to the door in time to see Miko stumble into view.

"Didn't think to bring a lamp?" he asked.

"No time," the other student gasped. "Kilraker sent me to get you. The others have gone back to the camp to pack up. We're leaving Mailand."

"Now?"

"Yes. *Now*," Miko replied.

Tyen looked back at the small tomb. Though Professor Kilraker liked to refer to these foreign trips as treasure hunts, his peers expected the students to bring back evidence that the journeys were also educational. Copying the faint decorations on the tomb walls would have given them something to mark. He thought wistfully of the new instant etchers that some of the richer professors and self-funded adventurers used to record their work. They were far beyond his meagre allowance. Even if they weren't, Kilraker wouldn't take them on expeditions because they were heavy and fragile.

Picking up his satchel, Tyen opened the flap. "Beetle. Inside." The insectoid scuttled down his arm into the bag. Tyen slung the strap over his head and shoulder and sent his flame into the passage.

"We have to hurry," Miko said, leading the way. "The locals heard about where you're digging. Must've been one of the boys Kilraker hired to deliver food who told them. A bunch are coming up the valley and they're sounding those battle horns they carry."

"They didn't want us digging here? Nobody told me that!"

"Kilraker said not to. He said you were bound to find something impressive, after all the research you did."

He reached the hole where Tyen had broken through into the passage and squeezed out. Tyen followed, letting the flame die as he climbed out into the bright afternoon sunlight. Dry heat enveloped him. Miko scrambled up the sides of the ditch. Following, Tyen looked back and surveyed his work. Nothing remained in the tomb that robbers would want, but he couldn't stand to leave it exposed to vermin and he felt guilty about unearthing a tomb the locals didn't wanted disturbed. Reaching out with his mind, he pulled magic to himself then moved the rocks and earth on either side back into the ditch.

"What are you *doing*?" Miko sounded exasperated.

"Filling it in."

"We don't have time!" Miko grabbed his arm and yanked him around so that they both looked down into the valley. He pointed. "See?"

The valley sides were near-vertical cliffs, and where the faces had crumbled over time piles of rubble had built up against the sides to form steep slopes. Tyen and Miko were standing atop of one of these.

At the bottom of the valley a long line of people was moving, faces tilted to search the scree above. One arm rose, pointing at Tyen and Miko. The rest stopped, then fists were raised.

A shiver went through Tyen, part fear, part guilt. Though the people inhabiting the remote valleys of Mailand were unrelated to the ancient race that had buried its dead in the tombs, they felt that such places of death should not be disturbed lest ghosts be awakened. They'd made this clear when Kilraker had arrived, and to previous archaeologists, but their protests had never been more than verbal and they'd indicated that some areas were less important than others. They must really be upset, if Kilraker had cut the expedition short.

Tyen opened his mouth to ask, when the ground beside him exploded. They both threw up their arms to shield their faces from the dust and stones.

"Can you protect us?" Miko asked.

"Yes. Give me a moment ... " Tyen gathered more magic. This time he stilled the air around them. Most of what a sorcerer did was either moving or stilling. Heating and cooling was another form of moving or stilling, only more intense and focused. As the dust settled beyond his shield he saw the locals had gathered together behind a brightly dressed woman who served as priestess and sorcerer to the locals. He took a step towards them.

"Are you mad?" Miko asked.

"What else can we do? We're trapped up here. We should just go talk to them. Explain that I didn't—"

The ground exploded again, this time much closer.

"They don't seem in the mood for talking."

"They won't hurt two sons of the Leratian Empire," Tyen reasoned. "Mailand gains a lot of profit from being one of the safer colonies."

Miko snorted. "Do you think the villagers care? They don't get any of the profit."

"Well ... the Governors will punish them."

"They don't look too worried about that right now." Miko turned to stare up at the face of the cliff behind them. "I'm not waiting to see if they're bluffing." He set off along the edge of the slope where it met the cliff.

Tyen followed, keeping as close as possible to Miko so that he didn't have to stretch his shield far to cover them both. Stealing glances at the people below, he saw that they were hurrying up the slope, but the loose scree was slowing them down. The sorceress walked along the bottom, following them. He hoped this meant that, after using magic, she needed to move from the area she had depleted to access more. That would mean her reach wasn't as good as his.

She stopped and the air rippled before her, a pulse that rushed towards him. Realising that Miko had drawn ahead, Tyen drew more magic and spread the shield out to protect him.

The scree exploded a short distance below their feet. Tyen ignored the stones and dust bounding off his shield and hurried to catch up with Miko. His friend reached a crack in the cliff face. Setting his feet in the rough sides of the narrow opening and grasping the edges, he began to climb. Tyen tilted his head back. Though the crack continued a long way up the cliff face it didn't reach the top. Instead, at a point about three times his height, it widened to form a narrow cave.

"This looks like a bad idea," he muttered. Even if they didn't slip and break a limb, or worse, once in the cave they'd be trapped.

"It's our only option. They'll catch us if we head downhill," Miko said in a tight voice, without taking his attention from climbing. "Don't look up. Don't look down either. Just climb."

Though the crack was almost vertical, the edges were pitted and uneven, providing plenty of hand- and footholds. Swallowing hard, Tyen swung his satchel around to his back so he wouldn't crush Beetle between himself and the wall. He set his fingers and toes in the rough surface and hoisted himself upward.

At first it was easier than he'd expected, but soon his fingers, arms and legs were tiring and hurting from the strain. *I should have exercised more before coming here. I should have joined a sports club.* Then he shook his head. *No, there's no exercise I could have done that would have boosted* these *muscles except climbing cliff walls, and I've not heard of any clubs that consider* that *a recreational activity.*

The shield behind him shuddered at a sudden impact. He fed more magic to it, trying not to picture himself squashed like a bug on the cliff wall. Was Miko right about the locals? Would they dare to kill him? Or was the priestess simply gambling that he was a good enough sorcerer to ward off her attacks?

"Nearly there," Miko called.

Ignoring the fire in his fingers and calves, Tyen glanced up and saw Miko disappear into the cave. *Not far now*, he told himself. He forced his aching limbs to push and pull, carrying him upward towards the dark shadow of safety. Glancing up again and again, he saw he was a body's length away, then close enough that an outstretched arm would reach it. A vibration went through the stone beneath his hand and chips flew off the wall nearby. He found another foothold, pushed up, grabbed a handhold, pulled, felt the cool shadow of the cave on his face . . .

. . . then hands grabbed his armpits and hauled him up.

Miko didn't stop pulling until Tyen's legs were inside the cave. It was so narrow that Tyen's shoulders scraped along the walls. Looking downward, he saw that there was no floor to the fissure. The walls on either side simply drew closer together to form a crack that continued beneath him. Miko was bracing his boots on the walls on either side.

That "floor" was not level either. It sloped downward as the cave deepened, so Tyen's head was now lower than his legs. He felt the book slide up the inside of his shirt and tried to grab it, but Miko's arms got in the way. The book dropped down into the crack. He cursed and quickly created a flame. The book had come to rest far beyond his reach even if his arms had been skinny enough to fit into the gap.

Miko let go and gingerly turned around to examine the cave. Ignoring him, Tyen pushed himself up into a crouch. He drew his bag around to the front and opened it. "Beetle," he hissed. The little machine stirred, then scurried out and up onto his arm. Tyen pointed at the crack. "Fetch book."

Beetle's wings buzzed an affirmative, then its body whirred as it scurried down Tyen's arm and into the crack. It had to spread its legs wide to fit in the narrow space where the book had lodged. Tyen breathed a sigh of relief as its tiny pincers seized the spine. As it emerged Tyen grabbed Vella and Beetle together and slipped them both inside his satchel.

"Hurry up! The professor's here!"

Tyen stood up. Miko looked upwards and pressed a finger to his lips. A faint, rhythmic sound echoed in the space.

"In the aircart?" Tyen shook his head. "I hope he knows the priestess is throwing rocks at us or it's going to be a very long journey home."

"I'm sure he's prepared for a fight." Miko turned away and continued along the crack. "I think we can climb up here. Come over and bring your light."

Standing up, Tyen made his way over. Past Miko the crack narrowed again, but rubble had filled the space, providing an uneven, steep, natural staircase. Above them was a slash of blue sky. Miko started to climb, but the rubble began to dislodge under his weight.

"So close," he said, looking up. "Can you lift me up there?"

"Maybe . . ." Tyen concentrated on the magical atmosphere. Nobody had used magic in the cave for a long time. It was as smoothly dispersed and still as a pool of water on a windless day. And it was plentiful. He'd still not grown used to how much stronger and *available* magic was outside towns and cities. Unlike in the metropolis, where magic was constantly surging towards a more important use, here power pooled and lapped around him like a gentle fog. He'd only encountered Soot, the residue of magic that lingered everywhere in the city, in small, quickly dissipating smudges. "Looks possible," Tyen said. "Ready?"

Miko nodded.

Tyen drew a deep breath. He gathered magic and used it to still the air before Miko in a small, flat square.

"Step forward," he instructed.

Miko obeyed. Strengthening the square to hold the young man's weight, Tyen moved it slowly upwards. Throwing his arms out to keep his balance, Miko laughed nervously.

"Let me check there's nobody waiting up there before you lift me out," he called down to Tyen. After peering out of the opening, he grinned. "All clear."

As Miko stepped off the square a shout came from the cave entrance. Tyen twisted around to see one of the locals climbing inside. He drew magic to push the man out again, then hesitated. The drop outside could kill him. Instead he created another shield inside the entrance.

Looking around, he sensed the scarring of the magical atmosphere where it had been depleted, but more magic was already beginning to flow in to replace it. He took a little more to form another square then, hoping the locals would do nothing to spoil his concentration, stepped onto it and moved it upwards.

He'd never liked lifting himself, or anyone else, like this. If he lost focus or ran out of magic he'd never have time to recreate the square. Though it was possible to move a person rather than still the air below them, a lack of concentration or moving parts of them at different rates could cause injury or even death.

Reaching the top of the crack, Tyen emerged into sunlight.

Past the edge of the cliff a large, lozenge-shaped hot-air-filled capsule hovered – the aircart. He stepped off the square onto the ground and hurried over to join Miko at the cliff edge.

The aircart was descending into the valley, the bulk of the capsule blocking the chassis hanging below it and its occupants from Tyen's view. Villagers were gathered at the base of the crack, some clinging to the cliff wall. The priestess was part way up the scree slope but her attention was now on the aircart.

"Professor!" he shouted, though he knew he was unlikely to be heard over the noise of the propellers. "Over here!"

The craft floated further from the cliff. Below, the priestess made a dramatic gesture, entirely for show since magic didn't require fancy physical movements. Tyen held his breath as a ripple of air rushed upward, then let it go as the force abruptly dispelled below the aircart with a dull thud that echoed through the valley.

The aircart began to rise. Soon Tyen could see below the capsule. The long, narrow chassis came into view, shaped rather like a canoe, with propeller arms extending to either side and a fan-like rudder at the rear. Professor Kilraker was in the driver's seat up front; his middle-aged servant, Drem, and the other student, Neel, stood clutching the rope railing and the struts that attached chassis to capsule. The trio would see him and Miko, if only they would turn around and look his way. He shouted and waved his arms, but they continued peering downward.

"Make a light or something," Miko said.

"They won't see it," Tyen said, but he took yet more magic and formed a new flame anyway, making it larger and brighter than the earlier ones in the hope it would be more visible in the bright sunlight. To his surprise, the professor looked over and saw them.

"Yes! Over here!" Miko shouted.

Kilraker turned the aircart to face the cliff edge, its propellers swivelling and buzzing. Bags and boxes had been strapped to either end of the chassis, suggesting there had not been time to pack their luggage in the hollow inside. At last the cart moved over the cliff top in a gust of familiar smells. Tyen breathed in the scent of resin-coated cloth, polished wood and pipe smoke and smiled. Miko grabbed the rope railing strung around the chassis, ducked under it and stepped on board.

"Sorry, boys," Kilraker said. "Expedition's over. No point sticking around when the locals get like this. Brace yourselves for some ear popping. We're going up."

As Tyen swung his satchel around to his back, ready to climb aboard, he thought of what lay inside. He didn't have any treasure to show off, but at least he had found something interesting. Ducking under the railing rope, he settled onto the narrow deck, legs dangling over the side. Miko sat down beside him. The aircart began to ascend rapidly, its nose slowly turning towards home.